INTEMPERANCE

Book I—Climbing the Rock

Alan G. Steiner

To my wife, Renee, who has stood by me and has always believed in me, even when I didn't believe in myself.

Printed in the United States of America

First Printing: August 2018

ISBN-9781983264047

CHAPTER 1

THE POWER OF MUSIC

September 13, 1980
Heritage, California

Heritage, California was certainly not the center of anything, especially not the rock music scene of the west coast in the year 1980. But little did the citizens of this moderate-sized metropolitan region in the most populous state know, the mediocre venue known as D Street West in downtown Heritage would one day become a Mecca for rock and roll music lovers worldwide because of the performance that would take place here tonight.

D Street West was arguably the most exclusive venue in the city, although that really was not saying a whole lot. It was a single-story building occupying a corner lot in downtown Heritage, at the corner of 3rd and D Streets, in a low-rent portion of the high-rise district. The bar could hold four hundred people, though on nights *The Boozehounds* played, it often held about two hundred more than the fire marshal would have legally allowed.

The Boozehounds were Heritage's most popular local rock group. Fond of songs about drinking and smoking pot and fornication and sometimes all at the same time, they were a competent band with a lead guitarist who knew most of the chords and could play them with something that resembled proficiency, a singer who had enough range to hit five or six high notes per set without his voice cracking, and a drummer and bass player who could keep time with the songs well enough to make what came out of their amps sound like actual music. Though *The Boozehounds* had been trying for eight years to secure a recording contract with one of many Los Angeles based record labels, they had been turned down at every turn, told they were "small time" and "great for a cow town, but not worth shit in a real city". And so, they stayed in Heritage, squeaking out a living by playing three nights a week at one of the ten or so clubs that featured live rock music.

At 5:00 on this Saturday afternoon, ninety minutes before the club would open, three and a half hours before *The Boozehounds* were scheduled to take the stage, two vehicles—a 1966 VW Microbus and a 1971 Ford van—pulled in the back parking lot of D Street West and parked near the backstage door. Five young men piled out of the two vehicles. All were dressed in blue jeans and dark colored T-shirts. All but one had long, shaggy hair. These were the members of the rock group *Intemperance*, a band that virtually no one in the Heritage area—or in fact the world—had ever heard of. They were opening for *The Boozehounds* tonight, their set to begin at 7:00 and last for forty-five minutes. It was to be their first performance before an audience.

Jake Kingsley was the lead singer and rhythm guitarist. He was tall and a bit on the thin side, his shoulder length hair dark brown. At twenty years old he still had the last vestiges of adolescent acne marring his face in a few places. He puffed a filtered cigarette thoughtfully as he examined the backstage door, still marvelling over the fact that they had an actual gig, that they were actually going to be paid to perform their music before an audience. And not just any audience either. They were at D Street West, opening for a band that had almost legendary status in the region. "Did you see our name out on the board out front?" he asked Matt Tisdale excitedly. "Right under *The Boozehounds*. Can you believe that shit?"

Matt was the lead guitarist. He was twenty-one, a little shorter than Jake and a little broader across the shoulders and the middle. His hair was dyed jet black and had not been cut since he was seventeen. It fell almost to his waist in the back and was constantly getting in his eyes in the front. It was he who had suggested they audition for the gig even though the flyer they'd found on the bulletin board at Heritage Community College had specified "only experienced acts need apply".

"Fuck *The Boozehounds*," Matt said contemptuously as he flicked his own cigarette into a nearby drain. "They ain't shit. If they were any good they wouldn't still be playin' in this fuckin' place after eight years."

"He does have a point there," said Bill Archer, the piano player. Bill was the one among them without long hair. His hair was in fact cut almost militarily short in an era where even businessmen sported their locks well below the ears. At nineteen years old, Bill was the youngest member of the band. He wore black, horned-rim glasses with lenses about as thick as they could come. In his spare time, he liked to study astrophysics, computer science, and the principals of electrical engineering. As far as the rest of the band knew, he had never been laid in his life, had never even had a girl's tongue in his mouth. He was also a prodigy on the piano, a fact that had been recognized by his parents well before his sixth birthday. Jake—who had known Bill all his life since he was the son of one of his mother's best friends—had been the one to convince the other band members that Bill needed to play with them. Though most hard-rock groups these days eschewed the piano on general principals, it had only taken one session with Bill accompanying them to convince the founding members of Intemperance that his skill and ability to blend the ivories with the crushing guitars and the pounding drum beat gave them a sound unlike any other group. Plus, he was fun to get stoned with. He could entertain them for hours with his large vocabulary and his lectures on just what E=MC squared actually meant.

"It could be that the music industry is deliberately keeping them down," suggested John Cooper, the drummer, who was known pretty much universally as "Coop". He had thick, naturally curly and naturally blonde hair that resembled that belonging to a poodle. It cascaded down across his shoulders and onto his back. Coop—who had been smoking pot at least once a day since approximately the age of ten—thought there was a deep, dark conspiracy for everything. He genuinely believed that men had never walked on the moon, that the government had killed John F. Kennedy, that fluoride in drinking water was intended to pacify the populace, and that the world was going to end in two years when all the planets aligned.

"Why would the music industry keep them down?" asked Darren Appleman, the bass player. He was twenty and perhaps the best looking of the group. His physique was well formed to begin with and made more impressive by the weight lifting he did five times a week. His dark hair was shoulder length only, always carefully styled. You would never catch Darren without a comb in his pocket. Though he wasn't any great shake as a bass player, he was very consistent with the rhythm, rarely missing a beat, and had a decent voice for back-up singing.

"You know how it is," Coop said, which was what he always said before launching into one of his conspiracy theories. "They probably didn't like a contract or something back when they first started and tried to change something. Now they've been blackballed. The industry keeps a list, you know."

"A list?" Matt said, raising his eyebrows, although with his hair you couldn't really tell he'd done it.

"Damn right," Coop assured him. "They only want the right kind of people in the industry. People they can control. If they think you're gonna try to push them too hard, boom, you're on the list and you'll never get a record contract no matter how good you are." He then ended his lecture with his signature end of lecture statement. "It's the way the world works, dude."

"Shit," said Matt, shaking his head. "Or it could be that they just suck ass, which they do. Singing about bonghits and boffing fat chicks. They're a fuckin' comedy act. That's why they don't get signed."

Matt was treading on what was considered sacred ground in the Heritage area. You just didn't talk shit about *The Boozehounds*. But of course, all of them knew he was right, even Coop. The truth was, *The Boozehounds* really weren't all that good. Matt could blow their lead guitar player away with one hand tied behind his back. And Jake could sing their lead singer under the table with laryngitis.

"C'mon," Jake said. "We'd better get our stuff inside. We need to get our sound tuned in. You know how long that takes."

"Fuckin' forever," Darren grumbled. Then something occurred to him and he brightened. "Do you think they'll give us some free drinks after our set?"

The backstage door was locked but pushing the button next to the jam soon produced the sound of footsteps and the clicking of numerous locks and security bars from the other side. The door swung open at last and there stood Chuck O'Donnell, the owner and manager of D Street West. He was a small, unassuming man with a bald scalp atop his head and a long ponytail in the back. A failed rock musician himself, he had purchased D Street West ten years before and had turned it into Heritage's premier rock and roll club. He wasn't a millionaire by any means but he wasn't hurting either. He had quite an ear for music. Though the inclusion of Intemperance on his audition schedule two weeks before had been a mistake—he had failed to check the bogus previous performance dates that Matt Tisdale had fabricated on their portfolio until just before the band arrived—he had allowed them to play for him anyway, partly because their deceit had left a twenty minute hole in his schedule, but mostly out of cruel amusement. His plan had been to let them start playing and then to cut the power to their amps shortly into their first song where he would then debase them as rudely and crudely as he could and humiliate them into never trying such a stunt again.

That had been his plan anyway. But then they had started to play and he discovered something astounding. They were good, very good in fact, perhaps the best new band he had ever heard. The lead guitarist was a magician with his instrument, able to play riffs of amazing complexity, to wail a solo that was right up there with Hendrix or Page and that fit in perfectly with the rhythm of the song. The lead singer—who played a pretty mean backing guitar himself—had a voice that was both rich and wide-ranging, a voice that would send a chill down the spine with a little more development. The kid could sing. And then there was the piano. There were many who believed a piano had no place in a hard rock group, that it was an instrument best left for the bubble-gum pop bands. O'Donnell himself had always believed this with all his heart. But goddamn if that nerdy kid on the keyboard didn't pull it off. This band knew how to play, had an instinct for music that could only get stronger as they matured, and perhaps most importantly, they had a distinct sound unlike anything that had been done before. They made *The Boozehounds*—his most valuable and popular band—sound like what they were: a bunch of hackers. He had a good feeling about these five young men.

"Hey, guys," he said, his salesman grin firmly upon his face. "How are you all doing today?"

They all mumbled that they were doing fine.

"Good, glad to hear it," Chuck told them. "You're right on time. I like that in a band. Why don't you go ahead and start bringing your equipment inside and setting up? You know where the power supply points are. Remember, have everything tuned and sound checked before we open."

Matt, acting as band spokesman, agreed that they would be dialled in long before the first customer pulled into the parking lot.

"Good," he said, patting Matt companionably on the back. "I'll just be doing some paperwork in my office. I'll drop in on you from time to time to see how you're doing."

With that, he disappeared, leaving the door wide open for them to find their own path to the stage. Once in his office he snorted two lines of cocaine and dreamed a little more about what he might have once been.

*****

It took the better part of twenty minutes just to get everything inside. The band had nine amplifiers, a fifteen piece double bass drum set, a sound board, five microphones with stands, an electric piano, two electric guitars, an electric bass guitar, six effects pedals, and nearly four hundred feet of electrical cord to connect everything together. The stage was a twenty by fifteen foot platform against the rear of the bar, raised four feet off the ground and covered in black boards. Lighting sets hung from scaffolding above. They stacked four amplifiers on one side and five on the other. They then set up the microphone stands and connected them to the master soundboard. While Coop assembled his drum set and Bill set up his piano, Jake, Matt, and Darren ran power lines to the amps and connected the effects pedals that helped twist and distort the sound of the guitars into music. They then opened up their guitar cases and removed their instruments.

Jake's guitar was a 1975 Les Paul in the classic sunburst pattern. It had cost him $250 dollars when he'd purchased it three years before and it was his most prized possession. It was a versatile guitar for the multiple roles he asked of it. It could produce a smooth acoustic sound that was about as close as one could get without actually having an acoustic guitar, or it could pump out a grinding electric distortion for backing Matt on the heavier tunes. He removed it gently from the case, lifting it as a father would lift his newborn infant from the crib, and then wiped it with a soft cloth until it shined. Only then did he sling it over his shoulder by the strap and carry it over to the length of cord leading to the string of effects pedals.

"Be sure you have enough picks," Matt told him. "Stick two in the guitar and a bunch in your right pocket in case you drop one or break one."

"What if I drop one in the middle of a song?" Jake asked, silently cursing Matt for giving him one more thing to be nervous about. When such a thing happened during rehearsal they would simply stop the song until the dropper could pick it back up or find another one. They wouldn't really be able to do that in front of an audience, would they?

"You'll have to use your fingers until the next song. Or at least until you get a break in the rhythm."

"Bitchin'," Jake said, frowning.

"The fuckin' show must go on, my man. The fuckin' show must go on. Remember that."

"Right," Jake told him, wishing for a beer or maybe a bonghit, just to calm his nerves a little.

Matt opened up his own guitar case and removed his favorite of the five electric guitars he owned, an instrument that he had vowed upon purchasing two years before would be the only one he would ever play onstage. Though he certainly didn't know or even suspect it at the time, it was an instrument that would one day, twenty-five years in the future, be placed in a display case in the Smithsonian Institute in Washington DC.

It was a 1977 Fender Stratocaster, the make and model that Matt considered the finest guitar in the history of music. It was deep black on the top, shiny white beneath the three pick-ups and the tuning knobs. It produced a rich, heavy sound and it was as familiar in Matt's hands as anything he had ever held before, including his penis. The "Strat", as he called it, was his baby, perhaps the most important thing in his life, the instrument he had dedicated his life to, and he treated it with all the reverence such an icon deserved. He would have been more upset at its loss or destruction than he would've been at the loss of his parents or his siblings. He even talked to it, usually when he was stoned or drunk, but also when he felt it had been played particularly well, beyond what he believed his own considerable talent could be responsible for alone. He talked to it now as he slung it over his shoulder, as his fingers ran lovingly over the frets, the strings, the whammy bar. "We're gonna kick some ass tonight," he whispered to it. "We're gonna kick some fuckin' ass."

Jake plugged his guitar in first. He set the pick-ups he wanted and adjusted the tuning knobs upward. Next, he turned on the amplifier it was connected to, keeping the master volume relatively low, the pre-amp about three quarters up, and bypassing the effects for the time being. He strummed a few times, listening to the tuning first and foremost. Though he had carefully tuned the instrument earlier in the day, before packing it up for the trip over here, he had a morbid fear that it had somehow come out of tune. It hadn't. The sound emitting from the amplifier was as rich as always, richer even since he'd put new strings on only two days before.

"It sounds like a freshly fucked pussy smells," Matt told him, plugging in his own cord and belting out a quick power chord that reverberated throughout the room. He squeezed his fingers down on the neck, stopping the vibration and, subsequently the music. "Now let's get our sound adjusted. You ready, Nerdly?"

"I'm ready," said Bill, who had long since accepted the unflattering nickname Matt had bestowed upon him and had even learned to like it.

"Then let's do it."

It took them the better part of forty minutes to get everything just right. Bill was the closest thing they had to a sound expert and he always made sure that when they played they sounded the best they possibly could with the equipment they had available to them. Each instrument and each microphone was hooked up to its own individual amplifier, which would be carefully positioned and then adjusted so everything would blend together harmoniously. The goal was to keep their music from simply coming out of the amps like most club bands' music—which was to say to keep it from sounding like a bunch of indecipherable noise dominated by overloud guitar riffs and bass that would distort the singing. He wanted those who watched them to hear and understand every word Jake sang, to be able to differentiate between the rhythm and lead guitar, to hear each piano key being struck, to hear the harmony they worked so hard at in their back-up vocals. All of this had to be matched carefully to Coop's drumming, which was strictly acoustic only. Everything was checked and adjusted one by one in a particular order. Darren's bass went first, with the sound being turned up and down to match the output of the bass drums. Next came Matt's guitar. Distortion levels were adjusted first, both with and without the effects, then the actual volume itself. The same process was repeated for Jake's guitar, only this took longer because he had to continually switch from the acoustic sound to the electric distortion, adjusting both individually. Then came Bill's piano, which was where perhaps the finest line existed between too loud and not loud enough. Once the instruments were properly adjusted the microphones could be set. The back-up microphones were the most difficult since they needed to be adjusted first individually and then as a group. Last was Jake's mic, which would transmit his resonant voice through the most expensive of their amps, a $400, top-of-the-line Marshall designed specifically to reproduce clear vocals in venues with poor acoustic conditions. For more than ten minutes Jake used standard singing exercises intermixed with snatches of their lyrics while Bill turned the knobs up and down, down and up, while he had each instrument strum a few bars, while he had the rest of the band sing into their own microphones. This, of course, led to other minute adjustments of the instruments and other mics themselves and even more adjustments of the main microphone.

"Gimmee some more, Jake," Bill would say as he kneeled next to the master soundboard, his ear tuned to the output. "Do the chorus from Descent."

And Jake would sing out the chorus from *Descent into Nothing*, their most recent composition and the song they planned to open with. "Falling without purpose," he would croon, carefully keeping his voice even, emitting from his diaphragm, as he'd been taught long before. "Sliding without cause."

"A little too high still," Bill would say and then make an adjustment. "More."

"No hands held out before me, no more hope for pause."

A nod from Bill, another minute adjustment. "Okay, now everyone."

And all five of them would sing the main part of the chorus, just as they did it in the actual song. "Descent into nothing, life forever changed. Descent into nothing. Can never be the same."

They did this again and again, sometimes using the chorus of one of the other sixteen songs in their repertoire, sometimes having one instrument or another chime in, sometimes having all five instruments chime in at once. Nobody joked. Nobody even talked if it wasn't necessary. They took their sound check as seriously as a cardiac surgeon took his pre-operation preparations.

"I think we got it, Nerdly," Jake finally said when he could no longer detect any differences from one of Bill's adjustments to the next.

"Damn straight," Matt agreed. "We're dialled in tighter than a nun's twat."

It was necessary for one or both of them to tell Bill this at some point. If they didn't, he would go on making adjustments to every single setting for another hour, maybe more.

"I guess it'll have to do," Bill replied with a sigh, knowing deep in his heart that if he could just play around a little longer he would achieve true audio perfection, but also knowing that Jake and Matt were tired of screwing around and were taking control back from him.

"What now?" asked Coop, who was nervously twirling a drumstick in his hand. "It's only ten after six. Should we run through a song or two, just to make sure?"

"That don't sound like a bad idea," agreed Jake. "Let's do Descent one more time since it's our newest piece. Just to make sure we got it right."

Darren and Coop both nodded in agreement. But Matt—the founding member of the band—utilized his unofficial veto power. "Fuck that," he said. "We've rehearsed Descent at least a hundred times over the last two weeks. We've rehearsed the whole goddamn set at least twenty times. We're dialled in, people. We rock! And if we fuck up tonight then we fuck up tonight, but pounding out a few more tunes in the last twenty minutes ain't gonna prevent it and just might encourage it. You dig?"

Jake wasn't so sure he dug. If nothing else it would've kept their mind off their apprehension for a little longer. But he kept his peace and agreed with Matt, as Matt expected him to do. "We dig," he said. "Why don't we go grab a smoke before they open?"

They unplugged the guitars, shut off the mics, the amps, and the soundboard, making sure not to accidentally move a single volume or tone knob on anything. Matt, Jake, and Darren put their instruments carefully on the ground, necks facing up. They then headed backstage as a group. There they met Chuck O'Donnell who was in the company of two men in their late twenties. Every member of Intemperance—being the veterans of the Heritage club scene that they were—instantly recognized the two men as Seth Michaels and Brad Hathaway, who were, respectively, the lead singer and the lead guitarist of *The Boozehounds*.

"Hey, guys," Chuck greeted, smiling in a way that only good cocaine could produce. "I heard you doing your sound check."

"Yeah," snorted Hathaway, not even bothering to hide his contempt. He was a greasy looking man flirting with morbid obesity. His large belly spilled out the bottom of his extra-large black T-shirt. His hair was tangled and matted and looked as if it hadn't been washed or combed in at least a month. "Over and fucking over again. Are we a little unsure of ourselves?"

"Hey, give 'em a break, Hath," Chuck said diplomatically. "It's their first gig. They were just trying to make sure everything's perfect."

"Perfect, huh?" said Michaels, who was a sharp contrast to his guitar player. Almost painfully skinny, his long, curly black hair appeared to have been painstakingly styled. He wore a tight, white, rhinestone studded shirt and leather pants. He looked at Darren, who was closest to him and who had the most intimidating physique. "It's like they think people actually give a shit what they sound like."

"C'mon, Mikey," Chuck said, shooting an apologetic look at Jake and Matt. "Don't come down on people for being over-careful with their sound check. Don't you remember your first gig?"

"Over-careful?" Michaels said with a chuckle. "This ain't Madison fucking Square Garden. It's a shitty little club in a shitty little city that's widely heralded as a hemorrhoid on the rectum of the world."

"That may be so," Matt said calmly. "But there's still gonna be an audience out there, ain't there? Shouldn't a group of musicians always strive to sound their very best whenever performing?"

Michaels looked at Matt now. "Performing," he snorted, rolling his eyes upward. "That's a fuckin' laugh. Nobody gives a rat's ass what you sound like. You're an opening band. Don't you know your job is just to kill the time until we come on? You don't think these people are here to see you, do you?"

Jake tensed up a little, preparing himself to grab Matt if he decided to choke the skinny little singer into oblivion. The only thing Matt liked more than his music was brawling. But Matt stayed mellow. "I'll give you that," he said quietly. "They're here to see you tonight. But that'll change, my mediocre friend. That'll change."

It took about fifteen seconds for Michaels to realize he had just been insulted. When it finally came home to him he turned red in the face. "Just finish your fucking set on time, hackers," he said, pointing a finger. "When you're done, you got fifteen minutes to clear your shit off the stage. Fifteen fuckin' minutes. Understand?"

"Perfectly," Matt told him. "Unless, of course, they ask for an encore. We can't really control that now, can we?"

Michaels, Hathaway, and Chuck all both broke out into laughter at this suggestion. It was clear they thought that Matt was joking, trying to mend the fence that had been so quickly erected between the two bands.

"Right," Michaels said, still chuckling. He actually clapped Matt on the shoulder. "If they do that we'll cut you a little slack, won't we, Hath?"

"Oh, you bet your ass," Hathaway said. "Do as many encores as you need."

"We'll do that," Matt told them with a smile.

The two *Boozehounds* members and the club owners then disappeared, heading in the direction of the bar, still chiding each other over the thought of their opening band getting an encore request.

Only Jake knew that Matt hadn't been joking.

*****

Ten minutes after the doors were opened, D Street West was about three quarters full of customers, most between the ages of nineteen and twenty-five, about an equal mix of males and females. Jake and Matt sat on either side of the back-stage door, looking out over the stage and the gathering crowd. Matt was smoking a cigarette and tapping the ashes into an empty soda can. Jake was fiddling with a guitar pick, dancing it back and forth across his knuckles, eyeing Matt's cigarette with envy. He desperately wanted a smoke to help calm his nerves, but he didn't want to risk drying out his throat before taking the microphone. Neither of the young men deluded themselves that the crowd was rushing in so early because they were the opening band. It was simply an accepted fact at D Street West that if you wanted to get a good seat to catch *The Boozehounds*, you had to show up at opening and stake your claim.

"You know what I'm looking forward to the most?" asked Matt. "Now that we're starting to get gigs, that is?"

"We have one gig only," Jake reminded him.

"We'll get more," Matt said confidently. "How many times I gotta tell you? We fuckin' rock, dude."

Jake nodded absently. While he agreed that they did indeed rock, his confidence level was never quite as high as Matt's. Just because one rocked did not automatically make one a sure success. Though he didn't put much stock in Coop's conspiracy theories, he instinctively knew it wasn't all that easy to make it in the music business, that the chips were stacked against them by default. He didn't want to have this argument now though. "What are you looking forward to?" he asked.

"Groupies," Matt said greedily. "How long do you think it takes until they start giving up the puss for us just because we're in a band? I could see it happening just after one set. How about you?"

Jake chuckled, shaking his head a little. "Not spreading your message to the masses, not fighting for social justice with your newly acquired voice, but groupies. That's why you want to be a rock star?"

"Social justice?" Matt scoffed. "Jesus, Jake. You fuckin' kill me with that shit. You're the one who writes songs about social justice and politics and love and respect. You ever hear me writing songs about that shit?"

Jake had to admit that Matt had a point there. They had both penned a roughly equal amount of the lyrics for their music but their styles were on quite opposite ends of the spectrum. While Jake enjoyed writing political and social lyrics—everything from songs about the proliferation of nuclear warheads to the angst one felt by growing up as a misfit—Matt favored hard-biting, almost angry lyrics about picking up women and using them for his own pleasure, partying until the sun came up, or taking advantage of society for one's own gain. When he did write songs about love, it was to put it in a negative context, such as his most poignant piece, *Who Needs Love?*, which was basically a rant about all the negative emotions a committed relationship would cause. "No," he said. "I guess I never have."

"Fuck no," Matt said. "Not that I don't respect your tunes, you understand? Your shit is just as good as my shit. It's good stoner rock, you know what I mean?"

"I know what you mean."

"So anyway, what do you think the odds are? One set and you get groupies? Some dingbat sluts that'll be so impressed with us they'll let us snort coke from between their ass cheeks?"

Jake laughed. It was hard not to when hearing how Matt described certain people, things, or sexual acts. "I suppose," he allowed, "that it's theoretically possible we might have an encounter with someone of the female persuasion who could technically qualify as a groupie, tonight. How's that for an answer?"

"It sounds like you been talkin' to Nerdly too much lately," Matt said, dropping his cigarette butt into the can. He immediately pulled out another one and sparked it up. "Next you'll be spouting off shit about how gravitational discrepancies prove the existence of Planet X."

"Hey now," Jake said in his oldest friend's defense, "I thought that was a pretty cool lecture. I mean, where else can you get that kind of entertainment when you're stoned?"

"On the fuckin' PBS channel," Matt said, though he was not serious. He enjoyed Bill's marijuana-fueled dissertations as much as anyone. "And speaking of stoned, my man came through for me this morning. I got an eighth of that bitchin' sensimilian for after the set tonight. The bong is already in my ride and ready for stoking."

Jake nodded happily. "Tell your man we'll save a groupie for him. I'll be ready for a nice bonghit after we get through this."

"That ain't no shit," Matt agreed, taking an especially deep drag off his smoke.

There was no discussion, or even thought of a discussion, about taking a few hits before the set. Though the members of Intemperance—in the tradition of musicians worldwide—enjoyed a variety of intoxicating substances with a regularity that bordered on addiction, Matt had long-since established and rigorously enforced a rule that they would neither rehearse nor perform under any condition but complete sobriety. In the early days of the band, before Jake and Bill had joined, when they were just a simple hard-rock garage band banging out simple covers of existing tunes, Matt had found that even a few beers, even a few bonghits of crappy homegrown weed, would seriously degenerate their performance. It was acceptable to write songs while stoned or drunk—in fact, that was the only way Matt could compose—and it was acceptable to jam a little after imbibing just for the sheer fun of it, but when they actually got together to rehearse, it was straight heads only. It was a rule that was certainly not going to be tampered with on their first gig.

They sat for a moment, watching the gathering crowd. Jake was finally able to take it no more and plucked the cigarette out of Matt's hand. He took a deep drag and blew it out slowly, feeling the soothing nicotine go rushing to his head. Matt frowned in disapproval but said nothing. He did take the smoke back, however, before the singer could steal another hit off it.

"Tell me the truth, Matt," Jake said, using his don't-fuck-around voice. "Are you nervous?"

"Me, nervous?" he asked.

"Yeah. You, nervous."

Matt didn't answer for a moment. Finally, he admitted, "I've never been so scared in my fucking life."

They both had a laugh at this. A little of the tension seemed to melt away with it. A little, but not much.

"Most of it is probably irrational fear," Matt said thoughtfully. "I'm worried that we're really not as bad-ass as I think we are, that the audience here is too immature for our sound, that this is all some kind of a practical joke that O'Donnell is pulling on us because we fucked with him to get the audition."

"Yeah," Jake said. "I got my share of that too."

"Some of it is real fear though. I worry about Darren sneaking off and doing a line or having a couple shots of booze because he's nervous. He's the kind that would do that. I worry that Nerdly didn't get the levels just right and we'll come across sounding like shit. My biggest fear, though, is about fucking up. I know we rehearsed the shit out of this set, but there's always the possibility that one of the five of us will choke now that the cock's in the pussy, you know what I mean?"

"Yeah," Jake agreed. "I know what you mean. I'm afraid my voice will crack, that I'll forget the words, that I'll drop my pick and not be able to use my finger, that I'll hit the wrong pedal at the wrong time or forget to hit it at the right time and have my guitar set for the wrong sound. Most of all, I wonder about whether I'm really cut out for this shit. Do people really want to hear me sing, man? Do they really?"

"Well, let me ask you something," Matt said. "Do you think Seth Michaels has a good voice?"

Jake shrugged. "It's not painful to listen to him. That's about the best you can say. His timbre is decent but he doesn't have much of a range."

Matt laughed. "Timbre and range," he said. "Do you think that skinny, pompous little fuck even knows what those words you used mean?"

"No. I'm thinking he probably doesn't."

"But you do," Matt said. "Not only do you know what they mean, but you make use of them. Your voice has been trained since you were what? Ten years old?"

"About that," Jake said. He had actually been nine when his parents, who had long since realized that their youngest child was a natural born vocalist, had sent him to the first of several voice teachers.

"Your voice is made for singing, dude. If I was a chick, I'd be spreading my legs the second I heard it. You can belt out these fuckin' tunes we do like nobody else could. My voice ain't bad—I think it's a shitload better than Michaels'—but I sound like a truck grinding its gears next to you. I realized the second you bellowed into our mic that first day that you were the singer for this group. The fuckin' second!"

"Yeah," Jake said, embarrassed. Matt was not typically the mushy complimentary type. "But..."

"No buts," he said. "You answered your own question. These people paid money to come in here and listen to Michaels sing. You're better than Michaels. No fuckin' question about it. So, don't you think they'd pay money to hear you?"

He took a drink of the ice water he'd helped himself to earlier. "Yeah," he said. "I guess maybe they would."

"And, of course," Matt added, "my guitar playing makes Hathaway's sound like some kid learning to play *Smoke on the Water* for the first time."

"Don't be modest now," Jake said. "Tell me what you really think."

"Fuck modesty. I've been playing guitar since I was twelve years old. I kick ass and I know it." He looked at Jake, his expression intent, not the least bit whimsical. "We got what it takes, Jake. We're gonna smoke those hackers right off their own stage. And it ain't gonna stop there. We're gonna put this shithole town on the map."

"It's already on the map," Jake replied, deadpan. "I've seen it there. In the Central Valley. Right between Redding and Sacramento."

"That may be so," Matt said. "But some day some enterprising motherfucker is gonna be bringing tourists by your old man's house to show them where the great Jake Kingsley grew up. Then they're gonna take 'em over to my old man's house and show them where the great Matt Tisdale grew up and the garage where we used to rehearse. Mark my fuckin' words, my man."

Jake thought this was funny, one of the funniest things he had heard all day. He would've been quite surprised to know that Matt was absolutely right.

*****

It was 6:50, ten minutes before they were to hit the stage, when Michelle Borrows, Jake's girlfriend, finally showed up. It was Matt who spotted her first, walking through the thickening crowd with two of her friends trailing unenthusiastically behind her. He, of course, pointed them out in his usual, elegant fashion.

"Hey," he said, nodding in the general direction of the three girls, "there's your bitch." He appraised her two friends with his usual eye. "Damn. Who are the sluts she's got with her? Very fuckable."

Jake had long since gotten over being offended by Matt's terms of endearment toward the female sex. He hardly noticed them anymore. "That would be Mindy and Rhonda," he replied. "Mindy's on the left. Rhonda's the one with the big tits."

"They the bitches that keep trying to tell her she's too good for you?"

"In the flesh," he said with a sigh, wondering why Michelle had brought them along. He had met Michelle the year before in a Sociology class they both shared at Heritage Community College. Two months ago, at the beginning of the new semester, he had asked her out for the first time, expecting to be shot down. She was a very classy looking young woman, clean-cut, well dressed, and good looking; someone he figured was far out of his league. She carried herself with an air of elitism he had become familiar with in high school. Why would such a beautiful creature want to go out with a longhaired, scruffy looking musician who had not even declared a major yet? It was only the prodding by Matt, who had tired of listening to him pine about her, that finally forced his hand. Matt told him he didn't have a hair on his ass if he didn't ask her out. So, just to prove his ass was as hairy as anyone else's, he did it. To his surprise, she said yes.

It was during this date that he discovered she had grown up in a sheltered and ultra-religious household. Her father was a teacher at Holy Assumption Parochial School in downtown Heritage—an all-girls Catholic school. Michelle had attended Holy Assumption from 9th grade until graduation.

Before that, she had attended Saint Mary's School for Girls from Kindergarten to eighth grade. She had no brothers, just three younger sisters. She had never learned to socialize with boys except for brief encounters at heavily chaperoned coed dances and dates arranged by her parents with boys as socially inept as she was. Jake had been the first boy to ever ask her out.

By being the first to ask, he had scored the first date by default. But at the end of the evening, when he asked her out for a second date, she had agreed to that as well. Since then, they went out at least once a week, sometimes two or three times, depending on his schedule, which, between working at the local newspaper driving a truck, or attending classes, or practicing with the band, was often a little tight. She seemed to genuinely enjoy his company, of that he had no doubt, but he was not so stupid as to think that was the only reason she was going out with him. Her teenage rebellion, which had been staunchly and thoroughly suppressed during her high school years, was now making itself known with a vengeance. Her parents absolutely hated Jake, hated everything he stood for and represented. Jake was the epitome of everything they had always tried to keep her away from when they kept her out of the public school system. He had long hair, he played guitar, he sang that evil rock and roll music, he had no goals in life other than some misguided dream of being a professional musician, and his upbringing... Good Lord, their precious daughter was going out with a kid who had never attended a church in his life! He was the son of a man who had protested against the war in Vietnam and who had marched for civil rights, who, worst of all, worked as a lawyer for the hated American Civil Liberties Union, the group that had helped remove prayer from public schools, that had helped legalize abortion! All of these tidbits about Jake's life and his father's past and present activities were gleefully passed onto Michelle's parents by Michelle herself on a weekly basis, for no reason other than to get a rise out of them. She reveled in the newfound freedom she had to tell them "no" when they demanded she stop seeing him, to shrug her shoulders in disregard when they threatened to cut off her school fund or to take her car away from her.

"I told them if they do that," she had said to Jake on one occasion, "that I'll just have to move out and get a job as a waitress or something to put myself through school. Maybe at one of those places where they make you wear short skirts."

Though Jake still wasn't sure whether he was all that keen on being a rebellion symbol so Michelle could get back at her parents, he had to admit that he'd laughed his ass off when she'd shared that with him. Especially when she described how red her father's face had become, how he hadn't been able to speak for the better part of five minutes, how her mother had dropped to her knees and begun praying right there in the middle of the living room.

Still, their relationship wasn't only about delayed rebellion and pissing off conservative Christian parents. If that were the case one or both of them would have undoubtedly made the decision to move on by now. That had only been what got them together. They stayed together because they genuinely enjoyed each other's company in a variety of ways. For Jake, he enjoyed rubbing away her naiveté, exposing her to things she had been denied while growing up. She got drunk for the first time with Jake. It was he who introduced her to the pleasures of smoking marijuana. He introduced her to rock and roll music—real rock and roll music instead of the filtered, popular crap she'd been fed in her school and in her home. And, of course, he introduced her to the pleasures of the flesh—or at least as much of it as she would allow him to share with her. He was not the first boy to French kiss her, but he was the first to put his hand on her bare breast, to slide his fingers up beneath her prim and proper skirt and play with her wet vaginal lips under her panties. His penis was the first she had touched, the first she had really even seen in the flesh. He had taught her how to give a proper hand-job without spilling a drop of the offering on the couch or the car seat or the movie theater seat. So far that was as far as her prudish upbringing would allow, but she had hinted on several occasions that it wouldn't exactly be a mortal sin for her to go all the way with him as long as she was truly repentant afterward.

"So," Matt asked as the trio worked their way a little closer to the stage, Michelle's eyes peering towards the darkness, searching for him, "you tapped into that shit yet, or what?"

"I'm getting there," Jake replied, standing up and brushing the dust off his jeans. "It'll be any night now."

This produced an immediate look of boredom on Matt's face. In his view of the world there was no such thing as a woman worth waiting more than two dates for sexual congress. And even that was stretching it. "Well, you go talk to your little virgin. I'll stay here and scope out the future groupies."

"Right," Jake said. He walked out of the alcove they were in and onto the side of the stage. Michelle spotted him immediately and began working her way forward. Her two friends followed listlessly behind her.

"Hi, sweetie," she said cheerfully when they met near the front of the stage. "How's everything going?"

"Good," he said, sliding down so he was sitting on the edge of the stage. He gave her a brief kiss on the lips. "Thanks for coming to see us tonight."

"I wouldn't miss it for the world," she told him. "It's so exciting. Your first concert. I know you're going to be just awesome. Besides, it pissed Daddy off something fierce when I told him we were coming here." She giggled a little in her ain't-I-being-the-rebel manner. "He called this place the Devil's seduction pit."

Jake chuckled, thinking that would actually make a cool name for a club. It certainly had a better ring to it than D Street West. He looked at Michelle's companions, who were both chewing wads of bubble gum and sniffing dramatically at the cigarette smoke in the room. "Rhonda, Mindy," he said politely, nodding at each of them. "Nice to see you both again."

They looked at him with identical expressions of contemptuous disgust, as if he were a cockroach on a shower floor. "What are friends for?" Rhonda asked with a roll of her eyes.

"Yeah," Mindy put in. "Someone has to keep Michelle from getting raped and murdered in this... this place."

"Oh, Mindy," Michelle scoffed. "It's just a different crowd than we usually run with. Jake has taken me here six or seven times and we've never had a problem."

"That's because he's one of..." she started, then seemed to realize she was about to go over the edge of propriety. "I mean, they know him here. We're here alone now."

"Yeah," Rhonda agreed. "What if one of these... guys tries picking us up?"

"Then you might actually have a good time," Jake suggested, making the two girls gasp and making Michelle giggle again.

"I don't think that's very funny," Mindy said.

"Look," Jake told them. "Why don't you just try to have fun? This is a bitchin' place. Have a few drinks. Loosen up."

"We're not twenty-one yet," Rhonda said, giving another eye roll.

"They don't give a rat's ass about that here," Jake told her. "If you got the green, they'll sell you the booze."

This perked their interest. "Really?" Mindy asked carefully, as if he were setting her up for a practical joke.

He turned to Michelle. "Am I lying?"

She shook her head. "We've never been carded here," she told her friends. "Not even once."

Understanding seemed to dawn on their faces. Jake could almost read the thoughts going on in their pretty little heads. Here, at last, was a possible explanation for why their friend was hanging out with a longhaired loser. He knew how to get drinks.

"Well, maybe we'll have just a couple," Rhonda said.

"Yeah, since we have to be here anyway," Mindy agreed graciously.

"That's the way to party," Jake said, his sarcastic tone quite over their heads.

"Buy us the first round, Shelly," Rhonda said. "So we can see how you do it."

"Yeah," Mindy said. "Let's go get some."

"I want a Tom Collins," Rhonda said excitedly. "I heard those are bitchin'."

"My sister made those for me once," Mindy squealed. "Oh my Gawd! They are like, so good!"

The two reluctant attendees continued to talk excitedly about what kind of drinks they were going to have, what kind of drinks they had had in the past, and in what order they were going to consume them tonight.

"I think you've finally impressed them," Michelle whispered with a smile.

"Yes," Jake said. "I seem to have a way of getting to you religious girls, don't I?"

This produced yet another giggle. "They don't know the half of it," she said, reaching out and stroking his hand.

"Should I show them?"

She laughed. "You're naughty."

"That's what they say."

She was about to say something else but Rhonda grabbed her by the arm. "Come on," she said. "Let's go get those drinks now."

"Yeah," Mindy said. "I'm really thirsty."

"Your entourage awaits," Jake said. "Do you need any money?"

He was just being polite and she knew it. Money was one thing Michelle never seemed to be lacking. "I can swing it," she said. She leaned forward and gave him another kiss, a long one this time, the tip of her tongue just reaching out to touch his. "I can't wait to see you play," she told him. "You've been working so hard for this."

"I'm glad you're here to see me," he replied.

They kissed one more time and then parted, Michelle heading through the crowd towards the bar. Jake watched her until she disappeared and then mounted the stage again. It was almost time to go on.

*****

The final minutes ticked by with agonizing slowness. By 6:55 all five band members were standing in the alcove, looking out at the audience they were to perform for. Matt, Coop, and Darren were all chain smoking to calm their nerves. Bill, who didn't smoke, chewed his fingernails. Jake sipped from his ice water and wished he could smoke. He still could not believe he was about to walk out on a stage, pick up his guitar, and sing for a group of people, that he and his comrades were going to be the center of attention, the entertainment for the first part of the evening. Jesus Christ, he thought, his hands shaking a little with stage fright. What in the hell am I doing here? I can't do this!

His anxiety was not really surprising. Jake had always been on the shy side. The second of two children, his older sister Pauline had always been the attractive one, the smart one, the one with the straight A's and all the friends. Though he had no doubt his parents loved him equally, Pauline had always been a tough act to follow. It was she who had competed in and won the Heritage County spelling bee in 1964, the year before Jake had even started kindergarten. It was Pauline who had won the school's speech contest in the sixth grade with her controversial discourse about how prayer really didn't belong in public schools. She shot through junior high and high school, her GPA never once dipping below 4.0, and graduated at the age of 17 in 1972. From there she had gone on to UCLA on a full academic scholarship where she had maintained a 3.9 GPA while taking twenty-one units a semester. In 1975, a full year before the rest of her class, she was awarded a bachelor's degree in Business. From there she applied for and was immediately accepted to Stanford University's School of Law where she focused heavily on corporate law. Now, at the ripe old age of twenty-five, she was a junior associate for one of the most prestigious law firms in the greater Heritage metropolitan area.

Jake, by contrast, had always been what was known as an underachiever. He was intelligent, with a tested IQ well above what was considered average, but his grades from junior high school on had been mostly C's and D's, with the occasional F thrown in when a subject was particularly boring to him. It wasn't that he couldn't do the work or that he didn't understand it, it was that the work was not stimulating enough to him, that he just didn't care very much about it. He had never been interested in playing sports, never interested in mathematics or any of the sciences. He entered no spelling bees, no speech contests, never ran for student council. The only school subjects he did enjoy were history, literature, and anything that even remotely applied to music or the arts. In these subjects he carried consistent A's and in fact often spent extra time doing research and reading on his own. By the age of fifteen he had developed strong, if occasionally naïve political opinions, most of them considerably left leaning. As he grew older these opinions strengthened and became more mature, more focused. Long before receiving his high school diploma he had grasped the fundamental unfairness of life, how things were tilted in favor of the rich, the whites, the males, how the catalyst and explanation for any act of any group could usually be found by examining who had what to gain from it.

This un-childlike depth of thinking was one thing that kept him isolated from his peers. Another was the substandard physical characteristics his genetic code had forced upon him during his formative years. He had been shorter than average until junior high school when a growth spurt began and quickly shot him up to his adult height of six feet, two inches by his sophomore year of high school. Unfortunately, his weight had lagged somewhat behind, leaving him skinny and almost gangly until well into his senior year, at which point he began to fill out a little bit. The school jocks—always the elite trendsetters in a high school society—assigned him the charming nickname of "Bone Rack" sometime during his freshman year. It wasn't long before the cheerleading clique and then the rest of the school picked up on this moniker as well and called him by it until virtually no one knew what his real name was. That was when they talked to him at all. Mostly he was simply ignored, the kind of kid who faded from memory the moment he passed out of view.

It was the stoner clique that accepted him as a member during his sophomore and junior years. The stoners didn't care what you looked like, as long as you liked to get stoned and would occasionally spring for a dimebag or an eighth and share it with the crowd. Jake, who discovered the joys of marijuana intoxication at age thirteen by breaking into his father's stash, embraced the stoner lifestyle with gratitude. Here he found something approximating friendship and kinship. But unlike the majority of the stoners, he seemed to have an instinctive grasp of where the edge was in the lifestyle and how to avoid going over it. He would cut school, but never enough to actually get into trouble or fail a class. He would smoke weed with them, drink beer with them, and occasionally do a little cocaine, but stayed away from those who enjoyed the harder drugs like PCP, acid, and the various forms of speed.

Even among the stoners, however, he didn't quite fit in, not completely. His deep thinking amused them at times but quickly gained him a reputation as being a little on the strange side and overly pompous with his knowledge. He did not repulse the stoner girls—many of whom were the biggest sluts in the school—but neither were they endeared to him either. He was just "Bone Rack" to them, a nice kid who didn't talk much when he was straight and who talked about weird, political shit they didn't understand when he was stoned or drunk. He wasn't a fighter or a comedian or a particularly prolific supplier of smoke. Nothing about him bespoke any type of sex appeal or mystery. At least not until the day of the kegger at Salinas Bend. That was a day that forever changed Jake's outlook on life. It was the day he was shown the power of music, the power of entertaining.

*****

It was not unreasonable for Tom and Mary Kingsley to expect that their two children would be musically inclined to some degree. It was a simple matter of genetics. Mary had a beautiful singing voice and had performed in church choirs during her childhood. She played several instruments, including the piano, the saxophone, and the flute, but her love had always been the violin. She could make a violin cry or sing or lull or hypnotize or do all at the same time. Her skill and mastery of the instrument had secured her a position with the Heritage Philharmonic Orchestra at the age of nineteen, a position she still held on the day her son sat nervously backstage at D Street West (It was also where she met her best friend, Lorraine Archer, Bill's piano playing mother). Tom had grown up with musical interest as well. He had a decent singing voice and played a mean blues guitar. He had even tried to make it as a rock and roll star before deciding to change his focus and settle on a career fighting injustice as an ACLU lawyer.

With Pauline, their firstborn, it could not be said that they were disappointed in her musical abilities. She took to her piano and violin lessons with the same determination she took to everything else and by the age of twelve or so she could produce palatable music with them. Her voice was pretty as well, the sort of voice that sounded good singing along with the radio or belting out a spontaneous tune in the shower. Pretty enough to listen to, to enjoy, but nothing exceptional. Music was something Pauline would always have a love for but that she would never have the drive to produce.

With Jake, however, the combination of musical genes passed down by his parents combined in a way that was staggering, almost scary at times. Even before he learned to talk, Jake learned to sing. As a baby boy crawling around the floor in diapers, still drawing milk from his mother's breast, he would stop whatever he was doing when he heard music on the radio, when he heard a voice engaged in song, and he would try to imitate it. Though no words would form, he would imitate the syllables, the changes in tone and pitch. He would hum to himself in his crib, babbling out snatches of song he had heard and memorized. As he grew older, his love of singing, of music intensified. By the time he was four, he was playing around with his mother's violin and piano, his father's harmonica and acoustic guitar, learning the rudimentary skills needed to make the sounds he desired with them. He parents encouraged his musical development as best they could. They taught him about scale and harmony and melody. As he learned to read the written word from his early grammar school teachers, he learned to read music from his mother and father.

By the age of ten he was able to play every instrument in the house to some degree but it was the battered old acoustic guitar his father strummed when he wanted to relax or when he was drunk (or, after he and his mother had disappeared into the bedroom for a bit and that funny, herbal smell came drifting out with them) that Jake was most taken with. He would pick at it for hours, imitating songs he heard on the radio, on his parents' record albums and then, by about his fourteenth year, he started making up his own melodies and then penning simple lyrics to go with them.

Jake was never given anything that could be termed "formal" musical training. His parents took care of that on their own. With his voice, however, they recognized early on that he had a gift of song, a gift that cried out for professional honing. He began to see voice teachers at the age of nine. He always thought the singing exercises great fun, taking to them like a duck to water. It was feared that his natural talent for vocalization would diminish or even disappear with the onset of puberty and the changing of his voice. Quite the opposite is what actually happened. As his speaking voice deepened his singing voice grew richer and developed considerable range. It was truly a joy to hear Jake sing a song, any song, and around the house he did so often, but his shyness kept him from sharing his gift with many. He would play his guitar and sing for his parents, his sister, his voice teachers, but he would clam up and refuse during family gatherings when his proud parents would try to cajole him into an impromptu performance. He never joined the band in school though he easily would have been the star player. He never joined a choir or entered a competition of any kind. Nobody outside his family had any idea that young Jake Kingsley was a bourgeoning musical genius.

Until that night at Salinas Bend.

Salinas Bend, in the 1970's, was a 200-acre Heritage city park located in the relatively rural southern section of the city. Situated along the Sacramento River, which formed Heritage's western boundary, its primary purpose was a boat launching facility and family picnic area. That was during the day. During the weekend night hours it served as a favored location for students from three local high schools to hold their keg parties. Hundreds of teenagers between the ages of fifteen and nineteen would descend upon the park after 10:00 PM, parking their cars in the boat trailer lot and setting up kegs that the more business oriented among them would purchase and then charge two dollars per person for an unlimited refill policy, at least until the keg ran out, which typically gave each purchaser an average of eight to ten plastic cups full of cheap beer per keg. Since the site was so isolated from the rest of the city—it was surrounded by dozens of square miles of farmland upon which onions and tomatoes were grown—the partygoers could be as loud and obnoxious as they liked with little risk of the Heritage Police making an appearance. The Heritage PD did, of course, occasionally show up to break things up, but this was more for form's sake than anything else. They actually liked having the majority of the south area's teens gathering in one, known spot in the middle of nowhere instead of breaking up into a dozen or more parties in more populated areas.

As a member of the stoner clique Jake was a regular attendee of the Salinas Bend keggers during his junior year. Typically, he just kind of hung out, sticking close to a few friends, watching the antics of others while he smoked a little weed and got pleasantly buzzed on beer. He was the quiet one, saying little unless he had something important to say, which wasn't often. He had long since learned that his peers were not terribly interested in politics.

On the night in question, Jake was a senior in high school, just turned eighteen years old, and still a virgin. He had made out with a few girls before, had even done some light petting, but such encounters were very few and very far between. Since getting his driver's license nine months before he had been borrowing his parents' 1972 Buick station wagon to get him to the weekly parties on the theory that having his own transportation would improve his success rate with the opposite sex. It was a sound theory that might have held water—even with the wood panel siding on the wagon—if not for the fact that Jake was so painfully shy around girls he rarely got one alone long enough to sustain a conversation. And so, on this evening, like so many others, he was just standing around in a group that consisted mostly of males, sipping beer and maintaining a stronger than average buzz, waiting for some kind soul to pass a joint in his direction, saying little, mostly just watching and dreaming.

And then he heard it. The sound of an acoustic guitar being strummed. His ears perked up and sought out the source of the sound. It was coming from the midst of a group of about twenty people on the other side of the parking lot. A bonfire had been built out of broken up pallets and was blazing away. A male figure was the center of this group's attention. He was sitting on the top of a picnic table holding a guitar, strumming open chords on it. Even over the babble of conversations and the sound of multiple car stereos belting out conflicting tunes, Jake could hear that the guitar was out of tune. He headed in that direction, no one in the group he had been with even noticing his departure.

He knew most of the people gathered around the picnic table. They were a mix of juniors and seniors from his school, about half girls and half guys. In the stoner clique, as with any clique, there are cliques within the clique. This group was the elite among the stoners, the hard-core and coolest, the rulers of the clique as far as such a thing existed. The guitar player was Eric Castro, one of the premier members of the ruling clique, one of the hardest of the hard-core. Castro fancied himself a musician because he owned a guitar and had learned to play a few chords. He and a few of the others in this group were always talking about how they were going to get a band together. The guitar he was playing was little more than a toy, a knock-off of a knock-off of a Fender Grand Concert. The strings were of the cheapest quality commercially available. The finish was scuffed and scratched. Jake thought that if he had paid more than $15 for it, he had been ripped off.

And yet, despite the out-of-tune sound, despite the toy-like quality of the instrument, everyone in the group was staring at Castro with rapt attention as he finished strumming the open chords and started to play the opening of *Simple Man* by Lynard Skynard. His playing was only barely palatable. His fingers moved clumsily over the strings as he picked out the first few bars over and over again, never launching into the heart of the song.

"That's, like... so cool," crooned Mandy Walker, a chubby, jiggly stoner girl sitting next to him.

"Yeah," agreed Cindy Stinson, a skinnier, younger girl who sat on the other side. "My brother can play, but nowhere near as good as you."

Castro shrugged modestly, obviously proud of his alleged skill. "It takes lots of practice and dedication," he said solemnly, having to stop playing while he talked since he could no longer look at his fingers. "I picked this acoustic up just to play around with at the park. You should hear me on my electric."

"I bet it's awesome," Mandy said. "You'll have to play for me sometime."

"One of these days," Castro said, inflecting just the right tone of non-committal. He began to pick at the strings again, playing the opening to *Love Hurts* by *Nazareth* this time. He made fewer mistakes on this riff but played a lot less of the song before starting over.

The Castro concert went on for almost fifteen minutes, which was the amount of time it took for him to go through his entire catalog of acoustic jams he'd been taught or had managed to pick up by looking at tablature charts. Jake watched in fascination the entire time, not at Castro himself since he was not good enough to even qualify as a hacker, but at the group of people watching him. They had abandoned the recorded and broadcast music to watch him play a few simple chords. They were not talking to each other or joking or engaging in the age-old game of flirtation, they were watching, enjoying. He was making something that approximated music and they were listening to it. There was a magic at work here. He could see that as plain as he could see the alluring bounce of Mandy's breasts beneath her halter. If Castro could produce magic by mangling a few popular songs, what would Jake be able to do? Even with the low self-esteem he had for his music producing abilities, he knew without a doubt that he was exponentially better than Castro. What would these people do if he were the one playing for them? No matter how his mind tried to degenerate this thought, to whisper that they would laugh at him and ridicule him, that they would take the guitar from his hands and throw him in the river just to see the splash, he knew it wasn't true. It couldn't be true.

"I need a hit," Castro announced, setting down the guitar behind him. "Who's got some fuckin' weed?"

While several people scrambled to pull out a joint to share with the rock god in their midst, Jake began to walk forward. Later he would tell himself that it was the alcohol coursing through his veins that made him do something so wildly out of character. And perhaps that had a little to do with it. But it was unquestionably more than just liquid courage. Jake *wanted* to play for these people, *wanted* to see the adoration in their eyes directed at him.

"Wassup, dude?" Castro greeted Jake as he saw him standing before him, giving the standard head nod one gives a lesser whose name one can't remember.

"Nice guitar," Jake told him. "Do you mind if I... you know... check it out?"

"Do you play?"

Jake shrugged shyly. "A little bit," he said.

Castro smirked. "No shit?" he said. He picked up the guitar and handed it to Jake. "Here you go. Let's hear what you got." The expression on his face implied that this was going to be amusing.

Jake took it, hefting it a few times, getting the feel of it. It really was a cheap piece of shit, hardly worthy of being called a musical instrument, but it was magic in the making all the same. He stepped a few feet to the right and sat down on the other side of Mandy, who was ignoring him as she usually did. He ran his finger across the strings, producing a strum.

"Oooh yeah, baby," Castro said with a laugh. "You fuckin' rock, man."

"Fuck yeah," some other wise-ass put in. "Jimmy Page, eat your fuckin' heart out."

This produced a round of laughter from the crowd, a brief and mildly contemptuous round. Jake ignored it and strummed the E string a few times, listening to the tone. He reached up and adjusted the tuning knob half a turn.

"Hey, what the fuck you doing?" Castro said. "I just tuned that thing."

"It must've come out of tune when you were playing it," Jake told him. "I'm just getting it back."

"It sounds okay to me."

"Well, it's hard to tell without a tuning fork and all this noise out here. I'll have it close in a minute."

"Now hold on a minute..." Castro started.

The pivotal moment in Jake's life might have ended right there. Castro didn't want a little dweeb messing with his guitar and was about to snatch it back. Jake would not have fought him for it. If it were taken from his hands he would simply go back to his original group and go on with his evening. But then Doug Biel, a fringe member of the ruling stoner clique vying for full membership, stepped forward with a hand carved marijuana pipe and a butane lighter. "Here, Castro," he said. "Hit some of this. My brother picked it up in Hawaii. Best shit you'll ever smoke."

"Maui Wowie?" Castro said, immediately losing interest in Jake and the guitar.

"Bet your ass," Doug assured him. "This shit goes for twenty-five an eighth."

"I haven't smoked any Maui Wowie in a couple of months."

"Well fire it up, brother. Fire it up."

Castro took the pipe and the lighter from his hands and took a tremendous hit. He then passed the pipe to Mandy, who sucked up a hit almost as big. She passed the pipe over the top of Jake, to John Standman, who was sitting on the other side of him.

Jake didn't mind. He continued to tune the guitar, striking each string a few times and then adjusting the knob, working entirely by ear. By the time the pipe was sucked dry and passed back to Doug, he had it about as tuned as the cheap, saggy strings would allow. He strummed a few open chords and then grabbed a G chord and began to play.

He picked out a simple medley at first, a slow simple piece of his own composition. His left hand moved slowly and surely over the unfamiliar frets, his calloused fingertips grabbing and pressing with exact pressure, drawing sweet vibration from the strings as the fingers of his right hand picked at them.

The conversation around him stopped. The re-stuffing of the marijuana pipe stopped as well. Eyes turned to him in surprise and wonder.

"Wow," Mandy said, looking at him and acknowledging his existence for perhaps the first time ever. "That's pretty good."

"Thanks," Jake said, giving a slight smile. "I use this as a warm-up exercise when I play."

"What is that?" asked Castro, his mouth open wide, his expression that of a man who has just seen his pet dog start to talk to him. "Is that *Kansas*?"

"No," Jake said. "It's nothing. Just a warm-up to get the fingers limber."

Castro seemed to have a hard time with this concept. It was nothing? How was that possible? The only thing that could come out of a guitar had to be either random noise or something that one heard on the radio, right?

Jake began to play faster and with more complexity, his left hand making chord changes, his right strumming harder. As always happened when he played, his digits seemed to act independently, without conscious thought, transforming the notes and rhythm in his head instantaneously into music emitting from the guitar.

"Wow," he heard Mandy whisper beside her, something like respect in her tone now. She turned her body so she could see him better.

He picked up the tempo a little more, his fingers hitting the strings harder, changing chords faster as his confidence increased. He looked at Castro and was gratified to see his mouth still hanging open. Nor was his the only one.

He did a brief solo of sorts, picking out a glowing trip up and down the neck and then settling back down into a strummed melody—an instrumental version of one of the songs he had written. He gradually worked that into an improvised riff that he played around with for a minute or two before working that into the opening bars of *All Along the Watchtower*.

"Yeah!" someone yelled out from the crowd.

"Play it, man!" someone else yelled.

Jake played it, his hands belting out the rhythm to one of his favorite songs like they had so many times before in the privacy of his bedroom. Later, he would not remember making a conscious decision to start singing. If told earlier in the day that he would break into song before a group of twenty people from school (a group that was growing bigger by the second as people from other groups heard the music and drifted over to see who was making it) he would have judged the teller a liar or insane or both. Singing was a secret thing he did, like masturbation, a private thing, like taking a shower. But when the opening bar of the song worked its way around again on the guitar, his mouth opened and he heard himself belting out about how there had to some method of getting out of there, said the man who joked to the man who stole.

His voice was as clear and crisp as it always had been, this despite the cigarettes and the beer he had imbibed in tonight. He wielded it perfectly, instinctively, utilizing all the lessons he had learned over the years and coupling it with his own natural ability. His audience did not make fun of him as he always feared they would. They did not laugh at him. They did not mock him in any way, not even those, like Castro, like John Standman, who were known for such behavior. They watched him, their eyes aglow, their mouths open as he made music for them and before he got to the second verse, many of them were tapping their feet to the rhythm, were nodding their heads towards each other in confused respect.

He sang out the verses and strummed along, mixing his voice and the guitar nicely, never missing a chord, never forgetting a word, never having to look at his fingers to find the right fret. When the last verse was complete he ground out an acoustic guitar solo, his left hand once more moving with blurring speed up and down the neck, his right hand finger-picking out each note. After about thirty seconds of this he began to strum again, a slower, heavier version of the opening bars before finally working up a fancy flourish of strings to bring the song to a conclusion.

And then it was over and silence descended. But only for a second.

They did not applaud him, but only because that was simply not done in such an informal setting. Instead he was greeted with a chorus of appreciative phrases. "Yeah!" the most common, followed closely by "bitchin'!", "nice!", and, that perennial favorite "fuck yeah!" He was clapped on the back by several people, asked where he had learned to do that by several others, told he was fuckin' radical by others yet. Mandy's reaction to him was quite gratifying as well. She leaned into him, her large breasts pushing into his upper arm, her Maui Wowie scented breath blowing softly in his ear.

"That was tight," she told him. "Really fuckin' tight."

This time it really was the beer that made him speak wildly out of character. "Just the way I like it," he told her. He started to blush automatically, started to berate himself for saying something so stupid, was preparing, in fact, to apologize to her out of simple instinct. And then he looked in her eyes. They were shining at him and it was she who was blushing.

"Do something else!" someone shouted out, demanded of him.

"Yeah," other voices chimed in. "Let's hear some more."

A chorus of agreements followed, followed by a few shouted requests. "Zepplin!" was of course the most frequently heard. "Do some fuckin' Zepplin, man!"

Led Zepplin, to the teenage stoner crowd of 1976, was revered about as much as Jesus Christ and the Virgin Mary were in the Vatican. Jake was no exception to this worshipfulness. While he didn't know how to play every song they had released, and some of them didn't translate very well to an unaccompanied acoustic guitar, he certainly had a vast and well-practiced regiment of their work in his head. So, brimming with the excitement of discovery, basking in the glow of something very like group adoration for the first time in his life, he gave the people what they wanted. His fingers began to move again, strumming up the opening chords of *Rock and Roll*.

He played it as effortlessly and as smoothly as he'd done *Watchtower* before, his voice ringing out in perfect harmony with the guitar chords. People were now swaying back and forth as they watched, some mouthing the words along with him. Mandy had now turned completely toward him, her knee touching his lower thigh, her boobs bouncing up and down alluringly as she moved to the rhythm. He cast appreciative glances at this sight as he played, noticing with black excitement that the friction of her movements (or perhaps something else?) had made her nipples erect beneath her shirt. She saw him looking at her but did not turn away in disgust as she probably would have only ten minutes before. Instead she smiled back at him, her eyes unabashedly looking him over and seeming to like what they were seeing.

Yes, he thought as he poured out the second chorus and prepared to launch into another solo, *I think maybe I like this. I think maybe I like it a lot.*

By the time he finished *Rock and Roll*, the crowd around him had grown to well over fifty people, with more still streaming in his direction. Nearby car stereos had been shut off so he could be heard better. The cries for more, more, more, continued, as did the shouted requests for particular bands. He played some *Foghat* next, churning out *Fool For The City* and *Slow Ride*. He then mellowed a little, showing off his fingerpicking skills by doing a rendition of *Dust in the Wind*. Some of the guys groaned a little at the slow tune but the effect on the girls was something he immediately catalogued and vowed to repeat as often as possible. They all but swooned over him as he used his voice to its best advantage. Remembering something his father had told him once during a lesson, a hint about performance technique, he made a point to look at his audience as he sang, making eye contact with several different girls, as if he were singing to them personally. Some blushed and looked away. Some smiled back at him. A few chewed their lips nervously as they held his gaze. None seemed to mind his eyes upon them, particularly not Mandy, whose gaze grew dreamy as they stared at each other all through the second chorus.

In all, he did twelve songs, going heavy on the *Led Zepplin* and Jimmy Hendrix. He did one more slow song—*Yesterday*, by *The Beatles*—near the end and then closed the set with the hard driving *Tush* by ZZ Top. His audience, which now included almost everyone present at Salinas Bend on that night, continued to shout out requests at him but he wisely elected to adhere to one of the golden rules of performing: Always leave your audience wanting more.

"I gotta take a break for now," he said, putting a pained expression on his face. "My hands are getting sore and my voice is getting kind of scratchy." This was not the least bit true. He often played and sang for two or more hours in his room and usually quit because of boredom instead of finger or voice fatigue, but it was a lie they bought and when he handed the cheap guitar back to Castro he took it from him without further protest.

"Dude," Castro said, looking at Jake as if he might be hot. "That was fuckin' cool. I didn't know you could play."

Jake shrugged, reverting back to his shy persona now that the performance was over. "I just mess around with it a little. Thanks for letting me borrow your guitar."

"Mess around a little? Shit. I mean I'm pretty good and all, but you're even better than I am." Castro said this as if this admission pained him greatly. "You play electric too?"

"A little bit," Jake said, not mentioning that he owned two electric guitars—cheap Les Paul knock-offs at this point in his life—in addition to having access to the four his father owned.

"We'll have to get together and jam sometime, you know what I mean? You ever think of joining a band?"

"Well..."

"Hey, dicknose!" Castro shouted to Doug before Jake could answer. "Where's that fuckin' pipe? Give my man here a goddamn hit!"

Jake was given not just one hit of the potent Hawaiian bud, he was given three and he was soon in the stratosphere. Someone else handed him a fresh cup of beer. The radios came back on and the majority of the crowd drifted away, but Castro and his immediate circle continued to talk to Jake, telling him about this concert they'd been to, that song they knew how to play, how famous their band was going to be once they got it together. Jake nodded and responded in all the right places but barely heard a word said to him. His attention was instead on Mandy, who had scooted even closer and was now almost snuggled up against him, her breasts making frequent and seemingly accidental contact with his arm.

Eventually the conversation shifted away from guitars and music and onto other things like cars and movies and drugs. The focus shifted off Jake as well, as Castro and the other ruling members fell back into their more natural patterns. It was then that Mandy tugged his arm.

"Let's go fill our cups up again before the keg runs out," she said.

"Uh... sure," he replied, standing up.

They walked over to the keg, taking up position at the end of a line of about thirty people. As they moved slowly forward towards the tap, Mandy held onto his arm possessively, cuddling close to him. She was not able stake her claim on his conversation as easily as she staked it on his person. All those around him in the line commented on his performance, asking the same questions he'd been asked back in the group, making the same observations. Two more people asked him if he would consider joining their band when they put one together. He answered politely and monosyllabically, more than a little overwhelmed with this sudden attention.

Finally, they reached the head of the line, where the keg was stored in a park services garbage can filled with half-melted ice. Jake primed the keg with the hand pump on the tap. He filled Mandy's cup and then his own.

"You wanna take a walk with me?" she asked as he handed her drink to her.

He swallowed a little nervously. "Sure," he replied, nodding a little too forcefully. "That's a good idea."

She led him away from the parking lots, toward the river. As they walked, Jake's mind reviewed what he knew about this girl he was going off alone with. She, like he, had just turned eighteen (although, since she'd been held back a grade in ninth, was only a junior) and, though not the best looking of the stoner girls, was one of the favorites among the guys, which accounted for her membership in the ruling clique. It was said that she loved making out, loved having her tits played with and would do both of these activities quite freely with anyone who could get her alone. Getting to third base was reputed to be a little more difficult but certainly within the realm of possibility if one did a decent job working his way to second base. Only a select few had actually fucked her. No one had ever claimed he'd scored a blowjob from her, although there were occasional, unconfirmed reports of hand-jobs. Jake wondered what he was in store for. Would he even get to first base? Sure, the power of music on her attitude had been quite magic, almost supernatural even, but he wasn't playing music any more. Would the spell last? Or would she suddenly remember that she was with a virtual nobody and storm off? He wasn't sure. This was well beyond his minimal experience. The other girls he'd made out with had been those as shy as or even shier then himself.

The boat launch area was one of the darker parts of the park. It consisted of a sloping concrete ramp and a fifty-foot dock that protruded out into the river. There were no streetlights here because the facility was not intended to be used at night. They walked out onto the dock and sat down at the end of it, both of them taking off their shoes and socks and rolling up their pant legs so their feet could dangle in the semi-warm water. The sound of crickets chirping easily overrode the sound of revelry coming from the parking lot.

"Nice and peaceful out here, isn't it?" Mandy asked as she snuggled up next to him, her warm, soft body pressing into his.

"Yeah," Jake said nervously, taking a drink of his beer in an attempt to quell his dry mouth. "Very nice."

Her foot began to rub against his under the water, her bare toes caressing him. "Romantic even," she whispered.

He was shy, but not dumb. He put his arm around her, pulling her closer to him. She cooed a little, laying her head on his shoulder.

"You have such a beautiful singing voice," she told him. "Who would've thought? And when you were singing *Dust in the Wind* to me..." she shivered a little. "Wow. When you were looking in my eyes while you sang it... I knew there was connection there. I mean... didn't you feel it?"

"Yeah," he said, putting his head even closer, snuggling his nose through her brown hair. "I felt it."

"That's such a romantic song," she crooned. "It just gets you, you know?"

"I know," he whispered, even though *Dust in the Wind* really wasn't a romantic song at all. Quite the opposite in fact. It was a dark song about the inevitability of death and about how meaningless the actions of mere humans really are in the great scheme of things. But Mandy really didn't need to be enlightened about this, did she? He thought not.

She tilted her face up to his and he kissed her. Her lips were full and soft, very sensuous. They exchanged slow, soft kisses for a few moments and then her tongue slid out of her mouth and into his. He swirled his own tongue against it, not caring that she tasted of beer and cigarettes. He tasted the same, he was sure. She was a great kisser, he discovered, which was hardly surprising considering the amount of practice she'd had at it.

It didn't take long before she lay back on the dock and he lay forward, half-atop her. They continued to kiss each other—deep, tongue dueling, spit swapping French kisses, the kind that gave "making out" its name. His hand rested on her hip for a while and then slid up and down her bare leg beneath the hem of her denim shorts, feeling the soft skin there. It felt very nice, very feminine.

He caressed here for the better part of five minutes before moving his hand back upward, onto her stomach.

"Mmmm," she cooed into his mouth as his hand rubbed her tummy through the Black Sabbath T-shirt she wore. He made larger and larger circles until he was just below her breasts on the upturn, just above her waistband on the downturn. He didn't risk going any further. Never before had a girl allowed him this much liberty on a first encounter.

Mandy came to his rescue. Seeming to sense his hesitation, she broke the kiss long enough to whisper, "You can touch them if you want. I like it."

He trembled a little but did as requested. His hand came up and landed softly on her left breast. He squeezed it experimentally. It was soft and pliable and oh so sexy.

Mandy broke the kiss again. "You can touch them *underneath* my shirt," she said softly. "That's kind of the best way."

"Yeah," he said, his mouth rendered otherwise speechless.

She giggled and pulled his face back down. Their lips connected and their tongues made contact once again. He brought his hand down to her waistband and began to tug on her shirt, trying to untuck it. Here he encountered problems. Her shorts were so tight upon her that the shirt didn't want to come free. He tugged harder and harder, moving it only a quarter inch or so at a time.

"Hold on," Mandy said. "You'll rip it."

"Sorry," he mumbled, embarrassed, feeling like what he was—inexperienced.

She giggled again. "It's okay," she said, pecking at his nose. And then, to his aroused astonishment, she reached down and unbuttoned her shorts. She then slid the zipper down, opening them wide. "There," she said, her tongue licking up the side of his face to his ear, where it swirled around the lobe. "That should help, shouldn't it?"

All he could do was nod. He reached down and pulled on the bottom of her shirt out of the shorts. As he did so, he was treated to a loin-stirring view of her white panties in the V of the unzipped zipper. His penis, which had been hard enough to jackhammer pavement ever since she suggested they go for a walk, suddenly throbbed a little deeper.

"Here," Mandy said, pulling her shirt up a little, revealing her belly. Though somewhat chubby, she was not fat. The skin here was smooth and sexy looking. She took his hand and put it under her shirt. "Touch me," she told him. "I like your hands on me."

He went back to kissing her as his hand slid even further beneath her shirt. When he encountered her bra, he shoved it underneath without waiting for permission. Now her bare breast was in his hand and he felt he was in heaven. Only once before had he actually touched a girl's naked tit, and that had been Gloria Canderson's back in the ninth grade. Gloria's had been barely large enough to require a brassiere. Mandy's was far too big for his entire hand to grasp at once. It was bigger than a softball, the nipple nearly the diameter of a dime. His fingers found that nipple and began to play with it. The effect on Mandy was impressive to behold.

"Yes, yes, I love that," she sighed against his mouth. "Kiss my neck while you do it."

He moved his mouth down and began kissing her neck, licking at the salty skin, occasionally offering a slight bite. He had no idea what he was doing but it seemed instinctive and he was certainly enjoying it.

And to think, he thought as his cock throbbed and his head spun with sensory overload, this all started because I played the guitar, because I sang. Music does have a power! A very potent power.

It wasn't long before her shirt was pushed all the way up along with her bra and his mouth found that engorged nipple. After less than a minute of his suckling, her hand grasped his again and positioned it where it was wanted, where it was needed. This time the direction was down. He felt the soft skin of her lower stomach as his knuckles forced their way under her shorts. He felt silky panties. He delved beneath them, feeling crinkly pubic hair and then wet, hot, slippery lips. He curled his finger inward, sliding between those lips, feeling the clutch of her body, and both of them moaned.

This was an entirely new experience for him and he reveled in it. His fingers, made limber and strong by years of guitar playing, pushed in and out, stroked up and down while his mouth continued to suckle on her engorged nipple. He had read about the clitoris in porno magazines he'd acquired over the years and in a mysterious publication he'd found in his parent's dresser drawer entitled *The Joy of Sex*. It took only a few minutes of probing around before he discovered a wet, slippery lump just atop Mandy's slit. He rubbed it a few times just to see what would happen. The effect was quite dramatic.

"Ohhhhh, ohhhh," Mandy moaned, a shudder working through her body.

"Are you okay?" he whispered.

"Uh... yeah," she said. "Do that again. Whatever you did, do it some more."

He did it some more, rubbing up and down, back and forth. Mandy continued to moan and soon her hips were bucking up and down.

He didn't make her orgasm, but only because she stopped him before he could get her there. She had other things in mind. She sat up suddenly and looked him in the eye.

"Take it out," she said softly.

"Take what out?" he asked, genuinely confused.

She giggled. "You know what I want out. C'mon. Sit on the edge of the dock again and I'll... you know... jack you off."

She wanted him to take his cock out! Right here. Right now! Holy shit! He took a moment to be self-conscious about his size. It wasn't small by any means but it wasn't huge either. This trepidation lasted only a moment though. She wanted to put her hands on him! To make him come with her hands! He wasn't about to turn this down.

He scrambled forward until his feet were in the water once again and then reached down for the button on his jeans. He undid it, pushed his zipper down, and then raised his hips up long enough to push his jeans and underwear down. His cock, hard and throbbing, popped out in all its glory.

"Mmmm," Mandy said, edging up close to him again. Her soft hand dropped down and closed around it, feeling it, testing its heft. "Very nice."

"Uhhh," was all he could manage to grunt out. It was the first hand other than his own to touch him there and it felt astoundingly good.

She began to stroke him up and down, softly at first and then with greater speed. As she did so she kissed the side of his face, his neck, his ear. It went on for no more than a minute or two before she whispered in his ear again. "Can you keep a secret?"

"Yes," he whispered back.

"I'll put my mouth on it if you promise not to tell anyone."

"What?" he asked, startled, convinced he hadn't heard her right.

"Do you promise?" she said. "Cross your heart and hope to die? Because I don't want a reputation as a... you know."

He had heard her right. And she was serious! "I promise," he said. "Cross my heart and hope to die."

She kissed him on the ear one more time. "Keep an eye out on top of the hill," she told him. "If someone starts to come down, tell me."

"Right," he said.

A moment later her head went down into his lap. Her mouth closed over his manhood and he felt the exquisite sensation of her lips and tongue slurping at him, moving up and down on him. It was even better than he'd imagined it would be.

"Oh, God," he groaned, fighting to keep his eyes where they belonged.

It didn't last long. After all the teasing and flirting and making out and breast feeling and vagina fingering, he was on quite the hair trigger. Within a minute of her starting, he felt the spasms start, felt the waves of pleasure building within him. He remained cognizant enough to warn her that he was going to come in case she didn't want him to go off in her mouth, but she kept right on sucking away, increased her pace in fact. A few seconds later he exploded. She kept sucking through it all, swallowing every drop.

They went back to the party a few minutes later, walking hand in hand up the hill. No one commented on their closeness. No one asked what had or had not happened while they'd been gone. He was talked into giving another brief performance. He played three more songs, *Fly by Night*, by Rush, *Satisfaction*, by The Rolling Stones, and, for Mandy, whom he stared at through most of it, *Tequila Sunrise*, by The Eagles—again, not exactly a romantic song when one analyzed the lyrics, but he'd already determined she was unable to make that distinction.

Shortly after that, Mandy, who had come to the party with John Standman, asked him if he would be kind enough to give her a ride home. He was kind enough, but they didn't go directly there. Instead, they stopped at Homestead Park just south of downtown. This was the largest of Heritage's city parks. It contained the city zoo, a nine-hole golf course, the city softball complex, a huge duck pond, and more than a thousand acres of general parkland. Access roads twisted and turned throughout the entire thing. Though all of the access gates were locked at 10:00 PM when the park closed, Mandy, whose father was a fireman for the Heritage County Fire Department, possessed a key that allowed them to open one of the gates and then close it behind them. They drove into the bowels of the facility and parked as near the exact center as they could get. Once there, they spread a blanket out on the seventh green of the golf course—a par four of 328 yards with a severe left dogleg. It wasn't long before they were both naked.

"Yessss!" Mandy yelled. "Oh God! No one has ever... ohhhhh!"

Jake's face was between her legs, lapping away at her swollen clitoris while his fingers plunged in and out of her. Though she was a bit ripe from the exertions of the past few hours, he found the taste and smell very much to his liking. He became addicted to cunnilingus on that night.

This time the orgasm came for Mandy, and it came with a power and violence he had never suspected. Her hips bucked up and down like she was in seizure. Her legs tightened around his neck to the point he could barely breathe. She screamed so loudly he feared that someone in one of the expensive houses that surrounded the park might hear and call the cops.

And when it finally ended she pulled him atop her, her hands grabbing at his naked ass, squeezing it, pulling on it.

"Fuck me!" she demanded, her mouth kissing his lips, her tongue licking at the vaginal secretions there. "Oh God, fuck me hard. Fuck me now!"

He was desperate to do just what she demanded. His cock was once again throbbing and begging to be used for its most important purpose. But he was just cognizant enough of what was going on to hesitate. "What about... you know... uh... I mean... I don't want to get you... you know... pregnant. I don't have any rub..."

"I'm on the pill!" she told him. "Now do it. Fuck me, Jake. Fuck me hard!"

That was all the convincing he needed. This being his first time, he fumbled around for a few moments, trying to find the exact angle he needed. But his fumbling was brief. She was so wet from his oral ministrations and her orgasm that once the head of his penis found the channel he slid right in with one smooth stroke.

"Oh, God yesssss!" she moaned as she felt it.

For his part, he was back to mumbled verbalizations. The feel of her tightness around him was even better than her mouth had been. This was nirvana. He began to thrust in and out of her, his butt rising and falling, a wet, squishing sound coming from the junction of their bodies with each stroke—a sound that disturbingly resembled that of macaroni and cheese being vigorously stirred prior to being served. It went on for five minutes, then ten, his orgasm kept at bay by the earlier one he'd had in her mouth. For the most part, Mandy just laid there beneath him, panting, kissing his mouth and his neck, her hands stroking his back, his ass, his face. She had nothing that resembled an orgasm, didn't seem to be anywhere near one. This was disturbing to him. He wanted to please her as much as she was pleasing him. He did not want to leave her high and dry.

And then she whispered the words in his ear. It was the first time he heard this in such circumstances. It would not be the last.

"Sing to me," she panted.

"Huh?" he panted back, sweat dripping from his face and onto hers.

"Sing to me again," she told him. "Look me in the eyes and sing! Do *Dust in the Wind*!"

This struck him as more than a little strange. Singing during sex? What kind of strange-ass shit was this? But the world was more than a little strange, wasn't it? It wasn't like she was asking him to choke her or pee on her or something like that. He focused his eyes on hers and began to sing, telling her about closing his eyes, about how he would only do it for a moment.

"Yesss, yesss!" Her hips were now thrusting upwards, meeting his every stroke.

He sang on, telling about how they were all just tiny particles of matter being transported in the currents of air generated by atmospheric variations.

"Oh Goddd!" she cried, clenching at him harder.

By the time he made it to the part about how nothing lasted forever but the surface of the planet and atmospheric layer above it, she was screaming again, her fingernails raking into his bare back, her pelvis battering into his. She came and came hard, violently in fact. Never in his life would he be fooled by a fake orgasm after this.

Her orgasm triggered his own. He poured himself out into her body.

*****

Chuck O'Donnell came back three minutes before they were to go on. His smile was now so wide it looked a bit maniacal. Apparently he had dipped deeper into his cocaine supply. He put one meaty arm around Matt's shoulder, the other meaty arm around Jake's, hugging them against him like a wise old father. "How you doing, guys?" he asked. "You ready to go out there and rock?"

"Fuckin-A," Matt told him, nodding calmly, taking a drag off his latest cigarette.

"Bet your ass," Jake responded, with more confidence than he felt.

The other band members chimed in with similar epitaphs, each making a point to include at least one profane word.

"Good, good," O'Donnell said, hugging the two front men just a little tighter for a moment before finally releasing them. He turned to Jake. "Now all I have to do to introduce you guys is turn on your main microphone amp, right?"

"Right," Jake said. "The mic itself will be hot once the amp comes on." He swallowed nervously, wondering if he should really mention this—it might offend O'Donnell—or just trust him to know. Finally, he decided to take no chances. "And... uh... if you could be careful to not touch any of the volume or tone knobs on the amp..."

O'Donnell gave him a look that was half amusement, half-irritation. "Son, I've been in this business since before you were even a protein molecule in your daddy's nut sack waiting to get made into a cumshot. I'm not gonna touch your settings or adjust your microphone stands or bump your guitars or kick loose one of your cables. Trust me."

"Sorry," Jake mumbled. "It's just that..."

"No need to be sorry," O'Donnell told him. "You were just making sure I didn't fuck up your sound check. I won't. Now then, as soon as I'm done introducing you, you guys walk out—walk, don't run unless you want to trip over your own cables or overbalance and fall on your face in the front row—pick up your instruments, turn on your amps, and start playing. Keep the between-song bullshit to a minimum. These people came to hear music, not to listen to you run your mouth. And if you do talk between songs, no political shit." He looked sharply at Jake as he said this. "It's okay to put your politics in your music, but don't preach to these people. They don't wanna fuckin' hear it, and I don't want to lose customers because someone was offended by your anti-nuclear bullshit or something like that. Understand?"

"Yeah," Jake said with a nod. "I understand." In fact, they had rehearsed very little between song banter into the act, nothing more than the usual "How you doing tonight?" and "Everyone having a good time?"

"Good," O'Donnell said. "That's what I want to hear. And I'm sorry Michaels and Hathaway gave you boys such a bad time. People get a little famous and they let it go to their heads. But do mind what they said. Forty-five minutes is your set and you have fifteen minutes to get your shit off the stage after that."

"Unless there are encore requests," Matt said.

O'Donnell chuckled. "Of course. Unless there are encore requests." He checked his watch. "I got one minute to seven. About time to get this show rolling. You boys ready?"

They agreed they were ready.

"Then let's do it. Give these people a hell of a show."

With that, he walked out onto the stage. The crowd was mostly sitting at tables or gathered around the bar. A few people were wandering from place to place. Most were veterans of the club scene and knew that O'Donnell's appearance on the stage meant the show was about to start. The babble of conversation grew quieter.

He walked over to Jake's microphone amp, examined it for about two seconds, and flipped on the main power switch. There was a slight pop from the amp as it came to life. He then walked over to the microphone itself. He did not tap it, knowing that to do so would potentially knock it out of alignment. Being almost six inches shorter than Jake's six-two, he had to stand on his toes to get his mouth close enough.

"Good evening," he said, his voice booming through the room, "and welcome to the Friday night live performance here at D Street West."

There was some scattered applause and a few whistles, nothing terribly enthusiastic however.

"As has been the case for the past six weekends," O'Donnell said next, "our main event for the night will be Heritage's most favored and respected local band, those crazy boys in leather, those wild advocators of the illegal and immoral, *The Boozehounds!*"

This time the applause was louder, longer, and had some enthusiasm to it.

"Morons," Matt said, just loud enough for Jake to hear. "They're cheering a bunch of hackers, not because they're any good, but just because they don't suck as much as every other local band."

Jake kept his mouth closed. He had heard Matt's argument about *The Boozehounds* many times before. Besides, his nervousness was now reaching a peak. Were they really about to walk out there and play for these people? Were they really?

"But first," O'Donnell went on, "I'm pleased to present to you our opening act. This is a new band doing their very first live performance for you tonight." He chuckled. "So, cut 'em a little slack, huh?"

There was some laughter at his words. A drunken voice from just behind the front row shouted out: "Fuck 'em! Bring on the Hounds!" A few other voices echoed this cry and a round of spontaneous applause erupted for a few seconds.

O'Donnell waited until it died down and then said, "Well, I'd love to, but the Hounds are still backstage warming up with their pre-set groupies. You know how it is? They get real cranky if they don't get a little skull before they come on."

More laughter greeted this.

"Jesus fucking Christ," Matt moaned. "Let's just get this shit over with."

"So anyway, I think you'll like these five young men I've slated for the opening slot. They're good musicians doing all original material and they're one hundred percent, bona fide Heritage grown, just like all the bands here at D Street West. Let me introduce to you now, for the first time in any venue, but certainly not the last... *Intemperance!*"

The applause was light, nothing more than a few people being polite. There were no whistles, no calls, no encouragement from anyone other than Michelle and her table and a few others, scattered around the club, who knew Matt or Coop or Darren (Bill had virtually no friends—certainly none he knew well enough to invite to a concert).

"C'mon guys," Matt said. "Let's fuckin' do it. Remember. We rock."

"We rock," everyone else repeated in unison.

Matt held out his right hand, palm down. Jake slapped his down atop it. Coop's hand landed atop Jake's. Darren's came down next. They all looked at Bill, who was staring at them, mesmerized.

"Put your fuckin' hand down, Nerdly," Matt growled. "We need to get out there."

Bill finally got the idea. He slapped his trembling hand down.

They held the position for a moment, a spontaneous act this time, but something that would be repeated every time they performed together after.

"Let's do it," Matt said.

"Let's do it," the rest echoed, drawing strength from this gesture of camaraderie.

They walked out on the stage. As they did, the stage lighting clicked on, bathing them in hot, white light. The crowd quieted a little, waiting, sizing them up.

It was Bill's job to power everything up. He stood by the master soundboard, his fingers hovering over the panel. To avoid a feedback whine he waited until Jake, Matt, and Darren had picked up their instruments and walked away from the amps they were leaning against. Once they were clear, he hit the switches one by one. There were a few pops and a slight hum. Jake swirled the guitar pick in his fingers, resisting the urge to strum the strings a few times to get the feel and check the sound, and walked to the microphone before him. He felt the heat of the lights burning into him, could see the dim faces of the crowd. They were all looking up at him, their expressions as widely varied as the people themselves.

From behind him came the ting of one of Coop's cymbals, an accidental strike as he sat down, Jake was sure. A muted bass string followed it as Darren took a grip on his instrument. Jake twirled the guitar pick in his hand once more. *We're gonna fuck this up*, a pessimistic part of his mind insisted. *No way we won't. We're too nervous, too inexperienced to pull off a forty-five minute set for a crowd like this. We're a fucking garage band*!

"No," he mumbled to himself, far enough away from the mic to keep the word from being picked up and broadcast. He took a deep breath. "We rock," he whispered. "We fuckin' rock."

He leaned forward, his mouth close to the mic now. "Good evening, D Street West," he said, his voice echoing through the venue. "We are *Intemperance*. Welcome to our show."

With that, it was out of Jake's hands. That was Matt's cue. He didn't hesitate a second. His pick came down and struck the open low E and A strings, the most basic of rock guitar sounds. It blared from the amp, the distortion and the effects giving it a somber, almost dark tone. He let it reverberate for a few moments, long enough for the crowd to realize things were starting, long enough for the more musically sophisticated among them to think, *Big Fucking Deal. So he can play an open chord.* And then his fingers clamped down on the neck at the sixth fret, halting the sound. The pick struck again and again, rapidly, surely, while his fingers danced over the low E, the A, and the D strings in a complex pattern, blasting the unique riff for *Descent Into Nothing* out into a crowd for the first, but certainly not the last, time.

This got the crowd's attention, as had been the intention when Matt and Jake decided to open with this song. It was a powerful riff, complex and moving at the same time. Attention grabbing. Matt played it four times in a row without accompaniment, ending the fourth with the open low E and A for a few seconds and then a brief mini-solo grind of the higher strings. As the guitar solo faded out Bill came in, playing a five second solo of his own on the piano. That too was allowed to fade out, leaving a brief silence in its wake. The crowd was looking at them, silent, considering, contemplative, their judgment now reserved, at least for the time being.

Please, Jake thought, staring out at the crowd, his fingers poised to start playing his part of the song, his nervousness and stage-fright now at its peak, *don't let me fuck this up.*

Coop hit his drumsticks together—one, two, three, four. On four, Jake's pick came down, hammering out the backing riff. Simultaneously, Matt began to play the main riff, Bill's piano backed the both of them up, and Coop and Darren began providing a solid beat for the rest of them to keep time to. It came out of the amps with a near-perfect blend, the combination of the five instruments producing sweet rock and roll music.

Jake's body began to move with the rhythm, his shoulders and head shaking back and forth as his fingers picked the strings and grabbed the frets, finding the right spot every time and at exactly the right moment by feel and instinct—feel and instinct instilled by practice and repetition. He looked out at the crowd, watching their faces, seeing heads nodding, seeing lips pursed in surprised respect, seeing the contemplation in many faces becoming deeper. So far, so good. Now it was time to see how they liked his singing.

The opening reached a minor crescendo and then settled into the main rhythm. As it did, Jake leaned forward, his mouth two inches from the microphone. He had another brief moment of sheer terror. *What if they hate my voice? What if my voice breaks? What if I forget the words?* But it was too late to back out now. He was committed. The only thing to do was the best he could. When the music reached the proper moment, his mouth opened and he began to sing.

"All at once it's upon you
"The pleasure and the need,
"You never know just when it begins
"Just when it starts to seed."

His voice did not break. It sounded as good as it always had, amplified with crisp reproduction by the voice amp. Nor did he forget the words. They flowed from him with ease, as easily as they did in rehearsal, or the shower, or while driving his car. His fingers continued to do their work on his guitar as the words came out of his mouth, dancing over the backing rhythm with hardly a thought, the movements actually helping him keep time.

"But it will take root within your soul
"And where it stops... nobody knows
"Compelling bliss, sweet sweet pain
"Down you fall, down the drain"

They changed tempo, Coop pounding out a roll on the drums, Bill hitting a flourish on his keys, Matt and Jake synchronizing a throbbing power chord atop it all. This led them into the chorus, that mixture of Jake's solo voice and five-part harmony.

"Falling without purpose
"Sliding without cause
"No hands held out before me
"No more hope for pause
"Descent into nothing
"Life forever changed
"Decent into nothing
"Can never be the same"

The bridge consisted of Matt pounding out the opening riff again, playing it four times in the raw, without accompaniment. The crowd cheered as he did it, erupting into a chorus of shouted yeah's and whistles. When Jake chimed back in to put them on the next verse, his nervousness was all but gone, his fears forgotten. They were doing it! The audience liked them!

They went through the second verse and the second chorus. There was another flurry of drums and piano and then Matt launched into his guitar solo. If there was any remaining doubt in the audience that *Intemperance* was a little more than your average opening band, it was dispelled right here. The solo was loud and complex, fitting in perfectly with the rhythm of the song. There seemed an emotion tied to it, emotion as strong as what Jake projected with his voice. Despair, helplessness, and inevitability—the theme of the song—came pouring from Matt's fingers, washing over the now-transfixed crowd.

Jake knew what they were experiencing. You could tell Matt was good by listening to him play a riff... any riff. He was fast, accurate, and almost supernaturally musically inclined. But when you heard him solo you knew you were not dealing with someone who was merely good. You knew you were not dealing with someone who was merely great. A Matt Tisdale solo showed you in the first few seconds that you were dealing with someone who was brilliant, genius even, someone on the same level as Eddie Van Halen or Clapton or Rhodes. Jake—now standing well behind Matt, shoulder to shoulder with Darren, his fingers still belting out the backing riff—could see expressions of awe in the crowd, could see guys leaning towards their friends and speaking into their ears, knew they were saying things like "Holy fucking shit! This guy can play!"

The guitar solo went on for almost ninety seconds. In the last ten seconds, the rest of the band halted their own instruments, allowing it to finish off as a true solo. Matt played it out flawlessly, his fingers whirring near the bottom of the neck, pressing and releasing the high strings and then holding the last note and engaging a slow pull on the whammy bar, increasing the pitch. Just before it faded out, Coop played a brief drum solo and then the rest of them launched back into the main rhythm.

Jake sang out the third verse and then the chorus once again, now totally into his performance. Sweat was starting to bead up on his forehead and under his arms as his legs moved him back and forth, as his shoulders kept time with the beat, as his fingers moved across his guitar. They repeated the entire chorus one more time and then settled into a coarse repetition of the last two lines.

"Descent into nothing, Descent into nothing,
"Life forever changed
"Descent into nothing, Descent into nothing,
"Can never be the same

They did this four times in a row, the backing music become louder, angrier with each one. Finally, on the very last line, Jake sang it out slowly, drawing the words out.

"Can never... never... nevvvvver be the saaaaaaammmmme."

As his voice stretched the final word Coop did a final flurry of drums, Matt did one last winding down solo, and then the five of them together hit a two-beat flourish and stopped, ending the tune.

The audience erupted immediately into applause, yells, whistles, shouted encouragements. It was not quite ear-splitting, but it was close. Jake let it wash over him, drawing power from it. There was absolutely no doubt that this was genuine applause, not the polite acknowledgment reserved for most of *The Boozehounds* other opening bands.

Listen to that, he told himself, a smile on his face, a lightness in his being. *They loved us, at least so far. They fucking loved us!* This was what performing was all about. The $250 they were getting for the gig wasn't shit compared to this feeling, the feeling of an entire roomful of music fans cheering for you, telling you that you rock! There really was a power here. A power and a magic.

When the applause began to die down Coop gave them another four-count with the drumsticks and they launched into *Who Needs Love?*, one of Matt's cynical pieces about the dark side of male-female relationships. It was a grinding, fast-paced song, the lead riff yet another impressive demonstration of Matt's guitar skills. Jake—though he had a more idealistic view of interpersonal relationships himself—nevertheless sang the lyrics with raw emotion and a hint of desperate anger, just as he knew Matt had intended them to be sung. Thanks to Bill's careful sound tuning before the show, the audience heard every word and responded to it, seeming to catch some of the emotion, particularly during the chorus.

"Who needs love?
"Love will force you to commit,
"Will make you feel that this is it,

"Life goes on and there you'll sit"

"Who needs love?
"A lie formed to make you choose,
"Just put your neck into the noose,
"Those who love will always lose."

The applause following this song was even louder, sustaining itself for longer. There were more cheers, more whistles, more yeahs and fuck yeahs. They played their third song and then their fourth with equal response. Before launching into number five—a slower song, almost a ballad, heavy on the piano and Jake's acoustic guitar sound—Jake asked them if they were having a good time tonight. They damn near hit the roof in their affirmative outpouring.

"We're having ourselves a hell of a time as well," he told the audience. "It's an honor to be playing here at D Street West and an honor to be opening for The Hounds."

"Fuck The Hounds!" someone yelled out.

"Yeah, fuck The Hounds!" a few others put in.

The applause that erupted from this was the loudest so far.

*****

In all, they did eleven of the sixteen original songs they had to date. By song number six Jake began to realize that he wasn't in as good of shape as he needed to be if this was going to be a regular habit. He was sweating freely, drops dripping down onto the stage and even into the front row of the audience. His shirt became damp, as if he'd run a mile. His heart pounded almost alarmingly. His breath became a little on the short side, though he did not allow it to become so short it would affect his singing voice. He sipped from a glass of water between songs and hung in there, driven on by the intoxicating sound of applause and cheers.

The last song of the set was one of Jake's, a tune called *Living By The Law*, which was a political piece about the proliferation of lawyers in society. They started it off with a musical duet of the two guitars, Jake finger-picking a beautiful acoustic backing while Matt played a mournful solo. They gradually increased the tempo of the duet until it reached a point where the acoustic could no longer keep up. At this point, Jake stomped on one of his petals, changing his sound over to full electric distortion, allowing him to grind out a riff instead. They kept this up for another minute, continuing to increase the tempo the entire time, building up to a peak at which point Jake stopped playing, allowing Matt to launch into a full-blown guitar solo that lasted four minutes and displayed every bit of his considerable genius to the crowd. That led him into the main riff of *Living By The Law*. The rest of the band chimed back in and they belted out the song perfectly. They ended with an extended flourish of guitars, drums, and piano that went on for almost a full minute and then it was over. The applause and cheers exploded through the venue once again.

"Thank you," Jake said, gratitude and pleasure plain as day in his voice. "Thank you so much. You're all great!"

They applauded even louder as the five of them linked their arms around each other and took a bow.

"Enjoy *The Boozehounds* and have a good night," Jake said into the microphone. "We'll see you again soon."

They walked off the stage, back into the alcove. Jake checked his watch. It was 7:43. They had finished up two minutes early.

"That was fuckin' awesome!" Darren yelled, clapping everyone within reach on the back. "They fuckin' loved us. Loved us!"

"We rocked!" Coop said, his grin ear to ear, his poodle-hair saturated with perspiration. "We really did!"

Bill looked overwhelmed, as if he couldn't really believe he had just performed before an audience—that he had in fact done a blistering two-minute solo of his own that had earned him a standing ovation (*a fuckin' standing-O from a hard rock crowd for a goddamn piano solo!* Jake thought in wonder). Matt simply looked thoughtful, a strange expression on his face that looked a little like expectation. They would now wait for the applause to die down and then they would start clearing their equipment off the stage.

Only the applause didn't die down. It grew louder. They began to clap rhythmically and shout a word out in unison, over and over. The word was more.

"They want an encore," Coop said in wonder. "Can you believe that shit?"

"Let's give the people what they want," Matt said. He turned back toward the stage.

"Wait a minute," Jake said, grabbing him by the shoulder. "We didn't rehearse an encore. What the fuck are we supposed to do?"

"*Almost Too Easy*," Matt said, naming off the first song—another of Matt's fuck 'em and leave 'em tunes about women—they had done together as a band, a song that pre-dated Jake and Bill's tenure. It was a grinding, simple song full of loud guitar riffs, frequent solos, and heavy backbeat. "We've done that one enough. We know it cold."

"Are you really sure we should do that?" Bill asked. "Won't it piss off O'Donnell?"

"I seriously doubt that," Matt said. "Come on. Let's do it."

They did it, walking back out onto the stage, back out into the hot spotlights. The crowd roared its appreciation at their reappearance. They picked up their instruments and took their positions. Another four-count by Coop and they launched into *Almost Too Easy*. Matt was right. They knew it cold and performed it flawlessly. The crowd loved it and demanded another.

"*Business as Usual*," Matt told them over the roar, naming a song they had initially rehearsed to be part of the set but had been forced to cut in the interests of time.

Everyone nodded and there was another four-count. The sound of *Intemperance* filled the hall one more time.

The crowd demanded even more after they left the stage but that was all they were going to get for tonight. They were following a golden rule, after all. Leave them wanting more.

The calls for the encore went on for some time, dying down only when someone turned off the stage lights and turned back up the house lights. A few minutes after this Michaels and Hathaway came stomping back, fury on their faces.

"What the fuck do you assholes think you were doing?" Michaels demanded. "Your set was supposed to be forty-five fucking minutes. It's five minutes to eight!"

"Just giving the people what they want," Matt told him with a shrug. "Just giving them what they want."

"Oh, you're real fuckin' funny," Hathaway said. "Now we're running late. Our set starts in thirty-five minutes and your shit is still on the stage!"

"What's the big deal?" Matt asked. "It's not like you guys do sound checks or tune your instruments or anything."

This infuriated both of them. "You fuckin' hackers!" Michaels screamed. "We were playing on this stage while you assholes were still listening to Sonny and Cher on your parents' eight track players! How dare you..."

"And you're *still* playing here, aren't you?" Matt said. "What's it been? Eight years? Eight years and you're still playing in Heritage and you have the nerve to call *us* hackers? Did you hear that applause they gave us tonight? Did you hear them calling for encores? Did you hear them yelling out 'Fuck The Hounds'?"

"Let's see what O'Donnell has to say about this," Hathaway said.

"Yes, why don't you do that?" Matt suggested. "In fact, here he comes now."

O'Donnell had a lot to say actually. None of it was what Hathaway and Michaels really wanted to hear however. He congratulated the members of *Intemperance* on an outstanding show, telling them it was the best performance by a first-time band he had ever seen in his life.

"You boys are going places," he gushed. "Holy fucking shit. Come to my office when you're done clearing the stage. I want to schedule you for the next couple of weekends if you're up for it."

"No," Michaels said firmly. "That ain't gonna happen."

O'Donnell turned slowly towards him, his face neutral. "How's that?" he asked softly.

"I don't want this band opening for us anymore. They're rude, unprofessional, and they ran far past their allotted time. If you want to sign them, sign them for nights we're not here."

O'Donnell seemed to think this over for a moment. Finally, he said, "There's gonna be a lot of nights you're not here if you ever tell me how to run my establishment again. These boys will be performing when I say they're performing. If you don't like it, you're free to play some other venue."

Michaels' face was so red it looked like he might explode. "We're *The Boozehounds!*" he shouted. "If we're not here, no one is gonna come to this fucking place. We're what brings the crowd in."

"For now," O'Donnell agreed. "But I think that's gonna change real soon."

CHAPTER 2

One Year Later

September 23, 1981
Heritage, California

Willie's Roadhouse was located five miles north of downtown Heritage, on the Eden Highway, which ran along the Sacramento River levee. The club was one of four businesses that sat atop a large wooden pier, built on stilts next to the levee, which jutted out over the east bank of the river. Stairs led down from the pier to the Heritage Marina, where dozens of boats were permanently berthed and dozens more had been parked in the temporary berthing for the concert that had taken place at Willie's tonight. Similarly the parking lot located adjacent to the pier was completely full, as was every available space alongside the twisting levee road for a quarter mile in both directions. There was only one thing that could draw a crowd like this out to the small roadhouse on a Wednesday night and that one thing was listed on the marquee.

PLAYING WEDNESDAY, 9-23, the sign read, *INTEMPERANCE*. There was a notation in smaller print that *The Stevedores*, a group of hackers with even less talent then *The Boozehounds*, would be opening the show, but no one gave a shit about that. *Tiny Tim* could have been opening for all the crowd cared. It was *Intemperance* they had come to see.

It had been just over a year since Jake and Matt and the boys had done their first live performance at D Street West. By now they were doing at least three shows a week—Friday and Saturday nights at D Street West and Wednesdays at Willie's Roadhouse. Often, they would pick up a Thursday or a Tuesday night performance at one of the other local venues. They were a household name in the greater Heritage area, even among those who disliked rock and roll music and those who never set foot in clubs. *The Boozehounds*, who had enjoyed a long reign as best local band, could hardly find a gig anymore, especially since they refused to degrade themselves by opening for *Intemperance*—the band who had kicked their asses so soundly out of the number one slot. Michaels, Hathaway, and the others had actually had to go out and find real jobs for the first time in their lives. Michaels was working at a UPS warehouse unloading trucks. Hathaway was flipping burgers on the night shift at a truck stop just outside of town.

One night after hearing this news, Matt and Jake, done up quite nicely on cocaine and beer supplied by O'Donnell after a particularly rousing performance, had driven out to the truck stop and parked themselves at the counter in direct view of the guitarist turned truck stop chef.

"Hey," Matt had yelled at him, a smirk firmly upon his face. "That's a nice hat you got there, Hathaway. It goes pretty good with the hairnet."

Hathaway had fumed at them as they'd chortled and snickered but refused to entertain them with a reply. At least not then.

The counter waitress—a young, bleached blonde girl of about nineteen—was an *Intemperance* fan and was quite enthralled to find herself in the presence of the lead singer and the lead guitarist. She went on and on for a while about how "awesome" they were and about how she'd seen them play a dozen or more times and how they sounded "more awesome" every time.

"Thanks, hon," Matt told her, his eyes unabashedly looking her up and down and liking what they saw. "You gonna be at the show tomorrow night?"

"I'm supposed to work," she said sadly.

"Call in sick," Matt said, reaching out and stroking the side of her hand with his finger. "Come to the show and hang out with us after it's over, you know what I mean?"

She knew what he meant. The smile on her face said so. "I'll be there," she told him. "Count on it."

Matt ran his hand a little higher up her arm, to her shoulder, sliding it slowly down over the top of her breast before finally withdrawing it. "I'll be looking forward to it," he said, kissing the tip of his finger.

This exchange between waitress and guitar player made Hathaway turn even redder, made his hands clench into fists. It was quite obvious that he had his own, unrealized romantic interests in the young waitress. Matt chuckled again, relishing the effect he was causing.

"What can I get you guys?" the flustered waitress asked them.

"I'll have the Chef's Burger," Jake said.

"Fuckin' A," Matt said, laughing out loud this time. "Hit me up with the same. I heard the chef makes a damn good burger. Is that true, Hathaway?"

Hathaway didn't say a word. He simply turned and threw a couple of patties on the grill.

When the burgers were set before them ten minutes later, Matt poked and prodded at his for a moment, examining it from all angles like it was a used car he was thinking about purchasing. Finally, he picked it up and took a bite, chewing thoughtfully for an extended time before swallowing. He took a drink of his water and then seesawed his hand back and forth.

"This is a pretty second-rate burger," he finally said. "I could do it a *lot* better."

This pushed Hathaway over the breaking point. He threw his spatula down, whipped off his tall white hat and his hairnet, and stormed over to the counter. "You and me," he said, pointing an angry finger at Matt. "Outside! Right fuckin now!"

Matt simply grinned and shrugged. "If that's the way you want it, hacker," he said. "But I think you're making a mistake."

"Now, pussy!" Hathaway screamed. "Come on! I'm gonna kick your fuckin' ass!"

They got up and headed for the door. A couple of truckers that had been watching the confrontation followed them out to watch the festivities. The fight didn't last long. Hathaway took a swing at Matt and Matt ducked easily under it. He then countered with an uppercut that took Hathaway right on the chin, stunning him long enough for Matt to drive a right cross into the side of his face. Hathaway fell to the pavement in a heap, where he lay there, moaning in pain.

Matt, who had not even broken a sweat, cracked his knuckles and then walked back inside. "Here ya go, hon," he said, dropping a twenty-dollar bill before the transfixed waitress. "Keep the change."

"Uh... thanks," she said numbly.

"See ya tomorrow night?"

She nodded. "You know it."

And he did. She came to the club dressed in a denim mini-skirt about six inches higher up the thighs than what was currently considered tasteful. She approached them after the show, two of her girlfriends in tow, and asked shyly if they remembered her.

"Of course we do," Matt said, putting his arm around her and drawing her close. "How could I forget the sexiest damn waitress I've ever met?"

She giggled and introduced her two friends, both of whom were equally attractive and dressed in an equally slutty manner. She then informed them that Hathaway had called the police on Matt shortly after they'd left that night but, thanks to the statements of herself and the two truckers, they basically told him to go pound some sand.

"Don't let your mouth write checks your body can't cash," had been their parting advice.

Matt ended up fucking the waitress in his van less than an hour later. Coop and Darren ended up fucking her friends at about the same time, doing it side by side in the backstage area of the club. In other words, it was a fairly typical end of set party at D Street West.

A similar party was going on now inside Willie's Roadhouse. The Wednesday night set had ended less than an hour before and most of the band members were mingling with the remaining crowd, evaluating the girls who fawned all over them and deciding which ones were going to be invited to the inevitable post-set gathering at Matt's house. It was there that the *true* action took place.

As Matt had prophesized before their first performance all those months ago, there was a seemingly endless supply of women and girls willing and able to do just about anything physically possible with the members of *Intemperance* simply because they were members of *Intemperance*. These girls hung around the band in hoards, sidling shamelessly up to any member they could find and making no bones about their willingness to be bedded.

"Sluts!" Matt called them with delight, sometimes right to their giggling faces. "They're all a bunch of fuckin' sluts. God bless and keep 'em!"

Even Bill—whom the rest of the band would have sworn at one time was going to die a virgin—got laid by their second gig at D Street West. It had been a little brunette groupie with a leather mini-skirt and black, calf-length boots who had taken Nerdly's cherry at the after-gig party that night. She enticed him into Matt's spare bedroom, sat him on the corner of the bed, made him take out his cock, and then demonstrated her lack of underwear beneath the skirt by sitting on him and grinding until he blasted off inside of her. Since then, Bill had been insatiable, his appetite geared towards the most exotically dressed and attractive groupies he could find—the more out of his former persona's league, the better.

Bill was having a little trouble deciding between two likely prospects on this night. The first was a gorgeous redhead in a green micro-mini. The second was a natural blonde in Calvin Kleins and a yellow halter that showed off her generous breasts. Both were aristocratic looking and rich. Red was a receptionist at a local law firm. Blondie was the daughter of a real estate developer. They looked at him with rapt attention as he explained to them the best way to go about producing cold fusion and why it had not yet been done in a controlled manner under laboratory conditions.

Across the room, where a group of cocktail tables had been pushed together, Darren and Coop were working as a team, entertaining a group of eight women—three of whom had abandoned their dates in the hopes of hooking up with one or both of the musicians. They had already invited the entire group to Matt's place and would cull two out of the herd there. They had no qualms about getting it on with their chosen groupie in each other's presence and had even been known to copulate with the same girl simultaneously on occasion, performing the maneuver they had termed "the rotisserie".

Matt was over at the bar, sipping out of his sixth Jack and Coke and talking to a young brunette dressed in a simple pair of Levi's and a blue pullover. Lately he had taken to finding one of the attractive but shy girls in the crowd, one of the girls who would never have approached him or any other band member on their own. It was more challenging for him that way, more gratifying as well as he saw the adoration and disbelief in their eyes as he fulfilled what he liked to think of as "the Cinderella Fantasy" by inviting them to *The Ball*—i.e. his place—and *making their dreams come true*—i.e. fucking the shit out of them in assorted unconventional positions in various parts of his house.

The only member of the band not working a groupie or groupies at the moment was Jake, who was currently not even in the building. So far, despite having performed live a total of 168 times before a combined total of approximately 65,000 people, 32,000 of whom were female, Jake had not bedded a single woman besides Michelle Borrows—who had finally given him her virginity at the after-gig party on the night of their first performance and had been supplying him with regular sex ever since. Not that he hadn't been tempted at times. In fact, he had found it best to stay away from the after-gig parties if Michelle was not with him, the temptation was *that* strong. But if there was one particular moral he had been raised with it was fidelity in love. And at some point along the way Michelle had ceased being a mere girlfriend to him and had started being the first woman he had fallen in love with.

Since that fateful day at Salinas Bend when he had lost his virginity to the jiggly and alluring Mandy, Jake had been with a respectable number of girls and women. Most of these relationships had been short and simple, based almost entirely on lust and the alleviation of horniness. Even in the longer-term relationships, those that lasted a month or more, he had never felt anything that could even remotely be termed love. With Michelle he would have sworn the same thing was taking place. He was wrong. Love had crept up on him, stealing so gradually into his mind that it had been fully entrenched before he recognized its presence. He adored her, adored everything about her. He liked the way she smiled, the cast of her eyes, the softness of her skin. He liked the sound of her voice and the conversations they had. He liked simply sitting with her on the couch in his apartment (an apartment he shared with Bill). There had been a point where he had even entertained the thought of proposing marriage to her. But that had been before her feelings towards him had started to take a turn for the worse.

The love he felt for Michelle was mutual, of that he had no doubt. He could see it in her eyes every time they were together, could hear it in her voice whenever her defenses fell long enough for it to creep out. She was in love with him but for the past two months, maybe a little more, she had been quietly starting to push him away from her, quietly hardening herself up for what seemed an inevitable parting of the ways. Jake knew it was coming and knew he was helpless to prevent it. But at the same time the irrational part of his brain, the part connected to his heart and emotions, continued to insist that she would come around, that she would be able to cast aside what her head was telling her to do and follow her own heart.

The gist of the problem she was having concerned her parents and the upbringing she had been subjected to. She was now twenty-one years old and had transferred over to California State University at Heritage where her third year of college was beginning. Her plan was to graduate next year with a degree in English and a teaching credential. Her dream was to teach at her alma mater, Holy Assumption, where she could help educate the next generation of Catholic girls. Her delayed teenage rebellion—the thing that had brought her and Jake together in the first place—was rapidly dying, allowing her upbringing and especially her faith to regain the ground it had lost.

It seemed like not a day would go by when she didn't nitpick at some aspect of his personality that didn't fit in with this upbringing. She had started to complain to him that his hair was too long, that his language was too coarse, that he drank too much, that he smoked too much. She admonished him every time he took the Lord's name in vain. She criticized his parents and their beliefs. She had even tried to get him to attend church with her (she herself had recently started going again) and to go to confession.

"We've been sinning," she told him during one argument. "Every time we make love without being married, we're sinning, Jake. Don't you see that? Don't you understand that?"

Round and round they would go on the subject of pre-marital sex, how wrong it was, how sinful, how they would burn in hell for it. But the interesting part was that despite her newly discovered views on the subject, she could not seem to get enough of it. She loved getting naked for him and rubbing her body against his. She loved bending over and lifting her skirt up so he could slide into her from behind, his hand slapping at her ass every once in a while. And she most especially loved when he put his mouth between her legs and sucked orgasm after orgasm from her.

That was, in fact, what he was doing to her right now, while the rest of the band was setting up their own random sex for the night. She had been there for the Wednesday night performance—something that was rare enough in its own right these days—and had seemed to be particularly hypercritical and aloof when they had talked immediately after the show. When he asked her what was wrong she fell back on her favorite excuse since school had started again in late August. "I'm behind in my studies. State's a lot harder than HCC was."

He didn't believe it for a minute, of course. Studying and schoolwork came as naturally to Michelle as it had for Pauline, Jake's sister. But, like usual, he allowed the excuse to stand, knowing that if he pushed the issue she would simply storm out and refuse to talk to him for a few days. Though the relationship was fading and fading fast, he could not help but love her and strive to keep her near him.

"Why don't we go check out Willie's yacht?" he'd suggested as a way of easing the tension. Willie Bradford, the owner of Willie's Roadhouse, kept a forty-footer down in the marina. There were few he allowed to access his precious boat without his presence but Jake, the lead singer of a band that drew 450 people paying a $5 cover charge and swilling down $1 beers every Wednesday night, was among that few. He had his own passkey to the marina entrance and the combination to the door lock on the main cabin. He and Michelle had *checked out* the yacht on more than one occasion.

"I don't really have the time," she'd snapped, although Jake had already been able to see a flicker of interest in her eyes.

"Come on," he'd goaded, taking her arm and leading her in that direction. "It's only 10:30. You can hang out for a little while, can't you?"

She had given a few more token protestations, but it was clear during the entire exchange that she wanted to go to the yacht. He could see it in the way her nipples poked through her cotton shirt at the very suggestion, in the way her tongue kept coming out and licking at her lips. She could go on and on about how wrong and sinful they were, but the simple fact remained that she had become addicted to the pleasures of the flesh.

"I'll eat your pussy for you," he'd whispered in her ear. "Stick my face right up under your dress and lick you until you come."

A shudder had worked her way through her body. "Let's go," she'd said.

Now, ten minutes later, they were in the cramped bedroom portion of the cabin, Michelle sitting on the tiny bed, her legs spread wide, Jake kneeling on the floor between them. Her calf-length skirt had been pulled up around her waist and he was holding her white, cotton panties to the side, his tongue lapping up and down her swollen vaginal lips. Her blond pubic hair was matted with his saliva and her secretions. Her clit was swollen and protruding proudly from its hood, demanding its own attention.

"Oh, God," she moaned, her fingers running through his long hair, her breath tearing in and out of her body.

"Mmmm," he responded, giving an extra-long lick, his hands running up and down her sexy legs.

Soon the fingers of his right hand found their way to her slit. She was tight here, very tight, so tight that the first time they'd gone all the way it had taken him almost ten minutes to work his way completely inside of her. Feeling the firm clutch of her body on his fingers never failed to kick his passion up a few notches. It didn't fail now. His cock throbbed in anticipation of nestling there. He made a quick check to see if the condom he planned to use was still in his pocket—it was—and then attached his mouth to her clit, intending to suck the first orgasm of the night out of her.

It was only seconds before she began bucking against him, her hands now pulling on his hair, drawing his face in tighter and tighter. Her legs wrapped around his back, her feet rubbing up and down. A continuous moan began to come from her mouth, the pitch going higher and higher as the spasms of orgasm began to build.

She came with a scream, muted slightly by her forearm in her mouth, but loud enough that a couple out for a walk through the marina heard it and looked knowingly at each other. No sooner had the spasms died that he was on his feet, standing between her legs, the condom wrapper in one hand, his other hand going to the snap on his jeans. In less than fifteen seconds he would be capped and thrusting within her, his mouth attached to hers, those legs wrapped around his back.

But it was not to be. She put her hand on his, halting him in mid-un-snap. "No," she said, her face still flushed and sweaty but determination in her eyes.

"No?" he asked, confused. "What do you mean, no?"

"I have to go, Jake," she said, pushing her hips back, pulling her skirt down. "I shouldn't have even stayed this long."

"You're going to leave... *now*?" he asked incredulously. "We're kind of in the middle of something."

"Yes," she said. "We're in the middle of sinning before God. Only this time I have the strength to stop."

"You've got to be fucking kidding," he said.

"You don't need to swear at me," she said. "You know my views on pre-marital sex. You know I feel guilty when I sin with you. I'm not going to do it this time. I can't and I won't."

He trembled in place for a moment, strongly considering just dropping his pants, putting on the condom, and taking her anyway. She might protest a little, but she would let him, especially once his cock entered her. She would wrap those legs around him and beg him for more. But in the end, he didn't do it, couldn't commit what would technically qualify as rape. Instead, he slumped backwards, sitting down on a small chair against the bulkhead.

"Why are you doing this?" he asked, putting the condom back in his pocket. "Is this some kind of punishment?"

"No, Jake," she said. "I told you, I have to leave. I have an 8:20 class in the morning and I'm already out too late."

He shook his head angrily. "Why don't we cut the bullshit?" he suggested. "Tell me what's really bothering you." He snorted a little. "What's bothering you that's not normally bothering you, that is."

She opened her mouth, undoubtedly to insist that her 8:20 class was all that was on her mind, and then closed it again. She sighed, her hands smoothing her skirt out. "That song you played tonight," she said. "The new one."

"*It's In The Book*?" he asked, although he knew that was the one. It was the only new song they'd performed. And he had a pretty good idea why she wasn't too keen on it.

"That's the one," she confirmed. "It's about The Bible, isn't it?"

Now it was he who sighed, slumping a little further against the bulkhead. He had known this was going to come up at some point, he just hadn't thought she would pick up on the meaning of the lyrics in *It's In The Book* so quickly. The song was about the negative lessons The Bible taught, a well-researched and poignant tune that Jake—who had penned it—was quite proud of, but that any person who identified himself or herself as "a good Christian" would probably take offense to.

"Intolerance and hatred, bigotry and pain
It's in The Book... It's in The Book
Violence, oppression, jealousy, shame
Persecution in God's name,
It's in The Book... It's in The Book"

That was just one verse of the song. There were six others plus a particularly vehement bridge just prior to the guitar solo that was a borderline rant. In short, the song was an angry condemnation of fundamental Christianity and organized religion.

"Yes," Jake said. "It's about The Bible."

Michelle's face tightened up, her eyes narrowing to slits. "You're making fun of The Bible, Jake," she said. "Sweet Mary, Mother of God! Do you think that's funny or something?"

"Funny?" he asked. "Did it sound like I was trying to be funny? There's nothing in that song that isn't true, hon. The Bible does teach intolerance and hatred. It does teach bigotry and pain. Do you deny this?"

"You're taking things out of context!" she shouted. "And you're doing it just so those Godless people out there will worship you even more. Don't you ever fear for your soul, Jake? Not even a little?"

"I'm not going to discuss religion with you," he told her. "We've already been over this again and again. My beliefs are not your beliefs. You've known that about me from the start. Why are you suddenly having a problem with it?"

"I've grown up since we started dating," she said. "You know, maturity? You ever heard of it? You certainly haven't developed any in this past year."

He took a deep breath, biting back on several hateful replies. Finally, he asked, "What is it you're trying to say?"

"I don't know," she said, a tear running down her face. "I've grown up, I've matured, and I'm working my butt off to try to achieve my goals in life. I love you, Jake. I love you dearly, but look at what you're doing with your life. Look at yourself! You've dropped out of school and you have no intention of going back, do you?"

"If there comes a time I need to go back, I'll go back," he said. "Right now we're pulling off three sets a week, sometimes four. We have rehearsals two days a week and jam sessions where we try to put together new songs on the other days. This band is my job, Michelle. Don't you get that?"

"Oh, I get it all right," she said. "And how much are you making at your job, Jake?"

"You know how much we make," he said. This was an old argument too. "Five hundred dollars a set at D Street and six hundred a set here at Willies. Other clubs usually pay us somewhere in between."

"All of which doesn't amount to squat when you divide it up among the five of you and take out taxes, does it?"

"No," he admitted. "It really isn't that much."

"It's less than what people on welfare make," she accused. This wasn't strictly true, of course, but it wasn't all that far off either.

Nor was Michelle the only one to have made this argument to him. His own parents, the two people in the world who he should have been able to count on to support him in anything he did, were constantly asking him when he was going to get this "rock band phase" out of his system and go back to school.

"I know you love making music, honey," his mother had told him the last time he'd been over for dinner. "And it's obvious you and your band are very good at it. I mean, we've seen you play, right? But I think your talent would be put to much better use as a music and voice teacher, don't you? Can you imagine, sharing your gift with the young? Wouldn't that be beautiful? But to do that you need to get your college degree and your teaching credential. And that means going *back to school*."

Nor was he the only one under such parental pressure. Bill's mother, who was Jake's mother's best friend and fellow philharmonic orchestra-mate, regularly instilled similar lectures on Bill, although her suggestions included using his piano skills to try to land a position with the Boston or the Philadelphia or—dare they dream—the *New York* Philharmonic.

"Look," Jake told Michelle now, "I know I barely got a pot to piss in right now. But I'm doing what I love to do, don't you understand that? I love being a musician. I love getting up on stage and hearing those people applaud and yell for more of the music that I'm playing, that I wrote and composed, that I fucking sing. There's nothing else in the world that feels like that. Nothing. And until the thrill I get by doing this goes away, or until the people stop wanting to hear my music, I'm going to keep doing it. Do I think I'll ever make it big? Probably not. Matt's sent that demo tape we made to about two dozen agents trying to get someone to represent us and we haven't even got so much as a rejection letter in return. Does that change my mind? No. Because right now I'm living exactly the life I want to live. I'm having the time of my life, Michelle, and how much money we're making doesn't have a goddamn thing to do with that. I'm sorry if that doesn't fit in with your plans of a decent boyfriend."

There were more tears running down her face now. "It doesn't," she said, shaking her head. "It doesn't fit in at all."

He didn't know what to say. There didn't seem to be a right reply here. God, how this hurt. He could feel the pain like a physical thing, welling up from his gut, spreading throughout his body. He felt a tear running down his own cheek now. He brushed it angrily away.

"I have to go now, Jake," she told him, standing up. "Will you think about what I said?"

"What's to think about?" he asked bitterly. "You're asking me to choose between my music and you."

She shrugged, sniffing a little. "If that's the way you want to look at it," she said. "When you're ready to be with me on my terms, give me a call."

"Yeah," he snorted. "And when you're ready to be with me on mine, you do the same."

She didn't answer. She gave him a sad smile and climbed the small ladder to the door. She opened it and slipped out into the night. Jake did not go after her. He knew when the point of futility had been reached.

He fumbled around in his pants pocket for a moment and finally came out with a crumpled pack of smokes. All of the cigarettes inside were bent and broken. He straightened the end of one and fitted it onto the filter of another. He dug in his pants again and finally came up with a lighter. He sparked up, smoking slowly while he cried.

"Point of futility," he mumbled to himself, a part of his mind already composing the barest beginnings of lyrics to go along with that phrase, that concept, while the rest of him grieved. "How's that for a fucking tune? The point of fucking futility."

He stayed down there for almost twenty minutes, long enough to rig together and inhale three cigarettes, each one shakier than the last. Finally—once he felt himself under control (and with that phrase, *The Point of Futility*, still dancing in his brain) he got up and cleaned up the mess he and Michelle had made, leaving the yacht more or less as he'd found it.

He locked up and walked slowly back to Willie's, towards the booming of bass from the jukebox, towards the sound of revelry in progress. When he entered the smoky room he didn't make it more than a dozen steps before five girls and a couple of guys surrounded him. All began babbling about how great of a show it had been, how he rocked, how they were good enough to "make it" if they could just get a break. He mumbled his thanks to them and separated himself as quickly as he could, finding his way to the bar, where Chris the bartender brought him a rum and coke without even being asked.

"Thanks, Chris," he said. "You got a pack of smokes back there for me too?"

"Bet your ass," Chris told him. He reached under the bar and came up with a red and white hard pack that contained Jake's favorite brand. He slapped it down before him along with a clean ashtray. "Should I put it on your tab?" he asked with a smirk.

Jake chuckled back. "By all means," he replied.

The "tab" he was referring to was non-existent. Willie supplied free drinks to the band members (but not their groupies) as long as they remained on the premises since their presence encouraged people to stick around after the show and order drinks of their own. Cigarettes and cheeseburgers and hotdogs had never actually been specified as being on the house but the bartenders all liked the band to hang out too for the tip volume they produced so they interpreted their instructions rather loosely.

Jake downed half of his drink in a shot and then fired up his first intact cigarette of the last hour. As he blew out the first plume of smoke and tapped the ashes into the glass tray, Matt came over, a cigarette hanging out of his own mouth.

"Hey, Chrissie," Matt shouted, banging an empty glass down on the bar, his words more than a little slurred. "Fire me up again, brother!"

"You got it, Matt," Chris replied. "Another Jack and Coke."

While his drink was being constructed Matt sat down on the stool next to Jake and put his arm around him, pulling him up against him. "What the fuck's the matter with you?" he asked. "You look like shit. Get ahold of some bad weed?"

"Naw," Jake said. "I'm all right."

"The fuck you are," he said, pulling him tighter against him before releasing him. "I've seen happier faces at a fuckin' funeral." He looked around for a minute. "Where's your bitch at? She bail on you?"

He nodded. "For good," he said. "We broke up."

Matt looked at him, his eyes widening a little. "You mean... like... broke up?" he asked. "You and the little Catholic girl?"

"Yep," he said, taking another drag. "She couldn't take being with the poor Bible-degrading musician any longer. She told me to call her when I decided to cut my hair and go back to school and be a respectable fucking member of society."

Matt absorbed that for a few seconds, nodding sympathetically. "That's some shit," he said.

"That it is," Jake agreed.

"Tell me something," Matt said.

"What's that?"

"Did you get to tear off one last piece before she went?"

Jake looked at him agog for a moment and then burst out laughing. "No," he finally said. "She got me to eat her pussy for her one last time and then went into her spiel right after."

Matt was truly appalled. "That is just fuckin *evil*," he declared.

"No shit."

"Well, at least you'll leave her with a happy memory, huh?"

"Yeah, I suppose."

"Well, don't trip too much on it," Matt told him. "Ain't no bitch worth it and that's the fuckin truth. Score yourself one of these groupies here and bring her back to my place when we leave. I'll reserve the spare bedroom just for you."

"Thanks," Jake said, "but I think I'll just head on home tonight. There's a new song I've been thinking about. Maybe I'll try to strum a little bit of it out."

"Suit yourself," Matt said. "But remember that horseshit about all work and no play and all that. You'd do yourself good to get your dick straightened by someone other than Miss Holier Than Thou."

And before he could reply Matt picked up his fresh drink and headed back the way he had come, leaving Jake to contemplate those words of wisdom while he sipped his own drink.

It wasn't more than a minute or two before one of the groupies came and sat next to him. She was about nineteen or so, a brunette, with long, straight hair styled after Brooke Shields. She wore a pair of Calvin Klein jeans that were so tight it appeared circulation might have been cut off to her legs. Covering her torso—barely—was a fluorescent pink tube top that allowed her large, obviously braless breasts to bounce and jiggle with every move she made. She carried what appeared to be a Long Island iced tea in one hand and a long, skinny cigarette stained with lipstick in the other.

"Hi," she said brightly, turning her body towards him and making sure her boobs gave a particularly expressive wobble in the process.

"Hi," he replied, keeping his expression neutral. He didn't really want to talk to anyone right now but she was a fan and it was bad business to be rude to one's fans.

"I'm Colette. Colette Jones."

He gave her a polite smile. "Jake Kingsley," he said.

She giggled. "I know *that*," she said. "Everyone in here knows that. I saw you sittin' here all by yourself and thought I'd... you know... come and join you. Keep you company, ya know."

"That was very nice of you," he told her.

"You guys did an awesome show tonight. Totally awesome."

"Thank you," he said. "I'm glad you enjoyed it."

"You have *such* a hot voice," she said, leaning a little closer. "I guess girls tell you that all the time, don't they?"

"I may have heard that once or twice," he allowed.

"I just love music," she said. "And you guys totally rock. This is like the fifth or sixth time I've seen you now. A couple of times here but mostly over at D Street. That's like my favorite club, ya know. Everyone knows me over there."

"Do they?"

"Oh yeah." She giggled again. "I guess I have something of a... ya know... a *reputation* there."

That was his opening of course. He was supposed to ask her just what sort of reputation she had. From there the sexual talk would begin, culminating in an invitation to the party at Matt's house. Though Jake had never participated in this dance before, he knew its steps well enough by listening to the tales of the other band members. But he wasn't really interested in dancing. "That's very... uh... interesting," he said.

"And very well earned, I'm told," she said saucily.

He suppressed a sigh. "Look, uh..."

"Colette," she provided.

"Right... Colette. I... uh... well I'm really having kind of a bad night. You see..."

"Did you have a fight with your girlfriend?" she asked, her eyes shining now.

This threw him off stride a bit. "What makes you say that?"

"Well, everyone knows you have a girlfriend. The girls are all jealous of her and the guys are all hot for her. She is pretty cute." She scowled a little as she said this. "Very wholesome looking, ya know, although she does need to learn how to dress a little better for the clubs. I mean, really... a cotton skirt and a peasant blouse? Puh-leeze. But anyway, we always see you here with her. If she's not with you than you leave early. So, since she was here with you earlier and now she's gone and you're still here, sitting by yourself and drinking at the bar, you must've had a fight, right?"

"You're a regular Sherlock Holmes," he told her.

She puzzled over that for a moment and then finally seemed to get the premise, or at least she pretended to. She laughed as if that was the funniest thing she'd ever heard. "Right," she said, leaning closer and slapping lightly at his arm. "So, what did you guys fight about?"

"Don't you think that's a little personal?" he asked.

She shrugged, her breasts jiggling distractingly from the motion. "It helps to talk about it. That's what they say."

"Is that what they say?"

She nodded seriously. "Oh yes."

"Well, if it's all the same to you, I kinda like to keep things penned up inside, you know? I'm an artist. Suffering is good for us. At least that's what they say."

This time his humor shot cleanly over her head, not so much as nicking a hair on its way. "I can respect that," she told him.

They sat in silence for a bit. Jake turned his attention back to his drink, swallowing it down and waving to Chris for another. He was hoping Colette would simply take the hint and leave him alone.

She may have done the former, but she was passing on the latter. She sat there next to him, puffing on her cigarette and sipping from her own drink, trying to think of a way to get the conversation rolling again. Finally, she just fell back on instinct.

"Do you like my boobs?" she suddenly blurted.

Jake looked slowly over at her. "Do I like them?"

She nodded, smiling sexily. "Most guys love them," she said. "That's why I wear these kind of tops. It shows them off. I mean... if ya got it, flaunt it, right?"

"I suppose that's a good philosophy," he said.

She puzzled over his words for a moment and then smiled. "Right," she agreed. "That's my philosophy. So... you wanna touch them?"

"Huh?"

"My boobs, silly," she said with feigned shyness. "I'll let you if you want. I'll let you do *anything* if you want."

"Umm, that's uh... very nice of you to offer, Colette, but..."

She stood up, taking a step closer to him, so she was standing between his outspread knees, close enough for him to feel the warmth radiating off of her body, close enough for him to smell the perfume she'd put on. "Look," she said softly, "I think you're totally hot, Jake. Your voice makes me so fuckin' wet and I'd give anything to make it with you."

"That's very flattering, but..."

She leaned forward, her hands coming down onto his shoulders, her thighs now touching his, her cleavage now less than eight inches from his face. She bent down and kissed him softly on the forehead. "Take me to the party tonight," she whispered. "You won't be sorry."

The feel of her softness against him coupled with the view down her halter was having an effect. His groin, after all, was throbbing mildly with blue balls from his earlier, unrelieved session with Michelle. The fact that she was basically offering him her admittedly gorgeous body did little to dissipate the horniness that had suddenly sprung up. But on the other hand, he had broken up with his girlfriend of nearly eighteen months less than an hour before. Wasn't it a little too early for this? Wasn't there some sort of decorum that should be observed? Especially since it was possible— unlikely perhaps, but possible—that Michelle might just have a change of heart and call him in the morning with an apology.

He probably would have maintained the willpower to refuse her if not for what happened next. After kissing his forehead, she leaned down a little more and kissed him again, just to the left of his left eye. As her soft lips made contact she sniffed a little and then smiled.

"You ate her pussy out tonight, didn't you?" she asked.

"What?" he asked, his voice not quite steady.

"I can smell her all over your face," she said with a pleasant sigh. "I love the smell of another girl's pussy."

"You... you do?" he asked, his cock taking a large lurch at the words.

"Mmmm hmmm. Me and my girlfriend from high school used to go down on each other when we had sleepovers at my house. Just to see what it was like. I used to love tasting her." She shuddered a little. "This is getting me so hot, Jake. Sooo hot."

With that she leaned down and licked him right across the lips, swirling her tongue over them, gathering up the taste of Michelle that had been left behind.

"Mmmm, no wonder you liked her. She tastes yummy."

Jake's cock was now an iron bar in his pants. Thoughts of Michelle, while not exactly driven from his mind, had moved into the back seat. "You like that, huh?" he asked her.

"Did you fuck her?" Colette asked him next. "Oh God, did you stick your cock in that pussy? I'd love to lick her taste off your cock. Please let me."

Of course, he hadn't, so she couldn't, but at this point that had ceased to matter. Whether she was making all of this up or not didn't matter. She had succeeded in breaking through the wall he had put up. He put his hand on her side, just above the waistband of her Calvin Kleins, feeling her hot skin, feeling the promise of what the rest of her would be like.

"So, you want to go to the party, huh?" he asked.

"Yeah," she whispered in his ear, following it up with a lick at his earlobe.

"You got it."

*****

It could technically be said that Matt—who at the age of twenty-two had been accorded the status of the best guitar player in Northern California by multiple independent sources including *The Heritage Register* and the *Heritage Weekly Review*—still lived with his parents.

It was true in that he lived on the same piece of property as they did and that he paid no rent. Matt's father was a self-made millionaire who had built his fortune in the well-digging business in nearby Cypress County, in the Sierra Nevada foothills. Most of the new housing developments that had been built there in the past thirty years got their water from wells that Tisdale Drilling Inc. had sunk into the ground. Matt had come into the world late in his parents' lives—an accident of birth control when they were in their late thirties—just as their first two children were getting ready to graduate high school and start off on lives of their own, just as they themselves were starting to enjoy the fruits of their labors.

Matt had been loved by his parents but had always been something of a guilty inconvenience in his formative years. He had been mostly raised by hired nannies and maids while his parents had been away on extended vacations in Europe or Palm Springs or Hawaii. To make up for this he had been provided with every indulgence his mind could come up with. One of those indulgences had been the guitar he'd asked for as a twelfth birthday present—a guitar that had become his friend, his companion, his obsession. Another was the mother-in-law quarters tucked away in the very back cornier of the five-acre plot in the exclusive suburb of Gardenia.

It was a fully equipped, self-contained house of nearly 1800 square feet, complete with a two-car garage where the band rehearsed. Since Matt's parents had no in-laws on either side that they cared to have visit them (they had pretty much broken all contact with their families about the time their net worth climbed over $250,000 and the begging started to get out of hand), Matt had basically been given the entire mother-in-law quarters as his bedroom when he turned fifteen. He had lived in it ever since, seeing his parents only when the two events of him needing money and they happening to be home coincided.

Now that the band Matt had founded—the fifth he had played in since junior high, the first to actually get a gig—was popular, his home in the corner of the property was being used to its absolute best advantage. It served as a party Mecca for the 18–25 crowd of the Heritage club scene. Without exception, after every gig *Intemperance* performed, a select group of their audience would come back to the house with them and spend most of the night cementing the band's moniker as a verb instead of a proper noun. The parties became legendary long before the band itself was ever heard of outside of Heritage. In later years—when Heritage was "on the map", as Matt liked to say—hordes would claim to have been present at them at one time or another for the mere storytelling status they would achieve if they could not be disproved.

In truth, only about a hundredth of those who would later claim to have "partied with Matt and Jake and the boys back in the day" would be telling the truth. For anyone other than band members or their closest friends who wanted to attend the after-gig get-togethers, the rules were simple. You could come by invite of an *Intemperance* member *only*, no exceptions. Friends of those invited were not allowed unless he or she had been specifically invited himself or herself by said *Intemperance* member or members.

Another rule was that any males invited had to supply booze, marijuana, or cocaine to the festivities. This was strictly enforced by Matt himself at the door. He would actually check to see that some sort of illicit material was being brought in and brought in in a decent amount. Women, of course, were not held to such a requirement since—in Matt's opinion—they had their own form of party favor built right in.

The third rule was that everyone who was not a band member was responsible for his or her own transportation to and from the scene of the party. No one was allowed to hitch rides with a band member and everyone had to get out and go somewhere else when Matt decided the party was over— which was usually around four or five in the morning. He didn't give a shit how drunk or stoned a person was, how incapable of driving they were, or even if they were unconscious, they and their cars had to go. Other than that, pretty much anything was cool with him.

When they arrived at the after-gig show on this night, a stream of twelve cars that contained eighteen females and six males trailed behind them, inching along the access road that bypassed the main house and parking in the driveway. The band left all of their equipment in Matt's microbus and Coop's van—they would unload it sometime the next day, when they were all sober—and trooped inside. Matt did his normal check of the male guests, finding that each had brought a satisfactory contribution of intoxicating material as their admission ticket. Ten minutes later music was blaring from the stereo system, beer was flowing, and the pot smoke was so thick you could cut it with a knife.

Jake and Colette found a corner of the house over by the bar and sat next to each other on a love seat where Jake made some small talk with a few of the girls and one of the guys. The guy—a Ticket-King employee who claimed he could get Jake free front row tickets for any concert in the Northern California region—fired up a potent joint of some Panama Red and passed it around. Jake smoked deeply from it, taking hits as big as he could stand and holding them in until no smoke was exhaled.

Soon he was as high as it was really possible to get and thoughts of Michelle, of the break-up, of her parting words, of the pain he was enduring, had been pushed far to the back of his head (although that phrase, *The Point of Futility*, kept popping back up).

Throughout the conversation and the smoking Colette remained snuggled up on his left side, her leg rubbing alluringly against his, her breasts pushing against his shoulder, her lips every once in a while, going to his earlobe to lick at it and to whisper how horny she was into his ear. By the time the joint was a roach in the ashtray Jake's cock was as hard as a spike.

"Why don't we go check out the bedroom?" he asked her when he could stand it no more.

She nodded quickly, her bloodshot eyes shining brightly. "Yeah," she agreed most enthusiastically. "Why don't we?"

Jake excused them from the ongoing conversation and they stood up, walking hand in hand down the hall, towards the spare bedroom at the end of it, the room Matt had declared off limits to all until "my brother Jake has christened the motherfucker for the night".

The spare room was a standard sized bedroom with standard furnishings. There was a small desk in one corner, a lamp on a nightstand in another. The bed was queen-sized, the linen fresh and clean, changed earlier in the day by Ruby, the maid who lived in the big house. No sooner had the door shut behind them then Colette was in his arms, rubbing herself against his body, her tongue in his mouth, her hands running up and down his back, down to his ass, up to his neck.

"Oh, God, I'm so hot for you, Jake," she panted when the kiss finally broke. "I've dreamed about this since the first time I saw you up on stage."

It was obvious she was not lying about being hot for him. Her nipples were protruding sharply from beneath her halter-top, her face was flushed with excitement, and her neck had broken out in goosebumps. Her hand dropped down to the bulge in his jeans and began to rub it expertly, squeezing and palpating, caressing and rubbing in such a way that he suspected she could make him come without him even opening his pants if she so desired.

But she did not desire. Before he even had a chance to respond to her statement, she sank slowly to her knees before him, so her head was even with that bulge. She leaned forward and put her mouth directly on it, exhaling her hot breath against it with enough force for him to feel it even through the layer of denim and cotton that made up his jeans and underwear.

"Ohhhh," he groaned as the sensation coursed through him. By now, Michelle was not even in the back of his mind. Perhaps the fact that he was currently at the peak of his marijuana high was distorting things, but Colette's actions seemed the hottest, most erotic thing he'd ever experienced.

She undid his jeans, popping the buttons one by one, and then pushed them down, taking the underwear with them. His erection popped out, actually striking her in the face and leaving a wet smear on her nose. She didn't mind. Before the pants were even on the floor her head came forward, her lips opened, and she sucked him into her hot mouth with a satisfied slurp.

She sucked him up and down, her lips and tongue working madly against his flesh, her hand jacking him. Every sixth or seventh stroke she would pull her hand free and swallow him to the base in a delicious deep throat maneuver. He groaned each time she did this. Never before had a girl taken him all the way in her mouth. She began to move faster, to suck more firmly, to deep throat more often. He was so stoned that time really had no meaning. There was only sensation. The pleasure of her mouth upon him, the sight of her head bobbing forward and back, the sound of her slurping. She interrupted her rhythm only once, to pull her halter off over the top of her head, baring those gorgeous mounds on her chest. Jake's hands reached down, finding them, caressing them, squeezing them.

After what seemed an eternity he felt the orgasm beginning to stir within him. His hips began to move without his telling them to, his head fell back a little on his neck, his legs began to tremble, the knees bowing toward each other. Colette picked up on these signs like the expert she was. Her brown eyes looked up at him, sexiness and adoration shining within them. She pulled her mouth free of his cock but her hand kept moving back and forth, squeezing and releasing with each stroke.

"You want to come on my face?" she asked.

"Huh?" Jake asked, arousingly surprised. Though a common male fantasy since the days of Adam and Eve, women who would consent to such a thing were fairly rare in the dim, dark days of 1981.

"Or how about my tits?" she countered, jacking a little faster now. "You can. I like it that way."

It turned out that he did both. Her words kicked the machinery of orgasm into high gear all by themselves and the spasms began working through his body. She continued to smile and jack him off with her hands, her face inches away from the head of his cock, her mouth open, her tongue sticking out suggestively. The first spurt shot directly into her mouth, trailing across her wet tongue. The second hit her in the right cheek, splattering and running downward. She leaned back and adjusted her body, allowing the remainder to shoot over the tops of her breasts, saturating them with his offering.

While his nerve endings were still tingling from orgasm, while his pot-enhanced mind was still trying to grapple with the total eroticism of what she'd just done, her face leaned forward again and began to suck on his half-deflated penis. She slurped him clean and began to bob her head back and forth, deep throating on each stroke this time. It didn't take long before the blood refilled his cylinder for whatever came next.

Satisfied that his fresh hard-on was there to stay, she stood up and kicked off her shoes. She unbuttoned her pants and, with considerable effort due to the tightness of them, pushed them down her legs. There were no panties beneath. Her pubic hair was pure black, a sharp disparity to Michelle's blonde bush. Her vaginal lips were swollen and glistening with moisture. She reached down and fingered herself a few times, smearing her juices around.

"What do you want to do to me?" she asked him softly.

"What do I want you to do?"

"I'll do *anything* for you, Jake. Anything. Do you want me to go get us another girl?"

"Another... another girl?" he squeaked, his mouth agape as he stared at her fingers playing with her wet lips. Was she serious?

"I'll do it," she said, her tone leaving little doubt that she was indeed serious. "I'll walk out there right now, naked, and I'll find another girl who wants to join us. There will be one. I guarantee it. I'll eat her pussy for you while you fuck me. Or I'll make her eat my pussy while you fuck her. Do you want me to?"

"Uh..." he stammered, his mouth refusing to form words. Was this really happening? Sure, Matt and Coop and Darren and even Bill had told him that the groupies would do anything, but he hadn't considered that anything meant... well... *anything*.

"Or maybe you'd just like to fuck me like a dog," she suggested next. "How does that sound?"

Without waiting for him to answer she turned her back to him and walked over to the bed. She climbed up onto it and leaned forward, her butt sticking up in the air right at the level of his crotch, her upper body supported by her elbows, her face—still dripping with his semen—up against the bedspread.

The sight of her offering herself to him in this manner, of her swollen, aroused vagina open for his pleasure, got the better of him. He stepped quickly out of his pants, kicking off his own shoes in the process (and nearly falling down two times) and stepped forward. His hands came down on the firm cheeks of her ass. His hips went forward until the head of his cock was touching the center of her wetness. He thrust forward, burying himself within her body in one brutal stroke. Both of them cried out at the intrusion.

He thrust himself in and out of her, not bothering with anything like a build-up, just lustfully fucking her with sharp, slapping strokes. She grunted and moaned continuously, pushing her bottom backwards to meet each of his strokes. After three or four minutes, she came, her hands ripping the bedspread free, her moans almost painful in intensity.

The moment her spasms died down she looked back at him with her sweaty face. "Do you want my ass?" she asked him.

"Your... your ass?" he asked slowly. That was something else that guys were always fantasizing about, dreaming about, wanting to try, claiming they had done, but that real girls rarely consented to in 1981.

"My ass," she confirmed, reaching back with her hands and grabbing her lower cheeks. She spread them widely, revealing the entrance to said ass to his overwhelmed brain. "It's yours if you want it. I *like* it up the ass."

Jake had never performed this act before. He didn't hesitate for more than a second or two. He pulled himself free from her pussy and put himself against her smaller hole. Soon, he was buried within her back passage, experiencing the tightest fit he had ever imagined.

As he pounded in and out of her, listening to her grunts of pleasure, feeling the soft skin of her hips as he leveraged himself, seeing the amazing sight of his cock disappearing and reappearing from her *ass* instead of her pussy, he could not help but compare and contrast the sex he had received from Michelle with the sex he was receiving from Colette. Granted, he had loved Michelle, had enjoyed her company apart from the sex, and therefore their couplings had been satisfying just because of the fact that they were together. And while their sex life had not been boring by any means, Michelle had never taken his cock into her mouth, had never let him spray his come all over her face and tits, had never spread her ass cheeks and told him to fuck her in the forbidden zone. Colette had done all of this unhesitantly and seemingly with real desire. She had even offered to get another woman and bring her into the room, to eat the woman out while Jake fucked her, to do things that, quite frankly, he'd thought were never really done in real life.

Jake didn't love Colette. He had no desire to converse with her outside of this bedroom. But the allure of what she had to offer, what the girls like her had to offer, was something that he could not deny. This woman was beautiful, sexy, light years out of what he considered to be his league, and she had given herself to him unconditionally and with un-faked enthusiasm simply because he was something of a celebrity, a musician in a band she happened to like. He could have a woman like Colette, maybe even two, after every gig if he wanted.

For the first time Jake suddenly realized the true magnitude of the gift his talent and efforts had bestowed upon him. For a twenty-one year old kid who had spent the bulk of his life being ignored and called Bone Rack, it was a powerful thought indeed.

*****

Los Angeles, California
October 1, 1981

Ronald Shaver's office was on the twenty-second floor of the Hedgerow Building in Hollywood. It was an office that was designed to intimidate and impress. The view out the large window was of the Hollywood Hills and the famous sign atop them. The desk that sat before this view was of genuine oak and contained nearly eighteen square feet of workspace. Next to the desk was a fully stocked wet bar, complete with polished mirror hanging behind it. There was a leather couch where he frequently balled his twenty-two-year-old female secretary. On the desk itself was a typewriter, two telephones, a large Rolodex, and a custom made blotter, atop which sat a jeweled frame mirror about six inches square. Sitting on this mirror were two lines of pure Bolivian flake cocaine that sold for $150 per gram. The coke had been lovingly chopped into a fine powder with a razor blade. Descending towards the line on the left was a rolled up $100 bill, the other end of which was attached to Ronald Shaver's right nostril.

Shaver was a talent agent specializing in musical acts. At the age of forty-two, his name was known and moderately well respected by most of the major recording labels based in southern California. He had cut his teeth in the business during the disco craze of the mid-seventies, signing six major groups and/or artists, including one who had managed to make the transition to more palatable music once that particular craze came to a swift and merciful end. These days his two major clients were *Earthstone*, a hard rock band from San Diego that had cut three gold records; and *The Two Lips*, a punk rock band from Indianapolis that had gone mainstream enough to make their fourth album actually shoot past gold and go platinum.

Shaver was successful enough at his trade to be more than a little pompous but privately he knew he was not as successful as he could be if he only had the right material to work with. *Earthstone* was a solid band that made good music and would probably continue to for some time, but there was nothing that particularly stood out about them, that made them appeal to more than a sub-section of the music market. And *The Two Lips*, while wildly popular at this particular moment in time, would undoubtedly flounder into nothingness as soon as the punk fad currently sweeping the nation died out and was replaced by something a little less abrasive (an event that couldn't come too soon as far as the part of Shaver that actually *appreciated* good music was concerned).

What he needed was to get his hands on an act that had some talent, some originality, and, most important, some long-term mass appeal. He longed to discover the next *Van Halen*, or *Led Zepplin*, or even the next *Hall and* fucking *Oats*. He wasn't particular.

He made a point to keep his ear close to the ground, to keep his nose sniffing about for such an act, but so far he'd encountered nothing but a bunch of second-rate one-hit pop types at best, out and out hackers at worst. Was he losing his touch or was the talent pool just shrinking? Either way he feared the consequences and so, with no idea that exactly what he was looking for was about to be carried into his office by his secretary, he snorted up the first line of cocaine and sniffed loudly as he felt it settle into his nasal passage.

"Hey, Trina," he said as she came through the door. He made no effort whatsoever to move his cocaine mirror or hide what he was doing.

"Hi, Ronnie," she replied, flashing her best smile at him. She was a beautiful, willowy blonde dressed in a tight, short business dress, her smooth, sexy legs clad in dark nylons. She set two envelopes down on his desk. "Mail's here."

"Thanks," he said, sniffing a few more times. He picked up the mirror and offered it to her. "Care for a little toot?"

"Sure," she said casually, taking the mirror from his hands. He handed her the $100 bill and she made the line disappear. She sniffed loudly a few times and then set both back on the desk. "Thanks, hon," she told him. "We still on for tonight?"

"Dinner and dancing at Aces and Spades," he assured her. "I'll pick you up at eight."

"Bitchin'," she said with a smile. "Should I call your wife and tell her you'll be working late?"

"No need," he assured her. "She's down in Palm Springs for a week with Loretta."

"She's still doing the LPGA girl, huh? Does she know you know that they're more than friends?"

He shook his head. "She's dumber than dirt. That's why I married her. She didn't even have her lawyer look over the pre-nup before she signed it."

They both had a laugh at the expense of Gina Shaver, the beautiful, sensuous, and dim-witted woman he had walked down the aisle with three years before.

"Ahh well, she is good breeding stock though," Shaver said. He turned his attention to the mail. "So, what came in today? Anything important?"

"That new copy of the preliminary contract for *Earthstone*'s next album. It's pretty much the same as the last prelim except the label cut the limo clause from the tour package and reduced the advance offer by another ten percent."

He sighed. That fuckstick Tim Johnson over at National Records' Business Affairs department was jerking him around again. It was obvious he understood the terminal mediocrity that *Earthstone* was condemned to and was trying to cut as much out of the artist's budget as he could in order to preserve more profit for the label. Well, what did you expect from a fucking accountant anyway? It was a wonder to him that the world held bean counters on some sort of higher plain than ambulance chasers when they were easily just as sleazy. "I'll call that asshole up and deal with him after I get a little more blow in my system," he told her. "What else we got?"

"Just this," she said, indicating a large brown envelope with multiple stamps on it. "Came from a return address in Heritage."

"Heritage?" he said with distaste. "I don't know anyone in Heritage. And if I did, I surely wouldn't admit it. What is it?"

"I don't know," she said. "It's addressed to you by name and labeled Personal and Confidential."

He picked up the envelope, hefting its weight, and knew immediately what it was. To confirm, he felt the outside of it, finding the shape of a cased cassette tape inside. "It's a fucking demo tape," he said in disgust. "An *unsolicited* demo tape by some talent-less hackers who found my name in the library. You know I don't accept unsolicited demos, Trina. Why are you bringing this crap to me?"

"And you know that I don't open envelopes labeled Personal and Confidential," she said huffily. "Jeez, just bitch me out for doing my job, why don't you?"

She did have a point. "Sorry," he said, more to preserve his copulation later that night than out of any real regret. "I guess you're right. But now that you've brought it to me, I guess I should give it my full and complete attention, shouldn't I?"

"I guess you should," she agreed.

And with that, the envelope ended up in the same place as the other twelve Matt Tisdale had sent to talent agents from Nashville to New York to Chicago to Los Angeles: Unopened in the round file next to someone's desk. And in fact, though he didn't know it, Matt should have been proud. This was only the second one that had actually made it into the office of the man it had been addressed to.

"So, anyway," Shaver said, "do you think you can dig me up some copies of those video rights agreements we signed with *Earthstone*? When Galahad gets here at ten I want to be well versed on what I'm talking about so he doesn't screw us on *The Two Lips* gig the same way." Steve Galahad was the head of the New Media department at National Records, the label that had signed *The Two Lips*. The New Media department was a relatively new subdivision of the recording industry hierarchy that had been formed by most of the larger labels in response to the popularity of music videos over the past year, a popularity that was becoming more of a force every week since the debut of MTV a few months before. The Galahads of the world all thought that videos were the wave of the future and that music was about to undergo a fundamental change as drastic as that caused by the invention of the electric guitar. The Shavers of the world, on the other hand, still thought of videos as just another pain in the ass thing they and their artists had to deal with.

"I'll have them and the notes you made on them on your desk by 9:30," Trina replied. "Anything else?"

"A blowjob?" he suggested.

She giggled. "How about in the car on the way to Aces and Spades?"

"Deal."

She left the office, closing the door and leaving him alone. The moment she was gone he opened the drawer on the front of his desk and removed the sterling silver container he kept his cocaine in. He dumped out a small amount and then went about the task of chopping it up into a fine dust and forming a line. Once this was done he snorted up and stashed his paraphernalia back where it belonged.

Before the latest dose even had a chance to work its way fully into his bloodstream, his office door opened again and Trina poked her head through. "Galahad just called," she said. "He cancelled his ten o'clock with you."

"Christ," Shaver said, shaking his head. "What the hell for?"

"His secretary said that one of his artists showed up drunk at a video shoot and tried to rape a dancer in the bathroom. He has to go deal with the fallout."

Shaver didn't disbelieve the excuse. On the contrary, to a man with as many years in the music business as he, it sounded all too plausible. "Okay," he said. "Is he going to reschedule?"

"She said she would call and set something up for early next week as soon as she can shuffle around his calendar. Anyway, it looks like you're free for the next two hours."

"Bitchin," he grumbled, wondering what he was going to do now. Before it occurred to him that a little rendezvous with Trina on his couch might be in order, she had already shut the door and disappeared. He could have called her back, of course, but he really wasn't that much in the mood himself. At least not at the moment, anyway.

As the cocaine finally hit his brain, filling him with cheerfulness and washing away his fatigue, he decided that maybe a drink was in order. True, it was only 9:15 in the morning, but it was lunchtime in New York, wasn't it? And didn't all the really important things in America happen in New York? He concluded that this was sound logic and walked over to the bar. He took down a water tumbler and filled it with ice from the machine in the freezer. On top of the ice he poured a quadruple shot of Chivas Regal. He then grabbed a Cuban cigar from the humidor next to the freezer and carried these acquisitions back to his desk.

He took a few sips of his drink and then sparked up the cigar. He leaned back in his chair and puffed thoughtfully for a few minutes, not thinking of anything in particular, just enjoying the effects of the coke and the sensation of the nicotine tingling his mouth. When the ash on the cigar grew to the point where it needed to be flicked off, he leaned forward again and opened the side drawer, reaching in to get the ashtray he kept in there for just such occasions. It wasn't there.

"Goddammit," he muttered, though in a good-natured manner. It was hard to be unpleasant when you had a couple lines of Bolivian flake coursing through your brain. He flicked on the intercom and buzzed Trina. She didn't answer until the third buzz.

"Yes?" she almost hissed, her voice impatient.

"I think you forgot to put my ashtray back in my desk last time you cleaned in here," he said. "Can you hunt one up for me?"

"Can it wait a few?" she asked. "I've got Galahad's secretary on the line and we're trying to come up with a time for the meeting."

"Oh, sure," he said. "Take your time."

"Thank you," she said, more than a hint of condescension in her tone.

With no ashtray to use, he leaned over the garbage can next to the desk and flicked his ash in there instead. It landed on the brown envelope that had been sent to him without his solicitation. He looked at this for a moment and had a momentary worry that he might accidentally start a fire. To avoid this he dug the envelope out, brushed the ash off it, and set it on his desk. He would throw it back in there when Trina finally brought him the ashtray. Until then, he would enjoy his illegal smoke.

He puffed away for a few more minutes, not thinking of anything in particular, occasionally dipping his ashes in the garbage can or sipping from his Chivas. Eventually his eyes found their way back to the envelope on his desk. He could read the return address in the upper left corner. Instead of a name there was only a word: *Intemperance*, presumably the name of the band.

"Fucking *Intemperance*," he mumbled. "What a stupid name." His eyes took in the city and zip code portion of the return address. "Fucking Heritage. What a dump." He had in fact never actually been to Heritage before, or anywhere in California that was north of Santa Barbara for that matter, but he assumed that any place that had a population of less than two million had to be a dump.

Impulsively, he decided to open the envelope. Unsolicited demos were usually accompanied by a cover letter of some sort—assuming the moron who had sent it knew that that was the custom—and they were often quite amusing to read. Maybe it would be one of those ones that was so full of misspellings and incorrect grammar that he could use it as an anecdote the next time he had lunch with a few of his colleagues. Hell, if it were lame enough to be amusing he would actually photocopy it and pass it around. After all, you took humor where you could get it in this life.

He picked up the envelope and used the switchblade letter opener in his pen jar to open it. He discovered that there was not just a cover letter inside, but an entire sheaf of papers, most of them copies. He glanced at the cover letter first, expecting the salutation to say: Dear Sir or Madam, or To Whom it May Concern, or something equally generic. Instead, he was surprised to see that it was properly headed with his full name and title, his address, and the first line was, Dear Mr. Shaver.

The text of the letter was professionally formatted and neatly typed. The gist of it was that the writer, a man named Matthew Tisdale, was the lead guitar player for a band called *Intemperance* and that the band had become very popular in the Heritage metropolitan region over the past year. The letter spoke of sold out shows and of receiving $500 per set plus fringe benefits.

"Five hundred per set?" Shaver mumbled. If that was true than it was marginally impressive. Most club owners wouldn't pay more than $250 per set, no matter how good the band was. And that was here in Los Angeles. In a cow town like Heritage that was some serious dough. A club owner wouldn't pay that much unless a band was bringing in significant business.

Shaver read on, learning that the band was playing three times a week minimum, introducing new songs once a month on average. Tisdale described them as a hard rock band that utilized a classically trained piano player to introduce a unique sound to their music.

"A fucking classical piano player?" Shaver said. "That's insane." While it was true that many rock bands utilized pianos in their music—*REO Speedwagon*, *Journey*, and *The Doobie Brothers* all came immediately to mind—they weren't *hard* rock bands like these *Intemperance* jokers were claiming to be. Hard rock and piano just didn't go together. It was like oil and water. But then, wasn't that what a British colleague of his had once said when a group had come before him explaining how their flute—a fucking *flute* for God's sake—mixed in nicely with the hard rock? That colleague had ended up representing the band *Jethro Tull* and had been on easy street ever since.

He read some more. The letter told him that he would find, enclosed, a collection of media reviews from popular Heritage County publications and letters of recommendation from various club owners, attesting to the popularity and skill of *Intemperance*. Tisdale closed by saying that he and the band were seeking an established agent so that they might expand their popularity beyond the Heritage area and possibly secure a recording contract at some point in the future. It gave a contact number, an address, and, lastly, a list of venues where the band could be seen if he should happen to be in the Heritage area any time soon. He thanked Shaver for his time and consideration in this matter and closed by wishing him a nice day.

Shaver had to admit to himself that he was impressed by the cover letter. Whoever this Tisdale joker was, he had at least done his research on how to correspond with a potential agent. He set it down and picked up the sheaf of papers that had been beneath it. The first was a music review from *The Heritage Register*, which was apparently what passed for a newspaper in that town. It was an articulate and gushing endorsement of the band *Intemperance*, who could be seen playing at D Street West and Willie's Roadhouse on a weekly basis.

"The soulful singing of lead singer Jake Kingsley mixed with the grueling riffs and grinding solos of lead guitarist Matt Tisdale would be more than enough to catch the attention of any rock music fan. But when you throw in the glorious melody of pianist Bill Archer you have a sound that's unique and refreshing on the rock music scene. You could do much worse than to sacrifice the five-dollar cover charge to see this band play. It's an experience that makes me proud to say I'm from Heritage."

The next article was from a publication called the *Heritage Weekly Review*. It also contained a glowing approval of *Intemperance* and their music, this time going on about the depth of the lyrical experience.

"The lyrics are written by either Kingsley or Tisdale and it is not hard to figure out which is which. Kingsley's songs are about hope, about the agony of love, about politics, while Tisdale's are hard driving, angry tunes about the futility of love, about living life to excess."

There were several other articles, all from one or the other of these papers. All of them expounded upon how good the band was, telling the readers about the mix of acoustic and electric guitar with piano, about Kingsley's voice, about Tisdale's solos and riffs. All of them mentioned sold-out shows.

"Hmm," Shaver said, licking his lips thoughtfully. He turned to the letters of recommendation, reading them over one by one. There were five of them in all, each one from a club owner in Heritage, each one telling of dedicated and talented musicians who regularly packed their establishment with paying customers, each one stating the price he was willing to pay to have *Intemperance* perform in his venue.

Finally, he reached into the envelope and pulled out the cassette case. It was an expensive name brand tape with the words: *Intemperance Demo* stenciled on the front. A song sheet named the songs that could be found on the tape. Shaver looked over the titles.

Descent Into Nothing
Who Needs Love?
Almost Too Easy
Living By The Law

He took the tape out of its case and stood up. Across the room, near the bar, was a stereo system. He popped out the *Beatles* tape that had been in there and put the *Intemperance* tape in. He shut the door and powered up the stereo. He pushed play and listened.

The tape was in mono and poorly mixed, probably done on the cheapest equipment available, possibly even rigged up entirely. Ordinarily he would have turned it off as soon as he'd heard the hiss prior to the first song starting. This time he didn't. It wasn't thirty seconds into *Descent Into Nothing* before he mumbled, "Holy shit," out loud.

He listened to the entire tape and then he listened to it again. After the second playing he walked to the door of his office and opened it. Trina was sitting at her desk, typing something on her IBM Selectric. She looked up at him guiltily.

"Sorry," she said. "I was supposed to bring you an ashtray, wasn't I?"

He hardly heard her. "What are you doing this weekend?" he asked.

"This weekend? I don't have any plans." She smiled in a naughty manner. "At least not yet."

"How would you like to go up to Heritage with me?"

Her look turned to confusion. "Heritage?" she asked. "What for?"

"There's something I need to look at."

CHAPTER 3

DISCOVERY

October 13, 1981
Heritage, California

It was Friday night and D Street West was packed with about as many people as it could physically hold. The air was hot and stale, choked with cigarette smoke, the odor of sweat and beer pervading every corner. The babble of hundreds of conversations and the shouts of drunken voices drowned out the recorded music playing from the overhead speakers. Behind the bar, six bartenders struggled to keep up with the hordes of customers pushing and shoving to get close enough to order another round. Occasionally, a fight would break out although they tended to be brief, mostly harmless struggles that were broken up by bystanders before they could escalate into something more dangerous. There simply wasn't the room to have a good fight. Not on a night that *Intemperance* was playing.

The opening band had been *Airburst*, a group that actually displayed something like talent. Jake had spent a few minutes talking to them before their set—something he made a point of doing with each band that opened for them—and had learned that their members were made up of the pick of the litter of three other bands that had been making the second-rate club circuit over the past year. They had a southern blues rock sound, sort of a cross between *Lynard Skynard* and *Molly Hatchet*, not exactly original, but not exactly a knock-off either since the lead singer was a woman. The crowd had cheered for them in a manner that seemed considerably more sincere than that displayed for most of the openers in this venue. But they did not ask for an encore. *Intemperance* remained the only opening act to have ever achieved that distinction.

At ten minutes to showtime Jake and Matt were in the backstage alcove looking out over the crowd. This was something both of them enjoyed doing, Matt so he could scope out likely groupie prospects for after the show, Jake because he never tired of marveling over the fact that so many people had come to see them play. He still felt some stage fright before each performance—some of those nagging, irrational fears refused to go away—but it was nothing like the intensity it had been before that first performance. They were now seasoned performers and they put on a damn good show. A thousand people had told them that a thousand times and they knew it to be true.

There had been a few mishaps of course. When you performed live, things got screwed up every now and then. It was just a fact of life. The most common thing to happen were dropped or broken guitar picks in the middle of a song. Matt and Jake had both done this several dozen times apiece now. There had also been the time that Jake's A string had snapped in the middle of *Worship Me*, a semi-ballad with lots of finger-picking of that particular string. Coop had broken drumsticks half a dozen times (though he had never, not even once, dropped one, not even while twirling them around or throwing them into the air and catching them). Darren had once stepped on his power cord, ripping it out of his bass and nearly falling to his face before recovering his balance. And Bill had once gone a little overboard while running his hands across his keyboard and had accidentally turned his volume switch all the way up, creating a feedback whine that had been nearly loud enough to shatter glass.

They had learned to recover from these mishaps quickly and professionally. In the case of the lost guitar picks, the band had gotten so good at covering for it that no one in the audience—save other experienced musicians—usually even noticed. Whoever lost it would switch to hitting their strings with their fingers for the remainder of the song. If there was no break planned between the song where the pick had been lost and the next, the band would insert a break, pausing long enough for Jake to throw out a "is everyone havin' a good time" and for a new pick to be produced. In the case of the drumstick, Coop would simply miss a beat with that hand long enough to reach down and grab another from a stash he kept in a pocket between the two bass drums. He had become so proficient at this maneuver that the audience usually never noticed this either.

The things the audience *did* notice—the volume on the piano, the broken guitar string, the forcible removal of the power cord—the band tried not to dwell on. They simply recovered as quickly and nonchalantly as possible and went on with the show. Jake, as the voice of the band, had discovered a natural talent for making humorous comments when such things occurred.

"That's a new step Darren's working on there," he'd said after the cord tripping incident, while Darren blushed and scrambled to plug himself back in. "As you can see, it needs just a little more work."

The audience had laughed, and a moment later Coop banged the sticks together and launched them into the next song.

When Bill created the feedback whine, making everyone in the house wince and cover their ears as 130 decibels washed over them, everything went quiet afterward, the audience stunned and a little shocked at this obvious malfunction of performance. Jake waited until things were at their quietest and then yelled into his mic, "Do we fuckin' *rock*, or what?"

Once again, laughter had erupted, followed by cheers, followed by resumption of the set as if nothing had happened.

Perhaps the most shining example of covering for a mistake had been when Jake's guitar string had broken. "Looks like I played that one to death," he told the audience—that after nearly two minutes of converting the remaining acoustic portions of the song into a rhythm that did not require the A string to be struck. He patted his Les Paul affectionately. "Can ya'll hang on a sec while I fix this thing up?"

And while he'd gone backstage and hurriedly installed a new A string, the rest of the band kept the crowd entertained with an impromptu jam session in which Matt and Bill played dueling solos while Darren and Coop kept rhythm. Once his string was in place and tuned as well as he could get it by listening without amplification, Jake had gone back out, plugged in, and joined them, inserting his own acoustic solos seamlessly into theirs and adjusting his tuning knob in between them. When he was tuned to his satisfaction, he gave a nod to the rest of the band and they wrapped up the unplanned, unrehearsed performance with an equally unplanned and unrehearsed flourish of instruments. The crowd had cheered wildly and given a standing ovation. When they quieted down, *Intemperance* fell back into the rest of the set they'd rehearsed, playing it out to perfection.

Such occurrences, however, were very much the exception to the rule. Most of their sets went off flawlessly, the music pouring out of them just as they'd rehearsed it. They changed their sets around every two weeks, usually cycling in new tunes they'd come up with once a month. They now had a bank of thirty-three original songs, all but two of which had been performed at least once before their fans. Tonight was the second night of a new cycle, the first night that *It's In The Book* would be performed for the D Street West crowd.

"Look at that one right there," Matt told Jake, pointing with his lit cigarette out into the crowd. "That brunette there in the purple blouse."

"Which one?" Jake asked. "There's like five hundred people out there."

"Over there by the bar," Matt said, pointing a little firmer. "Standing next to that fat bitch and that faggy-looking dude with the crew-cut. You see her?"

Jake dutifully turned his attention in that direction and, after a moment of searching, found the girl he was referring to. "I see her," he said. "And I believe that blouse is what the ladies call lavender, not purple."

Matt shook his head in disgust. "Fuckin' lavender? Jesus Christ, Jake. You smokin' dicks now? No dude should know what lavender is."

"Forgive me, Father, for I have sinned," Jake said. "Anyway, what about her?"

"She's my bitch for the night," Matt said. "I'm gonna fuck her."

"Does she know this yet?"

"No, but she will. Look how shy she looks. How innocent. She might even be a cherry."

"Awfully confident, aren't you?" Jake asked. "What if she doesn't stay for the after-gig festivities?"

Matt shrugged. "Then she'll miss out on her golden opportunity to have her furrow plowed by the great and powerful Matt Tisdale. Her loss. I have a Plan B already sighted in just in case." He pointed over at the other end of the barroom. "That blond librarian looking bitch. See her? Standing next to that slut in the red mini-skirt?"

Jake didn't see her but pretended like he did. "Uh huh," he said. "And what if the first chick does stay for the party but doesn't want to boff you? You ever think of that?"

Matt looked genuinely appalled by this suggestion. "No," he said simply. "I never thought of that. Why would I?"

Jake didn't press the point any further. He knew Matt was right. So far, he had never been turned down once he set his sights on a particular female. He had even gone through a period where he and Coop were betting twenty dollars on that very subject, with Coop picking a woman at the after-gig party and Matt having to fuck her before the night was out. Matt had a one hundred percent win rate so far and it had got to the point where he had to offer ten to one odds just to get Coop to take the bet.

"And what about you?" Matt asked. "You gonna get your weenie wet tonight?"

"I don't know," he sighed. "I'm still a little fucked over about the whole Michelle thing."

"That didn't stop you from nailing that Brooke Shields looking bitch on Wednesday. I was proud of you, man. Fucking proud. You finally took advantage of the pussy that's due people of our stature and talent. How was she, anyway? I've seen her at a couple of our shows and thought about giving her a ride myself."

"She was uh... well, very experienced at sexuality," he replied. "But I was drunk and stoned. I wouldn't have done it otherwise."

"You'll be drunk and stoned tonight too," Matt reminded him.

Jake thought that over for a second. "I guess you're right," he said, smiling.

"That's my fuckin' brother," Matt said, slapping him on the back. "I knew you were a man. You oughtta call up that Catholic bitch while you're fucking some slut tonight and put the phone down by her pussy so she can hear the squishing while you laugh at her. That'll show her she's been replaced."

"That would show her all right," Jake said, knowing he would never do such a thing no matter how drunk or how mad he was, also knowing that Matt *would* do it even if he were sober and only mildly peeved.

That sat in silence for a bit, Matt smoking, Jake drinking from his ice water. Finally, Jake brought up the subject that had been bothering both of them. "Darren is stoned out of his mind," he said.

"I know," Matt said. "I can smell it all over him for one thing, but that's not even it. I can tell just by looking at him. I mean, Jesus fucking Christ, we've gotten stoned together a thousand times. We know what he acts like, what he fuckin' looks like when he's flyin'. Does he really think he's fooling us?"

"Yeah, I think he does," Jake said.

"Moron," Matt said, shaking his head.

Throughout their year of playing together onstage, the members of *Intemperance* had changed and evolved in many ways. Their wardrobe, their playing styles, their onstage antics, the between-song banter, even their music itself had all undergone a shift as they gained experience performing. One thing that had not changed, however, was the rule about using intoxicating substances before rehearsing or performing. Matt and Jake both liked to think of this as a sacred decree. But over the past six weeks or so, they had noticed that Darren seemed to be throwing this rule to the wayside. He would show up for rehearsals higher than a kite, claiming that he had smoked some hours before but was fine now. Worse, he was now starting to slip out somewhere before their live performances and come back reeking of pot, his eyes half-lidded, his speech thick and slow in the way it only got when he was stoned. Tonight had been the first night that Matt—as the leader of the group—had actually called him on it. Darren had simply denied it absolutely and unwaveringly.

"Dude, I'm *not* stoned," he said. "I wouldn't burn before a show. You know that."

"I can smell it all over you, asshole!" Matt yelled back, exasperated and pissed.

"That doesn't mean I've been smoking it," Darren protested. "Jesus, man. I walked by some people out back that were toking up and the smoke got on me."

They had gone round and round about this for almost ten minutes before Matt finally walked away in frustration—an emotion that was almost foreign to him.

"What are we gonna do about it?" Jake asked now. "I mean, this can't go on. I'm pretty sure he was lit when he tripped over his power cord."

"Yeah," Matt said. "He was."

"And if this keeps up, he's gonna have Coop smoking out with him before long. You know how close those two are. You know how Darren's the fuckin epitome of peer pressure."

"I know," Matt agreed, dropping his cigarette into a soda can. "I've known Darren since we were freshmen in high school so I know what he's like and what he's capable of. This isn't going to continue. Mark my word."

"What are you going to do?"

"He's an old friend and I hate to do it, but I'm gonna have to lay down the law with him. I'll take him aside tonight and let him know that if he shows up stoned for either a rehearsal or a performance one more time... if we even *think* he might be stoned at a rehearsal or a performance, then he's out of the band."

Jake thought this was very harsh, but he didn't disagree. They couldn't afford to have anyone giving less than their all. "Do you think he'll believe you?"

"If he wants to push the issue, I'll let him know where he really stands. He's a fuckin' bass player. He's pretty good but he isn't outstanding or anything. He can easily be replaced. If we put an ad in the paper asking for a bass player to perform with *Intemperance*, we'll have two hundred applications the next day and I guarantee you that at least one out of every ten of them will be both better and more reliable than Darren."

"And what if he tries to get Coop to go with him if we kick him out?"

Another shrug. "If you were Coop, would you go with him?"

"No," Jake said immediately. "I wouldn't."

"And I don't think Coop will either. And even if he does, the same thing applies to him. Coop is better at drumming than Darren is at bass, but he's not Jon Bonham or anything. If we put an ad out for a drummer, we'd have five hundred applications and one out of every twenty would be as good as or better than Coop. When you come right down to it, those two positions in the band are nothing but support. Its you, me, and Nerdly that make this band what it is. Agree?"

"Yeah," Jake said. "I think that's a fair assessment."

"So if the fuckin' rhythm section is having a problem with the buds, then we can kick their asses out of here if they don't stay in line. And right now, that's the situation we face. I'll tell Darren how it is tonight, you support me, and this thing will work itself out. Trust me."

Jake nodded. "I'll support you," he said.

O'Donnell appeared a moment later, his signature cocaine glint firmly affixed upon his face. Darren, Coop, and Bill trailed behind him, Darren still looking sullen and hurt from the argument with Matt.

"You ready to do it, boys?" O'Donnell asked, putting his chubby arms around Jake and Matt's shoulders.

"We're ready," Matt said, casting an evil glare at Darren. "Aren't we?"

Darren refused to meet his eyes. Yeah," he muttered. "Ready for Freddie."

O'Donnell's smile faded a bit as he picked up on some of the tension. He seemed to debate saying something and then decided not to. "All right then," he said instead. "Let's get the show on."

The crowd cheered as he walked out on the stage, quieted while he made a lengthy and almost syrupy introduction, and then erupted into out and out pandemonium when the name *Intemperance* was spoken. The band did their now customary hands on hands symbol of camaraderie and then hit the stage. The cheers, whistles, and shouts intensified as they picked up their instruments and took their places.

"You ready to rock and roll?" Jake asked the crowd, serving the dual purpose of riling them up and performing a level check on his microphone. Since they were the headliner band they had no opportunity for a sound check prior to the show. They had to rely on pre-setting all of the equipment beforehand.

The crowd was ready to rock and roll. *Intemperance* obliged them. Coop did a four count with the drumsticks and they began to bang out their opening number for this cycle, *Waste Not, Want Not*—one of Matt's hard-driving tunes that dealt with the subject of never turning down sex or drugs when they were offered.

Jake's fingers picked out the backing riff with ease, moving from fret to fret. When the cue came around, his voice burst out of his mouth, the words flowing freely, effortlessly, the volume and timbre shaped to perfection. The crowd settled down a bit and enjoyed the music, most of them swaying to the beat and tapping their feet, more than a few actually singing along. When Matt played the first guitar solo of the night—a fast and furious finger-tapping number—the crowd stood and cheered, raising their arms and pumping them.

They ended the song as they did all of them—with a tremendous concerto of drums, guitars, piano, and bass chords. After a brief pause to let the crowd cheer in appreciation, there was another four count and they launched into *Descent Into Nothing*, a tried and true favorite at D Street West.

Matt, Jake, and Darren all moved around much more than they used to. In their earlier gigs they had tended to stay near their respective microphone stands, shuffling back and forth a little, but only shifting position during the guitar solos, when Jake would step back near Darren and Matt would step forward. These days both Matt and Darren kept their animation levels high while Jake sang, moving back and forth behind him, occasionally playing back to back or shoulder to shoulder. Jake did the same when his mouth was not required on the microphone, stepping back and joining the other two, occasionally doing a little spin maneuver. When it was time for a guitar solo, Matt would bend backward, or forward, or would force the neck of his instrument up or down, making it look as if the act of producing the music was a painful, difficult endeavor. This showmanship added an element of spontaneity to each performance, especially since Matt forbid them from choreographing or rehearsing such maneuvers in advance. They never went overboard—there was no dropping to the floor and scooting along on their buttocks, no licking of the guitar strings, no leaps from the amplifier stacks—instead, they simply let the rhythm and their instincts guide them. In this way, each *Intemperance* concert was unique.

As Jake performed, looking out over the crowd and making eye contact with person after person, the lyrics coming out of his mouth and transmitting through the amplifier, his hands moving up and down on his guitar, bending and pressing the steel strings with his left, his pick or his fingers hitting them in a series of complex rhythms with his right, all was copasetic in his world. Playing music for a crowd was what he loved doing most of all, making even sex pale in comparison. It was a difficult job—keeping his lyrics straight, keeping his riffs in time—but it was one he was good at and he thrilled with each song that went off without a hitch. The high it gave him was more powerful, more satisfying than even the best weed, the most potent cocaine, the smoothest booze. Thoughts of Michelle and their break-up, the sense of loss, pain, and incomprehension that had run through him constantly, they were gone while he played, as were thoughts of how he was going to make his next rent payment, how he was going to afford new tires for his car, whether or not his parents were right and he should start trying to put his talent to better use. There was no room in his mind for anything but the show, anything but the crowd he was playing for, for the music he was helping to make. Like a fighter pilot on a mission, an athlete in the middle of a game, he was in the bubble, and nothing else mattered.

By the halfway point of the set, after a solid thirty minutes of playing under the hot stage lights, Jake was dripping with sweat. His long hair was damp with it. His white, button-up shirt was sticking to his chest and back. He was not breathless, however. Not even close to it. After a year of dancing and jumping and singing and playing three nights a week for sixty to seventy minutes at a time, his body was actually in the best shape it had ever been in. Being a rock music performer was the equivalent of taking a high-impact aerobics class, complete with the endorphin rush that came when things really got smoking.

The endorphins were flowing freely as they did their last song of the set, *Who Needs Love?*—one of their most popular numbers. They ended the song with a longer and more potent flourish, drawing it out and then finally hitting the last chords. They let the last hums of the instruments slowly fade away as the crowd erupted into cheers and applause once again.

"Thank you," Jake said, tossing his guitar pick into the crowd. "Thank you very much and goodnight."

The band gathered together, linked arms, and took a bow. They walked back to the alcove and the cheering continued, growing louder even. This was followed by the stomping feet and the cries of more, more, more.

All five of them drank mightily from their water glasses, alleviating a little of their thirst. They allowed themselves two minutes to rest and to hear the glorious sound of the crowd calling for their return and then Matt said, "Let's do it." They hit the stage again.

Jake did a brief introduction of their new song—*It's In The Book*—and they launched into it, the fast-paced riff from Matt's guitar getting everyone's hands clapping and waving even before Jake began to sing. They then did their final number of the night, one of their raunchier and hard-driving tunes, Matt's *The Thrill of Doing Business*. Another drawn out, carefully rehearsed ending, another group bow, and they left the stage for good this time. There were shouts for another encore—there always were—but they died reluctantly away when O'Donnell turned up the houselights and took the stage himself.

"*Intemperance* everybody!" he shouted. "Let's hear it for them one more time!"

The crowd gave it up once more, as requested.

The band gathered backstage and sat down near their equipment cases. This was the cool down period, when they let their heartbeats return to normal, when they let some of the sweat dry up. They talked about how the show had gone—all thought it had gone exceptionally well tonight—while they guzzled water and smoked cigarettes (all except for Bill, who still hadn't picked up that particular habit).

"Well," Matt said after fifteen minutes, "let's go get it done."

"Yep," Coop said with a sigh. "This is the fun part."

They trudged back to the stage to clean up their mess. The crowd had thinned considerably with the end of the show but there was still upwards of three hundred people out there, smoking, drinking, and dancing to the jukebox music. As always, those remaining gave a cheer as the band reappeared. They all waved back casually, acknowledging it, and then went about the task of breaking down their show.

As part of his closing remarks each night, O'Donnell always asked the crowd to please refrain from disturbing the musicians during the stage clearing process. As a result, they were pretty much left alone as they disassembled the drum set and hefted amps and wound up electrical cable. Occasionally a fan near the stage would tell them "great show" or "you guys rocked tonight", but no one seemed to expect an extended conversation at this point in the evening.

Once all the equipment was packed into the two vans and secured, they went back inside through the backstage door. Adjacent to the bar supply storage room was a small locker room for the performing bands' use. Since it only contained two showerheads, the five of them matched quarters for bathing order. Jake and Coop came out first and second tonight, so they stripped off their sweaty stage clothes and fired up the nozzles.

Jake, who had never been a fan of the locker room environment, showered quickly, running a bar off soap over his skin, dumping some shampoo and conditioner on his hair, rinsing, and then vacating for Matt, who had drawn third place. He dried off and put on a fresh pair of jeans and a tattered black T-shirt. He combed out his long hair and then slipped back into the tennis shoes he had worn on stage.

As he was heading for the door Matt passed him, fresh out of the shower now, completely naked except for a towel slung over his shoulders. "We're gonna get us some fuckin' cherry pussy tonight," he said. "How's that sound?"

Jake didn't answer him. He knew Matt wasn't talking to him. He was talking to his own penis—an instrument he conversed with almost as much as his guitar. Jake shook his head, told his bandmates he would see them out there, and then slipped out the door and into the hallway.

When he walked through the service door that led from the backstage area into the main lounge, there was the usual crowd of people loitering around. Dozens of females and about half as many males made a point of staking out this location after the show in the hopes of being among the first to socialize with a band member. This used to overwhelm Jake in the early days—how everyone wanted to talk to him, to touch him, to be near him—but he was used to it now.

No less than twenty people called out his name in asynchronous harmony. Hands descended on his shoulders to pat him. He was told it had been a great show in a dozen different ways. They pressed all around him, mostly the girls, vying for his attention. Several of the closer girls made a point to "accidentally" rub their breasts on his arm or on his back. He acknowledged as many people as he could, shaking a few hands, throwing out a few words of thanks and a few other small commentaries. He kept a slight smile on his face—the signature shy smile people had come to love about him. As he walked towards his first priority—a stiff drink—the gathering moved with him. As he approached the bar, those in front of him and those who were not part of the gathering but were merely waiting at the bar for their own drinks, parted to either side, leaving him a clear path.

"Wassup, brother?" asked Mohammad Hazim, a full-time bartender for D Street West and a part-time struggling guitarist whom Jake had taken under his wing over the last few months. Mohammad's parents had come to Heritage from Iran in 1962, when he was just two years old. They were devout Muslims who still wore the dress of their native land and were quite horrified by their only son, who had gone to school in the Heritage Public School system and had become fully Americanized by the age of thirteen.

"Wassup, Mo?" Jake asked, holding out his right hand and exchanging a soul brother shake. "You comin' to the party tonight?" Mohammad was one of the select few who fell into the *personal friend of the band* category in regard to Matt's parties. As such, he had an open invite for every one and he did not need to bring an intoxicating substance along for admission (although he often did anyway).

"Bet your ass," he said, taking a water glass down from above the bar and filling it with ice. He poured a triple shot of 151 proof rum into it, filled the rest up with Coke, and then handed it over to Jake, not asking for payment on a drink that would've cost anyone else four bucks. "Here ya go. You good on smokes?"

"For the moment," Jake assured him.

"Yell me down if you need anything."

"I will," Jake said. "Thanks, Mo."

Mo moved off down the bar to serve some of the paying customers and Jake pulled out one of his cigarettes. Two of the guys moved forward to light it for him, both whipping out Zippos. The larger of the two—a blonde, surfer type in a *Van Halen* T-shirt—got his up and ignited first. Jake accepted the light from him and spent a few moments conversing with him. It turned out the guy was a guitarist as well—probably a hopeless hacker—and wanted to know details on several chords that Jake had played. Jake remained polite and cordial as he answered his questions.

"Thanks, dude," the surfer told him about halfway through the smoke. "Good fuckin' gig tonight. You guys rock."

"Thanks," Jake said. "We try."

The surfer had a laugh at that and disappeared into the crowd. He was instantly replaced by one of the girls, who wanted to know just how one went about securing an invitation to the after-gig party.

Over the next thirty minutes, Jake was promised sex ten times by ten different girls—one of whom had offered to take him out to her car right at that moment and fuck him in the backseat. During this time, he consumed two and a half of Mo's potent drinks and as the alcohol began to surge into his brain he went from politely deflecting each offer to seriously considering which one of the girls he was going to take to Matt's. After all, he'd done it the other night and had enjoyed it immensely, hadn't he? Why shouldn't he enjoy it tonight as well? It wasn't like he had a girlfriend any longer.

It was as he was working on his fourth drink and debating between Allison, the naughty looking short girl in the red mini-skirt, and Cindy, the exotic looking Asian in the Calvin Kleins, that a blonde woman worked her way through the throng and stood before him. She was wearing a conservative, businesslike dress, complete with nylons and high-heels. Her make-up was lightly applied and her eyes were a striking shade of blue. She seemed to be considerably classier than the average female who patronized this establishment.

"Hi," she said, flashing a brief smile. "You're Mr. Kingsley, right?"

"Mr. Kingsley?" he said with a laugh. "That's very formal. You can call me Jake."

She seemed to shrug in a manner that was almost condescending. "As you wish, Jake," she said. "My name is Trina. Trina Allen. I tried to get over to talk to Mr. Tisdale there, but he's got quite the crowd around him."

Jake glanced over in Matt's direction. There was indeed a huge crowd surrounding the lead guitar player. "Yeah, Matt's a friendly guy, all right. Anyway, it's nice to meet you, Trina." He held out his hand. "Did you like the show?"

She offered her hand and gave him a brief, businesslike shake. "Yeah," she said analytically. "It was good. Much better than I was expecting, really. But then I'm more of a soft rock fan. *Elton John, Billy Joel*, stuff like that."

"I see," Jake said slowly. This was certainly not the typical adoring groupie conversation. "Well, I'm glad we were able to keep you entertained."

"So am I," she said. "But anyway, I have a friend that would really like to speak to you and Mr. Tisdale, if that's all right."

"Of course it's all right. We're gonna be getting out of here pretty soon and heading over to Matt's place, but just bring her on over. I'm always happy to talk to a fan."

"Well, in the first place," she said, "she is a he. And in the second place, he's not really a fan, per se."

Jake began to get an uncomfortable sensation. "Really?" he said. "Well, whoever he is, just have him come on over and I'll say hello."

"He would like to speak to you and Mr. Tisdale together," she said. "And he's outside. In his car."

"Uh huh," Jake said. "Well... to tell you the truth, Trina, if he wants to meet us, he's just gonna have to come inside. We don't usually go meet people out in the parking lot."

"I think perhaps you should adjust your policy on that matter," she said. "The gentleman I represent is Ronald Shaver."

"Ronald Shaver?" Jake said, his mind spinning. That name sounded familiar, but he didn't know why.

"We're from Los Angeles, here in Heritage on business," Trina said. "Mr. Shaver is a talent agent whom Mr. Tisdale recently sent a correspondence. He caught your show tonight and would like to speak to the two of you before he goes back to the hotel." She gave him a calculating look. "That is, if you're not too busy engaging in your minor league debauchery preparations?"

Ten seconds later, Jake was forcing himself through the crowd of people surrounding Matt, shouldering scantily dressed girls and drunken men to either side, causing six spilled drinks, two extinguished cigarettes, and one drunken fall. Only the fact that he was Jake Kingsley saved him from getting his ass kicked on general principals. Finally, his target came into view, one hand wrapped around a tall Jack and Coke, the other wrapped around the girl he had vowed to fuck earlier, his fingertips caressing the top of her breast through her blouse.

"Jake!" Matt yelled in his three-quarters drunken voice. "How the hell ya doin', brother?" He turned to the admirers around him. "Do y'all know Jake? He's the singer for the band."

This caused a few laughs among the crowd. Jake ignored them. "I need to talk to you, Matt," he said.

"Well fuckin' talk, homey," Matt said. "What's got a bug up your ass?"

"The same thing that's gonna have a bug up your ass," Jake replied. "Come with me."

Matt responded to the serious tone of his voice. He looked around at his admirers. "If you will all excuse me for a few? It looks like Jake's got some serious shit he needs to talk." He turned to the virginal innocent on his arm. "Don't go nowhere, okay?"

She nodded shyly, blushing furiously and Matt released her. The two of them forced their way back through the crowd until they were standing near the side of the bar.

"What's up?" Matt asked him. "Is Darren fucking something up again?"

"No, nothing bad," Jake said. "Do you remember sending one of your envelopes to a man named Ronald Shaver?"

Matt searched his brain for a moment and then nodded. "Yeah, he was one of the ones I sent the demo tape to. He's the agent for *Earthstone*. What about him?"

"He's here," Jake said. "And he wants to speak to the two of us outside."

"Here?" Matt said, his eyes widening. "You mean, like, here here? Right here, right now, here?"

"Out in his car," Jake confirmed. "His secretary or girlfriend or whatever came up to me. She wants to take us to him."

"Well fuck my sister," Matt said. "Let's go."

Jake led him back over to Trina, who was waiting patiently by the front door. He introduced Matt to her. Matt was too excited to even make a sexist remark.

"Take us to the man," Matt said.

She led them outside, into the parking lot and out to the street. There was a black, stretch limousine parked in front of the fire hydrant there. The tinted windows were all up. A uniformed driver was standing by next to the rear door. As they approached, he mechanically opened it, revealing a plush, well-lit interior equipped with leather couch-like seats. A man in his forties was sitting against the rear of the passenger compartment. He was dressed in a black suit and tie. His hair was brown and professionally styled. A pair of Vuarnet sunglasses covered his eyes. A bottle of Chivas Regal was on the table before him as was a hefty glass filled with ice and the golden brown liquid.

"Gentlemen," he said, his voice rich and cultured. "Come in, please."

Matt and Jake looked at each other for a moment and then stepped inside, one by one. They sat down in extremely comfortable seats against the passenger side wall of the compartment. The driver closed the door after them, leaving Trina outside.

"My name is Ronald Shaver," the man said, holding out his hand to Jake. "You're Jake Kingsley, correct?"

"Yes," Jake said, shaking with him.

Shaver turned to Matt. "And you're the venerable Mr. Tisdale, are you not?" he asked.

"Yeah," Matt said. "I am."

Shaver took a sip from his drink. He did not offer the two musicians any. "I received your demo tape and your resume last week, Mr. Tisdale," he said. "I didn't think too much of it at the time. In fact, I only opened it because an appointment had cancelled on me and I had nothing better to do. But I did listen to your tape."

"Did you like it?" Matt asked.

Shaver frowned. "A very poor quality recording. What did you do, record it in your garage?"

"Something like that," Matt said. That was, in fact, exactly where it had been recorded, with Bill running their instruments through their soundboard into a series of cassette recorders and then mixing the whole thing together onto a master tape, with each volume level carefully adjusted.

"That's about what I figured," Shaver said. "In any case, though the recording was poor, the actual music was... shall we say... not terrible? You have a decent singing voice, Mr. Kingsley, and you seem to know your way around a guitar, Mr. Tisdale. And your piano player... well, he adds a certain uniqueness to the sound of your music. It was enough to keep me listening for a few minutes and to read over what you'd sent. It seems your little band has developed quite the following here in this... uh... city."

"We're the most popular band in Heritage," Matt said proudly. "We sell out every venue we play."

"Well... yeah," Shaver said. "But, unfortunately, that's a little like saying you're the most popular Chinese restaurant in Pocatello, Idaho. It's not really much of an accomplishment now, is it? The rarity of the medium makes for distorted analysis by the inhabitants. When you can say you're the most popular Chinese restaurant in Beijing, then you're getting up there. Right?"

Jake and Matt looked at each other for a moment, both trying to figure out if they'd just been insulted or not.

"Uh... look, Mr. Shaver," Matt said. "Maybe if you'd..."

"So anyway," Shaver interrupted. "I listened to your demo tape and read over your materials and then threw the whole thing in the garbage. That's a step further than most unsolicited demo tapes get, I might add. I forgot completely about you until earlier today. You see, I'm in town on some business and I happened to be leafing through your local newspaper." He said this last with particular disdain. "And there, in the entertainment session, I saw that your band was to perform tonight at this club. That reminded me of your tape. Since there really isn't anything that resembles entertainment in this town, I decided to take my secretary out to see what you were all about live." He took another sip from his drink. "You folks put on a decent show. As I was watching you I was thinking to myself that there might be something there. The crowd does seem to appreciate you."

"They love us," Matt said, a little defensively.

"That is obvious," Shaver agreed. "That's why I sent Ms. Allen in to retrieve you. Now, I'm probably being stupid and maybe I'm getting old and out of touch, but I've got this notion that your band stands a chance of moving beyond this... place. You're decent musicians and, most importantly, your sound is different than everything else out there. If you'd like to talk about my agency representing you, I'll meet with you in my hotel room tomorrow before I leave. We'll see if maybe we can work something out."

"Fuckin-A," Matt blurted.

Jake gave him a sharp look. "Yes," he interjected quickly. "That sounds like a very good idea."

"Wonderful," Shaver said. "How does eleven o'clock sound?"

"Perfect," Matt said, his composure returning.

"What hotel are you staying at?" Jake asked.

"It's in what passes for your downtown area," Shaver said. "I'll send the limo to come pick you all up. Just give the address to Trina and be waiting there at 10:30. Okay?"

"Yes sir!" Jake said. "We'll be there."

"Thank you, Mr. Shaver," Matt said. "You won't be sorry."

"Oh, I probably will," he muttered. "I probably will. I'll see you gentlemen tomorrow."

They exited the limo a moment later. Matt gave his address to Trina. She didn't write it down on anything, she simply nodded and repeated it back to him. With that, she climbed in the car and the driver shut the door. He then climbed in himself and the long black car drove off into the night.

*****

The limousine pulled up in front of Matt's house at precisely 10:30, gliding to a halt before the driveway. The driver was the same as the previous night, but his demeanor was markedly different. He did not wear his hat or call them sir. He simply knocked on the door and asked—in a rather impatient voice—if they were ready to go, his eyes looking at them with distaste. He did not open the back door for them. He just told them to wipe their feet before they got in and not to touch anything.

"Friendly guy," Jake said sourly as he settled into the rearmost seat.

"Hey, Jeeves!" Matt yelled as he looked at the bar. It was closed tightly and had a combination lock firmly affixed upon it. "What the fuck's up with the bar? I need a drink!"

The partition between front and back slid downward. "The bar is for paying customers," the driver said coldly. "You five most certainly do not fit that category."

The partition slid shut again and the limo took off, accelerating rather abruptly.

After a bouncing, jarring, twenty-minute ride full of centrifugal force and inertial changes, they pulled up before the Royal Gardens Hotel, a sixty-year-old, sixteen story hotel which was—until the Stovington Suites would be built in five more years—the nicest accommodations in Heritage County.

The partition came down again and the driver—who was munching on a deli sandwich and currently had a mouthful—told them, "Hop out here and go wait by the service entrance. Mr. Shaver's secretary will meet you there." He rolled his eyes a little. "If you tried going in the front looking like that, security would probably mace you."

Before any of them could reply, the partition slid back up.

"Asshole," Matt said, making sure his voice was loud enough to carry through the partition.

Coop fumbled around for a minute and was finally able to get the door open. They piled out one by one and walked towards the side entrance they had been directed to. There they found Trina, who was dressed in a pair of loose-fitting blue jeans and a maroon, sleeveless blouse. She looked tired, as if she might be hung over.

"Hey, guys," she greeted listlessly. "Follow me."

They followed her, entering through a little used door into a corner of the lobby where the security services and the housekeeping staff kept their offices. Matt and Darren both tried to engage her in conversation as they walked but she ignored them both, thoroughly and completely. At last they came to the elevators. They piled inside and rode up to the sixteenth floor. When the doors opened onto a spacious hallway there was a security guard manning a podium just outside. His eyes widened as he saw who the current passengers were.

"Miss Allen," the guard said slowly, his eyes flitting from one band member to the other. "Is... everything all right?"

"Everything is fine," she assured him with a wave of dismissal. "These are some guests of Mr. Shaver. They won't be staying long."

He looked them up and down again, quite disapprovingly, and then glanced up the hallway, obviously looking to see if any of the other hotel patrons were in sight. Finally, he nodded. "I guess its okay then," he said.

Trina offered him a slight smile and then exited the elevator. "Come on, guys," she said. "Almost there."

The band obediently followed. Shortly they came to a door numbered 1605. Trina used a key to open it and they entered the Presidential Suite.

"Holy fuckin' shit," Matt whispered as he took in the opulence.

Jake had to agree that that pretty much summed it up. There was a marble entryway that led into a spacious sitting room full of plush chairs. Beyond this was an oak wet bar. Beyond that, near the balcony door, was a hot tub that was bubbling and steaming. The balcony looked out over the Sacramento River. Off to the sides were closed doors that presumably led to a master bedroom and a bathroom. Sitting in one of the chairs, before an oak table large enough to hold a meeting at, was Ronald Shaver. He was dressed as casually as his secretary—in a pair of jeans and a button-up shirt. His feet were bare and his face was unshaven. A cigar smoldered in an ashtray before him. Next to this was a small serving tray with a silver lid over it.

Shaver had a phone pressed against his ear and was talking to someone named "Gary" about those "goddamn contract extension clauses". He looked up as they entered and waved towards the table he was at, inviting them to sit. They trooped over and grabbed seats, Matt and Jake sitting closest to Shaver, the rest spreading out to either side. Trina walked over to one of the seats not against the conference table. She sat down and began examining her manicured nails thoughtfully.

For nearly five minutes, they sat there in silence, listening to Shaver talk about some mysterious entity or entities that had tried to throw one of these mysterious contract extension clauses onto one of his artists. Shaver told Gary this was not even remotely acceptable and that he, Shaver, was going to recommend outright refusal of the contract in question if those fucksticks wanted to play hardball. He exclaimed that they needed to remember who held the power and who would end up sucking someone's asshole if things went to shit. He rounded out the conversation by asking Gary if he understood where he was coming from. Apparently, Gary did, as the conversation ended with the slamming down of the phone a few seconds later.

"Goddamn accountants," Shaver said, shaking his head in disgust. "Sometimes I think they're even *worse* than lawyers." He looked up at his guests, his eyes flitting from one to the next. "How you doing, boys?" he asked. "Glad you could make it."

They all said their various versions of hello and then Shaver introduced himself to Coop, Darren, and Bill, shaking each of their hands in turn. He then turned to Trina, who seemed lost in a world of her own.

"Trina," he said. "Maybe these boys would like a drink. Set us up with some glasses and some Chivas, please."

"Sure," Trina replied with a yawn. She slowly got to her feet and went over to the bar.

"Now then," Shaver said, while she filled glasses with ice, "I understand you boys are looking for an agent. Is that correct?"

"Yes," Matt said. "That is correct."

"Well, I'll tell you, I have a policy against representing unsigned bands and I especially have a policy against unsolicited demo tapes. But, you know, every policy should have an exception clause. You'll go far in life if you just keep that in mind. And in my case, I just might be inclined to invoke my exception clause with you fellows. I like the way you sound. You've got some raw talent among the five of you. I've been wrong before, but I think that with the right coaching, you just might be able to sell a couple of albums."

"Just give us that chance," Matt said. "You won't be sorry."

Shaver shrugged. "That remains to be seen. But before we go any further, do you boys understand exactly what an agent does for you?"

"You use your contacts in the recording industry to get us a contract," Matt said. "Without an agent, it's pretty much impossible to be heard. With a well-connected agent, such as you, it's almost a given."

Shaver smiled. "That's an oversimplified and somewhat cynical version of what I do, but yes, you have the basic gist of it. I also help you negotiate the most favorable recording contract if and when that time comes. In other words, I make sure you don't end up as poor slaves to the label. My job is to be your advocate. The relationship is mutually beneficial since what I am paid is tied into what you are paid."

Trina brought a tray over and set it down. On it were five crystal glasses with Chivas on the rocks. She distributed each glass, setting them down gently like a waitress.

Matt picked his up and took a small sniff of it. "Do you have any coke to go with this?" he asked.

Shaver kept his composure only by the sheerest force of will. He swallowed a few times and closed his eyes for a few seconds. Finally, he looked up at Trina. "Could you get a few cans of coke for these gentlemen?" he asked slowly.

She chewed her lip for a second and then said, "Sure." She went back to the bar and returned with three red and white cans from the refrigerator. She and Shaver watched with bemused revulsion as the members of *Intemperance* each poured healthy dollops of cola into their glasses.

"Good hooch," Coop said, after draining half of it at a swallow.

"Fuckin' A," Matt agreed. "Top rate."

"I'm glad you like it," Shaver said. "Would you boys care for a line to go with your drinks?" He reached over and lifted the top off the serving tray, revealing a large mirror with six fat rails of cocaine laid out side by side. He picked up the mirror and offered it to Matt.

"You are a good host, Mr. Shaver," Matt said, taking the mirror and setting it down before him.

Shaver shrugged, as if to say it was nothing more than putting out a bowl of chips and some salsa. He reached into his pocket and produced a $100 bill, which he quickly rolled into a tube. He passed this over to Matt. "Enjoy," he said.

Matt snorted up the first line and then sniffed loudly, his body shuddering a little. "Wow," he said, his eyes tearing up. "This is some killer blow."

"I'm sure you are used to cocaine that is at least sixty percent cut," Shaver said. "This is pure, uncut Bolivian flake. Perhaps the finest... uh... *blow*, as you put it, in the world."

"No shit?" Darren asked, grabbing for the mirror. "I gotta check this out." He picked up the bill and snorted noisily. When it was inside him he pounded the side of his head a few times and let out a yelp. "God-fucking-damn!" he declared. "It must be nice to be rich."

"It is," Shaver assured him. "Believe me, it is."

The mirror was passed the rest of the way around the table. When it came to Jake, he hesitated for a few seconds, thinking that maybe this meeting was just as important as a rehearsal or a performance—maybe more so—and that maybe someone should keep a clear head. In the end, however, his curiosity got the better of him. He simply had to see what the finest blow in the world was all about. He snorted, feeling a deep, satisfying burn deep in his nasal passage. The drug started to go to work on his head even before Shaver finished snorting up the last line.

"Now then," Shaver said, once everyone was feeling their finest. "To business."

"Fuckin A," Matt happily agreed. "To business. You gonna be our agent, or what?"

"Well, as I said, I may be willing to make an exception to my usual rules for you gentlemen. I think there may be some potential for commercial success with your music. I'm prepared to offer you a contract for representation. Now the terms..."

He was forced to stop his spiel because Darren and Coop began screaming in triumph and high-fiving each other.

"Darren, Coop," Jake said, shooting them a furious look. "Chill for now."

"Sorry," they mumbled together, but the grins remained on their face.

"As I was saying," Shaver continued, "the terms are that I will attempt to secure a recording contract for you and act as your negotiator with the record company in question. I will act as the representative for this band in all business matters. In return, I will receive thirty percent of all advances, royalties, and other revenue that this band produces. Does that sound like a fair deal?" He looked at Matt as he asked this.

"Thirty percent, huh?" Matt said. He glanced over at Jake and a look passed between the two of them. Both of them well knew that the standard rate for an agent was twenty percent. They had in fact had a lengthy discussion about this the previous night, over beers and cigarettes on Matt's back porch while the rest of the band had engaged in their usual activities. They had agreed that they would hold firm to this figure no matter what, neither one of them really believing that Shaver would try to deviate from it. After all, he was a respected agent. He knew the game. Only now, deviation was exactly what he was trying to do.

"Is that a problem, gentlemen?" Shaver asked softly, his tone implying that if it were he would be sending them on their way.

The silence stretched out as Jake and Matt continued to hold a telepathic conversation, their eyes and facial expressions sending the messages.

It's only an extra ten percent, Matt's eyes said. *If we try to push him, he won't represent us at all.*

He's trying to screw us, Jake's eyes shot back. *We agreed to twenty percent!*

"Matt?" Shaver asked. "Is everything okay here?"

"Yes," Matt said. "Sorry. Thirty percent is not a problem, Mr. Shaver."

"Good," Shaver said with a grin. "I thought you'd be happy with that."

Jake's instinct was to hold his tongue. Matt was the leader of the band and he knew more about how the music industry worked. And, after all, it was only an extra ten percent. That wasn't that much, was it? But that extra ten percent wasn't really the point. If they agreed to this they would be setting the wrong sort of relationship at the beginning, would be sending the wrong message. Someone had to stand firm here. If Matt, as their leader, wouldn't do it, then Jake would.

"No," Jake said, just as Shaver was reaching out to begin shaking hands. "I'm afraid that thirty percent *is* a problem."

Everyone looked at him with varying degrees of anger on their faces. Matt's version was perhaps the angriest. His eyes glared at the singer, sending not just daggers but tracer bullets dipped in cyanide.

"Jake," he hissed, "thirty percent is a lot, but it's fair."

"Yeah," Darren said. "That still leaves like sixty percent for us."

"Seventy percent, you fuckin moron," Coop told him. "And seventy percent is a lot of dough."

"No, it really isn't," Jake said. "Not when you divide it up among the five of us. And don't forget that all of our band expenses will come out of that seventy percent."

"Yeah, but still..." Coop started.

"Twenty percent is the standard cut for an agent," Jake interrupted, his words directed at Shaver.

"That *is* the industry standard," Shaver admitted, his face remaining expressionless, "but that is for established bands. You folks are a *garage* band looking to get a break. I can perhaps provide that break for you but I'll be taking a risk. Risky behavior means the reward needs to be bigger."

"Thirty percent is fine," Matt said, casting another evil glare at Jake. "Really. We all agree to that."

Jake shot an angry look back at Matt and held his ground. "No," he said. "We do not agree to that. Twenty percent is the agent's cut. I will not agree to anything more."

Shaver slumped backwards in his chair and sighed. "Look," he said. "I really don't have time for this shit. I brought you here to my room as a favor, because I thought that maybe I could help you boys get heard. I guess maybe you don't want to take a favor from me."

"Jake," Darren said menacingly. "Stop fucking around. You blow this for us and I'll kick your fuckin' ass."

"You're not in high school anymore, Darren," Jake said. "This is the real world. Threatening me is not gonna help." He turned back to Shaver. "And we're not in a whorehouse either, Mr. Shaver. So quit trying to screw us. I'm not asking for anything unreasonable, and you know it. If you thought enough of us to bring us up here and offer to represent us, than you're not going to kick us loose over a ten percent difference in your cut."

Shaver locked eyes with him, his face still blank. "You seem rather sure of yourself on that point, Mr. Kingsley. Are you sure enough to bet your career on it?"

Jake maintained eye contact. "It would seem that is exactly what I'm doing."

They continued to stare at each other for what seemed an eternity. Matt and the rest of the band watched in anxious silence. Even Trina, who had been laying out the supplies for a manicure, had stopped what she was doing to take in the battle of wills.

"Okay," Shaver said. "Maybe I was trying to take a little more than I was due. I'll come down to twenty-five percent."

The band breathed a sigh of relief. All except for Jake. He was shaking his head. "No," he said. "Twenty percent. That's the going rate. I won't accept anything else."

Now Shaver allowed his expression to slip a little. Annoyance filled his face, along with a tinge of anger. "Look, Jake," he said. "I dropped my percentage because I respect someone who has the balls to stand up for himself. But don't push me here. My patience is about at an end."

"How would you feel, Mr. Shaver, if I were telling you that I would give you a fifteen percent cut when the industry standard is twenty? Wouldn't you be inclined to disagree?"

"You're damn right I would if it were *you* telling me that. You are a nobody and I am a somebody. However, if I were in the position that you are in—if I was an unknown agent negotiating to represent say... *Van Halen*—then I would accept whatever they offered and be glad they even asked."

"Well, I guess that's where you and I differ then," Jake told him. "I'm not one to nitpick over a few percentage points, but I don't like being treated unfairly. That is what you are attempting to do. There's a principle involved here and I will not be dislodged from my principles. Treat us fairly or count me out of the equation."

The tense silence descended again as the two men stared at each other. It went for a longer period this time, the tension thicker. As before, it was Shaver who broke it.

"Twenty-one percent," he said. "And that's my final offer. Take it or leave it."

"Twenty-one percent," Jake said thoughtfully, mulling that over. He knew exactly why Shaver had named that figure. The one percent was symbolic, meant to indicate that a punk kid had not negotiated him all the way down to nothing. It was a face-saving measure, something important to

Shaver's ego and sense of control, and Jake instinctively knew that he would fight to the death over that final percentage point.

"Well?" Shaver said.

Jake nodded. "It sounds like a deal."

A collective sigh of relief was exhaled through the room. The tension began to evaporate almost immediately, like an ice cube on a hot sidewalk. Shaver shook each of their hands and welcomed them aboard.

"Trina," Shaver said. "Can you get one of those pre-printed contracts from my briefcase and bring it in here."

"Sure," she said, standing up. She shot Jake a look as she passed by. It was not a look of disrespect. She disappeared into the bedroom and shut the door behind her.

While she was gone, Shaver took the time to pass a few words with Coop and Bill while Darren sucked down the remainder of his Chivas and Coke. While they were doing that Jake looked over at Matt. Matt was staring at him, letting him know that this matter would be discussed later. Jake nodded slightly, acknowledging the telepathic communication.

*****

They signed a representation contract with Shaver Talent Agency Inc., all of them going over it line by line and initialing the part where Shaver's percentage of thirty percent had been crossed out and twenty-one percent written in instead. The rest of the contract was only two pages in length and had been written in pretty straightforward language. Jake and Matt were both able to satisfy themselves that there were no hidden pitfalls lurking within that collection of words and phrases. The complicated contracts, Shaver told them, were the ones they would sign with a record company, assuming things went that far.

"The very first priority," Shaver said, "is to get a real demo tape made. A professional tape, mixed and edited."

"Where are we going to do that?" Bill asked, speaking for the very first time since the initial introductory handshake.

"There's a studio down in Sacramento," he replied. "They usually use staff musicians to record tunes for local television and radio commercials, theme songs for shows, and stuff like that. Their techs aren't the best in the business, but they'll be able to get your music down on tape well enough for me to let the record company execs hear what you sound like. We'll do six songs, a cross-mix of your tunes. Matt, pick your three best and Jake, you do the same. Include one of your ballads in there somewhere too. The execs love ballads because they translate out into singles."

"How much is this going to cost?" Jake asked. They had looked into professional studios before and the average fee was in the neighborhood of fifty dollars for each hour of time. Recording and mixing each song generally took at least nine hours, which meant they were talking, for six songs, at least $2700. Money the *Intemperance* general fund was well short of.

"I have some connections there," Shaver told him. "I can get you sixty hours of studio time for free. Just be sure to get all the tunes recorded in that amount of time, will you? If you go over, you're paying for the extra time."

Sixty hours of studio time for free? Even Jake was impressed by this.

They left the hotel shortly after, each taking a copy of the contract they had signed with them (a room service employee had come up, taken the original, made seven copies, and then brought them all back up—for which Shaver had tipped him ten bucks). The limo was still waiting for them downstairs and as the driver took them back to Matt's house he seemed much friendlier than he had on the inbound trip, actually opening the doors for them and calling them "sir" now.

Coop, Darren, and Bill began to party immediately upon entering the house. The stereo came on, playing Led Zepplin's *Houses of the Holy*. Darren rolled a fat joint while Coop distributed mixed drinks. Matt and Jake abstained from the festivities, at least for the time being. They had business of their own to attend to.

"Don't get too fucked up," Matt warned the trio as he grabbed two beers out of the refrigerator. "Remember, we still have a gig tonight."

They promised they would maintain composure.

Matt handed one of the beers to Jake. "Come on," he said. "Let's take a walk."

"Right," Jake agreed.

They went outside, following a cement path over towards the main house. They ended up at the pool, which was too cold to swim in but which had not yet been covered for the coming winter and still had all the patio furniture laid out around it. They grabbed seats at one of the tables, both opening their beers and having a drink. Matt took out a pack of cigarettes and offered one to Jake. Jake accepted and they both lit up, smoking thoughtfully as they collected their thoughts.

"Jake," Matt said at last, "you ever hear people say that the ends justify the means?"

Jake nodded. "I've heard that a time or two. Can't say that I always agree with it."

"Exactly," Matt said. "The ends that you accomplished there with Shaver turned out to be a good thing. You got him down from thirty percent to twenty-one. I can't argue with that." He took a drag from his smoke, blowing it out thoughtfully. "But the means you utilized to get there, that was pretty fuckin foul, you dig?"

"I dig where you're coming from, Matt, but in this particular instance, I'm afraid that I do agree with the saying. I did what I needed to do there, what *you* should have done."

Matt's temper flared the smallest bit. He took another drag, calming himself. "I made a decision in there and I expected you to support me. You were putting our relationship with Shaver at risk and you were defying me in front of the rest of the band. Jake, I can't allow that to happen. This band has to have a leader and that leader is me. Don't cock-block one of my decisions like that ever again. Especially not in front of a roomful of people. You have any idea how fuckin embarrassing that was? How much you undermined my authority?"

Jake shook his head. "I'm not gonna promise that," he said.

"What?" Matt asked, his face coloring a little more.

"You pussed out in there. We agreed beforehand that twenty percent is what we would accept. Do you remember that conversation?"

"Yes, but..."

"Ain't no fuckin buts about it," Jake said. "You pussed out. You got overwhelmed because Shaver brought us in there and showed us how rich and powerful he was and how tiny and meaningless we are and he tried to screw us and you fuckin caved. You caved, man! I've never seen you do *anything* like that before. I did what I did because you didn't have the guts to."

"Hey fuck you!" Matt said, his temper boiling over. He stood up quickly, his chair falling over on his back. He pointed his finger angrily at Jake's chest. "I'm the fuckin founder of this band and I'm in charge of it. I don't give a shit what you think of my decisions or why I make them. I'm in charge and you will support what I do!"

Jake remained calm. "Or what, Matt? You gonna kick my ass? You gonna try to solve your problem with me the way you did with Hathaway? Go ahead. Kick my ass if it'll make you feel better. I won't even fight back. Of course, I probably won't be able to go on stage if I'm all bruised up, but maybe you and the rest of the boys can pull off the gig without me."

"Don't you fuckin play that card with me, Jake!"

"Then get the fuck out of my face," Jake told him. "Sit your ass back down and let's discuss this like the professionals we pretend to be. Like I told Darren, this isn't high school. The guy who can kick the other guy's ass doesn't win by default here."

Matt seemed to struggle with himself for a few seconds and Jake began to fear that he really was going to hit him. But finally, he seemed to get himself under something like control. He took a step back and lowered his hand. He picked up his chair and sat back down. "Okay," he said. "I guess you're right. I'm sorry I lost my temper."

"And I'm sorry I embarrassed you in front of everyone," Jake said. "That really was not my intention. I was doing what I thought I had to do. He was trying to screw us, Matt, and I didn't want to start off my music career by being played for a fool. Remember, we agreed to stick to our guns on this twenty percent thing. You were the one who folded without a fight, not me. Why did you do that? Why weren't *you* supporting *me*?"

Matt looked disgusted with himself now. He took another drag and then angrily snuffed out his cigarette. "I thought we were gonna lose him if we pushed. It seemed like he was looking for any reason to kick us loose."

"But he didn't," Jake said. "He was the one who caved in. Oh sure, he got his little one percent above standard so he can tell himself he still screwed us, but he caved in nonetheless. Just like I knew he would."

"How did you know?"

"A little deductive reasoning," Jake said. "Everything that happened seemed kind of contrived to me when I put it all together."

"What do you mean?"

"Well, he told us that he was in Heritage on business and that he just happened across our gig in the paper and decided to check it out. That sounds plausible but it really isn't. Did you ever stop to wonder just what sort of business a man like Shaver might have in Heritage?"

It was obvious Matt hadn't. Jake could see it in his face.

"He's a musical agent," Jake said. "There is no music industry in Heritage. There is no recording studio here, no famous band that's moved beyond here. There is no business he could be doing here. So, why do you think he's here?"

"You saying he was here specifically to see us play? To sign us up?"

Jake nodded. "That's the only explanation that makes sense. He came here to sign us up. I think that almost everything about our encounters with him and his little woman there was manufactured and rehearsed in advance. The limo driver was a big clue. I don't care what a limo driver personally thinks of the people he's driving, he wouldn't treat them the way we were treated unless he'd been told to. I mean, the dude was eating a sandwich behind the wheel. He was insulting us. But on the ride back, he was nice as could be."

"Yeah," Matt allowed.

"I think Shaver told that driver to be rude to us so we'd come up there feeling like losers, like an inconvenience."

"I don't know about that, man. You're starting to sound a little like Coop."

"Maybe," Jake said. "But sometimes paranoid suspicions are correct ones. For instance, there was that whole bit with Shaver being on the phone when we got up there. I don't think he was really talking to anyone at all."

"What?"

"When he called the front desk to get the copies of the contract made, I was able to hear the desk clerk's voice coming out of the speaker. It was low and tinny and I couldn't make out any of the actual words, but I could hear him, and that was with a conversation going on between Darren and Coop about how fuckin nice the hooch was."

"You're right," Matt said, now that he thought about it.

"But when he was talking to that Gary character when we first came in, I didn't hear shit. Not even a peep."

"Why would he make up a phone conversation?" Matt asked.

"To intimidate us," Jake said. "To try to make us believe that his time is valuable and that he was just barely squeezing us in and that, therefore, we should grateful that he was only asking for thirty percent."

"Shit," Matt said, shaking his head in wonder, his anger mostly forgotten.

"He gave us booze and coke when we got up there. Really good coke."

"You got that shit right," Matt said. "I can still feel it a little bit now."

"That was to break down any resistance we might have had. We need to make a vow not to get fucked up during any contract negotiations in the future. Seriously. Anyway, it backfired on him. The coke made me bold and confident. That's what gave me the courage to stand up to him like that. If I would've been straight I never would've done that."

Matt wasn't sure what to say to that. He was feeling a bit overwhelmed.

"You know what the biggest kicker here is though?" Jake asked.

"What's that?"

"The recording studio time. He doesn't have any fucking contacts up here. Those people who run that studio don't have any idea who he even is. And even if they did, there's no way in hell they would give away twenty-seven hundred bucks worth of studio time just to stay on his good side. After all, what could he do for them? What advantage would there be for a studio that makes commercials to do a twenty-seven hundred dollar favor for a talent agent?"

"So... what are you saying?" Matt asked.

"He paid for that studio time himself. That's how bad he wants to sign us. That's how confident he is in our music. He heard that demo tape we made and read that resume you put together and he knows how good we are and that people will love us. He *knows* that, Matt. Especially after he saw us play. He would've taken ten percent if we would've pushed him for it. He just wanted to try to keep the shoe on his foot and get a bigger chunk of us for the future."

Matt had to admit that what Jake was saying made sense.

"Look, man," Jake told him. "We need to make peace with this and come to an understanding, okay? I'm not trying to take over leading this band. I have no fuckin interest in that. But I also know I'm an integral part of this band. You yourself pointed that out last night. I'll let you call the shots. I have no problem with that. But if you're making a bad decision—and you were making a fucking horrible one in there with Shaver—I'm gonna let you know that, and if it means we butt heads, then we butt heads. If it means I need to step in and assert myself, then I'll do it. That's just the way it is. This is my ass, my future we're talking about here too. Do you dig?"

It took a long time before Matt answered. His face contorted into a variety of different positions as he grappled with anger and other negative emotions. Finally, he nodded. "Yeah," he said. "I guess I dig."

"Still friends?" Jake asked, holding out his hand.

Matt scoffed. "Like I was ever friends with a dick smoker like you," he said, slapping his hand down into Jake's.

They shook warmly and then went back up to the house. There was just enough left of the joint Darren had rolled to put them into the celebratory mood.

*****

Glockman Studios was located in the Del Paso Heights section of Sacramento, a neighborhood that was arguably the worst in the entire region. The parking lot of the establishment was surrounded by chain link topped with razor wire. The back of the studio itself looked out over a drainage canal filled with old shopping carts, old tires, and other bits of unidentifiable urban debris. The street outside was suffering a terminal infection of potholes. But inside the studio, all was clean, sterile, and professional.

Over the next three and a half weeks *Intemperance* used fifty-eight of the sixty hours they had been allotted, recording six of their best tunes—three of Jake's and three of Matt's, as requested. They made the ninety-mile trip from Heritage twice a week, on Mondays and Tuesdays, and worked under the direction of Brad Grotten, one of the sound engineers.

Brad was a skinny, chain-smoking, shorthaired man of thirty-six. He wore long sleeved, button-up shirts with pocket protectors. He seemed ecstatic to have actual rock and roll music to work on instead of advertisement tracks and he gave them his very best for the time he had available to them. He recorded each instrument individually, often making them repeat the song over and over again, dozens of times, until he felt the sound was correct. He recorded the drums first, then the bass, then Jake's rhythm guitar, then Matt's lead, then Bill's piano. He then recorded the back-up singing. Jake's lead singing came last and was the cause of the most numerous re-takes because Brad wanted the exact mix of tempo, pitch, and timbre for the recording. When this was all done, he would mix each individual track, adjusting volume and tone until everything blended together. He then reformatted the entire thing onto a single dual-track stereo magnetic reel-to-reel tape—which he called the "master recording". Once a tune made it to the master, they would start the entire process over with the next tune.

Jake would never forget hearing the first fully mixed copy of their first song. It was *Descent Into Nothing*, a song they had played perhaps a thousand times since he'd written it sixteen months before. But when Brad turned on the reel-to-reel tape to let them hear how the recording had come out, his mouth dropped as the guitar chords poured out of the speakers, as his own voice began to issue forth.

"You guys are pretty good," Brad said appreciatively.

"We really are," Jake agreed, listening to the near-perfect blending of instruments and voice, to the pounding drive of the backbeat. For the first time he was hearing their music as others heard it, and in a format that was much smoother and more articulate than a live performance. And they really were good. Not just a little bit, but a lot.

"We're gonna make it," said Matt from his seat next to him. Apparently, he was having a similar epiphany as he listened to the recording. "I always thought we would, but now I fuckin know. We really do rock."

"Goddamn right," said Bill, whose mouth was open in awe. "Goddamn fucking right."

When the recording sessions came to an end and all six tracks were captured on the master to the best of Brad's abilities, he went about making the actual demo tapes themselves. This was even simpler than pushing the record button on a home tape deck since the studio had extremely high speed dubbing equipment. It took less than thirty seconds to put the six tunes onto a blank high-quality cassette tape. He ran off twenty copies to send to Shaver (Brad had never actually admitted Shaver had paid for the session but had loosely implied it on more than one occasion) as demo tapes. He ran off another half a dozen for each of the five band members to do with as they pleased and told them that Glockman Studios would store the master recording for them for two years free of charge, but that after that they would have to pay sixty dollars a year to keep it in the vault.

"No problem," Matt told him. "Thanks for everything, Brad."

"You're more than welcome," Brad said. "It was fun working with you. You're good musicians and I think you're gonna go far."

And with that, they left the studio for the last time, leaving a master recording in its vault that would one day—because it contained two songs that *Intemperance* would never end up recording in any other forum—sell at an auction for almost half a million dollars.

*****

Life, such as it was, returned pretty much to normal in the weeks that followed. Winter came to Heritage and the band continued to play at least three times a week. They went back to working on new material, including a stirring new ballad from Jake entitled *The Point of Futility*. The crowds seemed to love this song with a passion that had so far been unmatched. It was tale of hopelessness in love, of the pain of letting go of someone, of the helplessness of not being able to change things. Ironically, the subject of the song—Jake's break-up with Michelle—was something he had pretty much gotten over by the time the song was performed before an audience for the first time.

Jake never tried to call Michelle and she, as far as he knew, had never tried to call him. He heard no rumors about her, spoke to none of her friends. It was as if she'd disappeared from the face of the Earth. As more time went by and he had time to put the relationship in perspective, he was able to conclude that it was probably for the best. They were incompatible personalities at the base. She would go on to be a bible-thumping teacher in a private religious school for the rich, and he would go on to whatever his destiny held in store. He stopped feeling guilty about bedding groupies after each show and learned to enjoy it almost as much as Matt and Darren did.

The subject of the demo tape they had made and what Shaver, their agent (it made them feel like rock stars just to say they *had* an agent) was doing with them, was always in the back of their minds and occasionally, when they were smoking weed prior to a jam session or drinking beer among themselves after a rehearsal, the topic of intense conversation. But when Matt would call Shaver to enquire on how things were going, all he would be told was that the tape had been sent out to various contacts in the industry and that it took time to get a response to them. Be patient, Matt was advised. Things will start moving soon.

And it turned out that Shaver was right. In mid-February of 1982, just as Jake was starting to think that the whole agent thing had been for nothing, he received a phone call from Matt.

"Wassup, Matt?" he asked, using the remote control to mute his television set. "You sound excited."

"I am," Matt said. "I'm about ready to come in my fuckin jeans, brother."

This got Jake's attention. "Shaver?" he asked.

"Bet your ass," Matt told him. "He came through for us. I just got off the phone with him. He's sending us some plane tickets and we're flying down to L.A. next Thursday."

"Who? Me and you?"

"No, the whole fuckin band, man. All of us."

"What for?"

"We're gonna meet with a guy from National Records."

"National Records," Jake said slowly, pondering. National Records was one of the largest names in the business.

"Fuckin A, homey," Matt told him happily. "Shaver says they want to discuss signing a recording contract with us."

"Holy shit," Jake said.

"Holy shit is right! Shaver did it. The motherfucker actually went and did it!"

CHAPTER 4

DESCENT INTO NOTHING

July 6, 1982
Los Angeles, California

Jake sat on a wooden chair with special padding on the legs to prevent it from making noise if it were accidentally moved across the tile floor. On his head were a set of high fidelity headphones known as *cans*, through which the sound techs could talk to him and through which the music he would be singing to would be piped. The room itself was fifteen feet square and completely sound insulated. Hanging from the ceiling by an adjustable bracket, directly in front of Jake's face, was a padded voice microphone that was wired into a socket in the ceiling. There was a window in the wall through which a large soundboard and two sound technicians could be seen.

"Okay, Jake," said a voice in the cans. This was Stan Lowry, the voice tech who was coaching him through this portion of the recording process. "We're cued up in here. Let's do it again. Remember, two inches from the foam, nice even timbre, and watch the lip popping."

Jake nodded and gave a thumbs up. By now, he knew not to talk back to them.

"*The Point of Futility*," Stan's voice said. "First verse, take twelve."

The music began to play in the headset, the gentle, melodic fingerpicking of an acoustic guitar with a piano in accompaniment. These were the tracks of the song they'd recorded over the last three weeks, mixed together but not finalized onto the master just yet. The song did not start from the beginning. Jake was given just enough lead to plug himself into the tune. He took a deep breath as his cue approached, making a check to see that his mouth was exactly two inches from the microphone, licking his lips a final a time to try to keep them from popping. The cue arrived—a long, mournful bending of the A string of Matt's guitar—and he began to sing, trying to project his voice perfectly.

"*There comes a time when it's over*

When souls have gone their own ways
When the things that brought you together
Now drive you apart, day after day

And you know that it's over
You've felt it go, there's been no mistake
It's the end of together
No more give, no more take"

"Hold up, Jake," Stan's voice cut in, overriding the music tracks. A second later they were turned off completely.

Jake sighed. After three and a half months of recording sessions, he was quite familiar with being interrupted like this. It meant something had fallen outside of parameters. Every strum of every guitar, every tick of every drumstick across every cymbal, every piano key, and, especially, every nuance of the lead vocal track, needed to be just right before it was considered a good take. And "just right" was a stringent specification in this place. The sound techs in charge of capturing *Intemperance* on tape were the most anal-retentive perfectionists Jake had ever met. Nothing the band had experienced while making the demo tape had prepared them for this constant litany of rejection of their efforts. *Let's try that one more time*, had become the most often heard and most hated phrase.

"A little too much on 'it's the end of together'," Stan said. "You red-lined the meter in the high end as you drew out 'together'. Try to keep that just under range or it might distort on the master."

Jake nodded.

"Okay then, let's try that one more time. *The Point of Futility*, first verse, take thirteen."

The music started and once more, Jake began to sing. This time he only made it through twelve syllables before Stan stopped him.

Eventually, on take twenty-three, Jake managed to croak out the entire first verse of the song without red-lining the meter or hesitating for a hundredth of a second or inhaling at the wrong time or not keeping exactly up with the timing. So far, after having recorded seven of the ten songs that would be on the album, this was about the average amount for vocal takes.

"Why don't we go ahead and break for lunch, Jake," Stan told him. "We'll start working on the second verse when you get back."

Jake looked at his watch. It was only 11:25. He looked at Stan through the window, pointed at his watch, and shrugged questioningly—his message: why don't we work on the second verse now? At least that way they could get the first six takes out of the way.

"I know it's early," Stan said, "but I want to mess around with the cueing tracks just a bit and Max is here and wants to see you."

Jake nodded and took off the cans, setting them carefully down on the chair. He went to the door and opened it, stepping out into the technician's room. There, by the door that led out into the hall, stood Max Acardio, the representative for National Records' artist and repertoire (A&R) department who had been assigned to work with *Intemperance*. Max was in his early thirties. He was a tall, artificially handsome guy with an expensive and well-fitted toupee atop his head. His teeth were capped and so white they could potentially cause blindness. And he showed those teeth a lot. Max was always grinning and smiling. He was dressed in his normal attire of a stylish but slightly loud Italian suit and a short, skinny tie. The grin widened to the point of alarm when he saw Jake emerge from the sound room.

"Jake," he said, holding out his hand. "How the hell you doing today? You sounded great in there. Just great. I can't wait until we get this project in release."

"Hey, Max," Jake replied, shaking with him and then submitting to the one armed hug that Max employed if it had been more than forty-eight hours since he'd seen you last.

"How you holdin' up in there, Jake?" Max asked him. "They tell me you're doing good and that production is on time and under budget."

"It gets a little tedious at times, but I'm hanging in there," Jake told him.

"Good, good," Max replied, obviously not having even heard what Jake had just said. "I have some good news for you."

"What's that?"

"I was just up in the Arts department. They've finished the album cover. You want to come see it? I have it up in my office."

"Sure," Jake said. "I'd love to see it. What about the rest of the guys?"

"Matt's in studio B re-doing some guitar tracks for *Who Needs Love?*, Bill is going over some of the mixes in the sound room, and Darren and Coop are setting up their equipment in the red room for the next song."

"Oh, okay," Jake said with a shrug. All of that was pretty typical. "Let's go check it out then."

The recording studio was located in the basement of the thirty-story National Records Building—a glittery, gaudy skyscraper on the edge of Hollywood. They rode the rickety, cramped elevator up to the eighteenth floor. Max's office was on the north side of the building, overlooking the squalor of Hollywood Boulevard and the tenement apartments beyond it. Max's desk stood against the outside window, presumably so he didn't have to actually look out there. He sat down in his chair and invited Jake to sit in a smaller chair across from him.

"Here it is," he said, pulling an album cover out from beneath his desk. He handed it over to Jake. "What do you think?"

Jake looked at it with mixed emotions. On the front of it was the scene that Acardio and Rick Bailey from the Artist Development Department had come up with. It was a picture of a hotel room with empty beer and liquor bottles laying everywhere, lamps knocked over, even the television set lying broken and battered on the floor. There were several sets of women's panties crumpled about with the rest of the debris as well as a small mirror with dusty residue clearly visible on it (though the mirror itself was something it took a few viewings to notice). Lying face down on the bed was a man that could have been Jake but was actually a model that resembled him. The man was naked but had his bare ass covered with the twisted sheets from the bed. He was presumably passed out, his left arm curled around an almost-empty whiskey bottle, his right resting on the bare back of an attractive female model, who was equally passed out and who also had her forbidden parts strategically covered by the placement of the sheet. On the top of the picture, in large, uneven pink letters that appeared to have been written with lipstick in a drunken hand, was: *Intemperance*. Beneath this, in smaller letters but still in the lipstick writing, was the name of the album: *Descent Into Nothing*.

Acardio and Bailey had discussed this album cover with the band but that had only been a courtesy. They didn't care what the band thought about it (Darren, Coop, and Matt all liked the idea, Bill and Jake hated it). As the band had come to learn since entering into the recording contract, the album belonged to National Records. Period. They would produce it, promote it, sell it, and package it any way they wished.

"It goes along with the image we're going to be pushing for you guys," Bailey had told them when they'd first discussed the album cover.

"The image?" Jake had asked.

"Right. Every band has to have an image. It's part of what sells you to the fans. In your case, your image is reflected in your very name. *Intemperance*. A lack of temperance. Temperance means sobriety, control, clean living. You boys are going to represent and portray yourselves as the very opposite of all that."

"Shit," Matt scoffed. "That shouldn't be too fuckin' hard. Why the hell do you think I named the band that?"

"Exactly," Bailey said. "And I want you to live up to that image—all of you. When you go out on the road to promote this album, I want you to party hard, to develop a reputation as total pagans, as ambassadors of debauchery. I want to hear stories circulating about drug and sex orgies from you. I want you to be notorious. As your publicity manager, I will do everything I can to get these stories into print. The more they print about you living up to the *Intemperance* name, the more popular you'll be and the more albums we'll sell."

"Shouldn't our music sell itself?" Jake had asked at this point. "I mean, we're a good band. People will want to hear our music because it's good music, right?"

"Well... having your music actually be good *is* a bonus," Bailey allowed. "And the promotion department will make sure your tunes are played on the radio nationwide, but trust me on this, your image will sell more albums than your music. That's always been true and always will be. Look at Ozzy Osbourne. The best thing he ever did for his career was biting the head off that bat."

"But Ozzy makes good music," Jake protested. "He has a good voice, good lyrics, and he had one of the best guitar players in the world."

"Until that little aircraft incident," Matt said solemnly, actually genuflecting as the memory was invoked. Matt had taken the death of Randy Rhodes four months before very hard. Part of it had been his worship of Ozzy's guitar player—who really was one of the best in the business. A bigger part, however, had undoubtedly been the circumstances of the death. Rhodes had been in an aircraft that their tour bus driver had stolen from a hanger to joyride in. They buzzed the tour bus a couple of times and then the plane had struck it, spinning it into a house. All inside had been smashed to pieces and burned beyond recognition. None of the news stories said so, but Jake was pretty sure that alcohol and/or cocaine had to have been involved. After all, how fucked up do you have to be before riding in a small plane with an unlicensed tour bus driver starts to seem like a good idea? The problem with Matt was that he could clearly see *himself* doing exactly what Randy Rhodes had done.

If he were drunk enough and someone suggested buzzing the tour bus with a stolen plane, Matt would be the first aboard.

"Yes, yes," Bailey said, waving his hands at what he saw as the irrelevancy of it all. "Ozzy and Rhodes were good. I'm not saying they weren't. But my point is that they didn't have to be. With Ozzy's reputation being what it is—the bat biting, the urination on the Alamo—people would buy his albums even if they sucked. It's his image they're in love with, not his music."

Jake, who was a music consumer as well as a musician, didn't agree with this image over quality argument. He didn't agree with it at all. He bought Ozzy Osbourne albums because he liked the music, not because Ozzy had once taken a piss on the Alamo or bitten the head off a bat. But the National Records executives all believed that image was the important thing. This was especially true now that MTV was up and running and gaining popularity across the country. Shaver had told once told Jake—over a few lines of his infamous Bolivian flake—that he, Shaver, was concerned about this new trend towards image and looks. For the first time in music history the A&R departments were starting to worry about what musicians *looked like* on camera instead of merely what they sounded like.

"Well?" Acardio asked when Jake had looked at the front cover art for almost thirty seconds.

"It's uh... very good photography," he finally said.

"I thought so too," Acardio told him. "We really do have the best graphic arts department here at National."

Jake flipped the album cover over to look at the back. Here, taking up the upper half of the space, was a group photograph of the band. Darren and Coop were sitting cross-legged in the foreground. Standing behind them were Matt, Bill, and Jake. All were dressed in their standard uniform of tattered and torn jeans and T-shirts. Matt was wearing dark shades. Jake had a two-day growth of stubble. Coop was holding a set of drumsticks in his hand. Darren had a cigarette in his mouth. None of them were smiling. The picture looked very natural, almost candid. It wasn't. Prior to the shoot, make-up artists had carefully applied coloring to their face, hair-stylists had gone to work on their manes, and wardrobe specialists had picked out their clothing. It had taken the better part of six hours to get the shot taken.

Below the picture was a listing of the band members and their roles. Darren Appleman-bass guitar, vocals; John "Coop" Cooper-percussion, vocals; Matt Tisdale-lead guitar, vocals; Bill "Nerdly" Archer-Piano, vocals; and finally, listed last due to his position in the picture, Jake Kingsley-lead vocals, rhythm guitar, acoustic guitar.

"I still think you boys should have listened to us about the name changes," Acardio said sadly. "Having stylish names helps with the band image. Look what it's doing for U2."

Jake bit back several nasty replies and simply shrugged. Jake and Matt had both gone around and around with Acardio, Bailey, and even Shaver on the subject of their names. Acardio was of the opinion that calling Coop *Coop* and calling Bill *Nerdly* was very hip, and that no one gave enough of a shit about bassists to have to change Darren Appleman's handle, but that the names Matt Tisdale and Jake Kingsley were just not interesting enough.

"It's what we do here in Hollywood," Bailey—who was the driving force behind the name-change effort—told them. "Why live with a plain name when you can change it to something that reflects your style and your outlook?" He looked at Matt, pursing his lips and thinking. "How about Rajin Storm?" he asked. "That's a good name for a guitarist of your caliber."

"Raging Storm?" Matt asked, his eyes wide. "Are you out of your fucking mind?"

"Not Raging Storm," Bailey said. "*Rajin* Storm!" He then spelled it out, as if that would change Matt's mind. "And you," he turned to Jake while Matt was still trying to process Rajin Storm. "I think something like... oh... say JD King."

"JD King?" Jake repeated.

"Right," Bailey said. "King is a simple name with powerful connotations. Invokes images of Elvis and shit like that. And JD is short, sweet, manly, and the fans will speculate endlessly on what it actually stands for. It's also an abbreviation for a popular alcoholic beverage." He looked up at the ceiling as an inspiration assaulted him. "Shit, maybe we can even get the Jack Daniels people to sign some sort of endorsement deal with you. We can say that your parents named you after their favorite booze and introduced you to drinking it at a young age. We can have you drink JD on stage! Holy shit, this is great. Eventually we can have them sponsor a tour and then..."

"Wait a minute," Jake said, holding up his hand. He was still calm but it was an effort. "You're suggesting that I lie and tell the public that my parents named me after a brand of whiskey? That they used to give me whiskey when I was young?"

"It's nothing against your parents, Jake. This is show business. You give the people what they want to hear."

Jake was shaking his head. "I *refuse* to dishonor my parents—who were goddamn good parents I might add—just so you can shape my image to your liking."

"Okay, okay," Bailey said, rolling his eyes a little at the naiveté of this young punk. "We'll keep the parents thing out of it. We'll say that..."

"We'll say that my name is Jake Kingsley," Jake said. "That's what we'll say. It may not be the most image-enhancing name in the world, but it's the one I was given, the one I like, the one I'm proud of, and I'm going to keep it."

"Fuckin-A," Matt put in. "I'm Matt Goddamn Tisdale and that ain't gonna change either. That's what Heritage knows me as, and that's what I'm gonna play under." He shook his head in disgust. "Rajin fuckin Storm. Holy shit, Bailey. What fuckin' world do you live in?"

This had of course pissed Bailey off and caused him to complain to both the National Records higher-ups and their agent, Shaver. It was implied that they were putting their entire recording contract in jeopardy by not going along with the name changes but they held firm. By that point in the process the album was already in production and neither Jake nor Matt thought they would cancel the whole thing over a Rajin Storm and a JD King. They were right. Though the pressure remained for the next few weeks, eventually Bailey and Acardio accepted that their artists were serious about keeping their Christian names for publicity and dropped the subject. Acardio's dig was the first time the subject had been mentioned in weeks.

Jake didn't take the bait. Instead he pointed to the portion of the cover below the picture and below the track listings. It was the part labeled: *Special thanks to:* He knew that he had never been asked who he would like to thank. He was pretty sure none of the other band members had been asked either.

"Who are all these people we're thanking?" Jake asked.

"Oh, the usual stuff," Acardio said. "Our production specialists, our technicians, our sound guys. They're all working hard on this project. Don't you *want* to thank them?"

"Sure," Jake said. "They are a good bunch. But what about these other people? What about these companies?" He let his finger trail down the list. "Brogan Guitars? Lexington Drums? Caldwell Pianos?"

"They're the people who supplied you with the instruments you play for the recording. You know that." And Jake did. The first thing they had been told when they came for the orientation session prior to starting the recording was that the battered old Les Paul Jake played and that the scratched and beaten Strat Matt played simply wouldn't do for recording quality play. Jake was given a brand new Brogan six string and a brand new Brogan mahogany finish electric/acoustic. Matt was given a top-of-the-line Brogan Battle-Axe guitar that he detested. Darren, who had already played a Brogan bass guitar was given nothing—apparently his scratched and battered bass was good enough. Coop's entire drum set had been replaced by a Lexington twenty-five piece set with the band's name on the dual bass drums. And Bill had been given both an electric piano and an actual acoustic grand piano from Caldwell.

"So, this is an endorsement thing?" Jake said. "Is that why you insisted we play those instruments?"

"No," Acardio scoffed. "Not at all. We've simply found over the years that those particular instruments sound better when recorded. It's nothing more sinister than that."

"But you're getting money from these people to mention these instruments on your album covers, aren't you?"

"Well... yes, but I assure you, that has nothing to do with why we pick those instruments. We pretty much figure that since we're using them anyway, why not pick up a few endorsement fees for the effort? And since we do have an endorsement contract of sorts, it means we get to supply you with those instruments for free. Isn't that nice? The cost of your guitars and that drum set is not included in the recoupable costs portion of your contract."

"Uh huh," Jake said sourly. He didn't want to get into the old recoupable costs argument again. That was a very sore subject for him and the rest of the band. He slid the album cover back across the desk. "Very nice, Max. Thanks for showing it to me." He started to stand.

"Uh... before you go, Jake, there is one thing I need to talk to you about."

Jake sat back down, wondering what it was this time. "Sure," he said. "What's up?"

Acardio gave an apologetic smile. "Well, it's about the outside work clause in your contract. I assume you remember the terms of that."

"Yeah," Jake said bitterly. "I remember the terms of it."

The outside work clause he was referring to was a portion of their contract that stated the band *Intemperance* and its individual members were forbidden from performing musically for anyone other than the record label without specific permission. And the label routinely denied such specific permission, as had been the case when Jake and Matt had asked Shaver to try to get them a few gigs down in the L.A. area so they could pick up a few bucks to help supplement the meager advance money they'd been given. Shaver had told them that the label would probably not give permission for such a thing and, of course, he was right.

"Nobody sees you in concert until we get this album finished and get you out on tour," had been Acardio's response to the request. He had not explained himself any further than this, nor was he required to.

"What's the problem with the outside work clause now?" Jake asked. "We haven't been doing any gigs. You should know that."

"Well," Acardio said, "I have some information to the contrary, Jake."

Jake raised his eyebrows up. "Someone told you that we have a gig somewhere?"

"Not the whole band, just you."

"Me?" Jake asked. "Someone told you I have a gig by *myself*."

"Had, not have," Acardio said. "I'm told that you engaged in a live musical performance yesterday evening before a crowd. Is that true?"

Jake's eyes widened. "Last night? Are you talking about the parking lot party we had after work? Is that what you're talking about?"

Since they were not able to work as musicians during the recording process, and since their advance money was hardly enough to live on, everyone but Matt (whose parents sent him generous allowance checks each week) had been forced to get night jobs to survive. Jake's night job was as a minimum wage dishwasher at The Main Course—a trendy yuppie eatery in downtown L.A. He worked from 7 PM to closing Monday, Tuesday, and Wednesday, and 5 PM to closing Saturday and Sunday. On Wednesday nights he and a few of the other staff members were in the habit of gathering in the back parking lot after closing to drink beer and smoke a little weed if someone had some. Last night Jake had happened to have his old acoustic in the car and had put on an impromptu performance for his friends. It had been a good time. He wowed them with his voice and his guitar skills, performing before a group for the first time since their last gig at D Street West all those months ago. Performance was like a drug and being able to play his guitar and sing, to have people appreciate his gift, had given him a badly needed fix. That couldn't seriously be what Acardio was talking about, could it?

"That's exactly what I'm talking about," Acardio confirmed. "You were in violation of your contract, Jake. This is a very serious matter."

"Max, I was playing my guitar for a couple of work friends. I hardly think that qualifies as a gig."

"You were performing live before an audience," Acardio said.

"There were like eight people there," Jake said, exasperated. "We were drinking beer. It's not like I was charging them money."

"Nevertheless, that constitutes an audience. I'm also told that you performed copywrited material from other musical acts. That's even more serious. You don't have permission to sing *Led Zepplin* songs live. They're not even on our label. Do you have any idea what sort of trouble we would be in if it came to light that one of our musicians was performing another label's songs without permission? I shudder to think of what would happen."

"Max, this was not a concert!" Jake almost yelled. "I sang *Stairway to Heaven* because one of the waitresses liked the song! I was trying to get laid, for God's sake!" Something else occurred to him.

"Wait a minute. How do you know that I was singing out in the parking lot last night? How do you know what fucking songs I was singing?"

"I see no reason to swear at me," Acardio told him. "And how I know is irrelevant. The fact is that you performed live before an audience last night in violation of the terms of your contract. Now, we're not going to fine you this time, but if something like this happens again I will be forced to penalize you monetarily by adding a five thousand dollar fine to your recoupable expenses. Do you understand?"

"You have a spy in the restaurant," Jake said in wonder, ignoring his question. "A fucking spy! That's why you recommended that job to me. That's why they hired me so quickly. They're on your goddamn payroll, aren't they?"

"The manager and I do have a certain arrangement," Acardio confirmed. "And he does have a network of people on his staff who keeps him informed about the activities of certain people. But that's neither here nor there. What I want to know from you, Jake, is if you understand that you are not to do this again and what the consequences are if you do?"

Jake took a deep breath, resisting the urge to clench his fists, to yell further. After all, it would be pointless. "I understand," he said.

"Very good," Acardio told him. "I'm glad we were able to clear this up. You may leave now."

Jake left, heading to the cafeteria where he would eat the bologna sandwich he'd made for himself. His anger and frustration followed him down.

*****

As they had been back in Heritage, Jake and Bill were roommates in Los Angeles as well, and for the same reason. They needed to split their living expenses in order to survive. Their apartment in L.A. cost almost one hundred dollars a month more than their apartment in Heritage had. And calling it a dump would have been giving it more credit than it was due.

It was in a squalid post-war era tenement building off Hollywood Boulevard, just two miles from the National Records building, but in a completely different world just the same. The complex was home to parolees and registered sex-offenders, to off-duty hookers and failed actors. It was the kind of place where nickel bags of marijuana were offered for sale to passing motorists out in front, where people sat on the stairs at all hours of the day and night drinking forty-ounce cans of malt liquor and smoking generic cigarettes. The sound of police helicopters hovering overhead and the sound of gunshots in the night were so frequently heard that they were rarely commented on. It was a complex that the LAPD visited at least three times in any given day, breaking up domestic disputes and handling overdose calls.

Their apartment was on the third floor of this building, tucked away in the rear. It was a two-bedroom and consisted of 642 square feet of living space. The carpet was a threadbare shit brown that radiated the faint odor of cat urine no matter how much they cleaned it. The bathroom featured a cracked and leaky toilet, a bathtub that was unusable because of the rust and mildew spots, and a showerhead that produced a pathetic trickle of lukewarm water at best. When Jake and Bill entered it after their recording session that day, it was stifling hot. There was, of course, nothing that resembled air conditioning available for their comfort.

"Damn, I hate this place," Jake said. "Let's get the fans turned on."

"Right," Bill agreed, setting down the twelve-pack of beer they'd purchased on the way home.

They opened all the windows and turned on all three of the fans they'd begged or borrowed when they'd moved here. That at least got the hot, sticky air circulating a bit and allowed fresh smog to be blown in from outside. They each grabbed a beer from the twelver and sat on their couch, which was pretty much the only piece of actual furniture they possessed.

"I hate L.A.," Jake said, taking a drink. "If we make it big with this recording deal I'm going to live anywhere but here. Hell, I'm not even going to come to this part of the state if I don't have to."

"This is a rather depressing existence," Bill said, taking a swig from his own can. "Do you really think we're gonna make it big?"

"Yeah," Jake said. "I do. The question is, are we going to be rich as well as famous?"

"Not under this contract we're not," Bill said. "That's for damn sure."

"What do you mean?"

"I've been doing some calculations."

"You, doing calculations?" Jake said with a grin. "Who'd have thought?"

Bill smiled briefly. "Make fun of me if you will, but know that I'm right as you do it. We've been screwed."

"I already know that."

"You may think you do," Bill told him. "But I don't think you appreciate the depth of our screwing. Our royalties are going to be ten percent, right?"

"Right."

"And that figure is based on a retail rate of five dollars per album, right?"

"Right," Jake said again. That had been a major negotiation point prior to signing the contract and the one thing that Shaver had fought tooth and nail for. The actual retail rate for an album was seven dollars but many first-time bands ended up having their royalties based on the wholesale rate, which was typically in the vicinity of two to three dollars. Shaver, wise to the ways of record contracts, had advised them to refuse to accept the wholesale rate. They did this but Acardio and the reps from the National Records business and legal departments had refused them a full retail rate. Five dollars per unit was the figure they'd eventually agreed upon.

"So, let's be optimistic here and suppose our album goes platinum," Bill said. "That's one million albums sold, right?"

"Right."

"Which means we would get fifty cents for each album, or five hundred grand as a base rate."

"Yes," Jake agreed. "And I know that the recoupable expenses and Shaver's fee all come out of that."

"But have you ever actually added all of this up? It's kind of depressing."

Jake sighed. He didn't want to hear this, but he supposed that he needed to know. "Okay," he told Bill. "Depress me. Let's hear it."

Bill pulled out a crumpled sheet of paper upon which his calculations were written. "Okay, assuming we go platinum, our base royalty is half a million bucks. However, there's that ten percent breakage deduction that they threw in there."

"Yeah," Jake said bitterly. That meant that the label was assuming that ten percent of all the records they shipped would end up broken and un-sellable in transit. So, if they sold a million copies, they would only be credited with nine hundred thousand for financial purposes.

"That brings our royalties down to $450,000. But then there is that 25% packaging fee."

Jake nodded. That was another figure the label wouldn't budge on, despite Shaver's wholehearted efforts to bring it down. The packaging fee was reported to be the costs associated with making the actual albums, the covers, putting them together and shipping them to the retail outlets where they would be sold.

"That's $112,000 off the top, which brings us down to $337,500. That also brings us to the biggest hit to our income, the recoupable expenses."

"The fuckin recoupables," Jake groaned. That had been the sorest part of the negotiations.

"The first thing is the advance they gave us when we signed. That was $50,000. Then there are the estimated studio time costs of $86,000, and the anticipated album promotion costs of $52,000. All of this is one hundred percent recoupable before a royalty check is ever issued and it adds up to $188,000. But it doesn't end there. We're responsible for half of the tour costs and half of the video production costs. That subtracts another $61,000, bringing us to a grand total of $249,000 in recoupable expenses. Do you know what that leaves us with?"

"How much?"

"$88,500," Bill said. "And don't forget Shaver's share. He gets twenty-one percent. That means we peel another $18,585 off, leaving us with $69,915. When you divide that figure up among the five of us, it comes out to $13,983 apiece. And that's assuming we go platinum. Cut that in half if we only go gold and sell half a million albums. If we do much worse than gold, we won't be able to cover the recoupable expenses at all and we'll be in the hole for the next album we do."

"Fourteen thousand bucks," Jake said, shaking his hand as he pondered the horror of that. "That's not even a living wage."

"You and Matt are entitled to extra royalties because you're the songwriters," Bill said. "But they don't amount to much. You can maybe add another thousand dollars apiece for that. And don't forget, we haven't even discussed taxes yet. Although they shouldn't be that bad since we would technically be below the poverty level."

"Jesus," Jake said. "That's what we get for all this work, all this sacrifice, for selling a million fucking albums? Fourteen grand?"

"Fourteen grand," Bill said sadly. "Hardly seems worth it, huh?"

*****

"You seem depressed tonight," said Angelina Hadley, the waitress whose pants Jake had been attempting to penetrate the other night when he did his illegal concert. "I've been flirting with you like mad every time I come back here and haven't gotten a single return flirt." Angelina, or Angie for short, was an aspiring actress. At twenty-two years old, her body was absolutely fantastic, with curves in all the right places, a set of breasts that were the epitome of perfection, and legs that any man yearned to have wrapped around his back. Unfortunately for her career, her face was not as perfect. She had some acne scars left over from her adolescence, a nose that was just a little longer than optimum, and a mole just right of center on her chin. She was not ugly by any means, but these imperfections precluded her from any role in which her face needed to be seen, which pretty much precluded her from the profession of acting in general. She had had a grand total of three parts in her two-year career, two of them as body doubles for other actresses where a nude scene was required and one in a weight loss product commercial where her legs and tummy were shown bare but her face was never seen.

"Sorry," Jake told her as he pulled the dirty dishes from her tray and put them in the industrial sink before him. "I've got a lot on my mind lately."

"Pondering life again, huh?" she asked, sidling up close to him, close enough that her leg was touching his. "I told you about that. Life sucks. The sooner you accept that, the sooner you'll be able to live it."

"Don't forget unfair," he said. "That's the big part. Life is unfair."

"That too," she agreed, putting her hand up on the back of his neck and giving him a caress.

He relished the sensation, letting his head fall back. He had not had an intimate relationship with a female since leaving Heritage and his body cried out for a woman's touch. And though he had not succeeded in bedding the luscious Angie after his illegal concert the other night, he had certainly made some inroads with her. Though they had shared a flirtatious relationship since he had been hired, it wasn't until he sang for her, had played his guitar for her, that she started to take him seriously. The power of music never failed to amaze him. "That feels good," he told her. "Can you keep it up for a few more hours?"

She laughed. "I wish I could. You want to talk about what's wrong with you?"

He shrugged, an action that caused her to put her other hand up to his neck as well. "It's about our recording contract," he said. "It's a long story."

"You want to know something?" she asked.

"What's that?"

"Don't be mad at me or nothing, but I didn't think you really had a recording contract until the other night."

"Really?" he asked, turning to look at her.

"Like I said, don't get me wrong. It's just that this place... this city, is so full of phonies. Hell, I may even be one of them. When someone tells you they have a role in a movie or that they're going to be getting one of their screenplays produced, well... usually they're just... you know... exaggerating."

"Yeah," he said. "I've noticed that." And he had. Never had he met so many liars, cheats, and outright con artists as he had here in L.A.

"I guess I figured that you were just the same," she said. "But then I heard you play and sing."

"And that changed your mind?"

"Oh my God," she said. "You're good, Jake. In fact, you're one of the best I've ever heard. You really do have a recording contract, don't you? You really are going to have an album come out."

He nodded. "We really are, although they pretty much screwed us on the contract. I had that pointed out to me the other day."

"Screwing people is what Hollywood is all about," she said sadly. "Look at me. Half the guys in America got boners looking at my naked body in a bathtub because they thought it was Lynn Harold's. And for this I got a two hundred dollar check and my name mentioned in the credits, but way down in the credits, the part just before the Dolby Surround Sound label, the part that shows up long after everyone's left the damn theater."

Jake knew the movie she was referring to. It was a second rate psychological thriller in which second-rate actress Lynn Harold's character had been pitted against a psychotic murderer. The bathtub scene in the beginning of the movie was legendary, mostly because it was one of the first R rated scenes to show, not just bare breasts, but pubic hair as well. And hardly anyone realized that the breasts and pubic hair in question were not really Lynn's, they were Angie's. "That always was one of my favorite scenes," he said slyly.

She giggled, removing her hands from his neck and slapping him on the butt. "You pervert," she said. "What are you doing after work tonight?"

"I don't know. I thought I'd go home, drink my last can of generic beer, and then hit the rack."

"That does sound like a lot of fun," she said. "But if you're interested, I got a joint back at my apartment. Some pretty good shit too."

"Yeah?" he asked, looking at her face, seeing a twinkle in her eye.

"Yeah," she confirmed. "Sound like a date?"

"You bet your cute little ass."

*****

Angie's apartment complex was just off Santa Monica Boulevard, in a part of Hollywood that was slightly more upscale than Jake and Bill's neighborhood. The LAPD only visited her complex once or twice a day and the number of parolees and sex offenders living there was in the single digits. The apartment itself was only a one bedroom, and a very small one-bedroom at that, but it was cozy and well decorated, the furnishings both feminine and practical.

They sat on her couch, *Saturday Night Live* playing on the television before them, and Angie brought out her tightly rolled marijuana cigarette. They smoked it slowly, relishing it. It was a fairly new variety of greenbud that was making the rounds of late, a high-quality domestic product known as Humboldt Skunkbud, named for the northern California county where it was grown. True to its name, its taste and aroma strongly resembled that which emitted from a skunk's scent glands, although not as potent. Once you got used to it, it was actually pleasant. And it was certainly potent. By the time the joint was a roach, both of them were quite annihilated.

"When are you going to sing for us again?" Angie asked as she leaned back on the couch, her eyes locked onto a framed Ansel Adams print over the television set.

"I can't," he told her, his eyes locked on her legs. She was still wearing her waitress uniform, which featured a skirt that fell several inches above her knees when she was standing. Now that she was slumped backwards the skirt had crept considerably higher, well above mid-thigh. And what lovely thighs they were. The very sight was making him extremely horny. "Not anymore."

Silence descended for a bit—how long, neither could be sure since their sense of time was horribly distorted. Finally, Angie asked him, "Why not?"

"Why not what?" he asked, having forgotten what it was they had been talking about.

She giggled, covering her mouth for a second and then slapping at his leg. "Wow, this is some good shit," she said. "Why can't you sing for us, you hoser?"

This gave him the giggles for a few moments as well, although just why, he was unsure. Finally, he got himself under control and answered her. "It would seem that playing my guitar and singing out in the parking lot after work is a breach of my recording contract. I'm not allowed to do any live performances without National Records' say-so."

"Wow," she said. "That's fuckin' trippy." She did not seem to be particularly surprised by this, however.

"Those assholes actually have a spy in the restaurant. That's why they got me a job there, so they could keep an eye on me." It suddenly occurred to him that Angie might be the spy. Was that possible? Hell, anything was possible in world where they implied they would ruin your career if you didn't say your name was JD King and that your parents were criminally negligent boozers.

"Tom's your spy," Angie said, as if reading his thoughts. "He and Marcus like to slip into the back room and suck each other's dicks every few days. Haven't you ever noticed how friendly the two of them are?"

Now that she mentioned, he had noticed that. And he knew she was not being figurative about them sucking each other's dicks. Tom was a flaming, flamboyant homosexual who had in fact made more than one pass at Jake since he arrived on the scene. And though Marcus, the manager, was not flamboyant or flaming, he was a forty-two year old, never-married man in a predominantly gay line of business.

Jake shook his head in bewilderment. "Spies and threats and positioning people where they can be watched. It's like Nazi Germany around here."

"Welcome to Hollywood," she told him. "Where any office boy or young mechanic can get fucked like a whore."

This too struck him as funny. They laughed together hysterically for the better part of two minutes.

"Oh wow," she said when they finally returned to normalcy. "I don't know what I'd do without good buds to get me through, or cheap beer." She slid over on the couch, until her leg was in contact with his. She turned toward him, a dreamy expression on her face. Her hand went to the side of his face, caressing him there, stroking him.

A moment later they were sharing their first kiss. It stretched out for some time, at first a gentle touching of lips, then a dance of tongues. She tasted of skunk bud and spearmint chewing gum and she radiated eroticism from every pore as she began to heat up. He let his hands roam up and down her back, whispering over the cotton of her blouse. Her fingers went to his long hair and began to run through it.

"You are so sexy, Jake," she whispered to him when the kiss finally broke. "I always thought that, ever since you started working with us... but when I heard you sing... mmmm, when I heard you sing..."

She seemed incapable of completing the thought. Instead, she covered his mouth with hers once more. Her tongue slid back between his lips. They moved closer together, so her firm, feminine body was pressed against his. He let his hand drop down to her leg, just below the hem of her skirt. It was a soft, smooth, sexy leg, one of the finest he'd ever felt, perhaps *the* finest. But when he tried to slide his hand up higher, to put it under her skirt, her hand dropped down onto it, stopping him.

"No," she whispered softly, breaking the kiss but keeping her lips only a few millimeters from his. "Not tonight. Not on the first date."

"No?" he whispered back, unable to determine if she were teasing or not.

"No," she repeated. "I'm not that kind of girl." And then, having said that, her tongue slid out and licked slowly, sensuously across his upper lip.

He sucked it into his mouth and their kiss resumed, quickly becoming passionate, intense. Her hand went back up to his neck, where it caressed the skin there, her nails scratching at him lightly. He concluded that she really had been kidding about the first date prohibition. And besides, this wasn't really a date, was it? They had just come over to smoke a joint. He tried to push his hand upward on her leg again. Once again, her hand slapped down on it, barring the ascension.

"Don't be naughty, Jake," she whispered, her tongue licking at his chin, sliding along the angle of his jaw to his ear. "First date gets first base only. That's the rule."

He groaned a little. His cock was rock-hard beneath his jeans and didn't much care for the idea that it would not get to play tonight. "Are there exceptions to the rule?" he asked her.

"No," she replied, licking at his earlobe, her fingers now scratching at the back of the hand that rested on her lower thigh. "Kissing only. No touching the private parts. No exceptions."

They continued to make out and she continued to deflect all of his efforts to move beyond first base. She allowed him to kiss her neck, to hold her by the waist, to run his hand up and down her legs below the skirt, but she refuted any attempts to touch her breasts or to slide his hands higher. Her hands were quite active as well. She ran them up and down his back, through his hair, even over his chest. But they went nowhere near his ass, let alone the bulge in his jeans. His erection was so intense that it was actually throbbing with the beat of his heart. He began to feel the sweet pain of blue balls for the first time since high school.

Finally, after nearly an hour, they broke apart. Jake was trembling with desire for her, especially since he could sense how turned-on she was as well. Her nipples were poking through her blouse. Her face and neck were flushed. Her lips were swollen and blood red even though her lipstick had long since been kissed clean off of them.

"Wasn't that fun, Jake?" she asked him, her breathing still heavy, her skirt still quite high on her legs.

He nodded. "Yeah," he breathed back. "But it could be funner."

She smiled sexily. "A second date might get you second base," she said. "If you're nice, that is."

"Is that a rule too?" he asked.

"That you have to be nice? That's always a rule."

"No," he said. "About second base."

"Don't you think second base is a good goal for a second date? I wouldn't want you to think I'm a slut or anything."

"I would never think that," he said.

"You guys all say that," she told him. "And you might even mean it, at least while you have a bulge like that in your jeans." She looked at it with interest, sighing a little.

"But..."

"I guess you're gonna have to take care of that yourself, aren't you?"

"Uh... yeah, I suppose," he replied.

"I'm gonna have to take care of myself too," she said. "I'm so wet right now, you wouldn't believe it. My panties are absolutely soaked."

A tremor worked its way through him at these words. God, what she doing? She had to be the worst cock-tease he had ever encountered.

"Tell me something," she said, her hand dropping to his knee and caressing there, almost absently. "Did you really like my bathtub scene?"

"Oh yes," he said truthfully. "It was very hot."

"Did it make your cock hard when you saw it?"

He nodded. "Yes." And it was true. It was hard not to get a hard-on while watching a woman with a beautiful body soap her breasts, stomach, and pubic region while reclining in a bathtub.

"It turns me on to think that I've made thousands of guys hard," she said. "Millions maybe. Does that make me sick?"

He shook his head. "No, not at all."

She gave her sexy smile again. "You know," she said, "I could use a bath about now. Maybe I could reenact that scene for you. Would you like that?"

"Re... reenact?" he asked. "You mean..."

"You can't touch me though," she said. "That would be going past first base and that's not allowed on a first date." She stood up. "But if you wanted to watch me do something I've already done on a movie set... well, that's not being a slut, is it?"

"Of course not," he blurted as an additional surge of blood went rushing into his nether regions.

"Wait until you hear the water turn off," she said. "And then come on in." She cast him a knowing look. "With your clothes on."

"Right," he said.

She sashayed into the bathroom. The door closed behind her. A second later he heard the sound of water running through the pipes. The minutes stretched out with agonizing slowness. Jake's mind whirred with thoughts of her undressing, of what he was going to see when he went in there, with thoughts of what might happen as a result. His cock did not deflate so much as an iota. Finally, after several forevers, the rush of water came to an end. He stood up and walked to the bathroom door, his hand coming down on the knob. He turned it and stepped inside.

The room was steamy and warm. The bathtub was smaller than the one that had been featured in the movie, but that detracted little from the eerily erotic deja vu he experienced as he looked down at her. She was posed just as she had been in the film, lying on her back in clear water, legs slightly apart, breasts just above the surface. She had a bar of soap in her hands and was rubbing it in lazy, opulent circles across her breasts, over her smooth belly, across the sparse black pubic hair. Her head was back, eyes half closed, a sexy, contented smile on her face.

"You're beautiful, Angie," he said, walking closer, staring at her unabashedly.

"Thank you," she said, making another circle with the soap, lingering near the pubic region this time, sighing a little as it passed lower, revealing just a hint of the pinkness beneath.

"God," Jake whispered, wanting more than anything to rip off his clothes and jump in the tub with her, to drive himself inside her body.

"That's close enough," she said when his knees touched the edge of the tub. "Just look at me. Just imagine what my body feels like, what my hands are feeling right now."

He did just that, watching as she soaped her breasts again. Her nipples were sticking up proudly, the areoles perfect circles the size of half dollars. How slick they would feel against his hands, how firm. She moved the soap lower again. Her tummy was flat and smooth, her belly button flawless. How he would love to run his tongue over it.

"Of course, you know what the implication of the scene was, don't you?" she asked, her hand trailing down into her pubic hair again, making lazy soap circles through it.

"Uh... I'm not sure," he said, hardly aware of what she was even talking about, so entranced was he by the visualization.

"Why masturbation of course," she said. "They couldn't actually show me playing with myself, but they could show me... getting ready to, you know what I mean?" She let go of the soap. It dropped beneath the water and disappeared. Her pelvis rose up out of the water, giving him an unimpeded view of her womanhood for the first time. Her lips were swollen and open. Her clitoris was erect and ready for pleasure. Her fingers dipped down, two of them sliding across those lips, touching them, delving inside for the briefest of seconds. "This," she said, her voice getting heavier, "is what the audience really wanted to see. What they were imagining. Mmmm, I wish I could've showed them this too."

"Oh God," Jake groaned. His hand dropped down to the bulge in his pants. He rubbed it a few times.

"But you can see it, Jake," she said, sliding her fingers a little faster. "You can see what I really wanted to do in that tub, what everyone really wanted me to do."

"Angie... Jesus," he said, rubbing the bulge a little more. He started to drop to his knees.

"No," she said, shaking her head. "Keep standing. No touching me. We stay at first base."

He grunted in frustration but stayed on his feet.

"But you can touch yourself," she said. "That's not going beyond first base." Her eyes locked onto his crotch. "Play with yourself while you watch me. I want to see it."

He didn't hesitate for a second. He ripped his jeans open and pushed them down, his underwear going with them. His hand went to his hard cock and began to stroke.

"Yessss," she said, licking her lips, her fingers moving faster against her lips. "That's right. Play with it. Jack off while you look at me."

He began to stroke faster, as did she. Her hands began to make circles around her clit. Her other hand went down there and slid first one and then two fingers inside of her body. They began to move in and out in short jabs.

Jake fought to keep his orgasm under control, employing every mental block he had learned over his sexual years. Despite this furious effort, he knew he wasn't going to last long. This was, without a doubt, the most erotic, sensual thing he'd ever experienced. And he wasn't even touching her.

"I'm gonna... gonna come, Jake," she panted, her fingers now a blur, her pelvis rising and falling, sending ripples of water out to either side of her. "And when I do, I want you to come too. I want you to come all over my body."

Jake's mental blocks crumbled in a smoking, sizzling wreck as he heard this. He began to tremble all over, his legs going weak, his own hand now a blur as well. "You better... better hurry," he grunted.

She hurried. With a drawn-out groan of pleasure, she began to come, her body nearly seizing as it released. He groaned as well, his orgasm slamming through his body, building and peaking with an intensity that was almost frightening.

"All over me," she panted, her fingers still working away. "All over meeeeeeee!"

His semen sprayed out of him with a power unlike anything he'd experienced before, spurt after spurt hitting her in the breasts, in the stomach, on her hands as they played, on her thighs. She moaned and jerked with each blast that struck her. When it was finally over she slumped down in the tub with enough force to send a wave of water splashing out. He slumped to his knees, landing in the puddle she'd created.

They sat in silence for a few moments, basking in their respective afterglows. Finally, he looked over at her. "How about we go out again tomorrow night?" he asked. "I've just got to find out what second base is like."

*****

They got together the next night after work. This time they drank a six-pack of beer before commencing with the make-out session. As promised, the second date led to a second base encounter. She allowed him to put his hand under her shirt and beneath her brassiere. Her breasts felt heavenly. Later, she allowed him to remove her shirt and suckle her nipples. They tasted as heavenly as they felt. Later still she stripped off her clothes and had him rub baby oil into her breasts. He used nearly half a bottle, his hands slipping and sliding over the perfect orbs but not allowed to venture below. The evening ended with her masturbating herself as he stroked her breasts with one hand and his cock with the other, until he ejaculated all over her oily boobs as she herself came.

Their third date was the following Tuesday. They actually went out to a restaurant and a movie that day and commenced making out in the back row of the movie theater. He soon had his hand up her skirt and in the tightness of her body, driving in and out. She played with his cock through his jeans and finally, just before the credits rolled, took it out and stroked it. He managed to give her two orgasms. She refused to allow him to come, however. She wanted to save that for later. Back at her place she dropped to her knees and elbows, pulled up her skirt, slid down her panties, and had him violently finger-fuck her from behind. As she approached orgasm she let him go to "third and a half base" and put his mouth on her pussy. He ate her to two orgasms, one from behind and one from the front. After, she opened his pants and gave him an agonizingly slow blowjob, teasing him unmercifully for the better part of thirty minutes before finally allowing him to blast a torrent of semen into her mouth.

The fourth date was not really a date at all. They spent eight hours in her apartment, screwing each other's brains out in every conceivable way.

Their relationship continued and was initially based primarily on passion and the alleviation of their considerable lust whenever they were able to be together outside of work. Often they would begin within minutes of finding themselves alone, sometimes the moment the door shut behind them. On one memorable occasion Jake fucked her as she stood against the door, while she was still wearing her waitress uniform and smelling of food and liquor and cigarette smoke from her shift. Their sessions lasted for hours at times as they basked in the pleasures of the flesh. Both of them happily accepted that it was a friends-with-benefits arrangement, concluding this was just what they were looking for. But as time went by and their lives went on, as Jake went to recording sessions and listened to endless bullshit from Acardio and Bailey and even Shaver, and as Angelina went to audition after audition and was turned down on the basis of her imperfect face time and time again, a strange thing began to happen, so slowly that they hardly realized it. The friendship part began to become more important than the benefits. Though their sex life remained active, varied, and even unconventional at times, they found themselves getting together just to talk more and more often. They began to call each other on the phone when they couldn't get together—Jake from the recording studio, Angelina from various studios or agent's offices. They began to go out to restaurants and to take weekend trips to the beach just because they wanted to be together. Before either of them realized it had happened, their booty-call relationship evolved into an actual lover's relationship, complete with passion, jealousy, longing, and trust.

*****

On August 28, 1982, the final voice track of the first *Intemperance* album was completed. The next day the dubbing and mixing began. The band was asked to redo individual portions of the songs—a ten second section of guitar here, a twenty-second portion of drums there, a piano section somewhere else, a bit of lead or backing vocal somewhere else still. Each of these dubs required an average of fifteen to twenty takes before the techs were satisfied it was right. In addition, they did a multitude of overdubs. Overdubs were extra instrumental tracks—usually guitars—that were laid down atop the existing music to make it blend smoother or sound better on tape.

Jake, Bill, and especially Matt had been vehemently opposed to doing this at first.

"*Intemperance* is a five-person band," Matt had protested. "You're suggesting we add another rhythm guitar over a song. That's more than five! That's not how we do things!"

"That *is* how we do things," Acardio told them, "and since you are under contract with us, you will do whatever the hell we tell you to do. If we want you to put a fucking Polka accordion track in one of your songs, you'll do it. If you don't, you're in breach of contract. Get it?"

They got it. They didn't like it, but they got it. They performed the overdubs when they were told to and when they got to the mixing process, everyone except Matt—who remained a stern traditionalist on the subject—had to admit that the overdubs did add quite a bit to the recording, giving it a smoother, more radio-friendly sound.

"We won't be able to reproduce it live though," Matt said. "Don't you guys understand that?"

Jake thought that maybe Matt was overexaggerating a bit. The overdubs were quite audible to professional musicians and sound techs, but most of the people buying the albums and going to the concerts would not fit into this category. Jake himself had never noticed such things in his favorite music before and this had never kept him from enjoying a concert.

In any case, the discussion was meaningless. Acardio was right. They were required to do what they were told.

The mixing process, which went on in conjunction with the overdubbing and the re-dubbing, was the very definition of tediousness. Day after day, for hours at a time, the sound techs would listen to each individual track of each individual song and blend them together piece by piece. Their perfectionism and anal retentiveness about this process was agonizing and made that displayed by Bill during their sound checks seem like hastiness personified in comparison. Only Bill himself found the process anything but boring. He was actually fascinated with it and would spend as much time with the techs as he could, asking hundreds of questions, listening to hundreds of nuances through the headphones, and learning the very basics of a skill that he would one day be counted among the world's best at.

On October 2, 1982, at long last, the mixing, dubbing, overdubbing, and re-dubbing was finally declared complete and the end result was put on a master tape. *Intemperance*'s first album was recorded and then copied onto another tape. That tape was sent to the manufacturer for production.

"They're going to run off one hundred thousand copies to start with," Shaver told them the following week, as they sat in their bi-monthly meeting with him. As usual, he had treated them to a few lines of his Bolivian flake and a round of Chivas and Coke. "In addition, they're going to run off about thirty thousand singles of *Descent Into Nothing*. That will be the first track that gets pushed. A few thousand of those copies will go off to radio stations all around the country, mostly in the bigger markets. National's promotion department is already talking to their contacts in the various cities about you guys and they'll start playing *Descent* even before the album and the singles are released for sale."

"So, we'll be on the radio soon?" Matt asked.

"Probably within the next three weeks," Shaver said.

"I can't fuckin' wait to hear us on the radio, dudes," Darren said wistfully. He had helped himself to a double dose of the cocaine and was working on his third Chivas and Coke. "That's gonna be bad-ass."

"Indeed, it will," Shaver said. "In any case, the tentative release date for the album and the single is December 7. I suspect it's going to do well as long as the radio stations keep up their end of the bargain and give it widespread and frequent airplay. *Descent* is a catchy tune and people will love it if they get to hear it."

"Yeah," Jake said, a little sourly. He didn't really care for one of his songs—the lyrics and melody of which represented some of his deepest emotions—to be referred to as "a catchy tune".

"When it starts to sell, they'll run off more copies of the album and the original single. They'll also release the next single which will be *Who Needs Love?*. Long before this happens though, you boys will be going out on tour. We're already starting to talk over the details of that."

"Oh yeah?" Matt asked, his ears perking up. "What do you mean?"

Shaver smiled, taking a sip of his Coke-less Chivas on the rocks. "Well, it just so happens that one of my other clients—*Earthstone*—is releasing an album mid-November. Acardio and I both believe it would be beneficial for all concerned if you went out on tour as their opening band."

"*Earthstone*," Matt said in awe. "You mean... The *Earthstone*. Richie Valentine and Brad Winston. That *Earthstone*?" *Earthstone* was a favorite band of all of the *Intemperance* members. They were solid musicians and good lyricists, hindered only by the fact that many of their tunes were too lengthy for radio airplay.

"Those are my boys," Shaver confirmed. "I discovered that band, you know. Just like I discovered you. This will be their fourth album. We're calling it *Losing Proposition*. Some damn catchy tunes on this one. I'm hoping this one will be their first platinum cut."

"So, we'll be on the *Losing Proposition* tour?" Jake asked, wondering if that was prophetic or not.

Shaver laughed. "It's just a name," he said. "You boys like *Earthstone*? They're great guys. You'll love touring with them. They really know how to party."

*****

NTV Television Studios, Los Angeles
October 25, 1982

The video producer was Norman Rutger. He was fifty years old but, thanks to multiple plastic surgeries on multiple portions of his body, looked an artificial thirty-five. He was a lecherous bisexual who came equally onto any man or woman who crossed his path. He had the habitual sniff of a habitual cocaine user and the trendy dress of a Hollywood insider. And he did not like being questioned, particularly in matters of one of his beloved music videos, which the members of *Intemperance* were here to film.

"I can't work with these people, Maxie," Rutger cried dramatically to Acardio. "How dare they question my choice of clothing. How dare they question my imagery!"

The band fumed as they watched this overdramatic tantrum. Matt, acting as spokesman, attempted a rare display of diplomacy. "Look, Max," he said, holding up the clothing in question. "We're not trying to be insulting; it's just that we don't wear stuff like this. I mean, leather pants?

And red ones at that? We wear jeans on stage. Old, faded jeans and T-shirts. They're comfortable and that's the image we want to project."

"Not anymore you don't," Acardio said without hesitation. "Leather pants are in and that's what you're going to wear, both in the video and out on tour."

"I'm not wearing any fuckin' leather pants on tour!" Darren interjected.

"You'll wear whatever the hell we tell you to wear," Acardio said, glaring at Darren and making him look away. "If we want you dressed in a goddamn tutu with crotchless panties and your dingus hanging out and flapping in the breeze, that's what you'll wear!"

Darren's fists clenched up, but he said nothing.

"Look," Jake said, stepping up to the bat. "The clothes are one thing. I suppose we can live with leather pants if we have to. But all this satanic imagery you're putting in this video. What is up with that?"

"It's the theme of the video," Acardio said, rolling his eyes. "Are you so dumb you don't realize that? Satanism sells! Look at *Black Sabbath*, Ozzy Osbourne, *Iron Maiden*. We're shooting a video called *Descent Into Nothing*! A perfect opportunity to inject a Satanist image towards our band. It's not overt of course, we just show you descending further and further towards a dark and flame-ridden place with each scene. What possible problem could you have with that?"

"Well... that's not what the song is about," Jake said. "*Descent* is about the struggles of growing up, about leaving childhood behind, about the disillusionment of becoming an adult. It has nothing whatsoever to do with Satanism."

Max rolled his eyes again. "Nobody cares what you think the song is about."

"What I *think* the song is about? I wrote it! I'm pretty fucking sure that's what it's about!"

Max waved this off. "Videos about the struggles of growing up don't sell albums and that's what we're here to do. Now I've had about as much of this shit as I'm going to take from you punks. Norman is producing this video and you are employees of National Records and you will do exactly what he tells you to do. Is that clear?"

It was clear. It took almost a week of ten-hour days, but they shot the video. They did what they were told, like good National Records employees.

CHAPTER 5

NEVER KISS A GROUPIE

January 1, 1983
Interstate 95, southern Maine

Jake woke up slowly, his head throbbing, his mouth dry and tasting of rum, his stomach knotted with hunger pains. He felt the familiar rocking of the bus, heard the familiar rumbling of its diesel engine as it pulled them up a hill, but he was not in the familiar confines of his fold-down bunk near the back. He opened his eyes slowly, wincing a little at the sunlight streaming in from the windshield up front. He found he was sitting at one of the tables adjacent to the bar. He was still dressed in the jeans and T-shirt he wore last night. He still felt a little drunk as well.

"Christ," he muttered. "What time is it?"

He raised his head up and looked around. The inside of the tour bus looked a little like the hotel room scene on the cover of their album. Empty booze bottles, beer cans, drink glasses, and overflowing ashtrays were everywhere. All that was missing was the naked woman. Matt was lying on the floor, his mouth open, snoring drunkenly. Coop and Darren were lying on the two couches. Only Bill was actually in his bunk, although his arms were hanging limply out.

Sitting across the table from Jake was Greg Gahn, the National Records Artist Development Department representative who had been assigned as *Intemperance*'s "tour manager". Greg was a short man, perpetually grinning, with a strong car salesman personality. His hair was cut short and always neatly styled. He always wore a suit and carried a copy of the Book of Mormon with him. He proclaimed himself a devout follower of the Principles of Mormonism.

"I don't drink, I don't smoke, I don't engage in fornication," he told them four days before, when they'd set out from Los Angeles to head for the opening date of the *Losing Proposition* Tour in Bangor, Maine. "That's why they send me out with you boys. I can keep the tour moving along without succumbing to the pleasures of the flesh or the gross alcohol intoxication that sometimes crops up on these things."

It seemed that the Principles of Mormonism did not cover cocaine use—or at least Greg pretended they did not. In the four days they had been on the road Greg had sniffed and snorted from a seemingly endless supply of high quality blow—blow he was more than happy to share with the five band members he was babysitting.

He was crunching up a few lines of it right now, as a matter of fact, going about it with the anal precision that drove all of his tasks. A bottle of expensive mineral water sat next to him. There was a slice of fresh lemon floating in it.

"Morning, Jake," he said cheerfully. "How you feeling?"

"Pretty shitty," Jake replied, running his hand across his face and feeling a two-day growth of beard there. "Where are we?"

"Within sight of our destination. We just crossed the Maine state line about twenty minutes ago. We should be in Bangor by noon."

"Bitchin," Jake said. "It'll be nice to get off this bus for awhile."

"I agree, although it seemed like you boys have been having a good enough time on our little trip from one corner of the country to the other. We had to stop twice to pick up more liquor for you."

Jake shrugged. Yes, they had partied rather hard since leaving Los Angeles. There was booze and cocaine and high-grade marijuana readily available for their pleasure and there was nothing else to do. There were portions of the trip that he didn't even remember. He would be the first to agree that they were off to a good start in the department of living up their band's name. It was very annoying, however, to have to listen to the self-righteous tripe this little coke-sniffing religious fanatic was always spouting at them during their brief interludes of sobriety.

"Well," Jake said, "you gotta keep the talent happy, don't you?"

Greg laughed as if that was the funniest thing he'd ever heard. "Yes indeed," he said, grinning wildly. "That is my job, after all." He leaned down and made the two lines disappear. He sniffed pertly, tapping the sides of his nose for a second and then looked at Jake. "Care for a little wake-up?" he asked him. "It'll probably get rid of your hangover."

He was right. A few lines would nicely erase the headache, the sour stomach, and the dark fatigue that was pulling on him. But he declined nevertheless. He had been snorting a considerable amount of cocaine for the last four days and he thought it might be a good idea to take a little break from it. "That's okay," he said. "I think I'll just grab some aspirin and drink a quart or two of water."

"Suit yourself," Greg replied, his grin remaining firmly affixed. "But don't hesitate to ask if you change your mind."

Jake nodded and stood up, doing it slowly to keep the nausea and the spins to a minimum. He made his way to the front of the bus, toward the small bathroom/shower room. His eyes were now more or less adjusted to the brightness and he took a glance out the window, seeing they were driving down a four-lane Interstate that had been cut through a thick forest. Though the sky was now a brilliant shade of blue that was never seen in Los Angeles or even Heritage, it was clear that a terrible blizzard had recently swept through this area. Snow covered the ground and the evergreen trees. Drifts thrown up by snowplows stood nearly six feet high on either shoulder. It looked cold out there, frighteningly cold. The kind of cold that killed if you ventured out in it without an Arctic protection suit.

"Wassup, Ken?" Jake asked as he approached the small door to the bathroom. Ken Adopolis was one of the two bus drivers assigned to the *Intemperance* tour bus. Robert Cranston, the other driver, was currently crashed out in his small bunk next to the bathroom.

"Jake, my man," Ken greeted, turning towards him for a few seconds before putting his eyes back on the road. "How you doing this morning? A little hung?"

"I've been worse," Jake said, looking at the mess that surrounded Ken's seat. There were several empty soda cans, the crumpled remains of various fast food and processed food wrappers, and, of course, the inevitable ashtray full of cigarette butts and marijuana ashes. Ken was a voracious smoker of pot. He claimed he didn't know how to drive the bus when he was straight.

Ken picked up a marijuana pipe that he always kept loaded. He offered it to Jake. "Care for a little hit?"

"Maybe later," Jake replied.

Ken nodded, putting the pipe back down. "I heard you guys' song three more times on the radio since I got on shift," he said. "They're playing it on all the rock stations I've been getting."

Jake smiled a little. "That's what I like to hear," he said, although by this point the novelty of hearing himself on the radio was starting to wear off, especially since during waking hours—which consisted of about eighteen out of every twenty-four so far—the drivers had made a point of blasting *Descent Into Nothing* at top volume whenever they happened across it on the radio waves. When this happened everything else that was going on would stop instantly and they would all sing along and play air guitars and cheer—their revelry proportionate to the amount of intoxicants they had in their systems. This was something that happened fairly frequently on the trip because *Descent* was fast becoming one of the most played hard rock songs in the nation. The single had been released to the radio stations on November 20, more than two weeks before being made available to the public. Thanks to the National Records Promotion Department—who had connections with pretty much every major radio station in the United States and Canada—rock DJ's across the country had started playing *Descent* the very next day, at first during new music segments and then as a regular part of their programming.

Jake would never forget the first time he'd heard the song on the radio. He had been in Angie's apartment and they had been naked in her bed, cuddling after an extended session of lovemaking. Both had just been drifting towards sleep, the radio alarm clock nothing but background noise, when Justin Adams, the night DJ for KRON had come back from a commercial break.

"New music here on the Krone bone," he said. "We just got this tune the other day. The album is not even in stores yet. It's a band from Heritage if you can believe that. You ever heard of Heritage? It's a little cow town up in northern Cali somewhere that makes Bakersfield look like friggin Beverly Hills from what I'm told. It's where they grow most of our tomatoes and our rice and where having a good time means shutting down the still for the night and going over to the grange hall."

Jake's eyes popped wide open and he sat up, startling Angie. "Holy shit," he said.

"What?" she asked, looking around.

"Shhh," he hushed her. "They're talking about us! They're gonna play our song!"

"Your song?"

He hushed her again.

"Anyway," Justin Adams continued, "I guess they're capable of producing something other than vegetables and cheap moonshine up in those parts because I gave this tune a listen and... well... it friggin rocks. Here it is for your listening pleasure. The band is called *Intemperance...*"

"That's you!" Angie had squealed. "Oh my God!"

"Shhhh!"

"...and the tune is the title cut from their up and coming album: *Descent Into Nothing.*"

And then the opening riff of Matt's guitar began to sound from the tinny speaker. Jake reached over and turned it up and both of them listened transfixed as the power riff began, as the piano chimed in, and then, finally, as Jake's voice began to issue from the speaker.

"It's really you," Angie whispered in awe. It was the first time she had heard the song.

"It really is," Jake agreed, just as awed, though he'd heard the song a thousand times.

They'd listened to it all the way through and then Angie looked at him seriously, a tear running down her face.

"What?" Jake had asked. "What are you crying about?"

"Nothing," she said. "Just love me."

He'd loved her, sliding into her naked body less than five minutes later.

On the day they left Los Angeles for Bangor, the album and the single had been in stores across the nation for twenty-three days. Album sales were less than twenty thousand at this point—well over ninety percent of those from the greater Heritage region—but sales of the *Descent Into Nothing* single had broken into Billboard's Hot One Hundred with a bullet. Quite a remarkable feat since techno and punk music were the current fads. It was projected that the song would be played on the Top Forty countdown the following week.

"Both the fifteen to eighteen and the eighteen to twenty-five crowd loves the song," Acardio had told them. "It's going just how we planned. As soon as the song peaks and starts heading back down the charts, we'll release *Who Needs Love* as a single and get the radio stations to start pushing that one. When that happens, album sales will start to pick up dramatically. It generally takes two hit songs before people start buying the album in droves. And if we can squeeze three hit songs out, the album is almost guaranteed to go platinum."

Platinum, Jake thought as he entered the bathroom and closed the door behind him. *So we can make an honest fourteen grand.* His mind wanted to be bitter at this, as it had so many times before, but it simply wouldn't take today. His hangover—which was really a four-day hangover—coupled with his nervousness at their first real concert, simply wouldn't allow it. And then there was his parting with Angie. That weighed heavily on his mind as well.

He had grown very close to Angie during the last few months, at least as close as he'd been to Michelle during the peak of their relationship. Parting with her had not been easy, especially since their tour schedule, which was quite grueling when you sat down and looked at it, would not even begin to approach the west coast any time soon. So far, the first leg was all that was planned out. Jake remembered reading it over for the first time.

Jan 1 – Bangor, Maine; Jan 2 – Concorde, New Hampshire; Jan 3 – Boston, Massachusetts; Jan 5 – Buffalo, New York; Jan 6 – Pittsburgh, Pennsylvania; Jan 7 – Cleveland, Ohio; Jan 10- Cincinnati, Ohio; Jan 11 – Indianapolis, Indiana; Jan 12 – Chicago, Illinois; Jan 13 – Minneapolis, Minnesota; Jan

14 – Des Moines, Iowa; Jan 15 – Peoria, Illinois; Jan 16 – Kansas City, Missouri; Jan 17 – St. Louis, Missouri; Jan 18 – Springfield, Missouri; Jan 20 – Oklahoma City, Oklahoma; Jan 21 – Amarillo, Texas; Jan 22 – Albuquerque, New Mexico; Jan 23 – El Paso, Texas; Jan 24 – Austin, Texas; Jan 25 – San Antonio, Texas; Jan 26 – Houston, Texas; Jan 27 – Dallas, Texas; Jan 29 – Little Rock, Arkansas; Jan 31 – Baton Rouge, Louisiana; Feb 01 – New Orleans, Louisiana; Feb 02 – Jackson, Mississippi; Feb 03 – Memphis, Tennessee; Feb 04 – Nashville, Tennessee; Feb 05 – Louisville, Kentucky

And that was just the first leg. Five legs were planned. There were days off included in there—occasional ones—but those were mostly due to particularly lengthy travel times between shows. It wouldn't be until at least the first week in February when he might get a chance to get back to Los Angeles to see Angie. A two-week break was included before the second leg of the tour began.

"I'll be back then," he told her at their last meeting, just hours before he climbed onto the tour bus for the first time.

"I know you will," she responded, kissing his face again, her arms around his body, hugging him tighter, not wanting to let go.

"And I'll call you every day," he added. "Twice a day when I can."

The tears had started to run at this point, glimmering drops that slid down her cheeks. "I know," she answered. "I know."

And then she reluctantly released him and walked back to her car, openly sobbing by that point. Jake had looked after her, puzzled, wondering why she was so emotional. It was only going to be about six weeks before he saw her again. She was acting like they were saying goodbye forever.

*****

The convoy *Intemperance* was traveling with consisted of six tractor-trailer rigs and six tour buses. The road crew, or "roadies" as they were known, occupied three of the tour buses. The other three were the two rock bands and their management staff. Contained within the trailers was a complete stage assembly, scaffolding to hang lights from, a complete stage lighting set with swivels, gimbals, and cooling systems, twenty-seven high performance amplifiers, more than a mile of electrical cable and power cords, and, of course, all of the instruments for both *Earthstone* and *Intemperance*. The convoy crossed the Bangor city limits just before noon on New Year's Day. The bulk of the vehicles headed towards Bangor Auditorium downtown, the site of tonight's show. The tour buses belonging to *Earthstone* and *Intemperance*, as well as one other that belonged to the management staff, peeled off and headed for the Bangor International Hotel near the airport.

The hotel was not nearly as classy as it sounded. It was, in fact, just a half step up from your standard Motel 6. The buses pulled around back and sat at idle, the heaters continuing to blow, the band members remaining onboard, while Greg and Joe Stafferson, who was *Earthstone*'s tour manager, went to check in. About twenty minutes passed before they returned.

"Okay, boys," Greg told them. "You have room 107 and 108. How you want to divide yourselves up is up to you."

"We only get two rooms?" Matt asked. He had imbibed in Greg's offer of a powdery wake-up/hangover potion and his eyes were glinting quite brightly. "The guys on *Earthstone* all get their own rooms. What's up with that?"

"It's *Earthstone*'s tour," Greg told him. "The headliner gets certain privileges. Now, as for your laundry, just bag it up and put it in the back of the bus. Ken and Robert will see that it's cleaned. Be sure to label your bags. This will be the procedure for laundry in every city we visit, so get in the habit."

As he had no doubt intended, the subject of what to do with their laundry distracted them from the subject of sharing rooms. He handed one key to Jake and one to Matt and then turned and headed out the door.

"I really don't like that guy," Jake said as they watched him go.

"He's not that bad," Matt said, clapping him on the shoulder. "He gets us some pretty bitchin' dope, doesn't he?"

"Fuckin' aye," Coop said.

"The coke's not as good as Shaver's," Darren pointed out.

Jake gave up. He went and gathered up his single suitcase, which contained pretty much everything he had been allowed to bring with him, and then stepped off the bus.

*****

They decided that Jake and Bill would share one room, Matt, Coop, and Darren the other. They would then rotate roommates from night to night as the tour progressed, the scheduling for this rotation automatically assigned to Bill, their resident scientist, nerd, and mathematician.

"Jesus fucking Christ, it's cold out there," Jake said as he emerged from the bathroom after shaving and showering, a towel wrapped around his waist. "What kind of morons live in a place where the temperature is three degrees at 12:30 in the afternoon?"

"I never felt wind like that before," Bill agreed as he stripped off clothes in anticipation of his own hot shower. "My dick isn't that big to begin with. I don't need a minus twelve wind chill factor to make it smaller."

Jake looked at him as he pulled a pair of underwear and a clean pair of sweat pants from his suitcase. "You know something, Bill? Not many people can work meteorological terminology into a witty retort, but somehow you pull it off."

Bill laughed his signature honking nerd laugh. "I guess it's just a gift," he said, pushing his underwear down and putting them with the rest of his dirty laundry. "And now, I'm going to shower and then catch a couple hours sleep before we go to the sound check."

"Amen to that," Jake agreed, dropping his towel on the bed so he could get dressed. "A little nap is just what I need. But first I'm gonna call Angie and let her know we got here safely. What time is it back in L.A? Is it three hours earlier?"

At that moment they heard the sound of a key turning in the door lock. The door swung open, letting in a cold blast of arctic wind, and Janice Boxer came into their room. Janice was a representative of National Record's Publicity Department. She had been assigned the position of *Intemperance* Publicity Manager. She was a tall, attractive, aristocratic woman in her late thirties, an almost perfect snob, and the wife of the head of the label's legal department. Rumor had it that Alvin Boxer sent her out on tour so he would have more time to spend with his various mistresses (and misters—but that was yet another rumor).

"Jesus!" Jake barked, quickly snatching up the towel and covering up. "Don't you know how to knock?"

Bill actually let out a squeal that was almost feminine. He had no towel handy. He grabbed his dirty shirt and held it over his genitals.

Janice looked startled for the briefest of seconds, but quickly recovered. "Sorry," she said, a hint of disgust in her voice. "I didn't know you were going to be..." A knowing look came across her face—with it, a little twinkle. "I wasn't uh... *interrupting* anything, was I?"

"Nothing but us taking showers and getting ready to crash out for a bit," Jake told her, irritated. "Is there some reason you came barging in here?"

His tone caused her expression to change to one of displeasure. "I do not barge anywhere," she replied. "I simply walked in. And as for 'crashing out', you can just put that thought out of your head. We're due at WZAP in forty-five minutes."

"WZAP?" Jake asked. "Forty-five minutes? What are you talking about?"

"It's part of the publicity campaign," she replied. "WZAP is one of the local rock music stations—one of the stations that has been playing that little song of yours and introducing our product to the people of Maine. You're going to go on the air with them for a ten-minute interview and then you're going to record some sound clips for them."

"On the air?" Bill asked, his eyes widening in terror. "You mean... live?"

"I mean live," she said. "It's standard in every city we go to."

"What do you mean, 'sound clips'?" Jake asked her. "Are you talking about musical stuff?"

"No," she said. "I'm talking about radio station plugs that they can play before songs, usually *your* songs. That too is standard. And after that, we're going to a local record store so you can sign autographs. I need you guys dressed and ready to go in ten minutes."

With that, she turned on her heal and went back out the door. They were dressed and ready to go in ten minutes. Jake decided he would have to wait until later to call Angie.

*****

The DJ's name was Mike Chesnay. They met him briefly when they first arrived, long enough to make introductions and shake hands, and then he disappeared from their sight. He interviewed them from a booth in one part of the radio station while they listened to him through headphones and responded to a microphone in a different booth next door. His questions were fairly generic and non-threatening. *How does it feel to be on your first tour? How does it feel to open for a band as great as*

Earthstone? *How does it feel to be doing your first show? What musical groups or individual musicians influenced you the most?*

Jake, as the voice of the band, was saddled with the responsibility of answering most of the questions. Though he was nervous about his voice being transmitted live to half of Maine, he did a respectable job. Part of that was the cocaine. In order to stave off the sheer exhaustion that threatened to pull him to sleep where he sat, he had accepted Greg's offer of a little pick-me-up on the way to the radio station.

Chesnay wrapped up the interview by thanking them for their time, telling them he would see them at the show tonight, and then playing *Descent Into Nothing* for the eighth time that day. While he did this Jake and Matt—the only two the station wanted sound clips from—were taken into yet another small booth where they spent half an hour saying things like: "This is Jake Kingsley from *Intemperance* and whenever I'm in town to party down, I listen to WZAP, Bangor's premier rock station."

Finally, they climbed back on the bus and headed for the local branch of Zimmer's Records where they were set up behind a small table in the middle of the store. Sitting before them was a stack of 45-rpm singles of *Descent Into Nothing*, which sold for $1.10 apiece. A sporadic stream of people came by to chat with the group for a few minutes. This came easy to them. They were all accustomed to fans talking them up, telling them how good they thought their music was, asking them questions that were sometimes intelligent but were usually inane. Many of these fans—about half were male and half female—purchased copies of the single and had the group sign the protective cover. In a future time, when a thing called the Internet swept the nation and a service called eBay came available there, some of these first release, group autographed singles would sell for more than a thousand dollars if they could be authenticated and were in good condition.

It was four o'clock in the afternoon when the autograph session came to an end. They climbed back in the bus and were transported across town to Bangor Auditorium. On the way there, Darren asked Greg if he could set up a few more lines of blow for him.

"Most certainly," Greg responded. "In fact, I could use a little more myself." He reached into the pocket of his suit jacket and removed his jeweled coke-sniffing and storage kit.

"I don't think so, Darren," Matt said, his eyes creaking open from the semi-dozing position they'd been in. "It's too close to showtime. You know the rules."

"Ahh, Matt, it's only coke," Darren whined. "Its three hours 'til showtime. It'll be worn off by then."

"You know the rules," Matt repeated. "You party after the show, not before it."

"Oh, come on, Matt," Greg said lightly, opening his case and pulling out the seemingly bottomless vial he stored the drug in. "A little pick-me-up never hurt anyone. You could probably use one yourself, couldn't you?"

For the first time since meeting him, Matt cast an irritated look at Greg. "Our rule is no mind-altering substances of any kind when it passes four hours to showtime or rehearsal. That rule has been with us since the beginning and we're not going to change it now."

Jake followed this exchange closely, half-expecting Greg to try to pull rank and say that Darren could have as much coke as he wanted whenever he wanted it. He wondered how Matt would react if

Greg did do such a thing. But Greg didn't. He simply shrugged, his car-salesman grin firmly affixed to his face.

"Sorry, Darren," he said. "The boss-man says no blow for you. I'll set you up after the show though. I promise."

Darren sulked but didn't try to push the issue. A few minutes later they arrived at their destination and the matter seemed forgotten.

*****

The bus parked in the loading dock area behind the auditorium. The tractor-trailers and the other tour buses were parked side by side near the service entrances. Before allowing them to exit, Greg handed each of them a laminated card with their picture on it and the words: *Earthstone-Intemperance* US Tour, 1983 – Unlimited Access Pass. Each card was attached to a nylon holder designed to be worn around the neck.

"These are your backstage passes," Greg told them. "You must wear them at all times when we are in the venue. Don't start thinking that just because you're a member of the band it's not necessary. Our tour security is augmented in every city by local security guards and/or law enforcement officers. A lot of these local security personnel are not rock music fans and will not know any of you from Adam no matter how famous you get. And in most venues, they will be the ones guarding the performance entrance and patrolling the backstage area. If you try to get in without your pass on, they will bar your entry. If they catch you wandering around inside without your pass on, they will eject you from the facility, by force if they have to. There have been cases of performers being handcuffed, maced, struck with nightsticks, and even arrested. It creates a big pain in the behind for all of us if that happens—not to mention delaying the show—so remember, if you're in the venue, this pass needs to be around your neck. The only exception is when you actually step out onto that stage. Do we all understand?"

They all understood. All of them dutifully hung their passes around their necks.

"And one other thing," Greg told them. "These passes are different from the ones we give out to the media and to radio station contest winners and people like that. Only members of the tour possess these. As such, memorabilia traders are willing to pay top money to get their greasy little hands on them. Keep your passes away from the trollops you fornicate with after the show. They will attempt to steal them right off of your neck while they're sticking their bosoms in your mouth."

"Oh, Greg," Matt said breathlessly, "you talk so fuckin' hot. You're giving me a boner."

Greg laughed at this of course. He laughed at everything one of them said if he sensed it was supposed to be funny. "Okay, okay," he said. "I think you boys got the point. Let's get inside."

The entrance was indeed guarded by a private security guard and he did indeed check their passes. Once the guard satisfied himself that they weren't terrorists or perhaps something even worse, he opened the door and allowed them entry. They passed through a narrow, ground level corridor and arrived a short time later before a door that led to the dressing and locker rooms. Another guard stood vigil before this entrance. This one had actually heard *Descent Into Nothing* a few times and told them how much he liked it.

There were several dressing rooms beyond the door. They were led to one of the smaller ones. It contained six sinks complete with lighted mirrors. The names of each band member were taped above one of the mirrors. A door in the back of the room led to a locker and showering area.

"This is where you'll get dressed prior to the show," Greg told them. "Reginald will lay the stage clothing you'll be wearing out on the chair before your mirror. Be sure to shower first. We'll need you dressed by 5:30 and then Doreen can get your hair done. They open the doors at 6:00. A little bit after that we'll take you backstage so you can meet the various DJs and media folks and winners of the radio contests. I'm sure I don't have to tell you to remain polite to these folks, but stay in character. Remember, you're the ambassadors of debauchery, so don't be afraid to make lewd, yet tasteful comments to any women who happened to be among the greeters."

"Lewd, yet tasteful?" Jake asked.

"You know," Matt said, "don't say shit like 'I'd really like to tap that ass of yours.' Say 'I'd really like to penetrate your anal orifice with my phallus'."

"Ahh," Jake said, grinning. "I see."

"Shit," Coop said, "Nerdly oughta be good at that. That's how he fuckin' talks anyway."

Greg gave his dutiful laugh and then went on. "Also, be sure to comment about how you plan to party hard and imbibe in alcohol after the show. You can imply that you'll be imbibing in other recreational pharmaceuticals, but don't actually come out and say it. We don't want to upset Nancy Reagan too much, do we?"

"No," Darren said. "We sure as shit wouldn't want to do that."

Greg had a brief conversation with the security guard outside the door. The guard spoke into a portable radio for a moment, received a squawky answer from whoever was on the other end, and then nodded to Greg. Greg then turned back to the band and told them that the roadies were ready for them to do the sound check.

They followed him back out of the dressing room and through the corridor to where they'd come in. Another security guard, this one a part of the tour's security force, was waiting for them. He led them through another door, another small corridor, and down another flight of steps into a dimly lit, claustrophobic tunnel about ten feet wide. The tunnel, the guard explained, was actually underneath the floor of the auditorium and served as the conduit to get to the backstage area.

"Did the roadies have to carry all the equipment through here?" Coop asked.

"No," Greg replied. "There's a freight entrance from the loading dock but it's only meant to be used when the auditorium is empty. This tunnel is to get you backstage from the dressing rooms without having to go through the audience."

They went up another two sets of concrete steps at the other end of the tunnel and emerged into the stage left portion of the backstage area. Here they encountered a considerable amount of activity. Roadies were moving everywhere, stringing cables and wires, climbing ladders to attach lighting sets, carrying boxes and crates from one place to the other or pushing them on dollies. All of them were wearing the tour member backstage passes around their necks. Many of them were smoking cigarettes and flicking the ashes carelessly on the floor. Security guards, about half tour personnel and half private, stood here and there, generally not socializing with each other. There was a large, plywood partition that separated stage left from the main stage. The door that had been cut in it was being held in the open position with a bungee cord. Jake could just see a microphone stand and a portion of Coop's new drum set through it.

"The sound guys are all ready for you," Greg told them. "Be extremely careful walking around back here. In fact, try not to come back here without an escort, and if you do, stand and sit where you're told. There's a thousand things that can hurt you back here; high voltage electricity, suspended sandbags, propped up scaffolding pieces, you name it."

None of them answered. They were all looking around in awe at the mechanics of putting on a rock show. Though all of them had been to dozens of concerts, none had ever been backstage of a professional tour.

Greg led them through the stage door and onto the actual stage they would be performing on. Constructed of one inch plywood supported by a frame of two by fours, it was forty feet wide and thirty feet from front to back. The entire thing could be broken down in less than thirty minutes and stowed in the back of one of the trailers, taking up barely ten feet of trailer space. The band knew its dimensions intimately. For nearly a month they had rehearsed their set on it in a rented warehouse in Burbank. On either side of the stage were the amplifier stacks—huge collections of commercial amps standing more than ten feet high. On the stage itself the drum set belonging to Gordon Strong of *Earthstone* had been assembled atop a wheeled platform and was pushed off to the very back corner. Coop's drum set was standing near the middle rear of the stage, a small collection of microphones placed in strategic locations to amplify the backbeat. In a venue of this size, going acoustic on the drums was no longer an option. Sitting in front of, and slightly to the left of the drum set, was the brand new grand piano graciously donated to Bill by the Caldwell Pianos Corporation. It was polished black and turned so the brand name was prominently displayed to the audience. Though an electric piano actually sounded superior when played through an amplification system, both National Records and Caldwell Pianos had insisted that Bill play an acoustic equipped with microphones onstage. All the better to advertise their brand with. At the very front and center of the stage was Jake's microphone. At stage left and slightly back was Matt's. At stage right and back even further, was Darren's. All of the various effects pedals were neatly arranged at the base of their respective microphones. Above their heads was a complex array of aluminum scaffolding, all constructed by the roadies, which supported more than a hundred high intensity lights.

Out beyond the stage was a flat auditorium floor surrounded on all sides by bleachers. About fifty feet out from the stage, in the middle of the floor, a large soundboard sat atop a four-foot plywood platform. Here the more technically savvy roadies would control all aspects of the sound and lighting. There were six of them out there now—longhaired men who looked like bikers—intently staring at a complex array of knobs, switches, and dials.

"Jake!" yelled a familiar voice from behind. "How was your trip across the country?"

Jake turned and beheld his friend Mohammad Hazim, the lapsed Muslim bartender from D Street West in Heritage. Part of the touring contract had specified that each band member could hire one person of his choosing as his personal assistant provided that person met the qualifications. The qualifications were fairly loose, only specifying that the employee be able to play and tune the band member's instrument and were passingly familiar with audio set-ups. Mohammad had jumped at the chance even though it meant leaving home for an indeterminate amount of time and even though the pay was only minimum wage—and it was only accrued when they were actually setting up, running the concert, or tearing down.

"Wassup, Mo," Jake greeted, giving him a hug of greeting and their customary handshake. "We were pretty much trashed the whole time. How was yours?"

"About the same," he said. "Lots of booze, lots of crank."

"Crank?" Jake asked, raising his eyebrows a bit. Crank was methamphetamine, a synthetic stimulant that was also known as poor man's cocaine. It had become popular the last few years and was widely regarded as the up and coming thing, particularly among those who needed to remain alert for long periods of time. Jake himself had never tried it, although Matt had and declared it 'a little too raunchy' for his tastes.

"They say if I wanna be a roadie I'd better get used to snortin' crank cause that's what fuels the show."

"No shit?"

"No shit," Mo confirmed. "I've been doing my damndest to get used to it." He grinned. "I don't think I've slept more than a few hours the whole trip."

"Be careful with that shit," Jake warned. "I hear it'll eat your face right off your head after a while."

Mo shrugged. "What's a man need a face for anyway?" he asked. "You ready for the sound check? I got your guitar all dialed in."

"We're ready," Jake said.

Mohammad disappeared through the stage left door and then returned a few moments later. In his hands he carried the Brogan six-string that Jake had agreed to play on the tour. Following behind him was Larry Milgan, Matt's personal assistant. Larry was one of Matt's friends from the Heritage Community College classes he'd been enrolled in before they started to get regular gigs at D Street West. He was carrying the black and white Stratocaster that Matt had successfully gambled their entire music career on.

The subject of their guitars had reached a quick and immediate head on the very first day of tour rehearsal. Jake had understood from the start that they didn't want him to play his old Les Paul. Though he hadn't been happy about this, he hadn't battled them too much. Brogan guitars—with whom National Records had an endorsement contract—were good instruments. The only problem he'd had was that they'd wanted him to play six different guitars during each set, to switch them out depending on which song was being performed. All the better to advertise the product with. They'd eventually agreed to allow him to play only one instrument, the Brogan AudioMaster 5000. This was a red and white model with dual humbucker pick-ups, basically a Les Paul knock-off, but a knock-off that was actually superior to the original. It could produce the distorted electric backing and the smooth acoustic finger picks that were Jake's signature sound.

Matt, on the other hand, absolutely refused to go onstage with any guitar other than his beloved Strat. He would not even rehearse the set with a Brogan guitar.

"I'll play the Brogans when we record," he told every National Records representative who tried to pressure him otherwise, "and I'll even spout about how fucking good they are when magazine and other media people interview us. But I made a vow when I bought my Strat that I would never play any other guitar on stage and I'm sticking to that vow. I tour with my Strat, or I don't tour at all."

"That will put you in breach of contract," he was told time and time again. "You'll be finished as a musician if you do that and we'll sue you for every penny you ever make doing whatever menial job you manage to get next."

But Matt didn't give a rat's ass about that. He was willing to trash his career and the careers of his bandmates over this issue and eventually, after threatening, pleading, trying to get Jake and the rest of the band to apply peer pressure, and even getting the actual CEO of National Records to talk to him on the phone and threaten him some more, Acardio was forced to conclude that Matt really was serious about this. They finally agreed to let him play the Strat onstage. But there had been a certain look in Acardio's eye when he'd given the agreement.

Matt had picked up on this. His eyes narrowed dangerously. "And there better not be any fucking accidents with my guitar either," he warned, his voice low and menacing. "That thing ends up with so much as a scratch on it, I'm walking away from this whole deal. And not only that, I'll come after your ass, Acardio. I know what fucking building you work in and what kind of fucking car you drive."

Apparently Acardio believed that Matt was crazy enough to do what he threatened, because when Matt looked the guitar over it was in the exact same condition it had been in when he'd surrendered it to Larry back in Los Angeles. He took it from Larry's hands and caressed it like a lover, putting a kiss on its neck and whispering words of endearment to it.

"What *is* it with him and that guitar?" Greg whispered to Jake.

Jake looked at him for a moment and then said, "It's the first really nice guitar, the first really nice *thing* he ever bought for himself. It's maybe the only thing he's ever cared enough about to even want to earn it himself. That guitar is his God and he worships it a lot more than you worship your God."

Greg looked immediately offended by this suggestion. He opened his mouth to say something.

"If I were you," Jake continued before he could, "I'd do whatever was within my power to make sure nothing happens to that guitar. You dig?"

Greg wandered off, shaking his head in disgust. Jake could tell that he dug though.

*****

The sound check took about an hour. They strummed guitars, sung into microphones, pounded on drums, hit piano keys, and then did all at once, their every action dictated by two of the longhaired biker types manning the soundboard. Levels were adjusted up and down and then up again. Through it all Jake could see Bill gritting his teeth in frustration that he was not allowed to participate more directly. He had been admonished way back in the rehearsal stage for interjecting his opinion on this matter.

"They're adjusting Matt's guitar and Jake's mic way too high," he'd complained during the very first sound check. "They're going to drown out the rest of the instruments!"

"People will be coming to hear Jake's voice and Matt's guitar," Acardio had told him. "The rest of the instruments are nothing but filler."

"*Filler?*" Bill had cried, his face turning red with anger. "A proper mix is what gives us our distinctive sound!"

"And we did that on the album," Acardio said. "A concert is different. It's impossible to recreate the intricate mixes of the instruments in a live venue."

"We used to do it at D Street West," Bill shot back. "Just let me dictate how to adjust the levels. I can..."

"You can play your goddamn piano when you're told and otherwise shut your ass," Acardio told him. "These are professional concert sound techs we have working those dials. They know a lot more about this shit than you do."

Bill played when told and shut his ass. He didn't like it, but he did it. As such, when the sound check was declared complete and they were sent back to their dressing rooms to chill out, Bill was complaining the entire way.

"Way too much volume on the bass," he mumbled. "Way too little higher freq on the other instruments. And the harmony mics..." He shook his head in disgust. "Don't even get me started on those."

They didn't get him started on those. By now they were used to his tirades. And, though they unanimously agreed that Nerdly probably could mix their sound better than the techs National had hired, it simply wasn't within their power to do anything about it.

*****

Jake's stage outfit consisted of tight red leather pants and a black, loose-fitting shirt that came down slightly below his waist and covered about half of his arms. For shoes he was given patent leather, ankle-length boots that had been polished to a high shine. The moment he got dressed he began to sweat. He knew it would only get worse out beneath the heat of the stage lighting.

"Fabulous," crooned Reginald Feeney, the wardrobe manager. "It accents that nice ass of yours but hides the skinny arms. Just fabulous!"

Jake said nothing. Reginald (who was to *never* be called Reggie) already knew the band's opinions of their stage clothing.

Reginald was undaunted. He turned to Matt, who was wearing black leather pants and a sleeveless black leather vest with metal studs protruding down the zipper line. "Now you," he said, fussing with a portion of the vest, "have the kind of arms we should be showing off. Nice solid muscle, bulging biceps..." He touched one of the biceps in question. "Mmmm, just beautiful."

Matt jerked his arm away. "Keep your fuckin' hands off me, faggot!" he barked.

Reginald huffed and turned away. "No need to start throwing labels around," he said. "Just because a man is a wardrobe specialist and likes to suck dicks you call him a faggot? How crude." He pranced over to Darren, who was also wearing black leather pants in addition to a white, wife-beater tank top that was extremely short on his torso. "Now you are the premium male specimen of the group." He ran his hand out and touched Darren's bare stomach. "Look at these abs. Just fabulous."

Darren slapped Reginald's hand away, almost panicked, too flustered to even say anything.

"You guys will all thank me when you win the best-dressed group award next year," Reginald told them. "And remember, after the show, get out of those clothes immediately so I can clean them before the tour bus leaves."

"You're gonna smell the crotches of these things, aren't you?" Matt asked him.

"And jack off while I do it," Reginald replied with a smile. "I just *love* the smell of male butt-sweat."

"That is fucking disgusting," Jake declared. He grabbed his water glass and took a tremendous drink.

Coop and Bill, since they were going to be seated during the performance, were allowed to wear jeans, normal T-shirts, and normal footwear, although Reginald insisted that Coop put on a red headband.

After getting dressed they sat down at their tables while Doreen Riolo worked on their hair. Doreen was almost sixty years old, a woman who had grandchildren older than Jake, but a woman who was dialed in as tight as a drum on the latest hair fashions. She clipped and trimmed, combed and sprayed, teased and tussled their manes until they were the very epitome of what she considered perfection. Through it all she hummed Frank Sinatra tunes under her breath or chatted to them about her long career fixing the hair of famous musicians. Jake and the rest of the band liked and respected her immensely, and none of them complained about the job she did.

"Now be sure you boys stay away from any pyrotechnics or open flames," she warned. "You each have enough hairspray in your hair to launch a small rocket."

They shared a group look of concern at this revelation, all of them imagining their hair going up in flames.

After Doreen retreated back to the roadie bus from which she came, they were finally allowed to sit down and relax for a few minutes. Darren, Matt, and Coop all sparked up cigarettes (being sure to keep the lighters well away from their hair). Jake and Bill simply sat and sipped from their water. Greg popped into the dressing room and whipped out his cocaine kit.

"You boys sure you don't want a little pick-me-up before the show?" he asked as he dumped a healthy amount onto the mirror. "You really look like you could use it."

Darren licked his lips longingly, but Matt answered for all of them. "We're sure."

Greg grinned away and then crunched up two lines. He made them disappear.

At 6:15 Greg told them it was time to head backstage for the public relations portion of the show. He reminded them once again to keep in character.

"Right," Jake said, vowing that he was going to be nothing but his normal self. After all, if Matt did the same thing, that would be in character enough for all of them.

As they exited the dressing room the four members of *Earthstone* were exiting from theirs as well, their tour manager leading them. This was only the second time the two groups had come into contact with each other. The first had been when they'd boarded the busses back in Los Angeles and that had not really been an official meeting. Jake looked at them, more than a little starstruck. He, like the rest of *Intemperance*, had been an *Earthstone* fan since their first album. He had seen them in concert twice. He knew their names, their faces by sight, what instrument each of them played, and their basic biographies. And here they were, standing in the flesh before him, all of them dressed in their concert garb. He walked over to Richie Valentine, the lead singer.

"How you doing, Richie?" he asked him, holding out his hand. "I'm Jake Kingsley."

Richie's head swiveled slowly toward him, revealing eyes that were bloodshot and swollen. "Wassup, Jake?" he replied, giving a brief handshake and then withdrawing his hand. "You got a pen?"

"A pen?" Jake asked.

"You want an autograph, right?"

"Uh... Jake's the singer for *Intemperance*," Greg spoke up. "Your opening band."

This struck Richie as deliciously funny. He broke up into peals of laughter. "Oh God, I'm fucked up," he said. "My fucking opening band. Jesus." With that, he continued down the hall.

Jake looked after him, his eyes wide. He was wasted! A little more than two hours before a show and Richie Valentine was wasted!

He quickly found out that this was not an isolated case. Greg decided that introductions were probably in order and did the honors. They all shook hands and muttered greetings and every one of the *Earthstone* members were reeking of alcohol and marijuana and were sniffing the frequent sniffs of recent cocaine use. Matt tried to engage Brad Winston, the guitar player, a man who had been a considerable influence on Matt's style, in some conversation but Brad was too far gone to even understand what was being said. He could barely walk without grabbing onto the walls for support. Mike Hamm, the bass player, was aggressive and tried to pick a fight with Darren. He had to be pulled away by his tour manager. Only Gordon Strong, the drummer, was amicable.

"I like that tune you guys got," he said. "That *Descent* thing. Good guitar work, good vocal range, good lyrics."

"Thanks," Matt said. "Are you gonna catch the show?"

Strong shrugged. "If I get enough blow in me I might. You guys any good live?"

"Yeah," Jake told him. "We're damn good."

Strong chuckled and clapped Jake on the shoulder. "Conceit," he said. "You gotta love it. Enjoy it while it's there, my man. Enjoy it while it's there."

The rest of the *Intemperance* members gathered around the drummer, since he was the only one who seemed to be capable of conversation at the moment.

"We've seen you in concert before," Bill told him. "Back in Heritage, California. The *Wandering Soul* tour and the *Lightening Strikes* tour."

"Yeah," Strong said whimsically. "I kinda remember them dates. Did you like us?"

"Fuckin' A," Matt said. "You guys rock."

"That drum solo you did in *Lightening Strikes* was bad-ass," Coop told him. "You gotta catch our show, man. I try to play like you do."

"I'll check it out," Strong promised. "If not tonight, then tomorrow, or some fucking night. Hell, we're gonna be playing together for months, right?"

"Right," Jake said. "Hey, you got any advice for us? Since this is our first tour and all?"

"Advice?" Strong said, his bleary eyes creaking open a little wider.

"Yeah," Jake said. "You've been on these tours through three albums now. This is our first tour, our first show. Anything you can tell us?"

Strong scratched his head for a moment and then grinned. "Yeah," he said at last. "There's one piece of advice I'll give you, one thing I've decided is more important than anything else when you're out on tour."

"What's that?" Jake asked eagerly. Darren, Coop, Bill, and Matt all leaned in to hear this as well.

"Never," Strong said, "and I mean *never*, kiss a groupie."

The rest of the *Earthstone* members cracked up at this advice. Greg did too for that matter.

"He ain't fuckin' with you there," Richie Valentine said between chortles. "Heed the man's words."

Earthstone and their manager continued down the hall, still laughing, leaving *Intemperance* to look at each other in confusion. Never kiss a groupie? What the hell was that supposed to mean?

*****

As soon as they emerged from the tunnel into the stage left area, they heard the crowd. There were no cheers at the moment, just the low-grade babble of hundreds, perhaps thousands, of conversations, loud enough to compete with the recorded rock music that was playing through the amplifiers.

"Listen to that," Jake said, feeling a little of his fatigue dropping away. "Our first big audience."

"How big is it?" Darren asked slowly, casting a nervous glance at the partition that separated them from the stage.

"This is one of the smaller venues," Greg replied. "We sold it out, so that means there are going to be about fifty-two hundred people."

"Fifty-two *hundred*?" Darren said, his eyes widening. "Wow... I mean... you know... wow."

"You okay, Darren?" Jake asked him.

"Yeah," he said, fumbling with his cigarette pack. He lit up with shaking hands.

There were about thirty people—locals, Greg called them—gathered near the rear of the backstage area awaiting the two bands. There were several DJs, reporters from both the Bangor and the Portland newspapers, even a television reporter who had been given permission to film small portions of the concert. The rest were fans, mostly of *Earthstone* since *Intemperance* was still somewhat unknown. They greeted people, shook hands, chatted, signed a few autographs, and gave a few impromptu interviews. Jake saw one of the female fans, an auburn haired beauty of about nineteen, pull up her shirt so Richie Fairview could sign her bare breast. He did so with a shaky hand and then leaned down and slurped the girl's nipple into his mouth, making her squeal in delight. Their road manager pulled the two of them apart before things could go any further.

Finally, the locals were hustled out of the backstage area by the tour security guards. The members of *Earthstone* left as well, descending back into the tunnel as they discussed how many more beers they could drink before the show.

"Twenty-five minutes until showtime," Greg told them. "Is everyone cool?"

Everyone said they were cool. They sat down on packing crates to wait. The roadies continued moving about from place to place, setting things up and doing double-checks on things that had already been set up. Jake heard the sound of his guitar being strummed by Mohammad, who was doing a final sound check. This elicited a muted cheer from the crowd, the first they'd heard so far.

"Jesus," Darren muttered, lighting up another cigarette. "Fifty-two hundred people."

"I gotta check this out," Matt said, standing up. He headed for the stage access door, through which the roadies were coming and going.

"Me too," Jake said, standing up and following him. After a moment, Darren got up as well.

They crowded around the door and creaked it open a few inches, staring out over the stage and into the crowd. As was the norm for venues such as this, the seating was general admission, which meant nothing was assigned. The bleachers were all about half-full, with people still streaming in, but the auditorium floor was packed with well over a thousand people. They were crammed in like sardines, pushing and shoving and fighting for the coveted spots near the stage.

"Oh my God," Darren whispered, backing away, his eyes wide.

"You okay?" Jake asked him again, looking at him with more than a little concern this time.

"I can't do this," Darren said. "I can't go on in front of that many people! Holy shit!"

"What the fuck are you talking about?" Matt asked. "You goddamned well better go on! It's a little late to get cold feet now!"

"Dude," Darren said, backing even further away, "it's just that... I mean... shit, dude. Five thousand fucking people! We ain't never been in front of that many before!"

"Darren," Jake started.

"What if we fuck up?" Darren yelled, approaching total panic now. "I mean, there are reporters and everything here. What if we go out there and just fucking bite?"

"If you chill out and play like we do in rehearsal, that ain't gonna happen," Jake said. "Get yourself under control, man."

"And do it fucking quick," Matt added.

All of this commotion attracted the attention of Greg, who had been over talking to the head of security about something. With a look of concern he came over. "What's the problem?" he asked.

"Nothing," Matt replied dismissively. "Darren's just getting a little stage fright. He'll be all right."

"He doesn't look all right," Greg observed.

"We'll get him chilled out. Don't worry."

But Greg wanted to worry. He stepped over to one of the tour security guards and whispered something to him. The guard nodded and spoke into his portable radio. Greg then stepped back over to Darren.

"Don't worry, Darren," he said. "I'll get you fixed up in no time."

"What do you mean?" Matt asked.

"You'll see."

Jake, meanwhile, continued to talk soothingly to Darren, telling him that everything was cool, that he needed to stop freaking out about the number of people out there, that he should pretend they were performing at D Street West instead of the Bangor Auditorium. Gradually, after two or three minutes, his words seemed to have an effect. Darren's breathing slowed. His hands stopped tremoring. He began to look a little less tense.

"Just like D Street West," Darren said, latching onto this thought.

"Fuckin' A," Jake said. "Just like D Street."

A security guard suddenly emerged from the tunnel entrance. He carried a black leather bag in his hands, a bag that looked like an old-fashioned doctor's bag. He brought it to Greg, who took it and walked over to Darren. He set the bag down and opened it, fishing through it for a few moments and finally coming up with a brown pill bottle. He opened it up and removed one of the pills.

"Here, Darren," he said. "Take this."

"What is it?" Darren asked.

"Just a little something to help you calm down. Use Jake's water."

Darren reached out to take it, but Matt grabbed his wrist, preventing the transfer.

"Wait a minute," Matt said. "What exactly are you giving him?"

"Just a mild anxiety pill," Greg said. "It's nothing."

"What is it called?" Matt demanded.

"Diazepam," Greg said. "It's a very common treatment for anxiety. It'll keep him from having a panic attack out on stage."

"Diazepam," Matt said, shaking his head. "That would be the generic name for Valium, correct?"

Greg's confident grin faded as he heard this. "Uh... yes, it is Valium, but..."

"Don't ever try to jerk me off about drugs, Greg. I've done too many of them. He ain't taking Valium before he goes on stage."

"Matt," Greg said, "this isn't an intoxicating drug. It's just to keep him cool."

"He'll keep himself cool."

"What if he doesn't? I've got the show to think about."

"So do I," Matt said. "No Valium. He's a professional musician. He'll have his shit together."

While they continued to argue about it, discussing Darren as if he weren't even there, Jake wandered over and sat down next to Greg's open bag. He looked inside to see what else was in there and found a variety of pharmaceutical vials lined up in little holders on one side of the bag, packaged syringes lined up on the other, and multiple pill bottles secured on the bottom. He read some of the vials. There was Narcan, morphine, epinephrine, Demerol, Versed, sodium pentothal, and a lot of Haldol. Jake didn't know what Haldol, epinephrine, or Versed was, but he certainly knew what the rest of those things were. They were narcotic painkillers, except for the pentothal, which was an anesthetic (*what the hell does he use* that *for?* Jake wondered) and the Narcan, which was a medicine that reversed the effects of narcotics. He glanced at the pill bottles next but there were far too many for him to read them all. He saw enough though. There was Dexedrine, Flexeril, Vicodin, codeine, Quaaludes, Phenobarbital, Percodan, morphine, Seconal, Nembutal.

"Look," Greg was saying. "You go onstage in twenty-five minutes. He needs to take the pill now or it won't have time to take effect before you start."

"He's not going to take the pill, Greg," Matt said forcefully. "I'm the leader of this band and I will not allow it!"

"And I'm the leader of this tour," Greg retorted, "and he will take what I tell him to take. I know what I'm doing here."

"Oh?" Jake interjected. "Are you a doctor?"

"What?" Greg asked, turning to Jake and blanching a little as he saw him going through his bag.

"You got some heavy-duty shit in this bag, Greg," Jake said. "I'm pretty sure you need a medical degree to dispense most of it."

Greg rushed over and snatched up the bag. "Don't worry about what's in there," he snapped, his grin fully gone for the first time.

Jake turned to Darren, who was sitting impassively, as if he were meditating. "Darren, you cool?"

"I'm getting there," Darren replied, his voice level. "I'll be okay."

"There you have it," Jake said. "He doesn't need your pill. Let him face his fears on his own. That's what the rest of us are doing."

"But..."

"That's the final word, Greg," Matt said. "He ain't taking the pill. If you want to push a breach of contract issue because someone didn't take a prescription medicine that wasn't prescribed to him, you go ahead and do that. I have a feeling the judge won't rule in your favor."

Greg sighed and bit his lip for a moment. Finally, a vestige of his signature grin returned. "All right then," he said, dropping the pill and the bottle back in the bag and closing it up. "Just don't screw up out there, Darren. Don't jeopardize the show."

"I won't," Darren said.

"He won't," Matt and Jake said in unison.

*****

The clock turned seven and the recorded music was turned off. The murmur of the crowd picked up a few notches as they sensed that the first portion of the show was about to begin. The band stood in a group near the stage access door, Coop holding his drumsticks, Matt and Jake fingering guitar picks, Bill chewing his fingernails, Darren taking a few last puffs from a cigarette. They had already taken off their backstage passes.

"Ten seconds 'til the lights go down," said Steve Langley, the production manager. "You guys ready?"

"We're ready," Jake said, looking at his bandmates.

They put their hands together, doing their customary show of camaraderie for the first time in months. Langley counted down the last few seconds and everything went dark. As it did, the crowd began to cheer, the sound dozens of decibels louder than any cheers they heard in the past.

Listen to that, Jake thought. *That's for us. Holy shit.*

"Okay, go!" Langley barked at them. "It's showtime."

They had rehearsed this a thousand times. It was not pitch black on the stage, just dim enough that the audience couldn't see what was happening. Each band member moved to his position, operating half by sight, half by feel. Jake found his guitar and picked it up. He checked to make sure his cord was plugged in and then turned the volume knob all the way up. He touched his microphone stand briefly, just to orient himself, and then put his lips near it, ready to speak. He took a deep breath, beginning to feel a little of what Darren had been feeling. It had been months since they'd performed live and there were *five thousand* people out there! *Five thousand*! Sure, they'd rehearsed this set endlessly, had taken dance lessons and done tri-weekly aerobic workouts to keep in shape. But still...

The nervousness had no time to really get a grip on him. Bill provided the opening cue, playing a brief piano solo that was amplified and sent out over the audience. They cheered louder, whistling and clapping.

The solo ended and Matt hit the first guitar chord. That was the final cue. Out on the soundboard one of the technicians hit a switch and the stage lighting blazed to life, showering them in bright white illumination. The moment it happened, Matt launched into the opening sequence of their first song: *Who Needs Love?*

Jake could hardly see the audience—the stage lights were too bright and the house lights were too dim—and he couldn't hear them at all over the music blaring from the amplifier stacks—but he knew they were there all the same, all fifty-two hundred of them, watching as he played his guitar, as he began to sing. He was nervous, as nervous as he'd been launching into that first show at D Street West, but he didn't let it show. On the contrary, he came across as almost cocky with self-assurance, projecting confidence with his every movement, his every facial expression, and especially with his voice. And as he performed, that nervousness gradually disappeared, replaced by wonder and awe. All of his doubts, fears, and frustrations about the recording contract, the tour, his relationship with Angie, melted away. He was doing what he loved more than anything, what he felt he had been put on this Earth to do. And while he was doing it, nothing else mattered to him.

The audience liked *Who Needs Love?* The cheers they gave when it was over were much louder than the polite enthusiasm they had shown at the beginning. It was almost deafening, the sound of respect, the sound of an audience expressing their realization that this band they'd only heard of for a few weeks, that they'd only heard one song from on the radio, was a band to be reckoned with. The next song – *Living By the Law*—only reinforced this. By the time it was done they had the audience's complete and adoring attention.

In all, they performed every song on the *Descent Into Nothing* album, intermixing them with four songs that had not been recorded yet. With each number they did, the cheers grew louder and lasted longer. When Matt did an extended guitar solo about halfway through, they went insane. The biggest cheers occurred when they performed the final number of the set, the only *Intemperance* song most of the audience had ever heard before, *Descent Into Nothing*. They played the song pretty much as it had been recorded, at least until the end. At that point they drew out the final flourish for nearly a minute, throwing in a final guitar solo, a final piano solo, a minor drum solo, and a gloriously stretched, operatic style vocal finish with Jake moaning out the final syllable for almost twenty seconds. The audience went wild, standing, cheering, raising their lit cigarette lighters into the air. Several bras and pairs of panties came flying up onto the stage, one of them hitting Jake squarely in the face.

"Thank you, Bangor!" Jake yelled into the microphone. "Thank you and goodnight!"

The five of them met at the front of the stage while the glorious applause continued to wash over them, while a few more pairs of panties came flying at them. All five of them were dripping with sweat, their skin flushed, their bodies approaching breathlessness. They linked arms and took a bow and then another. Jake, Matt, and Darren set their guitars down and threw their remaining picks into the crowd. Darren's drumsticks went into the crowd as well. They then walked off stage, going one by one through the access door. The cheers followed them and the calls for encore began.

Alas, there was to be no encore. This was not D Street West. It was *Earthstone*'s show and the stage needed to be cleared so they could go on in thirty minutes.

Mohammad was the first person Jake saw when he came into the relative dimness of the backstage area. He handed him a bottle of cold Gatorade and hung his backstage pass back around his neck.

"Awesome," Mohammad told him. "You guys were fucking awesome out there!"

Jake grinned and took a large drink of the Gatorade, swallowing half the bottle without taking the bottle from his mouth. He burped wetly and then drank some more. Finally, he had the breath to reply. "Thanks, Mo," he said. "Couldn't have done it without you."

Even before their eyes fully adjusted to the dimmer lighting, even before the roadies all had a chance to congratulate them on a premium performance, Greg appeared and led them back to the tunnel entrance.

"Let's get you boys out of the way," he said, "so they can get *Earthstone* rolling. I have cold drinks and other refreshments waiting for you in the dressing room."

Greg wasn't kidding. When they stepped into the dressing room the first thing they saw was a large ice chest filled with bottles of Budweiser, Coors, and Miller. On a folding card table next to the ice chest were bottles of Jack Daniels, Bacardi 151, Jose Cuervo tequila, a bucket of ice, and various mixers. On another table were a jeweled water bong and a sterling silver tray full of high-grade marijuana. Packs of cigarettes, Marlboro and Camel primarily, and monogrammed lighters sat next to this along with a sack of crystal ashtrays.

"Drink up, smoke up, party down," Greg told them. "You guys put on a pretty good show. You deserve it." He reached into the inner pocket of his suit and pulled out a small wooden box. "And if you want something to wake you up a bit, help yourselves to a few lines." He tossed it over to Matt. "Just be sure not to lose the box or I won't have one for tomorrow."

"Holy shit," Darren said, going over and grabbing a Coors out of the ice chest. "You're all right, Greg. Let's fuckin' party!"

"Hell yeah!" Coop said, making a beeline for the bong and the pot.

Jake would have preferred to drink a little more non-alcoholic refreshment to rehydrate himself but since that did not seem to be an option here, he finished up his Gatorade and then grabbed a beer. He sat down on one of the couches and smoked while he drank it. By the time the first bottle was in his empty stomach, he was already starting to buzz a little.

The five of them discussed the show while they cooled off and drank and while Matt crunched up some celebratory lines and passed the mirror around. When it came to Jake, he snorted two of them, one in each nostril. It was excellent coke and within a few minutes he was feeling very good indeed. He opened another beer, lit another cigarette, and then topped it all off with a couple of bonghits. He was starting to think that this really was the life.

Greg snorted up a few lines from his personal stash but did not converse with them or even sit with them. Instead, he sat off in the corner, writing something in a ledger he carried. The band didn't mind. Finally, as they were having an unmitigated and passionate discussion about the panties that had hit Jake in the face, Greg stood.

"Guys," he said, clapping his hands together like a kindergarten teacher trying to get the attention of his class, "I hate to break up your little debriefing here, but Gerald really needs your stage clothes. Why don't you go shower up and put your civvies back on?"

"Gladly," Jake said, standing and swallowing down the last of his second beer. A thought occurred to him. He really needed to call Angie. He still hadn't told her he'd arrived safely. "Hey, Greg. I need to make a call to L.A. Is there somewhere around here I can do that?"

"Nowhere here," Greg replied. "The only phones are the payphones in the front of the auditorium and we can't have you showing yourself out there. You'll get mobbed."

"Oh... okay," he said, frowning a little, trying to remember exactly what day of the week it was and whether or not Angie would be working tonight. "I'll wait until we get back to the hotel."

Greg made no further comment on the telephone call. He simply hustled them into the showers.

It was as they were all naked and soaping themselves under the locker-room style shower heads that they heard voices coming from outside the doorway, voices and feminine giggles.

"What the hell?" Jake had time to ask before the door swung open and five naked girls came strolling in. There were two dyed blondes, one natural blonde, and two brunettes. All were curvy, large breasted, and quite attractive. Jack Ferguson, the head of tour security, was with them. He was still fully dressed.

"There they are, girls," Jack said. "As promised."

The girls squealed in delight and came rushing into the room.

"Groupies!" Darren yelled excitedly.

"All fuckin' right!" Matt shouted. "I'm now officially impressed. One of you girls come over here and suck me off!"

The led to an eruption of giggles and a brief argument between one of the brunettes and one of the unnatural blondes. The brunette apparently won. She walked over to Matt, dropped to her knees at his feet, and sucked his soft, but rapidly expanding penis into her mouth.

"Fuck yeah!" Matt said, his hand dropping to the back of her head. "I don't even wanna know your name, hon. In fact, don't talk to me at all. You say a fuckin' word and I'm kicking your ass outta here."

The rest of the girls entered the shower area. Three of them raced towards Jake, who was still trying to process all of this with his intoxicated mind. The natural blonde reached him first, thus staking her official claim.

"That was a bitchin show," she told him, her hands going to his soapy shoulders and rubbing.

"Uh... thanks," he stammered, taking a step backwards. She stepped with him, keeping hands in place.

"Do you think I'm pretty?" she asked, her rubs going down a little further, onto his upper chest and back.

Involuntarily his eyes did a quick scan. She was nineteen or twenty, twenty-one at the very most. Her breasts were well above average size, yet perky due to her youth. Her nipples were pink, perfect, and gloriously erect. Her stomach was flat and smooth, her bush sparse and light brown in color. Her legs were nothing short of fabulous. The sight of her, combined with the sensuous feel of her soft hands caressing him, caused blood to go slamming into his penis, making it twitch and dance.

"Mmmm," she said, looking down at it. "It looks like you do."

He started to speak—he really did—started to tell her that he was flattered by the attention but that he had a girlfriend back in Los Angeles, a girlfriend who definitely wouldn't approve of him showering naked with an attractive female in an auditorium locker room. But the girl didn't hear word one of what he said. She leaned into him, pushing her breasts against his chest where they began to slip and slide against the layer of soap there, the nipples tracing circles and ovals. Her mouth went to his neck, where it began to kiss and nibble. And her hand, that lovely, soft hand with the manicured nails, dropped down to his penis and began to stroke it with a pressure that was almost unbearable. His words trailed off and his arms went around her, pulling her soft, sexy body tighter against him. He slid his hands down to her ass and began to squeeze it.

"I just love your voice," she whispered to him as she continued kissing and licking his neck and his ears, as she rubbed the head of his cock against her stomach. "And the way you move up on stage. I was in the front row. Did you see me flash my titties at you?"

"Was that you?" Jake asked, although he had seen no such thing.

She giggled. "That was me. And when some of your sweat came down and landed on my arm it turned me on sooooo much. I licked it off."

Jake had no reply for this, he only groaned as her fingers found his balls and began to gently squeeze them. He turned his head to her, meaning to put his lips against hers but stopped at the last second, remembering the advice from Gordon Strong. *Never kiss a groupie.* He had no idea why Strong had told them that and it was obvious that it had been meant as a joke of some kind, but it was also advice that seemed to contain a strong grain of truth. He diverted his lips at the last moment and kissed her on the nose instead. This produced another giggle and then she slowly slid down his body, until she was kneeling before him. She sucked his erect cock into her mouth and began to bob up and down on it.

Jake sighed, a sound of pleasure mixed with repressed guilt at his weakness. He looked around at the others to keep his mind occupied and saw that Matt was slapping his cock across his groupie's face. Bill had paired up with the other brunette and was currently palpating and squeezing every portion of her body while explaining to her the path that nerve impulses took from the surface of her flesh to her brain and how her Bartholin's gland was secreting slippery mucous to provide lubrication for sexual penetration. Coop, like Matt and Jake, was enjoying an enthusiastic blowjob from his groupie. Darren, however, had either forgotten the advice from Gordon Strong or was disregarding it. He was locked in a passionate embrace with one of the dyed blondes, his mouth firmly connected to hers, his tongue obviously driving as deep into her mouth as he could get it. Jack Ferguson, still fully dressed, was standing in the corner of the room, smoking a cigarette and drinking a bottle of beer. He was watching the whole thing impassively, with the eye of a man who had seen such shenanigans hundreds, maybe thousands of times before.

Darren suddenly broke the embrace he shared with his groupie. He put his hands on her shoulders and spun her around. "Bend over, bitch," he told her. "I'm gonna fuck you!"

The bitch in question obeyed without any sign of hesitation or offense. She even reached behind her and spread herself open. But before he could line himself up and enter her, Jack stood up and took a few steps forward.

"Stop right there, Darren," he yelled. "No fucking in the shower!"

"What?" Darren asked, turning angrily toward him. "What the fuck are you talking about? Where the fuck do you get off telling me..."

"You like paternity suits, do you?" Jack asked him calmly. "Or how about the drip? Or how about fucking AIDS?"

"I don't have any of that stuff," the groupie said haughtily.

"Maybe not, but you're of child-bearing age, aren't you? And getting knocked up by a rich rock star would get you out of this shitpot town you live in, wouldn't it? You were told the rules, sister. None of my musicians gets in your puss without a rubber."

"Well gimmee a fuckin' rubber then!" Darren pleaded.

"You son of a bitch!" his groupie yelled, standing up and turning angrily towards Jack, Darren forgotten. "How dare you talk to me like that—accuse me of that!"

"It's just my job, hon," Jack told her, blankly. "If you don't want to follow the rules, you can just get the fuck out of here. There's a hundred other girls out there who'd love to take your place."

"You can't do that!" the groupie yelled. "I sucked your fuckin' cock so I could get back here! We all sucked fuckin' cock to get back here! We had a fuckin' agreement!"

"And you just tried to violate the rules," Jack said.

"Wait a minute," Darren said, his face starting to turn a little green. "What do you mean you sucked his cock?" He turned to Jack. "What does she mean, she sucked your fuckin' cock?"

Jack shrugged. "The security boys and some of the higher seniority roadies are the ones who pick out a few girls to come meet you guys after the show," he told Darren. "It's been worked out over the years that there is a certain price to be paid for that privilege."

Darren looked like he was going to throw up now. "You mean... you mean..."

"You really shouldn't kiss groupies, Darren," Jack told him, a faint smile on his face. "Didn't anyone tell you that?"

A second later, Darren was rushing to the toilet, vomit spraying from his mouth.

*****

They didn't see *Earthstone*'s show. They didn't even hear it. They partied in the dressing room for a few hours, all of them smoking and drinking and snorting until all of them were quite obliterated. Jack allowed more groupies back to party with them (after they paid the admission price, of course) and soon there were twelve girls in addition to the original five. The entire group climbed onto the tour bus and were taken back to the hotel rooms where the party continued. At this point Greg passed out condoms to everyone, admonishing them to use them.

Jake ended up using two of them. He took his original groupie into the bathroom with him and had her sit on his cock while he sat on the toilet. She ground herself up and down while he suckled her breasts and felt her ass. The second girl was a tiny aspiring ballet dancer with short black hair and a heavy French accent. She gained his favor by asking him if he'd like to see her eat out another girl.

"Uh... yeah, sure," Jake had answered. By that point he'd done nine lines of cocaine, drank eleven beers and four rum and cokes, and had smoked half a gram of marijuana.

She pulled a random girl from the crowd, whispered in her ear for a few moments, and the girl nodded enthusiastically. They both took off their clothes and the second girl—a brown-haired, brown-eyed beauty—lay on her back on Jake's bed. The ballet dancer dived between her legs and began to lick her, running her tongue up and down, down and up, until the brown-haired girl was writhing in ecstasy. The rest of the partygoers who happened to be in Jake's room at the moment all stopped what they were doing to watch the spectacle.

"God damn I love being a rock star!" Matt yelled. "Look at that shit, Jake. Fuckin' look at it!"

"I am," Jake replied. He was in fact staring at in, transfixed, his cock hardening quite nicely despite the fact that he'd already come once in the first groupie's mouth and once in the condom while fucking her.

The dancer pulled her face out of the brown-haired girl's pussy long enough to look back and say, "Come on, Jake. I'm sooooo wet. Fuck me while I eat her."

One of the security guys—who were watching the festivities from the corner of the room without participating—walked over and put a condom in Jake's hand.

The rest of the room's inhabitants began to chant, "Jake, Jake, Jake, Jake," over and over again.

Jake's doubts and inhibitions were driven deeply into the back of his brain, so deep they couldn't even conceive of daylight, much less see it. He dropped his pants and put the rubber on his straining cock. He entered the dancer from behind and pounded almost violently into her for the better part of fifteen minutes while she continued to lick and suck on the brown-haired girl's clit.

By the time he finished there was a full-blown orgy going on in the room, the only non-participants the security guys.

At some point after that, Jake's brain stopped recording memories for the evening.

*****

A hand shook him awake some time later. His eyes creaked open to see Greg's face illuminated by sunlight streaming in through the windows.

"Wake up," Greg told him, his usual grin firmly affixed to his face. "We have to leave for Concord in forty-five minutes."

Jake groaned. He had a tremendous headache and his mouth was as dry as the Sahara. His lungs hurt and his body ached everywhere. And he was tired. God was he tired. He wanted nothing more than another six hours of sleep.

"I got your breakfast for you," Greg told him, putting his hands on Jake's shoulders and pulling him to a sitting position. "Come on. You need to eat."

Jake had never felt less like eating in his life. He shook his head. "No. No food."

"Yes food," Greg said. "I must insist." He put a fork in his hand.

Jake rode out a wave of dizziness and then looked down at himself, seeing that he was completely naked. He looked around the hotel room and saw that Bill, who was also naked, was unenthusiastically putting bites off egg and bacon into his mouth.

"Here," Greg said, handing him a bottle of Gatorade and a handful of pills. "Drink this down and take these."

"What are they?" Jake mumbled.

"Tylenol and a vitamin B12 supplement. They'll help you with your hangover."

Jake didn't argue. He drank down a huge swallow of the Gatorade and then washed down the pills with another huge swallow.

"Now eat," Greg insisted. "Every last bite of it. You need nourishment."

Jake ate, putting bite after bite into his mouth, fighting down the nausea the entire time. He did not feel better when he was done, nor did he feel any more awake.

"Now let's get you dressed and out of here," Greg said. "We've already packed up your belongings and put them on the bus. There are some clothes for you right there on the bed."

Jake looked over and saw that a pair of jeans, fresh underwear and socks, a T-shirt, and a sweater had been neatly laid out. He staggered over and began putting them on.

"Where did all the girls go?" he asked.

"They were taken back to the auditorium around five o'clock this morning when the party finally broke up."

"Five o'clock?" Jake asked. "What time is it now?"

Greg looked at his watch. "Seven-thirty," he said. "Now come on. We need to get on the road. There's a show tonight."

Ten minutes later the entire band was on the bus, all of them looking considerably worse for wear. They climbed into their bunks and were asleep before the bus even left the parking lot.

Four hours later Jake was shaken awake again.

"We're in Concord," Greg told him. "Let's get your stuff in the hotel and then we need to get you over to the local radio station for some interviews."

Jake groaned. It felt like he had only just closed his eyes. "Can't we get just a little more sleep?" he asked.

Greg shook his head. "It's time to go to work," he told him. "You got a show tonight."

CHAPTER 6

THE ROAD

January 29, 1983
Texarkana, Texas

The deputy was about as stereotypical of a Texas lawman as he could be. He was tall, white, had a gut that protruded over his belt, and he wore an actual Smokey the Bear hat upon his head. He had black leather gloves upon his hands. His light blue uniform featured an American flag on the shoulder and a five-pointed star pinned above the left pocket. His southern accent was so thick as to be nearly unintelligible.

"Y'all better eat up your chow now," he told them, pointing at two trays of watery powdered eggs and burnt toast that he had shoved through the bars. "Ya ain't getting nothin' else until supper time. And that's only if y'all are here and not down at the courthouse."

Jake glanced at the food, not just with disinterest but with actual repugnance, this despite the fact that he'd eaten nothing in the past twenty-four hours. "I'm not hungry," he said.

"Me either," replied Matt, who was sitting on the bench next to him.

They were in a holding cell in the Bowie County jail in downtown Texarkana, Texas, being held on charges of drunk and disorderly, multiple counts of assault and battery, and, most serious, assault with a deadly weapon. Both of them were quite battered. Jake had a spectacular black eye, two lacerations to his cheek and one to his forehead, and an array of bruises across his chest and back. Matt had a broken nose, two cracked ribs, and an impressive collection of body bruises as well. They were dressed in bright orange jumpsuits with BOWIE COUNTY PRISONER stenciled in black on the legs and back.

The deputy looked at them suspiciously. "Y'all on some kinda hunger strike or somethin'? Like them Irish terrorist pukes a few years ago?"

"No," Matt said. "We just don't want to eat that swill. We'll eat as soon as we get out of this shithole."

The deputy shook his head. "Y'all ain't gettin' outta here for a long time. Ain't you figured that out yet?"

Matt simply shrugged. Jake didn't respond at all.

They had been arrested just after four o'clock the previous afternoon, at a truck stop on Interstate 30 just inside the Texarkana city limits. The tour had been on its way from Dallas, where they'd done a show the night of January 27, to Little Rock, where they were scheduled to do a show tonight. It was one of their extended travel period days off and, as such, they had not left Dallas until almost eleven in the morning, which meant the entire band and crew had been able to sleep in and stock up on some much needed rest. Since they were reasonably well rested upon setting out that morning, the band had begun drinking and partying as the bus had rolled down the interstate, all of them eagerly anticipating arriving in Little Rock that night, a night when there was no show scheduled, where they would check into their hotel and lie around watching TV, where they would crash out about eleven and sleep through the night. Extended travel days were something everyone looked forward to, even Greg and Janice. But when they'd stopped at the Texarkana truck stop to refuel the busses and the trucks Jake and Matt—who both had the munchies and wanted to buy a pie—had begged some cash from Greg and then gone into the diner. There they'd encountered a group of truckers sitting at the counter eating their suppers. The trouble began within seconds.

"Hole-ee shit," one of them said, looking at the two musicians. "Look at the hair on these boys. What the hell you boys doing with hair like a girl's?"

"Maybe they *are* girls," another trucker said, causing them all to crack up at his wit.

"Y'all like to suck dicks, boys?" another put in. "That why you wears your hair so long?"

Things might have ended right there if they'd kept their mouths shut or just left the diner. But they did neither. Instead Matt looked them over and said, "Well God*damn*, if it ain't a bunch of garden variety shitkickers. Everyone named Billy Bob, raise your hand."

The biggest of the truckers stood up so fast his stool fell over. His was in his early forties, about six and a half feet tall, and at least three hundred pounds. Several prison tattoos decorated his arms. "You lookin' for trouble, boy?" he asked Matt. Meanwhile, the rest of the truckers stood up and sauntered over, forming a loose circle around them.

"Uhh... Matt," Jake said, looking from one to the other. "Maybe we should..."

"You think you can *give* me some trouble, Bubba?" Matt asked. "Come on and give it a shot. I'll kick your fat ass from here to the fuckin' Alamo."

And that had started it off. Bubba (or whatever his name was) swung a roundhouse at Matt, who easily ducked under it and drove a solid right into Bubba's stomach. The catcalls from the other truckers began. The waitress, who was actually named *Flo* and had an actual nametag on her pink uniform proclaiming this, told them to take it outside. But things were too far gone for that. Bubba launched an attack, driving at Matt with his fists. Matt, a veteran of many barroom brawls, blocked most of them, ducked away from a few others, and then launched a counter-attack, landing a solid right to Bubba's cheek and a solid left to his nose.

The other truckers stayed out of it at first, no doubt driven by some sort of Texas sense of fair play. But when Matt started to really hammer Bubba's face, splitting his lip open, breaking a tooth, making him gag on his blood, they tried to move in and break it up.

"That's enough, boy," one of them told him, grabbing at Matt's arm.

Matt then made his big mistake. Instead of stopping, he turned on the man trying to break it up and punched him in the face as well. All sense of fair play ended at the moment.

"Oh shit," Jake said, resigned, as the entire room rushed at the two of them.

Jake—who was not a veteran of barroom brawls, who in fact always tried to talk himself out of such situations if possible—held his own pretty well. He broke the nose of the first guy to come at him, felled the second with a kick to the balls, and held off the third by driving an elbow into his solar plexus. But then a fourth man slipped in from the right flank and delivered a solid blow to his face, stunning him. A fifth hit him with a shot to his kidneys that made him drop to his knees. And then there were fists pummeling him everywhere, hitting his face, his neck, his chest, his stomach. The adrenaline took over and he managed to pull himself out of there long enough to grab a plate from the counter which he promptly broke over someone's head (thus the assault with a deadly weapon charge). And then he was hit with a chair from behind, driving him back to his knees and opening him up for another furious attack.

Matt, meanwhile, had dropped two of the truckers to the ground, knocking them clean unconscious, but the rest had overwhelmed him and taken him down. They kicked him and punched him until he stopped fighting and was barely conscious himself.

Right about then, the cops showed up, pulling into the parking lot, red lights flashing, sirens blaring. And despite Greg's pleas, threats, and other reconciliatory attempts, Jake and Matt were both handcuffed and driven first to the local hospital where they were stitched and examined and then the jail cell where they were now residing. Not a single one of the truckers had joined them there.

"So, y'all are rock music stars, huh?" the deputy asked them now.

"Yeah," Jake said. "I guess we are."

"Y'all think that gives you the right to come into people's towns and start a bunch of trouble? Ya think 'cause you're rich and famous you kin do whatever you want?"

"No," Jake said. "We don't think that at all."

"Well, I guess them boys at the truck stop taught you a lesson or two, didn't they?"

"Yeah," Jake said. "I guess they did."

"I seen that video thing y'all put out," the deputy said next. "That thing about hell." He pronounced this *hay-all*.

Jake said nothing. He ached everywhere and just wanted this man to go away.

"Y'all think it's funny making music about the Devil?"

"The song's not about the Devil," Jake said. "Did you ever listen to it?"

"I caught my daughter watchin' that crap on the MTV," he said. "I seen all I needed to see. Why don't you boys try makin' some real music instead of damnin' your souls to hell by peddlin' that Satan worshipin' stuff?"

"Real music?" Jake asked. "What kind of music would that be?"

"There's two kinds of real music. Country *and* Western. You'll never catch Hank Junior or Waylon singin' about no Devil worshippin' crap."

"No, I don't suppose you would," Jake sighed.

"How old is your daughter?" Matt asked.

"She's eighteen," he said. "Just gettin' ready to graduate this year from high school."

"Yeah?" Matt said. "What's she look like? Would I do her?"

"Shit," Jake muttered as the deputy's face turned an infuriated red.

"Boy," the deputy said dangerously, "you say one more thing about my daughter and you gonna find out what an elevator ride is all about."

And of course, Matt didn't let it drop. "I can get her tickets for the show in Little Rock," he said. "I can even get her a backstage pass. Of course, there's a certain price she has to pay for that. Does she swallow? Or would she rather take it up the ass?"

"That's it," the deputy said. He spoke into his radio and less than twenty seconds later four more deputies were there with him. They opened the cell door and pounced on Matt, wrestling him down and handcuffing him. Jake made a move to help him, but two more deputies had arrived by then and held him back. Matt was dragged off down the hall, disappearing around the corner.

He was brought back twenty minutes later, barely conscious, and dumped back on the floor.

Slowly he became coherent enough to talk and relate to Jake just what the elevator ride entailed.

"They put me in the elevator," he said, "and put a football helmet on my head. And then they hit me across the head over and over again with a Dallas telephone book."

"Wow," Jake said, looking at Matt's face. Though he had been beaten to within an inch of his life, there wasn't a single mark on him that hadn't been there before. "Those guys have a little more imagination than I thought."

"No shit," Matt groaned.

"You know something?" Jake said. "You really need to learn to control your mouth a little."

Matt shrugged. "You can't change who you are, you know?"

"Yeah, I know."

They sat in there for another hour, watching flies eat their breakfast and listening to the catcalls, hoots, and yells of other prisoners. Eventually, the same deputy came back, his face red, his fists clenched. He seemed even more upset than he'd been when Matt had been talking about his daughter. He spoke into his radio and the cell door slid open on its track.

"Git your stinkin' asses outta there," he told them.

"Are we going for another elevator ride?" Matt asked, making no move to stand. "If so, you'd better get those other five guys in here to help, because I ain't going quietly."

"Shut your ass, rock star, and git the hell out of there," he said. "Your rich, faggot Hollywood friends bought your asses free."

Matt and Jake looked at each other carefully.

"Really?" Matt said.

It was true. A couple of high priced lawyers from Dallas had shown up and re-interviewed the "victims" in the case—the group of truckers who Jake and Matt had allegedly assaulted—and the witnesses to the fracas—Flo the waitress and the other non-involved patrons. All of them, the truckers included, had changed their stories around so that Jake and Matt were now portrayed as the victims and the truckers as the aggressors. Since they no longer had a case that the district attorney would be able to win a preliminary hearing on, much less successfully prosecute, the Texarkana Police Department was withdrawing all charges.

"Does it feel good?" the deputy asked them as he led them through the halls. "Does it feel good knowin' that your rich friends passed out a couple a envelopes full a money and got a whole group of honest men and women to lie before God just so you can make your next concert?"

"Yeah," Matt said. "It does, actually."

Jake had to agree with this sentiment as well. "Fuckin' A."

They were led into a changing room where they were given back their clothes and the few belongings they'd had on them when they were arrested. The clothes were tattered and bloody of course, but someone had arranged for them to have fresh clothing instead. They took off the orange jumpsuits, tossed them into a laundry hamper, and got dressed. They signed the forms that were put in front of them and were then taken to the discharge area.

"Y'all are free to go now," the deputy told them sourly.

Greg, dressed in his customary suit and wearing his customary grin, was waiting for them. "Thank you, officer," he said politely before turning to his musicians. "Boys. How are you doing? Did they treat you well?"

"Oh, they treated us really well," Matt said, casting an eye at the deputy. "In fact, this officer was telling me that his daughter is an *Intemperance* fan, can you believe that?"

"Oh really?" Greg said.

"Any chance you could set her up with a couple of tickets for the Little Rock show?" Matt asked. "And maybe some backstage passes for *after* the show?"

"Well sure," Greg replied, turning to the deputy. "Just tell me where I should send them and I'll..."

"Get out," the deputy said through clenched teeth. "All of you, get the hell out of this jail and God help you if I ever see you out on the streets of this or any other town again!"

Greg's grin faded. "Well..." he started.

"Uh... I think we should go now," Jake said. "Right now."

They went. There was a limousine waiting for them in front of the jail. It took them to the Texarkana airport where a rented helicopter was standing by, its rotors turning at idle. Forty-five minutes after lifting off, they landed at the Little Rock airport where another limo took them to their hotel, reuniting them with the rest of the band. Doreen fussed over them for the better part of two hours, covering all of their visible bruises with thick make-up. Not only did they make it to the show on time, they made their radio station interviews and their record store signings as well.

*****

It didn't happen very often, but the day following the Little Rock show was another extended travel period day off. They slept in until 10:30—which was good since they'd partied at the hotel room until almost four the previous morning—and were on the road by eleven, headed for Baton Rouge. They arrived at their hotel, yet another cheap, non-descript lodging facility, just after seven that evening.

Jake and Matt were paired together on this night and by 8:30 both of them were lying in their respective beds, shirtless and wearing sweatpants, watching *Simon and Simon* on the television.

"How's your ribs?" Jake asked, taking a final drag from his cigarette and then snubbing it out in the ashtray. He picked up a glass of soda, no booze in it tonight, and took a drink.

"Down to a mild throb," Matt told him. "Those codeine pills Greg gave me take the edge off." He yawned. "Make me tired too."

"I don't need codeine to make me tired. I'm wasted pretty much constantly."

"Yeah," Matt said, lighting a fresh cigarette of his own. "Life on the road."

"Yep."

They sat in silence for awhile, Matt smoking, Jake staring at the television without really seeing anything.

"Still haven't called her?" Matt finally asked.

He was talking about Angie of course. "No," Jake said. "Not yet."

He had had no communication with Angie at all since leaving Los Angeles. Not a letter or a phone call. God only knew what she thought about him now. He thought about how he'd promised to call her every day, twice if he could, how flippantly he'd made that promise, how naïve he'd been when it had passed his lips.

The first two weeks of their tour had passed in an unbelievable blur, a harsh and unforgiving routine of sound checks, bus rides, autograph sessions, radio station interviews, eating, drinking, getting wasted, and, briefly, for one hour every day, performing. The cities they visited passed one by one, some of them the most famous and historical cities in American history, and they saw nothing of them but hotel rooms, auditoriums, record stores, and freeway systems. From the bus windows they saw high rises, factories, parking lots, and fuel stations. Jake screamed out the names of these cities to their inhabitants, yelling them with enthusiasm, as if he were proud to be there, honored to be there, and with none of the residents realizing that he had to be reminded just what city he was currently in before he stepped out onto the stage each night. He fucked beautiful women in each city, sometimes two at a time, occasionally three at a time, and he never learned their names at all, never knew anything about them, never cared to know anything about them. And with each of these encounters he felt less and less guilt about his lack of fidelity, less and less guilt that he had not managed to call Angie yet.

Not that he hadn't tried, or at least made the effort. Their first extended travel break, after the Boston show but before the Buffalo show, he had actually picked up the hotel phone, his apology speech and excuses rehearsed and waiting on his lips. But the moment he began to dial, the busy signal started to sound in his ears. A retry produced the same result. A call to the hotel switchboard for assistance informed him that long distance calls were not authorized from his room.

"Who the hell asked for *that*?" Jake had asked.

"The person who made the reservations and paid for the rooms," he was told.

"Greg," he said, seething. He hung up and called Greg's room, demanding an explanation.

"We're on a strict budget for the hotel rooms," Greg told him. "They're paid in advance and we have no accommodation for extras like long distance calls."

"Are you kidding?" Jake asked. "What about all the room service we order? Isn't that an extra?"

"No, we pay a flat fee in advance for food service. It doesn't matter what you eat, it's all covered under a negotiated flat rate."

"But you can't do that same thing with phone calls?"

"All your local calls are free."

"I don't want to make a local call," he yelled. "Who the hell do I know in Buffalo? I need to call Los Angeles and talk to my girlfriend!"

"Well that's easy," Greg said. "Call her collect."

Jake slammed the phone down at that point. He knew that Greg's suggestion made sense, but he couldn't bring himself to call a girl collect to apologize to her for not calling. And so the phone call went unmade. The next day he fell back into the rabbit hole of consecutive tour dates and the next time he found himself in a hotel room in a relative state of sobriety and with the time to actually make the call, the thought of calling collect was even more repugnant.

"Would she even want to talk to me now?" Jake asked Matt as *Simon and Simon* reached the exciting conclusion for the week. "I mean, would she even accept the charges?"

"You're asking *me*? Matt replied with a laugh. "The man who has made a life out of not caring what women think? You're the fucking Romeo. You figure it out."

Jake looked at the phone. He didn't pick it up. "I don't even know what day it is," he said. "Is it Saturday?"

Matt stared at the television, thinking as hard as he ever did about anything. "I think it's Tuesday," he finally said.

"Tuesday? No way. We did the show in Houston on Wednesday and got arrested on Thursday. That means the Little Rock show was Friday and this is Saturday night."

"No," Matt said. "Houston was four days ago. We got arrested after Dallas, remember?"

"Oh yeah," Jake said, shaking his head. "So that would make it Sunday then, not Tuesday."

"No," Matt protested. "It has to be Tuesday because when we did the Austin show it was Thursday and Dallas was the next day."

"No," Jake disagreed. "We did San Antonio in between Houston and Dallas, remember?"

Matt thought that over. "Fuck, you're right," he said.

"And El Paso was in there somewhere too, wasn't it? Was that before or after Austin?"

"Or was it before San Antonio?" Matt asked.

This discussion went on for several more minutes, long enough for both of them to realize that they had no idea whatsoever what day it actually was and that they had no frame of reference they could agree upon in order to fix a day in the past. It was not the most comfortable realization.

"So, what about your bitch?" Matt asked when they finally stopped racking their brains about it. "You gonna call her, or what?"

"I don't even know if she's home," Jake said. "If I don't know what day it is, I don't know if she's at work or not."

Matt rolled his eyes upward. "If she's not home then no one will answer the fucking phone," he said. "It's not like a nuclear device is gonna go off under the White House if she's not there."

This was sound logic, but Jake uncharacteristically did not allow it to sway him. "I think it's been too long for a phone call," he said. "I need to talk to her face to face."

"And when are you going to do that?"

"After the Louisville show next week," he said. "That's the end of our first leg. We'll have two weeks off and Greg said they'll fly us back to LA."

"Really?" Matt said. "That's bitchin'."

"They're not doing it out of the kindness of their hearts," Jake replied. "It's cheaper to fly us home and then back to Hartford when we start the second leg than it is to pay for two weeks worth of hotel rooms somewhere."

"Ahhh," Matt said, nodding. "Of course."

Jake lit another cigarette, took another drink of his soda, his brain pondering. He looked over at Matt. "Home," he said. "That's a funny thing to be talking about right now."

"How's that?"

"I don't *have* a home."

"Huh?" Matt said, looking at him strangely.

"I'm not talking figuratively either," Jake explained. "I'm talking literally. I gave up my apartment in Heritage when we moved to LA. I gave up my apartment in LA when we went on the road. I don't live anywhere at all. My mail is going to some PO Box. If I left the tour right now, I wouldn't have anywhere to go to and no money to go there with."

"Are you thinking of leaving the tour?"

"No," Jake said. "But that's not my point. My point is that even if I wanted to, I couldn't. Not unless I wanted to be stranded in Baton Rouge or New Orleans or someplace like that without a dollar or even a quarter in my pocket. Did you ever wonder why they seem to make sure we don't have any money on us?"

"What's to wonder about?" Matt asked. "We haven't *made* any fucking money yet. The album has sold almost three hundred thousand copies but we're still a couple thousand fathoms in the hole because of the recoupable expenses."

This was all very true. *Descent Into Nothing*, the album, was selling like hotcakes all across the nation, much faster than the record execs had predicted. The biggest sales spikes were appearing in the cities that *Intemperance* had visited as part of the tour, spiking there in every case in the three days following the concert. And *Descent Into Nothing*, the single, was doing even better. When they'd listened to the top forty countdown on the radio during the bus ride to Baton Rouge earlier that day (and if either Jake or Matt would have remembered that the top forty countdown was always on Sunday, they would have realized what day it was) their song was spending its third week in the top ten, this time occupying the number six spot. Again, this was much higher than the record execs had expected since album sales were the moneymakers with hard rock bands and the individual songs usually didn't fare well on the charts. But even with all of these remarkable sales, the first of the four yearly royalty periods had passed with *Intemperance*, the band, still in the red, their recoupable expenses still being paid off. Though National Records was raking in the money, the band members had yet to see a penny beyond their initial advance.

"It's not just that though," Jake said. "Even if we were out of the recoupable expense hole and bringing in thousands, *millions* in royalties, we still wouldn't be able to get our hands on any of it out here on the road. Those checks would just be sitting in our PO boxes uncashed. I don't even have my checkbook with me and even if I did, who's going to cash an out of town check for us? They don't *want* us to have any money, Matt. They want us to have to rely on them for everything. Remember when we wanted to get the pie?"

"How could I forget?" he asked sourly. That had, after all, led to their beating, arrest, and general mistreatment by the Texas authorities.

"We had to beg for money from Greg in order to do that. And that was just a pie. What would happen if we wanted to go see some sights here in Baton Rouge and asked him to give us some cash for a rental car? Or what if we wanted to cruise New Orleans when we're there? After all, Mardi Gras is this week and we're gonna be in the Big Easy. You think he'd kick loose some cash for us?"

"No," Matt said at once, remembering how reluctant Greg had been to even give them money for the pie.

"Without money, we can't do anything," Jake said. "We can't even leave the hotel rooms. Food, booze, pot, coke, women—all of that is provided for us, but if we wanted to go hit some nice restaurant down on Bourbon Street... forget it. We couldn't even get a cab to take us down there. We couldn't even take the fucking city bus."

*****

The next few days passed in its usual consecutive shows blur. They performed in Baton Rouge, in New Orleans, in Jackson, in Memphis. They did drugs and drank alcohol and fucked groupies. They crashed hard and were awakened with cocaine instead of coffee. And then, on February 4, came Nashville, the heart and soul of the country and western music industry. You would hardly be able to tell that by the crowd that filed into the nine thousand seat Memphis Memorial Auditorium. *Intemperance* and *Earthstone* had sold it out weeks in advance and on the night of the show it was stuffed to the rafters with teenagers and young adults, most of the females in tight mini-skirts or tight jeans, most of the males sporting long hair and a variety of rock band T-shirts. A sea of lighters was held aloft when Jake, Matt, Bill, Darren, and Coop took the stage and began to play.

After the show, as they were sitting in their dressing room, sipping their first beers of the night, smoking their first post-show cigarettes, snorting their first post-show lines of cocaine, all of them were noticeably more gleeful than usual.

"Louisville, Kentucky tomorrow night and then two weeks off!" Jake said happily, taking the bong from Coop and inhaling a tremendous hit.

"I can't wait to go back to LA," Matt said. "By now we're famous there. The bitches will be throwing pussy at us. I'm gonna hit up every nightclub I can and fuck a bitch in every one. And the nightclubs that have B's as the first letter in any word of their name, I'm gonna either fuck two or fuck one up the ass."

Everyone cracked up at this, not only because it was funny but because they knew Matt took such vows seriously. If he said he was going to do that, then he meant to do just that.

Jake coughed out his hit. "Jesus, Matt," he said, still chortling. "Where do you come up with this shit?"

"It's the way my mind works."

Greg walked into the room. "Hey, guys," he said in his best glad-handed manner, the way he talked when he was pretending to be just one of the boys. "Great show tonight. You rocked hard and steadily."

"Thanks," Matt said blandly. "And you set up your usual impressive spread of hooch, blow, and smoke. So, what about the groupies?"

"Yeah," Bill said. "Is Jack gathering us a suitable cross-section of Nashville promiscuousness?"

This caused another outburst of laughter. They were in a good mood indeed.

"I know nothing about that," Greg said in his best conspiratorial voice. "You boys are aware of my views on fornication."

"Hey, Greg," Coop asked. "Tell us the truth. You been doing this gig for a few years. Ain't you ever slammed a groupie? Not even once?"

"Never," Greg said with righteous conviction. "My wife and I were sealed in the Temple. To violate our vows would be the utmost betrayal of my faith before Heavenly Father."

"But snorting a couple grams of coke a week is cool with The Man?" Jake asked.

Greg grinned. "That's just to keep me alert and responsive enough to do this trying job I've been assigned," he said. "It's a minor infraction and I'm sure I'll be forgiven come Judgment, especially in light of all the other temptations I avoid."

"Of course," Jake said.

"Anyway," Greg said, "I was on the phone with Mr. Acardio while you guys were playing. The results are in for the week and *Descent Into Nothing* has slipped back to number eight on the charts. Since it's reached its peak and is heading back down, we're going to release *Who Needs Love?* on Monday. The radio stations across the country will start receiving their copies of the song by next Friday and hopefully it'll start getting airplay over the weekend."

All five band members uttered some version of approval at this. *Cool, bitchin, awesome, groovy* (that contribution from Bill).

"A new release," Greg continued, "means we're going to need to get a new video out. Fortunately, there's a two-week break in the tour coming up after tomorrow's show. We're going to utilize that break to film videos for *Who Needs Love?* and for *The Point of Futility*, which will be the next release."

This time there were five different phrases of disapproval from the band members, most of them profanity-based.

"I'm sorry, guys," Greg said. "I'm just passing on orders."

"*Two* videos?" Matt asked. "Christ, it took us a week to shoot the *Descent* video. Our whole vacation is shot to shit."

"This is supposed to be a break," Jake said. "Is Acardio unaware of what the definition of that word is?"

Greg simply shrugged. "I'm just a small cog in the National Records machine," he said. "They don't consult me when they make these decisions."

"Why the fuck not?" Matt grumbled.

Greg wasn't sure whether he was supposed to answer that or not. You never could tell with Matt. He chose not to.

"Are they flying us out of Louisville then?" Bill asked.

"Does Louisville even have an airport?" Jake put in.

"We're not flying anywhere," Greg said. "We'll be taking the tour bus."

"The tour bus?" Matt asked. "We're driving all the way back Los Angeles? That'll take three days."

"We're not going to Los Angeles," Greg said. "We're going to Orlando, Florida."

"What?" Jake said, sitting up so fast his beer dumped onto the floor. "Orlando? Why the hell are we going to Orlando?"

"Well, because we're close by it and NTV maintains a studio there. Norman Rutger and his production staff are on their way there now to start setting up the pre-production details."

"Great," Jake said, kicking his beer bottle across the dressing room. It spun from one corner to the next, spraying beer the entire trip.

Greg's grin faded the tiniest bit. "Orlando's a great place, Jake," he said. "And I hear Mr. Rutger has some awesome themes for the videos. They're flying a complete wardrobe out for all of you!"

Jake grabbed another beer out of the ice chest. "I can't wait," he said. "I just can't fucking wait."

*****

They managed to film both videos in twelve days, although this meant the days in question were spent with them on the set at least twelve hours and sometimes as much as sixteen. If not for the cocaine—Matt and Jake had both decided that filming a video was not exactly performing so the no drugs rule was ruled not-applicable—they might very well have collapsed from sheer exhaustion.

None of the band was happy with the end results of their efforts. Once again they were forced into bizarre clothing and forced to act out a bizarre production that had little or nothing to do with what the songs were actually about. *Who Needs Love?* was about a man who simply enjoyed casual relationships because he didn't want to experience the lack of freedom that went with commitment. But the video for the song, utilizing Matt as the main character, was about a disturbed serial murderer who killed every woman who got into a relationship with him. It was full of images of beautiful women sliding notes to him or trying to move things into his house or displaying other signs of affection for him and then ending up as the starring feature of various crime scenes. And *The Point of Futility* came out as being an anti-nuclear weapons piece, complete with images of old nuclear tests, protests at various weapons productions facilities, and still photos of victims of the Hiroshima and Nagasaki bombings.

"My God, you freakin' moron!" Jake had screamed at Rutger, infuriated, when he first read the script. "This is a song about breaking up with a woman! It's about the point when you realize it's over and there's nothing more to be done to save the relationship! It's *not* about nuclear weapons! Not even remotely!"

This, of course led to a dramatic tantrum by Rutger and threats to end his relationship with National Records and NTV. "These are visionless buffoons you've sent to me!" he complained. "Buffoons!"

And this, of course, led to phone calls from Max Acardio and a few people even higher up the ladder, all of them issuing threats and reading provisions of the contract to him.

The videos were shot as scripted and the band members dressed as they were told and did what they were told.

The upshot was that they never saw anything of Orlando but the inside of cheap hotel rooms and the inside of the NTV Florida studios. Jake never got a chance to call Angie, and, in truth, his desire to do so was rapidly fading.

*****

The second leg of the *Earthstone/Intemperance* US tour started on February 20 in Hartford, Connecticut. The following night they played in Newark, New Jersey. The night after that brought them to New York City and a break in the routine. Though they would still be doing consecutive shows they would not have to travel in order to do them. They were playing Madison Square Garden—one of the most prestigious venues in the country—not just once but three times, every one of the shows a sell-out of the seventeen thousand seat facility.

The members of *Earthstone* were initially very proud of this fact and were quick to take credit for it. This was natural since they were the headliners of the show. On the day they got the news, just prior to the end of the first leg of the tour, all four of them had been strutting around like Gods, high-fiving each other, and proclaiming that this album had indeed been their shining jewel. Their attitude was understandable. On their three previous tours they had only sold out the smaller venues and had never been booked at Madison Square Garden at all.

It was Greg, in a fit of cocaine-induced tactlessness, who had been the one to burst their bubble. "You guys didn't have anything to do with the sell-outs," he told them. "It's *Intemperance* they're coming to see, not you."

They tried to scoff at this suggestion, but Greg scoffed at their scoffing.

"I'm not making this stuff up," he told them. "National has done the studies and the polls. *Intemperance* is hot and most of the people buying tickets are doing it to see *them* and not you. It seems like the word has spread about how good of a show they put on."

Earthstone had undoubtedly already suspected this fact but having it pointed out to them in such a fashion had been perhaps one of the unkindest things Greg could have done. From that point on the indifference *Earthstone* had shown towards the members of *Intemperance* changed to out and out hostility.

"Nice," Jake told Greg as he watched the four men he had once idolized go storming out of the backstage area, kicking over boxes and trashcans on the way. "Did you have to be so brutal with them?"

"Fuck 'em," Matt said with a shrug. "It's a brutal world."

Jake could not deny that it was indeed a brutal world.

For reasons they were initially unable to fathom, each member of *Intemperance* was put up in a luxury suite in the Park Avenue Towers Hotel for the duration of their stay in New York, this despite the fact that *Earthstone* was still assigned to what was little better than a motel across the river in Jersey City. Jake, though mystified, could not help but be impressed by the 1600 square foot room on the 43rd floor, a room that overlooked Central Park.

"To what do we owe this pleasure?" he asked Greg as they headed for the radio station interview of the day.

"Just a little reward for you boys for doing such a good job on the tour so far," Greg responded, grinning from ear to ear, of course.

It was the next morning, after playing before their largest crowd ever and then engaging in a night of New York debauchery, that the real reason became clear. A reporter from *Spinning Rock* magazine, the premier publication for rock music and everything associated with it, arrived to hang out with the band for twenty-four hours so she could do a story on them. Her name was Gloria Castle and she was an attractive, self-assured woman in her late thirties dressed in jeans and a T-shirt from the recent *Rolling Stones* world tour.

"As you can see," Greg told her after introducing her to the band in Jake's suite shortly after breakfast, "the band members demand only the best in their accommodations and we at the record company go to great lengths to keep them happy."

"I can see that," Gloria said, scratching a few things in a notebook she carried. "And do you guys enjoy this sort of treatment in every city you visit?"

"Of course they do," Greg said, before any of them could answer. "We treat our talent like royalty at National. Like the kings that they are."

"Jesus," Jake muttered, resisting the urge to roll his eyes.

"We're hip-deep in the bullshit here," Matt agreed.

If Gloria heard their comments, she made no indication so. She simply snapped a few pictures of the room, a few pictures of the band sitting at the dining room table, and then sat down.

"Would you care for a little party-favor?" Greg inquired, whipping out his fabled cocaine kit and cracking it open.

"By all means," Gloria replied, smiling for the first time.

Greg laid out a tremendous spread of the drug, covering nearly the entire mirror. It was passed from person to person, with no one abstaining. Once this ritual was complete, everyone was in a better mood.

"So, tell me," she asked no one in particular, "how did you guys get together in the first place? My understanding is that you all met in college in Heritage?"

"Well, kind of," Matt said, lighting a cigarette. "You see, Darren and I have been friends since junior high school. And Coop hooked up with us in high school, when we tried to get our first band together."

"What was the name of the high school?" she asked.

"Casa del Oro in Gardenia. That's a suburb of Heritage."

"The rich suburb," Jake said. "And Casa del Oro was where all the rich kids went."

"Hey, my family wasn't rich," Darren protested.

"No shit," Matt said. "That was why I hung out with you. I hated rich kids."

"You were one of the rich kids," Coop said.

"I know. That's why I hated them so much. A bunch of preppie faggots."

"So, you didn't know them in high school, Jake?" she asked.

"No," he said. "I grew up in South Heritage. I've known Bill since I was a kid though."

"Oh?" she said.

"Yes," he confirmed. He tried to explain how their mothers were best friends and fellow musicians in the Heritage Philharmonic Orchestra, but she wasn't interested.

"Tell me about how the five of you came together," she said after interrupting his story. "That's what the readers are really going to want to know."

"Well," Matt said, "Darren, Coop, and I had been playing together all through high school. Some other guys drifted in and out of the band, most of them sucked ass, a few were decent, but none of them wanted to make the band like... you know... the most important thing in their lives. They would get jobs or find girlfriends who didn't want them spending so much time rehearsing and shit. Anyway, after we graduated from high school we started doing some original songs together. I was singing at that time. I have a pretty good voice and..."

"So, you went to college?" she cut in, not wanting to hear about how good Matt thought his voice was.

He gave her an irritated look but kept his tongue civil. "Yeah," he said. "We couldn't get any gigs or nothing because we just didn't sound quite right. I decided to take some classes at Heritage Community College, some of the music courses just to... you know... get a little more educated in my field." He scoffed. "That was a joke. I had already studied most of that shit on my own. I knew more about music theory than most of the instructors. And I sure as shit played better than any of the guitar instructors who tried to..."

"So that was where you met Jake?" she interrupted again.

The look of irritation was a little stronger this time. "Yeah. That was where I met Jake."

"And what were you doing there, Jake?" she asked him.

"I was taking general ed classes," he replied. "After I graduated, I worked for about a year and just kind of drifted from job to job. I didn't know what I wanted to do with my life... other than be a musician of course, and that seemed like such a long shot I didn't gear myself too much towards it. So anyway, I got tired of my parents nagging at me to go to college and get a degree, so I signed up for some classes, thinking I'd start working towards an English degree and then kind of decide from there what I wanted to do. I had this vague thought that maybe I'd like to be a teacher. You know... so I could..."

"And then Matt crossed your path at some point?" she cut in.

This time the look of irritation came from Jake. "Yes," he said slowly. "Matt's path crossed mine. I took some of the music courses as a general elective for pretty much the same reason as Matt, because I thought I might learn something I didn't already know." He shook his head. "And like Matt, I didn't. I was already a better musician than anyone I encountered in those classes... except for Matt."

"We ended up in Advanced Guitar together," Matt said. "Everyone else in that class was a fuckin hacker, the instructor included. And then I heard Jake play." He took a drag off his smoke and nodded appreciatively. "I knew he was bad-ass from the start. Almost as good as me."

Jake chuckled a little. "Almost," he agreed. "So we gravitated towards each other and hit it off. And Matt told me he had a band with a good drummer and a good bass player but that they needed something else to make the sound a little richer. He asked if I would come jam with them and see about playing a little rhythm guitar."

"You had never been in a band before?" she asked.

"Never. I'd been playing and singing since I was a kid but I was kind of shy about doing it in front of other people. Usually the only time I would was when I was drunk and trying to... you know... catch the attention of a few females. I learned a long time before that singing and playing guitar was an almost certain way to get... uh... you know..."

"Laid?" she asked.

Jake chuckled again. "Yeah. It was an easy way to get laid. So anyway, I was a little nervous at first but I got together with Matt and Coop and Darren and we had a few sessions with me playing rhythm. Now up until this point, Matt didn't know that I was a singer too. I listened to him sing and he's not bad at all, but I knew that my voice would sound a little better."

"Just a little," Matt joked.

"Well, I had more range and endurance than Matt. I finally took him aside one day and asked him if he would let me take the microphone for one of the songs."

"And how did you react to this?" she asked Matt.

"I was kind of pissed off at him at first," Matt admitted. "I mean, he was treading on my fuckin' territory there, or at least that's what I thought. But I let him give it a shot. I'll never forget that moment, not if I live to be fuckin' ninety. He did *Who Needs Love?* – or at least the version of it we had before Bill." Matt shook his head. "It was fuckin' awesome, man. He belted out that song with all the emotion I'd put into writing it and it was perfect, just perfect. Before he even got to the first chorus I knew my days of singing for *Intemperance* were over."

"And does this ever bother you?" she asked him.

"Not a single bit," he said. "We wouldn't be sitting where we are today if it wasn't for Jake's voice. The man can sing, as I'm sure you heard."

"I will agree with that," she said. "And what about Bill? He is probably most responsible for the unique sound you have. Where did he come in?"

"Nerdly was Jake's doing," Matt said.

"Oh yeah?"

"Yeah," Jake said. "As I was saying earlier, Nerdly and I have been friends since we were little kids. We both come from musical families. He has always been something of a prodigy on the piano and I just had this feeling that mixing a classical piano in with the hard rock would sound good." He shrugged. "I guess my mind just thinks that way when it comes to music. I brought up the suggestion to Matt... who had the predictable reaction at first."

"I thought he was out of his fuckin' mind," Matt said. "I mean... a fucking piano? But we smoked a bunch of bud one day and Jake convinced me to at least give it a listen."

"Bill blew them away," Jake said. "Just like I knew he would."

They expected her to ask a few questions of Bill at this point but she didn't. She didn't even look in his direction. "And the rest is history," she concluded. "So, what's this rumor I hear about the tour splitting at the end of this leg?"

"Splitting?" Jake asked.

"What do you mean?" Matt asked.

"Well," she said, "I hear that you're going to be headlining your own show after this leg. That since you're responsible for selling out all the venues for *Earthstone*, National thinks it's time you went out on your own."

Matt, Jake, Coop, Darren, and Bill all shook their heads at this question. They had heard nothing whatsoever about this alleged rumor. But Greg popped up at this point.

"Actually, I just got word on that this morning," he said. "Starting March 15th *Intemperance* will be headlining a North American tour starting in Seattle."

"What?" Jake asked, forgetting about the journalist as he tried to absorb this information.

"We're going to be headlining a North American tour?" Matt asked. "Holy fucking shit! Why didn't you tell us this?"

"I was going to wait until after the interview," Greg said. "I guess Gloria has some pretty good sources.

"Yes I do," she confirmed, casting a knowing look at Greg.

The interview was put on hold for a few minutes as the band members swamped Greg with questions, most of which he put off for the moment claiming that all the details had not been worked out yet.

"The home office is busy at work as we speak, booking dates and working out a tour schedule," Greg told them. "All I know for certain is that we'll start in Seattle on March 15th and that *Voyeur* will be the opening band."

"*Voyeur*?" Matt scoffed. "They're a bunch of fuckin' hackers if I ever heard any. Can't you get anyone better than that to open for us?"

Greg's smile disappeared in an instant. "Uh... I think you're thinking of a different band, Matt," he said forcefully. "*Voyeur* is a fine band, one of National's best hard-rock groups."

Matt didn't notice Greg's look or his tone, nor did he notice the look of interest in Gloria's eyes. "They suck ass," he insisted. "They're nothing but an *AC/DC* sound-alike band. And they don't even do a good job of that. In fact, I bet..."

"Matt!" Greg hissed.

This finally got Matt's attention. He looked up to see Greg making throat-cutting gestures and casting his eyes towards Gloria. Finally, he got it. "Oh..." he said slowly. "You mean *Voyeur*! I'm sorry. I thought you meant... uh... that other group that... you know..."

"You don't care too much for *Voyeur*, do you Matt?" Gloria asked. "Would you care to elaborate on that?"

"No," Greg said. "He wouldn't."

Gloria smiled and penned a few notes while Matt became uncharacteristically quiet, at least until she changed the subject and asked him about another rumor she'd heard. "What's this I hear about a filing cabinet and a bunch of Polaroid shots?"

"Oh... you mean my map of the US?" Matt said proudly.

"You mean your map of sinfulness," Greg said with disapproval in his voice, although he was the only one Gloria could have received the information from unless she'd been talking to the bus drivers, which was unlikely.

"It's true then?" she asked. "You are actually taking photographs of all the girls you have sex with while you're on the road and pasting them in an album?"

"Fuckin' A," he replied. "You wanna see it?"

She did. He dashed out of the room and disappeared for a few minutes. When he returned he held an oversized United States road atlas in his hands. The atlas was tattered looking, the pages bulging unnaturally. He set it on the table and opened it up to the first state in which there were entries—Arkansas. Stapled up in the corners of the Arkansas map were two Polaroid pictures. Each was of a girl with Matt's penis in her mouth, looking up at him into the camera. On the bottom margin of the photos the date and city the picture had been taken in were neatly printed. In this case they both said the same thing: Little Rock, 1-29-83.

"I'm doing pretty good," Matt told her as she examined the shots. "So far I've gotten a piece of ass in twenty-three of the fifty states, not including California, my home state."

"You record every one of your... uh... conquests?" Gloria asked.

"Every one that I'm coherent enough to take a picture of," he said. "My goal is to nail some poon in every state of the union, plus at least two in the District of Columbia. I'm almost halfway there."

"I see that," she said, flipping through the atlas in wonder. On some of the states like Missouri and Ohio and particularly Texas, where they had visited multiple cities, there were up to fifteen pictures stapled, all of them showing the same thing—a groupie with her mouth around Matt's penis.

"None of these pictures have names on them," Gloria noted. "Why is that?"

"Groupies don't have names," Matt said. "They're just groupies."

"I see," she said, making a careful note of that particular quote.

The official interview went on for another fifteen minutes or so. Gloria then retreated to the corner telling the band to just do what they normally did and ignore her presence. "This is a day-in-the-life-of story," she said. "I'm here to chronicle your life on the road."

"Remember," Greg whispered to each of them individually when she was out of earshot, "debauchery, debauchery, and more debauchery. Let her see you living up to the *Intemperance* name. It's your image we're selling here. Your image is what sells your albums."

Jake simply rolled his eyes, his intent to do nothing different than he normally did. Of course, by this point in his career, he had already forgotten that what he normally did was well inside the definition of debauchery.

As for Matt, he openly proclaimed that if they wanted to see debauchery, then he was going to give them debauchery.

"What could you do that you haven't already done?" Jake asked him.

"I don't know," he replied. "But I'll think of something."

Jake had no doubt he was right.

Gloria rode in the bus with them when they went to another local radio station for interviews and two more local branches of Zimmer's Records to sign autographs. She rode with them to Madison Square Garden and watched as they did the sound check. She accompanied them to the dressing and locker room area, stepping out briefly while they actually put on their stage clothes and then stepping back in for the hairdressing portion. Through it all, she snapped pictures and made notes in her notebook. When the time came for them to head backstage to meet the locals, she followed them there as well. She snapped a few more pictures just before the lights went out prior to them taking the stage.

"Listen to that crowd," she commented to no one in particular. "Do you guys ever get nervous about going out in front of seventeen thousand people?"

"Naw," Darren answered, taking a final drag of his smoke. "It's just like D Street West back in Heritage. Just a few more people is all."

The crowd roared as they took the stage for their second night in New York City. The set went off without a hitch. And went it was over, the crowd screamed and cheered for an encore that would not be granted.

As the band opened their first post-show beers and snorted up their customary lines of post-show cocaine, Gloria was there, snapping a few more pictures of them with their hair sweaty, their shirts sticking to their skin, of the ice chests full of beer, of the liquor bottles on the tables. She accepted a few lines of cocaine when it was offered but declined when Matt offered to rub his naked body against hers.

And then they entered the shower area. As had become customary, five groupies were brought in to help the boys shower and get them in the mood for more partying. Gloria, still fully dressed, trailed in behind them and watched impassively as soapy female bodies were rubbed and palpated, as blowjobs were delivered.

"Never kiss a groupie!" Darren yelled at her as a particularly voluptuous redhead slurped and sucked and slobbered all over his knob. "That's the most important thing about being on tour! Never kiss a fucking groupie!"

"It would seem that would go without saying," she said blandly, snapping a picture of Jake as his head fell back in ecstasy.

When they returned to Jake's suite to continue the party, eighteen girls came with them, filling the tour bus to capacity. Gloria parked herself in the corner, trying, and mostly succeeding, at being as unobtrusive as possible.

Jake had had reservations about her presence ever since the first interview. Just how much of this shit was she actually going to write down? But with each drink he consumed, with each line of cocaine he snorted, with each bonghit he sucked into his lungs, his reservations diminished, finally disappearing into the haze of gross intoxication. It wasn't long before he forgot she was even there at all.

He coaxed two of the groupies into the sitting room with him where he had them kneel naked next to each other in the doggie-style position, side-by-side. He slid into one, gave her ten or fifteen thrusts with his condom-capped manhood, and then switched to the other. When the two girls—who had not known each other prior to ending up as part of the "whore brigade" as Matt always put it—began to tongue-kiss each other while he fucked them, he felt his second orgasm of the night starting to churn towards eruption. That was when Matt's voice interrupted him from the other room.

"Jake! Come out here, brother! You've got to check this shit out!"

"I'm busy!" he yelled back.

"Make yourself un-busy!" was the reply. "I got a fantasy coming true out here!"

That was enough to pique his interest. He withdrew from the girl on the left and patted both of them on their bare asses. "Keep yourselves occupied for a minute," he told them. "I'll be right back."

Still naked, his wet condom still on his fully erect penis, he walked back into the main living room of the suite. There, amid the full-blown orgy that was going on, a naked groupie was lying on her back on the carpet, her legs spread wide while another groupie—an Olivia Newton-John wannabe—also naked, was kneeling between her legs and licking her. Matt, equally naked, his penis capped with a rubber as well, was kneeling behind Olivia and dumping cocaine into her butt crack while yet another groupie was spreading it open for him.

"You've heard of body shots, right?" Matt asked Jake. "Well this is a fuckin' crack line! Check it out!"

And with that he leaned forward and stuck a drink straw into her crack and snorted up. The groupie raised her head up and giggled as she felt the sensation.

"That *is* something new," Jake said, impressed.

"Ahhh," Matt said, sniffing a few times and then dumping some more into the girl's crack. He handed the straw to the groupie holding the cheeks open. "You want in on this, hon?" he asked her.

She did. Matt took over the duty of holding the cheeks open while the groupie snorted up the cocaine.

"You want some of this, Jake?" Matt asked him, dumping some more into the valley.

"Hell yeah," Jake heard himself say. He walked over and took the straw in hand. He leaned in and snorted. It would be one of the last things he would remember doing that night.

*****

On February 12, 1983, *Descent Into Nothing*, the album, went gold when the five hundred thousandth copy was sold. Two days later the band opened for *Earthstone* in Miami, Florida. It was the last date of the second leg of the tour and it would be the last time in their existence that *Intemperance* would open for anyone. The following day *Earthstone* would be bussed back to Los Angeles for two weeks off prior to starting the third leg of their tour in Tucson, Arizona. *Intemperance* would be bussed to Seattle where a small auditorium had already been rented for them to begin rehearsing for the first leg of their North American tour.

After their set was over, the band did their normal cool-off routine in the dressing room. They cracked a cold beer, lit up smokes, and took a few bonghits to put them into the mood for their post-gig shower and the customary blowjobs from nameless, faceless groupies. No sooner had those first beers been consumed than Greg utilized his patented schoolmaster hand-clapping routine and told them it was time for them to get out of those clothes so they could be cleaned and put away. Right at that moment the dressing room door opened up and Gordon Strong, *Earthstone*'s drummer came strolling into the room. Dressed in his stage garb of parachute pants, a muscle shirt, and with a Kamikaze bandana around his neck, he was smoking a cigarette of his own and had a joint cocked behind his left ear.

The band fell silent as he looked them over. Relations between the two bands had remained strained since Greg's contemptuous comments and they had gone out of their way to avoid each other even more so than they had before.

Gordon took a thoughtful drag off his smoke and blew it out into the room. He looked at each one of them. "I caught your show tonight," he told them.

"Oh yeah?" Matt replied, not exactly politely. He had been on the receiving end of more than one insult by an *Earthstone* member.

"Yeah," Gordon said. "I thought it might be a good idea since... you know... this is our last gig together and none of us have even seen you yet."

The silence stretched out, quickly becoming uncomfortable. Jake finally broke it.

"What did you think?" he asked.

Gordon nodded. "Pretty fuckin' good," he said. "I can see why you sold out MSG and all the other venues. You guys rock."

"No shit, Sherlock," Matt said, unwilling to be appeased. "Sorry it hurts your feelings so much."

Gordon was undaunted by this. He simply shrugged. "Just thought I'd let you know that," he said. "If we don't see you again, have a good tour."

"Yeah," Matt said, standing up and passing threateningly close to Gordon. "You do the same." He looked at the rest of the band. "Come on guys. There are sluts waiting."

He walked out the door, heading for the locker room. Coop, Darren, and Bill got up and followed him. Jake stood but remained in place.

"You comin', Jake?" Bill asked.

"In a few," Jake replied. "Go ahead and start without me."

Bill nodded and disappeared through the door. Greg remained behind, watching the two musicians nervously.

Jake and Gordon stood looking at each other, ignoring Greg's presence.

"You really liked the show?" Jake asked Gordon.

"Yeah," he said. "I really did. Have you caught our show yet?"

Jake laughed. "I paid twenty bucks two years ago to catch your show. I paid sixteen the year before. But now that I've been touring with you for three months, I haven't even heard a single note of it."

Gordon nodded. "I know how it is, friend. Believe me. I know how it is. You want to catch it tonight?"

"Is this a lure to get me backstage so the rest of your band can kick my ass?"

Gordon laughed. "I can't guarantee an insult-free trip, but I think the boys are a little too wasted to kick anyone's ass right now. Come on. I'll burn one with you before we go on."

Jake smiled. "You talked me into it."

"Wait a minute," Greg said. "What about your clothes? What about your shower? What about getting back to the hotel? The bus leaves well before the main act is complete."

"Well," Jake said thoughtfully, "Reginald can just wait on my clothes. I won't need them again until Seattle, right?"

"Well... yes, but..."

"And you guys can give me a lift back to the hotel when your set is over, can't you?" Jake asked Gordon.

"I think we can squeeze you in," Gordon assured him.

"There you have it, Greg," Jake said. "Just leave my clothes in the locker room and I'll shower after the show."

This all made sense, but Greg didn't like it. His carefully orchestrated routine was being upset. "You really should stay with your band, Jake," he said. "I don't like the idea of leaving you alone here."

"I'm not a five-year-old child, Greg," Jake told him. "I'm a big boy. I'll be all right."

"But..."

"Goodbye, Greg," Jake said firmly. "I'll see you tomorrow."

Greg obviously wanted to say more but he held his tongue. Fuming, he stormed through the door and disappeared.

"You gotta love tour managers, huh?" Gordon asked. "Zed Golan, he's our tour manager, had the same shitfit when I told him I wanted to get dressed early and catch your show tonight."

"I'm surprised they let us go to the bathroom by ourselves," Jake said. He reached in the ice chest and grabbed another bottle of beer.

"Are those for anyone?" Gordon asked.

Jake smiled. "Help yourself."

Gordon did. To two of them.

They walked in silence to the stage left area, which was teeming with activity as *Intemperance*'s roadies were removing their band's equipment from the stage and stowing it in a back corner for later transfer to the trucks while *Earthstone*'s roadies were busy setting up their band's instruments and equipment on the stage. It was a dance no less delicate and intricate than that performed by the flight deck crews aboard an aircraft carrier during a launch and recovery cycle. And by this point in the show both sets of roadies had it down to a fine science.

"Hey, Jake," Mohammad greeted as he trotted by with a microphone stand in each hand, two lengths of guitar cord looped around his shoulders, and a cigarette poking out of his mouth. Mo had trimmed down considerably these last few months, but not just because of the hard work. He, like the other roadies, had been using a lot of crank, subsisting upon it for days at a time during the consecutive set periods. His face had thinned out and was showing an outbreak of acne. His hair had grown long and was suffering from an acute lack of combing.

"How you doing, Mo?" Jake asked him.

"I'm ready for a few weeks off," he said wearily. "What are you doing back here? Shouldn't you be getting your helmet polished about now?"

"Thought I'd catch the *Earthstone* gig tonight."

"Ahh," he said. "Well bang a groupie for me, later, will ya?"

"You know it," Jake told him.

Mohammad dumped off his load of equipment and then rushed back to the stage to get another. Jake and Gordon wandered over to the far side of the stage left area, where the packing cases were stacked. They found seats here, sitting on splintery boxes and leaning against the auditorium wall. From outside, the muted murmur of the crowd could be heard. Gordon pulled the joint from his ear and lit it up with a disposable lighter. He took a large hit and then passed it over to Jake.

"Thanks," Jake said, putting it in his mouth.

They smoked it until it was a roach and then Gordon simply threw it on the floor like it was a cigarette butt. He then took out a real cigarette and sparked that up. Jake lit one as well, enjoying the sensation of the marijuana surging through him and finding himself feeling an excitement he hadn't felt in a very long time. He was going to see a concert tonight! And a concert by one of his favorite bands. And he was, in fact, getting stoned with the drummer from that band and was going to watch it from backstage. How many times had he dreamed of such a thing?

"Wow," he said in amazement.

"Pretty good shit, huh?" Gordon asked, opening his own beer and draining half it at a swallow.

"Yeah," Jake said, grinning, feeling the best he had felt in months. "In fact, in a way, it made me feel like a kid again."

Gordon raised his eyebrows but offered no further comment on that. Instead, he commented on *Descent Into Nothing.* "Heard you went gold the other day. Congratulations."

"Thanks," Jake said.

"And in only four months. That's pretty damn fast for any album, especially a debut album. You guys will go platinum by mid-summer."

"You think so?"

"I know so," Gordon said. "And you'll go double-platinum by New Year's Day, maybe sooner if you get a few more songs on the radio."

"Too cool," Jake replied. "That means I'll make twenty-eight thousand in royalties for the year instead of fourteen." He shrugged. "Oh well. I guess that's better than a poke in the ass with a fireplace implement."

Gordon was laughing, but Jake could tell it wasn't at his joke.

"What?" he said.

"You think you're going to earn twenty-eight grand off a double platinum album?" Gordon asked him.

Jake was embarrassed. "I know it's not much, but that's what we calculated it out to. Maybe the next album we'll get a little better royalty rate. Especially if it sells as well as this one is doing."

Gordon's laughter trickled off and became a look of pity. "Jake," he said. "You ain't gonna make shit off this album and I mean that quite literally."

"Huh?"

"We've put out three gold albums in the last four years. And this album, which is our fastest seller yet, is probably going to go platinum. I'm the primary songwriter. And do you know how much I've made in royalties all this time?"

"How much?"

"Not a fucking dime," he said. "I have never seen a royalty check. Not even one. In fact, our recoupable expenses clause has got us more than a quarter of a million dollars in the hole."

"Jesus," Jake said. "How the hell did that happen? What kind of contract did you sign?"

"Pretty much the same contract that you signed," Gordon told him. "Twenty percent for Shaver, recording and promotion costs one hundred percent recoupable, tour costs and video costs fifty percent recoupable. That sound about like what you signed?"

"Yeah," Jake replied, not mentioning that Shaver was actually getting twenty-one percent out of them. "That's what we signed. But when we calculated it out we came out to fourteen grand apiece if we went platinum. Nerdly did the math on this and he never screws up math."

"I'm sure his math is correct," Gordon said. "He just didn't calculate in some of the incidental clauses in the contract."

"Incidental clauses?"

"All that pot you smoke, all that booze you drink, all that coke you stuff up your nose, all that coke your tour manager is stuffing up *his* nose. Who do you think is paying for all that?"

Jake's eyes widened a little. He had never really thought about who was paying for all of it. He had always just assumed it was part of the perks of being on tour. "That's all coming out of our recoupables?" he asked.

"Yep," Gordon confirmed.

"But isn't it included in the estimates of the tour costs?"

"Nope. It's completely separate. It doesn't fall under the category of 'tour costs'. It is considered part of the 'entertainment costs' clause and that, as you may or may not know, is one hundred percent recoupable."

"You're telling me that we're paying for that fuckhead Greg to snort coke day and night. We're paying for all of that?"

"Well, you're not physically paying for it, but it's being deducted from your royalties. You're also paying for all of that crank your roadies are snorting. You could make an argument that, since the roadies rely on that shit to put the show up and then tear it back down day after day, it is an operational cost and therefore subject to the fifty percent recoupable rate. Unfortunately, and unsurprisingly, National doesn't quite see it that way. They consider the crank to be part of the 'entertainment costs' as well."

"So, it wasn't included in the estimate either," Jake said numbly.

"You're starting to see the light," Gordon told him. "My guess is that you're about fifty grand in the hole at this point. It'll be close to a hundred grand by the time you're done touring for this album, maybe even a little more. You and your guitar player got arrested and thrown in jail, didn't you? The bribe money they used to get you out, the cost of the helicopter they rented to fly you out here, the lawyer fees, the limousine rides, all of that shit falls under the 'legal costs' clause of your contract. That too is one hundred percent recoupable."

Jake was shaking his head. "I'm not gonna put up with this," he said. "Paying for Greg's cocaine? Fuck that!"

"There's no way around it, Jake. There's absolutely nothing you can do about it. If you quit the tour, you'll be in breach of contract and the record company will sue you for everything they're losing, and they'll win. No lawyer would even take your case. And if you demanded that Greg snort less coke, all they'd do is jerk you off and say they'll have a word with him and nothing will change."

Jake was fuming now, his happy feeling of earlier shattered into a million pieces.

"Welcome to being a rock star," Gordon said. "Ain't it a glamorous life?"

"Jesus," Jake said, shaking his head.

"But look on the bright side," Gordon said.

"There's a bright side?"

"There's always a bright side. It just depends on how you look at things. Forget about the recoupable expenses. Forget about being in the hole. It doesn't matter."

"What do you mean, it doesn't matter?"

"You're a star, Jake, and you're going to be treated like one as long as you play their little games. So you don't have any money in your wallet? So you don't even have a fucking bank account? Who cares? The record company will take care of you as long as you're still hot."

"Take care of me?"

"You get to get wasted all the time," Gordon said. "You don't have to worry about going out and finding your dope or buying your booze. They do it for you. They get women for you—some of the most beautiful women in the world and they're just dying to fuck you. How many times have you been laid on this tour?"

"More than I can count," Jake admitted.

"And when the tour is over, they'll set you up in a nice pad somewhere in LA and keep you supplied with drugs and booze and broads and even some spending money for when you want to go out on the town. You'll get limo service wherever you want to go. You'll fly first class or maybe even private whenever you have to travel to another city. And you'll have a premium sound studio that you and your boys can rehearse in for your next album. Is that really all that bad?"

"But what about when you're not hot anymore?" Jake asked him. "What then?"

Gordon sighed. "Well, that's kind of when it all falls apart," he admitted. "If you stop selling albums and making money for them, they drop you like a rock and you'll be out on your own."

"Uh huh," Jake said.

Gordon shrugged. "It's the life we choose, Jake. It's the life we choose."

The rest of *Earthstone* emerged into the backstage area at that point. They cast hostile looks at Jake but said nothing to him. They gathered over on the other side, near the stage entrance, and their tour manager began crunching up some cocaine for them.

"Oops," Gordon said. "That's my cue." He stood up and clapped Jake on the shoulder. "Don't sweat it, Jake. Just go with the flow. You're a fuckin' rock star, man. It may not be what you thought it was, but it ain't that bad either."

Jake made no reply and Gordon walked away, heading for the table and the cocaine.

Jake watched the *Earthstone* members as the lines on the mirror were formed. They were all looking eagerly at it, reminding him strongly of dogs salivating as their canned food was being opened and dumped into a dish by an attentive master. He looked at their faces. They all looked years older than they really were, like men in their mid-forties instead of their late twenties.

"The life we choose," he muttered. "The life we choose."

CHAPTER 7

COMING HOME

March 25, 1883
Portland, Oregon

A soft spring rain was drizzling down as the band walked from their hotel room to the tour bus. As usual, they were looking a little haggard, their faces unshaven, all dealing with varying degrees of hangover. By this point in their careers, however, being hungover was an almost normal state, something that a few more hours of sleep on the bus and a few lines of coke and a few beers upon awakening would take care of. Their humor was good since they were not only starting an extended travel day off but the extended travel day was taking them home for the first time in nearly a year. They were scheduled to perform for two nights in Heritage.

"I think I like this whole having our own rooms thing," Matt was saying as they boarded. "Now that we have some privacy I was able to try out a few new things with my groupies last night."

"What kind of things?" Jake asked, wondering what there could possibly be that Matt was too embarrassed to do in front of others.

"Well," Matt said, "I always wanted to see what the whole water sports thing was about."

"Water sports?" Jake asked, folding down his bunk and tossing his bag up on it. "You tried water sports?"

"Yeah," Matt said. He shrugged. "It was all right. I don't see why all those weirdos in the porno mags get off on it though. I wasn't nothing spectacular."

"Wait a minute," Coop said, folding down his own bunk. "Are you talking about pissing? That kind of water sports?"

"Yeah," Matt said. "What's the big deal?"

"We're you pissing on the bitches or were they pissing on you?" Darren asked.

"I tried it all," Matt replied. "I had two of them up there last night. First I pissed on them."

"Where *at* on them?" Darren asked, seemingly fascinated.

"Their stomachs, their tits, their pussies."

"Did you do this on the bed?" Coop asked.

"No, in the fuckin bathtub, you moron," Matt told him. "Anyway, it didn't do much for me, other than relieve my bladder. So, then I had them piss on me. They squatted over me and let go all over my cock and balls."

"That is purely disgusting," Bill said, though he seemed fascinated by it as well.

"It wasn't that bad," Matt said. "It was a little hotter than me doing it to them but nothing mind-blowing or anything. The only part that actually gave me a boner though was when they pissed on each other. That was so nasty it was hot."

"How'd they do it?" Darren asked. He was nearly drooling.

"Well, first they were making out with each other and then they pissed while their pussies were rubbing together. Then, later, after I'd already drilled them a few times, they sixty-nined in the tub and pissed in each other's faces."

Greg had come on the bus during this story and had caught the tail end of the conversation. He seemed genuinely appalled. "That is the sickest thing I've ever heard of, Matt," he said. "That is truly abusing Heavenly Father's gift of sexuality for perverted ends."

"Hell yeah," Matt said. "Give me a gift, any gift, and I'll abuse it any way I can think of."

Greg shook his head, took a moment to compose himself, and then put his grin back on his face. "Before you all climb in your bunks to sleep off last night's licentiousness, I do have something you'll probably want to see." He held up a copy of *Spinning Rock* magazine from a stack he carried under his arms. "The latest issue just came out. And look who's on the cover."

The picture was one of the few the group had actually posed for during the twenty-four hours Gloria Castle had followed them around back in New York City. It had been taken just prior to their hitting the stage at Madison Square Garden. They were dressed in their stage garb, Jake and Matt standing in the center of the shot, the rest of the band gathered in the background. But it was not the picture that captured Jake's attention. It was the print below it.

DESCENT INTO DEPRAVITY, it read. A DAY IN THE LIFE OF WHAT MAY BE THE MOST DEGENERATE ROCK BAND OF ALL TIME.

"The most degenerate rock band of all time?" Jake asked.

"Isn't it beautiful?" Greg said. "I just read the article. I couldn't have written it better myself. You boys performed splendidly for her, just splendidly. The publicity you'll get from this will be better than any advertising we could have taken out. In fact, there is already an article in the Portland newspaper's entertainment session about it. They're outraged at you boys. Absolutely outraged! It's beautiful."

"They're outraged?" Bill asked.

"And that's good?" Coop chimed in.

"Of course, it's good," Greg said. "Negative publicity is the best kind for a rock and roll act. Remember Ozzy Osbourne and the bat? Well, that little trick you did with the cocaine in that trollop's buttock crack is going to be just as infamous. You'll be remembered forever for that thanks to this article and the follow-ups that will be done in the mainstream newspapers."

"She wrote about the coke in the groupie's ass crack?" Jake asked, horrified. His *parents* would see that article! Angie would see it!

"She wrote about the entire party at the hotel room," Greg confirmed. "The drinking, the drugs, the sex, everything! But the cocaine in the buttocks is the centerpiece of it all. And then there are the pictures!"

"The pictures?" Jake said, feeling a little sick to his stomach now.

"Oh yes indeed," Greg said. "The most gloriously depraved pictures I've ever seen in a mainstream publication. I imagine she had to get special permission to print some of them since they're borderline pornographic."

"Yeah?" Matt said, excited. He snatched a copy of *Spinning Rock* out of Greg's hands. "I need to check this shit out."

"Oh Jesus," Jake moaned as the rest of the band grabbed copies as well.

The bus pulled out of the hotel parking lot and began heading for the freeway. Jake listened to the hoots and yells of Matt, Coop, and Darren as they paged through the magazine, checking out the article and the photographs. He simply sat for a few minutes, staring at the caption on his copy, afraid to even open it. Finally, he decided he might as well get it over with. He opened it up and consulted the table of contents, turning to page 19, where it started.

The first thing he saw was a picture of himself in the shower. The shot was only from the stomach up but it was quite obvious what was going on. His head was back, an expression of bliss on his face, his hands reaching downward, disappearing at the bottom of the frame but set in the universal position of a man receiving a blowjob. The caption below read: *Lead singer Jake Kingsley enjoys the attention of a young female fan while showering after the show at Madison Square Garden. The group demands that five young ladies are brought back for such activities immediately following each performance.*

"Oh my God," Jake said. "I can't believe this."

"I know," Greg said, nearly orgasmic with joy. "Me either. People will be *outraged.* This might be one of the best selling issues of *Spinning Rock* of all time."

There were plenty of other pictures as well—shots of the beer and liquor table, shots of the groupies being led backstage after the show, shots of the hotel room with all the girls in it just before the clothing had started to come off. Each one had a caption beneath explaining just what had been going on when the shot was taken. Jake looked at each one and then returned to the beginning and started to read the article itself.

I was recently asked to spend twenty-four hours with one of the hottest upcoming bands of the year, Intemperance, *as they visited New York City for three sold-out shows at Madison Square Garden. I thought I would merely be interviewing another rock band, something I've done dozens, if not hundreds, of times in my ten years as a* Spinning Rock *journalist. What I encountered instead was a one-day trip into the darkest, most depraved recesses of gross intoxication and sexual perversion I have ever witnessed.*

And that was just the beginning. The entire article took up twelve pages of the issue; almost ten thousand words. She touched only briefly on the background of the band members and how they had come together, covering the entire subject in three paragraphs. And one of those paragraphs contained an out-of-context quote from Jake that seemed to say he had learned to play guitar only so he could get laid. The subjects of the album, the tour, and the show itself were covered by another six or seven paragraphs. The rest of the article was almost entirely dedicated to describing in graphic detail the events that took place after the show.

The members of Intemperance *are demanding and specific when it comes to their after-performance pleasures. After leaving the stage they return immediately to their dressing room where ice chests full of beer and a complete array of hard alcohol and mixers are laid out, along with a supply of both marijuana and cocaine. While cooling off after an hour of performing, they imbibe in all three of these substances, which puts them in the mood for phase two of their after-gig festivities: The shower. Now most bands simply get into the shower after their performance and get clean.* Intemperance, *however, likes to utilize their shower-time to get dirty. Their security force has orders to bring back a young female fan for each member of the group – that's five girls – and these girls then undress and join the band beneath the spray. The sex in the shower is usually oral in nature and the band members use terms such as "bitch" and "ho" and even the dreaded C-word as they instruct the girls on just how they like to be administered to.*

And that, like the actual events themselves, was just for the warm-up. She chronicled exactly what each band member drank, smoked, and snorted. She frequently quoted the banter that went on between them. She told how the security force brought in thirteen more girls to go with the original five and how they loaded onto the tour bus and went back to the *"opulent suite overlooking Central Park"* and engaged in a sex and drug party that *"defies description or terminology. Merely calling it an orgy is like saying the World Trade Center towers are merely tall buildings"*.

And then she got to the part that was going to make *Intemperance* a household name and put her article into the running for a Pulitzer Prize.

By this point in the party I was speechless, beyond appalled at the debauchery I was witnessing. All of my years of watching rock acts party after their shows had led me to believe I had seen it all, but it was obvious I hadn't. These musicians managed to shock me. But the greatest shock was still coming. It came when Tisdale, still completely naked and unashamed, ordered one of the girls to perform oral sex on another one of the girls. He then grabbed yet another girl and ordered her to hold open the buttock cheeks of the girl performing the oral sex. Once this was done he actually poured cocaine in between her buttock cheeks and snorted it out of there with a drink straw. He then offered the straw to the girl who was holding the cheeks apart. She seemed reluctant but she finally took it and did what she was told. After that, Tisdale called Kingsley in from the other room (where he had taken another two girls – presumably Kingsley has at least a little shame) and poured some more cocaine into her buttocks for him to snort. Kingsley's only remark was "this is different", before he took the straw and snorted his fill as well.

"Oh, man," Jake groaned as he read this. Yes, Greg was probably right. This story was going to make them infamous. But infamy was not exactly what he had been shooting for when he signed up for this gig.

*****

At 7:30 that night, Jake was sitting up in front of the bus next to Ken Adopolis, who was behind the wheel for this last stretch. He and Ken had just taken a few hits of marijuana from Ken's pipe and both of them were drinking from bottles of beer when the sign appeared out of the darkness in front of them.

HERITAGE CITY LIMITS
Population 343,316 Elevation 44

"There it is," Jake said, smiling as he saw it. "I never thought I'd be almost crying to see that sign."

"It must be like totally awesome, dude, to like come back to your hometown as a fuckin' star," Ken said.

"It's just nice to be home," Jake said. "To be able to see things I'm familiar with." He looked out the side window. "The river is right over there, and in a minute, we'll be able to see the buildings downtown. God, I missed this place."

"I can dig it, dude," Ken said. "I can really dig it."

Ken drove them to the Royal Gardens Hotel—the same place they had met with Shaver for the first time. Since this was their hometown and the local media attention was going to be quite intense, even without the controversial article in *Spinning Rock*, they had been given deluxe accommodations, the best available in Heritage, in fact. WELCOME HOME, INTEMPERANCE!!! read the marquee in front of the hotel. KEEP ON ROCKIN' AND ROLLIN'.

Their check-in was quiet and uneventful. They were handed their keys and led to the sixteenth floor and their individual suites. Jake found that he had been given the exact suite they had negotiated their representation with Shaver in. He found a strange sort of irony in this.

He lay down on his bed and picked up the phone, excited about calling a local number for once. He dialed from memory the number of his sister's house in Gardenia, a house not far from that of Matt's parents. It was the second time he'd contacted her since going out on tour, the first being a collect call from a Seattle hotel room while rehearsing for the opening night of their headline tour.

"What's up, overachiever?" he asked her when she picked up the phone.

"Well, if it isn't my little brother the rock star," she responded. "I've been reading about you today. Very interesting article in *Spinning Rock*."

"Oh great," he groaned. "I was hoping no one had seen that."

"Everyone has seen it," she told him. "You guys are all anyone talks about in this town since you got that first single on the air. They play your songs three or four times an hour on every radio station, even on stations that don't play rock music. The news has been reporting for a week that there was going to be an article about you in *Spinning Rock*. I hear every copy they sent to the Heritage area has sold out."

"Wow," he said. "I didn't realize people were that... you know... into us here."

"You're the first musical group from Heritage to gain nationwide popularity," she reminded. "What the hell else does this town have to be proud of?"

"I never thought of it that way," he said. "So... did... you know... Mom and Dad see it?"

"Their only son gets his picture on the cover of a famous national magazine and you want to know if they saw it?"

He sighed. "Well, when you put it that way... Did they say anything about it?"

"Dad didn't. You know how hard to read he can be. Mom seems to be hoping it's all just fabrication."

"This is *so* embarrassing," he said.

"So... did you do it?"

"Did I do what?"

"The butt-crack thing, you idiot. What do you think everyone's been talking about?"

"I thought the blowjob in the shower and the drugs might've taken precedence as the topic of conversation."

"Well, they're talking about all of it, of course, but it's the butt-crack that seems to stand out the most. It has a little bit of the sex and the drugs all in one story."

"I see," he said.

"So how much of the story is true?" she asked him.

He sighed again. "It was written in a slanted manner—very slanted actually—but the basic facts are pretty much true."

"Hmmm," she said thoughtfully. "I can see why you're concerned about the price of all that cocaine if you're dumping a quarter-gram at a time into some bimbo's ass. Does that sort of thing go on *every* night?"

"Usually not to that degree, but... yes. It goes on pretty much after every show."

"Well I have to admit, little brother, your job is certainly more interesting than mine."

"If not better paying," he agreed. "Were you able to get a copy of our contract?" That had been the subject of the first call from Seattle. He wanted a lawyer to look over the contract and see if everything Gordon Strong had told him was true, and, if so, if it were enforceable. And since Pauline was the only lawyer he knew, he had turned to her for assistance. In order for her to legally get her hands on a copy of the contract, she had instructed him to send her a signed, notarized piece of paper proclaiming that she was representing him in a legal capacity and that he authorized release of all documents to her. This had been embarrassing in and of itself because in order to do this she had to wire money to him.

"I got it," she said. "Finally. I had to send a notarized copy of your authorization twice because they claimed they'd lost the first one. Then I had to spend about two hours on the phone getting passed around from person to person like a joint. Eventually, I wore them down and got hold of that Acardio guy."

"A real prince, isn't he?"

"Yeah, about as fun as a yeast infection. Anyway, he tried to play some hardball with me but he finally sent me a copy after I threatened to fly down there and get a subpoena. It just arrived yesterday. Postage due no less."

"And what do you think?" he asked. "How screwed did we get?"

"Pretty damn screwed," she told him. "I'll go over it with you tomorrow. Are we still getting together for breakfast?"

"Fuckin' A," he replied. "I'm looking forward to it. I'm at the Royal Gardens, room 1602."

"A suite," she said. "I'm impressed."

"It's all for show," he said. "There's going to be a stream of media people interviewing us tomorrow and National wants them to be impressed with our decadence. Usually we stay in second rate hotels."

"Ahh," she said. "That makes sense. What time should I be there?"

"How about seven?" he suggested.

"That early?" she groaned.

"Sorry, we have to be over at KROT at nine for our first radio interview."

"I guess I can drag my ass out of bed then," she said. "Did you get tickets for all of us?"

"Yep," he confirmed. "Tickets and backstage passes for you and Mom and Dad." He hesitated. "Are you sure they still want to come? I mean... after the article and all?"

"Of course they want to come," she said. "You're still their only son, even if you *do* snort coke out of ass-cracks."

*****

Jake went to bed at ten o'clock that night, his mind troubled but his body fatigued enough to allow him to drift off. A wake-up call at six-twenty got him out of bed and, as was usually the case on the rare occasions when he went to bed sober and got a good night's sleep, he felt almost giddy with energy. It was getting so it felt strange *not* to wake up exhausted and hungover.

He shaved, showered, and took care of his other morning duties. By the time he finished this and got dressed in a clean pair of jeans and a fresh pullover sweater, the room phone began to ring. It was the front desk, inquiring if a "Ms. Pauline Kingsley" was authorized to visit him. Typical of Pauline, she was ten minutes early.

"Send her up," he said.

Less than five minutes later she was knocking on the door.

She was as beautiful as ever. Dressed in a fashionable pair of slacks and a tight sweater, her brunette hair neatly styled, her make-up just right, she smiled broadly as she saw him. Jake was surprised to find himself near tears as he looked at her. Hers was the first familiar face he'd seen outside the band since leaving Heritage. They hugged affectionately and sincerely. Jake then gave her a brief tour of the suite, suitably impressing her. They then retreated to the sitting room, taking seats on the couch where they perused the room service menu for a few minutes before Jake placed the order.

Jake wanted to get into the discussion of their contract right away but Pauline told him that he might want to tune into the morning news instead.

"The news?" he asked. "What for?"

"I caught the six o'clock edition while I was getting ready," she said. "You guys have been moved from the entertainment section to the top story."

He took a deep breath. "The *Spinning Rock* article?"

She nodded. "Turn it on and see."

He turned it on, getting a strange sense of satisfaction in knowing what channel to turn to. The timing was perfect. The seven o'clock edition of the Channel 4 Reports was just starting.

Again, he felt a sense of melancholy nostalgia when they introduced the two lead anchors for the news show. He knew their names and faces, had grown up watching them deliver their daily reports to the citizens of Heritage County. It was Maureen Steward and Mike Jacobs, faces he hadn't seen or even thought of in almost a year. His nostalgia withered, however, when Jacobs began discussing their top story of the day.

"Excitement over the return of Heritage's own *Intemperance* for two sold-out concerts at the Community Auditorium have been somewhat marred by an article that appeared in the latest edition of *Spinning Rock*," he read, his face staring solemnly at his audience. "In the article, penned by veteran *Spinning Rock* reporter Gloria Castle, who spent twenty-four hours with the band when they visited New York City in February, are allegations of heavy cocaine and marijuana use, gross alcohol intoxication, and sexual debauchery with a number of young girls in their hotel room after the show. Ms. Castle alleges that she witnessed a drug and sex orgy in which young girls were forced to strip naked and engage in lesbian sex as well as group sex with the band members."

"Forced?" Jake nearly yelled. "Where the hell did it say..."

"Shhh," Pauline hushed him. "Just listen."

"The most disturbing allegation made is that two of the band members—lead singer Jake Kingsley and lead guitar player Matt Tisdale—ingested cocaine from the nude buttocks of a young girl while she was performing oral sex upon another young girl. The descriptions of the activities in the hotel room that night are a little more graphic than we're able to go into on the air, but many people around the country, particularly here in Heritage, the band's hometown, and in New York City, where the alleged activities took place, are shocked and disgusted."

They cut to a series of interviews in which a reporter was asking people what they thought about the allegations. The first was an overweight, middle-aged woman. "I think it's completely disgusting," she opined. "I bought my daughter tickets to that show when they went on sale but now she's *certainly* not going to go."

"They're just a bunch of degenerates," said the next interviewee, a middle-aged man in a suit and tie. "I never liked their music to begin with, but now I truly find it revolting."

"Would you let your children go see an *Intemperance* show?" the reporter asked him.

"Never," he said. "I wouldn't let them within ten miles of those people."

"Jesus," Jake said, shaking his head.

The showed a few more clips of interviews, all of them negative in nature, and then Jacobs reappeared, still looking solemn. "*Intemperance* sold out both of the scheduled shows in Heritage within two hours of the tickets going on sale. However, reports now are that many parents who had given permission for their teenage children to attend one of the shows have revoked that permission in light of the allegations. It is also reported that a coalition of parents are attempting to get the shows at Community Auditorium canceled."

They cut to another interview, this one with a mid-thirties woman with a beehive hairdo and thick glasses covering her eyes. She was listed as Monica Toland, member of something called the Family Values Coalition of Heritage.

"This is just another symptom of the disease that these rock music personalities are inflicting upon the American youth," Ms. Toland said angrily. "This is a band that spits upon everything American families hold sacred. They make videos about Satanism and twisted serial killers. They advocate promiscuousness, homosexuality, and drug addiction. We are calling on the Heritage City Council to meet and pass an emergency decree revoking the performance permit for this band and to pass a further measure permanently banning any future performances. Lacking that, we will picket their performances tonight to show them just what they're up against."

The scene cut back to Jacobs. "Meanwhile, in New York City, the scene of the already infamous after-show party, the NYPD is opening an investigation into the events of that night. Captain Barry Stern, spokesperson for the NYPD, had this to say at a press conference outside New York City Police Headquarters just an hour ago."

A uniformed police officer appeared on the screen, the caption listing his name and title. There were several microphones before him as he addressed the issue for the citizens of his city. "Obviously we are very concerned about these allegations of illegal drug use and possibly of unlawful sex acts. Unfortunately, we are not able to pursue indictments regarding the drug use, as there is no way to get hold of any concrete evidence. However, we are attempting to locate some of the young ladies who were present at that party that night to determine if any of them were underage or if there were any issues of non-consent involved. If that is the case we will push for a grand jury indictment of any band members or their support staff who were involved and we will request arrest and extradition from whatever jurisdiction they happen to be in when the indictment is handed down."

"Holy shit," Jake said, his mouth wide open now. "Indictments? Can they really do that?"

"Were any of those girls underage?" Pauline asked him. "Or was there any... rape involved."

"They were all willing participants in everything that went on," Jake told her. "They're groupies. Nothing but common sluts who would do anything to get it on with a band member. They have to give blowjobs to the security staff just to get backstage with us."

"That's disgusting," Pauline proclaimed.

Jake shrugged. "I suppose you could see it that way when you come down to it," he said. "Anyway, I'm pretty sure none of them were underage."

"*Pretty* sure?"

"They have to get their ID checked in order to be issued a backstage pass. Our security guy is always careful to make sure we have rubbers and that they get used and that the girls don't have weapons and all that. I never actually asked, but I wouldn't think he would allow any underage girls to come back."

"Well, if that's the case you should be all right. Especially if he keeps a log of who the passes are issued to. If any underage girls tried to claim they were raped by you or one of the other band members, they would have to prove they were even there. Something they wouldn't likely be able to accomplish if they really weren't there."

"That's a relief," Jake said.

"My guess is that it's all just bluster on the NYPD's part. They get up there and jerk off the reporters and claim they're looking into it, but I imagine they actually have much better things to do with their time." She gave him a stern look. "However, I would be a little more careful if I were you, particularly when a damn reporter is in the room and taking pictures."

He nodded, ashamed. "Yeah," he said. "I think I'll keep that in mind."

Their breakfast came a few minutes later and Jake switched off the television set. When the room service waiter left they began to eat, talking of inconsequential things between bites. Pauline caught him up on family gossip. Jake shared some of his tamer anecdotes about life on the road. It was only when they were finished and the plates were put back in the tray and covered that she asked a serious question.

"How bad are you into the drugs, Jake?" she wanted to know. "No bullshit."

He thought it over for a moment, not completely sure of the answer himself. Finally, he said, "It could become a problem if I don't do something about it."

"It *could* become a problem?"

"Yeah," he said. "At this point, New York hotel rooms aside, I'm still in control. When we have days off I can go without it. In fact, I like going without it on my days off. But its kind of part of the routine on show nights. You just kind of get swept away by it. I mean, when everyone worships you and you get done with a show and there's cold beer and bonghits and coke just waiting for you, and when you get in the shower someone sends in a bunch of beautiful naked chicks..." He shrugged. "It's kind of hard to say no, you know?"

"Yeah," she said. "I suppose it would be."

"I think once the tour is over things will slow down. I think I have the willpower for that."

She looked doubtful but did not contradict him. Instead, she opened her briefcase and removed a large manila envelope. "Let's talk about your contract then," she said.

"Yes," he said, grateful for the change in subject. "Let's do that."

"I have to say," she told him, "I've only been practicing law for three years but corporate contracts are my specialty. I've read hundreds of them, maybe thousands. And never have I seen one as screwy and one-sided as this thing. There are clauses in here that even the most unethical and sleazy management wouldn't dream of trying to pull off, things that tilt this entire relationship horribly in the record company's favor. Didn't you read this thing before you signed it?"

"Yes," he said. "Most of it anyway. But it's written in lawyer language."

"Why didn't you have a lawyer go over it for you?"

"We didn't think we needed that," he said. "We had Shaver, our agent, who was *supposed* to be making sure we didn't get screwed."

She gave a sharp, cynical laugh. "He did a good job of making sure *he* didn't get screwed. He's raking in his portion of your royalties just fine. They take his twenty-one percent off the top before they start deducting your portion for all the recoupables."

Jake shook his head. "That asshole. No wonder he pushed us to sign once he got the royalty rate as high as he could."

"You guys were babes in the woods," she said. "You made the mistake of thinking that anyone gave a shit about you. Now you're going to be paying the price."

"Are you're saying that all that stuff Gordon Strong told me is true? They're making us pay for all the coke and booze and crank and all that?"

"You got it," she said. "Expenses related to entertaining the band, its road crew and its agents are considered entertainment expenses and are one hundred percent recoupable."

"But we're talking about illegal drugs. How can they justify that on an expense report?"

"I don't know for sure, but my guess would be that they're simply recording each drug purchase as a generic cash transaction for miscellaneous supplies."

"But what about if we ask for an audit of the books? Don't we have the right to do that?"

"Well... that's one of those screwy things I was telling you about. You have the right to demand an audit, but they don't have to grant it."

"They don't have to grant it? Is that legal?"

"Sure it is," she said. "You signed a contract that granted the right of refusal to them." She flipped through her copy of the contract for a moment until she came to a section she had highlighted. "Right here. '*Audit of expenses are done at the sole discretion of National Records. Requests for audit by the undersigned*'... that's you... '*will be considered, but National Records reserves exclusive rights and judgment as to the necessity of said audit*'." She put the contract back down. "In other words, if they don't think there's a need for an audit of the books, they don't have to grant one. And how often do you think they're going to decide there's a need for an audit?"

"Jesus," he said. "Is there any way out of it?"

"Not that I can see," she said. "Any failure to abide by the terms of the contract is considered a breach. If that happens, they have the right to sue you for any money they could have reasonably expected to make off of you through the terms of the contract. And at the rate you guys are selling records, that would be enough to have them garnisheeing your wages for the rest of your life."

"So, we got fucked without lube is what you're saying?"

"With a Louisville Slugger," she confirmed.

He picked up a cigarette from a pack on the table and lit up. Pauline gave him a disapproving look but said nothing.

"Oh well," he sighed. "Live and learn, I guess. At least with the success we're getting with this album we'll be able to negotiate from a position of strength for our next album."

"Uh... actually that's not true," she said. "This is a six year contract, Jake, calling for six albums, not including Greatest Hits re-releases or live albums. Are you telling me you didn't know that?"

"Well, I know it's a *potentially* six year contract," he said. "I'm not completely stupid. But there are those options for re-negotiation after each contract period. Didn't you read that part?"

"Oh, I read it all right," she said. "But apparently you didn't. Those options you're talking about all belong to the label, not you."

"Huh?" he asked, starting to get a sinking feeling in his stomach.

"Each option period is for one year and one new album," she explained. "You signed up for six option periods. At the end of this period the label has the option of retaining your contract for another period, which means another year and another album. If they didn't like the way your first album sold, *they* have the option of releasing you from the contract. You, however, do not have the option of doing anything but what they decide. If they want you to record another album, you are obligated under the contract to do so and the terms you signed up for on the first album will still apply."

"You mean we're stuck with a fifty thousand dollar advance and all the recoupable expenses?" he asked.

"You got it. And furthermore, any debt you incur as a result of those recoupable expenses will carry over to the next album. They'll still give you your advance, but you'll start out two or three hundred thousand in the hole and it'll only get worse. And once that second contract period is up, they can force you to exercise the third option, and then the fourth, and then the fifth and finally the sixth, all under the same terms. You're stuck with this deal, Jake, until 1988 at least."

*****

Every interview they did that day was longer than usual, both because it was their hometown and it was therefore felt they owed the local media a little more, and because of the *Spinning Rock* article and the tumult it had caused. The first of the day was with Brian Anderson of KROT, the local hard rock station. Anderson was a DJ they had all listened to for years, his voice as familiar to them as their mothers and fathers. The first question out of his mouth was one the band was already becoming intimately familiar with.

"Did you really snort cocaine out of a girl's butt?" he enquired.

"I would certainly never imbibe in illegal drug use," Jake responded with a forced laugh.

"And even if we did," Matt added. "It's not polite to snort and tell."

Anderson laughed, saying he understood. He then went on to a more conventional interview.

From KROT they were driven to the Channel 6 studios in South Heritage, very near Jake's old neighborhood. The interviewer here—a heavily made-up, impossibly Ken-doll like man named Nolan Starr—was not quite as friendly.

"You're denying the allegations?" he asked.

Jake tried to keep things on an even keel. "Well, I'm certainly not going to admit to them."

"Is that the same as denying?" Starr probed.

"We're taking the fifth on this, dude," Matt told him. "You dig?"

Starr dug, but he didn't let the issue drop. "What do you think about the efforts of the Family Values Coalition of Heritage to get the city council to revoke your auditorium permit?"

"Well, obviously I'm against that," Jake said. "This is our hometown and I'd hate to have our local fans miss out on our show just because a few people are overreacting to an entertainment article."

"Then you think the people who are upset by these allegations are overreacting?" Starr asked. "That the parents of many of your fans who believe you advocate Satanism and drug use and rampant, irresponsible sexuality are overreacting as well?"

"I'm just a musician," Jake said. "I don't advocate anything."

"Then you *do* think they're overreacting."

"Yeah," he said. "I guess I do."

"And what about the allegations that you had sex with minors?" Starr asked next.

"I have never had sex with a minor," Jake said forcefully.

That interview ended soon after. They were immediately driven across town to another one, this one for the Channel 9 news. It went pretty much the same as the Channel 6 one had.

From Channel 9 they went to the Lemon Hill branch of Zimmer's Records. There was the usual crowd of fans waiting outside to have their albums and singles signed but there was also a group of news crews with cameras set up and a group of hostile older people off to the side. When they got out of the bus this latter group pelted them with rolls of toilet paper and chanted, "Clean yourselves up or get out of our town!" The sheriff's department, which had been standing by to control the crowd, kept the angry mob away from them. And when they went inside and began signing autographs nearly ever person asked their own version of the same question: Did you really snort coke out of a girl's ass?

By the time they finished with all of this, it was after three o'clock. They were given bag lunches of sandwiches in the bus as they were driven downtown to Community Auditorium. They ate them in their seats, washing them down with cold beer since it was still over four hours until eight-thirty, the time they were scheduled to take the stage.

Since they'd been delayed so long with interviews the entire schedule was running behind. The members of *Voyeur* could not complete their sound-check because *Intemperance* needed to complete theirs first. As such, they were waiting impatiently just off-stage in the stage right bleacher section when Jake and the others emerged from the backstage area to finally get it done. None of the *Voyeur* members acknowledged the *Intemperance* members other than their lead singer, a short, skinny man who called himself Scott Bonner (though his real name was Steve Callman), who looked at his watch impatiently.

"Yeah yeah," Matt told him. "Keep your fuckin' pants on, hacker. We'll be done in a little while and then you can get up there and do your poor man's imitation of *AC/DC* again."

Callman, a.k.a Scott Bonner, fumed, but kept his mouth shut. He had already had his eye blackened and two of his ribs sprung when he'd made the mistake of getting in Matt's face for insulting their musical abilities and their unabashed (and poor) imitation of *AC/DC*. That had been prior to their second tour date together, just before *Voyeur* had taken the stage, just after Matt had accused him of sacrilege for having the audacity to call himself Scott Bonner—an obvious reference to the legendary Bon Scott, the original singer of *AC/DC* who had died of an alcohol overdose in 1980.

That had just been the culmination of the tension that had existed between the two bands even before they had met for the first time in Seattle. *Voyeur* was touring for their third album, having put out two gold albums prior to their latest effort, which was called *The Promised Land*. They thought it was demeaning to have to open for a band touring for their debut album, as if seniority carried any shit with the National Records executives. *Intemperance*, on the other hand, thought it was demeaning to have their very name on the same ticket as a group whose sole appeal was imitating another band. To any professional musician or true music aficionado their music was atrocious. Their guitar chords were hopelessly simple, their backbeats were unimaginative, and their lyrics were nothing but blatant rewrites of the concepts the band they were imitating had already covered.

"Look at this shit they're passing off as original music," Matt complained at one point. "*Road to Purgatory*, *Murder For Hire*, *Blown Out of the Sky*, *Black is the Color*, all played with repetitive three-chord riffs and that asshole singing in his quasi-evil voice. How do they get away with it? Why the hell doesn't *AC/DC* sue their asses?"

"As long as they don't duplicate the actual melodies or the actual lyrics, they're in the clear," explained Bill, who, among his other talents, was a semi-expert in copyright law.

"At least you can be assured that they're even further in the hole than we are," Jake put in. "They've barely made gold their first two releases."

"Proof that there are enough stupid-asses out there to buy anything as long as it's played on the radio enough," Matt said.

Voyeur's tour manager, a veteran at the post, knew that it was in everyone's best interest to keep the two groups as separated as possible at all times. As such, he gathered them up and whisked them away with the promise of some fresh cocaine lines while *Intemperance* mounted the stage and began their sound check.

As Mo handed Jake his Brogan guitar and as he stepped up to his microphone at the front of the stage, he looked out over the empty auditorium floor in wonder. Though he had done these same actions in dozens of auditoriums in dozens of cities across the country, this time it was different. This was Community Auditorium in Heritage! This was the auditorium where he'd attended his very first concert—*Rainbow*, in 1975. Since then, he'd seen scores of acts here. He'd seen *Black Sabbath* multiple times, with both Ozzy and Ronnie James Dio at the helm. He'd seen *Styx* and *Foghat* and *ZZ Top* and *AC/DC* with both Bon Scott and Brian Johnson. He'd seen *Journey*, *Foreigner*, *REO Speedwagon*, *Jethro Tull*, *Kansas*, *Rush*, *Blue Oyster Cult*, *Supertramp*, *Santana*, *The Doobie Brothers*. He'd camped out in line all night long in order to get tickets to see *Led Zepplin* in this auditorium. He'd seen concerts here from numerous other bands that had been mere flashes in the pan, bands whose names he couldn't even remember anymore. He'd attended concerts alone here, seeing acts he secretly enjoyed but wouldn't have admitted to under torture—acts like *Chicago*, Neil Diamond, Robert John, Johnny Cash, even, most embarrassing of all, *Abba*.

And at every single performance, he'd dreamed and fantasized that one day *he* would be up there on that stage in this auditorium, that one day *he* would be the one the citizens of his city were coming to see. And now, here he was, standing on that very stage, looking down at that very floor where he'd crowded in with thousands of others, pushing and shoving to get to the front, passing joints around. Tonight, they *were* coming to see him. This night was the quintessence of his dream coming true. He was performing at Community Auditorium.

It took only twenty minutes for the tech roadies to achieve what they considered the perfect mix of outputs for the various instruments to optimize the acoustic qualities of the auditorium. The positions of the various switches and dials were carefully noted down and the band left the stage, leaving the roadies to remove their guitars and cords from the sound system, to remove their microphones and stands, and to wheel the platform containing Coop's drum set off into the corner of the stage. *Voyeur*'s roadies then began assembling their drum set and stringing cables and placing microphones. Of course, long before the culmination of this process, *Intemperance* was back in their dressing room and enjoying their last beers before the onset of the four-hour pre-show moratorium.

They took their showers and put on their stage clothes just before five o'clock. As Doreen began fixing their hair they watched the nightly newscast on Channel 4. Once again, they were the lead story. This time it was read by Kimberly Caswell, another familiar and famous face in the Heritage television news community. She was hopelessly cute and cuddly looking, perhaps the most loved of all the local newscasters since she was the epitome of the girl-next-door who rises to fame and fortune and who, according to the reports in *Heritage Magazine* and in the local newspapers, never let it go to her head. She had started out as plain old Kimberly Morgan, the girl who read the weather and the traffic reports and then, about five years before, she had become very publicly engaged to and subsequently married Jonathan Caswell, the head of Caswell Development, the most successful real estate development firm in Heritage and a man whose reputation for philanthropy was almost saintly. Twice in the past three years they had been voted Heritage's cutest couple.

"She's so fuckin' innocent looking," Matt observed as the camera zoomed on her. "Just like a librarian or a kindergarten teacher. Wouldn't you just love to nut all over her face?"

"Matt," said Doreen in motherly disapproval. "*Must* you use such crude language in my presence?"

Matt actually blushed a little. "Sorry, Doreen," he mumbled, and she went back to teasing his hair with her brush.

"The Family Values Coalition of Heritage," Kimberly read, "failed to convince the Heritage City Council to revoke the concert permit for controversial local band, *Intemperance*, tonight and tomorrow. The controversy centers around an article in *Spinning Rock* in which the band's excessive drug use and sexual exploits are graphically detailed, including allegations that lead singer Jake Kingsley and lead guitarist Matt Tisdale snorted cocaine from between the naked buttocks of a young girl. The FVCH, citing concerns that many of *Intemperance*'s fans are teenage children, petitioned the city council to open an emergency meeting and to revoke the permits on the grounds that the band violates local standards of decency and therefore constitutes obscenity. Mayor Mary Bancroft refused to call for such a meeting and refused to meet with FVCH members. Her office did release a statement in which Mayor Bancroft stated, 'While I don't agree with the alleged actions of these band members, and while I believe their so-called music is indeed an unhealthy influence, charging them with obscenity based upon unsubstantiated reports in a magazine would never stand up. If we were to pass such a decree, *Intemperance*'s lawyers would have a court order for us to rescind it within two hours.'

"Monica Toland, leader and spokeswoman for the FVCH, expressed anger and disappointment at Mayor Bancroft and the city council for refusing to take up the issue." They cut to a shot of Toland outside city hall.

"I think it's a flagrant breach of accountability to the voters that our mayor and elected officials are unwilling to take steps to protect Heritage's children from obscenity simply because they think a judge will reverse their decision. I would call on every citizen concerned about this matter to place phone calls to Mayor Bancroft's office, *demanding* that these concerts be cancelled."

The shot cut back to Kimberly Caswell. "Since it is now after five o'clock and city hall closed for the day more than an hour before, members of the FVCH have moved their protest to Community Auditorium downtown, where the first concert is scheduled to begin in just over two hours. We have Bob Goldman on hand there. Bob, can you tell us what's happening?"

They cut to a live shot of a grinning, toupee-wearing man dressed in a suit and tie and holding a microphone. "Kimberly," he said, "as you can see behind me here, *Intemperance* fans began to line up some hours ago for admission to tonight's show." There was a pan of the camera and they were looking at a long line of fans stretching from the auditorium doors, down the steps, and down the street and out of sight. Many of the fans began to wave and cheer and hold their lighters up as they saw the camera looking at them. "And over here, on the other side of the entrance, members of the Family Values Coalition of Heritage and dozens of concerned parents have begun picketing."

The camera panned over there and, sure enough, there were nearly a hundred people holding up signs and chanting "*Intemperance* go away! Don't come back another day!" over and over. The camera panned over some of the signs, catching slogans like: GLORIFY TEMPERANCE INSTEAD, PROTECT OUR CHILDREN, INTEMPERANCE SUPPORTS DRUG USE, FRIENDS DON'T LET FRIENDS SEE INTEMPERANCE, or JUST SAY NO – TO INTEMPERANCE.

"Isn't this beautiful?" asked Greg, who was hovering just behind the band, nearly drooling as he saw the coverage. "You can't pay for this kind of publicity. I couldn't have planned this better myself."

"What's so great about it?" asked Coop. "The news in our own hometown is bagging on us. Our own mayor told people we were an unhealthy influence."

"It's publicity," Greg said. "When your target audience is teenagers and young adults, the best way to get them to buy your product is for their parents and elders to be against it. People who didn't even like you or that haven't even heard of you will go buy your albums now. They'll pay more attention when a DJ announces that one of your songs is about to play. Having that writer observe you in your after-show debauchery was brilliant, just brilliant!"

Jake sighed, watching as Bob Goldman walked over to interview a few of the sign carrying FVCH members. He found a fat, middle-aged redhead, and as she began explaining about obscenity and drugs and Satanism and how the band *Intemperance* was evil personified, the camera panned back a bit, showing some of the other protestors. Jake's breath froze as he caught sight of a familiar face. He leaned forward. "Holy shit!" he yelled. "There's Michelle!"

"Michelle?" asked Matt, leaning forward as well, which served to jerk some of his hair right out of Doreen's hands. "You mean that bible-thumper bitch you used to fuck?"

"That's her!" Jake said. "Right there!"

And it was. She looked a little older and more mature, but it was definitely her. She was nodding in agreement every time the interviewee said something negative about *Intemperance*. In her hands was a sign that said: INTEMPERANCE IS SATAN'S TOOL!

"Son of a bitch," said Darren. "That *is* her!"

"Satan's tool?" Bill said. "She really is a bible-thumper, isn't she?"

"She's the bitch that let Jake eat her pussy out one last time before she broke up with him, but then wouldn't let him tear one off in return," said Matt. "Remember that shit, Jake?"

"Yeah," Jake said sourly. "I remember."

"Did she really do that?" asked Doreen.

"She really did," he confirmed.

Doreen seemed appalled by this. "Some people just have no manners," she said.

*****

"Listen to that," Jake said in wonder as the sound of the audience filled the backstage area. It was 8:15 PM, fifteen minutes after *Voyeur* had finished their set, fifteen minutes before *Intemperance* was to take the stage, and everyone out there was shouting out *In-temp-erance*, *In-temp-erance*, at the top of their lungs and stamping their feet against the bleacher seats or the floor.

"I guess the fucking family values bitches didn't change that many minds, did they?" asked Matt.

"Nope, I guess not," Jake agreed.

He had glanced out at the audience a few minutes ago, peeking through the stage access door and out over the auditorium. It was packed to standing room only on the floor, which was the general admission area, and it was equally packed in the bleachers, which were reserved seating. Their fans had signs of their own, signs that said things like, HERITAGE *LOVES* INTEMPERANCE, ROCK ON INTEMPERANCE, and FUCK FAMILY VALUES!! He even saw one gorgeous young woman holding one that read, YOU CAN SNORT COKE OUT OF *MY* ASS ANYTIME!

Greg confirmed that not many people had stayed away. "We sold ninety-two hundred tickets for tonight's show," he said. "As of ten minutes ago, 8925 people have come through the doors, and there's still well over a hundred partying out in the parking lot. You see how it works? Even if a lot of parents did refuse to let their teenagers come see the show, the tickets were just sold to someone else. I checked a few back issues of the local paper and flipped through the classifieds. *Intemperance* tickets were selling for sixty to seventy dollars. And Jack tells me that the scalpers out front were charging ninety bucks for them. Ninety! Can you believe it? I haven't heard of tickets going on the black market for that much since the *Rolling Stones* tour!"

The time clicked by and the chants for *In-temp-erance* grew louder and louder. When the lights were finally turned down just before the show, the cheers grew deafening. Jake was grinning as he heard it, as he basked in it. True, he had played before seventeen thousand at Madison Square Garden, but that didn't have shit on this. That was Heritage out there! Those were his people!

"It's time," said Steve Langley. "Hit the stage."

They all took a deep breath, clasped hands in a circle, and then released. Moving in darkness they went through the door and out on the stage. They picked up their instruments and got ready. The cue came, the lights blared to life, and they began to play. The audience was so loud they nearly overrode the amplification system.

Since they were now the headliner, and since they now had two hit songs (*Who Needs Love?* was currently at number 16 on the chart and rising fast), their set had been changed around and an additional thirty minutes had been added to it. They opened with their first hit song, *Descent Into Nothing*. They closed with the hard driving *Who Needs Love?* And then came the encores. They did three more songs, *Point of Futility*, which was slated to be the next single released, *Living By The Law*, which hadn't been recorded yet but which any fan who used to catch *Intemperance* at D Street West would recognize, and *Almost Too Easy*, which was the last cut on the album and was slated to be released as a single after *Point of Futility* peaked. Through it all the audience cheered wildly and steadily, holding up their signs, holding up their lighters, dancing and singing along with the music, throwing panties, bras, and marijuana pipes up on stage. For once Jake didn't have to struggle to remember what city he was in during his between-song banter. He didn't have to fear that he would accidentally blurt out the name of the city they'd been in yesterday, or the one they would be in tomorrow. He was home and performing before people he actually knew: his parents, his sister, his friends from high school, girls he had slept with and guys he had drank beer and smoked pot with. This was his town and, though performing on stage was always the highlight of every long tedious day on the road, never had it felt this good, this real, this satisfying.

The set actually ran ten minutes longer than usual because of the extended cheerings after each number they did. And when it was finally over they were given a standing ovation that was still going on long after they left the stage and the house lights were turned back on. It died out only as the roadies took the stage and began disassembling the show.

*****

Jake had taken Greg aside before their set and asked him politely to keep the dressing room spread confined to only alcohol while they were in Heritage.

"My parents are going to be in there tonight," he explained, "and I'd just assume we maintain a little bit of an illusion for them."

"Of course," Greg had promised. "Consider it done." And it was. When they arrived there, still sweating and out of breath and sipping from their Gatorade, there was no marijuana bong or cocaine mirror in sight.

Actually, it wasn't just Jake's parents who came back, it was Bill's as well.

"Jake!" squealed his mother when they finally made it through the gauntlet of security and entered the room.

Smiling, Jake stood and walked to his mother, who was holding out her arms for a hug. "I wouldn't do that if I were you," he warned her. "I'm all sweaty from the show."

"Oh, I don't care about that," his mom told him. "I used to change your diapers, after all, didn't I? Now give me a hug."

He gave her a hug. Next his father came up and refused the handshake in favor of a hug of his own.

"Great show you put on," his dad told him. "You've gotten better since we saw you at that D Street place."

"Thanks, Dad," he said, looking over the two of them.

Pauline came up and punched him on the shoulder, just the way she used to when she wanted to annoy him as they were growing up. "I agree," she said. "You guys rock."

He was also hugged by Stan and Cynthia Archer, Bill's parents, whom had been his alternate family ever since he was a toddler. They both told him it had been a great show as well. While they were doing that his parents went over and hugged Bill before greeting the rest of the band.

"Good show, guys," his dad told Matt and Coop and Darren, who were all sipping from bottles of beer.

"Thanks, Mr. Kingsley," Matt said politely, in classic Eddie Haskell form. "Can we offer anyone a drink? The beer is nice and cold."

As it turned out, everyone wanted a drink. Bottles were passed around and opened and then everyone found seats.

"It's too bad you can't stay longer," Jake's mom said. "Can't they give you more than two short days here?"

"We have a tight schedule," Jake told her. "We have to be in Sacramento day after tomorrow, Oakland the day after that, and Los Angeles the day after that."

"Don't forget San Jose," Matt said. "That's between Oakland and LA."

"Oh yeah," Jake said.

"My goodness but they run you boys ragged, don't they?" his mom asked.

"It's the life we choose, Mom," Jake told her. "The life we choose."

"And what about that nice girl you said you were dating in Los Angeles?" she asked next. "Are you and she still an item?"

Jake felt the normal twinge of guilt at the mention of Angie. "Uh... well, we haven't talked too much since I went out on tour. It's kind of hard to maintain a long-distance relationship, you know."

"That's too bad," his dad said neutrally. "She sounded like a very sweet girl. You haven't found too many girls like that, have you?"

"I'm trying, Dad," he said.

"Uh huh," his dad replied, staring at him.

This, of course, led to the discussion of the *Spinning Rock* article and all the media publicity of the past twenty-four hours.

"All those things that woman said," his mom asked. "Well... that wasn't true... was it?"

"Of course not, Mom," he lied smoothly. "Our attorneys are looking into slander charges against that rag. We were just as shocked as anyone when we read that."

"Really?" Bill's mom said. "So, you boys didn't really... you know... do what they said?"

"Do you really think I would do anything like that, Mom?" Bill asked her. "Remember, I didn't even have a date until after high school."

"Well... I admit it didn't sound like something you would do," she said.

"He surely wouldn't, Mrs. Archer," Matt told her. "Bill here is straight as an arrow out there on the road. You would be proud of him."

She beamed as she heard this. Mr. Archer looked a little more doubtful, but his mind seemed to ease as well.

"Then you're not really doing all those other things the article said," Jake's mom asked next. "The things with those... you know... those women and the drugs."

"Nobody could do all those things, Mom," Jake assured her.

"There are those who would give it a try though," Jake's dad put in. "Are you sure there's no accuracy to that article, Jake? If you're starting to get yourself into trouble, we can help you."

"We're not in any trouble, Dad," Jake assured him. "I mean, sure, we smoke a little weed every once in a while. I mean, who doesn't, right?"

"Yeah," his dad said guiltily.

"And there's usually beer and stuff like that for after the show," Jake went on. "That is kind of standard."

"But what about the cocaine, honey?" his mom asked. "Pot and alcohol are one thing. Your father and I would be awful hypocrites to try to condemn you for that. But you're not getting into cocaine, are you?"

"Well, we've all tried it a few times you know," Jake said. "Just to see what its like. But using it after every show?" He shook his head vehemently. "No way. That reporter had it in for us."

"Then you didn't really... uh... snort it out of that girl's... out of her..."

"No way!" Matt said. "Not only is that sick, it's unsanitary."

"And all those... those... girls?" his mother asked next. "That's not true either?"

"Not even close," Jake said. "I mean, sure, we meet some girls every now and then while we're out on the road, but we're not having orgies or anything. That's just the record company and the media hyping us up to try to sell records. You see, if we get a reputation like that they feel we'll sell more albums. I don't agree with that concept but there isn't a whole lot I can do to stop them from spreading things like that. To tell you the truth, it embarrasses me."

"Then your security guards aren't bringing back five naked women for you when you take your showers?" Jake's dad asked.

"Absolutely not," Jake assured him.

"I don't think girls would even do that anyway," Matt put in.

At that very moment, before anyone else could even reply, the door banged open and Jack Ferguson came walking in. With him were five excited and giggling young groupies. He closed the door behind him, failing to notice that the band was sitting on the other side of the room. He turned to the groupies. "Okay, girls," he said. "You've earned your backstage passes. Now, the guys are in the shower by now so let's get those clothes off and get in there and start sucking some cock. Remember, no fighting over which band member you get and no letting any cock in your pussies until *after* the shower."

The girls giggled again and began pulling off shirts and pushing down skirts and pants while the parents of the band members watched with their mouths hanging open.

"Jesus," Jake groaned, dropping his head into his hands.

*****

"Do you think they bought your story?" Matt asked Jake an hour later, as the five of them, plus Greg, were riding the elevator to their rooms on the top of the Royal Gardens. The story he was referring to was the hastily concocted explanation Jake had given his and Bill's parents for the appearance of Jack Ferguson and the groupies.

"That it was just a practical joke on Jack's part, that he knew we were in the dressing room all along?" He shook his head. "No. I don't really think so."

"Me either," Matt agreed. "But that was some pretty quick thinking. You're pretty good at that."

"Yeah," Jake grumbled. "And at least they *pretended* to believe it."

"I'm sorry," Greg said for perhaps the twentieth time. "It's all my fault. I forgot to let Jack know that the routine in Heritage was to be a little different. At least I got rid of the cocaine, didn't I?"

"At least there's that," Jake had to agree.

The usual after-show party had been assembled, this time in Coop's suite. Nineteen groupies had been brought back with them and the alcohol, marijuana, and cocaine were flowing in their usual quantities. Jake opened a beer but before he could even take a drink of it and get a good look at the groupies for the night, Matt was beside him.

"Got a surprise for you," he said. "My old man paid a little visit to the hotel earlier."

"Oh yeah?" Jake asked. "Where is he?"

"I didn't want to socialize with him or anything, I just had Pops do a favor for me. Gather up some coke and enough pot for a couple of joints and meet me by the front door in five minutes."

"What are you up to?" Jake asked him.

"A little hometown celebration," Matt said. "Just do it."

Jake did it. He took the plastic wrappers from Coop's bathroom drinking glasses. He dumped some cocaine into one and some pot in the other. He then pocketed them and made his way to the front door. While Jack Ferguson and two of his underlings were watching Bill, Coop, and Darren get the orgy started, Matt and Jake slipped out the door and into the hallway. They went down the elevator to the lobby and out to the front of the hotel. A quick walk around the building brought them to the parking lot. After a few moments searching they came to a Mercedes convertible.

"Isn't this one of your dad's cars?" Jake asked.

"Bet your ass," Matt said. "We're going out for a night on the town."

"Where we going?"

Matt grinned. "Today is Wednesday," he said. "I actually confirmed that with a copy of the *Heritage Register*. I also confirmed that D Street West still has live entertainment on Wednesdays. Guess who is playing there tonight?"

"Who?" Jake asked, grinning, starting to like this idea.

"*Airburst*," he said. "Of course, the show is already over by now—it's almost 11:30—but we can still close out the bar, can't we?"

"I suppose we can," Jake agreed. "Do you have the keys?"

Matt opened the door of the driver's side. It wasn't locked. He leaned over and opened Jake's door. Jake sat down in the luxurious seat.

"Open the glove box," Matt told him.

Jake did so. Inside were the keys and a white envelope. Matt took both. The keys he put in the ignition. The envelope, he opened. Inside was a stack of bills.

"A thousand bucks," Matt said, smiling. "God, I love my old man. He does just what I tell him to do." He peeled off roughly half of the cash and handed it across to Jake. "Come on. Let's go have ourselves a good time."

Jake pocketed the money. Ten minutes later they were pulling up in front of D Street West.

*****

The hero worship Jake had experienced at D Street West in the past, when they were simply Heritage's most popular club band, was nothing compared to what they experienced that night. The bouncer guarding the door, a man both Jake and Matt knew well and had partied with many times, was hardly able to form an articulate sentence when he saw them. He absolutely refused to take the cover charge from them.

Within seconds of their walking through the door, everyone in the building knew they were there. A huge crowd formed around them, with people pushing and pulling and shoving and shouting, everyone trying to be the ones next to them, to be close enough to see them and converse with them.

Nor were they allowed to buy drinks. The bartenders—again, most of them people Jake and Matt knew on a first-name basis—fell all over themselves to give them free drinks. And not just them either, but anyone who happened to be officially in conversation with them at the moment.

While Matt reveled in the attention and privilege, Jake found it a bit disconcerting, especially when it was someone he knew who was acting so strangely. A good example of this was Chuck O'Donnell, the owner, the man who had booked them for that first gig and so many after it. He was almost slobbering with excitement at having Matt and Jake in his establishment. He hugged them repeatedly and offered them anything from the bar that they wanted.

"Thanks, Chuck," Jake told him. "But we're just regular customers. You don't have to treat us special."

Chuck scoffed at this suggestion as if it were sacrilege.

And then there was *Airburst*, a band that had opened for them dozens of times, that had partied with them even more than that, a band whose female lead singer Matt had once enjoyed a threesome with. They were just as awe-struck as everyone else, unable to converse on the same level they once had, able to do little more than blather out the same simple phrases like "we really love your music" and "you guys rock".

This bothered Jake for a while, especially since he'd once considered Dave Merlin, *Airburst*'s lead guitarist, one of his closest friends outside his own band. But, like with everything else, a few drinks and a few lines of coke made it all seem better.

Jake ended up running into a girl that he knew from high school. Her name was Sara Borne and she had been one of the elite back then, a girl who wouldn't have given him the time of day had he been the last boy on Earth. Now, she was doing anything she could think of to get into his good graces.

At closing time, she abandoned the group she had come to the club with in favor of leaving with Jake and Matt. Matt, of course, had picked up a girl of his own, a naïve and innocent looking nineteen year old named Julie. The four of them—Matt and Julie in the front, Jake and Sara in the back—went cruising through the city, passing a joint around from time to time, snorting a little coke from time to time. By the time they reached the rural area north of the city, they were feeling very loose.

"Do you want me?" Sara asked Jake when they finally parked off the road in a grove of walnut trees on someone's farm. Her eyes were shining and excited, as if she couldn't believe that she was actually doing this. Matt and Julie had already disappeared, having "gone for a walk" the moment they'd parked. They had been carrying a blanket with them.

"I used to fantasize about you," Jake told her, his hand reaching out to stroke her face. "You were one of the best looking girls in school."

She giggled. "I always thought you were pretty cute too," she said.

Jake frowned a little. "No lies," he said. "Let's keep things honest here. You used to call me 'Bone Rack' along with everyone else. You and your friends used to make fun of me because I had long hair and wore nothing but rock band T-shirts and I hung out with the losers."

She opened her mouth to deny this but then thought better of it. "I'm sorry," she said shamefully. "I've grown up since then."

He looked her up and down. "Yes," he said. "You certainly have. And you're just as hot as you ever were."

Another giggle. "So, you want me then?"

"Do you want me?" he asked.

"Yes," she said. "Very much."

"Why?" he asked. "What's different about me now? I've put on a few pounds, that's true, but I'm still the same person. I'm still have long hair. I still hang out with stoners. I'm still dressed in jeans and a rock band T-shirt. What's different?"

"I'm able to see you for who you really are now," she said. "I've listened to your music. You're deep, Jake. Incredibly deep. Deeper than any of us ever would have thought possible."

Jake digested this for a moment and then smiled. "Good answer," he said. "Damn good answer."

She laughed. "Shall we take a walk?" she asked him.

He reached out and stroked her face again. "Do you know what I really want to do with you?" he asked.

"What's that?" she asked, perhaps with a bit of nervousness. After all, she had to have heard about some of the things he had done with other women.

"I want to kiss you," he said. "I want to kiss you a lot."

"Kiss me?"

"Yeah," he said. "I haven't kissed a girl in months, since before we went out on the road."

"What?" she asked. "But those stories about you and the..."

"Oh, I've *fucked* dozens of girls," he said. "In every way, shape, and form. But I haven't kissed one. Not even a single time."

"How come?" she asked.

"It's a long story," he said. "But I want to kiss *you*. I want to kiss you very badly. Are you a good kisser?"

She licked her lips slowly. "I've never had any complaints," she said.

"I bet you haven't," he said.

They leaned into each other and kissed very softly. She had puffy lips, the kind of lips men dreamed of kissing. In fact, when he had fantasized about her back in his high school days, when she was a cheerleader and student council vice president, her puffy lips had been the body feature he used to dream about the most. Was that perhaps the reason he had focused on her tonight? He thought it probably was.

"Mmmm," she said softly when they broke the first kiss. "That was nice."

"Yes," he said, his arms going around her trim body. "It was very nice. Let's do it some more. A *lot* more."

They did it a lot more. They kissed deeply and softly, firmly and passionately, they enjoyed every kind of mouth-to-mouth contact it was possible to enjoy. Jake reveled in her mouth, in her lips, in the feel and taste of her tongue. He licked her lips and sucked on them. He nibbled on them and ran his tongue over them. He slid his tongue over her teeth and over the inside of her lips. He sucked on her tongue and encouraged her to suck on his. For more than twenty minutes they did nothing but kiss each other. His hands stayed on her waist or on her back. Her hands stayed around his neck. Both of them became very heated from this.

"We're making out," she panted at one point, while Jake ran his tongue over her lips, while he sucked the top one into his mouth. "I haven't done this in years. I mean, not like this... in a car."

"Me either," he said. "It makes me feel like a kid again. And I haven't felt like that in a while now."

They went back to kissing. Eventually, of course, they became heated enough to push things along a bit. His hand went to her breasts, first through her sweater and then beneath it. As he cupped her bare tit, her hand dropped to his lap, finding the bulge of his erection. She palpated and felt it for several minutes before finally finding the buttons of his jeans and opening them.

He pulled her sweater and bra up, baring one breast, which he put into his mouth and suckled. She jacked him with her hand the entire time. Finally, she kicked off her shoes and he pulled her pants and panties off, leaving her nude from the waist down. He dropped his own pants down around his ankles. He fumbled in his pocket for a moment, trying to find a condom, while she lay back on the back seat and put one leg up on the front seat, opening herself. At last, he found the package and capped his tool. He lay down upon her and they had sex, rutting in the uncomfortable, cramped, noisy, and oh-so-exciting manner of teenagers trying it out for the first time.

*****

They arrived back at the hotel just before 4 AM, parking the Mercedes back where they had found it and staggering to the hotel lobby. Greg was waiting for them upstairs and he was furious at them.

"Where in Heavenly Father's name have you two been?" he demanded. "I've been frantic! I thought you were kidnapped! I've even had the police out looking for you!"

"The police?" Jake asked. "Are you serious?"

"Of course I'm serious," he said. "You disappeared without a trace from the hotel. What am I supposed to do?"

"You're supposed to conclude that we went out on the town and had a good time," Matt told him. "We are adults, aren't we?"

"You can't do things like this!" Greg said. "Anything could have happened to you!"

"Is that in our contract, Greg?" Jake asked him.

"What?"

"Does it say somewhere in our contract that we aren't allowed to leave the hotel without permission?"

"Well... no, but..."

"Then fuck off," Jake told him. "Last time I checked, this was still America and I was still an American citizen."

"You have no reason to talk to me like this," Greg said. "All I'm trying to do is look out for your welfare."

"The record company is looking out for our welfare," Jake nearly spat. "Doesn't that make you feel better, Matt?"

"Yes," Matt said. "I'll sleep good knowing that they're looking out for me."

"Listen, you two," Greg said. "In the future..."

"Good night, Greg," Jake said. "I'm going to bed now. I think I have to get up in a few hours, don't I?"

"Yep," Matt agreed. "There's a show tonight."

They went into their rooms, leaving Greg standing in the hallway.

CHAPTER 8

IMAGERY

June 28, 1983
John F. Kennedy Airport
New York City, New York

The limousine stopped as close to the Nationwide Airlines terminal as possible. The driver had been instructed not to open the door for them. That would only attract attention. The hope was to get through the airport lobby and security checkpoint as anonymously and unobtrusively as possible. It was a slim hope at best, but a hope nonetheless.

Jake opened the door and stepped out. He was wearing a pair of blue jeans and a button up short-sleeve shirt. Dark sunglasses covered his eyes. His long hair was tucked up under a San Francisco Giants baseball cap. He carried a simple duffle bag in his right hand.

Stepping out behind him was Janice Boxer, the National Records publicity department agent who had accompanied the band on their tour, coordinating autograph session and radio station interviews. The end of the *Descent Into Nothing* tour of 1983 had apparently, and unfortunately, not been the end of the band's association with Janice. It had only been the beginning. She had been named as *Intemperance*'s head publicist. And even though the tour was over there was lots of publicity to cash in on.

Intemperance had the most popular song in the nation right now. After *Who Needs Love?* had peaked at number four *The Point of Futility* was released and had shot up the charts like it had been fired from a cannon. It had been at number one for the past three weeks and was showing no signs of giving up its position just yet. Nor was that the only chart *Intemperance* was atop of. *Descent Into Nothing*, the album, had been number one on the album sales chart for eleven weeks now and was still selling as fast as National Records could ship copies to the stores. It had gone platinum back in May, just six months after its release, and was predicted to go double platinum around late November.

This popularity, coupled with the morbid publicity that was still going strong from the *Spinning Rock* article meant that National Records was doing everything within its powers and within the vast boundaries of its contract with the band to keep *Intemperance* in the forefront of the public's mind. The band members were being flown all over the country—individually, in pairs, and all five at once—to attend everything from record store openings to local television news interviews to nationally syndicated telecasts. The band had appeared on *Saturday Night Live* and *American Bandstand*. Jake and Matt had been interviewed for two hours on *Rockline*. On this particular trip Jake had been sent solo to the seventy-two story NTV building in New York City where he was subjected to a particularly inflammatory and caustic interview by Brad Cummins of the renowned *Wake Up USA* show. He was still seething from the treatment he had received at the veteran interviewer's hands.

"Don't you believe that this so-called music you produce is a deliberate attempt to foment the corruption of the youth of America?" had been one question. And before Jake could even complete a sentence of his reply, Cummins began retorting. "Oh, come now! You make songs about drug use and Satanism. You make videos that glorify protest and serial killers and satanic rituals. Tell me something. Is it all just an act to sell records or do you really believe in all of this?"

And of course, Jake had stammered and stuttered at this point because there was no way to answer that question without seeming to admit that he was either in favor of Satanism or at least pretending to be. The end result of this was that he came across to a nationwide audience like a stoned out moron, which was exactly what Cummins had intended. The interview had only been five minutes, but it was five minutes that had been among the longest of Jake's life.

"Can you believe that asshole?" Jake asked Janice as they entered the terminal building. "Shouting a bunch of accusatory questions at me and then interrupting while I'm trying to respond? They call that journalism?"

"No," Janice said. "They call it entertainment. That's all television news is. He's not a journalist, he's an actor, and a damn good one at that. He was given his lines by the people who produce the show and he read them off to you, just like an actor is supposed to."

"Did you know he was going to do that?" Jake asked her.

"Well, of course," she said, rolling her eyes a little. "That's his style. Don't you ever watch *Wake Up USA*?"

"No, I don't."

"Don't feel too bad. He's done that same shtick to presidential candidates, heads of state, veteran actors and actresses, judges, lawyers, you name it. And some of them came off looking even worse than you did up there."

They began to walk through the terminal, heading toward the line at the security checkpoint. Other people milled around, moving in different direction, heading for different parts of the building. A voice overhead announced arrivals and departures.

"If you knew he was going to do that," Jake asked, "then why didn't you at least warn me beforehand?"

"Warn you?" she asked. "Why would I warn you? You performed perfectly. You came across exactly the way we wanted. I couldn't have scripted you any better than that."

"You *wanted* me to look like an idiot up there?" he asked, grappling with his temper.

"Idiot is not the word I would use," she said. "Disorganized, unremorseful, defiant. That's what we wanted."

"That's what you wanted?"

"Of course," she said. "It not your fans who are watching *Wake Up USA*—your fans are still in bed at that hour—it's their parents. We need to keep their parents outraged at you as much as possible. The more disgusted with you the parents are, the more albums the kids will buy."

This was an old subject for Jake and the rest of the band. The old *image is what sells your music* argument. Jake didn't hold to it anymore now than he had when they'd tried to change his name to JD King. They made good music, music that people liked to listen to over and over again. That was why *Descent Into Nothing* had sold 1.3 million copies. That was why *The Point of Futility* was sitting firmly at the number one position. Not because Jake had once snorted cocaine out of a groupie's ass or because that moron producer had made some horrible videos. And certainly not because some asshole actor on a television show had made him look like an idiot.

But you couldn't tell that to people like Acardio or Janice or even Shaver, their agent. They claimed complete and total credit for the runaway success of *Intemperance*, a success that had surpassed even their most optimistic imaginings during the early stages of the contract. In their view a band that was promoted correctly with the proper amount of parental outrage and controversy simply had to produce palatable music in order for success to occur. They would make the admittedly compelling argument of *Kiss* in order to make their point. Musically, *Kiss* was beyond simple, edging into the territory of hopelessly mundane. All of their songs used the same basic guitar riffs and employed the same style of bland, formulistic lyrics. If not for the make-up and the blood spitting and the outfits, *Kiss* wouldn't have sold a thousand albums nationwide. Jake knew this was true, of course. Any real lover of music looked at bands like *Kiss* with contempt. But *Kiss* was also an anomaly, the one true example of image overcoming artistic ability. Just because the formula had been successful once, record execs had mistakenly concluded that that was the key and tried to duplicate it with every band they signed. The popularity of MTV and music videos in general was only making this trend worse. When the record companies failed to successfully promote an image-only band successfully, they blamed it on poor publicity or on the public not being quite ready for that particular image. And when a band did become successful because of good music—like Ozzy, like *Dio*, like *Motley Crue*, like *Intemperance*—they assumed that their image shaping had simply been a success this time.

"Dude," a voice said on Jake's left. "Aren't you... like... Jake Kingsley, dude?"

Jake suppressed a sigh and put a smile on his face as he turned and beheld two young men in their late teens. They were dressed like college kids heading off somewhere for summer vacation, which was to say they were dressed similarly to Jake himself.

"That's me," Jake told them, already reaching for the pen he habitually kept in his back pocket for just such occasions.

"Dude," the first young man said, his eyes shining. "This is, like, so awesome. Can I get your autograph, dude?"

"Sure," Jake told him, pulling out the pen. "You got something for me to sign?"

The young man handed over his airline ticket stub. Jake asked his name.

"It's Mike," he said. "Mike Millen."

"How do you spell it?"

Mike looked at him strangely. "Uh... M–I–K–E, dude."

"No, I mean your *last* name," Jake said.

"Oh," Mike said, hitting himself in the forehead. "Like... duh." He spelled it out.

Jake scratched out a variation of his standard autograph scrawl: *To my friend Mike Millen, Keep rockin, dude. Jake Kingsley.*

Mike's friend was Jason. Jake signed his airline stub as well.

"Thanks, dude," Jason said. "You really rock, man. I was at your MSG gig. Heard you had a real good time after it, you know?"

"Yeah," Jake said. "I know. Take it easy, guys."

They thanked him, told him he rocked one last time and then wandered off, comparing each other's autographs. Jake hoped that would be the end of it, but of course it wasn't. Others had noticed the interaction and had homed in on it. Many had probably been asking themselves if that could be Jake Kingsley over there but had not been sure enough to approach and ask. Now that they had seen him signing autographs for Jason and Mike, their suspicions were confirmed and their fears of approaching a celebrity were assuaged. Within seconds there were more than twenty people clustered about him, all of them chattering away and pushing airline stubs or other scraps of paper in his face.

Jake started signing, asking each person's name and how to spell it and then scrawling out basically the same thing he'd scrawled for Jason and Mike. He passed a few words with each person, shook each hand, and remained polite and soft-spoken. When they asked questions, he answered as briefly and as vaguely as possible. And, of course, as always seemed to happen when he stepped out into public these days, the small crowd continued to swell as other people drifted over to see what all the fuss was about, as people leaving the crowd reported to those outside of it that it was Jake Kingsley in there. He began to get claustrophobic as they pushed in at him from all sides, as they all tried to speak at once. His hand began to cramp up after about the thirtieth signing. And, as always also happened, a few people pushed their way through not to get his autograph but to express their disapproval at what he was and what he represented.

"God will punish you harshly come the Judgment," said a middle-aged woman dressed in a frumpy ankle-length skirt. "You'll burn in the fires of hell for eternity!"

"Well, at least I won't have to worry about what to wear," he replied blandly.

"Rapist!" shouted another woman, this one college age and wearing a Cornhuskers T-shirt. "Stay away from this pig, girls. He's nothing but a common sex criminal."

Jake didn't have to answer this one. Several members of the crowd spoke up for him.

"He can sex crime me any time he wants," said one young lady.

"You're just mad he won't snort coke out of *your* fat ass," said a young man.

This led to a shouting match between the Cornhuskers girl and the actual fans, which quickly escalated into something like a pushing match. That was when Jake decided enough was enough.

"Listen, folks," he said, raising his voice loud enough for all to hear. "I really need to get checked in for my flight. Sorry I couldn't get to everyone."

With that he pushed his way out of the crowd and headed for the security checkpoint once again, Janice trailing silently behind him. There were a few pleas from those who had not gotten their autographs and even a few angry words about how Jake was forgetting where he came from. Jake didn't look back.

"You didn't have to be so huffy to them," Janice chided. "They are your fans, after all."

Jake ignored her. If she would've had her way he would've stayed there for six hours signing something for every person in the airport.

There was a short line at the security checkpoint. The people waiting in it all stared at him and whispered among themselves, but none of them talked to him. The two security guards manning the checkpoint, however, seemed very interested in him. One of them spoke into his phone, covering his mouth and glancing over at Jake as he came closer and closer.

When Jake and Janice got to the front of the line and put their bags on the conveyer the guards let them run through the machine and then took both of them off and set them to the side. After they walked through the metal detector the guard who had been on the phone asked them if they could step over to the side for a minute.

"Is there a problem?" Jake asked.

"I don't know," the guard asked arrogantly. "Is there?"

Jake sighed. Janice seemed about to say something but changed her mind.

Within a minute two uniformed police officers arrived, one of them a sergeant. They conferred in whispers with the two security guards for a moment and then walked over to Jake.

"I'm afraid we're going to have to search through your carry-on luggage," the sergeant told them.

"What for?" Janice asked.

"The officers noticed some strange items in the X-ray," they were told. "We just want to take a closer look."

"Bullshit," Jake said. "They were on the phone to you before we even put our bags through."

He looked at Jake mildly. "I don't know what you're talking about," he said. "But even if that was the case, you are subject to search in this airport. I believe you might've seen signs to that effect when you came in?"

Jake shrugged. "Go ahead," he said. "But there aren't any drugs in there. All you're gonna find are my dirty underwear and some shampoo samples I swiped from the hotel."

They went ahead, pawing through everything in both Jake's and Janice's bags in full view of the other people making their way through the checkpoint. They held up Janice's panties and even felt the lining. They opened up Jake's electric razor and sniffed the inside of it. When they failed to find anything incriminating, they had both of them submit to search of their person.

"I will certainly be sending a letter to your chief about this," Janice huffed as they made her turn out her pockets and dump the contents out onto a tray.

"You do that," the cop said as he commenced patting her down.

They did the same to Jake, who dumped his cigarettes, his lighter, his wallet, and two dollars in small change out for them. When it was over they didn't apologize for the inconvenience. They simply told them they could enter the terminal and then they left.

"The nerve of those people," Janice fumed as they made their way into the terminal. "Searching *me*. We'll just see what my husband has to say about all this when we get back."

"He'll just try to get it written up in the newspaper somewhere," Jake said. "Jake Kingsley suspected of drug smuggling at JFK. Cops unable to find his stash."

"Hey," Janet said, brightening. "That's not a bad idea."

Jake just shook his head and showed his boarding pass to the security agent guarding access to the first-class lounge.

They waited in the lounge for about twenty minutes. Through it all Jake could see people pointing at him, whispering about him, much of it, he was sure, disapproving in tone. The other first-class passengers were mostly older types wearing suits or business dresses. They probably weren't *Intemperance* fans. None of them came over to talk or ask for an autograph.

The aircraft was a Boeing 747 and the first-class section was on the upper deck, just behind the cockpit. They climbed up the steps and went to their assigned seats. Jake and Janice were in the second row on the left side. Janice claimed the window seat, leaving Jake on the aisle. He stretched out and tried to relax a little as the rest of the first-class passengers found their own seats. No sooner had he settled in than a tall, clean-cut man wearing a white uniform and cap emerged from the cockpit and walked directly over to him.

"You're Jake Kingsley, right?" the man asked, glaring down at him.

"Yeah," he said. "I am."

"I'm Captain Simmons," the man said. "I'm in command of this aircraft."

"Uh... okay," Jake said. "Nice to meet you, Captain." He held out his right hand.

Simmons just looked at it. "You're not going to cause any trouble on this flight, are you?"

Jake let his hand drop. "I wasn't planning on it," he said. "What sort of trouble was it that you were thinking I'd cause?"

"Drunken behavior, lecherousness, drugs, Satanism. I won't put up with any of that on my aircraft."

"Satanism?" Jake asked. "You were afraid I'd have a satanic ritual on your aircraft?"

"Don't be smart with me, boy," Simmons told him. "You just keep your nose clean up here. There's any trouble from you, I'll land at the nearest airport and have the FBI take you into custody."

Jake sighed. "I'll keep that in mind," he said.

"You do that," Simmons said. "My flight attendants have been instructed to keep an eye on you."

With that he turned and walked back into the cockpit, closing the door behind him.

He wasn't gone more than ten seconds before one of the flight attendants in question came over to him. She was a redhead, in her early twenties, and possessed a body that filled out her red and white uniform quite nicely.

"Hi," she told him, leaning down so close she was flirting with violating Jake's personal space. "I'm Laura. I'll be your flight attendant. I'd just like to tell you that I really love your music."

"Thanks," Jake said, giving her a smile.

"I tried to catch your show in LA but all three dates were sold out."

"Well, maybe next time," Jake said.

"Do you think you could sign your autograph for me?" she asked.

"You bet," Jake told her, taking out his pen. "Do you have something for me to sign?"

She giggled a little. "Oh, I got lots of things for you to sign," she said. "But for now, I guess we'll have to make do with this." She tore off a page from her order book and handed it to him.

"What's your last name, Laura?" he asked.

"Grover," she told him.

He had her spell it and then wrote, *To Laura Grover, the best damn flight attendant in the sky. Keep on rockin, Jake Kingsley.* He handed it back to her.

She read it and then giggled again and made it disappear into her pocket. "Thanks, Jake," she told him. "Now can I get either one of you a drink while we're waiting for the coach section to board?"

"I'll have a bloody Mary," Janice said. "A *strong* bloody Mary."

"You got it," she said, noting that down. "And what about you, Jake? Do you want a bloody Mary as well?"

"No, I'll just have..."

"How about some Chivas and Coke?" she offered. "I read in that article your agent put in *Rock Star* magazine that you love Chivas and Coke."

"Uh... no, thanks," he said. "I'll just have some coffee."

"Coffee?" she said, disappointed. "Just coffee?"

"It's only ten in the morning," he said. "I wouldn't want to get drunk this early. Who knows what might happen. I might start having a satanic ritual or something."

She giggled yet again, casting a knowing look towards the cockpit. "Right," she said, winking at him. "I get you."

When she returned four minutes later and set the steaming cup of coffee down before him she winked again. "Just the way you like it," she said. She then gave Janice her bloody Mary and headed off down the aisle to get more drink orders.

The coffee smelled funny to Jake. He found out why when he took the first sip. It was heavily spiked with whiskey, whiskey that tasted suspiciously like Chivas Regal. He shook his head in consternation and drank it anyway. *What the hell? It's what they expect of me.*

Ten minutes after they reached cruising altitude, Laura propositioned him.

"Do you want to come back and see the flight attendant quarters?" she whispered in his ear.

"Uh... no, thanks," he told her. "I thought maybe I'd just get a little sleep."

"But I'll show you *everything*," she said. She looked around and, seeing no one paying undo attention, added, "Including the bathroom that we use, if you know what I mean." She blew softly in his ear as she said this.

He, of course, knew what she meant. And, as intriguing as the thought of joining the mile-high club with a stewardess might be, he didn't think it would be a terribly good idea right now, not with the scrutiny the captain had told him he was under. "I don't think that's a good idea, Laura," he said. "We might get caught. And if we did, they'd fire you, wouldn't they? I wouldn't want to be responsible for that."

"We won't get caught," she said. "Trust me. And even if we did, it would be worth it."

"I'll... uh... have to take a rain check on that," he said. "Sorry."

She pouted a little but didn't push the issue any further. At least not yet.

What she did do was keep feeding him drinks. She gave him another cup of spiked coffee and then a Chivas and Coke. By the time he finished these he was starting to buzz, his better judgment retreating towards the back of his brain... again.

It was after his fifth drink, as they were cruising at 38,000 feet over central Missouri, and as Janice was snoring lightly beside him, that he gave in. He exchanged a few words with Laura, receiving his instructions, and then she disappeared. He waited five minutes and then stood up and walked back to the far end of the first-class section, past the staircase and into the flight attendant's quarters. There was a warming kitchen, several coffee pots, and a bar back here. The bartender was a fortyish woman who looked at him knowingly.

"I think you need the bathroom, don't you?" she asked him, giving a wink. "It's that door right there. Just go on in."

He went on in. Laura was waiting for him there, her pantyhose and panties wadded up and tossed into the small sink, lust in her eyes. She kissed him hotly, sticking her tongue into his mouth. He let his hands go to work, squeezing her bare ass with one, fingering her wet vagina with the other. She moaned into his mouth and then broke the embrace. She dropped to her knees, unbuttoning his jeans and tugging them to his feet. She took his hardness into her mouth and began to suck, delivering a blowjob with a precision and skill that equaled that of the best groupie he'd been with.

She brought him nearly to the brink and then suddenly pulled free.

"Sit on the toilet," she hissed at him. "I want to fuck you."

He sat on the toilet. She stepped forward and pulled up her skirt, showing him that she was indeed a natural redhead. She squatted over him and started to lower herself down. He grabbed her butt and stopped her.

"Wait a second," he told her.

"What?" she asked, panting.

"I need to put a rubber on," he said, reaching down to extract his wallet from his pants. He never left home without at least two condoms in there.

"You don't need that," she told him, trying to force herself down now that one of his hands had come free. "I'm on the pill."

"Actually, I do need it," he said, pushing her back up a little. "It's in my contract."

"In your contract?" she asked, confused.

"Yeah," he said, finally getting the wallet. "One of those clauses they put in. You know how it is?"

While she puzzled over this he extracted the wallet and then the condom from within it. It was not actually a part of his contract of course, but he'd had enough lectures on the horrors of sexually transmitted diseases and paternity suits to make sure he never rode bareback. He opened the condom and rolled it expertly into place.

Laura sighed a little. Though Jake would never know it, she actually was *not* on the pill and was in fact in the middle of the most fertile part of her cycle. Her vague hopes of getting herself pregnant by what she assumed was a filthy rich rock star were dashed, but at least she still could still get half of what she was after. She sank her body down on Jake's cock, engulfing him within her. She then began to buck up and down, moaning while she kissed him.

Jake knew there was little chance of actually giving her an orgasm in such a cramped and nervous environment. He held on for about five minutes—enough time to qualify as a respectable performance—kissing her, feeling her ass, whispering nasty things in her ear, before allowing himself to let go and fill the condom with his sperm.

When they stood back up he removed the rubber and tied a knot in it. He then personally flushed it down the toilet, adhering to another rule that had been ground into him by National's security experts: *If you're going to leave a used rubber lying around where some bitch can pick it up, you might as well just fuck 'em without it.* By this point in his career his mind was so jaded by his profession he didn't even stop to think that normal men did not have to worry about such things.

They cleaned up and then exited the bathroom. The bartender gave them both another wink but said nothing. They did not get caught.

Jake returned to his seat and was soon fast asleep. He didn't wake up until they were on final descent to LAX.

*****

A limousine dropped Jake off in front of the twenty-eight-story Esnob Pinchazo Tower building in downtown Los Angeles. The driver opened the door for him and he stepped out, duffel bag in hand.

"Now remember," Janice told him, "we have that movie premier on Saturday night."

"I remember," Jake told her. As if he could forget. He had been dreading the experience ever since being told about it two weeks ago.

"I'm sure Manny will remind you and see that you're dressed in the tux we're sending over." She was referring to Manny Mariposa, the live-in maid/butler/cook who had been hired for him.

"I'm sure he will," Jake said.

"And do try on that pentagram medallion we gave you," she said. "It would look so... you know... Satanic if you wore it with your tux."

"I threw the pentagram medallion in the garbage," Jake said. "Don't send another one."

Janice feigned hurt feelings. "That was a gift, Jake," she said. "Mr. Acardio himself picked that out for you."

"And deducted the cost of it from my recoupables, no doubt. I'm not wearing a pentagram or anything else besides the tux, Janice. That's final."

She shook her head. "Sometimes you're just so resistant to the image enhancement program we're running, Jake. Don't you know we're just trying to look out for your interests?"

Jake snorted in disgust. "Goodbye, Janice," he said. "Nice traveling with you."

Before she could say anything else, he walked away, heading for the main lobby door.

"Good afternoon, Mr. Kingsley," said the uniformed doorman who guarded the entrance to the upscale residential building. "Did you have a nice trip?"

"Did you catch *Wake Up USA* this morning?" Jake asked him.

"Yes sir, I did," he said.

"Then you know what kind of trip I had."

The doorman nodded, unfazed. "Can I get someone to help you with your bag, sir?"

"No, thanks," Jake said. "I think I can manage."

"Very good, sir," he said and held the door open.

Jake entered the plush lobby and walked directly to the elevators. There were two other residents of the building standing there waiting. One was Steve O'Riley, a flamboyant weatherman on one of the local news channels. The other was Tanya Harrigan, an aging character actress whose specialty was playing a mother in made-for-television movies and after school specials. They both nodded to him, displaying as little recognition as they could socially get away with. Though the building was full of two-bit actors, local television personalities, and other minor league celebrities, most of them chose to snub Jake when they ran into him. They seemed to think that a Satan-worshipping rock musician didn't belong in their beloved high-class building. Jake had been told by one of the doormen he was friendly with that there had even been a meeting of the owner's group in which they had tried—unsuccessfully—to initiate the eviction process on both him and Bill, who also lived in the building. The only time any of them talked to him at all was when they were out of cocaine and couldn't find their dealer and, assuming Jake was a raving coke-fiend, tried to beg some off of him.

Tanya got off the elevator on the sixth floor. O'Riley got off on the ninth. Jake then rode alone all the way up to the twenty-fourth floor, where the larger condos were. He stepped out into a spacious, lushly carpeted hallway that was lined with oil paintings and walked sixty feet to his front door. He opened it with a key and stepped inside the place he was currently calling home.

He had to admit, it was a really nice condo they'd set him up with. It had three bedrooms, including an eight hundred square foot master bedroom that featured an oversized bath, a separate shower, and a six-person Jacuzzi. The living room was quite large as well and was furnished in expensive leather. There was a sixty-two inch projection television with premium cable, a stereo VCR, and a laser-disc player. Next to that, in a separate cabinet, was a top-of-the-line stereo system that included a turntable, dual cassette players, a receiver, and even one of those new-fangled compact disc players, although this last was little more than a novelty since hardly any music was being released on CDs as of yet. All of these audio and visual components could be activated and adjusted by a variety of remote controls that stood on the smoked glass coffee table before the couch. On the far side of the living room were a huge picture window and a sliding glass door that led out to a spacious balcony that overlooked downtown LA. On the near side of the room was a fully stocked and operational oak wet bar.

Yes, it was a really nice place to stay and it was the only place Jake could refer to as "home" at the moment, but it wasn't really his. The luxury condo was leased by National Records and had been assigned to Jake as part of the "housing assistance" clause of his contract. What this clause stated was that if one of the undersigned was unable to secure housing between or during contract periods, the label would provide housing appropriate to the "perceived public status expected of a person of their stature". The label would also provide necessary groceries, clothing, toiletries, grooming supplies, and, of course, "entertainment items". There was also a clause in there about providing a "manservant" if such a thing was deemed appropriate.

It went without saying, of course, that the cost of all of this was being deducted from the recoupable expenses account. Jake had asked for and received a copy of one of his monthly expense reports and was unsurprised to find that all of this luxury was running him an average of eight thousand dollars a month. And that did not even account for the cost of the limousines he rode in whenever he went somewhere or the cash allowance of one thousand dollars he was given every two weeks.

"Can't you set me up in a smaller place?" he'd asked at one point. "Just a little apartment in Hollywood somewhere? I can drive my own car and use my cash allowance for groceries."

"Remember the contract clause, Jake," Acardio responded. "We need to keep you in a place appropriate to your stature. People don't want to see a famous rock star living in some shithole Hollywood Boulevard dive. They want to see you in luxury. They don't want to see you driving some piece of shit car. They want to see you in a limo."

"But what about that manservant guy," Jake asked next.

"Manny? You don't like Manny? He came highly recommended."

"And he comes highly expensive as well," Jake said. "He's costing me two grand a month in salary and god knows how much in food. I can do my own laundry and clean my own house."

"We've found it best over the years if our musicians have someone take care of those duties for them. After all, we do have guests come over to your condo from time to time. We prefer that things remain professionally clean when such occurrences happen."

"So I can't get rid of Manny?"

"You're looking at this the wrong way, Jake. You're living in the lap of luxury. You should be grateful we're providing all of this for you."

And that had pretty much been the end of the discussion. Jake had made a phone call to Pauline later that day and asked her to peruse her copy of the contract again.

"Can they force me to live in this place and make me have to pay for everything associated with it?" he asked her. "Isn't there any way I can demand they put me in some place cheaper?"

She'd looked it over while he'd waited on the phone and her answer had been, incredibly enough, yes, they could and no he couldn't.

"They could put you up in some apartment in the middle of Watts or in a six million dollar mansion in Malibu with a complete staff of servants if they wanted to. Unless you're able to independently secure your own housing and pay for it out of your pocket, you have to live where they say."

And of course, he couldn't pay for even the Watts apartment out of his own pocket. He had no cash flow of his own. Though the royalties were pouring in from the sales of the album and all the singles, and though the tour they'd completed had sold out every venue and had actually made money instead of losing it (a rarity among tours), the recoupable expenses were still eating up more than twice as much income as the royalties were bringing in. On the day *Descent Into Nothing* went platinum the band as a whole was more than ninety thousand dollars in the red. And now that the tour was over and the housing expenses were being deducted as well they were going even deeper into the hole.

As Jake closed the door behind him, Manny emerged through the kitchen door, smiling. Manny was forty years old but looked much younger. He was exquisitely fit, a flaming, lisping homosexual, and, like many menially employed people in the greater Los Angeles area, a frustrated actor. Though he was always polite, even when Jake wasn't, and though Jake had actually learned to like having a manservant, he instinctively knew where Manny's real loyalties lie. He was just another babysitter, just another spy for National Records who would report anything Jake said or did to Acardio if he deemed it something Acardio would want to know about.

"Jake," Manny greeted. "It's good to see you back. How was your trip?"

"Just groovy," Jake said, closing the door behind him and walking over to the couch. "What's that you're cooking? It smells funny."

"Hasenpfeffer," Manny said.

"A rabbit?" Jake asked. "You're cooking me a rabbit for dinner?"

"Oh, you've heard of it?"

Jake nodded. "Yeah, on a Bugs Bunny cartoon."

Manny looked at him strangely for a moment and then decided not to pursue the Bugs Bunny reference. Instead, he rushed over to take Jake's duffel bag. "Let me take this to the laundry room for you. I'll get everything washed up and put away before I go to bed tonight."

"Sure," Jake said, relinquishing possession of the bag.

"Can I get you a drink?"

"Naw," Jake told him. "You go back to stewing your rabbit. I'm gonna go take a shower and change. I'll get my own drink when I'm done."

"As you wish," Manny said, giving a polite little bow. With that, he whisked the duffel bag off towards the laundry room.

Jake locked the bedroom door behind him and then took a long, luxuriant shower, washing the smell of the redhead stewardess from his body. He dried off, dropping the towel into a laundry hamper Manny had installed and then put on a pair of baggy sweat pants and a loose fitting T-shirt. He sat down at his desk in the corner of the room and looked at the telephone. Like a Pavlov reaction, thoughts of Angie came flitting into his head. He still knew her telephone number. Assuming she was on the same schedule she had been on before the tour, he could dial that number right now and be talking to her in less than twenty seconds.

He sighed as he thought about it. "You're so pathetic," he told himself.

He still hadn't spoken to her since that last day, when they'd climbed on the bus to head for their first concert in Bangor. Even when they'd actually been in Los Angeles for three concerts, when he could have called her from the hotel room phone, he hadn't done it. That had been when the *Spinning Rock* article was all everyone was talking about. He'd told himself he couldn't face her after that, that she wouldn't want to speak to him. And then when they'd returned to Los Angeles after the tour, when they'd set him up in this condo, he hadn't called her then either. She lived less than six miles away and he couldn't bring himself to contact her.

Call her now, a part of his mind whispered. *Pick up that fucking phone and* call *her. She could come over tonight and you could talk to her. Maybe she'll be disgusted with what you've become, with the things you've done, but then, maybe she'll understand. Wasn't that always the best part of your relationship with her? She was a girlfriend, not just a slut you fucked. You could talk to her, relate to her, tell her your fears and frustrations and she would listen and commiserate.*

He picked up the phone. But he didn't dial Angie's number. Instead he called Bill, who lived in a smaller condo just three floors down.

"Hey, Jake," Bill said, his voice a little strained. "Caught you on the show this morning. Had to get up with this overindulgence syndrome to do it, but I caught you."

"Yeah, that asshole fucked me over pretty good," Jake said.

"It wasn't very aesthetic," Bill had to agree. "You just get back?"

"Yeah. You must've gone out last night if you got the overindulgence syndrome again."

"Indeed, I did," he said. "Matt and I went to the Pink Flamingo Club again."

The Pink Flamingo Club was a trendy Los Angeles nightclub near downtown. It was one of eleven such places they were allowed to frequent, which was to say that they were on the list of places their limo drivers would take them to. Though it had never been admitted to them, Jake was pretty sure that National Records had some sort of endorsement contract with the establishments on the list. If they tried to go someplace not on the list, the limo drivers would refuse. And it had been threatened that if any of them used their allowance money to call a cab and go someplace not on the list on their own, the allowance money would be cut off for a month.

"Did you get laid?" Jake asked.

"I think so," Bill said. "Two of my prophylactics were gone when I woke up and there was a pair of panties next to my bed."

"That's usually a reliable sign. Were they nice panties?"

"Pink bikini cut," Bill said. "Size small."

"Well, odds are she was hot. What're you doing now?"

"Laying around in my pajamas and waiting for my headache to go away."

"Why don't you come upstairs?" Jake asked. "We'll burn some and then eat the hasenpfeffer Manny is making for me."

"Hasenpfeffer?" Bill asked. "You mean like on Bugs Bunny?"

"That's the stuff," Jake said. "You in?"

"I'm in," Bill said.

Bill came up ten minutes later, unshaven, dressed in a pair of knee-length shorts that showed off his knobby knees and a tank top that showed off his skinny arms. His coke-bottle glasses were resting in their accustomed place and his crew cut was only two days old.

"Would you care for a drink, Mr. Archer?" Manny asked after inviting him inside.

"I'll get the drinks, Manny," Jake told him. "You go get the stash and load up the bong for us."

"As you wish," Manny said, disappearing into the kitchen.

Jake mixed Bill his favorite drink, Crown Royal and 7up. He mixed himself a potent concoction of coke and imported Jamaican rum. They settled in before the television set just as Manny came back carrying a hand-blown glass bong filled with ice water and a lemon slice. He set it down before them and then handed Jake a silver container filled with high-grade marijuana.

"Would you care for me to load the water pipe for you?" Manny asked.

"Naw, go stew your rabbit," Jake told him. "We'll manage on our own."

And they did. They took three hits apiece and then sipped quietly on their drinks. They talked about going out to one of the clubs but eventually decided not to. Instead they engaged in one of their more frequent activities, playing video games on the Atari 2600 console. They played Space Invaders and Missile Command until it was time to eat. After destroying Manny's hasenpfeffer they smoked some more weed and played for another three hours, drinking all the while.

It was a fulfilling evening.

*****

The next morning a limousine picked up Jake at 8:30 in the morning. He was clean-shaven and dressed in a pair of dress slacks and a dress shirt. The driver cruised through the congested downtown streets until he arrived at the Maton Pauvrete building, which was yet another higher end condominium building full of second rate celebrities. This was where Matt had been assigned to live. He had a huge suite up on the twenty-first floor of the twenty-three-story building.

The driver opened the door and Matt stepped inside, finding a seat directly across from Jake. He was dressed a little more casually for the meeting they were about to attend, as was typical. He wore stonewashed jeans and a T-shirt he'd picked up during a recent day-trip to Mexico. The logo on the shirt was an advertisement for a popular Tijuana brothel Matt had visited and eventually been kicked out of.

"Wassup, brother," he greeted as he lit up a cigarette. "Caught you on the tube yesterday. Pretty fucked up showing."

"Yeah," Jake agreed. "It was about as much fun as a rectal exam."

They were driven to Hollywood and dropped off in front of the National Records Building. A group of tourists that had been wandering by spotted them and quickly swarmed them. They signed ten or fifteen autographs apiece before managing to break free and make it to the main lobby entrance. There they were admitted to the elevator by an aging security guard. The rode up to the eighteenth floor and were led by yet another security guard into a conference room.

Sitting at the table in the room were Max Acardio, Shaver, Rick Bailey from the Artist Development Department, and, of course, Janice Boxer, their publicity manager. All had cups of coffee and plates of bagels before them. A cocaine mirror sat in the middle of the table, residue plainly visible on it.

"Matt, Jake," Acardio greeted, getting up to give them the obligatory hug of greeting. "How are you doing this morning?"

They both grunted that they were fine and then took a seat.

"We were just enjoying a little Bolivian flake while we waited for you," Shaver said. "Would you boys like me to set you up?"

"No, thanks," both answered, making a point to be as cool to Shaver as possible. While he was still technically their agent, they no longer met with him, sought out his advice, or even talked to him. While it was true he had opened the door for them in the recording industry their gratefulness for that was overridden by the fact that he had allowed them to be screwed by their contract while he himself had been nicely taken care of and was currently raking in twenty-one percent of all their royalties before any deductions were taken out. They had tried to fire him when National decided to exercise their second option on the contract, but they were unable. *Intemperance*'s contract with Shaver specified that he would be their agent for the duration of any contract he secured with the recording industry, including any option periods. It hadn't seemed like a big deal back in the beginning, when the goal had simply been to secure a contract in the first place, but it was certainly a big deal now.

"I will take some of that coffee though," Jake told Acardio. "If it's not too much trouble."

"Of course not," Acardio replied. He rang for his secretary.

The coffee was poured and Jake took a sip. It was excellent brew, imported directly from Costa Rica.

Acardio, the chairperson of the meeting, passed a few more preliminaries and then got to business. "Let me start off by saying that we at the label appreciate all of the traveling you two, as well as the rest of the band, have been doing in order to keep the album promotion machinery rolling. I know we've had some problems with each other, that we don't always see eye to eye on a lot of matters, but you've been very good sports about all this, particularly you, Jake. The way Brad Cummins treated you was appalling, absolutely un-called for."

"I thought you wanted him to treat me that way," Jake said.

"Well, we wanted controversy of course," Acardio said. "It does sell your albums, after all. But we weren't expecting him to be quite that brutal. I apologize for putting you into that particular position."

"Yeah," Jake said, not believing him for an instant.

"Anyway," Acardio said, "we've spent the last two weeks going over the recordings you boys made for us. I must say, you did a very good job with that primitive equipment."

The recordings he was referring to were a cassette tape full of music the band had recorded in the small warehouse the label had rented for them to rehearse and compose in (the cost of which was being deducted from their recoupables as well). The recording quality was only expected to be good enough for the National executive to hear what the raw songs sounded like so they could decide which to use. The lyrics did not even have to be discernable since lyric sheets were provided with the recording. As such, the only equipment they had been provided in order to produce the recording were an old mixing board and a commercial cassette recorder. No technicians of any kind had been assigned to assist them.

"It's very simple," Acardio had instructed. "Just plug everything into the mixing board, turn all the dials up to about mid-range, put the cassette in the machine, and start playing. Give us at least twelve songs, more if you got them. It shouldn't take you more than an afternoon."

It had actually taken three afternoons to record fifteen songs. Bill took control of the mixing board and sound checked and adjusted each and every input as carefully and anally as he used to oversee their sound checks at D Street West. The end result had been not exactly a studio-quality recording but about as close as it was possible to get without actually utilizing the resources of a studio.

"Thank you," Jake said. "We did work very hard on that, particularly Bill."

"There are some catchy tunes in there," Acardio said. "We're pretty sure we can use about half of them.

"Half?" Matt asked. "That's it?"

"That right," Acardio replied. "Here's a list of the songs we've decided on." He passed out slips of memo paper to Jake and Matt. They looked at them carefully, both noting that "about half" meant seven out of the fifteen selections.

"As you can see," Acardio said. "Most of the tunes we've selected were the un-recorded tunes you performed during the tour as filler. The audience response was good enough that we are almost obligated to include those selections on the next album. It's obvious, however, that we're going to need a few more songs from you before we start the recording process."

"We don't have any more songs," Jake said. This was literally the truth. The fifteen they'd presented were all songs they'd written and performed in the D Street West days. They had come up with nothing new since then, as they had had neither the time nor the inclination. Jake had not even sat down and strummed on his guitar—the process he used when composing new material—since before they'd released *Descent Into Nothing*.

"We need ten cuts for the album," Acardio said. "We can possibly get away with nine if you extend one of the less commercially viable tunes into a non-radio format length. That's what *Earthstone* generally does."

"Or we could use some of these songs you rejected," Jake said.

"No," Acardio said. "That's out of the question."

"What the fuck for?" Matt asked. "I mean, sure, a few of those are maybe a little simple—it's some of our earliest stuff—but you've also shitcanned some of our best work here. How about *It's In The Book*? The D Street crowd loved that one, but you keep rejecting it. You wouldn't let us record it for the first album, you wouldn't let us use it as filler on the tour, and now you don't want it on the second album either."

Janice fielded this one. "It is a reasonably catchy tune," she said, "but I'm afraid it's too controversial. The subject matter, you know."

"Excuse me?" Jake said. "Too controversial? Do you even know what the song is about?"

"Of course we know what it's about," Janice said. "It's a grotesque and highly offensive parody of the Bible."

"It's an examination of the negative values taught by the Bible," Jake corrected. "And a condemnation of religious hypocrisy."

"We can't release an anti-biblical piece," Acardio said. "The controversy would be too severe."

"Let me get this straight," Jake said carefully. "You're trying to make us out to be a bunch of Satan worshipping pagans because you think that sells albums, but you don't want an anti-bible song on our next album? Am I missing something here?"

"You're not following the context under which we're rejecting it," Janice said.

"Well, please enlighten us then," Jake said.

"It's too specifically insulting to the Bible," she explained. "Though you don't mention the scriptures by name, it's very obvious what you're talking about. We want any anti-religious or anti-biblical lyrics to be deniably vague. Like the lyrics for *Descent Into Nothing*. That's a perfect example of a deliberately vague satanic song."

"*Descent Into Nothing* is *not* about Satanism," Jake hissed angrily.

"Exactly," Janice said. "That's what we say when the censorship nuts or the family values people start complaining about it. The lyrics are vague enough so they can't point out a specific reference to the tenants of anti-religious doctrine."

"The song has nothing to do with religion," Jake said. "It's about..."

"It doesn't matter what your interpretation of the lyrics is," Acardio cut in (once again infuriating Jake with the suggestion that he didn't know what his own song was about). "The point is that *Descent* is vague and unspecific, only hinting at the Satanist theme that it encompasses. *It's In The Book*, on the other hand, is specific in its content and would give the censorship freaks something solid to latch onto. Our goal is to make you controversial, even hated by certain classes of people, but not to step over the line to the point where people might actually start to consider real censorship of music. If that happens, this entire industry could flounder."

"And that means less money for all of us," Bailey said.

"Oh, well we certainly wouldn't want to make less money, now, would we?" Jake said sarcastically.

"I'm not going to get into that discussion with you again, Jake," Acardio said firmly. "You are bound by the terms of your contract and that's all there is to it. You are also bound to produce another album for us and you're short a few songs. Now let's talk about what we're going to do about that, okay?"

"Fine," Jake said. "I guess we could try to compose a few more songs for you. There's a few ideas I've been mulling over in my head lately."

"Yeah," Matt said. "Me too. I've been thinking about doing a song about..."

"Uh, well actually," Acardio said, "I think we might have already solved the problem for you."

"Come again?" Jake said.

"Well, obviously it takes you guys a little while to compose and perfect a new tune," he said. "And quite frankly, we need to get you into the studio as soon as possible so we can get the second album finished and ready for release when *Descent Into Nothing* finally starts to fade off the charts. We're on the crest of a wave here and we want to stay up there. There should be little or no lag time between album successes. Before people start to get sick of hearing the songs from *Descent* on the radio, we need to be able to give them some new ones."

"I'm down with that," Matt said. "But how are you going to help?"

"Mr. Bailey can answer that," Acardio said.

"Right," Bailey said, opening his briefcase and pulling out two packets of papers. "Over the past two months I've been working with some of our songwriting teams to put together some new material for you. They came up with a selection of eight tunes that we feel would be both commercially viable as single releases while maintaining the *Intemperance* image."

"Whoa whoa whoa," Matt said. "Hold on just a goddamn second here. Are you saying you had songwriters come up with music that you want us to play and put on an album with our name on it? Is that what the fuck you're trying to say?"

"No need to get hostile, Matt," Acardio said. "We're not trying to insult you or anything; it's just that our songwriters have a better idea of what the public is after in an *Intemperance* style song than you do. They've been around a long time and they know what the demographic group you appeal to wants. It's a very common thing in the industry."

"Yes," Bailey agreed, "and I must say that we utilized our best people for this project and they outdid themselves both with the lyrics and the melodies. When people hear Jake sing this stuff and when they hear Matt grinding out the riffs in that quaint style of his, they're going to go insane. The next album is going to fly off the shelves. I guarantee it."

"They really are very good tunes," Janice added. "I looked them over yesterday. Quite frankly, I think they're much better than anything you did on *Descent* and look at how well that album is selling."

Matt was actually starting to turn red in the face. Jake wasn't too far behind him. Before either of them could say anything, however, Bailey pushed the papers over to each of them. They were music sheets that covered the basic melody and the lyrics. They each looked at the top sheet, which was for a song entitled, *Embrace of Darkness.*

"That first song is what we're thinking of naming the new album," Bailey said excitedly. "Look it over. Tell us what you think."

Matt clenched his fists a few times and then, more out of morbid curiosity than anything else, he looked at the sheet, ignoring the lyrics and checking out the music. "You call this a riff?" he asked after about two seconds. "It's a simple three-chord repetition, just like that crap *Voyeur* plays."

"Well, you'll be given a little bit of latitude in how you interpret the music," Bailey said. "I mean, you can't change the basic melody, but you can enhance it in that style you have."

Jake, meanwhile, had been looking at the lyrics. He was shaking his head in disbelief. "*Goodbye to light, goodbye to joy,*" he recited. "*The King of Darkness uses me like a toy?*"

"The fucking King of Darkness?" Matt said. "Uses me like a toy? Are you shitting me?"

Jake read a little further down. "*I feel his hands upon me, I feel him pulling me in. My awareness is full now, I'm jumping down into sin.*" He looked up at the record execs. "Isn't that a bit homo-erotic?"

"Well, in a vague sort of way, I suppose it is," Bailey said. "I mean, after all, you are *Intemperance* and you do represent lust and sin."

"You're suggesting that Jake sing about getting butt-fucked by the Devil?" Matt asked.

"It doesn't say anything in there about the Devil or about anal sex," Janice said. "Like Mr. Acardio said, the lyrics are kept deliberately vague."

"Well you can throw this shit deliberately in the trash can," Matt told her. "We ain't playing this crap."

"Amen to that," Jake said.

Acardio sighed. "Look guys," he said. "A lot of people worked a lot of hours to compose this music for you."

"I hope you didn't pay 'em too much," Matt said.

"They probably paid them as much as we get paid," Jake said, causing both of them to crack up.

"Look," Acardio said, losing his decorum just a bit, "we don't care whether you like the songs or not. You are employees of National Records and those are the songs we want you to do. So, my suggestion is that you pick out at least three you can live with and start rehearsing them. I'll want a preliminary recording of your efforts on my desk in two weeks."

"Oh, and I must insist that *Embrace of Darkness* be among the three," Bailey said. "We're already working on the premise that that will be the name of the album."

"Right," Acardio said. "Pick out two of your favorites in addition to *Embrace*, which will be mandatory."

"No," Matt said firmly. "I don't give a rat's ass what you want; we are not performing any of this crap. We write our own songs and compose our own melodies."

Acardio took a deep breath. He looked at Jake. "Jake," he said reasonably. "You need to try to talk some sense into Matt. If we don't have a complete set of songs from you by the end of the month some very unpleasant consequences might occur."

"What kind of consequences?" Jake asked.

"Breach of contract kind of consequences," Acardio said.

Matt stood up so fast his chair fell over backwards. His hand went to his crotch and gave it a large, contemptuous squeeze. "I got your fuckin' contract right here," he told Acardio. "We ain't performing that shit! Period! I don't care if the United States Supreme fucking Court calls me up and tells me I have to. It ain't gonna happen. I will not play a song that some ass-sucking hacker wrote for you."

"Matt, there's no need to get threatening," Janice said nervously.

"Who's threatening?" Matt responded. "I'm doing nothing but stating a plain fucking fact. We ain't gonna do it."

"Jake," Acardio said, appealing to the calmer head. "What do you have to say about this?"

Jake stood up next to Matt. "I say that any productivity we might've hoped to achieve in this meeting has probably been lost. I think it's time to adjourn for the day."

"We need to settle this *now*," Acardio said firmly.

"It's already settled," Matt said. "You can hold a fuckin' gun to my head and I ain't playing that shit."

"Why don't we meet on Monday?" Jake suggested.

"You aren't thinking about caving to this fuck, are you, Jake?" Matt suddenly asked. "Because even if you do, I still ain't doing this shit!"

"I'm not thinking of doing anything right now, Matt," Jake told him. "But I think it's time for us to go, okay?"

"We need to work this out," Bailey cried.

"There's nothing to work out," Acardio said. "You're doing the songs we tell you to do."

"I'll live in a skid-row flophouse before I play one of them songs," Matt said. "See if I'm kidding, Acardio. See if I'm fucking kidding!"

"You see if *I'm* fucking kidding," Acardio returned. "You will fall into line and do what you're told or your music career is over!"

"We're leaving now," Jake said, grabbing Matt by the arm. "We'll be back on Monday. Have your secretary call me to set up a time."

"You two need to get back here and..."

"Goodbye," Jake said, leading Matt out the door. Matt reluctantly allowed himself to be pulled from the room. The last thing they heard was Acardio yelling at them to take the fucking music sheets with them.

They didn't talk until they got into the elevator. At that point Matt turned on Jake with a fury.

"What the fuck do you think you're doing, dragging me out of there like that?" he demanded. "Why the fuck weren't you supporting me?"

"I am supporting you," Jake told him. "I have no intention of singing any of that crap they wrote for us."

"Then why the fuck didn't you say that? Why were you letting me just yell at those pricks by myself?"

"Because this isn't the time to make a stand on this," Jake told him.

"What?"

"We don't have enough facts right now."

"Facts? What the fuck are you..."

"Look," Jake interrupted, "I don't think they can really force us to sing those songs. I've read that entire contract now and, though I still don't understand a lot of it, I don't remember it saying anywhere that they have the right to force us to sing songs we don't want to sing."

"So why the fuck didn't you tell them that?" he asked.

"Because I want to be absolutely sure of what our legal position is before I start spouting off."

"So, what are you going to do?"

"I need to talk to Pauline," he said.

*****

The movie premier that Jake and Matt had been pretty much ordered to attend (their contract stated they were required to make themselves available for public appearances as arranged by the record company—this was without compensation, of course, with only travel being paid for) was for a film called *Thinner Than Water*. Neither Jake nor Matt knew anything about it other than it starred Mindy Snow and Veronica Julius, two of the hottest young female actors on the movie scene today, though two polar opposites as far as public image went.

Mindy Snow was the epitome of the innocent girl next door. She was beautiful, of course, but in a wholesome, family values sort of way. She had been one of the stars of a popular prime time series called *The Slow Lane*, which was about life in a small midwestern town in the fifties. She had played the churchgoing, overly religious younger sister of the family. America had watched her grow from a sweet and innocent twelve-year-old to a sweet and innocent sixteen year old during the four years the series had been on the air. She was now twenty years old and had been in two movies since then, her character always a copy of the sweet and innocent role she'd portrayed in the series.

Veronica Julius was also beautiful, but in a way that was not so innocent. She too had been in a popular prime-time series but she had played a troubled, street-wise teenager in a dysfunctional family. Her movie roles had become ever more risqué since then, with her playing a young drug addict, a young rape victim, and the villainous vamp in a horror flick.

"Tell me again why we have to go to this thing?" Jake asked Janice—who, naturally, had been sent to accompany them and act as their babysitter—as they rode in the limousine towards the Bentley Brooks Theater in Hollywood.

"Yeah," Matt agreed, tugging at the bowtie on his neck. "And why do we have to wear these fucking tuxedos? I think I'm breaking out in a rash from this thing."

Janice sighed, her patented *why do I have to put up with such uncouth barbarians* sigh. "You have to go because it will get your faces in the entertainment magazines and therefore give you publicity," she explained. "And you have to wear a tuxedo because that is simply how it is done in Hollywood. It's a black-tie affair."

"Well who invited us?" Jake asked. "Why do the people throwing this gig want us there?"

"This is a film aimed at the fifteen to eighteen and the eighteen to twenty-five female demographic," Janice replied.

"So, it's a teenybopper chick flick," Matt said.

Janice actually winced at that description but nodded. "Yes," she said. "And that particular demographic also happens to be a big part of the *Intemperance* fan base. Therefore, the girls who will be interested in this film are the same ones who buy your records. Your presence at this affair is helpful to National Records and to Galaxy Studios."

"I see," Matt said, nodding wisely. "W hat's this flick about, anyway?"

"It's about two sisters," Janice said. "One is wholesome and innocent, the other is somewhat of a... well, a girl without morals."

"A goody two shoes bitch and a slut?" Matt asked.

Janice winced again. "I suppose," she said. "Anyway, the story apparently centers around their uneasy relationship with each other, particularly when they both become attracted to the same guy. The guy is played by Mark Dennison."

"The guy who used to play the quarterback on that stupid-ass TV show about high school football?" Jake asked.

"That's him," Janice confirmed. "He's quite popular among that particular demographic as well."

"I heard he's a dick smoker," Matt said. "Is that true?"

"Well... yes, he is a homosexual, but that's a Hollywood secret. Don't go saying anything about that to any reporters you encounter."

"It ain't a very well-kept secret if Matt knows about it," Jake said.

Janice was starting to get flustered. "Look, you guys," she said. "This is a high society event you're attending here. Some of the elite of Hollywood will be there. Now just watch the movie and then we'll go into the lobby where a cocktail party has been set up. Try to mind your P's and Q's as much as possible, okay?"

"They gonna have any good blow at this party?" Matt asked.

"How about the bar?" Jake asked. "Are the drinks free, or do we have to pay for them?"

Janice sighed, already trying to figure out how big of a disaster this was going to be.

The limousine pulled up in front of the theater and the three of them emerged into a sea of onlookers. There were dozens of photographers and videographers stationed just on the other side of a purple velvet rope that separated the walkway into the theater from the sidewalk. Flashbulbs began to explode all around them, effectively blinding them as they made their way to the doors. Jake could hear astonished whispers as the crowd asked themselves if that was *really* Jake Kingsley and Matt Tisdale. A few of the reporters shouted questions at them but they overlapped each other to the point where they could understand nothing being said.

Two doormen were guarding the entrance. They asked for no passes or tickets from any of them. They simply greeted them all by name, including Janice, and stepped aside, allowing entry. Jake was so flash-blinded that it took a few moments for his vision to clear enough for him to make out the details of the room. When it did, he whistled in appreciation.

"Holy shit," Matt said. "Look at this fucking place."

"No shit," Jake agreed.

The entire lobby was covered in plush red carpet. Hors d'oeuvre tables covered in silk tablecloths were located in several strategic locations and featured a large variety of appetizers, everything from escargot to expensive salami and cheese to stuffed mushrooms. The smell alone was intoxicating. On the far side of the room a large bar had been set up (the drinks were indeed free, according to Janice, but they had been instructed to "please go easy"). Circulating through the crowd were two lovely young women in cocktail dresses. They carried trays upon which glasses of champagne were sitting. And everywhere were men in tuxedos and elegantly dressed and made-up women, most of them beautiful. Nor was that even the most amazing thing. A sizeable portion of the people were celebrities. Jake saw a multitude of actors and actresses he had seen in television shows and on movies. They were circulating around, sipping from champagne or mixed drinks, talking and hugging and giving fake little cheek kisses to each other. He stared from place to place in wonder, marveling over the fact that many of the actors looked much smaller than they did on screen.

"Oh man," Matt said, his eyes flitting from place to place. "We have got to score ourselves some pussy at this place, Jake. I need to tap me an actress. Talk about the fuckfest coup of the century."

"Matt," Janice warned, "you are not here for cheap fornication. This is a very public event."

"Don't worry, Janice," he said. "We'll be sure to fuck privately."

"Oh sweet Lord," Janice muttered, and then closed her mouth as a middle-aged woman in a hideous-looking strapless dress approached them.

"Janice," she said, holding out her hands for a hug. "How are you doing, darling? Thank you so much for coming."

As Janice and the woman hugged and exchanged one of the fake cheek kisses, Matt turned to Jake and asked, "Who the fuck is that?"

Jake shrugged.

"This is Georgette Minden," Janice said, shooting them a look. "She is Mindy Snow's agent and one of the hosts of this premier."

"Ahhh," Matt said. "I see. How you doing? Nice shindig you got going here."

"You would have to be Matt Tisdale," Georgette said, stepping forward and giving him a hug and a fake kiss. "I'm very glad you could show up tonight, Mr. Tisdale."

"Like I had a choice," Matt muttered.

"Matt," Janice hissed.

Georgette ignored this exchange. Instead, she turned to Jake. "And you, of course, are the somewhat infamous Jake Kingsley."

"That's me," Jake agreed, submitting to her as she pushed her ample bosom into his chest and made a smacking noise near his left ear.

"You know, Mindy is a big fan of your music," Georgette told them. "She absolutely adores you."

"Oh yeah?" Matt asked, a twinkle starting in his eye.

"Of course, we don't announce that to the public," Georgette said. "It would be bad for her image."

"Of course," Jake said.

"Anyway, why don't you all follow me and meet the stars of the show?"

"Why the fuck not?" Matt said.

The three stars in question were standing near the back of the room, just adjacent to the entrance of the actual theater. Mark Dennison was a handsome, exquisitely fit young man with capped teeth and a prize-winning smile. He was decked out in a custom fit tuxedo and wore a Rolex watch on his wrist. Mindy Snow and Veronica Julius, both of whom were wearing expensive and elaborate formal dresses, flanked him. Mindy's dress was very conservative, almost borderline prudish. It was light blue and completely covered her shoulders. Only the smallest amount of her ample bosom was showing. Veronica, on the other hand, was wearing a skimpy red dress that left very little to the imagination. Her back was bare, her breasts were nearly falling out of it, and her legs, clad in black nylon, were exposed well past the knees.

"They're certainly keeping up with their images, aren't they?" Jake whispered as they approached.

"Well, naturally," Georgette said. "Image is everything in Hollywood."

The introductions were made and handshakes were exchanged all around.

"I'm really glad you guys could come," Mindy told them. "I just love your music." She blushed a little. "Especially your voice, Jake."

"Uh... thanks," Jake said. "I'm glad I could entertain you."

"I think you guys are fabulous too," Dennison told them. "I own all of your albums."

"We only have *one* album, dude," Matt said sourly.

Dennison actually giggled. "Of course you do," he said. "And a great one it is."

Matt took a step away from him, and a step closer to Veronica, who he had been eyeing ever since she came into view. "How about you, Ronnie?" he asked. "Can I call you Ronnie?"

"No, you may not," she said, glaring at him.

"Forgive me," Matt said. "But do you listen to our music too?"

"I don't listen to music," she said. She turned to a woman who was hovering nearby. "Callie, get me a drink, will you? Scotch on the rocks."

"Of course, Ms. Julius," the woman said. "Coming right up."

"Six ice cubes," she called after her. "No more, no less."

"Yes, Ms. Julius. Six ice cubes."

Janice spoke up at that point and thanked them for the invite. She then led the two musicians away.

"Bye, guys," Mindy called after him as he went. "It was nice meeting you."

Jake looked over his shoulder and gave her a smile.

"What a fuckin' cunt that Veronica bitch is," Matt said when they were out of earshot.

"Matt, please keep your voice down," Janice hissed. "This place is crawling with print reporters. If they overhear you saying something like that it will be all over the tabloids tomorrow morning."

"Right," Matt returned, sounding anything but sincere.

One of the champagne girls came by and offered them all a glass. Janice and Jake declined but Matt took one.

"Is this the good shit?" Matt asked her.

She looked a little taken aback but answered politely. "It's Dom Perignon," she said. "Chilled to precisely forty-six degrees."

"Yeah?" Matt asked. With that, he swallowed the entire glass at a gulp. His eyes watered and he released a wet burp that resonated throughout the immediate vicinity. He pounded his chest a few times. "Not bad," he said. "That is some pretty good hooch." He set the glass back on her tray and walked off towards the bar while Jake smirked in amusement and Janice suppressed an expression of horror.

"Hey, Jeeves," Matt said to the tuxedoed bartender. "Set me up with a Jack and Coke, and don't be chintzy on me with the Jack."

"Right away, sir," he replied. He then looked at Jake. "And you, sir?"

"Rum and Coke," Jake said.

"What kind of rum would you prefer?"

"The most expensive you got," Jake said.

"Of course," the bartender said. He reached down below the bar and produced two glasses.

"No fuckin' way," Matt told him. "That simply will not do."

"Excuse me?" the bartender asked.

"Those glasses ain't big enough. I'll drink something that size in about fifteen seconds. Bust out the water glasses, homey. I want a fuckin' drink, not a shooter."

"Oh my God," Janice moaned. "Matt, this is not the local watering hole. This is a high society party."

"Then these pricks don't know how to drink," Matt said. "Fire me up, Jeeves. Just the way I asked."

He fired them up, taking down two water glasses, filling them with ice, and then concocting an alcohol to coke mixture with a ratio of about fifty-fifty. "Will these meet your requirements, sir?" he asked Matt when he was done.

"Bet your ass," Matt replied. He turned to Janice, who was still flushing in embarrassment. "Don't just stand there, Janice. Give the man a tip. A big one."

Janice kept her lips tightly pursed but did as she was told. She dug a five-dollar bill out of her purse and dropped it in the bartender's tip jar.

"Thank you, sirs," he said, assuming, as Matt had already figured out, that Janice was their servant.

"Matt," Janice chastised once they were away from the bar, "you simply must maintain some composure here."

"What the hell for?" he asked. "Aren't we supposed to be a bunch of boozing, drug addict, Satanist badasses? I'm only acting the part."

"You're *over*acting," she said. "This is not the place for such shenanigans."

"Okay," he said. "Sorry. I'll try to maintain."

"Thank you," she said.

He looked around, as if scoping out the crowd. "Now then," he asked, "where can we burn?"

"Burn?" Janice asked.

"Yeah," Matt said. "Me and Jake need to toke up one of these joints I brought."

Janice paled. "You brought marijuana *here*?"

"Of course," he said. "We're gonna watch a movie, ain't we? I don't ever watch movies without being stoned."

"You can't smoke marijuana here," Janet told him. "Go in the bathroom right now and flush it down the toilet!"

"The bathroom," Matt said. "What a brilliant idea. Thanks, Janice."

"What?" Janice said.

The other one of the champagne girls was passing by. Matt grabbed her arm. "Hey, beautiful," he said.

"Would you care for some champagne, sir?" she asked.

"Uh... sure," Matt said. He took a glass from her tray, quickly downed it, belched again, and then set it back down. "Thanks. But I what I really wanted, is for you to tell me where the shitter is."

The champagne girl pursed her lips for the briefest of seconds before answering. "The... uh... men's facilities are located over there." She pointed. "Just down that hallway."

"Thanks, sweetie," Matt said, giving her a little pat on the butt. "Come on, Jake. Let's go burn one."

Jake was suppressing his laughter by now. "You bet," he said. "Let's do it."

"Jake, Matt," Janice hissed. "You can't... I mean... come back here!"

"We'll be back," Jake told her. "Have yourself a drink while we're gone."

The men's restroom was sparkling clean and smelled of lemons. Three tuxedoed men were standing around the sink as they entered, taking turns snorting cocaine from a small mirror. Jake recognized two of them: Michael Quinn, a teen heartthrob who had starred in numerous tough guy flicks, and Anthony Rentworst, a renowned director of such teen heartthrob movies. None of the three even looked up when the two musicians entered the room.

"Wassup, homies?" Matt asked them. "Got any spare blow for me and Jake here?"

Three identical looks of contemptuous disgust met this question. "No," said Quinn. "I think not."

Matt nodded. "I know how it is," he said. "The shit's expensive. You can't be sharing it with just anybody."

"Right," Quinn said. He turned back to the mirror and snorted his fill.

"Pricks," Matt muttered under his breath. With that, he reached into the jacket pocket of his suit and pulled out a pack of cigarettes. He opened the box and removed a tightly rolled joint—a fat one. He put it in his mouth, put the cigarettes back in his pocket, and then pulled out a lighter that he used to spark up the joint. He took a tremendous and quite noisy hit.

The actor, the director, and the unknown person with them (he was Conner Bergman, another famous actor that neither Jake nor Matt recognized) all turned towards them as they heard the inhalation and smelled the pungent odor of the Humboldt Skunk Bud being burned. Their mouths dropped open in shock.

"You guys want a hit?" Matt squeaked, still holding the smoke in his lungs. "*I'm* not a Bogart."

They didn't answer. Keeping the look of shock and revulsion on their faces, they quickly gathered up their mirror, their straw, and their little silver box and made a beeline for the bathroom door. They didn't let it hit them in the ass on the way out.

"Fuckin' squares," Matt said as he passed the joint to Jake.

Jake took it but was laughing too hard to take a hit just yet. "You're fuckin' killing me, Matt," he said. "Oh shit. This is the most fun I've had since we went to that truck stop and you kicked Hathaway's ass."

They emerged from the restroom five minutes later, both of them reeking of skunk bud and red in the eyes, but in the proper mood for viewing a movie.

*****

Even stoned, the movie wasn't very good. It was as predictable as the sunrise, full of lame clichés, and suffered from a myriad of plot holes and suspension of disbelief problems. About the only redeeming quality it featured was the two actresses who starred in it. They really were talented at their trade and the strained and sometimes violent interaction between them came across as the most genuine aspect of the entire production. And they were both quite alluring in starkly contrasting ways. Mindy's character was cute and cuddly, syrupy sweet. The kind of girl who would like puppies and holding hands at sunset, who would wear a promise ring and actually keep the promise. Veronica's character was sultry and tempting, foul-mouthed, a risqué dresser, a girl who thought nothing of giving it up on a first date, or even before a first date. Of course, the predictable aspect of the movie guaranteed that Mindy's character was the one who ultimately ended up with Mark Dennison's character. And, of course, the Veronica character was shown the consequences of the lifestyle she was leading (in the form of an AIDS scare she got when a former lover told her he had tested positive) and vowed to become more like the Mindy character. And of course, all three of them became the best of friends and shared a group hug in the end, this despite the fact that the Veronica character had slept with the Mark Dennison character while he was the Mindy character's boyfriend and the Mark character had thought, for a short time, that he might have AIDS because of this.

The audience either didn't notice the film's shortcomings or pretended not to. Everyone applauded wildly when the closing credits began to roll. They even gave a standing ovation. And afterward, when they filtered back out into the lobby and began to sip from their drinks and munch on the appetizers, nobody had anything but praise for the film, especially when in earshot of one of the stars.

Once most of the party-goers had filtered through and congratulated all the cast members who were present, Mindy drifted across the room until she was standing next to Jake and Matt, who were in the process of sipping from their fourth drinks and annihilating the salami and cheese table.

"Hi, guys," she said brightly, her chocolate brown eyes shining in that innocent and endearing way. "What did you think of the film? Did you like it?"

"It was uh... not bad, overall," Jake said. "Your acting was superb."

"Thank you," she said, blushing a little. "And what about the storyline? Just 'not bad'?"

"Well, I'm sure the writers worked very hard on it," Jake said.

"I was disappointed," Matt said from around a mouthful of food.

"Oh?" Mindy asked. "Why is that?"

"There wasn't a single bare titty in the whole flick," he said. "There wasn't even an ass shot."

Mindy giggled. "Is that how you rate your movies, Matt?" she asked. "By how many nudity scenes are in them?"

"Fuckin' aye," he said. "I can't give a flick a thumbs-up unless they show some ass, tits, or gash."

"I'll keep that in mind for my next film," she said, smiling.

"You do that," Matt told her. "In fact, you and Veronica should think about doing a dyke-out scene. I bet that would get you a sold-out opening weekend."

"I'm sure you're right," she said. "But that wouldn't maintain my sweet innocent image very well, would it?"

"True," Matt agreed, "but what a way to let it die."

She took a sip from the mineral water she was drinking. "I heard you guys smoked some pot in the men's room," she said. "Is that true?"

"Well, you have your image to maintain, and we have ours," Jake replied.

She laughed, reaching out and slapping lightly at Jake's arm. "You guys are refreshing," she said. "These parties are so boring sometimes. Everyone is such a phony."

Matt suddenly stepped up to her, a serious expression on his face. "Tell me something, Mindy," he said.

"What's that?"

"Is there a chance in hell of my scoring with you tonight?"

She blushed again but held his gaze. "No," she said. "I'm a good girl, remember?"

"Yeah, I remember. How about Veronica? She was a bitch to me earlier, but maybe it was part of her act. Think I can score with her?"

"Well..." she said. "How to put this? Veronica is more into... oh, you know... the softer things in life, if you know what I mean."

"You mean she's a dyke?" Matt asked.

"Women *are* her preference," Mindy said. "Although she's not above sleeping with a man if he can do something for her career. Can you do anything for her career?"

"Her career? No."

"Then you have no chance," Mindy said.

Matt shrugged. "Oh well. It was a nice dream." He brightened as he thought of something. "Hey," he said to Mindy, "you know these people. Tell me what actress I *can* score with tonight."

"Hmmm," Mindy said, looking around the room. Finally, she pointed out a tall, willowy blonde in short black dress. "Her," she said.

"Isn't that Tana Kensington?" he asked. Tana Kensington was another former television star who was trying to make the jump to the big screen. She had played one of the supporting characters in *Thinner Than Water*—the Veronica character's best friend.

"That's her," she confirmed. "She's got quite the reputation among those of us on the inside."

"Yeah?"

"Yes indeed," Mindy assured him. "My guess is you would find her quite receptive to your advances."

"Well, off I go then," Matt said. He quickly downed the rest of his drink, left the empty glass on the side of the appetizer table, and headed that way. Since Janice was off talking to the producer of the film and since Georgette was off schmoozing some people of her own, this left Jake and Mindy relatively alone together. She made no move to excuse herself.

"Is that true, what you told him?" Jake asked her.

"I hardly ever lie," Mindy replied, flashing him her smile again.

"Because it doesn't fit your image?" he asked.

"Exactly."

"And does your real personality reflect your image?" Jake asked.

She giggled. "I like to think so," she said. "I grew up in a small town in Nebraska, raised by church-going parents who loved me. I used to sing in the school choir and act in the school plays. I played Annie in my junior high class play."

"I'm sure you were a very beautiful Annie," he told her.

She shrugged shyly. "We got good reviews, especially me. I tried not to let it go to my head. I still don't."

"Well I must say that you're quite refreshing too."

"No sense getting too much of an ego," she said. "If you're good at what you do then you're good at what you do. I know I'm good, so I don't have to over-inflate myself to prove it."

"You are a very talented actress," he said. "And you're cute as can be on top of it."

This brought another blush to her face. "And what about you?" she asked. "You asked me about my image. Does your image reflect your real personality?"

He laughed. "I don't think anybody could live up to *my* image," he said.

"Then you're not a Satan worshiping pagan?"

"Nope, not this week."

"And you're not a cocaine addicted sex maniac?"

"Well... I'm not a cocaine addict," he said.

She giggled. "And the sex maniac part?"

"Uh... well, it depends on what your definition of 'maniac' is."

She giggled again. Their talk turned a bit more serious. They swapped anecdotes about life on the road as a musician and about life as a sit-com star and then a movie star. The stories Jake told her were the tamer ones. He avoided references to groupies or drugs or the exploitation. The stories she told were of a similar vein, centering on fussy directors, practical jokes between cast members, and the basic routine of filming. As they conversed, Jake found himself awed by the fact he was actually standing here and talking to Mindy Snow—*the* Mindy Snow. And not only was he talking to her, there seemed to be a connection of some sort taking place. Her beautiful brown eyes were flirting gently with him as she spoke. She continually twirled a lock of her rich brunette hair as she listened.

She's interested in you, his mind kept insisting. *A movie star is actually interested in you.* Though his self-esteem had certainly improved over the years, particularly over the last two years as his music career took off, he still had a hard time listening to this part of his mind. *She's a movie star*, the more cynical portion of his brain whispered. *And a sweet and innocent one at that. Why would she want anything to do with a longhaired musician with a reputation for ass-crack snorting?*

"When are you going to make another album?" she asked.

"We'll be hitting the recording studio next month some time," he replied. "We're having a little spat with the label over some of the tunes, but I think that'll work itself out pretty soon."

"Will it?"

He smiled. "Yes, I think it will."

"That's good," she said brightly. "It's such a bummer when people don't get along, isn't it?"

"Indeed it is," he agreed, his heart lurching a bit more as she did a particularly aggressive twirl of her hair.

"Tell me," she said. "What do you do with yourself these days... since... you know... you're not in the studio?"

"They have us flying all over the country making public appearances."

"Oh yeah," she said. "I caught you on *Wake Up USA* the other morning. That man was so mean to you."

"Yeah," he said. "It's not up there among my fondest memories, that's for sure."

"I can relate to the whole publicity thing," she said. "This is only the first premier party we'll be doing. I get tomorrow off and then we do one in a different city every day until the movie is actually released to the public next Saturday."

"Yeah, I guess you can relate all right," he agreed.

"However, I'll have some free time when I get back."

"Oh?"

"Uh huh," she said softly. She began to blush again, her eyes dropping to the floor. "Maybe... you know... when I get back, you and I could... oh... you know... go out sometime."

It took him a moment to credit what he had heard. Go out? What did she mean by that? Surely she wasn't talking about a date, was she?

He didn't get a chance to find out. Before he could even open his mouth, Georgette appeared as if by magic. Her face was scowling.

"Mindy," she said, her voice low but authoritative, "I think it's time to start mingling a little more. You've been talking to Mr. Kingsley an awful long time."

"Oh, Georgette," Mindy said with a sigh. "We were having a really cool conversation."

"That was quite obvious by the way you were smiling and cooing and eye batting and hair twirling," Georgette said. "For God's sake, Mindy, there are reporters here. You can't be seen together with... *him*. It could destroy your image." She looked at Jake. "Uh... no offense, of course."

"Of course," Jake said sourly.

"Georgette, that's not very nice," Mindy said.

"I'm not paid to be nice," she replied. "I'm paid to look after you. Now come on. I fear you've already given them far too much to speculate about." She grabbed Mindy by the arm and began to gently tug her away. "Come on. Let's get you out of here."

Mindy was pouting but she allowed herself to be led away. As she went she took one last look over her shoulder. "Bye, Jake," she said. "Nice talking to you."

A second later she merged into the crowd and disappeared from sight. It wasn't more than a minute before a reporter approached Jake to ask what he and Mindy had been talking about.

"Where did you get the idea that our conversation was any of your business?" Jake asked her.

"The people have a right to know," she told him in all seriousness.

Jake opened and closed his mouth a few times, on the verge of saying several profane and inflammatory things. But in the end his better judgment kicked in. He said nothing and walked away.

Matt ended up leaving in the company of Tana Kensington thirty minutes later, a battalion of cameras clicking and flashing away as they walked hand in hand through the door and climbed into Tana's limousine.

"He can't do that," Janice cried to Jake. "He didn't even check with me first!"

"Check with you?" Jake asked.

"The gossip magazines will all be reporting on this tomorrow. This is just terrible. We'll have to come up with a statement about how they're just friends... and no one is going to believe it."

Jake sighed. "Can we go now?" he asked.

"Leave? Now? It's so early. They haven't even cut the cake yet."

"If we don't leave in the next five minutes I'm going to pick up on one of the champagne girls and bang her in the bathroom."

That made Janice suddenly very agreeable. She made the arrangements for their limo to come to the front of the building and then the two of them went to say their official goodbyes to the hostess and the stars. Veronica remained coolly polite as Jake shook her hand. Mark Dennison tried to score some tickets for the next *Intemperance* concert—a concert that wasn't even scheduled yet. Georgette had a look of warning in her eyes but said nothing. Mindy was smiling a little and sending warm messages with her eyes. When Jake shook hands with her he felt something pressed into his hand. When he got back into the limo he waited until Janice—who was still fretting about all the exploits her two charges had engaged in this night—was mixing herself a stiff drink. He opened his palm and looked to see what Mindy had slipped him. It was a cocktail napkin, folded into a small square. He opened it and saw, written in spiky, feminine handwriting: *479-1647. My personal number. Call me Sunday if you want to talk some more.*

*****

He called her Sunday afternoon. She answered on the first ring. They talked for more than an hour and made plans to try to arrange a circumspect date the following week. When Jake finally hung up he was in the best mood he'd been in for months.

*****

"How'd you do with Tana?" Jake asked Matt in the limo as they drove towards the National Records Building Monday morning.

Matt made a snort of disgust. "One of the crappiest fucks I've ever had, possibly *the* crappiest. She didn't do nothin' but get on her back and lay there. She didn't make any noise, didn't move the whole time. I had to feel her fuckin' pulse to make sure she was still alive."

"No shit?" Jake asked, somewhat disillusioned. He had assumed that a Hollywood actress would be outstanding in the sack.

"It sucked ass," he said. "It's like she thought she was doin' me a favor by letting me in her sacred clam. I got fed up with it after a few minutes."

"Yeah? What did you do?" Jake asked, knowing that when Matt got fed up he always did *something.*

"I pulled my shit out of her snatch and nutted all over her face and that pretty blonde hair she's so fuckin' fond of."

"And what did she do?"

"She started screaming about her make-up and her hair and ran into the bathroom. And then, just as I was finishing up dressing she came out with a blow drier and started hitting me with it. I was forced to make a strategic withdrawal from the building."

Jake laughed. "That's just so you, Matt."

"Ain't it though?"

They made more idle conversation but stayed well away from the subject of the meeting they were on their way to. It was assumed (quite correctly in fact) that the limousine drivers were all record company spies. It was only when they were actually in the elevator heading up that the subject was discussed.

"You're absolutely sure about this shit, right?" Matt asked.

"As sure as I can be," Jake said. "It's a simple equation. We don't have much to lose. They, on the other hand, have a lot to lose."

"I guess," Matt said, a little bit of doubt leaking through.

"Trust me on this," Jake said. "It'll work. The important thing is that we stand firm, no matter what."

"No matter fucking what," Matt said.

They entered the conference room and found the same players as before, all of them looking solemn and more than a little arrogant. The two musicians were invited to sit and were offered cocaine and a drink, which they politely declined. Acardio, acting as chairman, passed a few preliminaries and then launched right into his attack.

"I must say," he said, "that your behavior at the premier of *Thinner Than Water* was reprehensible."

"Reprehensible?" Matt asked. "That's a pretty strong word."

"Yeah," Jake agreed. "I think it was more in the category of dreadful, or maybe appalling at the very worst."

Acardio began to fume early today. "Don't play word games with me," he told them. "You embarrassed this record company and threatened the good will that exists between our organization and the movie industry. I cannot allow behavior like that to go unchecked."

"Well check it then," Jake said. "Stop sending us to shit like that and we can't embarrass you."

"Public appearances for album publicity are part of your job," Acardio said. "You will go where we tell you to go and you will behave the way we tell you to behave."

Jake shrugged. "You do have the right to send us to those things," he said. "But that last part—about how we have to behave the way you say—well, you're wrong about that one."

"What?" Acardio said, his face turning red now.

"It doesn't say anywhere in our contract that we have to behave in a certain manner. In fact, that subject is pretty much wide open."

"Have you been talking to that sister of yours again?" Acardio asked. "Is she filling your head with more of her lies and misinformation?"

The subject of Pauline's interpretations of their contract had come up before. Acardio and members of the legal department had gone to great lengths to try to discredit her and her advice.

"She's filling my head with knowledge and facts," Jake said. "But that's only on the main subject we've come to discuss today. On the subject of our behavior at public events, I didn't need her advice. We're just a bunch of wild and crazy guys, Max. You're the one who pushed that image, remember? So you gotta figure it's a public relations crapshoot when you send us to one of those things."

"Are you threatening us?" Acardio demanded. "Because if you are..."

"I'm just pointing out a reality to you, Max. Of course, we *might* be inclined to mind our manners a bit more if we were treated with a little more respect."

"He *is* trying to threaten you," Janice said.

"Jake, this is a bad idea," Shaver spoke up. "You're way out of your league here."

Acardio ignored the rest of the speakers. He just continued to stare at Jake. "Is this your little game, Jake?" he asked. "Is this what your sister told you to do? Well she really is a shyster if she thought that having you act up at a party was going to prevent you from fulfilling the contractual obligations you made. Sorry. You lose this round, boys." He reached into his briefcase and took out the music packets. He slid one to Jake and one to Matt. They were smaller than they'd been last week, only six pages instead of almost twenty. "You've lost your privileges of picking which songs you want. I've decided for you. You will rehearse and record *Embrace of Darkness*, *Loss of Control*, and *Evil Times*, in that order. I want preliminary efforts on tape by the end of the month."

Matt and Jake looked at each other. Slowly they picked up the music packets and ripped them in half. They then ripped the halves in half. They then ripped the quarters in half. They threw the pieces up into the air, allowing them to come drifting down like snow over the conference table.

"How dare you," Acardio said. "You will *not* defy me like this."

"We just did, Maxie," Matt said.

"You are doing those songs!" he yelled. "That is final!"

"We are *not* doing those songs," Jake said. "And that is final."

"Then you are in breach of contract!" Acardio yelled.

"No, not really," Jake said.

"What?" several voices asked at once.

Jake smiled. "Nowhere does it say that 'the label' can compel us to record any particular song. Now once we've recorded a song, any song, it does become your property and at that point you can order us to perform it live, or make a video out of it, or you can let some movie maker use it in his shitty-ass flick, or you can even let some other rock band do a cover of it. There's nothing we can do to stop you in any of those things once a song is recorded. But you cannot force us to record something we do not wish to do. And we flat out *refuse* to record or perform any song that we have not written and approved of ourselves."

"You idiots," Acardio said. "You are once again operating on bad advice. True, you can technically refuse to record these songs, but we, 'the label', have the right to refuse any song you present to us. We will simply refuse everything you present except for those three songs. And if you don't have a full complement of songs that are acceptable to us by the specified date—which is fast-approaching, I might add—then you are in breach of contract."

"I know," Jake said.

"You know?" Acardio cried. "Then what the hell are we having this discussion for? Christ, what a waste of time."

"We know," Jake went on, "and we are fully prepared to take the consequences of that."

"What?" Acardio screamed. "Are you insane? If you go breach of contract, we'll sue you for everything we could have expected to make from your albums. And even the most conservative judge and jury would have to agree that that figure is in the tens of millions for the length of the contract you're under. You would be giving any money you ever made to us for the rest of your miserable lives."

"And, Jake," Shaver said, "if you go breach you wouldn't be able to work as musicians in any capacity until this contract would have expired."

"Ahh," Jake said. "Then what you're saying is that if we breach our contract, we'll end up in menial jobs and wouldn't be making much money for you to take away from us?"

"That is irrelevant," Acardio said. "We'll take every penny from you even if you're working as a shithouse cleaner."

"Which is likely what we'd be doing if we couldn't work as musicians," Jake said. "What's minimum wage these days?"

"About three bucks an hour," Matt replied.

"That's not much," Jake said. "You wouldn't be making much money off us that way, Max."

"We don't care," Acardio said. "We'll take all your money just for the principle of it. Don't think we won't."

"I have no doubt you're shitheaded enough to do exactly that," Jake said, "but you're missing the point I'm trying to make. If you force us to go breach of contract, you'll be getting six thousand, maybe eight thousand apiece out of us for the next year, right? That's about fifty grand at best."

"I told you, we don't care," Acardio said. "It's the principal of the thing."

"Uh huh, but isn't your main principle to make money for your corporation?"

"What?" Acardio asked.

"We're not asking too terribly much here," Jake said. "We're asking that we not be told to perform some crappy music that you think is good for our image. We only want our own songs on the *Intemperance* label and believe me, Max, we will stand firm on this. Now, if you accept three more songs from that recording we made, we'll be in the studio on time and we'll have our next album out by November. If that happens, you'll make a little more than fifty thousand dollars from us next year, won't you?"

"This isn't going to work, Jake," Acardio said. "We'll breach you before we allow you to start dictating terms to us."

Jake shrugged. "Then I guess you'll have to breach us," he said. "You've heard our terms. Give us a call when you're ready to accept them."

"That will be *never*," Acardio told them. "You will do our songs, or your career is over!"

Jake and Matt stood up.

"Then I guess our career is over, isn't it?" Matt said.

Despite the threats and pleas, they walked out the door, not looking back. Five minutes later they were in their limo, heading for their respective homes.

CHAPTER 9

REBELLIOUS SOULS

July 8, 1983
Los Angeles, California

"Jake, where are you going?" Manny asked as Jake picked up his key ring and headed for the front door. It was 9:25 AM and Manny had just finished cleaning up the mess made from the light breakfast he'd served.

"Out," Jake said simply.

"But you didn't call a limo," Manny said.

"Just taking a little walk, Manny," Jake told him. "Don't worry about it."

"But, Jake, you can't just..."

"Don't worry about making lunch," Jake said as he opened the door. "I'll be eating elsewhere."

He stepped through the door and closed it behind him. He half-expected Manny to come chasing after him, but he didn't. Thank God for small favors.

He rode the elevator down to the lobby and encountered the day-shift doorman as he walked through the doors.

"Are you going somewhere, Mr. Kingsley?" he asked, concerned.

"Yes," Jake said, walking right by him.

"But I wasn't notified," the doorman told him. "There's no limousine out front for you."

"I'll be walking to my destination today."

"Walking?" the doorman said, appalled. "You can't do that!"

Jake turned and looked at him. "I can do whatever I want. I'm an American citizen, remember?"

"Well... yes, but..."

"See you later," Jake said, turning and heading out the door.

"But, Mr. Kingsley," the doorman called after him. The door slid shut, cutting off what came next.

Jake was dressed in a pair of tan shorts and a collared white shirt. He had a baseball cap on his head, sunglasses on his face, and a pair of old tennis shoes on his feet. He began to walk west. As he did so, the doorman—who was being paid one hundred dollars a week to keep an eye on Jake and Bill—got on the phone to Manny, his contact in the chain of command. "Jake just left on foot," he said. "Where is he going?"

"I don't know," Manny replied. "He just walked out of here and didn't tell me anything. I didn't even know he was planning to go out."

"He's up to something," the doorman opined.

"Yes," Manny agreed. "I'd better call Mr. Acardio."

Jake, meanwhile had gone two blocks west. He turned right at the next intersection and there, parked in front of a fire hydrant, was a candy apple red 1983 Porsche 911 convertible. Sitting in the front seat, dressed in white shorts and a sleeveless red blouse, her brunette hair pulled back in a simple ponytail, was Mindy Snow. The dark sunglasses she wore hid her eyes but she sported a huge smile as she saw him approaching. She opened her door and got out, holding out her arms to him for a hug.

"You made it," she said as they embraced.

"Mission successful," he reported, feeling himself flush as he felt her alluring body push against his.

She pulled back and looked him up and down for a minute. "It's good to see you," she said. "I'm glad we were able to get together."

"Me too," he said. And it was very true. They had talked to each other two more times on the telephone since that first conversation and he was finding himself increasingly infatuated with her. For the first time in months he had stopped thinking about Angie whenever he looked at a telephone and had started thinking about Mindy. Today was the first time they had actually been able to arrange to get together. Since neither her agent nor Jake's employers would care too much for them being seen together, they had been forced to resort to secret agent maneuvers in order to have an actual date.

"We'd better get going," Mindy said, looking around. "I think people are starting to take notice of us."

Jake looked around and saw she was right. Several people walking down the sidewalks or sitting on the benches were looking directly at them, whispering to each other, pointing fingers. It would only be a matter of seconds before someone came closer to see if their suspicions—that they were *really* looking at Jake Kingsley and Mindy Snow—were correct. "Yeah," he said. "Let's hit it."

"Why don't you drive?" Mindy suggested.

Jake shook his head. "It's your car," he said. "And you know the way."

She stepped a little closer to him, so her shoulder was pushed against his. "I'm an old fashioned girl, Jake," she said. "I believe the man should drive. I can tell you the way."

He smiled. "You talked me into it," he said.

He opened the passenger door for her, allowing her to sit, and then walked around to the driver's side and climbed in. He had to adjust the seat back since Mindy was considerably shorter. He then pushed in the clutch, fired up the engine, and listened with satisfaction to its finally engineered purr. He put it in first gear and pulled away from the curb, accelerating rapidly down the one-way street.

"Sweet," he said as he shifted gears. "This a beautiful car."

"It doesn't exactly fit my image," she said, "but I love it so. Get on 110 east and take that to I-5 north. From there, we'll go through the valley and catch Highway 14 out into the boonies."

"I'm on it," he said, changing lanes and getting ready to hit the onramp.

"You're a great driver," she told him as he rocketed onto the freeway and merged into the semi-thick mid-morning traffic.

"I don't get to do it very often these days," he said. "And I've never driven a Porsche before. It's very nice."

"Nothing handles better," she said. "Wait until we get to the winding roads up by my place. You'll really love it then."

"I can't wait," he said.

They drove in companionable silence for a while, just enjoying the smoggy air in their faces, the warmth of the summer morning sun on their backs. Jake took them through the interchange for Interstate 5 and into the San Fernando Valley, putting them in the fast lane and keeping their speed pegged at 75 miles per hour.

"So how are things going with you and your label?" Mindy asked as the traffic began to thin out a little. "Any signs of them giving in yet?"

"Not yet," he replied. "Acardio has called me up a few times, threatening me with everything he can think of to threaten me with. He seems particularly fond of telling me I'll be working as a portable lavatory maintenance technician at various construction sites throughout the greater Los Angeles area."

She laughed. "You have quite a way with words, Jake."

Jake shrugged. "It's a gift, I guess. Anyway, he's been calling up the other band members too, trying to do the old divide and conquer routine. We're all standing firm though."

"Are you?"

"Oh yes," he said. "The guys were willing to put up with the allowances and the assigned housing and the babysitters as long as they got to keep living the lifestyle, but when they wanted us to do those crappy songs, that crossed the line. There's no chink in our armor on this issue."

"You guys take your music very seriously, don't you?"

He nodded. "More seriously than anything else in life," he said.

He took the Highway 14 exit and within minutes the bustling, overcrowded Los Angeles metropolitan area seemed to disappear around them as they headed northeast into a canyon surrounded on both sides by rugged mountains. After about twenty miles Mindy directed him to turn right on a small, badly maintained, two-lane road. Here, as promised, Jake got to experience the handling of the Porsche as they twisted and turned upwards, into the mountains. His ears began to get stuffy and then popped as the altitude abruptly changed from near sea level to more than three thousand feet. The foliage turned from scrub brush and oaks to pine trees and firs. The smell changed from burned hydrocarbons to fresh, mountain-scented air.

"Isn't it beautiful up here?" Mindy asked him as he whisked around a fifteen mile per hour turn at thirty-five.

"It's gorgeous," he said. "You can almost forget that you're only a few miles from nasty old LA."

"It's a long drive into Hollywood but I'm glad to take it," she said. "I can feel my problems slipping away every time I drive home. It's like I leave them down below, you know what I mean?"

"I think I do," he said, smiling as they climbed higher and higher.

They turned off on another two-lane road, drove about two miles, and then pulled into an unmarked single-lane road cut through the thick pine trees. About a quarter mile down this road was a wrought iron gate. Mindy leaned forward and pushed a button on a remote control clipped to the driver's side sun visor. The gate swung slowly open. Jake drove through and it closed behind them.

He drove up to the top of a steep hill and the road made a sharp left. As he negotiated the turn, a large clearing opened up before them. In the midst of this clearing Mindy's house stood. It was a huge tri-level of classic Spanish architecture surrounded by a lush green lawn. Off to the side stood a smaller guest home and what appeared to be a stable.

"Here it is," Mindy said. "Home sweet home."

"Wow," Jake said, taking it in. "That's a nice pad."

"I had it custom built," she said. "I'm prouder of the land though. I own six hundred acres here. My property goes right to the edge of the Angeles National Forest."

"Not bad for a twenty-year-old," he said.

She shrugged. "It's my summer home," she said. "I keep a place on Molokai for the winter."

He parked the Porsche in a detached six-car garage. Parked in there with it was a Mercedes convertible, a Range Rover, and two horse trailers. They exited the vehicle and stepped out a door on the side of the garage. They walked up a cement path and entered the main house through a side door, which led into the kitchen.

A Hispanic woman of about thirty greeted them. She was dressed in blue jeans and a long T-shirt. She smiled when she saw Mindy enter.

"Carmella, this is Jake Kingsley," Mindy said to her. "The one I told you about."

"Welcome, Mr. Kingsley," Carmella said with a heavy Spanish accent. "I understand you are famous musician. Do you know Carlos?"

"Carlos?" Jake asked.

"Carlos Santana," she said. "He plays the guitar."

"No," Jake said. "I admire his music very much, I've even seen him in concert before, but I've never met him."

"Carlos is *great* musician," she said.

"I agree," Jake said truthfully.

"Did you enjoy the trip up the hill?"

"Uh... very much," Jake said.

Carmella turned to Mindy. "I have your picnic basket all packed, ma'am," she said. "And I gave it to Eduardo to mount to the saddle."

"Thank you, Carmella," Mindy said. "We'll be heading out soon. Why don't you go help Eduardo get the horses ready and then both of you can have some free time until we get back."

"Thank you, ma'am," Carmella said. She smiled at Jake one last time and then disappeared through the door.

"Your maid?" Jake asked when she was gone.

"Yes, and my cook. Her husband, Eduardo, takes care of the landscaping and the horses. They live in the guest quarters out back."

"Is there any chance they might... you know... tell your agent that we're together?"

She found this amusing. "No," she said. "I hired them myself and they are completely loyal to me. They'd better be for as much as I'm paying them."

"Wow, that's a concept," Jake said. "Servants that are actually loyal to you."

She gave him a tour of her house. It was even more impressive from the inside. She had an actual ballroom on the ground floor, a complete entertainment room, a library, a game room, and four large bedrooms, including a master bedroom of more than a thousand square feet that featured a large balcony that looked out over the mountains.

"I like it," Jake said when the tour was complete.

She shrugged modestly. "It's a far cry from the tract house I grew up in," she said. "Shall we go have our picnic now?"

"You bet."

"How are you at horseback riding?"

"I rode one once when I was a kid," he said.

She laughed. "I guess you'll need a few lessons then, won't you?"

Her stable was very modern, with climate control and automatic feeding and watering mechanisms. It contained eight horses. Two of them had been taken out of their stalls by Eduardo, a mid-thirties Hispanic man in a straw hat. His face was weathered but friendly. His grasp of the English language was almost non-existent. He simply smiled and nodded. If one wished to communicate with him, one had to go through Carmella.

"This is Annabelle," Mindy said, patting the nearer of the two horses. "You'll ride her. She's sweet and gentle."

"Okay," Jake said doubtfully. She was also huge, her massive shoulders nearly at the height of Jake's head.

"And this," Mindy said, walking to the other horse, "is Zarita. She's my pride and joy, aren't you, Zarita?" She patted her butt affectionately and then made a quick check of the picnic basket attached to her saddle.

Mindy thanked the two servants and dismissed them. She then led the two horses outside. "Climb aboard," she told Jake, smiling.

He managed to get into the saddle without too much difficulty. Mindy then climbed aboard her own mare and gave Jake a brief rundown on the command and control systems for operating these particular vehicles. They then started off on their ride, going at an easy walk out behind the back of the house to the large part of the clearing. Here, Mindy had him practice stopping and starting, turning and trotting until she deemed him skilled enough to take to the trail.

"Just follow me," she said, aiming Zarita towards an opening in the foliage at the back end of the clearing. Jake brought Annabelle around and got her moving. They entered a wooded trail that climbed gently before them.

"You don't really have to guide her anymore in this part," Mindy said. "The horses will follow the trail on their own."

And follow they did. They took their passengers through the thick woods, climbing higher and higher into the mountains. To Jake it was quite the novel experience. He was out in the middle of nowhere, surrounded by pine trees and the scent of fresh, smog-free air. Squirrels and chipmunks were everywhere. Birds called out from the trees. The occasional deer crossed their path, usually does and fawns but the occasional buck as well. He was in nature, in a square mile of land that did not contain another eight thousand people, as every square mile of the LA urban area did. And no one knew where he was. He had no babysitter with him. There was no phone to ring with an enquiring voice, asking him what he was doing or telling him to go somewhere or threatening him if he didn't record a bunch of crappy music that some sell-out hacker had written. There were no autograph seekers or religious fanatics. The only sounds were the sounds made by the animals.

"I see why you like to come out here, Mindy," he told her. "It's so... so peaceful."

"Yeah," she said dreamily. "It's a little slice of solitude. I paid a lot of money for it, but it's worth it."

They continued on, not talking much, just enjoying the outdoors. Jake found his eyes flitting back and forth from the beauty of the surroundings to the beauty of the girl sitting atop the horse beside him. She almost seemed to glow with an innocent splendor he had encountered in no one he'd met since he started performing live as a musician. She seemed like she had no idea how pretty she was. Her tanned legs were smooth, perfectly formed, with just enough muscling to give them shape. Her breasts jiggled softly beneath her shirt, not too large, not too small, rounded in a way that made men ache to look at them. And her face... it was simply exquisite, a terminally cute, terminally innocent face that conveyed gentle naiveté, wholesomeness, and stubborn purity all at the same time. This was Mindy Snow he was with. He could not get over this. He was riding into the mountains with Mindy Snow.

After about an hour of following various trails, branching left and right, going up hills and down until Jake, a city boy, was thoroughly and completely disoriented, they came to a small clearing about thirty yards across. Here, a mountain stream babbled and roiled its way down the side of the mountain.

"We're here," Mindy announced. "My top secret I-want-to-be-alone-place."

"I like it," Jake said, looking around, thinking that this place was about as isolated as it was possible to get within the territorial boundaries of Los Angeles County.

"Of course, it's not really *mine*," she said. "We left my property about a half hour ago. This is national forest property here."

"As long as they don't mind you using it."

"They haven't complained yet," she said. "In fact, I've never seen another person here in all the times I've been here."

She dismounted and stretched her back a little. Jake climbed down as well, finding it considerably harder than climbing up had been, and felt a definite soreness in his butt and legs. He stretched himself this way and that a few times, trying to work out the stiffness.

"It'll take your bottom a little while to get used to it," Mindy told him as she unstrapped the picnic basket. "Can you get the blanket from the back of your saddle?"

He figured out how to release the straps that held it in place and unfolded it. It was a large, soft cotton blanket, red and white checkered. At Mindy's direction he spread it out on the bank of the stream. While the horses wandered over and began to drink, Mindy opened the picnic basket and pulled out fried chicken, potato salad, corn on the cob, and ice-cold sodas. She filled two plates and they began to eat. The food was nothing short of spectacular.

"This is great," Jake said between chomps and chews. "Did your maid make this?"

"Yes," Mindy said. "She's really good at the kinds of food I like—fried chicken, chicken fried steak, gumbo, meatloaf. That's one of the reasons I hired her. Part of my interview process was having the candidates cook for me." She giggled. "I had to do a lot of extra hours with my trainer during that week to keep the pounds off, but it was worth it."

"Wow," Jake said. "You actually interviewed and hired your own servants. I can't get over that."

"I can't get over the fact that your servant was assigned by the record company and that he spies on you. Why don't you fire him if he's not loyal to you?"

He explained to her about their contract and their housing assignment clause and the assigned house staff clause.

"That's horrible," she said, genuinely shocked. "Are all musicians treated this way?"

"Well, I haven't talked to all musicians, obviously. And I doubt that once you reach a certain level that they *can* treat you that way, but I think that most musicians under their first contract experience pretty much what we're going through. We're so eager to get signed in the beginning we'll agree to damn near anything. And the record companies take horrific advantage of that."

"And you don't have a union or any sort of professional organization to help you?"

"Not that anyone has ever told me about," he said.

"You need one. We have the Screen Actors Guild. They make sure that even extras are paid fairly and treated fairly. And for those of us that do this for a living, we're very well protected and set up. They have health insurance and retirement plans for us. Most important, there's a whole list of exclusions that the movie producers are not allowed to try to put in our contracts."

"What a concept," Jake said sourly.

"Writers have a guild too," she said. "So do cartoonists and stuntmen and theater actors and television actors and even people who make commercials. Why don't musicians have one?"

"I don't know," he said.

"Well somebody should get one going, don't you think?"

"Yeah," he agreed. "I'd vote for it."

They ate in silence for a few minutes, finishing up the last of their food. Jake wiped his face with his napkin and took a drink of his soda. "Does it bother you?" he asked her.

"Does what bother me?"

"That I'm not really rich and powerful? That it's all just an illusion?"

She laughed. "You may not be rich, Jake, but I think you're very powerful."

"Oh?"

"Your songs are incredible. They're very moving. Your voice is hypnotic and very... you know..." She blushed furiously. "...sexy. And your lyrics are deep and meaningful. Your song *Descent Into Nothing* sounded like you wrote it about me, about what it was like to grow up in an adult world like a television studio, about how I felt like I'd been pushed too hard and too fast, that I... I don't know... learned things young that I wasn't meant to know about yet. You captured all of that in three verses and a bridge and then put it all to music. Don't tell me that's not powerful."

Jake was amazed. Mindy knew exactly what the song was about. Exactly. She was one of the few people he had talked to who had actually absorbed the message he had imparted into that song. "Thank you," he stammered.

"Like I said, I'm a fan of yours, Jake. And just because I'm famous myself doesn't mean I'm not in complete awe that I'm actually sitting here with you, talking to you, that *the* Jake Kingsley actually rode one of my horses out here. I keep wanting to pinch myself to see if I'm just dreaming all of this. I don't care that you don't really have any money. Why should I care about that? I have my own money. Lots of it."

"You're very mature for a twenty-year-old," he said, looking into her brown eyes again, feeling his infatuation for her deepening into something a little stronger.

She gave him her shy smile. "I went through the descent into nothing," she told him. "Just like you did."

"Yes," he said, "but somehow you came out just as cute and cuddly on the other side, didn't you?"

"Well," she said thoughtfully, "you can look at me and say whether or not I'm cute, so I'll have to take your judgment on that one. But you can't say I'm cuddly until you've actually cuddled me."

"No," he said, "I don't suppose I can. Maybe we should make the experiment?"

"For the sake of verbal accuracy," she said, "I suppose we probably should."

She spun her body around, so she was facing away from him. She then scooted backwards, until she was leaning backward against his chest. His arms went around her middle, coming together just below her ribs. Her stomach was unbelievably soft beneath her shirt. Her head lolled back onto his shoulder. She sighed contentedly. "This is nice," she said softly.

"Yes," he said, his mouth suddenly a little dry as he smelled the fresh aroma of her body, as he felt the silky softness of her hair caressing his cheek. "Very nice."

"So?" she asked. "What's the verdict? Am I cuddly?"

"Oh yes," he said. "It has been confirmed. We have cuddly here."

The light in her eyes took on a particular shine and he responded to it. He lowered his face and put his lips to hers. Their first kiss was soft and gentle. So was the second one. She cooed during the third one. During the fourth, his tongue probed out just a little and hers came out to meet it. After that, the rest of the kisses merged into one. Soon they were making out like teenagers in the movie theater. She eventually let him lay her down on the blanket and put himself on one elbow next to her. He rubbed her stomach as they kissed, feeling that rich softness of her abdomen, but when he tried to push his hand beneath her shirt to touch her bare flesh she stopped him.

"We're moving a little fast, Jake," she said somewhat breathlessly.

"I'm sorry," he said.

"It's okay," she said. "I liked your hand on me. It's just that... well... I'm an old fashioned girl. I don't like to jump into things like I'm sure you're used to doing."

"I'm sorry," he repeated.

"Don't be sorry," she said, disentangling herself from his embrace. "I like being together with you. We'll have time for moving things along later, won't we?"

"Will we?" he asked.

She leaned down and kissed the tip of his nose. "Do you want to see me again?"

"As much as I can," he assured her.

"And I want to see you again," she said. "We'll have lots of time for kissing and touching, and... you know... working our way onto other things, won't we?"

He agreed that they probably would. But there was one small problem. "What about your agent?" he asked. Jake knew from their phone conversations that Georgette had all but ordered Mindy to stay as far away from Jake as possible. Even a rumor that she was seeing a scrungy, coke-sniffing, womanizing, Satan worshipping rock musician would derail the sweet and wholesome image that was her trademark and could potentially cost her future parts in future movies.

"That does put a bit of a kink in things, doesn't it?" she pouted. "I wish we could date like everyone else in the world without having to worry about what the public thinks."

By "we", Jake knew, she didn't just mean the two of them, but all celebrities in general. "This is the life we choose," he told her. "And we have to play by its rules, don't we?"

She kissed him again, a soft, lingering kiss, breaking it just short of the tongues coming out. "We'll get together whenever we can," she said. "We'll talk on the phone and meet in secret like spies. And, most important, we'll deny everything if we get caught."

"Should we carry cyanide capsules with us too?" Jake asked.

She could have gotten angry at that comment, but she didn't. Instead she gave him another kiss. "Maybe when we get to know each other better."

*****

It was when they were about halfway back to her house, as the horses were working their way down one of the slopes, that she finally asked the question she had so far avoided posing. "Did you really snort cocaine out of a girl's... you know?"

He lied without even thinking about it. "No," he said. "That was Matt's gig. I just got carried along for the ride when the reporter wrote the article."

She nodded, seemingly relieved by his answer. She talked about that particular issue no more.

*****

She dropped him off in the same place she had picked him up. They said their goodbyes and they clasped hands affectionately, but they did not hug or kiss. There were too many potential eyes on them. When she drove off he stared after her, watching until she turned the corner and disappeared. He had a smile on his face and a lightness in his soul he hadn't felt in a long time. There was romance in his life, something that had been absent from it for a long time now. He wondered how Matt managed to live without such a thing. Was it because he'd never experienced it?

He pondered this thought as he walked back to his building. A different doorman was on duty when he went through the entryway, but he had apparently been briefed on Jake's AWOL status.

"Mr. Kingsley," he said. "Where have you been? We were worried about you."

"We?" Jake asked.

"Us on the staff," he said. "It's not like you to disappear on foot like that."

"Yeah? Well, you'll have to get used to it I'm afraid. It's going to be happening a lot."

"But, Mr. Kingsley," he said. "How will..."

"Here's a thought," Jake said. "How about you and your colleagues do this thing my mom taught me... oh... about kindergarten age or so."

"What's that?"

"It's called minding your own business," Jake said. "It's really easy if you try."

Jake continued into the building and went directly to the elevators. He pushed the call button. While he was waiting for the car to arrive he could see the doorman was already on the phone.

The lines of communication worked quickly. When he walked into his condo three minutes later, Manny was standing inside the doorway, waiting for him. He had the phone already in his hands. "It's Mr. Acardio," he said, handing the phone to Jake.

Jake took it and put it to his ear. "Wassup, Maxie?" he asked.

"Jake!" Acardio barked. "Do you know what *time* it is?"

Jake looked at his watch. "It's four twenty-eight," he said. With that, he hung up the phone and handed it back to Manny. "Here you go," he told the manservant/spy. "Can you mix me up a rum and coke? I think I'd like a stiff drink to relax with after this most interesting day."

Manny's eyes were wide with shock. "Jake, you hung up on Mr. Acardio!" He said this in the same tone a Christian would use when describing a particularly grotesque blasphemy.

"Yep," Jake said. "I sure did. So, how about that drink?"

The phone began to ring again.

"You get the phone," Jake said. "I'll mix my own drink."

"Jake," Manny hissed. "You're behaving like a buffoon."

Jake ignored him and walked over to the bar. He took out a water glass and filled it with ice. Before he could even select his rum, Manny came in, holding out the phone to him again.

"Mr. Acardio *insists* on talking to you," he said.

Jake sighed. "Just a sec," he said. "Let me get my drink going first."

And despite Manny's frantic gestures and whispers, Jake went about the task of constructing the perfect rum and coke. He took out two bottles of rum, opened them, and smelled each one. He thought it over for a few seconds, smelled them again, and then chose the Jamaican import. He used a shot glass and carefully measured out three individual ounces of the rum, one by one. He poured each over the ice in his glass. He added coke from the sprayer installed in the bar, waited for the bubbles to settle, and then added some more. He stirred slowly and carefully with a stainless steel stirrer. He had a sip and decided it wasn't strong enough, so he poured another half shot into the shot glass, poured that into his glass, and then spent a bit stirring again. He tasted it once more and then nodded his approval. Only then did he take the phone from Manny's hand and put it back to his ear.

He looked at his watch again. "It's four thirty-one now, Max," he said. "Did you know that there's a number you can call that is specifically dedicated to time-telling?"

Acardio was infuriated. "You watch how you talk to me, you ungrateful punk! How dare you hang up on me! You'd be nothing without me. Nothing! You'd still be playing for those banjo strumming hicks in that dreadful club in Heritage!"

"Uh huh," Jake said. "And strangely enough, I'd be making more money than I am now, wouldn't I?"

Acardio stammered for a moment, obviously unsure how to answer that one. Finally, he just changed the subject to the one he really wanted to discuss. "Where have you been all day, Jake?"

"Out," Jake said.

"That's not good enough," Acardio told him. "You sneak out of your condo, take off on foot without telling anyone where you're going, and then don't come back for seven hours? I'm afraid 'out' isn't going to cut it. Where were you, who were you with, and what were you doing?"

"None of that is any of your business, Max," Jake said calmly.

"Anything you do is my business," Acardio told him. "We can't allow you to just go wandering around the city wherever and whenever you please. Anything could happen to you!"

"Your concern is touching," Jake replied. "But you and your babysitters and your spies down in the lobby are just going to have to get used to it. I will be coming and going as I please from now on."

"You *can't* do that!" Acardio yelled.

"Sure I can. I believe we abolished slavery and indentured servitude a few years back, didn't we?"

"Your contract..."

"Doesn't say shit about me having to ask your permission to go out or about having to get your approval to see any particular person."

"That may be true," Acardio said, "but it doesn't say we have to give you a spending allowance either. That is completely at our discretion. If you do not abide by the rules we set down I will cut off your allowance."

"Do what you need to do, Max," Jake told him. "But since you're planning to declare a breach of contract anyway, that's not really much of a threat now, is it?"

"Jake," Acardio said, "you know as well as I do that you're not going to let us file a breach of contract on you. You're not going to give up this lifestyle we're allowing you to live for a life of poverty and misery. We've been over this before. You're not fooling us. We're calling your bluff."

"We're not bluffing, Max," Jake said. "I would have thought you'd realized that by now. All five of us are quite prepared to go down with the ship before we play any of that shit you call music."

"Listen, Jake," Acardio said. "You've had your little rebellion against our authority, okay? We've been treating you with kid gloves through it but it's getting old. Don't make us get nasty with you."

Jake sighed. "You know something, Max," he said. "I was in a really good mood when I came in my house just now, the best mood I've been in in years. That mood is starting to fade a little and this conversation is directly responsible for that."

"You need to face reality, Jake," Acardio said.

"So anyway," Jake continued, "before my mood fades even further, I'm going to end this conversation. Call me back when you're ready to talk about which three of our songs you want to record."

"Jake, I'm warning you..."

"And cut off my allowance if you think you need to," he added. "It'll probably do me some good to stay home at night more."

"Jake!" Acardio yelled. There might have been more, but Jake didn't hear it because he hung up the phone again.

"Jake," said Manny, who had been hovering nearby during the entire exchange, "I think you're making a big mistake. Nobody talks to Mr. Acardio that way."

Jake looked at him with contempt. "When I want advice from you, Manny, I'll ask for it. In the meantime, I'm accepting no calls from Acardio unless he tells you they've given in. Do you understand?"

"I can't refuse to..."

"Look, Manny," Jake told him. "I just had one of the best days of my entire life, you dig? And I refuse to have it spoiled. I refuse. Now I understand where you're coming from. You're an employee of Acardio and National Records and..."

"No, Jake," he said. "I'm not. I'm..."

"Let's not play games," Jake said. "You're an ass-sucking mole planted here by Acardio to keep an eye on me and babysit me. I've known that since the first day. I'm not stupid, okay? And while I can never respect you for what you do, I can at least understand your position. I'm sorry I'm forcing you to be in the middle of this dispute between myself and the executives at National Records, but it's the life *you* chose and you're going to have to deal with it. When he calls back you need to ask him if he's given in to our demands in full. If the answer is anything but yes, I will not talk to him. Period."

The phone began to ring.

"You'd better get that," Jake said. "In the meantime, I'm going to go out on the balcony, drink my drink, smoke a few cigarettes, and reflect upon my day."

And with that, he took his drink, grabbed a pack of cigarettes and a lighter, and walked across the room to the balcony door. He stepped outside and sat in his favorite chair. He stared out at the smog choked downtown buildings and sipped rum and coke. Manny did not disturb him.

*****

Eighteen hours later, Jake and Matt stepped out of limousine in front of the National Records building. They had been summoned to a meeting though told nothing about what the subject of it would be. Jake knew, however, that it could be only one of two things. They were either giving in, or they were announcing an official breach of contract.

"How was your date with the little cutesy actress?" Matt asked as they waited for the elevator.

"It was good," he said. "Very good. But my ass is so sore right now I can barely sit down."

"*Your* ass is sore?" Matt asked, interested. "What kind of kinky-ass shit were you doing with her?"

"It's from the horseback riding," he said. "She owns this huge piece of property up near the Angeles National Forest. We rode for a couple of hours and had a picnic."

"A picnic?" Matt asked, as if he'd never heard of such a thing.

"Yeah, by a stream. It was nice."

"It was nice?" Matt said. "What the hell does that mean? Did you nail her, or what?"

"I kissed her," Jake said.

"On her pussy?"

"On her lips."

"And then what?"

"And then we rode back to her house. Like I said, it was nice."

"You didn't bang her?" Matt asked, appalled.

"No, I didn't bang her. It was our first date. We had a picnic, we kissed a little, and I came home."

Matt shook his head in disbelief. "I thought you said you had a good time."

Jake chuckled, not bothering to explain any further. Matt simply wouldn't get it. Instead, he turned the subject over to more serious matters. "What's your guess?" he asked him. "Are they caving or not?"

Matt shrugged. "At this point I'd just be glad if they made a decision of some sort. I'm tired of having these fucks call me up and threaten me all the time."

In the end, it turned out to be almost anti-climactic. They were led into the office of James Doolittle, the head of National's A&R department, a man they had never met before in person but that both had talked to on the phone several times during the crisis over Matt's refusal to play anything but his Strat onstage.

"It's good to meet you boys at last," he said as they sat down in chairs before his large desk. He was a short man in his mid-forties, his graying hair neatly styled, his clothing a power-suit right out of *Dress for Success*.

They shook with him but did not return the sentiment that it was good to meet with him at last. Instead, Matt got right to the point.

"If you brought us in here to threaten us some more, we'll just leave now. We're not bluffing and we're not giving in on this. We will not perform any song we haven't written."

"I understand completely," Doolittle said.

"Oh you do, do you?" Matt asked.

"Yes," he said. "I do."

They waited for the punch line. Apparently, however, there wasn't one.

"You guys are artists," he said. "It's understandable that you're unwilling to compromise your art for strict commercialism. I get where you're coming from and I respect you for it."

"But...?" Jake asked.

Doolittle shook his head. "No buts here," he said. "As of today, I've removed Max Acardio from his position as your Artist and Repertoire rep. He will be reassigned to work with some of our other bands. From this point on, Steve Crow will be your rep from the A&R department. Steve's a little younger than Max, but he is a little more up on current trends in hard rock. I think he'll be able to work a little more harmoniously with you on this second album."

"Replacing our rep is not going to change anything," Jake said. "If he's just going to try to get us to record other people's music then we're still at square one here."

"He's not going to try to get you to record anything you don't want to," Doolittle told them. "It's obvious that you have very strong feelings about that. Now personally, I think those songs our writers came up for you would have been phenomenal had they been recorded but I would never force any of my artists to do things against their will. I only wish Max would have come to me with this problem earlier and we could have resolved it before so much bad blood developed between you all."

"Wait a fuckin' minute here," Matt said, leaning forward. "Are you saying you're *not* going to try to get us to record those shitty songs?"

"That's exactly what I'm saying," Doolittle said. "Steve has your preliminary recording and has been going over it since yesterday. He'll help you decide which of those songs to record in place of the three by our in-house writers that you've rejected. The important thing here is that we get you boys into the studio as soon as we can. We want that next album ready for release when *Descent* starts to fall off the charts."

Jake and Matt looked at each other, sharing a bit of telepathic communication. They turned back to Doolittle.

"Okay," Jake said. "If that's the way you want it, then we'll get to work."

"That's the way we want it," Doolittle told them. "Steve's office is on the sixteenth floor. I'll have my secretary let him know you're on the way. Matt, why don't you head over there now, meet him, and get the wheels turning."

"What about Jake?" Matt asked.

"He'll be along in a minute or two. I'd just like to have a word with him about another matter first."

Another look was shared between the two musicians. Jake gave an almost imperceptible nod. Matt returned it and walked out the door.

"I suppose you know what this is about," Doolittle said as soon as the door clicked shut.

"I suppose I do," Jake said. "And I'm standing firm on this as well. I will come and go from my condo as I please. I am not an inmate, I am not a slave, and I refuse to be treated like property."

"We're just trying to look out for your safety, Jake. Max may have been a bit over the top in his response to you, but that was all he was doing. You're a famous person and you're also controversial. There is a real danger of you getting hurt when you go off on your own like that."

"Well, that's a chance I'll just have to take," Jake said. "Cut my allowance off if you need to, but it doesn't matter. When I want to go out, I will go out and I will go out where I want to go and it's none of your business, or anyone else's business, where I'm going or what I'm doing."

Doolittle sighed. "Jake, I appreciate where you coming from with this, really I do, but the fact of the matter is that you have a history of unauthorized performances of music in violation of your contract. That is one concern."

"Unauthorized performances, huh?" Jake said. "That would be the time I played my guitar and sang for some of the employees of the restaurant I was working at. I still think calling that an unauthorized performance was a bit much, but I was told not to do it again and I didn't do it again. And I'm not going out and performing concerts behind your back now. I think you probably know that. Don't you suppose you might've heard about it if I were?"

"Nevertheless, we have a vested interest in keeping you safe and in knowing your whereabouts."

"I'm a big boy," Jake told him. "I can take care of myself."

"I'm sure you can, Jake, but what harm does it do to let us know where you're going and what you're doing? If you're not doing anything contrary to your contract, why should you mind letting us keep tabs on you?"

Jake looked up at the ceiling for a moment, taking some deep breaths. He then looked around the room and locked his eyes on an expensive leather briefcase sitting on a table behind Doolittle's desk. "Is that your briefcase?" he asked.

Doolittle looked back at it. "Uh... yes, it is."

"Can you bring it over here for a minute?"

"Why?"

"I want you to open it up for me, so I can look through it."

"What?" Doolittle said.

"You don't have anything illegal in there, do you?" Jake asked him.

"No, of course not, but..."

"If you don't have anything contrary to the law in there, then why should you mind me looking through it?"

Doolittle sighed. "That's not the same as what we're asking you to do, Jake."

"I know," he said. "What you're asking me to do is even worse. I just want to look through your papers. You want to stick your nose into my private life. That is offensive to me, Doolittle. Very offensive. And I will not allow it. Now you can accept that, or you cannot accept that, but that's the way it's going to be."

Doolittle seemed about to say something else but didn't. He raised his hands in surrender. "Okay, Jake," he said. "Have it your way."

It seemed he'd given in too easily, but Jake didn't press the issue. He simply said his goodbyes and left the room.

*****

They met with Steve Crow. He was a young, hip-talking man in a loud but fashionable suit. He had long platinum blonde hair styled in punk rock fashion. He wore sunglasses even though he was indoors. He was intelligent and articulate, and he sat and went over each of the previously rejected tracks with them, rating each on its relative merits.

"The only one you're absolutely forbidden to record is *Its In The Book*," he told them.

"Which is one of our best songs ever," Matt said sourly.

"Hey, guys," Steve said. "I'm trying to work with you here. I agree it's a bitchin tune, but the bosses say no go on that one. That's the only thing they're standing firm on."

In the end, they picked two of Matt's songs and one of Jake's, all of them the more recent numbers, the songs they'd written after maturing a bit by performing at D Street West. That gave them a complete list of ten tunes for the next album, every one of them an *Intemperance* original.

"Looks like we're set," Steve told them. "I'll get Bailey and his merry men working on a song order and an album title right away. In the meantime, I want you guys to be prepared to start hitting the studio in two weeks. That means lots of rehearsals, okay? Janice's publicity trips aside, I'd like you to do at least four hours a day in your warehouse. Tune that sound in tighter than a schoolgirl's ass."

"You got it," Matt said.

Steve smiled, shook their hands again, and then dismissed them.

As they rode the elevator down to the lobby level, Matt asked, "What do you think? Did they cave to us, or are they raising up a hammer to drop on our fuckin heads?"

"They caved," Jake said. "Doolittle was trying to make it seem that all of the resistance was just Acardio's little quirks."

"Which is a bunch of bullshit," Matt said.

"Agreed. But that was just their face-saving measure to make it seem like we didn't really win."

"But we did."

"Yeah," Jake said. "I think we did."

Matt grinned. "Let's get the rest of the guys together tonight and go hit the Flamingo. This is a cause for celebration."

*****

Jake and Mindy were not able to get together much. Mindy was still heavily promoting *Thinner Than Water*, which had been released across the country and was currently the most popular movie in theaters, and Jake was spending at least a portion of every day rehearsing the ten tunes they were to record. They were able to talk on the phone almost every night and usually spent at least an hour doing so. Manny no longer bothered enquiring who was calling when she called (she never told him) and had stopped trying to backhandedly pry the information out of Jake.

Still, there were a few times where their schedules did coincide and they were able to make each other's acquaintance. When this happened, she would always park a few blocks away from his building and he would simply walk out the door without giving anything like advanced notice to Manny. Manny learned not to ask or to try to stop him, although Jake had no doubt he was still calling up Steve Crow to let him know another AWOL session was taking place.

The two times they did get together, Mindy drove him up to her place. The first was an almost exact repeat of their first date. They went horseback riding up into the hills, had a picnic next to the stream, and spent a few minutes making out on the blanket. Though this make-out session was a little heavier and a little longer lasting, she allowed him to progress no further than kissing her neck and stroking her bare legs. He rode back for an hour with a throbbing case of blue balls.

The second time they skipped the horseback riding and instead went for a long drive in her Porsche through the hills and canyons of rural Los Angeles County. Jake took the wheel for this and she navigated, directing him from back road to back road until he was hopelessly lost and disoriented. She, however, seemed to know the area like the back of her hand and unerringly led him to a dead-end lookout eight hundred feet above a place called Fish Canyon. The view was very impressive. It was a rugged, narrow canyon with a small river running down the middle of it. They were also utterly alone. They spent a few minutes enjoying the view and nearly an hour enjoying the sensation of each other's bodies pressed together, their tongues in each other's mouths, their hands touching bare legs and bare stomachs, but staying well away from anything else. She did allow Jake to briefly feel her left breast through her shirt—and a fine breast it was—but she called an end to the session when he tried to unbutton her shirt.

He kept his humor up as they drove back to her house. Though it was frustrating beyond belief, and though his balls were not appreciating the forced congestion too much, he relished the challenge and the underlying romance of this relationship. It had been a very long time indeed since a girl had made him work his way up the sexual ladder and the novelty of it was something he both appreciated and respected.

On the way back to her house that day she did something that was slightly out of character. She stopped at a mom and pop restaurant in a small, rural town called Sleepy Valley and insisted that they go inside and have dinner.

"Do you think that's a good idea?" he asked. "I mean, I know it's a small town but people will see us together. Aren't we supposed to be avoiding that?"

"I stop here all the time," she said. "They know me in here. It's a nice older couple that runs the place. They would never tell anyone we were here."

And indeed the couple that ran the place did know her and Mindy addressed them affectionately by their first names. They doted over the two of them, setting them up with a farmhand style home-cooked meal complete with all the fixings. Jake had no trouble believing that the owners themselves would keep their mouths shut about their famous visitors but there were other customers in the restaurant too, and most of them spent their entire meal staring at the beautiful actress and the longhaired rock star, whispering behind closed hands. When Jake asked her about this on the drive back to his building, she simply shrugged it off.

"They're all small town folks," she said. "They know how to mind their own business. I grew up in a small town, remember?"

"I suppose," he said and then refused to worry about it any further.

And indeed, a week passed and there was no mention in the various tabloids and entertainment reports of a reported sighting of Mindy Snow and Jake Kingsley eating dinner together in a small town restaurant. Jake knew from personal experience that had there been even the slightest whisper of such a meeting to any of the various reporters who wrote for such rags that their names would have been on the front page. He should know. His name had been up there many times in the past. Whenever he went out to a club or to dinner or to virtually any other place in public, someone was always popping up out of nowhere and snapping his picture. If he met up with a girl, there would be a report on it, sometimes with a blow-by-blow description of their activities provided by the girl herself. These reports both infuriated and embarrassed Jake (although Matt – who encountered the same thing, relished them) but he knew there was nothing that could be done about it. It was yet another thing that fell under the heading of the life we choose.

During that week, Jake and Mindy were unable to get together at all, were in fact not even able to talk on the phone. Mindy had been whisked off on a tour of Florida to promote her movie and Jake took two trips himself, one to Atlanta to do a promo radio station interview, and one to Boise to sign autographs at a new record store.

The night after he returned from Boise—a Thursday night—Mindy called him at home just as he was getting to bed. She too had just got back into town and was very anxious to get together with him.

"Are you rehearsing tomorrow?" she asked.

"Yes, it's our final rehearsal day. Starting Monday, we go into the studio and start recording."

"And then your schedule gets a little busier?"

"A lot busier," he said sadly. "We'll be pulling ten-hour days Monday through Saturday for the foreseeable future."

"Rats," she said. "We'll hardly ever get to see each other then."

"I know," he said, a bit bummed about that himself.

"Well, what time are you going to be done tomorrow?" she asked.

"We're gonna start at nine," he said. "Since it's the last day we're not going to go the full four hours. We'll probably knock off around noon or so."

"I'm totally free tomorrow," she said. "How about I meet you after you rehearse and we go to the beach together?"

"The beach?" he asked. "Isn't that kind of... you know... public?"

"Have faith in me," she said. "I'm the queen of the greater LA rural area. I know all the places where no one else goes."

He took her at her word for that and they arranged for him to make another one of his mysterious departures, this time from the rehearsal warehouse.

*****

He climbed into her car at 12:10 PM, two blocks from the entrance to the warehouse where the two National employed security guards and the limousine driver were still puzzling over what they were supposed to do when one of their charges just walked off on them in the middle of a not-too-terribly-attractive neighborhood. While the rest of the band, all of whom knew what Jake was doing, explained that they should just mind their own fucking business, Jake drank in the sight of Mindy dressed in a pair of blue jean short shorts and a tank-top that clearly revealed the red bikini top beneath.

"You are gorgeous," Jake told her. Unable to resist, he leaned over and gave her a long, lingering kiss on the mouth.

"Mmmm," she said when the kiss finally broke. "That was nice. I missed you."

"I missed you too."

She drove off, winding expertly through gray and dingy streets, darting in and out of lunchtime traffic, and eventually accessing Interstate 10 heading west, toward the ocean. She rested her right hand on Jake's leg as she drove, removing it only when she had to change gears. They talked of their trips and the adventures they'd had on them. When they got to Santa Monica she took the offramp for Highway 1, the Pacific Coast Highway, or PCH, as it was known. She headed north on the winding, twisting coastal road, the sparkling blue Pacific to their left, a series of hills and cliffs with multi-million dollar mansions poised upon them on their right.

They drove for miles, passing out of the densely populated area and into the more undeveloped section of seacoast (as far as such a thing was possible in southern California anyway). Less than five miles from the Ventura County line, they came to a small turnoff that led to a place called Point Dume Beach. She turned here and descended down a steep road to a white stretch of beach. It wasn't completely deserted—there were a few people walking dogs, a few surfers down by the southern end, and a small family gathering near the northern end—but for the LA area it was about as deserted as a stretch of seacoast could possibly be.

"Do I know emptiness, or what?" she asked, parking the car in a small lot.

"I am impressed," Jake admitted.

They gathered a blanket, a picnic basket, their beach bags, and a small cooler and carried them down to the beach, finding a spot to deploy that was roughly in the middle of the biggest stretch of emptiness. The nearest person to them was more than three hundred yards away.

Jake had showered, shaved, and changed his clothes before leaving the warehouse. As such, he was now wearing his swimming trunks, a pair of sandals, and a Corona T-shirt. He took the T-shirt off and tossed it in his beach bag. Mindy whistled appreciatively as he bared his chest and ran her hand softly over it.

"Nice," she said, pinching a little on his upper abdomen.

"It's all those aerobic classes and personal trainer sessions they make us go to," he said, enjoying her touch upon him.

"I know how that is," she assured him. "I go three times a week for two hours. That's why I can eat all that fried food and ice cream." She shrugged. "It beats anorexia or bulimia. That's how a lot of the actresses keep their shape. That's how Veronica does it."

"Really?"

"Oh yeah," she said. "While we were filming *Thinner Than Water* she was off barfing in her trailer six or seven times a day sometimes. When she wasn't getting it on with her agent, that is."

Jake pondered that little bit of inside Hollywood information for a moment but lost the image of Veronica puking and munching muff the moment Mindy grasped the bottom of her tank top and pulled it over her head.

"Wow," was all he could say as he gazed upon more flesh than any Mindy Snow fan had ever seen on the big screen or on television. Her bikini top was certainly not risqué, but it wasn't terribly conservative either. Her perfectly rounded breasts molded the red cups with a form that could only be considered excellence personified. And when she undid her shorts and pushed them down, showing the almost skimpy bikini bottoms, Jake had to fight to keep from drooling.

"What do you think?" Mindy asked, seeing his interest. "Is my workout regiment effective?"

"You're beautiful," Jake said. "You're an absolute work of art."

She gave him her shy smile. "Would you mind rubbing some sunscreen on this work of art? I wouldn't want to burn it."

He didn't mind at all. In fact, he had to fight furiously to keep from springing an embarrassing bulge in his shorts as he slathered the coconut scented liquid over her shoulders and back, going from her neck all the way down to the top of her bikini bottoms. Her skin was soft and silky and oh so smooth. He longed to put his mouth on it but held off for the time being.

"Should I do the front too?" he asked when he'd rubbed and touched her as much as he could get away with.

She giggled. "I think I can get that part myself," she said. And she did, but the sight of her rubbing lotion into the tops of her breasts and her smooth stomach and her sexy legs was almost more erotic than touching her with his hands.

When she was completely covered with sun block, she offered to do him as well. He gladly turned his back to her and spent a very pleasurable five minutes feeling her soft hands slide over his flesh, rubbing oil on his shoulders, his back, his neck.

"You can do *my* front," he offered once the job was complete.

She smiled and dropped the bottle of lotion into his hands. "I would," she said, "but you might think I was taking advantage of you."

"Spoilsport," he said.

Once he was as oiled as she, they broke into the picnic basket. Inside they found roasted turkey sandwiches, potato salad, and fresh cantaloupe slices, all prepared by Carmella. That ate the food and washed it all down with ice cold cokes. They then lay down next to each other and listened to the crashing of the waves on the shore. Jake wanted to hold her hand, but she kept it firmly atop her stomach, out of his reach.

In all, they stayed for almost three hours, mostly just laying around and talking, but occasionally going out into the surf to play a little. They dodged waves and picked up shells. They did some body surfing until a particularly ferocious wave picked Jake up and slammed him down into the sand hard enough to knock the wind out of him. They walked up and down the length of the beach a few times, taking care to stay as far away as possible from any of the other beachgoers, outside of what Mindy called the "zone of recognition". And while they touched each other a few times while in the surf, they did not kiss or make out. And while they held hands while walking on the beach, they did not embrace here either.

"It's too public of a setting," Mindy told him the one time he'd tried to kiss her.

"But there's nobody else around," he said.

"I know, but its better safe than sorry." She offered him a seductive look. "There will be time for that later."

He tried no further, pacified by the implied promise she'd offered.

*****

They climbed into the Porsche just after four o'clock, Jake behind the wheel this time. They were still wearing their wet bathing suits—although Mindy had put her tank top back on—so they sat on their towels to protect the seats.

"Let's go to my place," Mindy told him. "Do you know the way?"

He didn't actually, but she was glad to direct him. As he piloted the car through the winding roads Mindy snuggled up next to him, resting her head on his shoulder, her hand on his leg. A few times, during the straightaway portions, she would angle her head upward and give him soft, drawn out kisses on the mouth. They talked little, and what conversation they did have was of unimportant things. Jake didn't mind. He was immensely enjoying the feel of her body against his.

They pulled into her garage just before five o'clock. When they entered the house, Carmella was nowhere to be found but the smell of roasting meat came from the kitchen.

"Mmmm," Mindy said, sniffing the air. "Her pot roast. It's one of my favorites."

"It smells delicious," Jake said.

"Wait until you taste it. But in the meantime, I really need a shower. I'm all icky with sunscreen."

"Me too," Jake said. "Do you mind if I hit your guest bathroom?"

"You could," she said thoughtfully, "but we *are* in the middle of a drought, you know."

"Huh?"

She blushed, her eyes looking downward shyly. "Well... in the interests of water conservation, maybe we should... you know... shower together."

Jake felt a flush passing through his body, along with a surge of blood rushing into his nether regions. "Uh... sure," he said. "I think that would be very environmental of us."

She led him upstairs, to her bedroom, closing the door behind her. They went to the master bathroom just beyond it. The shower stall was huge, encased by glass, tiled in dark granite. She opened the door and turned on the water taps, bringing it to life. Within seconds, steam began rise.

After taking two large, fluffy towels from the linen shelf and hanging them on hooks just outside the shower door, she turned to him, her shy look still upon her face.

"Shall we get in?" she asked.

"Yes," he replied. "I think we should."

She gave a slight smile and reached behind her, unfastening her bikini top. She let it drop to the floor, baring her perfect breasts to his eyes. They were uniformly tan, the tone matching the rest of her skin. Her nipples were erect, pushing outward insistently. While he was still drinking in the sight of them, she put her hands on her hips and pushed her bikini bottoms down, kicking them off with her foot. Her flesh here was tanned as well, her pubic hair black but sparse, the edges neatly trimmed.

"There *is* a God," Jake said, his eyes looking her up and down while she blushed.

"Now it's your turn," she whispered.

He pulled the string on his trunks, untying the knot, and then pushed them down. His penis was about three quarters erect and rapidly working towards full-blown diamond cutter status. Her eyes dropped to it and she smiled. She turned and stepped into the shower, putting her body beneath the spray. He stepped in behind her and closed the door.

The water was hot and stinging, almost hot enough to burn. He put his arms around her and pulled her against him, kissing her hotly on the lips, feeling her breasts against his chest, feeling his hard-on pushing into her stomach, feeling her sexy legs touching his. She slid her tongue into his mouth, returning the kiss with passion, her own hands dropping to touch his ass, her fingernails scratching over it. She only held the kiss for a few moments however, before she pushed him away.

"Let's get clean," she said, grabbing a large sponge from a shelf and a bar of soap that smelled like fresh watermelon. She handed them to him. "Would you do the honors?"

"By all means," he said.

He soaped up the sponge and ran it over her body, soaping her thoroughly and completely, washing between her breasts, atop her breasts, and feeling her hard, slippery nipples gliding across his forearm. He soaped her smooth stomach, dipping all the way down to the top of her pubic hair, watching as rivulets of soap ran down through her bush and onto her thighs. She held her arms up and he washed her armpits. She then turned around so he could do her back. He kissed the back of her neck as he soaped her back. She pulled her hair out of the way so he could have better access. She hummed contentedly as his tongue licked at her, as his teeth nipped at her, as his erection nestled into the top of her butt.

She turned around in his arms, her body now flushed, her breath a little ragged. "The top half is clean," she told him.

"Yeah," he said. "Guess I should do the bottom half now."

She smiled and he sank to his knees before her.

He started at the bottom here, doing her left leg and then her right, moving from the toes all the way up to the hips. She then spread her legs a little, opening her stance and giving him access to her womanhood. Her lips were swollen and bright red, as appetizing a set as he'd ever seen. He put the soapy sponge between her legs and rubbed it across, cleaning her here, watching as the spray from the shower rinsed her clean. He then dropped the sponge to the ground and put his hands on her firm ass. He pulled her forward and put his mouth directly on her vaginal lips.

"Oh... God," she moaned as he began to lick up and down. "Yes. Eat me. *Eat* me."

She put her right leg up on the side of the shower, opening herself up for his ministrations. He took full advantage of the situation, plunging his tongue inside of her, rubbing his face back and forth, pushing his nose into her swollen clitoris.

Her hand dropped down to the back of his head, pulling him more firmly into his target. Her legs grew wobbly, seeming like they were going to collapse before him. Somehow, she hung on, grunts and squeals and moans passing her lips as he licked and plunged with his tongue. When he took her clitoris between his lips and began to suck on it she shuddered all over.

"Oh, fuck yeah!" she squealed. "Eat that fucking clit!"

This was the first profanity he had ever heard come from her mouth. He had actually thought her incapable of uttering such words. So shocking was it that he stopped what he was doing and looked up at her.

"What the fuck are you doing?" she panted, pushing his head back between her legs. "Don't stop!"

"Sorry," he mumbled and went back to work. He began to work on her clit in earnest, lashing it with his tongue, moving his head back and forth, all the while maintaining a constant, ever-increasing suction. This action made short work of her. In less than a minute she was trembling all over. The trembles grew worse and her pelvis began to mash back and forth. Her fingers tightened in his hair and she screamed at the top of her lungs, "Oh my fucking God, yesssss! *Fuck* yes!"

She jerked him to his feet and attacked his mouth with hers, kissing him hotly, licking at his lips, sucking on them. Her hand dropped to his cock and began to jack it up and down, squeezing it all the while.

"That was fuckin' fab," she told him when she finally broke the kiss. "Don't ever let anyone tell you that you don't know how to eat a pussy."

"Actually, no one ever *has* told me that," he said, with a certain amount of pride.

She laughed and kissed him again. "Now it's my turn," she said. She bent over and picked up the sponge. "Let's get you nice and clean now."

She soaped up the sponge and then rubbed it softly, sensuously over his chest and arms. When he was well lathered she stepped forward, pushing her body against his, grinding her breasts into his chest, rubbing them through the soap, tracing arcs with her nipples. He groaned in pleasure. She brought the soapy sponge to his back and began to wash there, all the while continuing to press and rub her soft flesh against his.

When she was satisfied that the upper portion of his body was clean, which took a considerable amount of time, she slowly dropped to her knees before him. With a soft smile she washed his legs one by one and then reached around to get his ass. She put a fresh application of soap on the sponge and then went after the main target. She soaped his testicles and then the shaft of his cock.

"You like that?" she asked as her slippery hand jacked up and down upon him.

"Uh huh," he agreed.

She dropped the sponge and turned him a little, so the water ran over his groin and washed all the soap away.

"There," she said. "Nice and clean now. Let's see if it passes the taste test."

She licked slowly up the shaft, swirled her tongue a few times around the head, and then licked down the other side. She sucked his balls into her mouth one by one, tonguing them a few times before releasing them. She then put her mouth back on his cock and slowly deep-throated him.

"Ohhhh," Jake moaned as he felt her bottom out. "Nice."

"Mmmm hmmm," she hummed as she pulled her mouth back off and softly sucked on the head.

She put her hands on his ass and squeezed while her mouth started to suck and release, suck and release, applying just the right amount of friction and suction to impart a delicious sensation. Jake began to suspect that this was not the first time she had performed this particular act. She began to speed up her actions, sucking a little harder, bobbing her head faster and faster, sucking further down with each stroke she made, developing a rhythm designed not just to pleasure but to bring him off.

"You're gonna make me come," Jake warned, just in case that was not her goal.

"Mmmm hmmm," she repeated, increasing her suction and her speed yet again.

Jake had learned a considerable amount about the art of sexuality over the years, including how to maintain tight control over his orgasm. Through practice he had learned to hold himself at bay almost indefinitely. But he also knew that when a woman was giving a blowjob, and expressed intent to perform said blowjob to completion, that was not the proper time to be holding one's self off. In fact, the faster you could let yourself go, the better. With Mindy, it didn't take very long. She already knew to keep up a constant, steady rhythm with lots of stimulation to the head. Jake employed no mental blocks to keep himself under control and he moved rapidly towards orgasm, his hips starting to thrust against her after less than two minutes.

And then he looked down at her. Her pretty, innocent face was looking directly up at him as she sucked, her eyes staring into his. This was the face of Mindy Snow—*the* Mindy Snow! It was not a woman who resembled her, it was actually *her*! This was the cute girl in the long hoop skirts he had watched grow up on that campy, family values show *The Slow Lane*, a show in which she had been known to use phrases such as "gee willikers" and "goodness gracious" and, occasionally, when she was really mad, "for Pete's sake!". A girl whose greatest dilemma with the opposite sex in five seasons was whether or not she should allow Dustin Jerkins, the boy she had a crush on, to hold her hand when they went to the movies. This was that girl, that image of innocence and small town America personified, and she was down on her knees in the shower stall, sucking his cock like a professional. It was that face looking up at him now, that innocent face with those chocolate brown eyes and she was... she was...

"Oh shit," he grunted as the orgasm fired through his body like a nuclear reaction. His knees wobbled and he had to hold onto the sides of the shower to keep from falling. His sperm fired from his cock in hot jets and she kept sucking the entire time, never taking her eyes off his face, never letting that sweet, innocent sensation slip from her own.

When the last vestiges of his climax faded away, when he was finally able to maintain his feet beneath him without holding onto something, she pulled her mouth from his member and stood up. She licked her lips a few times and kissed him.

"Do I make the grade?" she asked sweetly.

"You set the standard for the grade," he told her. "Holy shit."

She smiled again, this time not so innocently. She reached over and turned off the shower. "Let's get dried off and go to the bedroom," she told him. "We've only just begun."

They retired to the bedroom. Once there she lay naked on her back, her legs spread widely, opening herself up almost obscenely for his inspection. "Eat me some more," she told him. "Eat me raw."

He ate her raw. He put his face between her legs and did not remove it for almost thirty minutes. He licked and sucked and slurped and tongued. He slid his fingers into her body, first one and then two and then three. He brought her to orgasm after orgasm, with her screaming out guttural obscenities as each one took her over, and still she kept begging for more, *demanding* more. He ate her until his tongue was numb, his jaw cramping, his neck stiff and threatening to lock up on him.

Finally, after orgasm number six or so, she pulled him out of her crotch. She sat up and kissed his face, licking her own juices from his mouth, his chin, his cheeks. When she finished drinking her fill of this bounty, she rolled over, positioning herself on her hands and knees, presenting her backside to him, her head facing the front of the bed, her swollen vagina gaping open for his plunder.

"Fuck me," she told him, looking over her shoulder.

He nodded, but instead of moving forward, he stood up and turned towards the bedroom door.

"What the hell are you doing?" she asked. "Fuck me!"

"I need to get a rubber," he said.

She shook her head almost violently. "No," she told him. "You don't need a rubber. I'm on the pill! It's safe!"

"But..."

"Come on!" she demanded. "I need you in me, Jake. Get up here!"

Ordinarily he would have ignored such pleas, but this was not an ordinary situation. This was Mindy, the girl he had been talking to and dating, for lack of a better term, for almost a month now. Mindy was trustworthy, wasn't she? And even if she wasn't, she certainly wouldn't have any reason to lie about being on the pill, would she? Getting pregnant by Jake would be much more damaging to her than it would be to him.

He turned and climbed back on the bed.

"Yes," Mindy said. "Oh yes. Now fuck me hard! Fuck me like you *hate* me!"

Fuck me like you hate me? Jake wondered, a bit taken aback. What the hell kind of shit was that?

"Come on!" she demanded. "Get that cock in me! Pound me! Use me! Treat me like a fuckin' slut!"

His cock was, of course, quite hard and had been so for the past twenty-seven minutes. He didn't pause any longer to ponder the meaning of her words. He positioned himself behind her, grabbed her roughly by her hips, and slid into her body in one fluid stroke. He began to fuck her, pistoning his hips rapidly and strongly.

"Yes," Mindy cried in sheer pleasure. "Slap those balls against my ass. Oh fuck yes!"

She fucked back at him expertly and well, matching his rhythm exactly, never missing a stroke. After ten minutes of rear-entry, she pulled free and lay on her back again, this time pulling her knees up to her shoulders, opening herself as wide as possible. He fucked her in this position until both of them were sweaty and panting. For the finale she rolled Jake onto his back and climbed atop him, mounting him in the female superior position. She ground herself to one more orgasm and then began to slam her body up and down on him in a frenzy, sweat flying off her face, her breasts bouncing deliciously.

"Come, Jake," she panted, her fingers pinching at his nipples. "Come for me! Shoot in my body!"

He stopped holding his orgasm at bay and it only took a few seconds before he did as she asked. Like before, it was looking at her face that sent him over the edge, the sweaty, lustful, ecstatic face that belonged to the cute girl on *The Slow Lane*. His second orgasm was almost as powerful as the first.

*****

They cuddled afterward, both of them naked atop the covers, letting the sweat dry from their skin. The Mindy he was familiar with—the Mindy who spoke no profane words, her voice soft and sweet— returned within minutes.

"That was some good lovemaking," she observed. "I can see that all that practice you get in on the road really pays off."

"You were pretty good yourself," he said. "Very... uh... energetic."

She blushed furiously, unable to meet his eyes. "I do get a bit of a potty mouth when I'm... you know... doing it, don't I?"

He kissed her cheek, which still smelled very strongly of her vaginal secretions. "I wasn't quite expecting that," he admitted. "But I liked it."

She ran her fingers through the sparse hair on his chest. "You didn't think that I was... uh... a virgin or anything, did you?"

"Uhh, well... I wasn't expecting that actually, but I wouldn't have been surprised if you *had* been."

"My sweet, wholesome image," she said, this time with a hint of bitterness in her tone. "A lot of it just image, Jake, sad to say. I adore having sex, absolutely adore it. I haven't been a virgin since I was fourteen and the producer of *The Slow Lane* seduced me on the couch in his office." She shrugged. "He was pretty good too. Not as good as you, though. You're up in the top five category, I'm telling you."

"What else is just image?" he asked her.

She giggled. "I guess you'll just have to figure that out for yourself as we go along, won't you?"

That wasn't quite the answer he was looking for, but he accepted it. What else was there to do?

CHAPTER 10

EXPOSURES

The Next Day
Los Angeles, California

It was eleven o'clock the next morning when Mindy dropped Jake off in the usual place. As was the usual routine, they did not kiss or hug or show any sort of affection toward each other. They simply smiled, said their goodbyes, and parted company.

Jake was limping as he made his way back to his building. He was tired, having had less than two hours of broken sleep the night before. He and Mindy had spent the entire night naked in her bedroom, lustfully boffing each other's brains out. Her appetite for sex was incredible, something one had to experience to believe. She could scream out four, five, even six orgasms and still she wanted more. Jake's jaw was so stiff from performing oral sex on her he could barely open it. He had fingernail scratches all over his back and buttocks. His lower back and groin muscles ached with a dull soreness that throbbed outward with each step he took. His penis was shriveled and raw, with abrasions in several places. It had done its duty well, performing all that was asked of it without faltering, ejaculating no less than six times in the past eighteen hours, but it was letting him know about it now.

In all, aches, pains, and abrasions aside, he had to note this down as a successful date. All he had been hoping for, after all, was to finally get his hand on Mindy's bare breast. At the same time, however, the sweet and wholesome image he had held of her had been altered a bit by the sixteen-hour sex marathon. But, all in all, it was not really a bad alteration. She was certainly better in bed—and on the floor, and in the shower, and in the tub, and over the sink—than he had been expecting when he'd started the relationship.

"Good morning, Mr. Kingsley," the doorman greeted as Jake came limping into the lobby. They no longer bothered enquiring where he'd been.

"Morning," Jake mumbled, going right past without slowing. As always, however, while he waited for the elevator to arrive he saw the doorman speaking into his phone, informing Manny that their wandering subject was home.

He rode up to his floor, limped down the hall, and then used his key to open the door to his condo. Manny was there to greet him, a worried expression on his face.

"Welcome home, sir," he said politely, sniffing the air and wrinkling his nose a little as he caught the unmistakable odor of Mindy's musk clinging to him. He had taken a shower before coming home but she had grabbed him as he'd come out of it, laying him down on the bathroom floor for one last ride.

Jake grunted an unintelligible response and closed the door behind him. As he stepped out of the entryway and into the living room he saw Shaver sitting on the couch, dressed in his usual tailored suit and sipping a Chivas on the rocks.

"What the hell is he doing here?" Jake asked Manny. "He's not welcome in this house. Is there anyone you won't let in?"

Manny chewed his lips nervously but before he could answer, Shaver did.

"Mr. Crow instructed him to let me in," he said. "There's something of importance I need to speak with you about, Jake."

"I have nothing to say to you, Shaver," Jake told him. "I thought we made that clear some time ago. You fucked us with your contract. You're raking in millions off of us while we're going deeper in the hole every day. I know we can't get rid of you, but we're done dealing with you."

"Jake..." Shaver said.

"If Crow or anyone else from National has anything to say to me, they can say it themselves. They already know that."

"This has to do with Mindy Snow," Shaver said.

Jake froze, feeling a burst of adrenaline go shooting through him at the mention of her name. What did they know? Obviously, *something*. "What are you talking about?"

"Your girlfriend, Mindy Snow, the actress," Shaver said. "The story about you two is going to break in the next few days. Since I'm your agent, it's me the reporters are going to be calling. Like it or not, Jake, you're going to have to deal with me on this."

Jake sighed, shaking his head. He wanted nothing more than to collapse on his bed and get four or five hours of sleep, but it looked like that wasn't in the cards just yet. "All right," he said. He looked at Manny. "Manny, fix me up a rum and coke, heavy on the rum, and bring me a pack of smokes and a lighter."

"Yes, sir," Manny said, almost skittering away.

Jake walked over to the easy chair and sat down. "All right, Shaver," he said. "Tell me what's going on."

"You were at Point Dume beach with Ms. Snow yesterday," Shaver said. "There was a photographer there as well. He used a high magnification telephoto lens and shot almost a dozen rolls of film of the two of you lying on the beach, holding hands, rubbing suntan oil on each other, and playing in the surf. The photographer has been identified as Paul Peterson, a well-known independent who specializes in celebrity shots."

"A paparazzi?" Jake asked.

"Correct. We have yet to hear who he will be selling the shots to, but the most likely is the *American Watcher* tabloid. They have the biggest budget for shots such as this and he has a long history with them."

This was all just a little too much for Jake to process at once. He decided to take things one at a time, starting with the most obvious question first. "How do you know about all this?" he asked.

"Steve Crow called me and told me," he said.

Jake resisted the urge to yell. "Okay," he said. "And how does Steve Crow know about all this?"

"I'm not really at liberty to say. The information is accurate, however. I have no doubt about..."

Jake leaned forward, his eyes burning into Shaver. "How does he know?" he said, a hint of menace in his voice.

"Jake..."

"How?" Jake barked.

Shaver took a deep breath. "A private investigator in the employ of National Records was there on the beach watching the two of you," he finally said.

Jake shook his head in disgust. "A private investigator was following me?" he asked. Had he really thought that Doolittle was really going to let him live his own life? Had he *really*?

"Jake, I had nothing to do with that," Shaver said. "Had I been asked, I would have advised against it."

"Sure you would've," Jake said. "How long has this asshole been following me?"

"Ever since you met with Mr. Doolittle about which songs you would be recording."

"So they've followed Mindy and I everywhere we've been since our second date?"

"They know everything, Jake," Shaver confirmed. "They know she picks you up three blocks from here and you usually drive to her house. They know you drove up to her house once, that you drove around the rural part of the county on another occasion and had dinner in a restaurant together, and they know you went to the beach and then spent the night at her house last night."

"Those fucks," Jake said, enraged.

"Here," Shaver said, whipping out his little silver case. "Let me set you up a couple of lines. That way you'll be able to..."

"I don't want any of your blow, Shaver," Jake told him.

He seemed hurt, but he put his case away. "Look, Jake. All they're trying to do is protect you. They've invested a lot of money in you and they just want to know that you're not putting yourself in any danger—physical danger or professional danger. And you have to know that this relationship you're in with Mindy Snow certainly falls into the professional danger category."

"Professional danger?"

"The relationship is bad for both of you. Your images are incompatible. It would be bad for her for it to be known she was seeing a rock musician and it would be bad for you for it to be known you're seeing a... well... a character actor known for family values roles."

"I'm not going to stop seeing Mindy because National Records doesn't like what it does to my image," Jake said. "Nor does their concern for all of this give them the right to send detectives after me." He shook his head in anger. "That fucker followed us *everywhere*?"

"Everywhere," Shaver confirmed again. "But you're missing the point. What we need to do is start worrying about damage control."

Jake wasn't listening. "How in the hell did this snooping fuck even know…" He stopped mid-question as Manny came into the room, carrying Jake's drink, a pack of cigarettes, a lighter, and a crystal ashtray.

"How did he know what?" Shaver asked, ignoring Manny as he set his bounty down before Jake, at least until he noticed Jake glaring at the manservant in a knowing way.

"Is there something wrong, sir?" Manny asked, catching the glare as well.

"No," Jake said. "Nothing at all."

"Will there be anything else?"

"No," Jake told him. "Go find something to do."

"How about you, Mr. Shaver?" Manny asked. "Can I refresh your…"

"He won't be staying long," Jake interrupted. "Go find something to do."

"Of course, sir," Manny said. He bid a hasty retreat.

"What were you going to ask, Jake?" Shaver enquired once he was gone.

"Nothing," Jake said. "Don't worry about it."

Shaver nodded. "Okay then," he said. "Let's talk damage control. My suggestion is that when the press calls to ask about this we simply tell them that you and Ms. Snow are nothing more than friends. You met initially at her movie premier, correct?"

"Yes," Jake said.

"You decided to get together and go to the beach after that," Shaver said. "My understanding is that there are no… well… compromising pictures. About the worst they have are the shots of you holding hands and rubbing oil on each other. That's something that two people who are friends would conceivably do, right? Of course, we should touch bases with Ms. Snow's agent and let her know the pictures are coming out as well. That way, we can coordinate the story so it matches. I can't imagine Ms. Snow's people will have any problem with the denial."

"Right," Jake said. "Sounds good. Do it."

Shaver seemed surprised. He had obviously been expecting some sort of a fight over this. "Really?"

"Really," Jake said. "I'm sure you're an expert in this sort of thing. I don't give a shit if the whole world knows I'm dating Mindy, but I don't want to hurt her career. But don't contact her or her agent until I get a chance to talk to her."

"When will you do that?" Shaver asked.

"As soon as she gets home. That should be in about forty minutes or so."

"Uh… okay," Shaver said. "Can I wait with you until…"

"No," Jake said. "I don't want to look at your lying, cheating face any more than I have to. I'll call you at your office."

Shaver looked like he wanted to say something but decided not to. Instead, he simply said, "Okay, I'll do that."

"One other thing, before you go," Jake said.

"What's that?"

"How did that paparazzi prick know we were going to be at that beach?"

"We don't know," Shaver said. "You can be sure that nobody at National tipped him off. They were horrified when they heard about these photos. I suppose it's possible that it was nothing more than bad luck. You know? That he just coincidentally happened to be there for reasons of his own and saw you with Mindy."

Jake shook his head. "No way. That's an isolated beach out in the middle of nowhere. The only way he could've just happened to be there at the same time we were was for someone to have told him we were going to be there. Now who might've done that?"

Shaver shrugged. "I see where you're coming from, but who would have the motivation to do that? It doesn't make sense."

"No," Jake said. "It doesn't. But someone called him up and tipped him off. Someone wanted pictures of us together."

But as hard as they stretched their imaginations, neither could think of a single person who had anything to gain by having the relationship go public.

*****

Shaver left, or rather was ejected from the premises. Jake sat and finished his drink. It was the first alcohol he'd had in two days and it imparted his body with a slight buzz. He stood up, taking his empty glass, and walked into the kitchen, where Manny was chopping up onions.

"What you making, Manny?" Jake asked him.

"Chicken Bourgeois," he said, over-pronouncing the French. "It's a casserole with..."

"Cool," Jake said, setting his empty glass down next to the cutting board. "How about you fire me up with another drink?"

"Uh... sure," Manny said, a funny look on his face. Generally, if Jake came in and found him busy with something he would make his own drink, or fetch his own cigarettes, or do whatever other minor task he wished done. "As you wish."

"And hang out in the living room when you're done," Jake told him. "I need to talk to you about something."

"Yes, sir," Manny said, the funny look turning to a slightly troubled one.

Jake left him and went into the office. Here, in addition to a desk, a filing cabinet, a phone, and a water cooler, was a wall safe. He dialed the combination from memory—a number that Manny knew as well—and opened it. Inside was half an ounce of premium marijuana, a few pill bottles with things such as Valium and morphine and codeine in them (items that Jake never bothered with), and a gold plated case that contained several grams of cocaine and all of the paraphernalia for ingesting it. He took the case down and set it on the desk.

He sat down in the chair and opened the case up. He didn't use cocaine very much now that he was off tour. Realizing how dangerous the stuff was, how he had come to rely on it to get him awake in the mornings and to get him into the mood for the nightly festivities, he had made a conscious and successful effort to slow way down on the white powder. These days he used it maybe once a week, sometimes less, imbibing only when he was going out to a club or when he was having a party. But he needed some now to fortify himself for his coming discussion with Manny.

He dumped out two small lines on the mirror, crushed them up into a fine powder, and then snorted them with the gold-plated straw that was part of the kit. He sniffed a few times and then closed up the kit and put it away. By the time he was done with this task he could feel the drug surging through his system. Though not quite as good as Shaver's Bolivian flake, it was still, as the saying went, some pretty good shit, lovingly produced in the illicit warehouses of Columbia, smuggled across the border in shipping containers, and delivered to Jake's safe completely uncut. His aches and pains faded away like an afterimage, his fatigue disappeared and was replaced by elation and energy, and his heart rate, which had been chugging along at a sedate seventy-two beats per minute, kicked up to a hundred and twenty. He felt *good*, like he could take on the world, which was the proper frame of mind for what needed to be done.

He found Manny sitting on the couch expectantly, as ordered. His fresh drink sat next to the ashtray. Jake sat down and lit a smoke, taking a few deep drags. He then turned to Manny and stared at him.

Manny grew nervous under his gaze, as was the intent. "What's the matter, sir?" he asked. "You seem... uh... upset."

Jake took a sip from his drink and another drag from his cigarette. He blew the smoke directly in Manny's face and then set the smoke in the ashtray. "You tapped my phone for them, didn't you?" he asked.

Manny managed to look appalled by this accusation. "Excuse me, sir?" he asked. "Tapped your phone? I would never do anything like that."

"Then how did the snooping little fuck they hired to follow me around know when and where Mindy would be picking me up? How did he just happen to be there when I climbed in her car?"

"He probably staked you out," Manny said. "That's what people like that do."

Jake chuckled a little, though it was far from a friendly chuckle. "You just made your first mistake in the interrogation, Manny," he told him. "You should've asked what snooping little fuck I was talking about, shouldn't you have? After all, you weren't in here for any of the conversation about him. So how do you even know about him unless the people who pay you told you about him?"

Manny blanched as this was pointed out to him. He did recover quickly though. "Mr. Shaver told me about it," he said.

"Uh huh," Jake said. "I believe that about as much as I believe in Santa Clause. But that's not my concern at the moment. My concern is the tap that has been placed on my phone. I want you to show me where it is and then to show me the tape recorder or whatever you're using that is capturing everything I say."

"Jake, you're being paranoid. I would never tap your phone."

"Well somebody has," Jake said. "I might be able to believe that the private eye was staking out my building to follow us when we leave—just maybe—but I can't buy that he just happened to have been in position yesterday when Mindy picked me up at the warehouse. Sorry, that ain't gonna fly. Someone told him that we planned to meet there and the only way that information could have gotten to him was for someone to have been listening in on our phone conversations. Now I know you didn't do something as amateurish as picking up the extension and listening in that way. I was sort of expecting that and listening for the click and it never came. That means there's a tap somewhere."

Manny shook his head. "I suppose it's possible, but I didn't do it. Maybe the private investigator tapped the phone himself."

"Oh, I have no doubt that he is the one who installed it," Jake said. "But he had to have been let in here by you, and you are the one who is listening to the tapes and reporting to him."

"Jake," he said. "He doesn't need me to do that. Surely you know that taps can be very sophisticated. He could be receiving radio transmissions of your conversations."

"He could be, but he's not," Jake said. "It would be expensive to do that, and he would have to monitor the transmission twenty-four hours a day, seven days a week, to be sure he caught everything. Wouldn't it be a lot easier for them to use the sneaking little mole they already have in the residence to monitor tapes for them? I mean, what would it take you? A couple of hours a day?"

"I'm not a spy, Jake. I don't know how many times I have to..."

Jake stood up suddenly and grabbed Manny by the front of his shirt. He pulled him bodily to his feet, spun him around, and then slammed him into the nearest wall hard enough to knock two pictures to the floor. Manny's expression registered shocked surprise and the first hints of fear.

"What are you doing?" Manny yelled. "You can't..."

Jake pulled him back and then slammed him into the wall again, harder this time. Another picture went down, the glass in the frame shattering on impact. "I can and I *am*," Jake yelled at him. "You're going to take me to that fucking tap right now or I'm going to beat the living shit out of you. You want a few scars on that pretty face of yours? I can give them to you."

"I'll call the cops!" Manny threatened, a little breathlessly since the wind had been driven from his lungs. "They'll arrest you!"

"Maybe," Jake said. "And then what? National will put one of their high-priced lawyers on the case and get me off. After all, I'm someone who makes millions of dollars for them, ain't I? What do you do for them? You spy on me and stew fucking rabbits for me. You don't make them any money. Anyone could do what you're doing. You are a replaceable asset. And the way the high-priced lawyer will get me off is by finding out every sordid thing you've ever done and bringing it out in open court. The media will be all over the case since I'm a celebrity. They'll expose you for the flaming faggot you are and any hope you ever had of being an actor will be destroyed. So go ahead and call the fucking cops. But first, you're going to tell me where that goddamned phone tap is!"

"Jake, there is no..."

Jake spun him around and threw him into the couch. He caught the back of it with his legs, flipped upside down, bounced onto the coffee table, knocking over Jake's drink and the ashtray, and then crashed to the floor. Before he could even begin to get up, Jake was upon him, pushing him back into the floor.

"Where's the fucking tap at?" Jake asked. "That's the last time I ask. You say there isn't one again, I start punching that pretty face."

Manny was now quite terrified. His eyes were bugging out in fear. "All right," he said. "All right! Let go of me!"

"Are you gonna show me where it is?" Jake asked.

"Yes," he said, crying now. "I'll show you. Just don't hit my *face*."

Jake stood up, jerking Manny to his feet. He pushed him towards the phone in the living room. "This one first. Did he put one in there?"

"They're not in the phones," Manny sobbed. "My God, did you have to be so violent?"

"Apparently I did," Jake said, without remorse. "And what do you mean they're not in the phones?"

"You don't have to put them in the phones," Manny said. "You just have to tap into the line."

"Oh," Jake said. "Guess I've been watching too many spy movies. Show me where the shit is."

Manny, still sobbing, led Jake to the back bedroom of the house, where Manny slept. The room was neat and tastefully decorated. Manny went to his bed and pulled it away from the wall. He picked up a small handheld tape recorder, which was plugged into a socket that had been installed in the wall.

"I thought you had your own phone line," Jake said.

"I do," Manny said. "But the main phone line is back here too. He just cut a hole in the wall, tapped into it, and then installed the tape recorder."

"And you've listened to all of my phone conversations on that thing?" Jake asked. "Listened to them and reported everything to this investigator asshole?"

"Yes," Manny blubbered. "I'm sorry, Jake. I had to do it. It's my *job*!"

"Uh huh," Jake said. "That's what the boys at Nuremberg all said too." He took the recorder out of Manny's hand and yanked it forcefully out of the wall. He dropped it to the floor and stomped on it with his foot, until it was nothing more than a smashed piece of components and plastic. "You can give that back to them now. Are there any more?"

"No," Manny said. "Why would there be?"

Jake nodded. He believed him. "And is there anything else in this house I need to know about? Bugs in my bedroom? Cameras in the fuckin bathroom?"

Manny shook his head. "They just wanted to know where you were going and what you were doing."

"Okay, and now for the big question. Did you play a little double agent on National and tip off that paparazzi fuck that Mindy and I were going to be at the beach yesterday?"

Again, Manny showed just how far into the loop he was by not expressing any surprise over the fact that a paparazzi had taken shots of the two lovers. Obviously Shaver or, more likely, Crow had already briefed him on that. "Of course not," he said. "That would be career suicide for me to do something like that. Besides, I didn't know what beach you were going to. Ms. Snow never mentioned that on the phone."

He did have a point there. "Okay," Jake said. "This is the deal. You tell Crow and that PI whatever the fuck you need to tell them. I would suggest the truth—that I beat the information out of your snooping ass—but that's up to you. In the future, you will allow no more recording devices or snooping devices of any kind to be installed in this house. You can keep informing on me like you're supposed to, but stick to your own observations. If I find out you're bugging or tapping or doing anything else along those lines, I will throw your ass off the fucking balcony. Do I make myself clear?"

He nodded. "Yes, Jake," he said. "You make yourself clear."

"And do you believe me?"

Manny shuddered. "I believe you."

*****

He called Mindy thirty minutes later. She expressed shock and embarrassment when he told her they had been captured on film, especially when he told her how he knew they had been captured.

"They tapped your phone?" she cried. "Oh my God, Jake. All those things I said to you. All those private conversations! They know *everything* we said to each other?"

"Well, Manny heard them all," he said. "I don't think he made a transcript though. He just reported the who and the where of the meetings."

"I still feel violated," she said. "My God. Listening in on private phone calls? What kind of people do you work for?"

"I think we've been over that one," he said. "But trust me when I say that it won't be happening again."

"How did you get him to admit it?" she asked. He had left his interrogation method out of the story.

"We had a heart to heart talk," Jake told her. "But enough about me. What's this going to do to you? What's our next move?"

She sighed. "I suppose I'm going to have to call Georgette and make a confession to her. It's her they're going to be calling when they decide to break the story. I think the best thing to do is to tell them that you and I are friends, that we met at the premier and found out we both liked the beach so we decided to go there together. After all, they didn't film us doing anything... you know... naughty. We didn't even kiss." She giggled. "Not there anyway."

Jake smiled despite everything that had happened. "Yes, it's a good thing they didn't catch our action a little later that day. Anyway, that's the same thing Shaver said we should tell them. Just good friends, nothing more. But will anyone believe it?"

"Of course not," she said. "People always want to assume the worst."

Jake did not point out that in this case, the assumption would be right. "Won't that hurt your image?"

"Maybe a little," she said. "I don't think it will be a fatal blow though. What about your image?"

"Well, they might not invite me to the next convention on Satanism and Practical Human Sacrifice, but I didn't have anything to wear to it anyway."

She laughed. "Oh you," she said. "Really though, is this going to hurt you?"

"No," he said. "It won't hurt a bit. I told you, I don't give a crap about my image. I'm just a musician. I try to let my music speak for itself."

"But your record company isn't happy."

"Screw them. They're never happy about anything. There is one thing I'm wondering about though."

"What's that?" she asked.

"How did that photographer know we were going to be there? Manny couldn't have told him because he didn't know where we were going. Did you tell anyone you were going to that particular beach?"

"Well, I told Carmella to pack me up to go to *the* beach, but I didn't tell her which one. And even if I did, Carmella would never snitch me out to the paparazzi. Not in a million years."

"Does anyone else know that you go there?"

"A couple of girlfriends of mine, but I didn't tell any of them I would be there that day, let alone that I would be there with Jake Kingsley."

"Hmm," he said, shaking his head. "It's just weird that he knew to be there. Someone had to have tipped him off."

"Unless he really was there completely by coincidence," she said. "Who knows? Stranger things have happened."

"I suppose," Jake said. "But it just doesn't ring true."

*****

It turned out that Shaver's prediction was the correct one. A reporter from *American Watcher* called Shaver's office early Monday morning, letting him know that certain photographs of Jake Kingsley in the company of Mindy Snow on a certain isolated beach were in his possession and the tabloid was planning on printing some of them along with a story in the following Friday's edition. Would Mr. Kingsley care to comment for the record? Shaver told the reporter that Mr. Kingsley would not care to comment and that the only comment he, Shaver, was offering was that Jake and Mindy had met at the premier of *Thinner Than Water* and had since become friends—and only friends.

"Are you denying that there is a romantic relationship between them?" the reporter asked.

"I am absolutely denying it," Shaver said firmly.

"But the pictures show them rubbing suntan lotion on each other and walking hand in hand."

"Those are things that male and female friends are known to do," Shaver said. "There is no romantic involvement between the two of them at all."

The reporter pestered a little more, but Shaver refused to comment further.

Georgette, Mindy's agent, received a call from the same reporter only minutes later. She too denied any romantic involvement between the two stars. She expanded a little bit on Shaver's friendship explanation by stating that Jake had mentioned to Mindy at the movie premier that he loved the beach but had a hard time finding one that wasn't swarming with people. Since Mindy knew about the isolation of Point Dume, she offered to take him there.

"But what about the hand-holding and the suntan oil rubbing?" he asked her. "That seems a little more than friendly."

"Mindy is a little naïve about men's attention toward her," Georgette replied. "I'm sure that Mr. Kingsley had something other than friendship on *his* mind, but with Mindy, I assure you that she was treating such gestures of affection as nothing more than a brother-sister type of interaction. She took Mr. Kingsley back to his home afterward and that was the end of it."

"Did Jake try anything with her?" the reporter asked.

"I am not at liberty to say what Mr. Kingsley might have attempted or not attempted," she said. "But I can state with absolute certainty that he would have been shot down in flames if he did. Mindy would never become romantically involved with such a person as Jake Kingsley."

By Tuesday afternoon word had leaked about the upcoming article and pictures. The entertainment shows, the celebrity gossip rags, and even the legitimate national news programs were all reporting that pictures of Jake Kingsley with Mindy Snow on an isolated beach were forthcoming in the next issue of *American Watcher*. Descriptions of what the pictures would show were part of the leak and the public grew excited at the prospect of seeing Mindy Snow in a bikini.

Wednesday was the third day of *Intemperance*'s recording session. When the limousine dropped the band members off in front of the National Records building that morning, a group of paparazzi, news reporters, and print reporters were gathered out front waiting for them. Flashbulbs exploded and questions were shouted.

"Tell us about you and Mindy Snow," one demanded.

"Did you kiss her?" asked another.

"Did you try anything with her?" asked another.

"How long have you and Mindy been seeing each other?"

Jake weaved his way through the throng like a halfback on a running play. Only when he reached the door did he turn around and give a brief statement.

"Mindy and I are just friends," he said. "Nothing more. I didn't try anything with her and she didn't try anything with me. That is all."

The same throng was there when they left at 6:30 that evening. And they were there the next morning as well. Jake talked to them no further, but they didn't give up. They showed up everywhere he went, asking, shouting, and snapping pictures. Matt was even cornered by them at the Pink Flamingo on Thursday night, while he was partying and scoping out the likely groupie prospects for his enjoyment that evening. He offered perhaps the most colorful statement on the matter.

"There ain't nothing between Jake and Mindy Snow," he told them. "I guarantee it."

When asked how he could be so sure, he replied, "Because me and Jake are tight with each other, you know? If he would've tapped into something as juicy as that, he damn sure would've given me all the stinky details."

Advertising rates for that week's *American Watcher* were jacked up to almost double what they normally were and they sold out every square inch within hours. On Friday morning the issue was released for sale. All across the country it was placed in the usual locations: supermarket checkout displays, newsstands, convenience store shelves. The issues flew off the stands almost as fast as they could be stocked. Extra printings were ordered and they sold out as well. More than three million were bought in the first twenty-four hours—a new record. By week's end more than nine million copies were purchased—another record.

The headline on the front page proclaimed, in extra-large print, JAKE KINGSLEY AND MINDY SNOW PHOTOGRAPHED ON DESERTED BEACH! In smaller print, below this, was a sub-headline that read, THE YOUNG CELEBS DENY ANY ROMANTIC INVOLVMENT. WHAT DO *YOU* THINK?? Below this, taking up most of the available space, was a high-resolution picture of the two of them walking hand in hand in the breaking waves. The shot had been taken from the front and had caught them gazing at each other and smiling in that goofy way that lovers smile at each other. It was the perfect teaser shot. Mindy looked alluring and gorgeous in her red bikini, her young breasts, which a generation of adolescents had drooled over while watching *The Slow Lane*, pushing the cups out in a most appetizing way. FULL PHOTO SPREAD INSIDE! promised yet another headline at the bottom of the page.

And indeed there was a full photo spread. It took up five pages of the issue, starting with Mindy removing her shirt and pants. There was a shot of Jake rubbing oil on her back and one of Mindy rubbing oil on his back. There was one of them lying on their backs on the beach, the angle suggesting it had been taken from the dunes behind them. There were several hand-in-hand shots as they walked in the waves. There were shots of them playing in the surf, one in which Jake had his hands on her waist and was lifting her in the air. Each shot had a caption beneath which explained for the visually impaired exactly what was taking place.

The article that accompanied the pictures was short—less than a thousand words. It claimed that world-renowned photojournalist Paul Peterson had been on "sabbatical" at his favorite beach when, to his utter surprise, Jake Kingsley and Mindy Snow had shown up in a Porsche 911 convertible and set up camp less than fifty yards from him. Mr. Peterson stated for the record that the two "celebs" frolicked on the beach for more than three hours, eating a picnic lunch, rubbing oil on each other's body, and playing in the surf like two people who are intimately familiar with each other. They then "climbed back in Mr. Kingsley's sports car" (apparently, they didn't realize it was Mindy's car, or if they did, they thought it sounded better if they didn't) and "headed off into the sunset, looking like they had further business to attend to". There was then a brief background about Jake in which the cocaine from the butt-crack allegations were rehashed (in case anyone had forgotten about that) and a notation that the two celebs had been seen talking together for an extended time during the premier of *Thinner Than Water* in Los Angeles (a story which had been printed in *American Watcher* the week after the premier but had been largely forgotten at this point). The official statements from Shaver and Georgette rounded out the story.

"Goddamn," Matt said that Friday morning as the band, having just arrived at the recording studio, looked at the pictures for the first time. "She really *is* a tasty piece of poontang."

"I used to masturbate to her on *The Slow Lane*," Bill added. "I can see now that I was justified and correct in doing such."

"Did she let you spooge on her tits, Jake?" Coop asked. "Tell me you did that at least once."

"Yeah," said Jake, who had shared the fact of his all night copulation with the band but not the details. "I did that at least once."

While they were all holding up their hands for high-fives at this revelation, Crow came in the room, his dark sunglasses hiding his expression. "Those fucking reporters are everywhere out there," he proclaimed. "You didn't say anything to them, did you, Jake?"

"Just the standard, 'no comment'."

"Good," Crow said. "Keep that up and hopefully this will blow over in a few weeks. The most important thing is for you to stay well away from that girl from here on out."

"Excuse me?" Jake said, his eyes starting to glare a little. He and Crow had already had a long and heartfelt discussion about the tap on his phone and the PI hired to tail him (Crow had assured him it was all Acardio's idea and that it wouldn't happen again).

Crow looked at him strangely. "Well, obviously you can't take the risk of being seen with her anymore. The photos they got are damaging enough."

"If she wants to continue seeing me, then we will continue seeing each other," Jake told him. "You will not dictate who I do and do not socialize with. We've already been over this."

"Jake," Crow said, "try to think of Matt and Bill and Coop and Darren. You may not care about your own career, but you're hurting the rest of the band too. Dating little Miss Sweet and Innocent will cause your fans to lose respect for the entire band."

"Whoa there," Matt spoke up. "Hold the fucking phone, dickweed. Don't go invoking *my* fuckin name in this shit and trying to claim that *I* have a problem with who Jake is slipping his salami to. If he wants to hose down Snow White with all the fuckin forest animals singing to the rhythm of his balls slapping, that's his business. It won't do shit for our image, either good or bad. Our music is what sells the albums and that ain't changing."

"Yeah," Darren said righteously. "What he fuckin said!"

"Goddamn right," said Coop. "I'm proud of Jake for scoring with her! Don't be telling me what I should and shouldn't mind him doing."

"I agree as well," Bill said. "Who Jake chooses to fornicate with is his prerogative. I fail to see any intrinsic harm in our popular image secondary to his choice of carnal companionship."

"Well said, Nerdly," Matt said.

"Thank you," Bill replied.

Crow next tried to play on Jake's sensitivities toward Mindy herself. "What about *her* career?" he asked. "Did you ever think of that? However badly this revelation harms your image, it's ten times worse for her. She's supposed to be a respectable girl-next-door. If a sexual relationship with you becomes confirmed her fans won't take her seriously anymore. Parents won't let their kids watch her movies."

This did pull on Jake's conscience the tiniest bit. After all, he had developed rather strong feelings for Mindy and did not like to think he was doing irreparable harm to her career. He did not let Crow know this however, nor did he let Crow's argument sway him.

"It's nice of you to think of Mindy's image," he said, "but how about we let Mindy be the one to worry about that? If she thinks it's too much, she'll call me and tell me it's over. If she does that, I'll respect her wishes. Until then, you can just keep your nose out of my business."

Crow wanted to argue further but he'd already learned enough about Jake's stubbornness to know it would be futile. "Will you at least try to be discrete?" he asked.

"Sure," Jake promised. "For Mindy's sake, I will be discrete. I'll be the epitome of discretion."

*****

Jake was actually quite concerned that Mindy would do just as he'd suggested and call an end to the relationship in the name of imagery. He knew, based on phone calls the two of them had shared, that Georgette was pressuring her to stay as far away from Jake as possible and to start repairing the damage the photos had inflicted.

"She's trying to set me up with Joseph Clark," Mindy told him during one such conversation. "Can you believe that?"

"Joseph Clark?" Jake asked, lying in bed in his underwear and smoking a cigarette, the phone pushed to his ear. "Are you serious?"

Joseph Clark was the young, fair-haired lead singer of a musical group called *The Marchers*—a group that performed Christian tunes. They were one of the most popular of the genre, which meant that their last album had sold almost two hundred thousand copies, and had been nominated for a Grammy the previous year in the "Best Gospel Performance" category.

"I'm dead serious," she said. "She even had the arrangements half made. She got in touch with Clark's agent and suggested we be seen together in public. She had this whole campaign mapped out where we would be America's sweethearts. There would be shots of us sitting in ice cream stores together or going to movies or where I would attend his concerts and clap for him. We'd release press statement saying that we were both virgins and were committed to remaining so until we were married. She was even suggesting we tour high schools and lecture kids on abstinence."

"Do you even know Joseph Clark?" he asked.

"Never met him in my life," she said. "From what I hear though, he's very fond of the young Christian girls who attend his concerts. *Extremely* fond, if you know what I mean. There have been quite a few abortions paid for by Savior Music two months after *The Marchers* did a concert."

In the end, however, Mindy did what Jake had hoped she would do and told Georgette to go pound sand. There would be no contrived romance with Joseph Clark. She would keep seeing Jake as long as she wished, and she would not give in to pressure to discontinue the relationship. Georgette threatened to quit being her agent, which was of course a bluff that Mindy called, and she eventually extracted from her the same promise Jake had given to Crow—the promise of discretion.

The first time they were able to get together after the release of the photos was the following Sunday. Jake ordered a limo driver to take him to one of his favorite lunch spots. Halfway there he suddenly commanded the driver to stop. He stepped out and walked away, disappearing down a downtown Los Angeles street, cutting through an alley, and stepping into Mindy's Mercedes. They went directly to her place, ate a quick and satisfying lunch prepared by Marcella, and then rode the horses up to Mindy's secret place in the mountains. There they fell into each other's arms and were soon lustfully screwing atop the checkered blanket, Mindy shouting out her profane encouragements the entire time.

After Jake emptied himself into her they lay twined together for a few moments, enjoying the closeness of their sweaty bodies. When their breathing returned to normal Mindy squirmed out from beneath and walked over to the horses, who had watched their naked, noisy antics impassively, and reached into a compartment on her saddle. When she returned to the blanket Jake saw she had a pack of cigarettes and a lighter. Jake's eyes widened in surprise as she put one in her mouth and sparked up.

"You smoke?" he asked.

She smiled guiltily. "Yes," she said. "I have for years. I've been avoiding it when I'm around you, you know? The image thing? But the one after sex is just *so* divine. I couldn't hold off any more."

Jake shook his head in bemused amazement.

"What?" she asked. "Did I finally manage to spoil your vision of me?"

"Not at all. It's just that all this time I've been not smoking around you because I thought you didn't approve of it. I've been dying for a smoke for hours."

They laughed together. She gave Jake one of her cigarettes and they lay back on the blanket, smoking and staring up at the sky.

Later, after riding back to her house, she revealed another of her vices by mixing them up a pitcher of vodka martinis. They were very strong and not much to Jake's liking, but Mindy downed them like they were water. Soon she was drunk, giggly, and very affectionate. They retired to the bedroom where she became profane and extremely nasty—nastier than her usual level of bedroom nastiness.

While engaging her in the classic rear-entry position on the floor at the foot of the bed and breathing heavily from her demands to do it faster and harder, she suddenly reached back and spread her own butt cheeks as widely as physically possible.

"Put it up my ass!" she yelled.

"Are you sure?" Jake asked doubtfully. Her anal opening looked awfully small.

"Fuck yeah I'm sure," she told him. "Get it in there!"

And so, ever the obedient soul, Jake pulled himself out of her dripping vagina and put himself against her puckered anus. He pushed slowly, intending to work himself inside over a few minutes, but Mindy was having none of this.

"Cram it in there!" she ordered. "Rape that fucking ass!"

He did as she asked, finding at once that she wasn't nearly as tight here as he thought she'd be. She moaned blissfully at the intrusion and immediately began telling him to fuck harder.

"Oh yeah," she cried as he pistoned in and out. "Now hold me down by the neck... Yeah... like that! Pull my fuckin hair... harder... harder! Oh yeah... *fuck* yeah!"

Late the next morning Jake was once again tired, scratched up, sore, abraded, and quite satiated. Instead of dropping him off around the corner, Mindy pulled right into the circular drop-off in front of his building.

"Are you sure this is a good idea?" he asked her, already seeing the astonished faces of the doorman and two of the minor league celebrities as they stared at them from the lobby.

"Well, they already know we're seeing each other, don't they?"

"True," he said. "But what about that discretion we promised?"

She leaned over and kissed him firmly on the mouth. "I'm being discrete by not sticking my tongue down your throat," she told him.

"I see."

"Call me tonight?"

"You bet."

And he did. They talked for more than an hour and made plans for the following Sunday. Mindy suggested that since it was already known by the various National Records spies that inhabited the building that they were seeing each other there would be no harm in her visiting him in his condo. She was dying, she said, to try one of the exotic dinners his manservant was known for. Jake was forced to agree with this logic and extended a formal invitation.

Crow was not terribly happy about it when he found out (and Jake didn't even bother asking *how* he'd found out—the information had come to him less than twelve hours after Jake had told Manny he would be having Mindy for dinner on Sunday).

"This is your idea of being discrete?" Crow asked after calling Jake up to his office. "You invite her into your very building, where anyone and everyone can see that she's going up to your condo? How long do you think it will be until one of those local newscasters that lives in that place starts to think they're real reporters and feeds that to the news desk?"

Jake, knowing that there was little Crow was willing or able to do about it, simply shrugged off his concerns and told him to mind his own business. And, of course, Crow was right. When Mindy entered the Esnob Pinchazo building on Sunday afternoon she found herself waiting at the elevator with none other than Steve O'Riley, the flamboyant local weatherman. O'Riley pretended to make small talk with her for a moment and then, just as the elevator arrived, flat out asked her if she was here to visit Jake Kingsley.

"Whatever would make you think that?" she replied.

This confused O'Riley for a moment. "Uh... well... because it's been reported that you two are seeing each other and he lives in this building."

"Does he?" she asked innocently. "I didn't know that."

"You didn't?"

"No. Isn't that a fantastic coincidence? I'm here to see one of my girlfriends though."

"Oh," he said, disappointed. "I see."

O'Riley pushed the button for his floor. Mindy pushed the button for number twenty-four.

O'Riley chewed his lip for a moment. "Your friend lives on the twenty-fourth floor?" he asked.

She nodded. "Yep. She sure does."

"That's Jake Kingsley's floor as well."

"Is it?" she said. "That's another amazing coincidence, isn't it?"

When the doors opened at number nine O'Riley stepped reluctantly out. He cast one last glance at Mindy Snow, who was smiling her friendly smile at him.

"Bye now," she told him. "And if you see Jake around tell him I said hi, okay?"

"Okay," O'Riley said, his head spinning. He walked slowly down the hall and had put his key in the door when it occurred to him that maybe it really wasn't just a fantastic coincidence. Could it be that Mindy Snow really *was* up there with Jake Kingsley?

When he got inside he made a phone call to the television station. The news director agreed with his logic. Within an hour a news crew, packing a telephoto video recorder, was discretely staking out the lobby.

Meanwhile Jake was having another of his illusions of Mindy's innocence shattered. She had just been introduced to Manny and had just given her drink order to him (a double Vodka martini). As Manny went off to the bar to construct it, she turned to Jake and asked: "You got any pot? I really want to get stoned."

He did. They smoked several hits out of his bong and then retired to Jake's bedroom for a long, luxuriant session of sex, during which Mindy presented her bare ass to him and ordered him to spank her.

"Harder!" she said at his first feeble swats. "Leave some fucking marks on me, goddammit!"

He left some marks and produced a few shocked looks from Manny when they finally emerged from the bedroom. The sharp cracks of his hand hitting her flesh had been clearly audible to him as he'd fussed over his shrimp soup and Parisian chicken.

They ate Manny's meal, drank some more alcohol, smoked some more weed, and then engaged in a two hour sex session in Jake's bedroom. Mindy slipped out the door just before eleven that night, leaving a snoring Jake naked beneath the covers. Reeking of sexual musk she found Manny watching television in the main living room. She kissed his cheek, thanked him for a wonderful meal, and let herself out the door. Down in the lobby the news crew spotted her the moment she emerged from the elevator. They filmed her as she walked across the lobby to the valet and while she waited for her Mercedes to be brought around. The moment it was parked in front of the door and she stepped outside, they fell upon her like vampires.

"Mindy," the heavily made-up female reporter shouted, stepping forward and shoving her microphone in Mindy's face. "Do you have a minute?"

"No," she said, taking her keys from the valet and slipping him a ten-dollar bill.

"I understand you've been up on the twenty-fourth floor for the past eight hours. Was it Jake Kingsley you were visiting?"

"No comment," she said, pushing her way around the woman and getting into her car.

"But Mindy," the reporter persisted. "In light of the recent pictures of you and Jake Kingsley together, it could hardly be a coincidence that you just happened to be in the same building where he lives for eight hours, could it?"

"No comment," she repeated, closing her door and locking it.

The cameraman stepped close and zoomed on her through the window as she put the car in drive and pulled away. He continued to film the vehicle until it disappeared from sight around the next corner.

The next morning Jake, who had no idea that any of this had transpired, came limping out the front door to get into his limousine for the trip to the recording studio. A large group of reporters, paparazzi, photographers, and news cameramen swarmed him, blocking his access.

"What the fuck?" Jake muttered, blinded by the flashbulbs, his ears ringing from a hundred shouted questions. His confusion was understandable. Though the press hounded him endlessly wherever he went, this was the first time he'd actually encountered them outside of his building. They either hadn't known where he lived before, or they had been observing some unwritten rule about not disturbing celebrities at their house—he knew not which. But whichever, they were certainly bothering him now. He strained to listen to what they were shouting.

"Was Mindy here last night?"

"What were you two doing up there all night?"

"Are you going to acknowledge a romantic relationship with Mindy?"

"Were the two of you intimate?"

Jake sighed, keeping his expression as neutral as possible. "No comment, no comment," he said as he pushed his way through the crowd and dove into the back of the limo. They continued to shout questions at him as the car pulled away. And when he arrived at the National Records building, there was a similar throng waiting there as well.

Crow was infuriated. "Why the hell don't you just take out a goddamn ad in the *LA Times* and announce that you're banging Mindy Snow? The whole fucking world knows about it now anyway!"

Jake refused to feel apologetic towards Crow or anyone else at National Records. He did touch bases with Mindy and with Shaver, both of whom advised that the best thing to do was to deny everything and to hide behind a wall of "no comment". When contacted later that day Shaver and Georgette both stated for the record—with straight faces no less—that Mindy and Jake had not been together last night, that Mindy had merely been visiting another, unnamed friend, who coincidentally lived in the same building.

The story, the film of Mindy in Jake's building, and the pathetic, unbelievable denials, were played throughout the day on nearly every channel in the United States. Newspaper entertainment sections printed the story the following day. The following week several entertainment magazines had full-length articles about the growing rumors of a Kingsley/Snow relationship. The number of reporters and paparazzi stalking the two of them doubled.

*****

A month went by and things settled down a bit. There was still endless speculation and rumors printed in a variety of magazines or touted on a variety of entertainment shows, but nothing new added to the fever. Jake and the rest of the band were locked into the grueling routine of recording and Mindy had several public relations jaunts she had to undergo in addition to two readings for upcoming film roles.

"They turned me down for the part in *Focus On The Dream*," Mindy told Jake during one of the few phone conversations they managed. *Focus* was a teen-oriented film about a girls' softball team and their struggle for respect and recognition in an early seventies college known for its football team. It was just the sort of cutesy feel-good movie that exploited the Mindy Snow image to the maximum. The lead role had in fact been written with the specific intent that Mindy would play it. She had been told beforehand that the reading was nothing more than a formality. Apparently, however, that had not been the case.

"What happened?" Jake asked. "Was it because of... you know... you and me?"

"Yeah," she said. "It was. The producer told me that with the recent controversy that has cropped up between me and 'that lowlife musician', they decided to go with Jessica Coriander instead."

Jake felt horrible about this. He had cost her a part that would have paid eight million dollars. "I'm so sorry," he told her. "This is exactly what Georgette told you would happen. And she was right."

"Don't worry about it," she said. "It's not *your* fault."

"Maybe we should think about... uh... not seeing each other anymore," he suggested. "I don't want to..."

"Don't you like me anymore, Jake?" she asked, her voice quivering.

"Yes," he said. "I like you very much. I love spending time with you, but I'm hurting your career."

"Let me worry about my career," she said. "That was just another wholesome little girl part anyway. Fuck them if they're afraid my personal life will detract from it."

"But, Mindy..."

"There will be other parts for me," she said. "Trust me. Now when can we see each other again? I'm having a severe case of Jake-withdrawal."

That turned out to be the following Sunday. She gave him cryptic instructions to have a limousine drop him off at an intersection in Beverly Hills at ten o'clock in the morning. He followed the directions and found himself standing in front of a high-end Chevrolet dealership. Mindy's car was not parked out front as he was expecting. While he was puzzling over this, Mindy came walking out from within the showroom wearing a red spaghetti strap top and a pair of white shorts. She ran up to him and gave him a big hug, kissing him repeatedly on the mouth.

"Mindy," he hissed at her. "We're in public. There are people watching us."

"Fuck 'em," she said. "They all know we're together anyway, don't they? Is there any point in pretending?"

This threw him for a bit of a loop. "Are you saying we should go public?"

"No," she said, "but I'm tired of sneaking around like a teenager trying to hide something from my parents. Let's just get together when we want, do what we want, and say nothing to the vultures. Let them draw their own conclusions."

"It's not too hard to draw one when we're kissing in front of a car dealership."

She smiled her sexy smile, the one she usually only displayed during foreplay. "Like I said, fuck 'em. They can make of it what they will." And with that, she kissed him soundly, sticking her tongue in his mouth this time.

He was a bit breathless when she released him, and more than a little aroused. But he was curious as well. "What are we doing here?" he asked. "Where's your car?"

"It's at home," she said. "I had a limo drop me here."

"How come?"

"Because it's becoming quite the pain in the ass to pick you up from your condo," she said. "And as I told you before, I'm an old-fashioned girl. I like my man to pick me up for a date at *my* place, in his own car."

"But I don't have a car," he said, although that wasn't strictly true. His battered old 1976 Datsun sub-compact was still in a storage facility outside Hollywood, rotting along with all of his other pre-fame belongings. By now, its battery was undoubtedly dead and corroded beyond repair, its engine gummed up with disuse. Nor was it currently registered or insured. Even if it were running, however, he certainly wouldn't use it to transport Mindy around in.

"I know you don't," Mindy said. "And that's what we're going to fix today."

"Excuse me?" he asked. She wasn't suggesting what he thought she was suggesting, was she?

She was. "Didn't you tell me once that you always wanted a Corvette? Well they got a butt-load of them here. The eighty-fours are out now. That's the new re-vamped model, you know. I was just looking at them. They're bad-ass."

"Mindy, I can't afford a Corvette," he said. "I can't even afford a used beater car."

"But *I* can," she said. "Come on. Let's go get you one."

"Wait a minute," he said. "You're saying you want to buy me a Corvette?"

"You got it," she said. "What color do you want?"

He was shaking his head. "Nope, sorry," he told her. "I mean, I appreciate the offer and all, but there's no way I'm going to let you buy me a car."

She seemed undaunted by his refusal. "Why not?"

"Well... because... I just can't," he said. "A Corvette runs more than twenty grand. That's way too expensive of a gift."

"Jake," she said, "I'm a multi-millionaire, remember? You hooked up with a rich bitch who likes to spend. Twenty grand is pocket change to me. Now come on. I won't take no for an answer. We are leaving here in your new Corvette or we're not leaving here at all."

She wore him down. In truth, it didn't take too much. The moment he laid his eyes on the new Corvette his resolve started crumbling. When the sales manager—who was the only person Mindy would deal with—took him out for a test drive, his resolve disintegrated to dust. He picked out a metallic blue model with all the bells and whistles. The out-the-door price turned out to be $24,688. Mindy called her accountant and had him wire the money directly to the car dealership's account.

"Put the registration in Mr. Kingsley's name," she told the sales manager as he filled out the final paperwork.

"Yes, Ms. Snow," he said.

"And I trust that you and your employees will employ complete discretion about the details of this purchase?"

"Of course, Ms. Snow," he said, seemingly appalled that she would even suggest otherwise.

"Up to and including the fact that we were even here in the first place," Jake added.

"Of course," he said. He paused in his paperworking. "So... it's true what they say about the two of you?" he asked.

"No comment," they both said, smiling.

They left the lot less than ninety minutes after Jake's arrival, tearing out of the parking lot in his new car. Jake drove to the PCH and headed north. The moment they were out of the city Mindy reached in her purse and pulled out a baggie of high-grade marijuana and a marble pipe.

"Let's burn, baby," she said, stuffing a large load into the pipe. "A new car isn't properly broken in until you've done two things in it. And one of them is hotboxing it."

Jake laughed as she lit up and took a tremendous hit. "Mindy," he said, "you never fail to amaze me."

Ten minutes later they were both quite stoned. It was then that she showed him the second thing that needed to be done to break in a new car. She leaned over, opened his pants, and gave him a slow, sensuous blowjob while he twisted and turned along the winding coast highway. Somehow he managed to avoid driving his new car over a cliff while she sucked and slurped and eventually brought him to a powerful orgasm.

They drove on, following the PCH all the way to Ventura where they had lunch in a small café and then checked into a pricey hotel for four hours of enthusiastic sex. Jake then drove Mindy home and spent the night in her bed. The next morning, he phoned the doorman at his building and told him to tell the limo driver he wouldn't be requiring a ride today. He drove himself to the recording studio only to find that the entire world already knew about his new Corvette.

No one on the staff of the dealership had squealed, but there had been plenty of customers in the dealership while the two celebrities had conducted their business and more than one of them had felt compelled to call a reporter and tell all they'd seen. As a result, it was assumed that Jake had been the one to purchase the car. Having the world know that Mindy had bought it for him was the only indignity he was spared.

"After purchasing the new car," an entertainment reporter narrated on *Celebrity News*, a ten o'clock gossip show aimed at housewives, "the couple showed up an hour and a half later at a small Ventura restaurant, where staff members tell us they dined on cheeseburgers, fries, and chocolate milkshakes. From there they went to the Oceanside Resort Hotel, where an anonymous staff member informs us they rented a suite and spent the better part of four hours in there."

"Well," Crow sighed as he watched the show with Jake, Matt, and Bill, "it's as good as official now. There's really no way to deny you two are screwing each other."

"I guess not," Jake said.

"Did she get all freaky on you again, Jake?" Matt asked.

"Actually, she was pretty tame, relatively that is. I'm not even limping today."

Matt laughed. "God, I love this shit." He turned to Bill. "Has he been telling you what this bitch is into? Holy fucking shit!"

"Yes, he's given me a few details," Bill said. "She is quite the unorthodox sexual companion, that's for sure."

"Would you save your locker room talk for later?" Crow cried, exasperated. "What the hell am I going to do with you, Jake? You got Mindy Snow buying you a damn Corvette and then checking into a hotel with you! Did you guys really think no one was going to find out about this?"

Jake shrugged. "I guess we didn't really care," he said. "Should we get back to work now?"

Crow let his head drop to his desk. "Yes," he mumbled. "Get back to work."

*****

They got back to work and the recording of their second album continued with remarkably little strife between the band and the record company. Having mostly gotten their way in the matter of the album's content, Jake and Matt and the others kept their discontent to themselves about such things as the overdubs and extra rhythm guitar tracks. What strife there was had to do with the cover art and the proposed videos.

It was decided that the title of the album would be *The Thrill of Doing Business*, named for one of Matt's songs, the subject of which had to do with buying and selling drugs and sex. Of course, the National Records art department, sticking with the Satanism theme, had designed a bleak album cover in which the five band members were dressed in black and sitting around a table with candles, a pentagram, and a yellow scroll with the word CONTRACT on top, indecipherable calligraphy covering the middle, and the small but legible signatures of the band members on the bottom. All five of them were leaning to the left. On that side of the album cover a wicked looking hand with pale skin and long, claw-like nails, was protruding from a black cape, beckoning to the five of them. The implication, of course, was that the five of them had just sold their souls to Satan and were having them removed. The band protested this cover as sternly as they could.

"The song is not about doing business with the fucking devil," Matt had screamed at Crow. "It's about creeping through alleys to buy pot and blow. It's about hiring hookers to suck my fucking dick for me!"

Crow stood firm, however, spouting the same line as Acardio before him. "It doesn't matter what your perception of the song is. The title goes along with the satanic imagery *Intemperance* is associated with. This will be the cover, guys. Get used to it."

They didn't get used to it, but they didn't protest anymore. The photo-shoot for the cover took almost an entire day to complete because the band members had a difficult time putting the proper expressions on their faces, but it was completed and sent to the manufacturer for mass production, with a quarter of a million ordered for the first printing.

During the recording process itself, all five of them paid a lot more attention to the actual mechanics of putting music on tape than they had during the making of *Descent Into Nothing*. Since they were no longer intimidated or awed by the mere fact they were making an album, and since they had garnered the respect and admiration of the technical crew by virtue of the continuing success of *Descent Into Nothing* (it was still holding firm at number one on the album sales chart, although *Point of Futility* had finally dropped out of the top 40), they had more time, inclination, and cooperation to pay attention to the ins and outs of production. Bill and Jake were both prodigious in this pursuit, spending every free moment they had observing how the sound board and the mixing board were used, learning the finer points of levels and how to best combine them. They learned so much, in fact, that by the time they started working on the third track of the album the techs were actually taking suggestions from the two of them, not out of hero worship or complicity, but because they were actually good suggestions, garnered from their newfound knowledge of the process of recording coupled with their considerable pre-existing musical knowledge.

"We're actually ahead of schedule," Stuart Myers, the head technician who was producing the album, reported to Crow during a staff meeting just before the Labor Day weekend. "At this rate we'll be done by late October."

"Beautiful," Crow said. "Although we won't release the album until *Descent* starts to fall off the chart. It wouldn't be prudent of us to have the new album knock the old album out of number one."

"Are we gonna get a break between recording and hitting the road?" asked Coop.

"Fuck yeah," Matt said. "I'm down with a little vacation myself. I was thinking Mazatlán or even Rio."

"Let's go to Rio, dude," Darren said. "They have cheap pot there and all the bitches walk around on the beach with their fuckin titties hangin' out."

"I was thinking Hawaii myself," Jake said whimsically. Mindy had a winter home on Molokai and had already invited him to stay in it with her whenever he got the chance.

"Well, there will probably be a window available for a brief vacation period," Crow said. "Say a week or maybe ten days. And we do have some resorts we can set you up with in all of the above mentioned destinations, and quite a few others as well."

"Only ten days?" Coop asked.

"That will be all we can spare," Crow said. "We'll need you to start putting together the tour even if we won't be sending you out just yet. This tour is going to be much more elaborate than the first."

"It is?" Darren asked.

"Indeed," Crow replied. "We're planning on lots of fizz and sparkle, as well as some advanced technology. There will be pyrotechnics and a video screen. We're also working on a laser light display. It's all the latest rage."

"That sounds kind of expensive," Jake said. "That money comes out of our recoupables."

"We're paying for half of it," Crow said reasonably. "Besides, you made money on the last tour. That's almost unheard of. We might as well spend some of the surplus on production."

"Yeah," Jake said bitterly. "You might as well."

*****

As Mindy had suggested, she and Jake no longer bothered trying to sneak around and keep their relationship a secret. They had dinner together and went out to clubs together. They lounged on public beaches and took walks in public parks. At each place they went they were swarmed by fans snapping pictures, asking for autographs, and enquiring what exactly the relationship between the two of them was. Swarms of paparazzi and other media hounds converged upon them as well, asking the same questions.

"We're just *friends*," both would insist whenever it was asked. This was the official line from Shaver and Georgette as well (as appalled as both were over the publicity and the refusal of their clients to have a little shame).

"What about the hotel room in Ventura?" they were always asked.

"That never happened," was the standard reply. Shaver and Georgette both expanded on this denial by damning it as a false rumor started by a lowlife hotel staff member trying to cash in by selling completely made-up information. Since the hotel itself refused to release any registration information, or even to confirm that the couple had actually checked in, a seed of doubt remained in the minds of the public and a good number of people continued to believe that there was no sexual relationship between the two of them.

"Like Mindy Snow would have anything to do with *that* loser," was the common argument advanced by the hard-core Mindy fans.

"Like Jake Kingsley would be tappin' *that* goody two shoes bitch," argued the hard-core *Intemperance* fans. "You damn sure know she ain't gonna let him snort no coke out of *her* ass."

Even though there were shots of the two of them kissing each other—one taken on a dance floor at the Flamingo club, one taken as they climbed into Jake's car at a popular restaurant—they were not considered proof that the two celebrities were getting it on.

"They're very good friends," Georgette explained in each instance. "And Mindy is very affectionate with her friends. I assure you, those kisses are no more than sisterly in nature."

"Sisterly?" Matt laughed when he heard this one. "Holy fucking shit. I wish I had me a sister like that."

And then came the Labor Day weekend. Jake and Mindy left early on Sunday morning (after spending the previous night at Mindy's house, boffing themselves silly) and drove in Jake's Corvette to Lake Casitas, a large, fairly isolated man-made lake twenty miles northwest of Ventura. There, Mindy rented a cabin cruiser and they spent the day cruising around, drinking beer and smoking weed. They worked their way to the western edge of a large island that stood in the middle of the lake and anchored the boat about two hundred yards offshore. This was by far the emptiest portion of the lake. They ate a picnic lunch on the bow of the boat and then retired to the cabin where they stripped off their bathing suits and spent an hour pleasuring each other in a variety of ways.

After enjoying their after-sex smokes and drinking another beer—by now they were both quite intoxicated—Mindy suggested they jump in the water to wash themselves off.

"Let's do it," Jake agreed, standing and picking up his swimming trunks.

Mindy scoffed at him. "Don't be a puss," she said. "There's no one around. Let's swim naked."

And before he could protest she walked out of the cabin, perched herself on the edge of the boat, and dove into the water on the island side.

Jake looked around outside and saw no other signs of human habitation within a mile. "What the hell?" he mumbled. He dropped his suit back on the deck and then cannonballed in after her.

They swam around in the warm water for about twenty minutes, splashing each other and playing like teenagers. At one point Jake picked her up by the waist and hoisted her over his shoulders, sending her crashing back into the water behind him. Finally, their energy waning, they floated near the stern of the boat, Jake holding onto the ladder with one hand while Mindy snuggled herself up against him, her bare breasts pushing into his chest. Soon they were kissing each other, the exchange starting out friendly and playful but quickly working its way up to passionate.

"I want you again," Mindy whispered as he fondled her breast with his free hand and she stroked his erection beneath the water.

"Let's go back inside," he told her.

"Lets."

They went back inside and had another extended session. Later, they had dinner and, though it was illegal to camp on the lake, they slept the night away in the cabin, holding each other's naked body.

It was Tuesday morning, when Jake returned to the recording studio to start the new week, that he found out their little love nest was not as isolated as he'd thought. Crow called him into his office about ten o'clock, interrupting his session at the microphone.

"What's up?" he asked as he sat down in the chair before Crow's desk. Crow did not look happy.

"I just got a call from Shaver," Crow said. "*The American Watcher* just contacted him, enquiring about pictures they reportedly have of you and Mindy Snow swimming naked at Lake Casitas this weekend."

Jake was shocked. How the hell had they gotten pictures of that? There had been no one anywhere near them!

"It seems," Crow explained, "that they have shots of the two of you walking around naked on the deck of a cabin cruiser, jumping naked into the water, splashing and playing and throwing each other's naked bodies into the air, and then having a serious make-out session next to the boat. Although they can't print an unedited picture of this, they do have a shot of you climbing back into the boat after her, still naked, and with a 'raging erection' as I'm told."

"Jesus," Jake said. "This is kind of embarrassing."

"No shit," Crow said. "When they print those pictures and release the story of what was seen next Friday, there will no longer be any doubt whatsoever that you and Mindy are getting it on."

"No," Jake said. "I don't suppose there will be."

Crow started to get mad. "Is that all you have to say?"

Jake shrugged. "What do you want me to say?" he asked. "I'd rather not have my dick or my girlfriend's naked body plastered all over the fucking *Watcher*, but what's there to do about it? Who took the shots anyway? The only place someone could have been close enough was that island."

"I don't know who the fuck took the shots!" Crow yelled. "What the fuck difference does that make? I want to know what we're going to do about this!"

Jake longed for a cigarette, but since he was singing today he resisted the temptation. Instead, he took a piece of gum from his pocket and put it in his mouth. "Let me talk to Mindy, but I think it's probably about time that we just go ahead and tell the truth."

"Are you mad?" Crow asked, appalled. "The truth? You want to admit that you're having a sexual relationship with the girl from *The Slow Lane*? That will destroy both of you!"

Jake hummed the verse from *Que Sera, Sera* and then sang softly, "Whatever will be, will be."

This did not make Crow feel any better.

*****

At lunchtime Jake called Mindy. She already knew about the shots. Georgette had called her about an hour earlier after a reporter from *American Watcher* called her.

"We're totally busted," Mindy agreed. "And there's nothing to do now but come clean. Even Georgette agrees with that."

"Yeah, Shaver pretty much said the same thing," Jake said. "When do we do it?"

"We wait until after the next issue comes out," Mindy said. "Then we have Shaver and Georgette admit our involvement. We throw in a bunch of stuff about how we're appalled at the lack of privacy and all that."

"Why do we wait until after the issue comes out?"

"It gives us a little of the moral high ground," she said. "We can claim we were only trying to be a normal couple and that the evil press forced our relationship into the light."

"Ahh, I see," he said. He sighed. "I'm sorry about all this, Mindy. If I would've known it was going to cost you movie roles to be involved with me, I never would have done it."

She remained cheerful. "Don't worry about it, Jake. Things will work out. They always do."

*****

The rumors and reports of the next issue of *American Watcher* began to circulate before the end of the day. Every publication, every news channel, every gossip network began to talk about naked pictures of Jake Kingsley and Mindy Snow.

When the actual issue came out on Friday morning, it broke all previous sales records within hours.

The headline, printed in huge typeface, read: JAKE KINGSLEY AND MINDY SNOW CAPTURED IN THE BUFF AT SECLUDED LAKESIDE LOVENEST!! The picture on the front was one of the two of them against the boat, kissing with open-mouthed passion, their naked shoulders sticking up, the top of Mindy's obviously naked breasts just visible. The inside shots were a collection of near pornographic images that had been carefully censored to avoid obscenity charges. There was one of Mindy standing on the edge of the boat, about to dive in. There was one of Jake throwing Mindy over his shoulders. There were several of the two of them kissing hotly next to the boat. There were two of them climbing out to get back in the boat. In all of the shots black lines had been added to cover butts and genitals and Mindy's breasts, but what was shown left little to the imagination. There could be little doubt, especially in light of the previous sightings, that the two of them were very intimate with each other.

Jake had been expecting all of this when he opened the issue at the recording studio on Friday morning. He knew what the two of them had done and the angle of the shots did nothing but confirm his suspicion that they had been taken from a hidden enclave on the island they'd anchored next to. What he wasn't expecting were the words in the article that accompanied the photos.

World renowned photojournalist Paul Peterson, acting on a tip, followed the two lovers to their secluded love nest and took a series of shots of the two of them frolicking naked in the placid waters of Lake Casitas.

Paul Peterson? He had taken the shots of them on the beach too, had supposedly just happened across them by coincidence. And now he had just happened to receive a tip that Mindy and Jake were going to be at this particular lake?

"Something smells funny here," Jake mumbled.

"What's that?" Crow asked.

"Jake!" Matt yelled from his own copy of the tabloid. "These are some premium fucking shots, brother! Do you think you can get your stinky little hands on some copies that don't have these fucking lines across her snatch and titties?"

Jake ignored him. "I need to go," he told Crow.

"Go? What are you talking about?"

"I'll come in on Sunday if you want and make up for the lost time, but I need to take the rest of the day off."

"For what?" Crow yelled. "Jake, we have a crisis here!"

He said no further. He left the building, climbed in his Corvette, and started heading towards the freeway.

CHAPTER 11

THE RAZOR

Jake stopped the Corvette before the closed gate that guarded access to Mindy's property. There was a mailbox, a newspaper delivery box, and a small intercom box that could be used to communicate with the inside of the house. Jake pushed the intercom button, holding it down for several seconds.

He hoped he was wrong about what he was thinking—he hoped that sincerely and with all his heart—but he rather suspected that he wasn't. No matter how hard his brain tried to twist and distort the information into something favorable, there were still two irrefutable damnations it could not get around. Mindy was the only person who had known that she and Jake were going to be at Point Dume and she was the only person who had known they were going to be at Lake Casita. And Paul Peterson, the "world renowned photojournalist" had somehow shown up, camera in hand, at both places.

It was conceivable that coincidence was at work here. Peterson *might* have just happened to be on sabbatical at Point Dume at that particular moment in time and it was within the realm of possibility that one of the boat rental employees had tipped him off about Jake and Mindy renting a cabin cruiser and heading out onto the lake. If Jake were trying to prove his suspicions in a court of law he would certainly be shot down at the preliminary hearing stage. But this was not a court of law. This was real life and in real life Jake believed in a thing called Occam's Razor—a concept which stated: *when presented with two (or more) possible explanations for an event, and with all other things being equal, the most likely explanation is usually the correct one.*

It had been the application of this concept to the question of how National Records' private snoop had been able to follow Jake and Mindy around that had led Jake to the correct conclusion that his phone had been tapped and that Manny had not just assisted in the placement of this tap but was also actively monitoring it. And when he applied Occam's Razor to the question of how Paul Peterson was mysteriously finding his way to the secluded meeting places of Jake and Mindy—meeting places that only Mindy knew about in advance—the simplest and most likely explanation, and therefore most likely the correct one, was that Mindy herself was contacting the photographer and tipping him off.

Jake had no idea why Mindy would do such a thing but that was irrelevant to Occam and his razor. The why would be answered later perhaps.

There was no answer to his first intercom buzz. He pushed it again, holding the button down for a full ten seconds this time. This did the trick.

"Hello?" came Carmella's heavily accented voice. "Can I help you?"

He pushed the talk button. "It's Jake, Carmella," he said. "I need to see Mindy right away."

"Jake?" she said, her accent thinning considerably now that she knew who was there. "We weren't expecting you. Did you call?"

"No, I didn't," he replied. "Is Mindy there? This is really kind of important."

"Hold on," she said. There was silence on the box for the better part of two minutes. Finally, a click and Carmella's voice again. "Jake?"

"Still here," he said.

"Come on up."

The gate opened, and he drove through, following the narrow access road up to the guest slot in front of the house. He left the keys in the car and walked to the front door. Carmella opened it before he could knock. She looked nervous and slightly guilty for some reason, her cheerfulness at greeting him somewhat forced.

"Where's Mindy?" he asked.

"She's in her bedroom," she said. "She said to go ahead and send you back."

"Thank you," he said, heading that way.

"Would you like anything to drink, Jake?" Carmella asked him. "Or perhaps a snack?"

"No thanks," he said curtly, not looking back at her.

He opened the door to the bedroom, a room where he'd spent many an hour in sexual overload, and beheld the enigmatic actress sitting on her bed. She was dressed in a red velour robe, her pretty legs crossed in a lady-like manner. Her hair was wrapped in a white towel and her face was void of make-up though still quite beautiful. She had a serious expression on her face.

"Hey, Jake," she said, looking at him. "What brings you here unannounced? Aren't you supposed to be recording?"

"I left early today," he said, closing the door behind him and entering the room.

She nodded, unsurprised. "I assume you saw this week's *American Watcher*?"

"Oh yes," he said. "I found it quite interesting, especially the article."

"The article?"

"Uh huh. It tells a lot when one reads between the lines."

Her expression soured a little and then she shrugged. "Well, I guess the jig is up. You figured me out, didn't you? I was kind of expecting you to."

He stared at her. "You're not going to deny it? That you were the one who tipped off Paul Peterson about the beach and the lake?"

She shook her head. "Not really much point in denying it, is there? Yes, I tipped him off both times. I arranged for those photos of us to be taken. Georgette figured it out this morning too. I got off the phone with her about an hour ago. Man, was she pissed off."

"I can sympathize with her," Jake said. "I'm a bit pissed off myself."

She shrugged again. "Sorry," she said. "I wasn't doing it to piss you off, or to piss Georgette off. I hope you'll understand that."

Her casual, matter-of-fact tone was infuriating. She had just admitted to lying and deceit and was shrugging it off like it was nothing. He gritted his teeth, clenched his fists, and took a deep breath, commanding himself to keep his temper under control. It held for the time being.

"Why?" he asked her. "Why would you do such a thing?"

"Why do we do anything in Hollywood?" she replied. "For publicity."

"Publicity?" he asked. "You just destroyed your image! You've already lost one film role because you're seeing me and you'll probably lose any others they were considering you for now that there are photos of you traipsing around naked with the satanic, butt-crack sniffing rock musician."

She scoffed disgustedly, shaking her head. "You don't understand, do you?"

"No," he said. "I don't. Please make me understand."

She patted the bed next to her. "Why don't you come and sit down?"

"I'll stand," he said.

She frowned a little but didn't push the issue. "All right," she said. "The reason I arranged for those photos was because I didn't want any of those stupid roles they were trying to set me up in."

"You didn't want them?"

"No," she said. "Jesus, you heard what those fucking flicks were about. A film about a girl's softball team? A film about a girl and her horse? They're a bunch of cutesy, do-gooder, feel good films that no one but teenagers will ever watch. Meanwhile there are dozens of other films that will start production soon that are worth a shit. Films about gambling and war and nuclear weapons and hot, torrid love affairs between people who are not supposed to be having them. Films that are going to be nominated for academy awards next year, that will *win* academy awards next year. Films that need strong female leads and supports. Films that *I* can't even get a reading for because I'm cutesy little Mindy Snow who used to be on *The Slow Lane*, who looks like a fucking spokesgirl for the abstinence movement and the good Christian lifestyle. I'm tired of that shit, Jake. I'm tired of being trapped by my own image. So, I'm forcing the world to accept my new image. I'm a sexy, provocative girl and I'm a damn good actress. I deserve more than just fuzzy little family movies."

"So you used me for this?" he said, though it was not a question. "You set me up and displayed me like a prop in one of your films?"

"Well, that's kind of a harsh way of putting it," she said, "but... yeah, I guess I did."

He clenched his fists again, took another deep breath. When he was semi-composed once more he asked, "So when did you decide to do this?"

"Quite some time ago," she said. "When you were on all the front pages for snorting coke out of that girl's ass and when all the parents who love my movies were carrying signs out in front of your concerts, that's when I knew you were the one. I insisted that Georgette invite you to the premier. She didn't want to at first but I convinced her that it was a good idea since we do have some fan demographic crossover."

"You were planning this before you ever met me?" he asked.

"Yes," she said. "You were the perfect bad-boy to change my image. I thought about going after Matt since he's got an even worse reputation than you, but that would've been too much, too shocking. That probably would have had the opposite effect than I intended."

"So... so the wholesome, old-fashioned girl bit you hit me with at the premier, and on the phone, and on our dates. That wasn't real?"

"Oh, Jake," she said with pity in her voice. "I'm an actress, remember? I figured out in our first conversation that you enjoyed the little miss innocent act I was putting on at the premier so I just carried it out a little further until I had you hooked on me. It was easy."

Jake was stunned by the casual, almost off-handed way she admitted her deceit. He had thought he was falling in love with her and she had just been pretending the entire time in order to help her career along. "This is unbelievable," he said to her.

"I'm sorry, Jake," she said. "I wasn't doing any of this to hurt you."

"You know," he said, "I've been used by women before. What man hasn't? I gave a year of my life to a girl who dated me because it pissed off her dad. I've slept with a hundred groupies who were just using me to say they fucked a rock star. But you..." He shook his head. "My god, Mindy. The coldness and the calculation that you put into it is beyond anything I've ever had to deal with before. I'm just a tool to you, nothing more. You played with my emotions and manipulated me just so you could position me in front of a camera for you. I don't think there's even a word for a girl like you."

"Jake," she said, softly, "you don't understand."

"I do understand," he said. "I'm gonna go call for a limo to come pick me up. I'll leave the Corvette outside with the key in it. When they send me the pink slip, I'll sign it over to you and have Shaver mail it to you." He turned to go.

"Jake," she said, "let me finish what I have to say."

"You have finished," he told her.

"No, I haven't, Jake. For God's sake, stop being so dramatic. That's *my* job! Turn around and look at me."

He stopped his trek toward the door. Slowly he turned around.

"I'm being honest now," she said. "Would you prefer that I lie to you and try to tell you a big bullshit story about how it was all a spur-of-the-moment thing to call Peterson up? I lied to you in the beginning and I started this relationship with you for less than honorable reasons. I admit that freely and I'm sorry that life is so unfair that people like me have to do things like that to people like you."

He said nothing, just continued to stare at her.

"But I'm not cold and emotionless, Jake. I started this relationship for the publicity, that's true, but as we went along I really learned to like you. I like you a lot, Jake. I like being with you, talking to you, and I especially like fucking you. You're the first man I've ever met who is able to keep up with me in bed. I didn't intend to fuck you after that day on the beach but having your hands all over me all day made me so horny for you that I had to have you. I was never faking anything in the bedroom with you. In fact, I'm wet right now just looking at you."

Jake had to fight down a tinge of desire that tried to flood him at her words. Looking at her beautiful face, seeing those smooth, sexy legs, the painted toenails, seeing the jiggling bulges beneath her short robe that told him there was nothing on beneath it, knowing the sensuousness and aggressive sexuality she was capable of, it was hard not to become aroused when she told him he was making her wet, but he kept his composure.

"It's over, Mindy," he told her. "I'm not a puppet on a string who jumps when you tell me to. I'm sorry that I'm screwing up your little plan, but you can count me out."

"Jake," she said, her brown eyes peering meaningfully into his, "you're being dramatic again. My plan has already been successful. There are naked pictures of you and I together. If you leave right now, it won't matter. The damage I wished to inflict upon my image has already been done."

"Good," he said. "Then you don't need me anymore."

"Exactly," she said. "You just made my point for me."

Jake stared at her in confusion. "How's that?"

"I don't need you anymore for what I originally intended," she said. "It's over and done. The pictures have been taken, my reputation has been irrevocably altered to what I wish. There is no reason for me to continue seeing you except for the obvious one."

"The obvious one?"

She smiled seductively. "I want to keep seeing you because I like you," she said. "I am in a state of incredible infatuation over you. I long to hear your voice every day, to feel your body against mine, to feel your cock driving into my body. Why do you think I bought you that car? I didn't have to do that in order for my plan to work. I mean, sure, it helped to create another sighting of us together, but I could've done that anywhere. I bought you the car because I'm hot for you and because I wanted to do something for you... something to make you... to make you like me."

He shook his head violently. "I can't be with you after this, Mindy. You took advantage of me, played me, made a fool out of me. I'm done playing games with you. It's time for me to go."

"You don't have to be faithful to me," she said, uncrossing her legs, letting her robe ride up a bit on her thighs. "I know you're going to go out on the road again. I know there are women you'll want to fuck. I'm not going to stop you from doing that. In fact, I encourage you to do it. Hell, its more practice for when you come back to me."

Jake looked at her, mouth agape. "This is insane," he said. "You think I'm going to keep seeing you after what you've just told me?"

"You don't have to love me or anything," she said. "You just have to fuck me. Admit it, I'm the best you've ever had, aren't I?"

He could hardly deny that. "You are very... enthusiastic about sex, but that doesn't change the fact that..."

"Why don't you fuck me right now, Jake?" she asked, letting her legs fall apart a little, just enough to let him visualize her upper thighs.

"Mindy," he said, dragging his eyes away from the appetizing sight. "I don't think you understand what I'm trying to say."

"I understand," she told him. "I understand everything. I had myself shaved today."

This threw him off track a bit. "Shaved?" he said.

"My pussy," she said. "It's all nice and smooth now. Not a hair on it. It's something I like to do every now and then. Today seemed to be the proper occasion. Would you like to see it?"

"No," he said. "I wouldn't."

But she knew otherwise. She slowly pulled the tie on her robe and let it fall open, baring her body to his gaze. She slowly spread her legs, showing him her swollen vaginal lips. Her entire crotch was indeed completely bare of hair.

"Jesus," he muttered, unable to drag his eyes away from it. In 1983 it was very rare for a woman to shave her genitals. Jake, despite all of the women he'd enjoyed over the past year and in his pre-fame life, had never seen a shaved pubis in the flesh. He found himself licking his lips, felt his manhood stirring in his jeans.

"You like it?" Mindy asked, opening her legs a little wider. "I think it's sexy."

"Its very nice," he said, his voice sounding far away. "But it doesn't change anything. You're just trying to use sex to get what you want from me."

"Did you notice," she asked, "that I said, 'I *had* myself shaved'? I didn't do it myself."

"You... you didn't?"

She shook her head, letting the manicured middle finger of her left hand dip down and slide between her lips. She slid it slowly upward, over her clit and up onto the bare skin just above her slit. It left a trail of moisture behind. "Nope," she said. "Carmella does it for me." She put her finger in her mouth and licked the juices off.

Jake's little head was now quite in the game and was calling for a strategic huddle. He tried to fight the rebellion but his eyes could not stop staring at her smooth, sexy, *aroused* vagina. His mind had locked onto the thought of Carmella kneeling between Mindy's naked thighs and shaving her.

"That's right," Mindy said, putting her finger back down and stroking herself again. "Carmella was in here doing the deed for me. In fact, she was just finishing up when you buzzed the intercom. She took my razor and ran it all over me, from my ass to the top, and along the sides of my lips. She had to take my lips in her hands in order to pull them tight."

"Mindy..." he said, but he couldn't think of anything to say after it.

"I'm not into having sex with women, of course," she said, letting the tip of her finger slide between her lips. "Its been offered. Veronica wanted to eat me out in my trailer while we were filming *Thinner Than Water*. I turned her down... politely. But there is something about a woman's *hands* on my body that I like, even if I don't want their mouth and tongue on me. I let Veronica feel my tits once while we were showering. It felt nice. She played with herself while she squeezed them. Made herself come right there in the shower stall." She smiled with sexual nostalgia and slid her finger a little further inside of her. "I will admit that was hot. I played with myself when she was done, right in front of her. She tried to kiss me but I wouldn't let her."

"Jesus Christ," Jake said, licking his lips unconsciously, knowing he should just turn around and leave but unable to muster the willpower to do so.

"But anyway, back to Carmella," Mindy said, her right hand going to her nipple where it started to pull and twist it. Her left began to slide a finger in and out of her vagina, almost casually. "I think she knows how much I like feeling her touch me. She's always gentle and she never complains when I ask her to shave me. And when she's done... mmmm... you know what she does?"

"What?" Jake squeaked.

"She takes baby oil and she rubs it all over my pussy. You notice how soft and silky it looks right now? That's because she just got done rubbing it down before you came in. She slid her fingers in and out of me to make sure it got everywhere. It felt so good, Jake. I almost came all over her hand. In fact, I bet if you would've gotten close enough to her, you would have smelled my pussy all over her fingers."

Jake broke at this point. The visual image of Carmella fingering her coupled with the actual image of her playing with her shaven pussy was too much for him to take. He fell on her, burying his face between her legs, his tongue stabbing out and licking her juices. She squealed in delight at the contact.

He ended up staying for dinner and for a long, extended dessert. When he left at eleven o'clock that night he was behind the wheel of his Corvette and they had plans to get together the following weekend.

*****

On the following Monday morning, Shaver and Georgette, meeting each other in person for the first time, gave an impromptu press conference in front of the National Records building shortly after Jake and the rest of the band arrived and fought their way through the throng awaiting them. The statements the two agents gave were short and to the point. They admitted that Jake and Mindy were indeed involved in a romantic relationship with each other and that their previous denials regarding this relationship were out of a desire to keep their private lives private. Both Shaver and Georgette managed to sound indignant and angry as they chastised the media for sticking their noses into the business of two consenting adults. Neither Jake nor Mindy were present at the press conference although prepared statements—again having primarily to do with their wish for privacy—were read. There was no question period after the statements were given, but that did not stop the press from shouting them at the retreating agents.

"When did they first become intimate?"

"Did they have sex together the night of the *Thinner Than Water* premier?"

"Does Mindy snort cocaine with Jake?"

"Are they considering marriage?"

Strangely enough, or perhaps not so strangely, the number of paparazzi and media people hounding Jake and Mindy decreased dramatically once the admission of their involvement was released. There were still paparazzi popping up whenever they were together, and there were occasional groups of reporters and videographers shouting at them and trying to catch them on tape, but they stopped showing up in front of Jake's building and at the National Records building. They stopped hounding them when they went out to clubs or restaurants together. Now that the world knew they were together and they had acknowledged it, the focus turned from merely catching them in each other's presence to simply keeping a loose eye out for scandalous behavior.

Jake went back to ignoring Shaver, talking to him only when there was something new to release to the public, which wasn't often. Georgette, however, like any good agent, quickly embraced the new reality her client had forged and began seeking ways to shape it for the best advantage. Jake noticed their efforts the first time they went to a club together after the admission. Mindy wore a red dress that was short in the legs and displayed an impressive amount of her very impressive cleavage. Instead of sipping demurely from a glass of diet cola like she usually did in public, she ordered Long Island iced teas and drank several of them in rapid succession. She also chain smoked cigarettes from Jake's pack and made a point of swearing whenever a likely member of the press was near.

"All this is going to get you better movie roles?" he asked her after her third drink and her sixth cigarette.

"Goddamn right," she told him. "The public needs to see me as an adult. A hot, sexy, alluring adult. Actresses who look like adults get adult roles." She put out her latest cigarette. "Come on. Let's dance. Let's show these people what we can do."

What they could do on the dance floor was quite a lot. Jake, like most musicians, had natural rhythm. He had also been forced to take an intense accelerated course in modern dance before going out on the *Descent Into Nothing* tour. His body, used to brutal aerobic workouts and grueling ninety-minute sets on the stage was in excellent shape despite the cigarettes and the booze he imbibed in. And he certainly knew how to move his body to the music. Mindy, though not a musician, had more than three years of dance lessons under her belt as part of her dramatic arts training. She too was in superb shape secondary to thrice weekly workout sessions. The first tune they danced to was *We Got the Beat*, by The Go-Go's. They moved against and around each other with a fluid-like precision, their shoulders, hips, legs, and feet moving almost in unison.

The crowd was impressed with the two of them, so impressed, in fact, that for the next song—*Physical*, by Olivia Newton-John—they did something that Jake thought was only done on movies like *Saturday Night Fever* and *Flashdance*. They formed a circle around the two celebrities, clapping their hands to the beat, and letting them dance alone in the middle of the floor. Jake felt exposed like he never did onstage, felt all the eyes looking at him, staring at him. He prayed he wouldn't do anything stupid or nerdy. He kept the neutral expression on his face and let his body and his instincts for music take over. He didn't particularly care for *Physical*—not in a million years would he have chosen it as the song to dance to before a crowd—but he at least knew it well since the American public had been inundated with it over the past eighteen months far beyond what a reasonable culture could be expected to tolerate.

Mindy knew the song well too, and the two of them twisted and turned, spun and swayed, doing what they did best: performing. As the song played out they began to get more daring, more risqué. Their bodies moved closer together, so Mindy's breasts were virtually dragging up and down his chest, their pelvic regions ground together, and their hands moved up and down each other's backs, dipping dangerously close to the border between lower back and ass. Flashbulbs began to fire off around them but neither noticed, so intent were they upon their dancing. And when the song finally ended the entire club erupted in spontaneous applause, cheering and whistling at them.

"That was fuckin' fab!" Mindy yelled, loud enough for anyone within twenty feet to hear. "Let's go get another drink."

They went back to his place after the club that night and he took her less than thirty seconds after they walked in the door, pushing her against his couch, lifting her red dress above her waist, pulling her matching red panties to the side, and slamming into her while she panted and yelled obscenities to the room.

In the very next issue of *Celebrity News* magazine, there was a picture on the cover of the two of them on the dance floor, Mindy's breasts pushed against his lower chest, her lips less than two inches from his neck, his hands just above her ass. JAKE AND MINDY GET 'PHYSICAL' read the caption. The article that accompanied it was four pages long and described every detail of their dance.

"Is that what you were after?" Jake asked her the following Sunday, as they paddled surfboards out beyond the breakers at Point Dume. "Pictures of innocent Mindy Snow dancing dirty?"

"That's exactly what I was after," she said. "You did good."

"I'm glad I make such a good prop," he said sourly.

She gave him a hurt look. "Jake," she said, "we've been over this. You know I'm not seeing you just for the publicity. I told you that the day you found out. I'm with you because I like being with you. The publicity is now just a pleasant side-effect."

"Yeah," he said, partially mollified. "I guess so. Come on. Let's catch a wave."

In truth, he wasn't quite sure what to think of Mindy anymore. He couldn't tell from day to day, from minute to minute, whether this entire thing was just an act or whether, as she claimed, it had merely started out that way and had evolved into a real relationship. She was as passionate as she could possibly be in the bedroom and when they were alone together—completely alone, out of the public eye—she was just as sweet and caring as she'd always been. They still talked on the phone for hours at a time during the week when they couldn't get together.

It was when they were in public, however, or when there was even the slightest possibility that a member of the public might be watching them, that the whole relationship seemed contrived and scripted. Even now, as they were floating a hundred yards offshore of a relatively isolated beach, her mannerisms, her movements, even her clothing, were all designed to project the image she was fomenting. She was wearing a skimpy blue bikini that flirted with the local community standards of decency. She frequently held hands with him, or rubbed his back, or stole kisses, or grabbed his butt, not out of spontaneity or affection, he was sure, but out of the hope that someone back on shore was seeing her do it or even photographing it.

Subsequently, when he began to get irritated with these phony overtures of affection, as he was getting quicker and quicker to do with each public appearance, he would try to reject them. He would twist away from her kissing mouth, or pull his hand from her questing fingers, or grow surly and silent to her conversational gambits. At this point she would usually chastise him, hissing words through clenched teeth that he was "spoiling the image."

Sometimes, usually in the midst of one of these public put-ons, he would swear he couldn't take it anymore. *I'm not an actor*, he would tell himself, *and I'm tired of pretending*. Several times he had decided it was time to put a stop to it. *That's it*, he would vow, *as soon as we get home I'm breaking up with her. I can't take this anymore.* And then they would get back to his place, or her place, depending on what they had been doing and where they had been doing it, and she would turn her raw sexuality, her deviant nastiness full force upon him and his will would wither, his resolve crumble, under the onslaught of black eroticism. That was where she had him and she knew it, and she had no compunctions about using it.

On one occasion she had gone out onto his balcony, pushed off her pants and panties, and then sat on the balcony rail, her legs spread widely. He fucked her right there, holding onto her waist and pounding in and out, knowing that a simple mis-balance would send her careening downward to crash on the sidewalk three hundred feet below. On another occasion she had dressed in the white blouse and hoop skirt she used to wear on *The Slow Lane*, her hair done in exactly the fashion her character had been known for, the standard naïve clichés like "gee willikers" and "goodness gracious" coming out of her lips in exactly the right tone and inflection as he lifted the skirt and slid into her body. No matter how old the public posturing and contrived mannerisms got, the sex remained quite fresh and Jake, led by the penis, remained an official part of her life.

*****

Recording for *The Thrill of Doing Business* was officially and totally completed on October 28. Since *Descent Into Nothing* was still holding firm in the top ten of album sales—it had slipped from number one but was steady at number three—and since four of the songs from *Descent* were still enjoying saturation airplay nationwide, Crow told the band *Thrill* would not be released until at least January 31, and possibly not until the beginning of March.

"Now we're going to shoot three videos for the first three scheduled single releases," he told them, "and we're going to have you do an extensive rehearsal for the upcoming tour, but we won't start any of that until November 16. Until then, you boys are officially on vacation. Tell us where you want to go and we'll arrange for it. You've earned it."

They were glad for the vacation, but no one wasted any sentimentality on National's generosity. Their vacation expenses would be deducted from their recoupable expenses accounts.

Matt, Coop, and Darren all elected to go to an exclusive resort in Rio de Janeiro. Jake and Bill made different plans. They both wanted to go home and visit their families. Crow, when given this request, attempted to veto it on the grounds that there would be no favorable publicity resulting from such a trip.

"Going home is boring," he told them. "We want shots of you running rampant through some tropical beach somewhere, getting in trouble with the tourist girls and the locals. Visiting your mom and dad is just a little too wholesome, don't you think?"

"Oh, I'm sorry," Jake said. "I thought this vacation thing was supposed to be so we could rest and relax before going out on the road. I wasn't aware it was nothing but a publicity angle for you."

"Everything is a publicity angle," Crow told him. "You know that. Now look, why don't we set you two up at a resort down in Mazatlán? If you really want to see your parents, I'll arrange to have them flown up here for a couple of days when you get back."

They declined his kind offer and Mindy came to their rescue. Stating that she thought it was high time she met her boyfriend's parents, she booked the three of them on a private jet and they flew to Heritage County airport on November 1. The trip was a disaster pretty much from the point they landed.

Jake looked out the aircraft window as they taxied to the general aviation terminal and saw no less than six news vans, their antennas poking up into the sky, and nearly fifty reporters, photographers, and videographers standing between them and the terminal entrance.

"Holy shit," he said as the plane came to a stop and all the cameras pointed at the door. "How did they know we were going to be here?"

Mindy gave a nervous little giggle. "Well... uh... actually, I think Georgette might've... you know... tipped them a little."

"Georgette told them we were coming here?" he asked, feeling his anger start to rise.

"She thought it might be a good idea for the press to know I was coming home with you to meet your parents," she said. "You know? It gives the relationship a little more weight, makes it seem serious. It's one of those milestone things."

"Oh my God," Jake said, shaking his head.

"I'm sorry," she said, sounding anything but. "I didn't know there would be that many of them out there."

He held his tongue for the time being. They stepped out into the throng and the cameras began to fire like machine guns. The reporters began shouting their inane questions.

"Are you going to meet Jake's parent's right now, Mindy?"

"Is it true you're going to announce your engagement to them?"

"What about the reports that you're pregnant?"

"Do you think your mother will approve of Mindy, Jake?"

They kept their heads down, their expressions blank, and their mouths shut as they pushed through the throng and entered the terminal building. Inside were hundreds of fans and onlookers, all of them crowding around the group, shouting their own questions, snapping their own pictures, asking for autographs. Another group of people stood near the doors holding up protest signs that said things like HERITAGE SAYS NO TO INTEMPERANCE and HERITAGE HOLDS NO PRIDE IN THE SINNER and GO BACK TO HOLLYWOOD, FREAKS (and take your corrupt whore with you).

They signed no autographs, talked to no one as they worked their way to the rental car counter to sign out the two Mercedes that Mindy had reserved for them. Throughout the entire process the mob remained behind them, shouting, photographing, protesting, and filming. A fight broke out between a few of the protesters and the fans and airport security came rushing in to try to break it up. The counter girl, meanwhile, was so starstruck by the presence of the musicians and the actress, and so nervous by the presence of the cameras filming her every move, she was fumbling and stuttering through the paperwork and was speaking so softly they couldn't understand her.

At last they were given their keys and they worked their way out to the lot. The crowd, newly reinforced by the media, followed behind them, still shouting, fighting, and pleading for autographs. Jake and Mindy climbed in one car and Bill into the other. They had to honk their horns and rudely force their way through all of the people in order to get out of the lot.

"Well," Jake said, his fists clenched on the steering wheel in anger, "you got your publicity... again."

"I'm sorry, Jake," she said, utilizing her patented little-girl-who-has-done-wrong voice. "I really didn't know it was going to be like this."

He said no more.

Jake's parents had invited Bill's parents over for a homecoming party for their two celebrity sons. As they drove down the freeway and through the suburban streets, two news helicopters shadowed them, no doubt broadcasting their progress live to the noontime viewing audience. When they pulled onto the street where Jake had grown up, they found it lined with even more news vans, reporters, and hundreds of people. They were on the neighbors' lawns, parked in their driveways, milling about in the street. There were more sign holders as well. They had occupied the driveway of the Williams family, who lived next door to the Kingsley's.

"Jesus fucking Christ," Jake said as they forced their way down the street. "Is nothing sacred to these people?"

"It would seem not," Bill said.

The warmth of the family reunion was somewhat cooled by the need to make a mad rush from the driveway into the home. The horde rushed at them as they emerged from the cars, trampling through his mother's flowerbed, stomping over his father's immaculately landscaped front lawn. Jake's dad ripped open the front door as they approached and practically dragged them inside.

"You people are on private property!" his dad yelled from the doorway. "Get back out to the street or I'll be forced to call the sheriff's department."

"You're an ACLU lawyer," one of the reporters shouted back. "Would you really call a law enforcement agency on someone?"

His dad slammed the door without answering.

Jake looked around, seeing the stunned faces of his parents, his sister, and Bill's parents. They were all gathered around the television, which was showing a live view of the outside of the house as taken from one of the news helicopters.

"Well," Jake said, "I see how you knew we were here."

Jake's dad shook his head wearily. "It's been like this since yesterday," he said. "They've been calling us and showing up here sporadically ever since that article about... you know... the cocaine and the butt thing. But now they've been swarming us mercilessly."

Jake cast an angry look at Mindy, who at least had the decency to blush and look ashamed, although it was probably her acting skills he was seeing instead of sincerity. "I'm sorry," he said. "They were tipped off that I was bringing Mindy here."

"Who would do such a thing?" his mother asked. "Was it the airplane people?"

"Something like that," Jake said, casting one more angry glance at Mindy.

Now that things had settled a bit, they were finally able to complete the ritual of reunion. Jake hugged his mother, his father, his sister (who whispered, "your job is still a lot more interesting than mine" in his ear) and Bill's parents. Bill did the same in reverse order. Jake then formally introduced Mindy to everyone.

Mindy blushed and cooed and responded with a charming amount of shyness as her hand was shaken by Bill's parents, her person was hugged by Jake's mother and sister, and her cheek was kissed by Jake's dad. She told them she was happy to meet them and that she'd heard a lot about them. She charmed everyone completely and totally without even breaking a sweat. She awed them in a way they had never been awed by Jake or Bill. Jake and Bill were merely their sons, their brothers, their family friends. No matter how famous they were, each person in this house had changed Bill's or Jake's diapers at some point in their lives. But Mindy was the first actual celebrity any of them had ever met. She was plied with questions about life in the movie studio, about episodes of *The Slow Lane*, and about her current career. Jake was astounded to find that his own family had bought into many of the rumors that were floating around about the two of them.

"Is it true that you're going to announce your engagement?" his father asked.

"I heard that Mindy is... you know... *expecting*." That from his mother.

They denied all the various speculations and Mindy answered all of the questions posed of her with exactly what the asker wanted to hear. Eventually they were able to settle down in the family room and sip from drinks while they waited for the food to be served.

And as they talked, the continuous clatter of helicopter blades came from overhead, sometimes so loudly that the windows rattled in their frames. While they were eating, one of the news photographers suddenly appeared in the kitchen window, his camera snapping away through the glass.

Jake felt horrible as he saw his mother near tears, as he heard his father lapsing into uncharacteristic anger and profanity as he stormed across the room and ripped the curtains shut.

"I'm sorry," he said for perhaps the twentieth time. "I'm really sorry about all this."

*****

Their intent had been to stay overnight at his parent's house. At the suggestion of three sheriff's deputies, their sergeant and their lieutenant, all of whom showed up in response to neighbor complaints about the unruly mob that had taken over their quiet street, Jake, Mindy and Bill elected to get hotel rooms instead. Mindy made one phone call to Georgette in Los Angeles and an hour later they had two suites at the Royal Gardens. They ran the gauntlet to their rental cars and fought their way out of the driveway and down the street, cameras filming and snapping, questions shouted, protesters screaming the entire time. Half of the mob climbed into their vehicles and followed the celebrities downtown. The other half remained in front of Jake's parent's house, where they continually knocked on the door and called on the phone, demanding to know what had taken place within those walls.

Tom Kingsley finally stepped out onto the porch and addressed them. "Look," he said angrily, "Mindy is not pregnant, they are not engaged, and nothing of interest took place in here. We are a simple family who has not seen our son in months and we tried to have a reunion with him and meet his girlfriend. That is all I have to say. Now all of you, please get out of here."

"Mr. Kingsley," someone shouted, "what do you think of the corrupting influence your son is having on Mindy?"

"Did they mention any *possibility* of becoming engaged?" shouted another.

"Did you raise your son to be a Satanist?" enquired one of the protestors.

"Jesus fucking Christ," Tom said, shaking his head. He turned his back and walked back into the house, slamming the door behind him.

About an hour later, the crowd slowly drifted away, one by one, returning peace to the neighborhood.

By this point Jake, Mindy, and Bill had arrived at the Royal Gardens. Bill was in his suite enjoying the company of a nineteen-year-old cocktail waitress he'd met downstairs in the bar. He was stroking her hair and explaining to her the finer points of hydrogen bonding as it related to the mixing of alcoholic beverages. The waitress was nodding vigorously, understanding only one out of every three words he said and wondering when she could stop listening to the eccentric rock star and start fucking him.

Jake and Mindy were in the suite next door. Mindy was crying and Jake was red-faced with anger.

"I can't take this anymore," he told her. "You've gone too far this time! This was supposed to be a nice, relaxing visit with my family. I came here to Heritage to get away from all the goddamn photographers and news people! I wanted to just be a normal person for a few days, to introduce you to my parents, to show you around my hometown. And what did you do? You turned it into a fucking circus!"

"Jake, I'm sorry," she sobbed. "I didn't know the Heritage media was going to be so aggressive. I just wanted it known that you were bringing me home to meet your parents."

"Yes," he said. "You did it for that sacred image of yours. Just like you do everything! I'm tired of this shit, Mindy. For God's sake, the fucking cops kicked me out of my parents' house!"

"They didn't kick you out," she said. "They just asked us to..."

"Don't tell me what the fuck they asked me to do!" he screamed, causing her to back up in fear. "Cops came to my parents' house, Mindy! A whole bunch of fucking cops! They came in and they said their piece and I had to leave that house! Do you know how that makes me feel? Do you know how embarrassed I am about that? And do you know why that happened? Because of you and your need to have every fucking thing we do chronicled in those tabloid rags!"

"Jake..."

"There's nothing more to say," he told her. "This is the last fucking straw."

"Don't say that, Jake," she said, still sobbing. "I'm sorry. I don't know how many times I have to tell you that. I made a mistake by tipping them off. I realize that now. I was completely out of line. Please forgive me."

"It's not that easy, Mindy," he told her, trying not to look at her tear-streaked face because it was dampening his anger, something he didn't really want done right now.

"Please, Jake, don't leave me because of *this*," she pleaded. "I'll make it up to you."

"No," he said firmly. "This has got to end. I've been played for a fool long enough."

"No, Jake, no!" she sobbed, breaking down completely. She threw herself into his arms, burying her face in his neck. Her tears were hot against his skin, her body soft against him.

He tried to push her away but he simply could not find the will to do it. Her tears were getting to him, burrowing right under his resolve and lifting it from its moorings inch by inch. Soon instead of pushing at her, his arms went around her.

"Please don't leave me, Jake," she repeated, over and over. "Please don't."

"This has got to stop, Mindy," he said, his hands running up and down her back. "I can't go on like this."

"I'll make it up to you, Jake," she cried, more tears spilling onto his neck. "I swear! Just don't leave me. Give me another chance! Let me make it up to you!"

He didn't agree to this, but he didn't disagree either. And soon her soft lips were putting gentle kisses on his tear-stained neck as she kept muttering "please, please". Her soft body kept grinding into his, her breasts to his chest, her thighs to his. And, as she no doubt intended, the blood began to rush from one head to the other. Once this began to occur it was only a matter of seconds before her lips were on his mouth, her tongue probing gently outward, touching his. And then the clothing began to come off, piece by piece. Soon they were naked, flesh-to-flesh, grinding against each other on the King-sized bed.

*****

Afterward, as they lay naked on their backs, staring up at the ceiling, smoking their cigarettes, she turned to him.

"I really am going to make it up to you," she said.

He grunted in response, feeling his usual post-coital guilt at giving into her emotional blackmail.

She gently kissed his ear. "Jake," she said, "I know I've been unfair to you. I've been parading you around like a toy, exposing you to all kinds of things and people you don't want to be exposed to. I've ruined your trip home. It's time we went somewhere where we can be anonymous."

"Where?" he asked, a note of bitterness plainly evident. "Madagascar? Or maybe Indonesia?"

"No," she said. "Somewhere close by, about an hour and a half from here by plane. Georgette can make the arrangements tonight and we can be there by noon tomorrow."

"Where?" he repeated.

"Las Vegas," she said.

"Vegas?" he said. "You think we can be anonymous in Vegas? Are you insane? They'll be crawling over us from the moment we walk into the first casino."

"Au contraire," she said. "I've been there many times without anyone knowing. When you're considered one of the 'high rollers', as I am, they can be very discreet."

"I'm sure they can," he said, "but that still doesn't stop everyone in the casino from recognizing us and swarming us."

"Actually, it does," she said. "There are special parts of the casino set aside just for the high rollers, parts the ordinary people never see. And the staff in this part of the casino will do anything for you. Forget about waiting for a cocktail waitress. There's one assigned to your table. And forget about some moron on third base while you're playing blackjack. No one is allowed at your table without your invite."

"Really?" he said, interested in spite of himself. "And you've done this a lot?"

She smiled. "Gambling is yet another one of my vices. I'm pretty good at it, too."

"But you're not twenty-one yet."

She chuckled. "When you take out enough in chips they don't give a rat's ass how old you are, they just give you the signature sheet and a gold-plated fountain pen. And they stuff you with free food, free drinks, free everything. Go with me, Jake. Let me show you what the high life is all about. I don't think you'll be disappointed."

"I don't know," he said.

"Know," she told him. "We'll bring Bill along too, he'll have a blast. In fact, let's invite your whole family. Bill's too. It's all on me."

"Mindy," he said, "my family is never going to let you pay for a trip to Vegas for them. Neither is Bill's."

She shrugged. "I wouldn't be paying for anything, really. They'll fly us out there and give us suites in the hotel. All I'll be providing them with is their casino chips."

"How much in casino chips?"

"Don't worry about that," she said. "I can afford it. You know that."

"They won't go for it."

"You never know until you ask, do you? Give them a call."

He did. Bill was happy to try out the Las Vegas experience. His parents were not, for exactly the reason that Jake had surmised. Jake's parents said it sounded like fun but they both had to work the next day—Tom on a court brief he was preparing regarding a young man who lost vision in one eye after being struck by a Heritage Police baton, Mary on a rehearsal for the Philharmonic Orchestra's coming winter concert series. Pauline was supposed to work the next day as well, but she decided that she'd just had a sudden onset of the flu and called in sick.

"High roller treatment in Vegas?" she said. "Count me in."

Mindy made another phone call to Georgette. Their conversation lasted less than thirty seconds but that was all it took to get the wheels rolling.

*****

Jake, Mindy, and Bill drove to the airport (a smaller throng of reporters following behind them the entire way). They turned in their rental cars and found a place of relative privacy near the back of the general aviation terminal. Pauline arrived ten minutes later, stepping out of a limousine sent to her house and paid for by Hammurabi's Palace. She was giggly and wide-eyed— the result of drinking two bloody Marys in the limo—as she joined them in the lounge. She thanked Mindy profusely for inviting her along.

"It's my pleasure," Mindy assured her.

And Jake could see that it really was her pleasure. This little trip was probably going to cost her more than the average person earned in a year, but it was money she was glad to spend. She *liked* lavishing people with horribly expensive gifts. It was one of the things she lived for. And the more people she could lavish, the better.

Less than fifteen minutes after Pauline's arrival a uniformed stewardess told them their flight was ready. They followed her through the terminal, the reporters all screaming after them, demanding to know where they were going, what they were doing. No one answered or even acknowledged them.

They were led across the tarmac—the reporters were held back at the terminal exit by the security guards—to an idling Lear jet. The inside was cramped but luxurious, with padded leather seats, an entertainment center, and a full-service bar. They found seats and the stewardess served a round of drinks while the plane was sealed up and began to taxi.

They roared into the sky, climbing steeply to forty-two thousand feet. As soon as they leveled off the stewardess presented them with a silver tray upon which white lines had been neatly formed.

"Can I offer anyone some cocaine?" she asked in the same tone of voice with which she'd offered the drinks.

They all took her up on the offer, Pauline included. She snorted up two of the lines in a manner that told Jake this was not her first time. "This is some really good shit."

"Naturally," Mindy said.

They all had two more drinks and destroyed an ounce of Beluga caviar before the plane touched down at the Las Vegas airport. A limousine was standing by waiting for them and they piled in for the short trip to the opulent Hammurabi's Palace Casino. Instead of going to the main entrance, they were taken around to the side where three nearly identical looking tuxedoed men politely greeted them before escorting them to a small elevator that they rode to the top floor.

Pauline and Bill were each given their own suites. Jake and Mindy were given one to share. All were packed with every luxury that could conceivably be provided and had spectacular views of Las Vegas. Their tuxedoed man, who held the title of 'butler', Jake discovered, pointed out the various features of the room—the hot tub, the wet bar, the projection television set—and then let them know of some of the other services that were available to them.

"If you would care for a massage simply let me know, or, if you're down in the casino level, you can call extension 2976 from any phone and I will make the arrangements for a masseuse to come up to your room. Adult movies are available for your enjoyment as well. There is a menu of the selections inside the bar. If you fancy some intoxicating substances I can arrange for both cocaine and marijuana to be supplied to you. And, if you are desirous of some... uh... adult companionship, I can make those arrangements as well."

"Do you have a menu for that too?" Jake asked.

Mindy giggled. "Thank you, Roberto," she told him. "We'll let you know if we need any of those things. For now, I think we'll go hit the tables. Where might we find them?"

"Take the elevator you used to access this floor down to level seven. Turn right and your assigned casino room will be 703. Gaming and cocktail staff is already on duty."

"Thank you, Roberto," Mindy said, reaching in her purse and passing him a piece of currency. Jake didn't get a good look at it but he was pretty sure he'd seen a picture of Benjamin Franklin on its face.

Bill was suitably impressed with the services being offered. So impressed, in fact, that he wasn't quite ready to leave the room yet. "I'm going to imbibe in some of that adult companionship first," he told them. "Compensation is not required from *me*, correct?"

"Well, you are expected to tip your... uh... adult companion," Mindy told him. "You can use casino chips for that but you won't have any until you go down to the casino."

"Hmm," Bill said thoughtfully. "That does present a minor quandary. I wouldn't want to commit a breach of etiquette."

"Here," Mindy said, digging in her purse and coming out with another picture of Benjamin Franklin. "Give her this when she's done. That should suffice. You *are* only having one adult companion come up, right?"

"I can get *more* than one?"

"Oh yes," Mindy said. "There's plenty of companionship to go around."

"Hmmm," Bill said thoughtfully.

"You better give him another one," Jake told Mindy. "He's too shy to ask for it."

She laughed and dug out another bill. "Enjoy yourself, Bill. We'll see you down in the casino later?"

"Yes," he said, taking the money. "Thank you, Mindy. This is shaping up to be a superior vacation."

"My pleasure," she said, leaning in and giving him a kiss on the cheek, which made him blush.

If Bill was impressed, Pauline was completely dumbfounded. They found her wandering around her room, looking at everything, trying everything. She had a tall drink in her hand as she turned on the bathtub taps, fired up the hot tub jets, changed channels on the television.

"This is incredible!" she exclaimed, sounding like a child on Christmas morning. "My whole friggin' house isn't this big. And the view! My God! Do you live like this all the time, Mindy?"

"When I come to Vegas I do. It's one of the privileges of being a high roller."

"I need to make myself into a high roller then," she said, more than a hint of determination in her voice.

They went down the elevator, emerging into a wide, spacious hallway on the seventh floor. The section of the building they were in was completely isolated from the rest of the casino, the few entrances guarded by armed security personnel. There were several tinted glass doors on each side of the hallway, spaced every forty or fifty feet. Each one had a number on it. When they reached 703 Jake held the door open for the ladies. Another security guard stood just inside, manning a podium much like a maitre d's in a restaurant. He smiled and greeted them by name, waving them inside.

"Wow," Jake and Pauline said together as they entered, both of them looking around in awe. It was a windowless circular room, about two thousand square feet or so, done up in rich red carpeting that stretched from wall to wall. Standing upon this carpet, arranged symmetrically in a pattern that was pleasing to the eye, was every kind of gambling table the casino offered. There was a blackjack table, a craps table, two roulette wheels, and a pai gow table, all of them ready for action, all of them empty of players. There were three rows of slot machines, each with a padded leather chair before it. There were another two rows of video poker machines, each of them with the same chairs before them. A bar stood against the far wall, a bartender and a cocktail waitresses on duty. From hidden speakers in the wall soft music was playing.

"All this is for us?" Pauline asked.

"All for us," Mindy confirmed. "Our own private casino."

"Would you care to sign for your chips, Ms. Snow?" asked the security guard.

"You bet your ass," she said, taking a gold-plated pen from his hands and signing a form on his clipboard.

The guard passed out plastic racks to each of them, racks that contained nothing but black, purple, and yellow casino chips, the denominations of which were $100, $500, and $1000 respectively.

"This is fifteen thousand dollars worth," Pauline gasped as her accountant-like mind quickly added up the colors and came to a result.

"Oh, this is just for starters," Mindy said. "When you lose it all there will be more."

Pauline's mouth was agape.

"And what kind of music would you like to hear this evening?" the guard asked Mindy.

"Give us a variety," she told him. "A little hard rock, a little soft rock, a little country. Mix it up."

"Yes, ma'am," he said.

"Jake," Pauline whispered in his ear, "this is a *third* of my yearly salary she just handed me. Fifteen thousand dollars!"

"She can afford it," Jake whispered back. "Just go with the flow and have a good time."

"Shall we start out with some blackjack?" Mindy asked them. "That's always been my favorite."

"Uhhh, sure," Pauline said, still trying to come to grips. "Sounds good."

The sat down at the blackjack table, Mindy at third base, Jake at second, Pauline at first. The dealer, a buxom blonde of about twenty-five, greeted them by name. The cocktail waitress, a buxom brunette of about twenty-five, came over and offered them drinks. While they gave their drink orders Jake looked around again and saw that every one of the employees catering to them, man or woman, was physically attractive. Even the security guard was a buffed out male that most woman would describe as "a hunk".

"And would you like some cocaine to go with your drinks?" the cocktail waitress offered next.

"You know it," Mindy said. "Line us up."

"We're featuring Bolivian, Peruvian, and Venezuelan flake today. Do you have a preference?"

"Can we get a blend?" Mindy asked her.

"You can get anything you want," was the answer.

"I want a blend," Mindy said.

"I'll uh... have the same," Jake replied, wondering if there was some advantage to blending varieties of coke.

"No blend for me," Pauline said with a giggle. She was obviously starting to get into the experience. "I want Bolivian for the left nostril and Peruvian for the right."

"As you wish," the waitress replied. She headed off to the bar.

"The minimum bet is a hundred," Mindy told them, "but that's for pussies as far as I'm concerned." With that she dropped a purple chip down on the circle. "Oh, and no card counting in here. Its kind of easy for them to catch it, isn't it, hon?"

"I'm sure none of you would do something like that," the dealer replied.

"Just stick to basic strategy," Mindy said. "It's a slight house advantage, that's true, but I've walked out of here with almost a hundred grand before." She giggled. "Of course, I've also walked out of here missing nearly a quarter mil."

Mindy and the dealer shared a laugh at this. Jake and Pauline both began to look a little nervous however. They both put down black chips.

"Pussies," Mindy said with kind contempt.

Over the next hour they drank four potent drinks apiece and snorted four lines of potent, uncut cocaine. Mindy was a skillful and nerveless player, increasing her bets with every win to the point she was plopping down the thousand dollar chips five and six at a time. Her pile of chips grew from fifteen grand to more than sixty. Pauline was much more conservative with her betting, and not quite as skillful a player, but luck seemed to be with her. When she would hit on sixteen, the dealer would plop down a five or a four. When she would stand on seventeen with the dealer showing a ten, the dealer's down card would be four and the next hit would break her. She was up by more than ten thousand.

"Come on, sis," Mindy chided her companionably every time she plunked down another hundred-dollar chip, or, when she was feeling particularly daring, two or three of them. "Strap on a pair. Throw down one of them yellows."

Pauline, however, could not quite bring herself to plop down a thousand dollar chip on a turn of the cards. Not yet anyway.

Jake was the loser of the group. Though he fancied himself well versed in basic blackjack strategy, nothing seemed to be going his way. When he would hit on a fourteen with the dealer showing a face card, it seemed inevitable that he would receive a face card as well. When he would stand on eighteen with the dealer showing a three, she would flip up a seven and then toss down a nine to go with it. Even though he was sticking to one and two hundred dollar bets, he was quickly down almost ten grand.

"I'm gonna go play some craps," he finally said, standing and gathering his remaining chips. "Anyone want to join me?"

"I will," said Bill, who had just come in and received his own share of chips. He was looking like he was in a fine mood.

"All right, Nerdly," Jake said. "Let's do it. Do you know how to play?"

Bill scoffed at him. "Of course I know how to play," he said. "Craps is the one game in the entire casino where it's mathematically possible to negate the house advantage down to almost even odds."

Everyone stared at him for a moment. Jake finally clapped him on the shoulder. "Does this guy know how to fuckin' party, or what?"

They partied on, drinking, snorting, and gambling while music played endlessly from the overhead sound system. Bill, putting down purple chips one and two at a time, playing the pass and don't pass lines exclusively, and utilizing a system that Jake couldn't even begin to guess at, stayed safely within three thousand dollars of his original fifteen grand. Jake tried playing the odds a little and quickly lost the remnants of his first fifteen grand. Mindy simply blew him a kiss and signed him out another fifteen thousand. She and Pauline, meanwhile, remained at the blackjack table, now sitting companionably together and giggling like old friends. Pauline's luck took a turn for the worse and she whittled away her stake on a series of poorly thought-out plays. Mindy signed her out another fifteen grand as well.

Before they knew it, it was six o'clock in the evening. Mindy suggested it was time for dinner. They were led to a private dining area two floors down and served a huge meal of filet mignon, cracked Alaskan crab legs, artichokes, spinach salad, and a bottle of 1969 Cabernet Sauvignon that went down smooth as silk. For dessert there was Cappuccino Chocolate Mousse Roulade. All were served by well-dressed, attentive wait staff who said little.

"Well," Mindy asked, as she lit her after-meal cigarette and sipped from her water, "what do you think? Do they know how to treat you in Vegas?"

Everyone had to agree that they certainly knew how to treat people.

"Do you know what I like about it?" Jake asked, his head reeling with alcohol and cocaine, his spirits unsurprisingly quite high.

"What's that?" Mindy asked, her hand caressing his thigh.

"Not a single person has asked me for my autograph or told me how great they think my music is or told me I was going to hell as a sinner or even tried sidling up to me so they could tell their friends about it. They're catering to me without seeming to care who I am."

"Everyone who works in the VIP portion of the casino has been instructed on how to act," Mindy said. "They are expected to be friendly, efficient, and discreet."

"Discreet?" Bill asked. "Does that mean they will not give reports to the press about our presence here? Or about the things we did here?"

"What happens in Vegas stays in Vegas," Mindy said. "That's the prime directive of the VIP staff. It has to be that way or we wouldn't come here and gamble a hundred grand at a time. The casino won't even admit we are guests here, let alone what we do here. And if any of the staff leaked anything to a reporter, security would investigate with everything they had until they found the leaker and fired him or her."

"So Nerdly's mom won't hear about two hookers he had up in his room?" Jake asked.

Mindy laughed and Bill blushed.

"No," Mindy replied. "His mom won't hear about it."

"You had *two* hookers up in your room?" Pauline asked him. "You? William Michael Archer? Computer nerd and piano geek who was so shy you once threw up when you accidentally walked in on me in the bathroom?"

Bill blushed even darker. It was well known by both Kingsley siblings (as well as their parents) that Bill had always had a crush on the unobtainable Pauline, a crush that had started at roughly the age of four and continued probably to this day.

"When was that?" Mindy wanted to know.

"When he was about twelve," Pauline said, laughing at the memory. "I was sixteen. His mom had come over to visit our mom and had brought Bill along. I went in to go pee and must've forgot to lock the door. Bill forgot to knock and came walking right in on me." She laughed harder and had to take a moment to get herself under control. "You should've seen the look on his face. It was just like he'd seen the birth of the universe and the face of God all in one glance. And then he started to tremble all over and threw up in the sink."

"Wow, that must be some puss you have," Mindy said. She turned to Bill. "Did you get to see her bush?"

"Can we change the topic of conversation to something less discomforting?" Bill pleaded. "How about Grenada? I hear our troops will be coming home by December."

"Oh, fuck Grenada," Mindy said. "Let's hear about Pauline's bush."

"Uh, actually," Jake said, "the subject of my sister's bush is a bit disconcerting for me as well."

"You prude," Mindy admonished. "What's the matter? Didn't you ever get to see it?"

"Mindy, Jesus," Jake said, blushing a little himself now. Of course, he had seen it on a few occasions during their teen years—growing up in a household where modesty was only loosely encouraged made that inevitable—but the memory certainly didn't have the lustful power over his masturbation fantasies that the one brief glimpse Bill had gotten had over his, even to this day.

"There's nothing interesting about my bush," Pauline said wistfully. "Except maybe the cobwebs in it."

"Been a while since you got hosed down, huh?" Mindy asked sympathetically.

"Oh, it's an old story," Pauline said. "All work and no play means no play, if you know what I mean."

"Well, let's get you laid," Mindy said. "How about that craps dealer? I saw you giving him the eye. He'll clean your cobwebs out for you."

Pauline laughed, shaking her head. "He *is* kind of cute," she said.

"Damn straight he is," Mindy said. "Everyone who works the VIP room is cute. It's a requirement."

"So what do I do? Just go up to him and say, 'excuse me, Mr. Handsome Craps Dealer, but I find you attractive and would like you to lay me'?"

"Actually," Mindy said, "you go to the pit boss and let him know that you're interested and he'll make the arrangements for you."

Everyone laughed for a moment until they realized that Mindy was not joking.

"Wait a minute," Pauline said. "You're serious about this?"

"I don't joke about cobweb clearing," Mindy said. "If you want the craps dealer, he's yours. At least if you catch him before he goes off shift. If that happens you'll have to pick someone from the night shift."

"You mean everyone who works in the VIP room is a... a... prostitute?" Pauline asked, both shocked and aroused by this thought.

"No, they're not prostitutes," Mindy said. "At least not in the strict sense of the word. But one of the unwritten requirements for working in the VIP rooms is that you make yourself available for the customers if they request it. Everyone who accepts the position understands this and accepts it."

"Are you serious?" Jake asked, feeling his own mixture of discomfort and intrigue.

"Uh... does this mean that the women are available as well?" asked Bill, who had been eyeing the cocktail waitress all night.

"This is just too weird," said Pauline.

"Nothing weird about it," Mindy said. "It's part of the high-roller services. Naturally, there is some etiquette involved. That's where the pit boss comes in. You ask him to ask the person or persons you're interested in if they would mind joining you in your suite for a drink later. He then forwards the request to them and they say yes."

"What if they don't say yes?" Pauline asked.

Mindy smiled. "That doesn't happen," she said. "Trust me."

Jake was thinking that Mindy knew an awful lot about this particular high-roller service. How many times had she been here? How many times had she used such services? Obviously she'd used them enough to know the ins and outs of it.

Pauline, meanwhile, was shaking her head. "Sorry," she said, "that's just not me. I'm a respected corporate lawyer. I can't see myself asking a pit boss to arrange for some stud to come up to my room with me."

"You want me to do it for you then?" Mindy asked.

"No," she said firmly. "It's just not my style."

"Vegas is all about changing your style," Mindy said. "That's why they call it Sin City. And no one will find out. Remember, what happens in Vegas stays in Vegas."

"No," Pauline said, with something that sounded like conviction. "It's just too weird for me. I'll get my cobwebs cleaned out the natural way."

Mindy shrugged. "Let me know if you change your mind," she told her.

The subject changed to something neutral and about fifteen minutes later they went back to the casino to do more gambling. They weren't there thirty minutes before Bill went to the pit boss and held a short conversation with him. The pit boss then went to the buxom cocktail waitress and held a short conversation with her. He then went back to Bill and conversed even more. Five minutes later the cocktail waitress and Bill were leaving the casino together.

"Ahh, young love," Mindy said, gleaming at them. "Isn't it a beautiful thing?"

Jake was sitting next to her at the blackjack table, his pile of chips slowly shrinking down under a fresh onslaught of bad luck. Pauline was over at the craps table, rolling the dice under the watchful eye of the young stud Mindy had offered to get for him. "I can't believe you were trying to get my sister to hook up with that guy," he said, keeping his voice low so the blonde dealer couldn't hear it.

Mindy simply shrugged. "I'm just trying to get her to take advantage of all the services the casino has to offer."

"Yes," Jake said, "but this is my *sister*. Don't you understand how weird that is?"

"No, actually I don't," she said. "But you might as well get used to the idea. She'll be over here soon to ask me to make the arrangements for her."

"She will not," Jake said. "You don't know who you're talking about here."

"I think maybe *you* don't know who we're talking about here. I give her fifteen more minutes."

As it turned out, Mindy was wrong. It actually took twenty-four minutes and the consumption of two more drinks and two more lines of cocaine before Pauline came strolling over, her gait just a bit unsteady. "All right," she said, wafting her scotch scented breath in Mindy's face, "I think I'll try it. Can you talk to the pit boss for me?"

"Pauline," Jake said, "have you thought about this?"

"It's all I have been thinking about," she replied. "What's the protocol here? Do I tip him afterward, or what?"

"No," Mindy said. "His VIP room salary is compensation enough for these special services. Tipping implies he's a common gigolo, which he isn't."

"Wait a minute," Jake said. "Pauline, you're not seriously going to do this, are you?"

"Oh, look who's talking," she said, a hint of anger in her voice. "I'm getting a morality lecture from a man who snorts cocaine out of a girl's ass."

"I thought you said you didn't do that," Mindy said, turning to him.

"I *didn't*," Jake hissed, shooting a furious look at his sister.

"Oh... sorry," she said with a giggle. "Of course you didn't. Forget I said that." She turned back to Mindy. "So, are you gonna talk to the man, or what?"

She stood up, grinning from ear to ear. "I'll talk to the man," she said.

She talked to the man. Two minutes later Pauline left the casino on the arm of the handsome craps dealer.

"All right then," Mindy said when she returned. "That just leaves the two of us."

"Yep," Jake agreed, his mood still a little sour at the thought of his sister getting pounded by an ambiguously labeled male prostitute.

Mindy leaned close and whispered in his ear. "Why don't we pick one out for you now?"

His eyes widened as he looked at her. "Excuse me?"

"You heard me quite well," she whispered. "Which one? I've seen you eyeing our dealer. How about her?"

Jake looked up at the dealer, who had laid out their latest hands and was patiently waiting for them to pick up their cards. "Will you excuse us for just a minute?"

"Of course," she said.

Jake stood and dragged Mindy over to the corner of the room. "What are you trying to do?" he asked her.

"I'm trying to get you some pussy," she said. "Do you have a problem with that?"

"You want me to have sex with another woman?" he asked.

Her eyes took on a certain shine. "Yes," she said. "I want you to fuck the shit out of another woman."

"Why, Mindy?" he asked. "Are you going to be getting a stud for yourself?"

She shook her head. "No," she said. "I'm going to be up in our room with you... watching you fuck her."

"You want to *watch* me fuck another woman?"

"Yes," she said. "I'm a bit of a voyeur, Jake, in case you haven't figured that out. It would turn me on tremendously to watch your cock sliding in and out of another girl's pussy."

Jake shook his head. "I don't believe this," he said.

"You don't have to believe it," she responded. "Just do it. Now which one will it be? The blonde dealer? Or do you prefer the new cocktail waitress they sent in to replace Bill's squeeze? She's pretty hot too."

"Mindy, you're telling me to be unfaithful to you. You're encouraging it."

"Faithful?" she scoffed. "Jesus Christ, Jake, we're not married. You're going to be heading out on tour soon. Are you trying to tell me you were planning on staying celibate all those months? That you weren't going to be sinking your cock into any of those groupies?"

"Well..." he started, unsure how to answer that. In truth, he hadn't really thought too much about that. When he did, it was always with the assumption that he and Mindy would be broken up by then anyway.

"Remember, Jake," she said, leaning in and sliding her tongue along his neck in a way she knew turned him on tremendously, "what happens in Vegas stays in Vegas. Now which one?"

He picked the blonde blackjack dealer. Mindy was right, he had been ogling her the entire day. She led him over to the pit boss, insisting he come with her so he could see how the ritual was performed.

"Is there something I can help you with?" he asked politely when they approached.

"Yes," Mindy said. "As a matter of fact, there is. Mr. Kingsley is quite taken with that young blackjack dealer who has been putting down the cards for us."

"Ahh, I can certainly understand that," he replied. "Her name is Alisha. She's a fine dealer."

"Yes, she is," Mindy agreed. "Very fine. Do you suppose you could ask Alisha if she would be willing to accompany us up to our room so we could enjoy her companionship in a less formal setting?"

"I will ask," the pit boss agreed. With that, he walked over to her and held a brief conversation.

"Are you sure you want to do this, Mindy?" Jake asked.

She smiled, unbuttoning her shorts and unzipping them, paying no attention to the dealers and cocktail servers in the room. She took his hand and pushed it down the front of her shorts.

"Mindy," he started.

"Feel me," she told him, sidling a little closer, pushing her breasts into his arm.

He licked his lips and pushed his fingers downward, across her smoothly shaven pubis to her vaginal lips, which were hot, swollen, and extremely wet.

"You feel how wet I am?" she asked him.

"Yes," he muttered, feeling the usual lust beginning to course through his body.

"Do you think I'm sure about this?"

"I guess you are," he replied.

The pit boss came back. He did an admirable job of pretending not to notice that Jake's hand was down Mindy's pants.

"Alisha would be honored to join you in your room," he told them.

"And we would be honored to have her," Mindy said. "Can you have her bring a deck of cards up with her?"

Alisha played her part well. She feigned shyness and uncertainty as they went upstairs in the elevator and then became giggly and seductive after Roberto set her up with a drink and two lines of cocaine.

"Thank you, Roberto," Mindy told him. "You can go now. Leave us a little of that wonderful cocaine and we'll make our own drinks from here on out."

"As you wish," Roberto said, departing with a smile and a bow.

"You ever play strip poker?" Mindy asked Alisha once he was gone.

She giggled again. "Maybe once or twice," she said.

"Up for a game with Jake and I?"

"I'm up for just about anything," she said.

Jake did much better at strip poker than he had at blackjack. This was not so much because of a turn in his luck as it was the fact that the two females seemed to be deliberately losing. Mindy's blouse and shorts went in the first ten minutes. Jake lost his shirt (to the appreciative whistles of both girls) and then Alisha lost her pants, shirt, and bra.

"Nice," was all Jake could say after getting his first look at those huge, natural breasts he had been ogling all night.

"Thank you," Alisha responded, her shy persona coming forth as she dropped the brassiere to the floor.

Mindy's bra came next and then her panties, leaving her completely naked and exposed. "I guess I'm out," she said. "Now you two play to the death."

It didn't take much longer. Jake lost the next hand and sacrificed his pants. Alisha lost the next and there went her underwear. She stood up to take them off, revealing a neatly trimmed bush of hair that was considerably darker than that on her head.

"What now?" she asked coyly as the underwear hit the floor.

"Now," Mindy said, "I guess we should give a little reward to the winner, shouldn't we?"

"That would only seem proper," Alisha agreed.

The reward was an agonizingly slow double blowjob. They had him remove his underwear and sit on the table before them. They then took turns sucking his cock, each one mouthing it for thirty or forty seconds before passing it over. After ten minutes of this constant stop and start treatment he was trembling with unfulfilled need, beads of sweat standing out on his forehead. Mindy sensed when he was at the end of his string and stood up from her latest round of slurping and sucking, her hand still gripping him.

"I think he needs to come, Alisha," she said, her hand moving slowly up and down upon him.

"Yeah?" she asked.

"Yeah," Mindy said. "I think he needs to come all over those big titties of yours."

That was exactly what he needed to do. Mindy jacked him faster and faster while Alisha positioned herself before him, squeezing and palpating her orbs to provide visual stimulation. It was less than a minute before he was spurting all over her.

"Now he needs to recharge," Mindy said sadly as she removed her semen soaked hands from his member. "Whatever shall we do while we're waiting for that?"

"I don't know," Alisha responded, her hazel eyes looking adoringly at Mindy's naked body. "I guess we'll have to think of something."

Mindy smiled apologetically. "You like girls, do you?" she asked her.

Alisha nodded enthusiastically. "I like them a *lot*," she said.

"Unfortunately," Mindy told her, "I don't. At least not in the way you're thinking."

"Oh," Alisha said, somewhat taken aback.

"However, I do like the feel of a woman's hands on me," she said. "Would you like to put your hands on me, Alisha?"

"Oh yes," she said, the sincerity in her voice unmistakable. "I'd love it, Mindy. Can I?"

"Let's go to the bedroom," Mindy said.

They went to the bedroom, Jake trailing behind them. He sat in a chair and watched as Mindy lay on her back on the large bed and Alisha proceeded to feel and stroke and squeeze and touch every square inch of her body. She played with her nipples for more than ten minutes and then stroked her way down her smooth stomach to her hairless crotch.

"It's so beautiful," Alisha told her, gazing at it with something like worship. "Are you sure you don't want me to kiss it just a little?"

"No," Mindy told her firmly. "No girly mouths on me. That turns me off. Girly hands, however, turn me on." She spread her legs.

Alisha went to work on her, stroking her outer lips and then plunging her fingers inside. She began to harshly finger-fuck her with three fingers while her thumb spun around Mindy's clitoris. Soon Mindy was bucking and panting her way through a powerful orgasm.

Jake, watching all this, recharged fairly quickly. In fact, by the time Alisha asked if she could eat her, his penis was swollen and straining. He looked around and saw a glass tray full of lambskin condoms, provided, no doubt, by Roberto once he'd been informed Alisha would be coming upstairs with them. He tore one open and safed his weapon. Just as Mindy finished her first orgasm, he slid into Alisha's body from behind, his hands going to her breasts as he thrust in and out of her. She moaned her enthusiastic approval at this action.

*****

There wasn't much talk the next day as the Lear Jet cruised at forty-four thousand feet on its way back to Heritage. All four of them were quite hung-over, their bodies tired, wasted, satiated. Bill was sleeping in his seat, soft snores coming from his mouth with each exhalation. He had worked his way through three hookers and two casino employees and had finally called it a night around five in the morning.

Mindy and Jake sat snuggled together on the couch, her resting her head on his shoulder, he with his arm around her.

"Did I make it up to you?" she asked him.

"Yeah," he told her, kissing her forehead. "I think we'll call it even for the time being."

They both looked over at Pauline, who was looking out the window at the scenery far below, a blank expression on her face. She had been the quietest of them, not having said more than a dozen words since breakfast. Jake was worried that she was having regrets about her trip to Sin City now that she had sobered up.

"Pauline?" he asked her.

She looked over at him. "Yeah?"

"Are you... uh... doing okay?"

She gave a weak smile. "Why wouldn't I be?"

"You're not... you know... embarrassed about what happened last night, are you?" Mindy asked her.

"Embarrassed?" she asked. "Not in the least."

"Are you sure?" Jake asked.

She chuckled a little. "I'm not quite the prude you think I am, little brother," she said.

"No," he agreed. "I guess you're not. So, what's eating you? Is it the hangover?"

She shook her head. "I've had worse," she said. "I guess its kind of a depression of sorts."

"Depression?" Mindy asked. "You just got laid. What's there to be depressed about?"

"It's the lifestyle I've just been exposed to," she told them. "I've just gotten a taste of what its like to be filthy, stinking rich."

"And that's depressing?" Jake asked, not following her.

"It's depressing because it's only a taste," she said. "Tomorrow I go back to my normal life. I'll file briefs and research contracts. I'll work sixty-hour weeks and get paid a relative pittance. I won't be able to fly off to Las Vegas and live like a pagan whenever I want to."

"Is that what's bothering you?" Mindy asked. "That's no problem. We'll go again. Whenever you want."

"No, you don't understand," she said. "I don't want to have to rely on Jake's girlfriend to show me that life. I want it for myself. I want it for myself and there's no way I'm going to get it for myself."

Mindy opened her mouth to say something but Jake beat her to it. "Don't be so sure about that, sis."

"Huh? What do you mean?"

He gave her a conspiratorial look. "Just an idea I have."

"What is it?"

"It's not the time right now," he said. "But I don't want to have to rely on others to get me into the high-roller section either—no offense Mindy. And I think you'll be a great help when its time to make that move towards independence."

She hounded him about what he was talking about for the next twenty minutes. Mindy, her curiosity piqued, hounded him as well. But he would say no further on the subject. The vague plan he held in his head was only starting to form. It was enough to know that Pauline would be open to helping him with it. He sure as hell was going to need her.

CHAPTER 12

ON THE ROAD AGAIN

February 24, 1984
Los Angeles, California

"God, I hate these fucking leather pants," Matt barked as they emerged from the makeshift dressing room and made their way towards the back-stage area of the rehearsal warehouse.

"That ain't no shit," Jake agreed, pulling at his for the twentieth time to keep it from constricting his testicles. "I forgot how hot and uncomfortable these get-ups are."

This grumbling was met by more grumbling from the rest of the band. Coop complained about the goddamn kamikaze headband and the dark shades. Bill complained about the preppie button-up shirt and the pocket protector, complete with pens and a protractor. Darren complained loudest of all. They had him dressed up like a Chippendale dancer, with gray leather shorts, spiked leather boots, and no shirt at all.

"What are you talking about?" asked Greg Gahn, who had been assigned once again to the role of tour manager. "You guys look great. This is the look your fans are expecting of you."

No one answered him, which was the usual response to any statements made by him.

There were no fans out in the audience today, at least not in the strict sense of the word. This was a dress rehearsal, the first of six such events scheduled before they headed for Miami and the first date of the *The Thrill of Doing Business* tour. There was a small audience out there that consisted of a half dozen National Records executives, some cronies these executives had brought along so they could be impressed by the up-close look at the band, and Mindy, who had brought Georgette and a small entourage of publicists and photographers who planned to further enhance the young actress's evolving image by releasing a story about her attending her boyfriend's concert. In all, *Intemperance* would be performing their set for about sixty people this first time, not including the roadies and the techies who ran the show. It wasn't much of an audience, but it was enough to give Jake the familiar pre-show jitters and worries that were as much a part of performing as applause and sweat.

They entered the stage left portion of the warehouse. It was larger than it had been in their previous tour, with almost twice as many roadies moving about from place to place, putting the final touches on a performance that would be considerably more complex than their previous shows. The stage itself was larger, with more area for the three guitar players—Jake, Darren, and Matt—to move about in. Coop's drum set had also been expanded with more snare and trap drums, more cymbals, and even a set of bongos which would be used for a short time on *Lost in the Silence*, one of the ballads on the new album. Bill's grand piano had also become grander as well. He was now sporting the largest and most expensive model available from the Caldwell Piano Corporation.

Most of the additional personnel were technicians who were needed to run some of the more high-tech additions to the show. There were sixteen additional lighting techs to go with the more than two hundred stage lights that hung from movable scaffolding suspended above the stage. There were the laser technicians who would set up and control the laser show that took place behind the band during various numbers throughout the set. There was also the pyrotechnic crew, headed by a somewhat frightening man named Dave Warden.

"Okay," Greg said, waving to the band to sit down on the packing boxes well out of the way. "Fifteen minutes to show time. Everyone do a final wardrobe check."

The band did a variety of eye rolling and then dutifully looked each other up and down, looking for torn leather, unsightly stains, or anything else that was out of place.

"You know something, Jake?" Matt asked as Jake held his arms up and turned slowly around.

"What's that?"

"Your ass looks really juicy in that leather." He reached forward and gave Jake's left cheek a squeeze.

Jake and the rest of the band laughed while Greg blanched in disgust.

"In the name of Heavenly Father," Greg barked. "Be careful doing things like that!"

"We're just joking around, Greg," Matt said. "You know? Camaraderie? You ever heard of it?"

"Camaraderie is one thing," Greg said. "Homosexual behavior is something else. All it takes is one person to say that Matt grabbed Jake's buttocks and the next thing you know there's a rumor floating around that you two are engaging in oral copulation."

"Oral copulation?" Jake said. "You been hanging out with Nerdly? You're starting to talk like him."

"What's wrong with the way I talk?" Bill asked, indignantly.

"You seem awfully uptight about this homosexuality thing, Greg," Matt said. "Are you compensating for something?"

"What?" Greg asked.

"You ever smoke the old Havana?" Matt asked him. "Just to see what it was like?"

"Now you're being disgusting!" Greg spat. "I have engaged in sexual congress with exactly one person in my life and I think the subject of homosexual congress is both disgusting and sinful!"

"One person?" Jake asked. "Who was she?"

Greg turned red in the face and stormed off. He found one of the roadies and began yelling at him about a cable that wasn't properly taped down.

"I love that guy," Matt said, lighting a cigarette and inhaling deeply. "Should we make a point to fuck with him at least three times a day while we're on the road?"

"At least," Jake agreed, sipping from his water.

Dave Warden, the head pyrotechnician, came in through the stage door. He saw the band gathered in the corner and headed directly over. Dave was a tall guy, with brownish-gray hair and a scraggly mustache. An unlit cigar stump hung from the corner of his mouth. He was dressed like most of the roadies, in a pair of tattered jeans and a dirty T-shirt. He wore a tool belt around his waist that contained a variety of wire cutters, rolls of wire, and electrical connectors.

"You guys ready to go live with the pyro?" he asked them, his voice stern and unforgiving, much like a marine drill instructor's.

"Bring on the boom-boom," Matt said.

"Yeah," Jake agreed. "Nothing like a good blow."

"Hey," Darren said, "is it possible to light a smoke off one of them charges? I mean, wouldn't that be fuckin' cool? As the final boom goes off, me and Matt use it to light up our after-show smokes?"

Dave's face took on an expression of angry alarm. "Are you crazy?" he asked. "You're joking about pyrotechnic charges?"

The band looked at each other and then back at Dave. "We joke about everything, Dave," Matt told him. "Lighten up a little."

"Lighten up?" Dave asked, his eyes narrowing to slits. "You don't joke about pyrotechnics. You treat them will all the respect and caution you would a nuclear weapon."

"A nuclear weapon?" Jake said, raising his eyebrows.

"Hell, we joke about those too," Matt said.

"Really, Dave," said Bill, "don't you think it's a bit of a non-sequiturous analogy to compare destructive thermonuclear fusion to simple decorative flashes?"

Dave glared at Bill. "What the hell does that mean?" he asked.

"He's saying," Jake translated, "that it seems kind of ludicrous to compare your little pop charges to an ICBM warhead leveling Los Angeles."

"Little pop charges?" Dave barked, his eyes turning angry. "Is that what you think my pyrotechnics are?"

All five of them shrugged. "Aren't they?" Jake asked.

"Let me tell you something, you little punks," Dave said, looking from one to the other. "Those charges are made of some of the same high explosive components that the VC used on us over in Nam. Where do you think I learned this trade? It was my job to take those homemade booby-traps the gooks laid out for our boys and reverse engineer them to figure out how they worked. And I'm here to tell you, those gooks knew what the hell they were doing, and they blew off the legs, arms, faces, and testicles of many a good man over in that living hell of a jungle. Why, I remember this one time one of them booby traps blew up beneath this guy's legs and tore a hole so big in him that his intestines were hanging out where his cock used to be. You don't see shit like that in Los Angeles now, do you?"

"Uh... no, I guess you don't," Matt said slowly.

"Can't say as I've ever seen anything like that in LA," Jake had to agree.

"So... uh... are you saying," asked Darren, "that those charges you have set on the stage could blow my cock off? Because I'm not really sure I'm down with that, you know?"

"There's no shrapnel in my charges," Dave responded. "And they're shaped to produce noise and flash instead of bodily damage, but you lose respect for them, you treat them the wrong way, you bet your ass they'll blow your cock off. Remember that safety margin I told you about?"

"Yeah," Jake said. "We've been rehearsing our way around your charges the whole time."

"We'll make sure we're back at least six feet whenever one is supposed to go off," said Matt.

"You'd better make that safety margin your God, you ever-loving Jesus right down from the cross. Love my charges, love everything they'll do for you—hell, they're what's going to make your show— but never lose respect for them, and never, I mean *never*, let me hear you joking about them. That's just tempting the Almighty."

They all agreed to retain the utmost respect for his beloved charges. Satisfied, he left them to go man his detonation station. And, of course, the moment he was gone, they erupted into laughter and made fun of him for the better part of five minutes.

"Oh man," Darren said with dying laughter after the last round of listening to Matt and Jake imitate Dave's voice and speech, "I gotta go take a shit."

"A shit?" asked Matt. "Right now?"

"Darren, it's only six minutes until we hit the stage," Jake said. "Can't you hold it?"

"Naw," he said, standing up. "I gotta go bad. I'll be back in time."

"You fuckin' well better be," Matt said. "Jesus Christ, dude. Why didn't you shit before you got dressed?"

"I didn't have to go then," Darren said.

"Then go," Matt told him. "Hurry."

Darren scampered off, disappearing back through the stage left access door.

"Freakin' moron," Matt muttered.

"Oh, cut him a little slack," Jake said. "There's nothing worse than having your bowels want to let go while you're up on stage. Remember that time in Santa Fe when you got the shits right before we went on?"

"I remember," Matt said. "And if you'll recall, I fuckin' held it until the encore break. I was cramped and sweating and miserable the whole time, but I goddamn well held it."

"That is a singularly miserable experience," Bill said. "The passage of time seems to reduce in fluidity to the point where it seems to evolve from a liquid to a solid."

"Actually," Matt said, "my feces evolved from a solid to a liquid. That was kind of the problem, Nerdly."

They had a chuckle about this and then looked at the clock up on the wall. Five minutes to go.

"How was your fishing trip yesterday?" Jake asked Matt. "Did you get your limit?"

During his vacation in Rio de Janeiro Matt had gone on a deep-sea sport fishing expedition offered by the resort they'd stayed in. He had gone mostly on a whim, having become a little bored with the endless drinking and fornication that had marked his first week in Brazil. Prior to that trip, he'd never even been on a boat before, let alone one that went out into the open ocean. To his surprise, he'd not only not gotten seasick, as he'd feared, he'd had the time of his life. He went two more times before the vacation ended, catching fifty and sixty pound sailfish, and had come back with a new obsession, one that seemed nearly as strong as the obsession he had for his guitar and for fornication itself. Since the return, he had been out twice more, saving up his allowance and booking private charter boats out of Marina del Ray.

"Not even close," Matt said. "We got four rock cod and a yellowtail. I hooked into what was probably a ling cod but the motherfucker snapped my line before I could bring him into gaffing range."

"That's too bad," Jake said.

"No shit," Matt agreed. "And to make it worse, the bitch I took with me got seasick before we even left the harbor."

"You didn't get any puss?"

Matt looked at him like he was an idiot. "As if," he said. "Like I give a rat's ass if she's sick. Shit, I paid two grand to book that goddamn boat and have it all to myself. I'll be damned if the slut I took with me ain't gonna give it up."

"You fucked a girl while she was seasick?" Jake asked, half appalled and half amused.

"Goddamn right. I just bent her over the railing and nailed her from behind while she barfed in the fuckin' ocean."

"Wow," said Bill, a touch of awe in his tone. "You are truly one of the most depraved people I've ever met, Matt."

"Thanks," Matt said. "And I'm here to tell you, a chick's pussy muscles do some interesting shit while they're barfing. You all oughta try it some time."

They all pondered that while another two minutes clicked by. Just as they were starting to get nervous about Darren, he came back, strolling in through the stage door and heading over to them. Jake knew immediately that he hadn't gone out to take a shit. His eyes were half-lidded and reddened, the look on his face one he only got when he was stoned. And though he had tried to cover the odor of the marijuana with a mouthful of breath mints, it wasn't quite cutting it. The smell of greenbud was reeking off of him in waves.

Jake looked at Matt and saw that he'd realized the same thing. Matt's face was getting red with anger. They had had this problem with Darren before back in their early days, while they were still doing the club scene in Heritage. A heart to heart talk in which Matt and Jake had threatened to replace him had seemed to cure Darren of this violation of their internal code of conduct. But now here he was again, smoking out before a performance.

"You fucking asshole," Matt said. "What the fuck do you think you're doing?"

"What?" Darren said defensively. "I was just taking a shit. I'm back in time, ain't I?"

"You were smoking weed back there!" Matt barked. "You're stoned to the fuckin' eyeballs!"

"I am not!" Darren protested. "Jesus Christ, Matt! You know I wouldn't do nothin' like that!"

Matt looked at Jake, searching for backup. Jake nodded.

"You look pretty stoned to me, Darren," he said. "You smell like it, too."

"I'm not stoned!" Darren insisted, feigning anger at the accusation and doing a poor job of it.

"Really?" Matt said. "So, if I were to go back to the bathroom you just used am I going to smell your stinking shit or am I going to smell greenbud? Or were you at least smart enough to step outside before you hit your fucking pipe?"

"You guys are paranoid," Darren said. "I had to take a shit, that's all. My stomach hasn't been feeling too good today. You know how it is? Remember that time in Santa Fe, Matt?"

"Listen, asshole," Matt said. But before he could go any further, Steve Langley, the production manager, walked over.

"It's time, guys," he said. "Let's get lined up by the access door."

"Right," Matt said. He took a few deep breaths and then looked at Darren. "You'd better not fuck up out there."

"I'm not gonna fuck up," Darren said. "I'm telling you, man, I'm not stoned!"

"Uh huh," Matt said. "And you'd better believe we're going to be talking about this after the show."

"There's nothing to talk about," Darren said stubbornly.

Steve seemed a bit uncomfortable with the tension between the band members. "Is everything all right?" he asked carefully.

"I hope so," Matt said. "Come on. Let's do it."

"Let's do it," the rest of them echoed.

The lights in the warehouse had been dimmed down to near blackness. Playing from the amplifiers was a deep, ominous synthesizer melody, swelling in volume, intensifying in depth.

The band did their ritual slapping of hands. By the time they were done, their cue was upon them.

"Go," Steve told them. "And remember, stay clear of the pyro charges."

They went, walking into the darkness and finding their positions by feel and repetition. Jake picked up his guitar, a brand new Brogan Les Paul knock-off that had been re-strung and exactly tuned earlier that day by Mohammed, his personal assistant. He pulled a pick from the inlay and gripped it. He then backed up four paces, clearing himself from the danger zone of the pyrotechnic charge that would soon be exploding before him.

The synthesized recording built to a crescendo, held, and then cut-off. The moment it did, Matt hit an open low E and A string. The sound crunched out over the warehouse, blasting from the amplifiers and slowly fading away. Just as it was about to fade to nothing, Matt did a fast, finger-tapping solo, ending with a repetitive hammering of the whammy bar on the high-E string.

This was the cue for Dave, the maniacal pyrotechnician, to fire off the first of his explosives. He did it exactly and well. There was a flash of bright light and a resounding BOOM. Jake felt it hammer into his chest, smelled the smoke from the powder. His eyes were momentarily blinded, but he was safe and sound, his testicles still attached to his body. The spotlights came on, illuminating them brightly to the audience, and, as one, the band launched into the first song of the set, *The Thrill of Doing Business*.

Thrill had an extended session of hard, heavy guitar work prior to the first vocals. Matt crunched out the lead, working the tempo up faster and louder while Jake produced a solid backing riff. As they played they moved about the front of the stage, letting the pounding beat laid down by Coop and Darren guide their body motions. They came shoulder to shoulder a few times but made sure not to cross over each other and switch sides since that would quickly tangle their guitar cords like the leashes of two dogs. At last came the final build up to the main riff. It was a furious symphony of drumbeats, piano chords, bass, and dual guitars that worked their way into a simultaneous, heavy-handed production of the main riff. Matt moved backwards, sliding in a dancing, shuffling motion that went exactly to the beat. Jake moved forward, timing his approach to the microphone so that the second he reached it, it was time for him to sing.

His voice belted out the lyrics, the words coming from his mouth smooth and sure, with exacting emotion. He sang the verses and the chorus, changed timbre for the bridge, all the while his fingers playing his guitar and his body moving and swaying to the beat. When it was time for the guitar solo he stepped back, going shoulder to shoulder with Darren in a dizzying overlay of lighting effects as Matt twisted and turned while his incredibly fast and agile fingers hammered on the neck of his guitar and tapped surely at the strings. The song ended with another furious crunch of instruments followed by a brief period of silence—the short applause break as it was called. The applause did not wash over them as it would during a full performance—after all, there were only sixty or so people out there—but they did get a resounding session of appreciation. There were lots of hand clapping and a few whistles.

"Yeah, Jake!" Jake heard Mindy scream up at him. "Damn you're good, baby!"

Jake couldn't see her, or anyone else in the audience for that matter, since the stage was as bright as daylight and the seating area was in darkness. Still, he smiled and looked at the place where he thought she was sitting. He then stepped back to his microphone just as Coop did the four count and launched them into the next song.

They played solidly for the next seventy-six minutes, working their way through a mixed combination of tunes from *Descent Into Nothing* and the new album. Their motions on stage remained as spontaneous and improvised as they'd always been, though this was only because of another battle fought with the National Records executives, who had hired a choreography team and had tried to turn the entire production into a complex, coordinated dance in which every on-stage motion was pre-planned and carefully rehearsed.

"It's the way concerts are evolving," Crow told them when the idea was first explained. "It's part of the MTV effect on the industry. People don't want to see you just going up there and playing your instruments and singing. That's boring. They want to see production, flair, *performance*. This choreography team is the best in the business. They'll work with you step by step until every concert you do will be exactly the same, with everyone in an exact place at any particular time. You'll move in synchronicity up there, with new modern dance steps, some jumps, and even some basic gymnastic moves."

"Uh... no, sorry," Matt replied. "Not gonna happen. We'll keep doing our shows the way we've always done them."

This refusal of course led to arguments, threats of contract breach lawsuits, profane declarations by Crow and Doolittle about how they (the band) would do whatever the fuck they were told to do and like it, but by now Jake and Matt, with the help of Pauline, knew the wording of their contract inside and out.

"You have the right to plan a tour for us," Jake told Doolittle during a meeting on the issue, "you have the right to compel us to perform on the tour, you have the right to schedule the tour any way you see fit, you have the right to choose the songs we play during our concerts and in what order we perform them in, you have the right to arrange for all this laser lighting and explosive crap, and you even have the right to make us pay for half of the expenses of all this. But *nowhere* in our contract does it say anything about you having the right to choreograph our actual performance on stage. So take your choreographers and shove them up your ass. We'll continue performing our songs the way we always have."

This led to another meeting, this time with National Records' lawyers, who tried to tell Jake and Matt that they were misinterpreting the contract, that the order of musical performance clause gave National every right in the world to dictate just *how* the songs would be performed, up to and including the assignment of dance moves.

"Then take us to court," Jake said calmly, puffing on a cigarette while Matt, who had said little, was making a big production out of rolling a joint on the lawyer's desk.

"We don't want it to come to that, Jake," the head lawyer said. "It makes for bad publicity and hard feelings."

"We already have the fuckin' hard feelings," Matt said. He held up his joint for Jake's perusal. "What do you think of this one? Too tight for the greenbud to burn? You know how wet that shit is."

"Maybe a little less twisting on the end," Jake said. "And if you leave a big opening on the flame end, it'll let in enough oxygen to get the bud burning instead of just the paper."

"Does that solve the clogging problem, though? I mean, with all the resin in this greenbud, it chokes off the airflow by about the third hit."

"Gentlemen!" the lawyer said, exasperated, as, of course, had been the intention. "Could you put away your illegal substances so we can concentrate on the matter at hand?"

Matt shrugged and put the joint behind his ear. "Not much to concentrate on," he said. "I think our position is pretty clear."

"Your position is untenable," the lawyer said.

"Hey," Matt said, "that's a Nerdly word."

"A what?" the lawyer asked, appalled. "Are you calling me a nerd?"

"Look," Jake said, "it's very simple. We will not allow our performance to be choreographed unless you bring us a decision from a Superior Court judge proclaiming that we have to. Take us to court if you think the contract allows this sort of direction, but meanwhile that's going to delay the start of the tour, isn't it?"

"And that might affect album sales," Matt added.

National gave in. This didn't stop Crow and Doolittle and Greg and Janice from constantly whining and complaining about the decision, or from making snide little remarks about how much better the performance would be if it were only choreographed, but they gave in none-the-less. As *Intemperance* performed at the dress rehearsal before their audience of thirty, their moves on stage came from their hearts and souls, forged by their musical instinct and talent, and not from a choreographer's idea of what a rock audience was looking for in a show.

The stage effects, however, were something else entirely. The lighting was impressive, that was to be sure, but it was both dizzying and occasionally nauseating as multi-colored spotlights spun back and forth, over and across, and flicked on and off. Individual spotlights would blare onto Matt while he was doing a solo, or Bill while he was doing a piano solo, or Jake while he was strumming out the opening acoustical portion of one of the ballads. When this happened, the heat generated was almost unbearable and by the time they were halfway done Jake and Matt were both pouring sweat down their faces, their shirts saturated, their bodies screaming out for rehydration.

And then there was the laser show. At three points during the performance—during the ballads *Point of Futility* and *Crossing the Line* and during the hard-rocking *Descent Into Nothing*—a superfluity of blue and red beams crossed ten feet over their heads, whipping back and forth, forming patterns and pulsations that moved to the beat of the music. In order to make these patterns visible to the audience, a sparse fog of carbon dioxide was created with dry ice and water and blown gently out over the stage. Though most of the gas stayed up above them, enough drifted down to fill their mouths with the biting dryness, their noses with the acrid aroma. And though it was the sort of thing that probably looked really cool when one was stoned, Jake and Matt both thought it did more to detract from the music than to enhance it. They tried their best to ignore it while the performance was taking place.

What they could not ignore were the explosions. The opening pyrotechnic was only the first of three detonations throughout the show. The closing song was *Almost Too Easy*, a hard-rocker from the *Descent* album that enjoyed copious airplay after the fade of *Point of Futility* from the charts but had that had only climbed to the low thirties itself. They did a crashing crescendo to end the song and then the second explosion went off just as the final chords were being struck. The third explosion came at the end of the two song encore set, as the finale to *Who Needs Love?* This set of detonations, they had been warned by Dave Warden, was to be nearly three times the size and length of the previous two. He was not exaggerating, they found. The cue came and four separate devices went off at the front of the stage, followed by six more on either side and then two more mounted just in front of Coop's drum set. The concussions hammered into Jake's chest, into his ears, jarring his teeth and rattling his eardrums. But, as before, all band members remained in the safe zone and came out of it no worse for wear.

"Thank you," Jake said into the microphone as the sixty people stood and applauded. "Thank you and good night."

And that concluded the dress rehearsal.

*****

Jake and Mindy met that night at Flamer's Steakhouse on restaurant row. Flamer's was one of the most exclusive eateries in the greater Los Angeles region, with a waiting list for reservations more than three months long, but Jake had gotten them a table with a single phone call made less than four hours before. This was one of the perks to being a celebrity. Another was that they would not have to pay for their meal (although, of course, they would leave a hefty tip for their server). The reasoning for this was that Flamer's was one of those restaurants with a reputation for having the famous frequently dine there, which, of course, drew a steady stream of non-famous diners who were willing to spring for eighteen to thirty dollar entrees.

Their table sat in the middle of the main dining room, within easy view of most of the other diners. Jake wore a dark suit and a red necktie, Mindy a low-cut lavender gown. Though there were lots of whispers behind closed hands, nonchalant nods in their direction, and staring eyes cast upon them, no one actually came over to them. There was an unstated but well-understood rule that those granted precious seating at Flamer's were to treat any celebrities who happened to be present like museum artifacts in a display case. You could look and admire but not touch or interact with. Jake sipped from a glass of 1972 Merlot. Since the trip to Las Vegas he had developed a taste for both caviar and fine wine. Mindy munched on a cracker topped with goose liver pate while drinking a Long Island iced tea. Both had just placed their entrée orders.

"What was the problem with Darren?" Mindy asked. Jake had mentioned to her after the dress rehearsal that there had been a problem but had not gone into details about what it was.

He explained about the sudden trip to the bathroom before hitting the stage, the reddened eyes, the mint-enhanced odor of greenbud, and, most damning, the familiar mannerisms and speech of Darren stoned.

"What happened when you talked to him about it?" she asked.

"Nothing," Jake responded. "He kept denying it and denying it and denying it some more, no matter what we said to him. It's the same thing he did before, back when he was pulling that shit at D Street West in Heritage, but at least he stopped doing it when we threatened to kick his ass out of the band."

"Do you think that will work now?"

He shrugged. "Hopefully. I'm not sure what we'll actually do if it doesn't. It would be a little harder to get rid of him now. The way our contract is written we would need the record company's permission to fire a band member."

"Wouldn't they go along with you? I mean, he's using drugs before performing."

Jake grunted and took another sip of his wine. "Actually, they'd love to find out he's getting loaded before hitting the stage. They'd probably hold a press conference to announce it. It would fit in with this whole image they're trying to push on us."

"Image *is* important," Mindy said. "I'll be the first to agree with that."

"Yeah," Jake said, holding his tongue. He was well aware how much she agreed with that particular statement.

"But," she said, "it's a lot more important to have your head straight when you perform. Look at me. I take my acting every bit as seriously as you and Matt take your music and I wouldn't dream of trying to do a scene or even a rehearsal while I was stoned, or drunk, or coked out. It's just impossible to give your all, to do your best that way, no matter how much you're used to it. And doing your best is how you get to the top and stay there, right?"

"Right," Jake said, surprised again, as he often was, at her eerily accurate common sense insight into certain things.

"In the movie industry if an actor or actress is showing up to work under the influence of something, the producer will put a stop to it immediately. It doesn't matter how famous the actor is, how much money has been advanced, how much pull the actor has, it will be stopped or the actor will be fired from the project because the producers realize that you can't perform your best that way. I just don't see why your record producers aren't the same way."

"They are a different breed, that's for sure," Jake said. "Unlike your movie producers, they are convinced that image is more important than quality. The image they want of rock stars is of drugged out, strung out lowlifes and they do everything they can to promote that image. That's why they supply us with endless amounts of booze and coke and pot. They want us to be addicts. They want us to get fucked up before we go onstage. If we screw up a performance because we're wasted, they see that as an asset, a reinforcement of what they think is the most important thing."

"It's sad," Mindy said, draining the last of her drink and signaling to the waiter for another.

"Yeah," he agreed, "and hopefully Darren will get back into line. As long as he doesn't realize that we can't really fire him, he should."

Their dinner came and they ate slowly, relishing the tender cuts of filet mignon and the recently deceased Maine lobsters. For desert they had baked Alaska served with kahlua and cream.

"Well," said Mindy after the last bite went down her throat, "there's another twenty minutes of workout for the next two days. I can feel all this food trying to work its way into my butt as we speak."

"It's worth it though," Jake said, his stomach just below the threshold of being uncomfortably full.

"Agreed," she said. She twirled the remnants of her drink for a moment. "So when do I get my copy of your new album?"

"I told you," he said, "they're not giving us our complimentary copies until the last day of February. Once they do, I'll personally deliver it to you."

"That's only one day before it's released in stores," she pouted. "Doesn't being your girlfriend get me any privileges?"

"Not with National it doesn't," he said. "They sent out about thirty copies of the first single to some of the radio stations they have close ties to but the album itself is locked up solid. They're not even pre-shipping it to the record stores until the 27th."

"I guess everything fits in with some master plan," she said.

"Of course."

"And you're leaving for Miami on what day?" she asked.

"We climb on the bus March 12 and drive across the country again," he said. "The first show is on the 15th. We'll be up and down the east coast and the Midwest for two and a half months after that."

"They've got quite a schedule for you."

He nodded. "Lots of consecutive dates, lots of smaller cities we didn't hit before in addition to the ones that we did. It's going to be brutal, but I'm looking forward to it. Performing is why I got into this business, after all."

"Not just for the free food?"

"Not just for the free food," he confirmed.

"Jake," she said, "there's something I need to talk to you about."

He looked up warily. "What's that?"

"It's nothing bad," she said. "Not really, anyway. It's just that... well... Georgette and I have been talking about what this tour is going to mean to our images... yours and mine."

"To our images?"

"Yes," she said. "You see, you're going to be gone for months, almost six of them, right?"

"About five and a half before the whole tour is over," he confirmed.

"And you're going to be... you know... doing your thing with the groupies and the drugs and all that while you're out there."

"Mindy..."

"Hold on a second," she said. "Let me talk. I told you before that it doesn't bother me when you do that and it doesn't. You can screw all the groupies you want. I expect you to. But you see... the media is going to be reporting that you're doing that, aren't they?"

He tried to formulate several responses to this question and failed. Finally, he just asked, "What is it you're trying to say?"

"Well, it would look really bad for both of us if, in the eyes of the public, we were a couple and the media was constantly reporting that you were out there getting it on with a bunch of sluts after your concerts night after night. They'd portray you as a heartless womanizer and they'd portray me as a suffering abused woman. Every time they got pictures or reports of you with some groupie, they'd start hounding me and asking me what I thought about it. It would be a zoo. You have to agree with that, don't you?"

"I suppose that would be a source of negative imagery," Jake allowed. "So, what are you saying? You want to break up with me?"

"Not in real life," she said. "But on the record, yes, I think we should."

"On the record?"

"It's simple," she said. "We have Georgette and Shaver announce that we have decided to end our romantic relationship with each other for personal reasons. We don't make it ugly or anything, we just say that we decided to remain friends only and go our separate ways. That way, you'll be free to do your thing with the groupies while you're out on tour and it won't reflect negatively on either one of us. I'm sure Shaver and the executives at National would agree that this is the only way."

Jake was unsure what to say, what to think. This was a rather large bombshell for her to drop on him without any warning. "What if I told you," he suggested, "that I would stay away from the groupies while I'm on tour."

She was shaking her head before he even finished this statement. "That will never work," she said. "In the first place, do you really think you could do that?"

"Yes," he said. "I could."

"Jake, I wouldn't want you to do that," she said. "You would be miserable out there if your friends were always getting it on and you were being left out."

"I did it before," he said. "When Michelle and I were together I never slept with a single groupie."

"And look how that ended," she said. "She still broke up with you. But that's a moot point anyway, because look what happened with Angie. You were committed to her when you left on your first tour, weren't you? And didn't you tell me that you fucked a groupie after your very first show?"

The mention of Angie still had the power to send waves of guilt trudging through him. "Yes," he said softly.

"In fact, you never even talked to her again, did you? Never said goodbye? Never gave her an explanation?"

"No," he said. "I didn't."

"Don't you see the difference, Jake? With Michelle, you were performing in your own town all the time. She was always there for you. With Angie, she wasn't. You were away from her for months and you knew that. You would do the same thing if we stayed together. Be honest with yourself."

He did as requested and knew that, in all likelihood, she was right. He might hold off for a month or maybe six weeks, but in the end, he would probably give at some point. "Okay," he said. "I get your point."

"And even if you were faithful to me, something I don't want you to have to be, the media would still see Matt and Darren and Bill and Coop doing all those things with their groupies and they would assume that you were doing the same anyway. It wouldn't matter if you were faithful because they wouldn't want to report that. They love scandal and they would use every piece of innuendo they could come up with. Jake, honey, I love you dearly, really I do, but this is the only way."

He sighed, his pleasant evening suddenly turned morose. "Okay," he said, resigned. "If you want to break up, I'm certainly not going to stop you."

"But we're not *really* breaking up," she said. "That's the best part of this. We're just *pretending* to break up. We'll still see each other when we can. It'll just have to be secret. Really secret this time."

Jake nodded. "Sure," he said. "Really secret this time."

"You understand, don't you?" she asked, her eyes giving the innocent puppy gaze she was so famous for.

"I understand that the image wins again," he told her. "Shall we get out of here now?"

They got out of there. Jake tried to remain aloof with her as they rode in the limo back to his place. His intention was to dismiss her. If she wanted to break up, then they would break up. His intentions lasted only as long as it took her to open the fly of his dress pants and start sucking him while they drove through the streets of Hollywood.

*****

The break-up went down as discussed and scheduled. Georgette and Shaver gave their press conferences and read brief statements written by Jake and Mindy in which both proclaimed that the reason for their break-up was personal and that they were still "dear friends" and would always remain so. The media went into a frenzy over the announcement, with headline stories and analysis taking up more room in some local publications than the stories about the pull-out of the US Marines from Beirut in the wake of the suicide bombing or the alleged use of chemical weapons by Iraq in their war with Iran.

On March 10, two days before *Intemperance*'s departure for Miami, Mindy showed up at Jake's condo unexpectedly. She found him dressed in an old pair of jeans and a sweat-stained t-shirt, his hair in disarray. He was in a foul mood, the living room full of cardboard boxes in which he was packing all of his belongings.

"What are you doing here?" he asked. "I thought we weren't supposed to be seen together."

"It's okay," she told him, looking around the condo in amazement. "The official story is that I'm picking up a few belongings I left at your place. What the hell is going on here?"

"I'm being evicted," he told her. "Since we're going to be gone for almost six months, National decided it was cheaper to stop paying for this place and keep my stuff in storage until I get back."

"They're kicking you out of your home?" she asked, appalled.

"It's not my home," he said bitterly. "It's the record company's. All five of us are getting the boot. They say they'll find different lodging for us when we get back."

"That's horrible," she said, genuinely appalled.

"That's life in the music biz," he responded. "What did you really come here for?"

"I just wanted to see you one more time before you went," she said. "I have to fly to New York tomorrow for an audition." She smiled. "It's for a new movie they're going to start filming in a few months. A real movie. It's called *Back to the Future*."

"Yeah?" he asked. "What's it about?"

"It's going to have Michael J. Fox as the lead," she said. "He'll play a high school student who goes back in time and accidentally interferes with his parent's romance because his mom falls in love with him."

"His *mom* falls in love with him?" Jake asked.

"Yes... isn't it deliciously kinky? I'm trying out for the part of the teenage mom in 1955. She's going to be a little slut from what I understand."

"I guess she'd have to be if she wants to bang her own son."

"She doesn't *know* he's her son," she said, rolling her eyes. "Anyway, it's the first role with the least bit of sexuality in it that I've ever been offered. I just wanted to properly thank you for helping me get a chance at it before you went. We probably won't be able to see each other again for awhile."

"You're welcome," he said. "Just call me the image enhancer."

"Oh, come on, Jake," she said. "Don't be like that. You know this is the right thing to do, don't you?"

"Yeah," he said, tired of the whole subject. "The right thing."

"I've got a few minutes before people start to wonder why I'm up here so long," she said. "Shall we visit your bedroom one last time?"

He made the obligatory protests but within five minutes they were retiring to his bedroom. By the time they were done he needed a shower in order to go back to the dirty, grimy work of packing up his life.

*****

The convoy formed up on the morning of March 12 for the long trip to Miami. It was larger and more impressive than the convoy that had formed the *Earthstone/Intemperance* tour of 1983, or the *Intemperance/Voyeur* tour of later that same year. There were eleven tour buses forming the vanguard of the convoy. One for *Intemperance*, one for *Birmingham*—the rookie Southern rock band who would be opening for them—and nine for the roadies, technical specialists, and tour management who would be accompanying them. There were ten tractor-trailer rigs following behind the tour buses, four more than the last tour, including one with high-explosive placards pasted all over it. This particular tractor-trailer, which contained all of the pyrotechnic equipment and charges, was a particular pain in the ass to the planners of the tour because whenever the route took them over a large bridge or through a tunnel, it would have to divert around and rejoin later.

Jake, Matt, and the rest of the band were assigned to the exact same tour bus that had been their home during the last tour. The same two drivers were assigned to pilot it. And, of course, Greg Gahn, the hypocritical, Book of Mormon thumping, coke sniffing, drug pushing tour manager was assigned to accompany, intoxify, pacify, and generally babysit them.

"It won't be like last time," he told them as the convoy left the assembly area and started rolling towards the freeway. "We have nothing but luxury suites booked for you guys. You're big time now."

"That's real big of you," Jake responded, sipping from his first beer of the trip even though it was only seven in the morning, "considering that we're paying half the bill for those luxury suites."

"And *all* of your fuckin' nose candy," Matt added.

Greg wisely kept his mouth shut until the band was a little more into the spirit of things.

This didn't take long. They rolled down Interstate 10, leaving Los Angeles and its suburbs behind. By the time the bus entered the desert of Riverside County a thick haze of marijuana smoke hung in the air, the trash was full of empty beer bottles, and the mood among the band members was almost festive.

This mood remained as they rolled across the southern edge of the country. The bus sound system was turned on and, like before, whenever the new *Intemperance* single was found on a radio station, it was cranked loudly and out came the air guitars and the improvised dance moves. There was reason to be festive about this. Only fifteen days after *The Thrill of Doing Business* was released across the country for sale, the album had already sold eighty thousand copies and the single had already debuted on the Hot One Hundred chart. It was the most requested song on rock radio stations coast to coast and the first twenty venues they were scheduled for had already sold out in advance.

"Listen to this," said Bill on the second day of the trip, as he read from a newspaper he had picked up in an El Paso truck stop while the convoy had been fueling. "It's a record review of *Thrill*. 'It is clear when you listen to the cuts on the new album that the band has both matured and become more sophisticated in songwriting and musical composition. The lyrics by Tisdale and especially Kingsley are an obvious reflection of the life lessons both have learned in the rough and tumble music business. The ballad *Crossing the Line*, by Kingsley, is quite clearly influenced by his tumultuous, now-defunct relationship with television and screen actress Mindy Snow.'"

"That's some funny shit, Nerdly," Matt said. "We've matured and applied our life lessons. I guess they don't know that every last one of the tunes on *Thrill* are leftover material from D Street West days."

"Mindy and I only broke up a week ago," Jake said in wonder. "They think I composed a tune about it and that we rehearsed it up and recorded it since then?"

"Who is the song about then?" asked Greg, who was hovering nearby and preparing his latest nose candy feast.

"It isn't about anybody," Jake said. "It's not a love song at all. It's about taking risks in your life, about going beyond the point where your instincts are telling you to stop something. The line is where you can turn back from a decision and still walk away. Crossing it means you put everything at risk, expose yourself, flirt with failure in the name of a new achievement."

"Yeah," Coop said. "It's like when you're with a new bitch and you want to ass fuck her or have her dyke out with another bitch while you fuck them both. If you don't ask her, you'll never get to do it. But if you do ask her, she might dump your ass and start fucking one of your friends instead. That's the danger. But the reward you can get by crossing the line is that she might be down with it and you can get yourself into some ass or get a threesome."

Everyone stared at Coop for a moment, long enough to make him uncomfortable.

"What?" he asked.

"That's fuckin' deep, Coop," Matt said.

"Hell yeah," agreed Jake. "You nailed that concept right on the head."

Greg, as was his custom when the talked turned in this direction, simply shook his head in disgust and found another portion of the bus to occupy.

They rolled into Miami just after ten o'clock in the morning on March 15, ten and a half hours before they were to hit the stage for the first time. All five were hungover and strung out, badly in need of sleep. They stopped at their hotel long enough to check in and take a shower and then Janice Boxer gathered them all up for their first session of radio station interviews, sound byte recordings, and an autograph session at a local record store. They met the members of *Birmingham* for the first time when they reported for the sound check at four-thirty that afternoon.

Birmingham was a five-man band whose album had been released two months earlier and was selling moderately well with decent airplay of their single *Texas Hold-em*. Jake had heard their song on the radio many times and had also scored a copy of the album from Crow when he first found out they would be opening for them. They were obviously heavily influenced by *.38 Special* and *Molly Hatchet*, but not to the point where they were a complete sound-alike band like *Voyeur* had been for *AC/DC*. All in all, Jake thought their music wasn't bad and he told them so when the lead singer, who seemed awe-struck to be in their presence, introduced himself and his cohorts.

And of course, they asked if the veteran band had any advice to give to the rookies. They looked puzzled when all five members of *Intemperance* burst out in laughter.

"The best advice we can give," said Jake, "is the same advice *Earthstone* gave us when we opened for them the first time."

"What's that?"

Jake looked at Darren. "You want to lay it on 'em?" he asked him.

"Hell yeah," Darren said sourly. He looked at the members of *Birmingham*. "No matter what you do, no matter how much you might think you want to, *never* kiss a groupie."

And, as *Earthstone* had done before them, they said no further on that matter, leaving it to the newbies to find out how solid that advice was on their own.

In their dressing rooms they were assisted with their wardrobe by Reginald Feeney and had their hair done by Delores Riolo, just as before. Once dressed and presentable they went backstage for the obligatory autograph sessions and photo-ops for the various radio station contest winners and the other dignitaries who had scored back-stage passes.

"I'm sorry to hear about you and Mindy Snow," Jake was told no less than six times. Twice he was pressed for details of why they had broken up. He politely deflected these inquiries with vague statements.

Finally, they were led back to the dressing room so *Birmingham* could hit the stage. By this point they were really dragging ass, all of them wishing they had spent last night sleeping instead of partying.

"Does anyone want a little pick-me-up?" asked Greg, waving his cocaine kit before their eyes. "It would be therapeutic at this point, don't you think?"

"Don't start, Greg," Matt growled. "I was afraid of offending the record company last tour, so I went easy on you. I'm no longer quite so afraid of them."

Greg put a nervous look on his face and slinked off, taking his cocaine with him.

The thumping of *Birmingham*'s bass guitar could be heard but little else as they went through their set. After an hour it came to an end. Jake and Matt drank three bottles of Gatorade apiece to stave off the dehydration they knew was coming. Conversation was little. Finally, it was time to go forward. They made their way through the tunnel and into the stage left area. As soon as they opened the door the sound of the crowd hit them.

Jake felt his fatigue slipping away as he heard that sound, replaced by nervous excitement. It was time to perform.

The lights went down and the sell-out crowd of fourteen thousand began to roar. The synthesized intro began. They were warned one last time to stay clear of the pyro charges. They clasped hands and hit the stage. Matt ground out the opening chords, the explosions fired, and their first set of the tour began.

It went off flawlessly, just as it had in the dress rehearsals. Jake played and sang, giving himself fully to the performance, feeling everything else in his life slip from his thoughts as he heard the crowd screaming out their approval, as he heard them singing along with their songs. The ninety-minute set flew by, seeming to take only minutes, and when it was finally over, when the grand finale explosion finally ripped across the stage and the last chord was struck, when the five of them stood together at the front of the stage and took their bow, received their enthusiastic standing ovation, Jake felt that all was right in his world. He was doing what he was put on Earth to do and he couldn't wait to do it again.

The groupies in the shower routine of the last tour did not manifest itself on this tour. Instead, there was group of about thirty of them in the dressing room when the band emerged in their civilian clothing. Jake wasn't sure he was ready just yet to engage in the usual debauchery, but his misgivings were neatly squashed after three rum and cokes and two bonghits. He hooked up with a young Cuban girl with a lush, exotic body and large, pillow-soft breasts. She gave him a blowjob in the dressing room while he finished his fifth drink and then accompanied him to the party in Darren's suite. Later, around one in the morning, he took her back to his suite and undressed her like a Christmas present. He capped his weapon and slid into her alluring body, feeling no guilt during or after, but also feeling no real fulfillment at the conquest. He was giving her a memory that would last a lifetime—the night she fucked Jake Kingsley, *the* Jake Kingsley—but a week from now he wouldn't even remember her, not her name, not her face, not her scent, not even her existence.

*****

They fell back into the routine of touring with practiced ease. The days and then the weeks went by in a haze of long bus rides, greasy hotel and truck stop food, screaming fans and sign-carrying protestors at record stores, interviews (some quite caustic, touching on the Satanism or the Mindy Snow topic), sound byte deliveries, roaring crowds and the exquisite thrill of performing live, and late-night after-show parties marked by gross intoxication and naked, willing, nameless groupies. It wasn't long before Jake had to be reminded what city they were performing in before stepping onto the stage. It wasn't long before they lost complete track of the day of the week, even the month of the year.

They moved northward along the eastern seaboard, working their way city by city, arena by arena, to New England. They then moved west to the Great Lake cities, and then south, through the Midwest. Though their performances became more focused and more automatic through sheer repetition, the joy of performing never faded and the spontaneity of each show held firm, thrilling and delighting each audience. The word traveled in many forms—through print-media, through television, through word of mouth—but it remained essentially the same: *Intemperance* knew how to put on a show. Venues continued to sell out weeks in advance and there were reports of people camping out for two days to get tickets, of riots started by people trying to cut in line at such campouts, of record-high prices being charged by scalpers.

Another thing spread about by the media, usually in tabloids like *American Watcher*, was Jake's trysts with groupies. This was very big in the first month of the tour, while news of the Jake and Mindy break-up was still reverberating across the country. JAKE COPING WELL WITHOUT MINDY read one headline in the *Watcher*. Inside the issue was a lengthy interview with a nineteen-year-old girl who claimed to have had an extended sexual encounter with Jake in Atlanta after the *Intemperance* concert there.

"Is that the bitch you fucked in Atlanta?" Matt asked as they perused the issue during one of the bus rides.

Jake looked at the picture of her carefully. She was certainly attractive, with brunette hair, a trim body, and pouty lips. "Could be," he said. "She does look a little familiar."

Other such articles followed this one, but all shared the same theme. There would be pictures of a groupie that Jake had allegedly been involved with in some city or another, an interview with the groupie telling all that had occurred (at least within the bounds of the community standard of decency), and quotes from Georgette to the effect that Mindy was glad that Jake was moving on with his life and she wished him the best, and from Shaver, acting as Jake's spokesman (and raking his twenty-one percent off the top of their album sales) that Jake was living his own life and hoping that Mindy was doing the same.

It was only when they reached New York City when the articles finally came to an end, their monotonous theme replaced by one even more exciting, that of the arrest of the entire band on drug and indecency charges.

*****

Since it was the scene of the infamous coke sniffing from the butt-crack episode of the last tour, the protestations by the anti-*Intemperance* crowd were especially vigorous in the Big Apple in the weeks preceding their appearance there. There were petitions to revoke *Intemperance*'s concert permit, marches before city hall by local Christian and women's rights groups, even a candlelight vigil by an anti-drug coalition. None of it did any good. Madison Square Garden was sold out for three consecutive shows and the city council and mayor's office, citing first amendment issues as their basis for decision, refused to take any steps to prevent *Intemperance* from playing.

After the final MSG performance, the band was in Matt's room engaging in their usual post-performance activities. Jake, now fully back in the swing of the touring lifestyle, was on the couch in the suite's sitting room, fucking a young Chinese groupie from behind while her face was buried in the widely spread crotch of a young Japanese groupie. Resting on the Chinese groupie's lower back was a three-quarter full rum and coke. The challenge Jake had put upon his two lovers was to complete their act without spilling the drink. It was starting to look like the challenge would be lost when the front door of the suite suddenly boomed open and a dozen uniformed NYPD officers came bursting in, their guns drawn, their eyes wide.

"Everyone, get down on the fuckin' floor, now!" screamed a voice.

"I'm already on the fuckin' floor," replied Matt, who was on his back while two groupies took turns blowing him.

Chaos erupted for the next ten minutes as more cops came rushing in. Girls screamed, cops yelled, band members yelled back. Matt tried to get up and was pushed roughly back down. In his drunken and coked out state he did what came naturally to him. He hit the cop that had pushed him in the balls. The cops responded by pummeling Matt with their batons until he fell unconscious to the floor. Jake tried to get up and was pounced upon by three cops. He felt kicks to his ribs and a baton strike to the top of his head. His hands were wrenched behind his back and handcuffs were applied and wrenched down brutally tight. He was left to lay there, completely naked, a condom still on his penis, bleeding from his head, each breath a ragged stab of pain in his right side, a cop's foot on the back of his neck.

All the girls were gathered in one place and told to identify themselves. This took the better part of twenty minutes since they had to find their clothes first. Jake heard the two plainclothes cops who seemed to be in charge of the raid discussing them.

"None of them are underage," cop number one reported.

"*None* of them? Are you sure?"

"We've checked all their ID's, Lou."

"What about consent? Any of them say they're here against their will, or that they were being sexually assaulted."

"No. In fact, they're all quite proud to say they were here. Some of them were asking the CSI team to photograph 'em."

"Oh well," Lou sighed. "At least there's the drugs. Let's start searching."

The search took another hour. During it, the cops confiscated eight grams of cocaine and more than an ounce of high-grade marijuana. Jake and Matt were covered with blankets and transported to the hospital. Coop, Darren, and Bill were transported to jail. No one else was arrested.

Jake had six stitches put in the top of his head. An x-ray revealed three broken ribs. Matt was a bit worse. He had a major concussion, a bruised kidney, and required twenty-eight stitches to close off the bleeders in his head. He was held overnight, under guard, in a hospital room.

Late the next morning all five of them were brought before a magistrate and were formally charged with possession of cocaine for sale, possession of marijuana for sale, and being under the influence of cocaine and marijuana. In addition, Matt and Jake were both charged with resisting arrest and assaulting a police officer. None of the five made any statements, all invoking their right to an attorney. And attorneys were what they got. A veritable team of high-priced mouthpieces arrived to represent them.

The prosecution asked for the defendants to be held without bail, citing the seriousness of the drug trafficking charges and the high flight risk a traveling band entailed. *Intemperance*'s attorneys then had their say and, in the end, all five were released on ten thousand dollars bail and with special permission to leave the State of New York and continue their tour.

"This is outrageous!" proclaimed the prosecuting attorney when the ruling was handed down. "These men are sex criminals, drug traffickers, and complete menaces to society! Furthermore, your acquiescence to their request to leave the jurisdiction while out on bail is unprecedented. I must protest you allowing them to continue performing their concerts and receiving twenty to thirty thousand dollars a show while these heinous charges are pending against them."

Matt, wearing an orange jumpsuit, his face a kaleidoscope of bruises, stitches, and hematomas, his hands and legs in shackles, suddenly stood up. "Protest *this*, motherfucker!" he yelled, reaching his shackled hands down just far enough to grab his crotch and squeeze it.

The judge banged his gavel and angrily found Matt in contempt of court, but he also rejected the prosecutor's plea. "The ruling stands," he said. "This court is adjourned."

All five of them were bailed out of jail less than thirty minutes later. Though their performance was a bit more sedate than usual, they managed to go on stage, as scheduled, in Philadelphia that night.

Meanwhile, the team of lawyers went to work on their case. The first thing they looked at was the writ that had led to the warrant that had allowed the NYPD narcotics and sex crimes units to search the hotel room. It took them only two days to expose the entire thing as a collection of lies, innuendo, and speculation designed to do no more than get a judge to allow them to raid a hotel room without probable cause. A motion to dismiss all charges on the grounds of illegal search and seizure was filed with a superior court judge. The judge looked over the evidence presented to him and not only dismissed the charges, he charged two police investigators with perjury, requested an investigation by the New York state BAR of the judge who had signed the warrant, and ordered the New York City police commissioner himself to extend a public apology to the members of *Intemperance.*

Of course, the entire episode was reported on with glee by the national media. INTEMPERANCE MEMBERS ARRESTED ON DRUG CHARGES read the first headline. This was followed by KINGSLEY AND TISDALE WENT DOWN FIGHTING. Next came ROCK AND ROLL HEROES FACING TEN TO TWENTY FOR DRUG TRAFFICKING. And then, as things started to wind down, there was INTEMPERANCE OUT ON BAIL AFTER SEX ORGY. Finally, ALL CHARGES AGAINST INTEMPERANCE DROPPED ON A TECHNICALITY. Glittering descriptions of the orgy the police found upon entering the room were described over and over, as was the inventory of the drugs found in their possession. When the dismissals came there were cries of outrage from the law and order types about the liberal search and seizure restrictions in the United States constitution.

Greg, of course, loved every bit of the entire thing. "You can't pay for this kind of publicity! I swear to Heavenly Father, you boys don't even have to put music on those records for them to sell!" His attitude was undoubtedly a reflection of the rest of National Records' executives.

Two days after watching the NYPD commissioner's televised apology to the members of *Intemperance,* Jake was lying in his hotel bed in Boston. They had just enjoyed one of the rare extended travel days off and he was well rested and sober for the first time in two weeks. His phone began to ring. He picked it up, expecting it to be Greg, or Janice, or maybe Matt, but it wasn't. It was Mindy.

"How did you know where to get hold of me?" he asked her, surprised, and a bit trepidatious to hear her voice.

"I have a copy of your tour schedule, remember?" she asked. "I knew you just had a day off and were probably relaxing and I had some people I know find out where you were staying."

"I see," he said slowly.

"So, how are you doing?" she asked him. "It looks like you ran into a little trouble there in New York, huh?"

"That's a good way of putting it," he allowed.

"I heard you got banged up a bit by the cops. Are you okay?"

"I'm healing," he said. "Matt's worse than I am, but we still manage to get out there on stage every night."

"The show must go on," she said, uttering the sacred decree of performers.

"The show must go on," he agreed. "So how are you doing? Did you get that role you were after? That incestuous time-travel movie?"

"No, they turned me down for it. I did great at the audition but they decided to cast an unknown in the part. They said they didn't want to overshadow Michael J. Fox. It's understandable I suppose. I'm trying out for a part in another movie this weekend. This one looks a lot better."

"I'm glad to hear it," he told her.

"Listen," she said, "the reason I called is that I'm going to do an interview on *The Nightly Show.*"

"With Frank Wilson?" he asked, surprised.

"The one and only," she giggled. "I'm scheduled for next Friday. The subject of our relationship is going to be discussed."

"I see," he said slowly.

"Neither one of us has talked about our break-up or our relationship to the media. I just wanted to let you know what I was going to say before I said it. It's nothing bad or anything."

"Okay," he said. "And what are you going to say?"

"That we felt a strong infatuation for each other and fell into a hot, torrid love affair."

"It starts off good," Jake told her.

"And truthful," she said. "Anyway, I'm going to tell him that we just weren't compatible in the long run and that we both realized that. We couldn't spend enough time together, we were both too into our careers to make sacrifices for the other, and, since we knew you were going to be heading out on tour we thought it best to just be friends from that point on. Does that sound good?"

"It sounds more than good," he said. "It sounds perfect."

They talked for a few more minutes and said their good-byes. That Friday night, after the show in Montpellier, Jake left the party in Bill's suite after enjoying only a quick blowjob from a redheaded groupie and went back to his own suite alone. He tuned in *The Nightly Show* on the large screen television and watched as Frank went through his monologue and then introduced his first guest of the evening: Mindy Snow. She was wearing a sequined gown and looked absolutely stunning. He felt a tinge of black desire for her as he watched her take her seat. And, as usual, she hadn't told him everything about what her intentions were.

Frank asked her early in the discussion about what attracted her to Jake. "What makes a beautiful, innocent, successful young actress hook up with a scrungy, bad-boy rock star like Jake Kingsley?"

"Passion," she told him. "Jake is dangerous, and a horrible influence, and everything else that he's accused of. He drinks too much, he smokes too much, he does drugs and gets irrational at times, sometimes even belligerent, but he's an incredibly passionate, *alive* man all the same."

"Is he abusive?" Frank asked.

"Well... I wouldn't exactly use that word," she said, indicating with her face that she was withholding something. "I mean, he can be downright ugly at times, especially when he's been drinking, but he doesn't hit or anything like that."

"Well, that a relief," Frank said.

"It's the whole bad-boy image that attracts us girls to people like Jake," she said. "You know your mother wouldn't approve of him so it's kind of a rebellion of sorts. Eventually, however, you realize that maybe your mother was right after all."

The audience laughed. So did Frank.

"Truthfully though," Mindy went on, "I don't regret my little experiment with Jake. I'll always remember him with fondness even though he scared me sometimes, you know? I wish nothing but the best for him and I hope he gets the problems he has with drugs and alcohol under control before it's too late. I mean, we all saw what happened to him in New York, right? He has to realize that he's heading for nowhere good and in a hurry at that."

The rest of the interview only took ten minutes. The subject of Jake was dropped in favor of the subject of Mindy's up and coming auditions and her hope to soon appear in a major feature film.

The next morning the headlines in the entertainment sections read MINDY CITES JAKE'S DRUG ADDICTION AND ABUSIVENESS AS REASON FOR BREAK-UP.

Two weeks later Mindy was in the news once again. It was announced by newspapers and entertainment shows across the land that she had been given the lead in a new movie called *Handle With Caution*, which was about an abused wife trying to pull herself out of a violent relationship. Mindy was quoted as saying that she was perfect for this particular role since she had intimate experience with such a topic. A week after that it was announced that Mindy and John Carlisle, a twenty-eight year old actor who had been nominated for an Oscar the year before for his role as tough street cop, had been seen in each other's company on multiple occasions. By the end of the month both actors had confirmed to the press that they were romantically involved.

*****

On May 2, as *Intemperance* was halfway through the second leg of their tour, *The Thrill of Doing Business*, the album, went gold. At the same time *The Thrill of Doing Business*, the single, peaked at number eight on the top forty chart and began to work its way back down. *Crossing the Line* was the next single to be released for sale. It quickly began selling off the shelves as radio stations throughout the country began playing it six to ten times a day.

On May 4, the convoy rolled into Detroit and set up for three consecutive shows. The capacity of the arena here was almost twenty-two thousand and boasted some of the best acoustics in the country. In addition, Detroit fans were reputed to be among the most enthusiastic in the nation. For this reason, Detroit was often chosen as a favored place to record live shows for later release as live albums. Bob Seger had recorded his famous live album here, as had *Journey*, Peter Frampton, and even *Kiss* (although hopefully the reader will not hold that against the motor city). National Records, anticipating such a live album by their new hit band *Intemperance*, decided to follow suit and capture the live tracks from all three days. Extra sound equipment was brought in for high-quality recording. Video crews were hired and their equipment was strewn about the auditorium.

As the time approached for them to hit the stage for the first recorded show, the tension level among the five band members was considerably higher than normal. At fifteen minutes to stage time, while they were sitting in the dressing room, twirling guitar picks and drumsticks, drinking from Gatorade and smoking cigarettes, Darren suddenly upped the tension by pulling out a joint and lighting it up.

Everyone stared at this in complete disbelief as he took a huge hit of the greenbud they were supplied with for after-show festivities and held it in, a defiant look on his face. Matt was the first to react. He jumped up from his chair, dropping his guitar pick and his cigarette, took three steps across the room, and slapped the joint out of Darren's hand.

"What the *fuck* do you think you're doing, dickweed?" Matt demanded. "Cough that fuckin' hit out!"

Darren refused to cough it out, so Matt stepped behind him and did a Heimlich maneuver on him, which forced him to exhale, and quite forcefully at that. Pungent smoke was propelled across the room at more or less the speed of sound.

"Motherfucker!" Darren yelled, spinning around quickly. He pushed Matt roughly, shoving him back down into a seat. "Don't you ever put your fuckin' hands on me again!"

Matt was up in flash, his hand forming into a fist. He cocked back and drove a solid right towards Darren's face. Jake got there before it could hit. He caught it neatly in his right hand, the sound of the slap echoing throughout the room. He then pushed himself between his colleagues, preventing them from further violence.

"Sit the fuck down!" Jake shouted. "Both of you! Right now!"

It took a moment of angry looks cast back and forth, but both did as he commanded. Jake then turned to Darren, his eyes glaring at him.

"Okay," he said, trying to stay calm. "What the hell do you think you're doing?"

"I'm getting stoned," Darren said stubbornly. "What the fuck does it look like I'm doing?"

"You got a lot of fuckin' nerve sparking that shit up right in front of me!" Matt yelled from behind. "Where the fuck do you get off..."

He stopped as Jake held up his hand.

"Explain yourself, Darren," Jake said. "You know we have a rule about getting high in any capacity before we hit the stage. So why are you all of a sudden defying that rule by busting out a fucking joint fifteen minutes before we go on?"

"That's *your* fucking rule," Darren said. "Yours and Matt's. And I'm tired of living by it. I play better when I'm stoned, man. Don't you fuckin' know that?"

"Didn't you trip over your own goddamn guitar cord when you were stoned?" Matt spat.

"I wasn't stoned then," Darren said. "If I was, I never would've done that!"

Another shouting match developed over this subject, with Coop and Bill getting involved too. It went on for the better part of a minute before Jake yelled at everyone to shut the fuck up. Reluctantly, everyone did.

"Why you tripped over your cord is immaterial right now," Jake said. "Whether or not you play better while stoned is immaterial as well. The fact is, we have a rule about using drugs or alcohol before performing. This rule has been in effect ever since you joined this band, since before I joined the band as a matter of fact. We've had issues with you on this before. You are not allowed to smoke weed before we hit the stage. Period. End of discussion."

"No," Darren said. "That ain't the end of the fuckin' discussion. I want to get stoned before I go on and I'm going to get stoned before I go on. *That's* the end of the fuckin' discussion!" He started heading for the joint, which was lying on the floor about five feet away.

"Asshole!" Matt yelled. "I'll kick your stoned-out ass out of this fuckin' band if you pick up that joint."

Darren didn't hesitate for a second. He picked up the joint and faced Matt. "You ain't my boss anymore, Matt," he said. "You been pretending like you are all this time, but you ain't. You can't fire me. Greg told me that a couple days ago. As far as the record company is concerned, we're all equals here, we're all *their* fuckin' employees! And since my boss don't mind if I smoke out, I'm smoking out and you can't stop me!"

Greg—no doubt alerted by the security staff that trouble was brewing—appeared as if by magic, strolling through the door to the dressing room. "Is there a problem here?" he asked.

He wasn't answered verbally. He was answered by having Matt's hands grab him by the front of his shirt and lift him bodily off the ground. Before he even had a chance to let out a startled squeak, he was flying through the air with the greatest of ease and crashing into the tub of ice and Gatorade in the corner of the room. Matt walked over and picked him up again, slamming him into the nearest wall and driving the breath from his lungs. Matt's hand reared back to strike again and the only thing that prevented Greg from having his nasal bones smashed into his brain was Jake grabbing Matt's hand before it could strike. Even so, it was a close thing. Jake was lifted six inches off the ground before his sheer weight ended the forward motion.

"Let go of me, Jake," Matt said, trying to squirm free. "It's time I sent this coke-sniffing freak to see his Heavenly fucking Father!"

"Chill, Matt," Jake said soothingly, refusing to let go. "Chill. This isn't the answer."

"Who cares what the answer is?" Matt responded. "I just want to see his teeth sticking out of my knuckles!"

Jake, with the help of Coop, finally managed to wrestle Matt free and propel him back into his chair. Greg, still trying to get his breath back, glared at the guitar player, fire and brimstone in his eyes.

"Don't ever touch me again, Matt," he finally gasped when he was able to talk. "You may be able to get away with a lot out here on the road, but I'm a National Records executive and you will keep your filthy hands off of *me*!"

"Did you tell that asshole he could smoke weed before we went on?" Matt demanded. "Did you fuckin' tell him that?"

"Yes, he fuckin' told me that!" Darren said, still holding his joint in one hand, his lighter in the other. "Tell 'em, Greg. Tell 'em who's the fucking boss of this show."

"I am the boss of this show," Greg said. "And I don't see any problem with..."

"I'm the boss of this fucking band!" Matt yelled, standing up again. Jake and Coop were both forced to shove him back down.

"No," Greg said. "I'm sorry, but you're not. You are all National Records employees of equal stature. Steve Crow is your immediate superior and, while out on the road, I am your supervising agent, instilled with decision making authority and ultimate say-so on daily activities. Check your contract, Matt. I'm afraid that's the way it is."

"And so," Matt said, "using your decision making authority, you thought it would be a good idea to tell Darren to go ahead and smoke out before stepping onstage for a live video and audio recording? You told him this in spite of a long-standing band rule that specifically forbids this? What the fuck are you trying to do?"

"I'm not trying to do anything," Greg said. "I'm only here to make things flow smoothly. Darren told me that he performs better if he smokes a little marijuana first. I don't see any harm in doing that."

Matt actually became incoherent he was so mad. "You don't..." he stammered. "He doesn't... you won't..." He turned and cocked his fist back to hit the dressing room wall. Once again Jake jumped forward and grabbed it, preventing a broken hand this time instead of a broken bass player or a dead tour manager.

"Let me go!" Matt yelled. "I need to hit something!"

"I'm hitting something right now," Darren said defiantly. "Fuck all this shit." He put the joint in his mouth.

"Don't hit that fuckin' thing, Darren!" Matt yelled at him.

"Darren," Jake said. "Please. Don't start doing what these record company fucks want. It ain't good for us."

"Yeah, man," said Coop. "We need to stick together."

"You're moving in a starkly counterproductive direction, Darren," said Bill.

Darren looked at them all for a minute. For a second or two, it looked like he might put it down. And then Greg spoke up.

"Do what you want, Darren," he said. "If you need something to mellow you out before we go on, that's your business."

"I do what the fuck I want," Darren said. With that he sparked up his disposable lighter and took a tremendous hit.

They hit the stage a few minutes later, barely managing their pre-show display of camaraderie, all of them sullen and uncommunicative. But as they began to play, as they heard the impressive roar of the Detroit crowd screaming at them, they went to work and performed their best.

Darren played perfectly, as did everyone else.

CHAPTER 13

LINES OF PERSUASION

June 7, 1984
Austin, Texas

They moved about the stage, their motions pulsing, frantic, as they closed out *Almost Too Easy*. As the last beats were hit in a carefully timed crescendo, Jake, Matt, and Darren moved backwards, entering the safety perimeter that would keep them untouched by the coming explosion. By now they were well practiced in this maneuver and there had been no mishaps. The last beat was hit, the last strings strummed, and the two canisters detonated, sending a boom and a flash of light out. The audience of 11,224 cheered wildly.

"Thank you, Austin!" Jake shouted after stepping back to the microphone. Before him, the pyrotechnic canisters were still smoking. "Thank you and goodnight!"

He put his guitar down and stepped backwards, letting the applause wash over him, relishing it, basking in it. Darren and Matt appeared on either side of him, their arms on his shoulders. Bill and Coop formed up on the outside. They bowed one time to the crowd and walked off the stage, exiting through the stage left door.

This wasn't really the end of the show and the crowd knew it. There was still the encore. They screamed for it, stomped their feet for it, sending noise and vibration through the arena.

The roadies had placed cold quart bottles of Gatorade on a table just inside the stage door. All five band members picked one up and drank deeply, throats working frantically, green liquid running down their chins onto their chests. They took deep breaths after the first long drink and then drank some more. Jake forced himself to stop after consuming half the bottle. He didn't want his stomach to cramp when he went back out there for the last two songs.

The thundering of the crowd was too loud for conversation to take place, especially since the band's ears were still ringing from seventy-eight minutes in front of the amps and from the concussion of the explosion. But Bobby Lorenzo, Darren's personal assistant, had no problem understanding sign language. Darren mimed the act of lighting a lighter and Bobby brought him one, along with a marble pipe stuffed with greenbud. Darren put the pipe in his mouth and fired up, inhaling deeply and expertly. He then passed the pipe and lighter across to Coop, who took them and did the same.

In had been a month since Greg, using the authority vested in him by the *Intemperance* contract with National Records, had repealed the long-standing prohibition against getting high before performing. In that month, things had led exactly where Matt and Jake had always feared they would if this rule were relaxed. At first it was just Darren taking a few hits before the start of the night's show and then he began slipping out during his breaks in the performance—Matt's extended guitar solo, Coop's drum solo, and Jake and Bill's duet—and reinforcing his high with a few more hits. Then came the further hits during the encore break. Then, starting about six shows ago, Coop, unable to take it anymore, began to join him in the indulgence.

"Look, guys," Coop said when Matt and Jake called Coop on this after the first time. "I can handle it just like Darren does. It's just weed. It ain't like we're getting drunk before we go on."

But of course, once the precedent was set, neither Darren or Coop saw the need to stop drinking alcohol four hours prior to a show, or to keep from snorting a few lines of coke when the effects of drinking alcohol all day long had them a little weary. As a result of all this, tensions among the band members were high and there had been some screw-ups onstage. In San Antonio the week before, Darren tried to do a fancy twist maneuver and knocked over his own microphone stand. In the last show, in El Paso, Coop actually started playing the wrong song at one point in the set, forcing the rest of the band to quickly change gears and play out of the sequence they'd rehearsed. When confronted after the show following these mistakes by an angry Matt and Jake, both had simply claimed that it was road fatigue and over-repetition that had caused the mishaps, not the drugs and alcohol.

"That's fucking bullshit and you know it!" Matt thundered both times. "There's a goddamned reason why we had that rule, and *this* is fucking it!"

Unfortunately, whenever they tried to argue, or demand, or even plead for a return to the sobriety rule, Greg would step in and remind the two members of the rhythm section that they were free to do what they wanted before a show or even during it. "I'm your boss," he would tell them. "Matt and Jake are your peers. You don't have to give in to peer pressure. You can just say no to them."

"I don't think that is exactly what Nancy Reagan had in mind when she wrote that little catch phrase," Jake said sourly the fist time he heard this.

Darren and Coop were certainly saying no to no drugs on this night. Upon arriving in Austin at two that afternoon, they'd forgone the coffee in favor of three lines of coke. Throughout the day, as the band rode from place to place, signing autographs and greeting fans and talking to Austin disc jockeys at the local hard rock station, the two of them drank beers and took pipe hits and snorted line after line of cocaine. After the sound check, as the hour to hit the stage rolled closer and closer, they kept it up, draining bottles of beer and tossing them in the trash, hitting the pipe whenever their high started to dissipate, and begging another line from Greg whenever these first two indulgences started to make them feel tired. By the time they hit the stage both of them were keyed up and sweating, their eyes dilated and sluggish, their movements alternately clumsy and over-fast. They were, to put it mildly, fucked up beyond recognition, in the stratosphere, annihilated to the gills.

Coop screwed up his drumbeats three times during the set. Twice the rest of the band had been able to cover for it without the audience noticing, but the third time he played the drum roll build-up to the bridge of a song after the first verse instead of after the second, throwing the entire song out of whack and causing all of them to fumble around for the better part of ten seconds, their instruments jangling in opposition as Bill and Matt tried to blend and follow the mistake while Jake and Darren tried to transition them back on track. The audience emitted a shocked laugh and even a few boos before they were able to pull themselves back together and continue the song. The applause after that song was the most muted they had ever heard.

More embarrassing, however, was Darren. Though he hadn't made a mistake in his actual playing, he was still creating quite a spectacle of himself by trying out new dance moves to his routine. He was jumping up and down, kicking his feet out, making leering faces at the crowd, spinning back and forth, and generally doing everything he could to draw attention to himself. Jake supposed he thought he was being cool but in reality, he was looking like an intoxicated dork, the performing arts version of putting a lampshade on your head at a party.

As the cries for encore reached their peak, Jake and Matt shared a look of anger and helplessness, both knowing they had put in a substandard performance because of the two fuck-ups and both hating the fact that there was little they could do about it. Neither could know that the worst was yet to come.

Darren took a final hit from the pipe, actually burning the resin in the pipe-stem since the pot had all been smoked away. He handed it and the lighter back to Bobby, blew his hit out, and then took a last drink of his Gatorade. He smiled as he felt the latest surge of THC working its way through his brain, restoring the coveted high. Yes, he was ready to go knock off the last two songs now. And he was determined to show these Texas fans what he was all about. Jake and Matt thought they had some moves? They didn't have shit. He was the really important one in the band, him and his bass. After all, without the bass, the rest of them wouldn't have a rhythm to play to, would they? Why did those two prima donna assholes—three if you included that nerdy dickwad Bill—get all the credit for *Intemperance*'s success?

So intent was he on these thoughts that he didn't notice that the other four had already gone back through the stage left door and onto the stage. Not even the applause roaring back from the crowd clued him in. It took a slap on the back by Bobby and a shouted "Go!" into his ear to get him moving. He stepped through the door to find the rest of the band already in position, instruments in hand. There was another burst of laughter from the crowd at his late arrival and both Matt and Jake were glaring at him.

He didn't acknowledge them. He simply picked up his bass and put it in position. Just to show who was the real talent of the band he strummed out a quick, twelve note bass solo, something that was most definitely not part of the encore performance. He expected applause at this but what he got was a gasp of confusion from the crowd instead. Obviously, his talent was a little too sophisticated for these Texas assholes.

Coop hit the four count and they launched into the first encore song: *Rules of the Road*, from the new album. It was one of Jake's songs and one of Darren's least favorite to perform. Jake was fond of changes in tempo in his songs and this one was absolutely full of them. It started out fast, slowed down during the first verse, sped up to almost heavy-metal intensity during the chorus, and then slowed back down for the second verse and the bridge. Jake himself had to keep switching from acoustical sound during the slow parts back to distortion on the faster parts, said switch being accomplished by hitting one of the effects pedals arrayed around his mic stand. The rapid and constant changing in tempo meant that Darren couldn't perform a lot of the new badass moves he was trying to incorporate into his stagecraft.

When *Rules of the Road* ended, Darren perked up considerably. The final song was his absolute favorite that they did: *Who Needs Love?* It was a true rock masterpiece with a fast, heavy, and fairly consistent beat that he could truly pound out on his bass like rock music was meant to be pounded out. They launched into it with a roar of approval from the crowd. Darren's hands did their work automatically, his left hand pushing on the frets and moving up and down the neck, his left picking at the thick strings with perfect precision. He jumped up and down as he played, moving back and forth, making harsh faces that he thought were just the coolest fucking thing ever. Twice as the song progressed he was so intent on his jumping and moving and face making that he forgot to go back to his microphone and sing the backing to the chorus. *Oops*, he thought when this happened. *So fucking sue me then.* It wasn't like his voice was actually needed anyway with Matt, Coop, and Bill chiming in their parts. In fact, maybe he would talk to Greg about taking him off singing duty completely. Having to hit the microphone all the time detracted from his stagecraft.

As Matt launched into the main solo of the song and Jake backed off to give him the spotlight, Darren stayed at the front of the stage, deciding that more moves were in order. He jumped up and down a few more times and then bounced his way to the right to get next to Matt. His intention was to bump shoulders with the guitarist, one of those camaraderie type of moves that looked so cool, but instead he slammed into Matt with considerable force. Matt flew sideways from the impact, stumbling twice and nearly falling down. At the last second, he managed to keep his feet and, though he shot a murderous glare at Darren his fingers never missed a string and the solo went unbroken.

Oops, Darren thought again. *That probably didn't look good.* But then, if Matt wasn't so fucking clumsy on his feet he probably would've been braced a little better. Hopefully he'll learn from it. *Maybe if he smoked out a little and let himself chill like Coop and I, he'd do better up here.*

Darren worked his way back toward his microphone, bouncing all the way. Halfway there he crossed over Jake's guitar cord, caught it with his foot, and ripped it cleanly out of Jake's guitar, instantly silencing the backing riff just before the end of the solo and the beginning of dual riff portion of the song. He didn't even notice that he'd done it. When he heard Jake's guitar go quiet he turned and saw the singer frantically moving across the stage to pick up the end of the cord and plug it back in and concluded that Jake himself had been the one to cause the mishap.

And they give me *shit for stepping on my cord that one time*, Darren thought. *I'm never gonna let his ass hear the end of this one.*

Matt covered for Jake the best he could by extending the solo for another ten seconds, long enough for Jake to plug back in. He then repeated the ending, leading them back to the cue for the next section of the song. They hit the dual riff and then separated back into lead and backing. Jake sang out the third verse and the final chorus grouping and they worked their way into the final crescendo. This was what Darren had been waiting for.

Darren longed to perfect a move for the final moments of the last song. He wanted to do a double jump and then twist three hundred and sixty degrees in a circle on the third jump. The first time he'd tried it he had been too close to his microphone stand and had knocked it over. The second time his three-sixty had ended up being a one-eighty and he had been facing the wrong direction. This time, he was determined he would get it right. He had the rhythm, he was back far enough from his mic, and it just felt like something that was meant to be. He would pull this off just before the final climax of explosions and the crowd would go wild, would scream his name, and the next day, in the Austin papers, it would *his* name the concert reviewers would mention instead of Jake's or Matt's or Bill's.

The moment came. To his right, Matt and Jake pounded off the final notes. He jumped twice with the ending beat and then leapt high in the air for the third leap. As soon as his feet left the ground he spun violently to the left, imparting himself with enough force to make it all the way around before his feet came back down. The maneuver might have gone off as planned but he forgot one little thing. He forgot to make sure he cleared his own guitar cord. It wrapped neatly around his legs, effectively binding them together, and when he came back down he was unable to spread them to keep his balance. He pitched forward, feeling himself falling towards the stage. Instinctively he tried to counter this by giving one more hop forward and, in doing so, he jumped right into the midst of the danger zone surrounding the pyrotechnic charge situated in front of his microphone. The cord pulled tight as he reached the end of his slack and he pitched forward again, the neck of his bass knocking over his microphone stand, his body achieving a horizontal orientation. He found himself looking directly down into the pyrotechnic charge and, in sudden terror, he managed to turn his head to the left.

He heard the boom, louder than it had ever been before. A bright flash of light blinded him even through his closed eyelids and burning pain seared up the right side of his body. The air was blasted out of his lungs and he felt himself flying through the air, twisting around and around like a football thrown in an awkward spiral. And then he was crashing down on a sea of human bodies, hearing the faint sounds of screaming through his violently ringing ears.

*****

Holy fucking shit! Jake's mind screamed as he watched Darren go flying eight feet into the air, spiraling around and around, and landing somewhere in the darkness of the mosh pit in front of the stage. The cheers of the audience cut off in an instant, as if a mute button had been pushed. From the mosh pit itself, he could hear screaming over the ringing in his ears.

He spun the volume knob on his guitar to the zero position and dropped it to the ground, rushing forward, grabbing the main microphone as he went by. He looked down but could see nothing but a squirming mass of bodies in the darkness.

"Everyone," he said into the mic, "please back away from him. Give us some room. Stay back!"

Matt came rushing by on his right. He leapt off the stage and into the mosh pit and began pushing his way through.

"House lights!" Jake said into the mic. "Turn on the house lights, please. We need to see down there."

The lights clicked on, illuminating the chaos below. Jake dropped the microphone and jumped off the stage as well, finding himself surrounded by sweating bodies. He began pushing through. "Back away," he said. "Back away. Let me through."

He worked his way to Darren's position, elbowing and forcing his way through the gathered crowd, none of whom were heeding his pleas to back away. At last, he stood looking down at the bass player. He was on his back, eyes closed, smoke rising from his body, particularly his head where a good portion of his hair had been burned off. The right side of his face, his right arm, portions of his exposed right flank and stomach, and a good portion of his right leg were bright red in color, like sunburn only much worse. His bass guitar was lying next to him, the neck broken in half, the strings snapped and hanging free, the body charred and smoking. Matt was kneeling next to him, shaking him.

"Is he dead?" Jake yelled.

"If he's not, I'm gonna fuckin' kill him!" Matt yelled back. He gave an extra-hard shake. "Darren!"

Darren's eyes flew open, gazing around, unseeing. "My cock!" he yelled, panicked. "Did it blow off my fuckin' cock?"

*****

It did not blow off his fuckin' cock. The leather shorts he wore had protected that portion of his body. Nor did he suffer any broken bones from either the concussion or the spectacular flight through the air (although three members of the audience *were* injured when his two hundred and thirty pound, smoking bulk landed atop them). What he did suffer were second-degree burns all over his right leg, right arm, right chest and abdominal wall, and the right side of his face and neck. He also suffered a massively ruptured right eardrum, which left it doubtful that he would ever regain full hearing on that side. His hair was flat out gone, most of it burned off in the explosion, the rest shaved off in the Austin burn center later that night. For the next forty-eight hours he lay in a hospital bed, a morphine drip keeping the worst of the pain under control while blisters rose and fell on his burned skin.

They discharged him with a prescription for heavy-duty pain pills and strict instructions to change his dressings once a day and to maintain bedrest until the skin healed. They wanted him in for check-ups every three days for the next two weeks. But this was simply not to be.

"We had to cancel the first two shows in Dallas," Greg said as they climbed on the bus in the hospital parking lot, "but they're setting up for the third right now. We should make it there by three o'clock this afternoon. We won't have time for the usual interviews and autograph sessions, but we should be able to make the sound check on time."

"Wait a minute," Jake said as he heard this. "Are you saying we're not going home?"

"The show must go on," Greg replied. "It's bad enough we had to cancel two dates in one of our biggest cities. Do you have any idea how much revenue we lost?"

"Darren can't play like that," Matt said. "He looks like a fuckin' cartoon character who got shot with a cannon."

"And his eardrum is ruptured," Jake added. "Didn't they tell him to avoid loud noises until it healed up?"

"He could lose his hearing in that ear for good if he doesn't," said Coop.

"I really don't think I can play," Darren agreed. "These burns hurt real bad. All the fuckin' time, man."

"Nonsense," said Greg dismissively. "I'll make sure everything goes well. I'll get him an earplug for that ear and keep his injuries covered with moist bandages when he goes on stage."

"But my hair!" Darren cried. "I ain't got no fuckin' hair!"

"We'll get a hat for you," Greg said. "Trust me on this. I know what I'm doing."

"No," Matt said. "This is too much, Greg. The man is burned and has blisters all over his body. We ain't doing any more shows until he's healed."

"Then you will be responsible for all the lost revenue for any dates that are missed," Greg said. "All of it. That includes merchandising sales and all fees of inconvenience associated with refunded ticket sales. You think you're in the red now? Taking two or three weeks off from the tour will push you another half a million or so into the hole. Is that what you want?"

"What fuckin' difference does it make?" Matt yelled. "We're already a quarter mil in the hole. What's another half mil on top of it? Take us home until Darren recuperates. If you don't want to do that, put us up in a hotel here in Austin. You can tack that onto our account as well."

"Why don't we let Darren decide this?" Greg asked. "After all, it is his name you're speaking in." He turned to Darren and put his best smile on his face. "Darren? What do you think? If I can make you comfortable enough, do you think you can carry on?"

"Tell him no, Darren," Jake said. "This is bullshit!"

Darren looked miserable. "I want to," he said, "but I don't think I can. I'm really hurtin', you know?"

"I'll give you pain medicine before you go on," Greg promised.

"Oh, that's a fuckin' brilliant idea," Matt said. "Aren't the fucking drugs what got us into this situation in the first place?"

"What's that supposed to mean?" Darren demanded.

"It means you were trashed up there on the stage and that's why you tripped over your own cord and landed on top of an explosive charge!" yelled Matt. "If Mr. I Want To Suck Joseph Smith's Dick here hadn't of told you that you don't have to listen to me anymore none of this shit would've happened!"

"That's a fucking lie!" Darren yelled. "He just told me I could do what I want. Smoking weed had nothing to do with what happened!"

"I agree," said Greg. "I'm more inclined to think the accident was caused by a lack of choreography to your sets. If you would have let us train those dance moves into you before we went out on the road, Darren wouldn't have been trying to improvise moves on his own."

"Christ," Matt said. "Round and fucking round we go with this shit."

"If I do go on," Darren said, "I won't be able to do any of my moves at all. Will that be okay?"

"Do us a favor, Darren," Matt said. "Keep your moves to yourself in the future."

Darren looked hurt and then angry. "What's wrong with my moves? Are you just jealous because you can't do 'em? The audience loves them, man. They fuckin' love 'em!"

"Yeah," Matt said. "Especially those three people you landed on after one of your moves got you blown through the air like a fuckin' circus performer."

"It *was* a good demonstration of a ballistic arc," said Bill, in all seriousness.

"Look," said Greg, "I understand that you won't be able to do your moves for a while. The audience will understand that too. It was in all the papers about how you were burned by a mishap with the pyrotechnic charges. All you have to do is stand by your microphone and play your bass. Try to back up when Matt is doing a solo. The important thing is that you go on. You'll be applauded just for doing that. They'll understand why you can't move about with your normal enthusiasm."

"Okay," Darren said. "I'll try it."

It looked doubtful at first. During the sound check Darren had to sit in a chair and hold his new Brogan bass away from his body. The back of his right hand was burned and each stroke of the strings sent pain slamming up and down his arm. And even with the earplugs in place the concert level sound blasting out of the amps was making it feel like someone was sticking an ice pick in his right ear.

"I don't know about this, Greg," he said when the sound check was complete. "Even after the pills I took, this is fuckin' agony, man."

"Don't worry," Greg told him. "You'll be more comfortable for showtime."

And he was. His burned lag and arm were wrapped in moistened bandages imbedded with lidocaine jelly. He was dressed in a pair of loose fitting black sweatpants and a looser fitting white sweater. They put a lidocaine soaked bandana over his head, ear, and neck and then covered it with an *Intemperance* baseball cap from the merchandising stocks.

"How's it feel?" Greg asked him.

"Better," Darren said. "It still hurts when I move, but not as bad."

"Well, let's take care of that right now," Greg replied, opening up his little black bag. He pulled out a syringe and a vial of medicine.

"Dude," Darren said as he watched Greg draw the clear liquid into the syringe. "I don't really dig needles, you know."

"It's just a little needle," Greg said. "It'll be over in a second."

"What exactly are you giving him?" Matt asked.

"It's a standard pharmaceutical painkiller," Greg replied, taking out an alcohol swab. He pulled down the shoulder of Darren's sweater, baring his unburned left arm.

"The *name*, Greg," Matt insisted. "What's the shit called?"

"Demerol," Greg replied. "As I said, a standard painkiller used in hospitals all over the country."

"Ahh, Demerol," said Matt with a knowing nod. "One of the more potent narcotics commercially available." He looked directly at Darren. "It's like heroin, but lasts longer."

Darren looked from the needle to Matt's face to Greg's. "Like heroin?" he said. "I don't know about this shit, man. I don't wanna do no heroin."

"It's *not* like heroin," Greg insisted. "Demerol is a painkiller produced in the finest American pharmaceutical plants and used by doctors nationwide for the relief of pain. Heroin is an illegal street drug that you melt in a spoon and inject into your veins. They are quite different. Now hold still."

"But…" Darren started.

"Just relax," Greg soothed. "I know what I'm doing." He stabbed the needle into Darren's upper arm and depressed the plunger. Darren kept his eyes closed the entire time. Finally, he let them creak open.

"I don't feel any different," he said.

"I gave it to you intramuscularly instead of intravenously," Greg said. "It will take fifteen or twenty minutes to start working but it will last longer—probably for the entire show."

Darren looked doubtful but, as the minutes ticked closer and closer to showtime and the drug seeped into his venules and capillaries, gradually working its way through his bloodstream to receptors in his brain, the look of doubt was replaced with something like exaltation. "Wow," he said, smiling and nodding his head. "This is some cool-ass shit."

"Yeah?" asked Coop. "Better than weed?"

"Not better," Darren replied, "but different."

"Never mind how it feels," Matt said. "Will you be able to play like that?"

Darren stood up. He was a bit unsteady at first but as he got used to it he was able to walk back and forth with ease. He flexed his burned hand a few times. "It still hurts a little," he said, "but it doesn't bother me that bad, you dig?"

"That's exactly what it's supposed to do," Greg said with a smile. "I think you're going to do just fine out there."

Just fine was probably not the best description for what Darren did, but he did manage to make it through the show. He walked steadily out to his microphone, picked up his bass, and when the lights came up, when the first explosion of the night ripped across the stage, he didn't even flinch. The audience cheered loudly, louder than normal even. And he played. His hands moved like they were supposed to, hitting the right strings in the right order at the right time. He sang the back-up lyrics he was supposed to sing. He made no mistakes. But through the entire show, he hardly moved at all. He didn't sway his body to the beat he was helping to set. He didn't shuffle his feet, shrug his shoulders, or twist back and forth. He most certainly didn't jump or spin or make faces. When the time came for Matt's solos, he would back up a few steps, clearing the spotlight area. When the time came for the explosions, he backed up a little faster. In effect, he appeared to be nothing more than an animatronic bass player, or perhaps a holographic one, while the rest of the band moved and turned and swayed and played their usual enthusiastic performance. It wasn't pretty, but the show went on and when it was finally over the audience cheered as they usually did.

"Good job, Darren," Greg congratulated him when they left the stage after the final encore. "You did just great up there."

Darren simply nodded, his face drenched in acrid sweat. "That shot you gave me wore off," he said. "Can I get another one?"

He got another one. Greg shot him up and sent him back to the hotel in a limousine hired especially for the occasion. While the rest of the band engaged in their normal post-show groupie action, Darren crashed out in his bed and slept until eight the next morning.

*****

The next two weeks went by in a haze of consecutive dates. They worked their way out of Texas and into New Mexico, Arizona, and Colorado. Gradually, Darren's burns healed and he began to move around a little more on stage. The lidocaine soaked bandages went away but the earplug, the bandana, and the hat remained. So did the Demerol shots. Even though the blisters on his skin all popped and disappeared, he insisted upon getting his "pain shot", as he called it, before and after each performance.

"Why the fuck do you still need that shit?" Matt demanded of him as Greg drew up the proper dosage prior to the first of three Denver shows. "You're not burned anymore. You fuckin' hair is even growing back!"

"It's my *ear*," Darren insisted. "It hurts like hell whenever I hear something loud. I won't be able to make it through a show if something doesn't dampen the pain down."

"Christ," Matt said in disgust. "Your fucking ear my ass. You're getting addicted to that shit, Darren. Don't you realize what this asshole is doing to you? He's turning you into a fucking heroin addict."

"It's not heroin!" Darren yelled. "And I'm not addicted to it. It's only for the pain. The fuckin' show must go on, man. You know that!"

The shows went on. Soon, Darren's hair had grown back enough for him to lose the hat and the bandana. But he continued to complain about his ear and demand shots before and after each performance. In addition to the pain shots, he began to drink beer again and to smoke marijuana and snort cocaine before hitting the stage. Coop joined him in all of these endeavors with the exception of the pain shots. There were occasional mistakes on the stage as a result of all this, but they remained minor since both seemed to have learned to keep things at a certain level. Still, mistakes were mistakes and each one earned a furious screaming and yelling response by Matt and pleas from Jake to refrain from getting intoxicated before performing. The pleas and yells went unheard, however, since Greg was always there to let the drummer and the bassist know that he was their boss, not Matt or Jake.

*****

The Thrill of Doing Business tour came to an end on September 3, 1984 with the last of four sold-out shows in Los Angeles. *Intemperance* had played 126 shows in 96 American cities before a combined total of 1,308,297 paying ticket holders. Meanwhile, *The Thrill of Doing Business*, the album, went platinum and continued on past, heading rapidly towards double-platinum status, which would be easily achieved, if current sale rates continued, by Christmas. *Crossing the Line*, the second single released, shot rapidly up the charts into the top ten and then spent nearly a month clawing its way upward from there.

As the tour wrapped up, *CTL*—as it was referred to by the music professionals associated with it— was locked in a furious battle for number one with three other songs, all of them the pop-music staples of the Top Forty chart. *Ghostbusters* by Ray Parker Jr., *What's Love Got To Do With It* by Tina Turner, and, the stiffest of the competitors, a song called *I Love To Dance* by a group called *La Diferencia*, which was a pop-band from Venezuela that had released an American album on the Los Angeles based Aristocrat Records label.

As *Intemperance* spent their first week back in Los Angeles, moving into their new condos and recuperating from the long, torturous road trip just completed, *CTL* finally peaked at number two on the charts, aced out of the number one spot by *I Love To Dance*. It held there for another two weeks, trying and trying to dislodge the Venezuelan group's hit—during the second week the difference in single sales was less than five hundred—but ultimately, they were unable. *CTL* began to fall off and *I Want To Dance* held on, staying at the top spot for what would turn out to be another six weeks.

"What in the fuck is wrong with the music consumer these days?" ranted Matt on the day *CTL* began to fall. He, Bill, and Jake were sipping drinks on the balcony of Jake's new condo, out of earshot of Manny, who had been once again employed as Jake's manservant. "I mean really, I could understand if Tina Turner had aced us out of number one because Tina's at least a real musician with a rockin' voice and that song she's got going has got some fuckin' soul to it, you know what I mean?"

"I know what you mean," Jake said, and he in fact agreed with this assessment.

"But what's this *I Want To Dance* crap? So she wants to fuckin' dance? Who gives a flying fuck? I'm telling you, MTV did this shit to us. That and the public's fascination with goddamn third world countries."

"Actually," said Bill, "Venezuela has a standard of living quite close to that of the United States and Canada."

"What?" asked Matt.

"Oh yes," Bill said. "They have copious reserves of petroleum. They've been the largest supplier of foreign oil to the United States ever since the Arab oil embargo of 1973. They're also the only western hemisphere member of OPEC. All of this oil revenue amounts to a gross domestic product that is nearly as high as..."

"Nerdly," Matt said, taking a drag off his cigarette.

"What?"

"I don't give a fuck about their oil revenue."

Bill looked hurt. "I was just trying to tell you that Venezuela is not a third world country," he said.

Matt's face went through a few contortions as angry outbursts were formed and then headed off. Eventually, he nodded. "I apologize," he said. "Can we call them a second world country then?"

"That *would* be a more accurate portrayal," Bill agreed.

"Good," Matt said. "Anyway, that Venezuelan bitch with her hokey little accent and her fuckin' crucifix around her neck comes out of this *second* world country, sings about how she wants to dance, makes a video where her titties are bouncing all over the place under a tight shirt, and everyone eats it up. Nobody notices that the song itself bites ass."

"How do her titties look in the video?" asked Jake, who had not actually seen it, since he despised the whole concept of music videos, nor had he heard anything other than snatches of the actual song since it was not played on stations he typically listened to.

"They *are* nice titties," Matt admitted. "Kind of grapefruit sized with lots of good bounce to 'em. And the bitch herself is kind of exotic looking. Dark hair, light skin. The kind of skin you'd like to nut on."

"Light skin, huh?" Jake said, considering. "Is she actually a native of Venezuela or are they making all that shit up?"

"I'm sure they're sincere about her geographic origin," Bill said. "Light skin tone is not all that unusual among Venezuelans. As a nation, they retain a much higher percentage of Spanish blood in their citizenry than the more familiar Latin American nations like Mexico and Cuba."

"Then you'd nut on her too?" Jake asked him.

"Does all molecular motion stop at absolute zero?" Bill replied.

Jake looked at him for a second. "Does that mean yes?" he asked.

"Fuckin' A," Nerdly agreed.

"I thought so," Jake said.

"Okay," said Matt. "Now that we all agree we would nut on her, let's continue our shit-talking session about her and her crappy pop band and how the stupidity and complete lack of musical taste among the American public allowed them to keep us from our rightful place on top of the goddamn music chart."

"You already know the answer to that, Matt," Jake said. "It's a demographic thing. They sing pop music. Do you remember what 'pop' stands for? It means popular. The crap they produce is designed to reach out across the entire demographic spectrum. It's not harsh like rock and heavy metal, it doesn't twang like country."

"Country?" Matt said. "Don't even mention that word in my presence!"

"Forgive me," Jake said. "But anyway, pop bands specialize in catchy tunes that the musically unsophisticated—which, I'm sad to say, make up the majority of the American public—can bop and sing along to. They don't have to have strong lyrics or good guitarists or musical depth of any kind.

They just have to have a backbeat you can dance to and a catchy chorus that will stick in your head. If they can get that formula down, two-thirds of the goddamn country will buy their shit, and that crosses pretty much all of the demographics. They're just as likely to have a twelve-year-old boy buying their shit as they are to have a sixty-year-old woman. It's amazing that we've held our own against them with as many songs as we have. You ask me, it's a testament to our musical ability that we're even on the single charts at all, let alone vying for the number one spot."

"Are you saying that we're falling into the pop music category?" Matt asked, appalled at the very thought.

"No, not at all," Jake said. "I'm saying that our core audience are the late teen to mid-twenties crowd, the high school and college age demographic. Those are the ones who like hard rock music and we've dominated that demographic ever since they started playing *Descent* on the radio. However, our stuff is so musical, so enjoyable to listen to, that we've crossed demographics into the traditional pop music crowd. Most of these people buying *CTL* singles would never buy a *Van Halen* single, have never even heard a *Led Zepplin* or an *AC/DC* tune, and are only buying our songs because, through no fault of our own, our lyrical and back-beat formula are meeting the requirements they want in pop music."

"So you're saying," said Matt, "that *Crossing The Line* and *The Thrill of Doing Business* are being played by people because they like the beat and the chorus?"

"Most of them are probably not even listening to the verses," Jake said. "And if they are, they're not comprehending the meaning of them. Our core demographic catches our meaning and appreciates us both musically and lyrically, but then our core demographic are the people buying the entire album, not the singles."

And so far, that demographic was keeping *The Thrill of Doing Business*, the album, number one on the album charts for its ninth straight week, with no sign of dropping anytime soon. They had neatly dislodged the albums put out by both Tina Turner and Lionel Richie, both of whom had formerly held the number one spot.

"The singles don't mean shit in the great scheme of things," Jake said. "I mean, sure, they're making some money for National and they amount to prestige for the individual songs, but it's the album sales that are first and foremost here. By Christmas, we'll have sold two million copies of *Thrill* and almost three million copies of *Descent*. That's where hard rock pays for itself. Our fans—not the pop music faggots who are buying the singles—but the real fans, the guys and girls in jeans and leather, with long hair, the ones smoking pot and chewing shrooms, they buy albums, not singles. Our strength here is that our first album was full of good music. It didn't just have two or three songs that were good and the rest that were shit. People heard *Descent* the song, then they heard *Who Needs Love*. That's when the album sales started picking up in the cities we hadn't toured in. Now that we've established ourselves as a group that makes good music, our core fans snatched up copies of *Thrill*, the album, the moment it went on sale. *Thrill* is full of good music too. The core fans will develop favorites out of the tracks that aren't even played on the radio at all. That's what we need to focus on in the future. Keeping our core fans happy, not the pop fans."

"And the way to keep the core fans happy," Matt said, seeing where he was coming from, "is to keep making albums full of good music instead of albums with a couple of catchy tracks that will sell singles."

"Exactly," Jake said. "The worst mistake we could make is to start catering to the pop fans. If we start making music that's catchy instead of deep, if we start writing songs with the thought of what the video will look like when it's produced, or with the thought of how it will sound on the radio, we're going to fade into obscurity within two more albums. I don't want that."

"Fuck that," said Matt, horrified by the very thought.

"I agree," said Bill. "We need to be our own quality control. But how do we do that?"

"We need to keep doing what we did before Shaver and National Records came along," Jake said. "We need to write our songs and produce our music without interference, to do it from our hearts, just like we used to."

"Crow isn't going to like that," Matt said. "It'll take too long."

They knew this to be true. They had had a meeting with Crow just the day before and he had already started pushing them to get into the recording studio for their next album as soon as possible.

"If we can get you in there by the first of December," he told them, "we could realistically expect to release the next album by the first of April."

"The first of December?" Jake asked incredulously. "Are you serious?"

"Is that a problem?" Crow responded. "I'm already working on reserving the studio time."

"There's the small matter of us not having any fucking material to record," Matt said. "Since you won't let us record *It's In The Book* and since the other four tunes we got in the hopper aren't album quality, I'd say that's a pretty big problem."

"We haven't worked on anything new since we signed with you," Jake said. "It takes some time to come up with ten tunes."

"More like fifteen since you assholes reject at least a third of what we come up with," Matt said.

"Well," Crow said thoughtfully, "there's always those numbers our songwriting teams came up with as filler for the last album. There are eight of them, including *Embrace of Darkness*, which is a really good tune. We haven't farmed those songs out to anyone yet so all of them are available to you. That means you would only have to come up with two songs of your own."

"Ahhh," said Matt, "I was wondering when we would get back to this."

"Look, guys," Crow said, "I know you don't like the tunes. We gave into you last time—very much against our better judgment I assure you—but this time we're going to have to stand firm on this. We need ten songs from you by December 1. If you can't come up with them on your own..."

"We're not doing your songs," Jake interrupted. "Period. End of story. That's the final word. I thought we established that the last time we butted heads with you people. We would rather have you sue us for breach of contract, ruin our entire careers, and garnishee every wage we ever earn for the rest of our lives than record a song that someone other than me or Matt has written and composed."

"It ain't gonna happen," Matt agreed. "Let's just cut the bullshit and not rehash this stupid argument again, you down with it?"

Crow sighed, managing to look like his feelings had been hurt. "Okay," he said. "Just thought I'd throw that out there. But the fact remains we need to get you into the studio early in December. That means you need to submit at least twelve songs for our approval by mid-November. That's a little over a month away."

"It's also a little bit impossible," Matt said. "There ain't no way in hell we're gonna be able to come up with twelve tunes by then. We'd be lucky to get three or four going."

"That's all the more reason to consider utilizing some of our pre-written material," Crow said.

Matt got mad. He stood up and slammed his hands down on Crow's desk, hard enough to echo through the room and make Crow back up in fear. "Listen up, fuckdick!" Matt yelled at him. "You don't seem to be absorbing the point here about this pre-written shit your hackers whipped up for us. It will *never* be recorded by *Intemperance*! Never! I swear before all that I hold holy and sacred, I swear on my fucking Strat! We will never do it. Never! Do you catch my fucking drift now?"

"Okay, okay," Crow said, his hands trembling a bit. "No need to yell. I think you've made your point quite nicely."

Matt sat back down. He pulled out a cigarette and sparked up. Crow did the same, his hand still shaking.

"Now that we've settled that," Jake said. "We're left with the problem of not enough time to come up with new material. As Matt said, you're asking the impossible here. You need to extend the deadline."

"Now *you* are asking the impossible," Crow replied. "We can't allow any lag time between the decline of *Thrill* and the launch of the next album."

"Why not?" Jake asked.

"Well... because you just can't!" Crow said. "Everyone knows that. If you don't keep your name constantly at the top of the charts you fade into obscurity in no time. We need to have that next album out by mid-April at the latest."

They went round and round on this issue for the next twenty minutes but eventually Crow—after having a private conversation with Doolittle like a car salesman consulting with his sales manager— grudgingly gave some ground.

"All right," he said. "We don't usually do this, but Mr. Doolittle has agreed to give you a little more time to come up with new material."

"How much more time?" Jake asked.

"An extra month," Crow said. "We'll put off the start of the recording session until the first week in January. That means we'll expect twelve new tunes out of you by mid-December. Do you think you can meet that deadline?"

"That's still a little bit tight," Jake said.

"We're working with you all we can here, Jake," Crow said. "Really we are. But that's the absolute best we can do. Now all of the songs don't have to be masterpieces. Just give us two or three quality pieces for radio play and video production and the rest can be filler. Remember, your image is selling for you now."

Matt opened his mouth to say something, something that undoubtedly would have been profanity-laden and angry, but Jake put his hand on his shoulder, restraining him.

"We'll see what we can do," Jake said.

The meeting came to an end a few minutes later.

"Fuckin' filler," Matt said now, as they sipped from fresh drinks Manny had delivered to them. "I hate the very sound of that word. I do not produce filler. I will not play guitar for a song that is merely filler."

"I agree," Jake said. "I've done a lot of shit in the name of advancing my career. I've put on tight leather pants to play in front of an audience. I've lip-synched to my own music in front of cameras to make crappy music videos. I've given up my Les Paul for a Brogan. But none of that has actually affected the music itself. Pumping out filler tunes or playing crap that other people have written crosses a line that I'm not willing to cross."

"It would be an unacceptable compromise," Bill said. "Absolutely and completely deplorable."

"Let's make a pact," Jake suggested.

"A pact?" asked Matt.

"Yeah," Jake said. "We're the core members of this group, correct? You and I write the tunes and concoct the basic melodies. Nerdly, you're the one who knows the best way to polish those melodies into perfection. We are *Intemperance*. We are the ones who control the music we put out, agree?"

"Agree," said Bill.

"Damn right," said Matt. "Those two fuckin' druggies in the rhythm section are replaceable assets. I would've replaced Darren's ass a long time ago if they'd let me."

"I understand," Jake said. "And since we're the core of the group and since we control the music, we need to make this pact among the three of us. We need to vow that we will hold to our musical ideals in the production of new music. No filler tunes allowed. We will not allow our music to be compromised by the constraints of time or record company interference. Remember the standard we used before using new material at D Street West?"

They both nodded. The standard back then was that if the three core members were not drooling to play a tune before the audience for the first time, it would not be played. Any doubts about the quality of a new song by either Bill, Matt, or Jake, would be enough to get it banned. It was a rule that was unwritten and undiscussed, but a rule that carried the same weight as the Ten Commandments did for the bible thumpers.

"If we wouldn't play a song in front of D Street West," Jake said, "it doesn't go on an *Intemperance* album. That's the pact. Any one of us have unquestioned veto power over a tune. It has to be unanimous approval or we shitcan it. And no pressure by Crow or Doolittle or any of those other fuckheads will change our mind. Agreed?"

"Agreed," said Matt.

"Agreed," said Bill.

They sealed the pact the way the sealed any agreement between them. They drank on it and then smoked a joint in celebration.

*****

That night, after eating the dinner Manny had prepared for him—something with an unpronounceable French name that was made out of chicken breast and rich white wine gravy—Jake walked into the office of his new place. There, beside the computer desk and the filing cabinet was a black case that had been moved from his apartment in Heritage to his apartment in Hollywood to a storage house during his first tour to his first condo after it to another storage house during the second tour and now here, to his office in his second condo. The case hadn't been opened in more than two years.

He picked it up and sat on the couch across from the computer desk. He set the case down next to him and opened it. Inside was his old acoustic guitar—a Fender Grand Concert he'd purchased in a Heritage music store way back in 1977. Of course, the Brogan guitar company, his official sponsor, had given him several high-quality acoustic guitars as well as five electrics, but he had never even opened the boxes they'd come in. This guitar was the one he'd always used to compose with, the one he'd always strummed for the sheer pleasure of strumming, for the thrill of making music, for translating the rhythm and melody in his head into the air around him. He looked at it now. It was covered in a layer of dust despite the case. He strummed his thumb over the strings. The sound was muted and out of tune. He felt horrible as he looked at its condition, as he listened to its imperfection. It was almost like he'd abandoned a child.

Gently he lifted it from the case and set it on the couch. He spent the next thirty minutes polishing it, cleaning it inside and out and restringing it with a set of strings that had been stuffed into the box. He then took out his tuning fork and spent another fifteen minutes tuning it to perfection. He strummed it again, listening in satisfaction as the rich, perfect sound poured out.

"You sound good, old friend," he said with a smile, unaware that he was speaking aloud. "I promise to never leave you in the case that long again."

He sat back on the couch and put the guitar in his lap, his left hand going to the neck, his right twirling a guitar pick. The room was silent, the only sound the muted roar of a vacuum cleaner from somewhere else in the condo as Manny did his housework. He strummed a few times and then grabbed a G chord—his favorite for improvisation—and picked out a brief rhythm. He winced as he heard it.

"That really sucked," he muttered.

He sat back, staring at the blank computer monitor on the desk across the room. Had he lost the ability to compose music? Had he been out of practice at it so long that he no longer had the knack? How had he begun before, back in the days before National Records, before Shaver and his Bolivian flake cocaine, before national fame and groupies in every city?

"A concept," he said. "I began with a concept."

He let his mind flow over everything he'd been through in the past two years, over everything that had been going on in the world, just and unjust, good and bad. Images and emotions flashed by as if projected by a kaleidoscope, images of Angie and their brief relationship, emotions of leaving her to go on tour and never speaking to her again, never contacting her again. He thought of the giddy elation of leaving Heritage to go to Los Angeles and record their first album, of the thought that they'd actually been signed to a record label, that they were really going to be rock and roll stars. He thought of the gradual realization that was brutally slammed home when the lifestyle of the rock star turned out to be far from what he'd expected. He thought of long bus rides and the boredom that went with them. He thought of the road fatigue that settled in after a few weeks on tour, when you could no longer remember where you were or what day it was. He thought of the absolute thrill of performing on stage in front of thousands, sometimes *tens* of thousands of people, of hearing their cheers and adoration. He thought of the groupies he encountered out there, of the difficulty in resisting the primal urges the sight of their young bodies and willing sexuality invoked. He thought of horrid fatigue ridden hangovers after the post-show partying, hangovers that could only be driven back by the hair of the dog, by a few more drinks, by a few lines, a few hits. He thought of Mindy and the raw sexual infatuation she still invoked in him to this day, of the sweltering, drug-like allure of being with her, of touching her, of knowing that she wanted him to touch her, that she craved him as he craved her, of the glorious knowledge that he was fucking a woman that most of America would *kill* to fuck. And then his mind turned away from his own life and onto other things. He thought of marines in Beirut, blown to pieces by a suicide bomber. He thought of the marines who had survived this bombing being pulled out of Lebanon in response. He thought of other marines in another part of the world, landing in helicopters on the island of Grenada. He thought of a Korean Airlines 747 being blown out of the sky by Russian jet fighters, how the terrified passengers must have endured five or six minutes of still-living, horribly conscious terror before the spinning aircraft mercifully crashed into the sea. He thought of protestors lining up in front of nuclear power plants and nuclear weapons production facilities. He thought of the constant threat of sudden, extinction level nuclear war that hung over the world like a pall.

"Too much," he said, shaking his head, closing his eyes in frustration. "There's too much in there."

He lit a cigarette and smoked it slowly, keeping the guitar on his lap but keeping his hands off of it. Yes, there were too many concepts to consider, too many ideas for him to focus on a single one. Maybe he should just give this up for the night and try again tomorrow. It was obvious that the conditions were not right for composition.

But he didn't get up. Instead, he let his mind go a little bit further, releasing the brakes and restrictions on it, letting it drop into a mode it hadn't been in for two years now. And soon, as it always had back in the day, it picked a concept out of the maelstrom of thoughts and began to focus on it.

It was a pleasant thought, one of the most pleasurable, perhaps *the* most pleasurable, he'd experienced over the past two years, something he experienced every night out on the road. It was the moment when they first stepped onto the stage at each performance, when the lights came on, when the crowd saw them for the first time and they began to play. To Jake, the applause, the screams, the appreciative yells and whistles that took place at this instant of the show were the best, the most gratifying. They were the yells and screams and applause of people that had been waiting for days, weeks even for this moment. And every night, when he heard this, it didn't matter how tired he was, how hungover or pissed off or burned-out, it always brought him to life. It was like... like... like he'd found himself again, his purpose, his reason for being.

"Found myself," he muttered, setting his half-smoked cigarette in the ashtray. "Yeah."

He picked up the guitar and grabbed the G chord again. He began to pick at the strings, throwing out a simple melody as it formed in his head.

"Found myself," he said, half-singing those words this time.

But it wasn't just that he'd found himself at the moment, was it? No, not at all. It happened every night, every performance anyway. And no matter how many times it did happen, the sensation remained strong, the feeling of finding one's purpose.

"Again," he said. "Found myself again. I've found myself *again*."

He repeated this phrase, fully singing it now, emphasizing the last word, and strumming out the developing rhythm as he did so. "I've found myself *again*."

He liked that thought, could see the potential it held. His mind focused more intently on it and while it did so, his fingers continued to strum the melody over and over, twisting it a little, throwing in some chord changes, firming it up. And, as always, the music focused his mind even tighter, letting him recall everything about that moment, letting him put into words exactly what that moment felt like.

"The lights come on..." he sang, slowing the melody a bit. "The lights come on, I hear that roar... and I've found myself again." A furious bit of guitar strumming and then, "I've found myself *again*!"

He stopped, taking a few breaths, the words he'd just composed running over and over in his head along with the melody.

"Yeah," he whispered, smiling, grinning from ear to ear in fact. "*Fuck* yeah!"

He set the guitar down and walked over to the desk, pulling open one of the drawers. He took out a pen and a notepad and scratched out the lyrics he had come up with so far. True, it was only thirteen words, but more would soon join it, of that he had every confidence. He knew, of course, that his efforts might be in vain, that the song, the concept he was now working on might end up sucking ass when all was said and done, might end up a balled-up piece of paper in the wastebasket, but that didn't matter. He was composing. He hadn't lost it after all.

He went back to the couch, setting the notepad and pen down next to him and picking up the guitar. The melody and the words were still dominating the forefront of his brain. He began to play again, singing out the words he had so far.

"The lights come on, I hear that roar, and I've found myself again. I've found myself again!"

It was twelve-thirty when he finally went to bed. For the past three hours he had sat there on the couch, strumming and singing, thinking and composing, changing and changing back. During that time, he didn't smoke, he didn't get up to go to the bathroom, he didn't drink or eat. The notebook, which he locked in the safe next to his marijuana and cocaine, now had the first three pages covered with lyrics and musical notes. The first verse, the chorus, and the beginning of the bridge were already composed.

*****

While Jake was finding himself again, sixteen blocks away, on the twenty-eighth floor of another upper-class high-rise condo building, Matt was doing the same. He did things a little differently than Jake. In the first place, he was incapable of composing new material while sober. To prepare for this first attempt in two years he smoked six hits of potent greenbud from the old plastic bong he used to use when he was a teenager.

"All right," he said, grinning on his living room couch as he felt the massive surge of THC obliterating his higher brain functions. "Now let's write some fuckin' music!"

The instrument he used to compose with was different from Jake's as well. Jake's tunes were all acoustic guitar based and any one of them could be translated back to its base form if so desired. Even the hardest rocking of Jake's songs, like *Descent Into Nothing* or *Living By The Law*, could be sung around a campfire by a single guitarist or even played out on a piano. Matt's songs, on the other hand, were all based on power chords on a distorted electric guitar and virtually none of them could be translated into an unaccompanied acoustic format, at least not without changing the basic melody.

What this all meant was that while Jake was sitting in relative quiet with his old acoustic on his lap, Matt had taken down his beloved Stratocaster and plugged it into a thirty-five watt amplifier and connected a series of effects pedals. He spent almost thirty minutes playing with the distortion levels and the effects and then turned the volume on the amp itself up to eight. He began to play, warming up with a series of riffs and solos that were loud enough to cause the pictures on his wall to vibrate on their hooks.

His new manservant, Emil (his last manservant had refused to serve him again) came rushing out of his bedroom within seconds of Matt's initial solo. He had to scream "Mr. Tisdale!" six times before his voice finally made it to Matt's ears.

"What the fuck you want?" demanded Matt after silencing the guitar. "Can't you see I'm composing?"

"Begging your pardon, sir," Emil said, "but the noise! The neighbors will complain."

"Fuck the neighbors," Matt said. "And don't ever refer to my music as *noise* again, you dig?"

"Uh... yeah, I dig," he said. "But, sir, the... uh... music you're making is sure to..."

"I'll stop when the cops show up," Matt said. "That's a rule that's always worked for me in the past. Now tell me what you think of this riff. Too heavy? Or not heavy enough?"

And with that, he ground out a crunching, multifaceted riff that reverberated throughout the floor above and below his.

Emil didn't answer. He simply fled back to his bedroom, worried for his immigration status when the cops finally did arrive.

Matt chuckled under his breath and continued playing. He played with different riffs, trying to come up with something new, something original, something that sounded like nothing he or anyone else had ever done before. After about twenty minutes he hit upon such a thing. It was a complex five-chord riff that blasted out of the amp like lightning from a storm cloud. He tweaked it a little here and there, refining and modifying, increasing the power in some parts and decreasing in other, playing with the distortion levels until he had something that made him smile with accomplishment.

"Yeah," he said, his ears ringing from the amp, his head nodding in satisfaction. "Now *that* is what I'm fuckin' talkin' about!"

He began to play again, doing it over and over, getting it down, imprinting it in his brain for all time. Once the base riff was there, he began to modify it again, to make it even more complex. Through it all, in his mind, he envisioned what the riff would sound like backed by Jake's guitar, by Nerdly's piano, and with the drum and bass beat keeping time. Once that was done, he knew he had another hit on his hands, something that a crowd would scream for. Now it was time to come up with some lyrics to go with it.

What to write about? he wondered as he put the guitar down and took another three hits of greenbud. *What to write about?* His mind automatically turned towards the three things he loved to write about more than anything: sex, gross intoxication, and violence. Like Jake, he cast his mind backwards over the last two years, trying to focus on a concept that fit into one of these categories. And, also like Jake, he eventually locked onto an aspect that had to do with life on the road.

The groupies. For him, this was one of the most enjoyable aspects of being on the road. He loved playing before a crowd, loved the applause—initial and final—and loved the adoration that swept over him at such moments, but he also loved the gratuitous sex that he was provided at the end of each show by the young, slutty, and gloriously attractive groupies the security team picked and chose and admitted to the backstage area. He loved everything about them, their namelessness, their youth, their willingness to do anything and everything, up to and including dyking out with each other or even pissing on each other for his pleasure.

"They serve me," he said, ripping out his new riff again. "They fuckin' *serve* me!"

He played the riff a few more times, variations of this phrase running through his head, searching for a lyrical rhythm that went with the music. At last he came up with one.

"You're here to service me," he sang as the riff ground out. "You're here to service me. You're here to ser-vice me! You're here to ser-vice me!"

He could hardly hear his own voice over the sound of the guitar, but that didn't matter. He heard it in his mind and he liked it. He envisioned that phrase as a repetitive lyric, sung primarily by the back-up singers—himself, Bill, Coop, and Darren. Jake would sing other lyrics in between the repetitions. Other lyrics... other lyrics... like...

"I want you down on your knees," Matt sang, imagining Jake's voice and then imagining his own again, mixed with the others. "You're here to ser-vice me." He nodded in satisfaction and then stopped long enough to write that down on a piece of paper. He then began working on more Jake lyrics to go between the service me lines.

"Bring your girl-friend please," he sang. "Just don't bring no disease. Yeah, you're here to ser-vice me! You're here to ser-vice me! No talking, no names, please! You're here to ser-vice me! I like to come clean you see! You're here to ser-vice me!"

He played and sang, pausing every few minutes to write down the particular lyrics he thought were keepers (he rejected the ones about "no cottage cheese" and "watch those teeth if you please"). By the time the LAPD finally pushed their way into the condo, assisted by the building manager (who had pounded on the door, unheard for more than twenty minutes) and his passkey, he had all of the chorus sequences written and had started on the main lyrics.

*****

The entire band got together two days later for their first official jam session in more than two years. They met in their rehearsal warehouse where all of their touring equipment had been set up and attached to the soundboard and their basic recording set. Jake plugged his old Les Paul into the amps while Matt plugged in one of the Brogan brand Stratocaster knock-offs he'd been provided. Bill's piano was the electric one instead of the grand, the idea being simplicity in sound reproduction instead of showmanship.

Darren was ten minutes late and looking a little haggard. Most of his hair had grown back, although it wasn't as long as it had been before, and he had only minimal scarring from his encounter with the explosives. He still wore the earplug in his right ear, however, because loud noise allegedly still bothered him, as did a rampant, chronic case of tinnitus (ringing in the ear) from his damaged eardrum. He was also quite obviously stoned and under the influence of narcotic painkillers. Neither Jake nor Matt commented on it and didn't really care anyway. This was a jam session, after all, not a rehearsal, and during jam sessions, marijuana intoxication was not only allowed, it was mandatory.

They smoked out, passing Matt's old plastic bong around their little circle just like in the old days. When they were sufficiently stoned they climbed up on their makeshift stage and began to play around with their instruments.

"Check this out, guys," Matt said when he finally got his guitar adjusted to the sound he wanted. "This is what I've been working on for the past two days. It's called *Service Me*."

"Cool name," said Darren, sitting in a chair, his bass in his lap.

"Sounds like a fuckin' commercial for Tune-up Masters," said Coop.

"But it's not," said Matt. "Now check it out. Here's the riff I came up with for it."

He began to play the riff over and over, grinding it out of the amps and letting all of them absorb it. They liked what they heard—which wasn't the case with all of the riffs he came up with—and began to nod their heads in time to it. After ten or fifteen repetitions, he stopped and asked opinions.

"That's got a good flow to it," said Jake. "It's loud and authoritative, but it isn't harsh at all."

"Indeed," agreed Bill. "I like the step-up progression between four and five."

"Sounds good to me," said Darren. "Let's try it with some back-beat. It'll sound good with heavy."

"You always fuckin' say that," Coop told him. "Let's try it with moderate back-beat first and then we can step it up or down from there."

"Okay," said Matt. "Sounds like it might be a keeper. Let's do some mixing."

He launched into the riff again, doing it repetitively. After the third repeat, Darren began hitting his bass strings, adapting to the timing of the riff and then enhancing it. Then Coop began to hit the drums, playing offset from Darren's bass strokes. They played around a little, experimenting with different formats and powers, with different combinations of drum strikes and bass string progressions but finally were able to lock in something that just *sounded* right.

"That's it," Matt said, nodding enthusiastically. "That's fuckin' it! Now let's get Jake and Nerdly in on it. What do you think, Jake? Too heavy for strong acoustic backing?"

"Yeah," Jake agreed. "You need me to go distortion for this one. The acoustic strokes wouldn't do anything but get lost behind the bass and the drums, and there does seem to be something needed between two and three and between five and one."

"How about a three-chord mock-up of the main riff?" suggested Bill.

"Hmm," Jake said, considering. He walked over to his effects pedals and stomped on one of them. He hit an open chord and listened to the distortion that emitted. With a nod, he put his palm against the strings, silencing them. "How about something like this?" he said, and then began to play. The riff that came out was a much simpler version of what Matt had been doing. He played around with it a little, upping the tempo and decreasing the overall power.

"What do you think?" he asked.

"I think it'll work," Matt said. "Let's try it out."

Matt began to play the riff again. Darren and Coop chimed right back in with the rhythm they'd worked out. Jake let them go through a few repetitions and then he began to play as well, inserting his backing riff just beneath it all. It sounded good but not great. Jake changed his riff around a little, playing it stronger at the onset, a little weaker at the offset, and this seemed to do the trick.

"Fuck yeah," Matt said into his microphone. "This has got some balls. I like it."

"Get in on this thing, Nerdly," Jake said into his mic. "Let's put some frosting on it."

No one bothered suggesting to Bill just how he should incorporate his piano into the mix. Jake and Matt were both adept at the piano and Darren was passable on it, but none of them could even come close to matching Bill's mastery of both the instrument and its best use in a hard-rock song. Bill could always find a way to plug in, to give his playing soul, and he did so now, picking at a few keys for a moment but finally going full out and mixing the ivories just beneath the sound of the main riff and just above the sound of the backing riff.

"Fuck yeah, Nerdly," Matt said. "That's the shit right there."

"The fuckin' frosting, man," Jake said, smiling, enthralled by the music they were making. "You got the knack for that."

They played some more, solidifying the sound until all of them could do it without thinking. Then it was time to introduce the lyrics.

"Okay," Matt said into the mic while they continued to play. "Here's what I got for words. When you pick up on the main chorus lines, everyone sing them together. In between lines go to the lead. Got it?"

They all got it. Matt took on the lead vocal for the time being. "This is the chorus," he said, waiting for the riff to come around to the beginning again. When it did, he sang: "You're here to ser-vice me. You're here to ser-vice me!"

After five repetitions of this, Jake, Darren, Coop, and Bill all began to sing it in unison. When they had it dialed in, Matt began to sing out the in between lyrics for the first chorus.

"I hear you wanna meet me."

"You're here to ser-vice me," sang the back-ups.

"So come on back, babe, and see."

"You're here to ser-vice me."

"Just drop right down on those knees..."

"You're here to ser-vice me."

"...And show how you earned your SG."

They had to stop for a few moments as Jake and Coop both started laughing out loud at the last lyric Matt had sung. The SG he was referring to were the large blue letters on the Special Guest backstage passes that the groupies were typically issued. And everyone, of course, knew how they earned those passes.

"Oh my god, Matt," Jake said. "Those are some classic Matt Tisdale lyrics you got going there."

"It only gets better," Matt promised. "From the top?"

"From the top," Jake agreed.

They began to play again.

They went solid for the next two hours, first perfecting the chorus of the song—there were five in all, and all had different in between lyrics—and then starting in on the verses. After the entire song was introduced to everyone, Jake took over the job of lead vocals and Matt went back to singing back up. Jake read the lyrics off a piece of notepaper taped to the bottom of his microphone but by the end of the second hour he hardly had to refer to it at all.

The song was far from together when they finally decided to take a break. On the contrary, they had only the basic riffs and melody and the basic lyrical formula down. They would still have to work on the bridge, the intro, the changeovers, and the merges. But all of that would have to come later. They were burned out on *Service Me* for the day and it was time to work on something else.

They smoked some more bonghits, reinforcing their jamming demeanor and then Jake introduced them to the new song he had been working on. As had been the case with the initial composition itself, the introduction was also different. Jake put his guitar back into acoustic mode and played out the song for them exactly as he had been practicing it on his guitar at home. By this point he had a complete set of lyrics to go along with the basic melody and a strong bridge section as well. He still had to refer to his notes to keep from stumbling on the verses, but the guitar work itself had been committed to memory. It was a rough draft, of that there was no doubt, but the consensus was unanimous. They liked it.

"Classic Jake Kingsley lyrics touching on a new subject," said Matt.

"It's deep, man," agreed Coop. "I'm down with it intensely, you know?"

Jake was pleased at their praise. His opinion of the song was the same, of course, but one always needed the approval of others before one could surely know he wasn't deluding himself.

"Do the melody for me again," said Matt. "Let's get it into rock mode."

Jake did it again, naming off the chord changes and progression as he did them. Matt played around with the distortion levels on his guitar for a few minutes, adjusting the sound and adding another effects pedal.

"Okay, let's see how this comes out," Matt said. He began to play, translating the melody into distorted electric. It sounded like crap at first but, with suggestions from them all, they upped the tempo a bit and eventually dialed in something that everyone liked. A riff was born.

"I'm thinking strong acoustic for the backing," suggested Bill when this process was complete.

"Definitely," said Matt. "The only fuckin' way to go. Play the original acoustic base but up-tempo to match the distortion."

Jake hit another pedal and switched to a sound that was still acoustic in nature but on the edge of achieving electric distortion. It was the same sound he used to back several other *Intemperance* songs, like *Point of Futility* and *Crossing The Line*. He began to play the original score faster and harder and the sound was good. After a moment, Matt joined in, playing the new riff, which was a different version of what Jake was now doing, on top of it. All of them liked the combo at once.

"Bad ass," said Matt. "Now let's throw in the rhythm section and then Nerdly can plug himself in on top of it."

They worked on this song for the next three hours, changing and modifying, suggesting and rejecting, but eventually coming up with the bare bones of a tune they knew they would be proud to play before a D Street West audience or to put on an album. As they went through all of this, as they sang and played, as they complimented, derided, and occasionally argued, all of them forgot about everything else that was going on in their lives. In their minds, they were back in Matt's garage in Heritage, getting ready to put together another performance for their small group of fans.

*****

This amnesia to their current lifestyles did not last, however. They called it a day just before four o'clock in the afternoon, their plans to meet again at nine the next morning for some more jamming. Jake and Bill once again lived in the same building, so they climbed in Jake's Corvette and headed home. Matt climbed into a limo so he could go home, take a shower, snort a few lines of coke, and then go out for a night of drinking and carousing at the nightclubs. Darren and Coop, who had also been assigned to the same building together like before, climbed in their own limo.

"I don't know about this, dude," Coop was saying as they crawled through the congested downtown streets. "I mean... I wanna try it and all, but I don't wanna play around with no monkey, you know what I fuckin' mean?"

"There ain't no fuckin' monkey involved," Darren scoffed. "I'm telling you, if you do it the way I do it, it's harmless. It ain't nothing more than smoking some weed."

They arrived home just before five o'clock. Both went to their separate condos and enjoyed meals provided by their respective manservants. At six o'clock Darren called Coop on the phone.

"You comin' up, or what?" he asked. "It don't make no fuckin' difference to me."

"Yeah," Coop said. "I'll come up."

He went up. There he found Darren sitting on the couch before MTV, the manservant dismissed for the night. On the table before him was a polished, stainless steel kit known on the streets as an "outfit". It had been removed from a felt lined case and all of its pieces glistened with sterility and the air of medicinal necessity, but it was really no different than the paraphernalia of a homeless street bum with the same habit. It was a kit that was used for preparing and injecting heroin.

"I'll do myself up first, so you can see how it works," Darren said when Coop took a seat.

Darren now had a week's worth of experience with the process. When they'd come home from the tour Greg had disappeared from his life and so had the Demerol he'd been injecting the bass player with to "keep the pain under control". Darren had asked Crow to keep him supplied with the drug in order to get through the day, but Crow had refused.

"You're healed up now, Darren," he'd explained. "You don't need it anymore."

This led to a begging, pleading, and threatening session in which Darren had pulled out all the stops. "My ear still hurts!" he whined. "All the fuckin' time, man. Don't you understand that?"

"The Vicodin and codeine tablets in your safe should take care of those problems at this point," Crow responded. "Demerol is expensive and hard to get hold of. There's only so much we can provide you with. It's time you weaned yourself off of it."

For a week he'd suffered. The pills helped keep the withdrawal symptoms mild, but they were still there. He had constant body aches and rampant diarrhea. His appetite was next to nothing, as was his fluid intake. He vomited up everything that he did manage to put in his stomach. Not even marijuana—his previous best friend—seemed to help the aching and the depression.

And then Cedric, his faithful manservant, introduced him to the magical white powder that would soon consume his life. He didn't call it heroin, he called it "China White", implying that it was an ancient natural substitute for narcotic painkillers.

"Isn't China White a kind of heroin?" Darren asked him, uncomfortable with the thought of injecting an addictive drug into his veins.

"Well... I suppose that *technically* it is," Cedric replied. "It comes from the opium poppy, like heroin does, like morphine itself does, but it's as different from that black, sticky tar heroin the street bums use as a fine cabernet is from Mad Dog 20/20."

"I see," Darren said wisely. After all, Jake was always going on and on about those fine wines he liked to drink, almost as much as Matt went on and on about that fucking deep sea fishing shit, so he knew that cabernet was considered high class shit. Premium hooch. Something that only people with taste and class consumed. It was about as different from Mad Dog—which Darren had been known to swill down on occasion—as night and day.

"All right," he said at that point, thrilled that he would be enjoying a drug of the elite. "I'll try it."

What he didn't realize, however, was that whatever the class distinction between cabernet and Mad Dog 20/20, both were still wine, the active ingredient still alcohol, the effect of drinking either identical. Such was the case with tar heroin and China White.

"You don't have to put it in my veins, do you?" Darren asked Cedric as he watched him dump a small amount of the white powder, finer in consistency than the most carefully chopped Bolivian flake cocaine, into a stainless steel reservoir and light a butane lighter.

"Of course not," Cedric scoffed. "That's what the addicts do. You'll get this the same way you got the Demerol—intramuscularly."

And with that he'd injected Darren in the upper arm. Twenty minutes later, the cramps and nausea were gone, as were the shakes and the diarrhea and the longing and the fear.

Coop watched now as Darren expertly went through the steps of preparing the China White for injection. He measured out a small portion of it—very small, no larger than a pea—and put it in the oval spoon-like device. The cooker, as it was called, sat atop a stand, allowing the bottom of it to rest about four inches above the tabletop. Darren applied the butane lighter to the bottom of it and sparked up, holding the flame steady. The white powder slowly liquefied and began to boil. When it was at the perfect consistency, he dropped the lighter and picked up the syringe, drawing ever last drop of the bounty up into the body.

"It sure the fuck looks like heroin to me," said Coop, who had stared at the entire operation with a mixture of horror and fascination.

"It's *not* heroin," Darren insisted. "Heroin is for scumbags. And you can't get addicted to it when you take it like this." With that he rolled up the sleeve of his shirt and plunged the needle into his upper arm. He sighed, smiling even though he knew the drug wouldn't take effect for another twenty minutes or so. It was on its way and that was what was important.

"You sure about this, man?" Coop asked.

"Dude, I've been doing this for a week and I'm not addicted or nothin'. It's just like gettin' stoned, only better an' shit."

Coop allowed himself to be convinced. He watched Darren prepare another hit, his eyes taking in everything. When Darren used the same syringe to draw up the hit Coop had another moment of doubt.

"Dude, you just used that fuckin' needle on yourself," he said. "I shouldn't be usin' the same needle, should I?"

"Dude," Darren said, "we fuck the same bitches all the time. I ain't got AIDS or none of that shit and neither do you. It ain't no different than drinking out of the same beer."

"Oh... I guess," Coop said, still looking for a way to get out of this.

But Darren didn't give him a chance. He reached over and rolled up Coop's sleeve. Before the drummer even realized what was happening, the needle was buried in his bicep and the plunger was depressed.

"I don't feel no different," Coop said.

"Wait for it," Darren told him. "It takes a little bit. In about twenty minutes or so you'll be feeling fine."

And of course, he was right. The drug kicked in and Coop enjoyed it immensely. The two of them spent the next four hours sitting on the couch, side by side, smoking cigarettes and watching Bugs Bunny and Roadrunner cartoons on Darren's VCR.

CHAPTER 14

THE CORE

November 19, 1984
Los Angeles, California

Jake's Corvette moved slowly down Hollywood Boulevard, caught in the thick Monday afternoon traffic. Jake was behind the wheel, feeling the usual frustration that came with driving a high-performance vehicle he could rarely get out of second gear. Bill sat next to him, his thick glasses perched firmly upon his face, his hand playing with his crewcut, trying to determine if it was time to get another haircut or not. They had just finished a jam session, or rather, they had been forcibly pulled out of a jam session early by a National Records gopher who had shown up at their warehouse to give them a message. They were now on their way to the National Records building in Hollywood. Several blocks behind them were the two limousines carrying the rest of the band. The summons had asked for all of them, citing a "status meeting" as the reason.

"That asshole Crow keeps pressuring us to work harder, work longer, work faster," Jake complained as they sat through another red light for the second time. "He yells at us for wanting to take Thursday and Friday off so we can go home for Thanksgiving. And now, what does he do? He orders us to wrap up *early* today so he can tell us in an official meeting that we're not working fast enough."

"He does have a marked tendency to be counter-productive to our efforts," agreed Bill.

"We could have dialed in that new tune if we'd hit it just a little longer. We were getting there, you know what I mean? Now we'll have to spend an hour plugging back into it tomorrow." He sighed. "Oh well. What the fuck can you do?"

"Yep," said Bill with a nod. "Sometimes we're helpless before the actions of osmotic migration."

Jake interpreted that in his mind for a few seconds and finally decided—mostly through long experience of translating Bill's statements for others—that this meant 'what the fuck can you do?' as well. "Damn right, Bill," he said. "Well put."

The light turned green and they surged forward again, just clearing the intersection before the light turned back to yellow. Almost immediately, however, they were trapped in another section of gridlock waiting for the next light to turn.

"Coop and Darren are getting worse," Bill said.

"Yeah," Jake agreed. "They are. I don't think either one of them said a damn thing during the whole session today. They just did what they were told and played like they were told. It's making it harder to dial these tunes in."

Over the past few weeks, as the band tried frantically to come up with more tunes and to perfect them before the mid-December deadline for submission, Coop and Darren had become gradually but persistently less involved in the process. They would show up late, moving slowly, their actions lethargic and mechanical, their words few and far between. They had all but stopped contributing suggestions towards how the music should be played and mixed and, when asked to come up with a beat or a rhythm to back a particular beat, they would inevitably choose the simplest, least complex beat or rhythm possible.

"I never realized how much we relied on those two fuckheads to help set the backbeat for us until they stopped doing it," complained Matt during one of the multiple discussions the core members of the band had had on the subject. "It's hard enough coming up with the riffs and the mixes. Now we have to move their fucking fingers and hands for them as well to set the rhythm."

Both had been confronted on what the problem was, and both had denied that there was a problem.

"We're doing everything we've always done," Darren would respond.

"Yeah," Coop would agree. "I don't see no problem. We're getting these tunes done, ain't we?"

They were, but the quality was starting to suffer, as was the speed of progression. There was also an insidious decline in the feeling of teamwork and camaraderie that had always marked their jam sessions in the past. It was starting to feel like a battle was being set up—a battle between the core and the rhythm.

"I think they're using heavy narcotics," Bill said now as the light turned green and they crept forward another fifty yards before it turned red again.

"Narcotics?" Jake asked, looking over at him. "Why do you say that?"

"Mostly the way they're acting," Bill replied. "We've all seen each other stoned and coked-out and drunk a multitude of times so I think we'd all know if any one or two or three of those things were the problem. Instead, they're acting quite atypically for the normal intoxicants we use. But remember when Darren was getting shot up with the Demerol before the shows?"

"How could I forget?"

"That's the way both of them are acting now," Bill said. "They move slowly, and they don't talk much. They're almost falling asleep sometimes while the rest of us are arguing over something. When you do talk to them, it's like they're not completely cognizant of the words you're speaking to them."

"Hmm," Jake said, thinking about what Bill was saying and, now that it was pointed out to him, finding he was right. They *were* acting a lot like that.

"And then there's the physical symptoms of narcotic intoxication," Bill said.

"The physical symptoms?"

He nodded. "Their pupils are always pinpoint sized now," he said. "It's not dark in the warehouse by any means, but it's not bright either. Their pupils should be fairly normal sized, like yours and Matt's—about three millimeters, right?"

"You know what the normal pupil size is in millimeters?" Jake asked.

"Of course. Doesn't everyone?"

Jake let this go. "Go on," he said.

"Well... my point is, that your pupils and Matt's pupils, and, presumably, mine as well, tend to hover around three millimeters in the lighting conditions prevalent in the warehouse. Darren and Coop's pupils, however, tend to stay around a millimeter and a half no matter what the lighting is like. That's pretty small. It's also a side-effect of narcotic use."

Jake had never actually noticed this before, but now that it was mentioned to him, he did recall both Coop and Darren complaining at various times that the lights were too dim in the warehouse, that they were having a hard time seeing things because of this. Following his own train of logic, he concluded that having your pupils be half the size that they were supposed to be would serve to make it seem dim when it really wasn't. It would be kind of like walking out of the bright sunshine into a normally lit room, only this wouldn't go away.

"There are a few other things too," Bill said.

"Such as?"

"I've noticed both of them have burns on their fingers and burn holes in their clothes. That's from cigarettes that they've forgotten about because they were too zonked-out to remember or that they've dropped the embers from. They don't notice it right away because of the pain-killing effects of the narcotic and the sedation of the drug effect and they end up with burns. I bet if you lifted their shirts up you'd see a dozen cigarette burns on their stomachs and chest."

"Hmm," Jake said. Again, now that it was mentioned, he had noticed several nasty looking burns on both of their hands, including nearly identical blistering burns between the index and middle fingers of their right hands—right where a cigarette would normally be held.

"And then there's their shirts," Bill said. "Have you noticed they're both always wearing long-sleeved shirts now?"

"Yeah," Jake said. "I guess I have."

"They wear them even though it gets a bit warm in the warehouse. They don't want us to see their arms."

"So, when you're talking heavy narcotics here," Jake said, "you're not talking about just pills, are you?"

Bill shook his head. "Heroin," he said. "It's the only thing that makes sense."

"Jesus fucking Christ," Jake said. "And you can bet who is supplying them with it."

"And who is ultimately paying for it," Bill added.

The National Records building was now in sight, rising above the concrete of Hollywood Boulevard ahead. They made it through the next light and then settled in to wait for the next.

"A couple of heroin addicts in the band," Jake said. "That's just beautiful."

"I just thought you should know what I suspect is taking place," Bill said apologetically.

"Yeah, I know," Jake replied. "And there's not a goddamn thing we can do about it either."

*****

By the time the five of them assembled in Crow's office for the meeting, Darren and Coop were a little livelier than they had been at the jam session. Though they were still quite a bit on the lethargic side, they were at least talking now, and in sentences of more than six syllables even. Their liveliness kicked up a few notches when Crow, as was his custom preliminary to any meeting, offered them a few lines of cocaine. Matt, Jake, and Bill all respectfully declined, as was their custom during official meetings of any kind with any record company representative, but Coop and Darren both snorted right up.

"Good fuckin' shit, Steve," Darren complimented as the drug began to take effect.

"Fuck yeah," agreed Coop. "You got anything to drink in this place?"

Coop and Darren were served twelve-year-old scotch over ice cubes with coke. Matt, Jake, and Bill all accepted alcohol-free drinks, not even bothering to cast discouraging looks at their companions. Things had gone way beyond that now.

"First of all," said Crow once the preliminaries were complete, "let me congratulate you all on the continuing success of *Thrill*, the album. As of ten o'clock this morning, total sales were just one hundred and fifty thousand shy of two million. My guess is that you'll go double-platinum late next week or early the week after."

"No shit?" said Matt.

"No shit," confirmed Crow.

"Wow," Matt said. "And you told us our songs sucked ass, didn't you? I bet we'd be at quadruple platinum by now if we would just listened to you and used those hacker songs."

Crow cast a mildly contemptuous look at Matt but didn't bother to answer him. "And as for *Crossing The Line*," he continued. "It's still hanging in at number thirty-two on the Top Forty and is still in the top ten most requested on rock radio stations nationwide. There's even some talk of it being nominated for Record of the Year at the Grammy Awards."

"We'd never win it," Jake opined. "Tina Turner has it in the bag."

"Nevertheless," Crow said, "it would be a great honor just to be nominated, wouldn't it? The publicity angle alone would be almost priceless."

"Isn't *Crossing The Line* one of those songs you initially rejected?" Matt asked. "You know? One of the ones we fought and struggled and issued ultimatums to get included?"

"I seem to recall something like that," said Jake. "I'm not sure though. My memory gets fuzzy at times."

"Yes," confirmed Bill. "It was definitely among the forbidden artistic efforts we initially presented for consideration."

Crow sighed, shaking his head and feeling the ulcer in his stomach start to flair, as it always did when he had to deal with this troublesome but hugely profitable group of musicians. "All right, guys," he said. "You've made your point and hammered it home quite nicely. We were wrong about those tunes. Are you happy?"

"Rapturous," said Matt. "Now, what else is up?"

"Well, as you know," Crow said, "*Rules Of The Road* has been moving up the charts as well. This week it cracked the top ten at the number nine position."

"*Rules Of The Road*?" asked Matt. "No shit? Hey, Jake, isn't that another one of those songs that they initially rejected? I mean, there were so many of them I can't keep track. Refresh my memory for me."

"Yes," said Jake. "I believe they said it was too complex of a song, that there were too many changes in tempo for the average consumer to appreciate it."

"There *is* a lot of fucking tempo changes in it," Darren muttered.

Jake and Matt gave him a dirty look this time but otherwise ignored him. Crow did as well.

"Can we let the past drop?" Crow asked them.

"Who's bringing it up?" Jake asked innocently.

"In any case," Crow said, letting a little of his irritation slip through, "*Rules* is finding itself locked into the same stiff competition as *Thrill*. Namely, a tune by *La Diferencia* just happens to be moving up the chart at the same time."

This was a sour spot with Matt. "That fuckin' Venezuelan bitch again. Her and her crappy ass happy tunes."

"Uh... please don't say something like that in front of a member of the press, Matt," Crow warned. "But yes, *La Diferencia* seems to be acing you out of positioning yet again. Their new tune is called *Young Love* and the pop demographic are buying it up like mad. It's only been played on the radio for the past three weeks and already it's in the top ten—at number eight, I might add. That's one of the fastest selling singles of all time."

"And it's a stupid fucking song," Matt said. "Holy shit, have you heard this thing?" He sang, viciously mimicking the accent of the female lead singer. "Young love, burns like a fast flame. Hot and strong, but dies without tending."

Jake hadn't heard the song, but he had to agree that the lyrics—if Matt had sung them accurately—were pretty simplistic. But then, pop music was simplistic, wasn't it? He had, however, finally listened to *La Diferencia*'s first hit, *I Love To Dance*, which had aced *CTL* out of the number one spot back in September. As much as he hated to admit it (and he *hadn't* admitted it, at least not to anyone other than himself) he had actually found himself liking the tune a little bit. Not just not hating it, but *liking* it, singing along with it after a few repetitions, and even appreciating some of the musical qualities of it. The most striking thing about the tune was the vocals put down by Celia Valdez, the lead singer. Her voice was beautiful. There was no other way to describe it. It was rich and pure, sweet sounding, with considerable range for a pop singer. She had a strong Hispanic accent that was noticeable in her vocals but not to the point of distraction. It came through just enough to remind you that she was not American or English. And though the rest of the song consisted of a bland, formulistic backbeat, passable piano, weak lead guitar, and the inevitable synthesizers, there was a strong acoustic guitar backing that spoke of someone with some talent strumming the strings.

"What do we know about this band?" Jake asked. "Where'd they come from? How'd they get here? Are they really Venezuelans or is Aristocrat making all that shit up?"

"No," said Crow, "*La Diferencia* is really from Venezuela from what I understand. They come from some small town in the middle of nowhere and got noticed by the Venezuelan music industry. They put out an album of traditional Latin tunes early last year and it sold well enough in Venezuela that some record exec from Aristocrat decided to meet with them. They did up some tunes in English with more Americanized musical backing and the rest is pretty much history. They're a hit."

"They're a flash in the pan," Matt opined. "Just like most of the rest of the crap you record people put out."

Crow didn't even bother denying this. Flashes in the pan, after all, translated to lots of money for the music industry, so they were not really considered a bad thing.

"What about the band itself?" Jake asked. "How many people are in it? Who plays what?"

"Why are you so interested in these suck-ass pop assholes?" Matt asked.

Jake shrugged. "Know thy enemy," he said.

"Well," said Crow, "it should be quite obvious that the talent of the band is Celia Valdez. Without her, the rest of them would still be herding cattle or processing cocaine or whatever it is they do in that place. She sings and plays acoustic guitar. Her brother—I don't know his name—is the lead guitarist."

"Lead guitar my ass," Matt said. "He can't even play a simple three chord riff. It's a bunch of repetitive two-chord shit that just backs up the piano and the synthesizers. He doesn't do any solos, intros, or even mixes. The acoustic is the real lead in those tunes and the electric is the backing."

"He's her brother?" Jake asked.

"Oh yes," said Crow. "And the piano player is her sister. It's kind of a family band, you see."

"They keep that sister on the piano in the background in the videos," Matt said. "Her face ain't bad—though not as good as the lead singer bitch—but they never show her body at all. I bet she's a fuckin' whale."

"And she's certainly no great talent on the piano either," put in Bill. "She sounds like a first-year student reading from a piano book."

"It's just like the lead guitar," Matt agreed. "Simple, repetitive melodies over and over."

"Are the rest of the band members relatives?" asked Jake.

"The guy playing the drums is a second cousin from what I understand," Crow said. "The bass player is a family friend and the gossip columns have been hinting that he and Celia are romantically involved."

"You gotta respect *him* if he's tappin' into that shit," said Matt.

"Hell yeah," said Coop. "I'd buy him a drink for that."

"The synthesizer player is the only one who was not an original member of the group. They got him from some band in Caracas when Aristocrat signed them. They originally had two acoustic guitar players and a bongo player to go with the drummer. They kicked them out and replaced them with the synthesizer guy in order to convert to American style tunes."

"Then their material was fed to them by Aristocrat?" Jake asked.

Crow didn't like that particular terminology very much, but he nodded. "Most of it," he agreed. "I think they have two of their own songs on the album and the rest are composed by American songwriters who work for Aristocrat."

"Including the two hits they've had so far?"

"Exactly," said Crow, smiling. "Do you see now why we encourage you to utilize our songwriters for some of your material? Look what they're doing for *La Diferencia*."

"Let's not even start down this fucking road again," Matt said. "If Jake is done gathering his intelligence on the beaner band, maybe we can talk about the reason you dragged us out of a fairly productive rehearsal session?"

"I'm done," said Jake.

"Okay then," said Crow. "Let's get to the meat of the matter. How are we coming along with new compositions? Do you have at least ten songs composed yet?"

"Hardly," Matt said. "As of this afternoon, we have three tunes we're pretty happy with, although we're still tweaking them a little here and there, and three more we're in the beginning stages of."

Crow's face turned to instant unhappiness. "Just three?" he asked. "And only three more you're working with?"

"I believe I spoke plain English there, didn't I?" Matt returned.

Crow shook his head. "Gentlemen," he said, "I'm afraid that's not acceptable. You need to work faster. Your deadline is only three weeks away."

"We're doing the best we can, Steve," Jake said. "We told you back when we started this thing that you were pushing us a little too fast."

"But you also agreed you'd meet the deadline," he said. "At this rate you'll have, what? Maybe six songs complete? That's simply not good enough."

"We can only work so fast," said Matt. "We're not machines."

"I've already reserved studio time for you," Crow said. "You're scheduled to enter the studio for full-time recording duties on January 3. And even with that late date and working six ten-hour days a week it will be a chore to be able to finish the album by mid-April."

"We *could* be jamming right now," said Matt, "but instead, we're in here listening to you tell us we're not doing it fast enough."

"I hardly think three hours off from your schedule is the cause of this delay," Crow said. "You have to work longer and faster. You simply have to. I'm afraid I'm going to have to insist you work through the Thanksgiving holiday period. I know you all have plans, but the show must go on. We need those tunes by mid-December so we can start working on an order of recording and an album theme."

"Fuck that," said Matt. "We've been going eight hours a day without a break for the last three weeks. And that doesn't include the time Jake and I spend at night coming up with the new tunes in the first place. I haven't even scored any puss in a week and Jake here hasn't been laid in God knows how long."

"Three and a half weeks," Jake said sourly. "I've had to resort to porno mags."

"Me too," said Bill. "Did you see this month's *Hustler*? That punk-rock model on the cover is a premium self-stimulation visual."

"Oh fuck yeah," said Coop. "I got that one. She's hot."

"Did you see that other bitch in there?" asked Darren. "The one who can tie her pussy lips in a knot?"

"She tied her pussy lips in a knot?" Jake said, amazed. He hadn't got that far into the magazine yet.

"That's some seriously over-used pussy if she can do that," said Matt.

"Gentlemen!" Crow yelled, exasperated. "Could we keep on topic here?"

"Forgive us," said Matt. "But I'm sure you can see by our conversation that we're all seriously in need of a break. We need one and we're going to take one."

"I forbid it," Crow said.

"Yeah?" said Jake. "And I forbid the proliferation of nuclear warheads, but guess what? They still keep proliferating anyway. Sorry, Steve. Bill and I have our plane tickets already paid for—out of our allowance I might add—and we're going. Our families are getting together for the holiday at my parent's house, and we're going to be there."

"And I've got myself booked on a private two-day deep-sea fishing charter out of Marina Del Ray," Matt said. "I've also got a premium piece of puss scheduled to go with me. So, you can suck my hairy ass if you think I'm gonna hang out in a warehouse."

"Yeah," said Darren, emboldened by his peers' defiance. "Coop and I got shit to do too."

Crow looked up at the ceiling for a moment and took a few breaths. Finally, he looked down at his musicians. "All right," he said. "I guess I can't stop you from taking your little vacation. But we still need those tunes. The three you have ready. Are they decent tunes?"

"They're more than decent," Jake said. "They're bad ass."

"That's the only fuckin' thing we put out," Matt said.

"Good enough," Crow said. "How about you focus on perfecting those tunes prior to leaving on your holiday. When you get back, work out the other three as quick as you can. They don't have to be perfect, they just have to be palatable."

"Palatable?" Matt asked, hating that very word.

"The three main tunes can be the releases, if they're as good as you claim. The other three can be the filler. For the other four..."

"Don't even *think* about suggesting your hacker tunes again," Matt warned.

Crow held up his hand in a gesture of peace. "I understand your position on that and I respect it. What I was about to suggest was that you do some cover tunes to fill in the rest of the album."

"Cover tunes?" Jake asked.

"That's right," Crow said. "You can even pick them out yourselves. We don't care what they are. Pick three or four tunes from the old days and re-work them into something new. Do some country and turn it into rock and roll. Do some polka and turn that into rock. We don't care. Just let us know what they are as soon as you decide on them and we'll start working on the legalities of letting you perform them. There are a few songs you are not allowed to do—*Stairway to Heaven*, *Hotel California*, and stuff like that—but pretty much anything else can be arranged. Is that acceptable?"

"No," Jake and Matt said in unison.

Crow let his head fall onto his desk. Slowly he lifted it back up. "Why not?" he asked wearily.

"We don't do cover tunes," Matt said simply. "That's not what we're about."

"Everyone does cover tunes when they're short on material!" Crow screamed. "Fucking everyone! Look at *Van Halen*! They had cover tunes on their very first album! *Diver Down* was full of them! Look at *Motley Crue*! They did a cover of *Helter Skelter* on *Shout At The Devil*! Even *AC/DC* and *Led Zepplin* did covers! There's not a goddamn thing in the world wrong with it!"

Jake and Matt were both shaking their heads.

"Sorry, Steve," Jake said. "We don't do covers."

"Nothing but original Jake Kingsley or Matt Tisdale material will ever appear on an *Intemperance* album," said Matt. "I swore that on my *Strat*, man! Don't you understand that?"

"Christ," Crow groaned, feeling his ulcer flaring up again. "Do you guys know what you're doing to me?"

None of them apologized. "I'm pretty sure that none of us care what we're doing to you," said Matt.

"We're just holding to our ideals, Steve," said Jake. "You ever heard of ideals?"

"Maybe in some philosophy class I took once," he said. "What's the solution here, guys? You tell me how we're going to resolve this. I've got studio time reserved for January 3 and that is set in concrete. You have a deadline to provide me with at least twelve tunes by December 15. How are you going to do it?"

"We'll give you what we got on December 15," Matt told him. "As I told you, we're working as fast as we can here."

"But we're also not going to rush ourselves and come up with sub-standard material," Jake said.

"Exactly," said Bill. "One does not hurry the structural engineer into premature erection of his steel girders, does one?"

"Premature erection?" asked Darren. "Is there such a thing?"

"Yeah," said Coop. "I would think that the earlier you could get your girder up, the better."

"Otherwise it might not come up at all," said Darren, who had been having just that problem with his own girder since he'd started using the heroin more than three times a day.

Crow was now at his wit's end. "Look," he said. "I don't know how to put it any more plainly than this. I need those tunes from you—any tunes. I don't care if they're crappier than *Queensrhyche* covering *Scarborough Fair*. You can scream 'fuck the establishment' over and over again while Bill plays Beethoven tunes and Matt plays a goddamn electric harp. Just get the shit done so we can get this album in production. If we wait too long, you're going to fade and everyone will forget about you. I don't want that, National doesn't want that, and I know for damn sure that you guys don't want that. Do I make myself clear?"

"Crystal clear," Matt said.

"Then you'll get it done?" Crow asked.

Matt smiled. "We'll do the best we can."

This wasn't really an answer and Crow knew it, but his ulcer was making his stomach feel like a blowtorch had been lit within it and he knew that further discussion would gain nothing while only making the burning worse. "All right then," he said. "I'll hold you to that."

"You do that," said Matt.

They passed a few parting preliminaries, including Darren and Coop trying unsuccessfully to score a few more lines of coke from Crow, and the meeting came to an end. The five band members stood up to leave.

"Oh, by the way, guys," Crow said as they headed for the door. "Stop at Darlene's desk on the way out. She has some envelopes for you."

"What kind of envelopes?" Matt asked.

"Nothing big," Crow said. "Just a summary of your end-of-tour financial status. The same thing you got at the end of the last tour."

*****

They opened their envelopes in the elevator as they descended toward the lobby. Each contained a sheaf of financial sheets listing the expenses and revenue during the tour and correlated it with the total expenses and revenue. They were all slightly different—Jake and Matt earned a little more in revenue since they were the songwriters, Coop, Matt, and Darren had all burned a little more in "entertainment expenses" while off tour—but all were printed in bold red ink. It was the grand totals that were shocking to behold.

Jake looked at his numbly. It was worse than he'd imagined. "Damn," he said.

"Holy fucking shit," Matt said, shaking his head angrily as he looked at his own.

"Is this shit accurate?" asked Coop.

"It's about what I calculated it would be," said Bill.

"Are they gonna keep giving us our booze and shit?" asked Darren.

The elevator reached the lobby. Instead of exiting to their waiting limos and car, they grabbed a seat in some of the chairs around the lobby fountain where, oblivious to the pointing and gesturing of the tourists snapping pictures of them, they compared each other's sheets.

Jake looked at the bottom line, ignoring the rest. Since signing their contract with National Records and recording their first album, *Intemperance* had sold a grand total of 4,608,279 albums and 6,356,721 singles. This had generated a total of almost $5.2 million in royalties for the band, or, about a million bucks for each band member. However, between Shaver, who collected twenty-one percent, and the basic recoupable expenses like recording fees, breakage fees, tour costs, and promotion costs, that revenue had been cut down to a total of $240,000, or, about $48,000 per band member.

But then the other expenses began to come in. The 'entertainment expenses', which meant drugs and alcohol for the band, roadies, and management while on tour; the 'legal expenses', which meant the lawyers and the bail and the fines and the helicopter trip; the 'housing expenses', which was their condo rent and groceries and drugs and alcohol and manservants while off-tour; and, of course, the infamous 'miscellaneous expenses', which included airplane tickets, vacation expenses, limousine service, their allowances, their pre-paid cover charges at the nightclubs they frequented, and a hundred other things they'd found a way to charge to the band. The grand total of these other expenses—of which the 'entertainment expenses' made up a significant portion—totaled just a hair over $900,000, or, about $180,000 per band member. The net result was that each of them was about $132,000 in the hole and falling further with each passing day.

Coop and Darren, after getting over their initial shock at seeing a six-figure number with a minus sign in front of it, seemed to take it in stride.

"Well, it ain't like we didn't know this shit," said Darren. "Now we just have an itemized list of it."

"Yeah," said Coop with a shrug. "It ain't like it means anything."

"What do you mean it doesn't mean anything?" Jake asked him. "You're almost a hundred and fifty grand in the hole. How can that not mean anything?"

"But I'm still living in a premo fucking condo in downtown LA, ain't I?" Coop countered. "I still got a butler who cooks my food for me and cleans the shit stains out of my underwear, don't I? I still get a thousand bucks every two weeks to blow on bitches and booze, don't I? And I still get to ride a limo everywhere I go, don't I? So we're in the hole? What's the big deal?"

"Yeah," said Darren. "It ain't like there's a way out of it, is there? Might as well just enjoy all the shit they're giving us and not worry about a bunch of fuckin' numbers on a piece of paper."

"Don't you want to have your own shit, Darren?" Jake asked him. "Your own house, your own car?"

"I got my own house," Darren said.

"No," Jake reminded, "you live in a condo leased by National Records, and everything inside of it, the furniture, the TV, the sound system, the fucking groceries in the refrigerator, all of that shit belongs to National too."

"That just means we don't have to pay to get the shit fixed," Darren said.

Jake shook his head in frustration.

Matt patted his shoulder companionably. "You're fightin' a losing battle here, brother," he told Jake.

"There ain't no battle to fight," Coop said. "Why are you guys even trippin' about this shit? Aren't both of you always telling us to not worry about things we can't change because it's fuckin' pointless. Well ain't this one of them things? We can't change this shit, can we?"

"That remains to be seen," Jake said.

"In my house," said Darren, "whenever my dad said some shit like that, it meant 'no'."

"Mine too," said Coop.

Darren stood up. "Look, guys," he said. "We got screwed with our contract and we ain't making any money. That's just the way it is. Now I'm gonna go home and enjoy all the shit they give me so I don't have think about that, you dig?"

They dug, especially Coop who stood up and followed him towards the lobby doors and their waiting limousine.

"Sheep," Jake said contemptuously. "Those two are just a couple of sheep."

"Yeah," agreed Matt. He flipped his sheaf of financial papers in disgust. "And it's just like that prick Crow to have his fuckin' secretary give us these things as we're leaving. He's such a pussy."

"Hey, guys," said Bill, who had been furiously punching the keys on a pocket calculator (he habitually carried one with him everywhere but up on stage) during the entire discussion. "You want to hear something that will truly invoke anger within you?"

"Not really," said Jake, "but I'm sure you're going to tell us anyway."

"There's smoke coming off that calculator, Nerdly," Matt said. "What were you doing? Calculating Pi out to ten to the twentieth decimal?"

"Naw," said Bill. "This calculator isn't big enough for that, although I *did* calculate it out to ten to the tenth on my Commodore in my condo, just to see if the statistical randomness of the numerical assignments holds steady."

"You are a fuckin' party animal, Nerdly," Matt said.

"So what were you doing?" Jake asked. "Go ahead and hit us with it."

"I was trying to come up with a loose estimation of what National Records and Shaver are making off of us while we're going deeper and deeper into the red."

"And?" asked Matt.

"Shaver was easy," Bill said. "We made $5.2 million in royalties. Shaver got twenty-one percent of that. That's $1,092,000 that went to his agency from *Intemperance* album and single sales alone."

"Christ," Matt said in disgust. "And all he's done for us since we signed is act as spokesman for Jake when he started feeding his beef to Mindy Snow."

"And he's actually worked against us on several issues," Jake said. "He tried to talk us into doing the pre-written crap songs, he tried to get you to play that Brogan guitar during the first tour, and he went against us on the whole choreography issue too."

"Shaver is nothing though," said Bill. "National is the real robber baron here. It was a little harder to figure out what they're making since our royalties are based on the retail rate of five dollars an album, right?"

"Right," said Jake. "That means we get fifty cents in royalties for every album sold."

"But that was a negotiated rate, remember?" said Bill. "The actual retail rate of an album is more like eight dollars. In actuality, our royalties are only about six percent of the true retail rate."

"That means they're actually getting ninety-four percent of the money?" asked Matt.

"No, it's not quite that bad," Bill said. "Remember, they're not selling the albums and the singles for retail rate. That's what the record stores charge for it. National sells them to the record stores and Wal-Mart and all those places at the wholesale rate, which, to my understanding, is actually more like four dollars for albums and sixty cents for singles."

"Then it sounds like we actually are getting one over on them," Matt said. "If they're only getting four bucks for each album and they have to pay fifty cents of that in royalties, doesn't that mean we're really getting twelve and a half percent?"

"It does," agreed Bill, "but don't let that fool you. That still means National is collecting three dollars and fifty cents for each album sold and fifty cents for each single. Now I went ahead and knocked off ten percent of the total sales of both albums and singles for my calculations in order to account for things like breakage, theft, and giveaways. Even with that thrown in, they pulled in about $14.5 million in album sales and $2.9 million in single sales. That's almost seventeen and a half million dollars they've made off us so far strictly in music revenue."

"Seventeen and a half million bucks?" Matt said angrily.

"What about overhead costs though?" asked Jake. "They must eat away quite a bit of that."

"Unfortunately," said Bill, "I don't have a breakdown of their overhead costs relating to our albums and singles, but I don't think they're too terribly high. Remember, they have *us* paying for a lot of the traditional overhead costs out of our royalties. Our cut of the money paid for the cost of recording the albums, packaging the albums, marketing the albums, and shipping the albums. That includes the singles as well. We pay for half of the tour and half of the costs of making those abhorrent videos they insist on putting out. If their total overhead costs amounted to more than fifteen percent, I would be surprised."

"So, they're rakin' it in while we're closing in on being a million in the hole," said Jake.

"Now we know how they can afford this big-ass building," said Matt.

"That's not the only revenue they're getting either," said Bill. "Let's talk about the tours for a minute."

"What about the tours?" Jake asked.

"They're making a considerable amount of money off them as well. The *Descent* tour ended up generating a profit of more than three million dollars in ticket revenue alone. The *Thrill* tour was a little more expensive to put on, but it was still profitable. It made about a million in ticket revenue. Even though we paid for half of the costs of putting on the tours, they are not required to share any of the profit with us. And then there's merchandising. All those hats, T-shirts, sweaters, guitar picks, and other trinkets they sell at the concerts or in the department stores. We have no cut of any of that whatsoever. It is completely separate from our contract in every way."

"How much do you think they're making from that?" asked Jake.

Bill shrugged. "Your guess is as good as mine."

"I hardly think so," Jake said. "Come on, tell me what you think they're pulling in."

"Okay," said Bill. "Mind you, this is only an estimate."

"Of course."

"Those T-shirts they sell go for eight bucks. I'd be surprised if they actually paid more than a dollar apiece for them wholesale. Hats go for twelve and probably cost about two bucks wholesale. Sweaters go for sixteen and probably cost three wholesale. Let's assume that forty percent of the raw profit goes to operating expenses like shipping and paying for the employees who sell the stuff. That would mean they're clearing about $4.20 for each T-shirt, $6.00 for each hat, and $5.20 for each sweater. Now let's start with the T-shirts since they're the biggest sellers. How many T-shirts do you think they move in each show?"

Jake thought about that for a few seconds. "I wouldn't think it unreasonable to say they're selling about five hundred of them at every show."

"That sounds about right to me," agreed Matt.

"Okay," said Bill. "We'll plug in that figure then." He punched a few keys on his calculator. "That means for each show they're clearing $2100 in T-shirt sales. That's the *net*, remember. We did

126 shows on the *Thrill* tour. We did 110 on the *Descent* tour. $2100 times 236 shows is..." He pushed the buttons. "$495,600 in net T-shirt profit alone, none of which is shared with us in any way. Now the sweaters and the hats don't sell as well, but I think that a hundred apiece at each show is a conservative estimate, right?"

"Right," Jake agreed.

Bill punched up some more numbers on his calculator. "Assuming a hundred of each item times 236 total shows means they've generated $264,320 in hats and sweaters—give or take a few dollars because of uncertain variables."

"So basically, we're talking about almost three-quarters of a million or so in net merchandising profits," said Jake.

"I'm sure the grand total is closer to a million," said Bill. "Maybe even a little more. We just figured out the totals for T-shirts, hats, and sweaters. Don't forget, they sell dozens of other things with the *Intemperance* name on them. Lighters, stickers, baby-doll shirts, rolling papers, ashtrays, key-chains, pictures of us with our autographs copied on by a machine, fan club memberships. All of that stuff adds up to more revenue. And we also only did the concert sales. Don't forget, they're selling all this merchandise in malls and department stores across the country as well. I'm sure the profit margin is decreased in the mall sales, but you can bet your protractor it's still significant, otherwise they wouldn't be doing it."

"What's the bottom line here, Nerdly?" Matt asked. "How much money has National pulled in from us in total?"

"Well," he said, "as I told you, there are a number of variables that I just can't confirm, but I would think that somewhere in the neighborhood of twenty million dollars is about accurate."

"Twenty million dollars," said Matt, his eyes narrowing in anger.

"That's not fair," said Jake.

Bill and Matt both looked at him strangely.

"Well no fuckin' shit it's not fair," Matt said. "Now do you have anything constructive to say?"

"You don't understand," said Jake, "I mean it's not fair. We are not being treated fairly here." He looked at both of them. "I cannot condone being treated unfairly."

"What's your solution then?" Matt asked. "Should we march in there and tell Crow and Doolittle that we don't like being treated unfairly and that they should change our contract around so they can give us a little bigger cut of that twenty fucking million they've made off of us?"

"We're locked into this contract for four more albums, guys," Jake said. "Do you know what that means? If things keep going at this rate, we'll be about five million in the hole and National will have made more than a hundred million." He shook his head angrily as that worked its way around his brain. "A *hundred million* dollars," he said. "I refuse to go along with that. I *refuse*! It's unacceptable."

Matt groaned in frustration. "But it's the reality we're faced with now, isn't it?"

"Reality can be changed," said Jake. "I think it's time we tried to change it."

"How?" asked Bill. "We've signed a contract. We don't have a leg to stand on."

"A hundred million dollars is a lot of money," Jake said. "National won't want to risk losing that."

"What are you saying?" Matt asked.

"I've had an idea I've been tossing around for a while," Jake said. "I think the time has come to start firming it up a little, to start thinking about putting it into motion."

"What's the idea?" asked Matt.

"It's kind of drastic," Jake said. "But if it works, we'll have ourselves a new contract, one where the terms will guarantee some positive cash flow for us, the band members, and will put a little bit of the control of our destiny back in our hands."

"What is it?" asked Bill.

"National will not want to jeopardize the future revenue stream that *Intemperance* will give them."

"And how will we jeopardize it?"

"Simply by the possibility of them losing it," Jake said.

Matt grunted. "Speak, Jake. Fucking speak. Quit talking in mysterious Zen Buddha language here and get to the point."

"It's simple," Jake said. "National caves to us every time we demand something that we really want and threaten to do something that will hamper production of their albums or their tour or anything else that generates revenue for them. They caved when you took a stand on playing your Strat instead of a Brogan. They caved when we refused to perform those hacker songs. They caved when we refused to do their little choreography moves on the *Thrill* tour. In each case they could have pushed the issue and possibly come out the winner, especially with your Strat and with the hacker tunes, but they didn't. And do you know why they didn't?"

"Because they'd lose money doing it," said Bill. "They would've been able to get a breach of contract ruling against us with the hacker tunes, but they knew they would end up losing money."

"Right," said Jake. "They don't care about losing face, about being humiliated, about revenge, about making a point. All they care about is the bottom line. They will try to intimidate us, threaten us, manipulate us, and do a thousand other things to control what we do so they can produce more revenue out of us, but when push comes to shove, they *always* take the option that makes the most money for them. *Always*."

"That's true," agreed Matt. "But I don't see how that's going to help us here. What exactly is the plan?"

Jake looked at them both, his expression deadly serious. "The plan," he said, "is for us to cross the line."

Neither Bill nor Matt responded at first. They both knew the concept of his song and they both knew exactly what he meant. He wanted to go on strike, to cease all song composition and recording activities until National agreed to re-negotiate their contract.

"I don't know, Jake," Matt said. "You're talking about a blatant violation of our contract here."

"We really wouldn't have a leg to stand on if they decided to take legal action against us," said Bill.

"I don't think they'll take legal action though," Jake said. "They'll threaten it, and they'll bluster and they'll have us meet with their lawyers and they'll do everything else in their power to get us to cave in to them, but if we stand firm on this—if we stand really firm and united—they'll eventually get around to concluding that they would make more money by doing what we want then they would by filing a breach of contract suit and ruining us. Remember, all they care about is money, not saving face or making an example."

"We'd be gambling everything, Jake," Matt said. "Literally everything."

Jake nodded. "That's what crossing the line is all about, isn't it?"

Matt and Bill were clearly not keen on this idea at all. Jake could tell by the looks they were passing back and forth. He himself had already decided on the matter. He was not going to produce another album for National under their current contract. They were being treated unfairly and he was not going to tolerate it not matter what his fellow core members decided to do. If they wanted to keep working on this album under their current terms, they would have to do it without him. But he didn't want to tell Bill and Matt that unless he had to. It would be much easier if he could convince them to go along with this daring scheme of their own volition.

"Look, guys," he said. "We're rock stars, right? And not just any rock stars, but among the top five acts in the nation right now. We make badass music and we sell millions of records and singles. We sell out every auditorium we're booked in. Scalpers are charging eighty to a hundred dollars a ticket and people are paying that just to see us. Don't you think we deserve to get our fair share of that money? Aren't you tired of living in condos provided to us by the record company, waiting for your weekly allowance so you can go fishing or go out to the clubs? Wouldn't it be nice to buy your own house, hire your own servants, buy your own fishing boat perhaps?"

"My own fishing boat," Matt said, pondering that thought.

"Wouldn't it also be nice to have some say in what tunes we put on the albums? In how the tunes are mixed and mastered? Wouldn't it be nice to have some say in what our live show is going to look like? Or how about our music videos? We could stop letting that asshole producer make videos of what he thinks our songs are about and start making them about what they really *are* all about."

"How about our concert sound?" asked Bill. "Would we be able to make them let me be in charge of it?"

"Anything is possible," Jake said. "It would be a complete re-negotiation of the contract."

"The rewards would be great," Matt said.

"Yes," agreed Bill. "I must say he makes an intriguing argument."

"So what do you think?" asked Jake.

"Let's do it," said Matt. "Let's cross the line."

"Yeah," said Bill. "It's time for action."

*****

They put in their normal jam sessions on Tuesday and Wednesday, with none of the core members speaking of the conspiracy they were hatching to Darren or to Coop. Not that it was likely to matter if they did. The drummer and the bassist were both so strung out on what Matt, Jake, and Bill were increasingly coming to suspect was heroin that it was chore enough just to keep them focused on their musical tasks. On Wednesday, Coop actually fell asleep a few times—nodded off you might say—during some of the longer discussion periods of the jam.

"If this scheme of yours actually works," said Matt when they finally wound up and got ready to depart the warehouse to start their Thanksgiving break, "the first change we make is to put band member discipline back in our hands."

"Agreed," said Jake, watching as Darren and Coop stumbled and staggered their way into their limousine.

Jake and Bill climbed into a limo of their own, their suitcases already loaded into the trunk by the driver. They were driven to LAX where they waited for an hour in the first-class lounge before boarding a 737 bound for Heritage County Airport. They landed at 7:10 PM and were off the plane, luggage in hand by 7:25. A small mob formed around them as they were recognized in the terminal and they spent another fifteen minutes signing autographs, deflecting questions, and ignoring caustic remarks about Satanism and sexism.

When they were finally able to break free they parted company. Bill went with his mother and Jake went with his father. They would not see each other again until the Archer family arrived at the Kingsley house late the next morning for the annual Thanksgiving feast.

Jake gave his dad a hug when they finally made it through the mob and out into the relative sanctuary of the airport parking garage. As before, the emotion of actually seeing a family member, a familiar face that did not belong to someone who lived in Hollywood, was intense and he found himself near tears. His dad seemed equally glad to see him alive and safe. They made small talk until they climbed into the car. It was then that Tom Kingsley turned to him and asked, "How are you doing, Jake? Really?"

Jake knew this question entailed a lot more than a simple enquiry into his health and well-being. They had not seen each other since *The Thrill Of Doing Business* tour had made a single stop in Heritage a month and a half ago, and even then it had only been for a few minutes during the chaos of the post-show backstage area. He had spoken to his parents a few times on the phone during the last week but that had only been to make arrangements for coming home. He had not sat down in the same room and actually talked to them since that chaotic visit with Mindy more than a year ago.

His parents worried about him incessantly, with good reason he had to admit. Since *Intemperance* was the first musical act from Heritage to gain national fame, virtually everything their son did or was involved in ended up splashed across the headlines of *The Heritage Register*. When Jake and the rest of the band were busted in New York City, charged with possession of cocaine and lewd behavior, every detail had been reported, including the police reports themselves. When Darren had been blown off the stage in Austin, everything about that incident had been reported as well, including the fact that Darren was reported to be "under the influence of alcohol and cocaine".

"I'm doing fine, Dad," Jake said. "Really, I am."

"Are you sure?" he asked, probing a little, his voice flirting with disbelief.

Jake gave a reassuring smile. "Well, we're still locked into a crappy contract that keeps us from making any actual money..."

"Yes. Pauline told us about that. You really should have had her look that over before you signed it."

Jake gave a bitter laugh. "Yeah," he said. "Anyway, we're having some problems with that but hopefully we'll be working them out soon."

"What do you mean?"

"Well, we have a little weight to swing now. We're thinking that maybe it's time to start swinging it."

"I see," Tom said thoughtfully. "And what about the drugs?"

Jake looked down at his feet, uncomfortable. "What about them?"

They had reached the parking kiosk. Tom stopped before the closed crossing gate and handed a longhaired attendant his ticket. The attendant—who was listening to track three of *The Thrill Of Doing Business* album on a boom box—took it and ran it. He named his price and Tom paid it. As the attendant took the money he peered closely in the car at the passenger.

"Hey, dude," he said. "Anyone ever tell you that you look like Jake Kingsley?"

Jake shook his head. "Naw," he said. "No one's ever said that."

"It's true, dude," the attendant assured him. "You're dead on him. You could totally score some babes lookin' like that."

"I'll keep that in mind," Jake said.

Tom drove away, ending the conversation. He turned down the access road that led to the freeway and continued *his* conversation. "Look," he said, "your mother and I know you're an adult now and you make your own choices. But we're also still your parents and we always will be. Parents don't like to open the newspaper and read that their son was busted in a New York City hotel room with cocaine in his possession and an orgy in progress."

"It wasn't really an *orgy* per se," Jake said.

"The definition of an orgy *is* a bit dependent upon the interpretation of the participants and the observers," Tom allowed.

"Exactly," Jake said.

"But the definition of cocaine is not."

"We were set up, Dad," Jake said. "They threw out the case and made the police commissioner apologize to us."

"Yes, I read the details on that. It was perhaps the most flagrant falsification of probable cause I've ever seen, and believe me, I've seen a lot of trumped up probable cause writs."

"Damn right," Jake said. "They made everything up."

"But there *was* cocaine in the room, wasn't there?"

"Well... uh... yeah," Jake admitted.

"About eight grams of it if I remember correctly." He turned his head and stared hard at his son. "That's a lot of blow, Jake. A hell of a lot of blow."

"Yeah," Jake said softly, feeling like he was fifteen years old again and had just been caught smoking cigarettes in the backyard. "It is."

"Are you a cocaine addict?" Tom asked him. "Don't give me the answer you think I want to hear, tell me the truth."

"No, Dad," he said.

"No, you're not going to tell me the truth, or no, you're not a cocaine addict?"

This broke the tension just a little bit. "No, I'm not a cocaine addict," he said.

"You're sure about that?"

"I'm sure," Jake said. "I'm not going to tell you I don't use it because, obviously, I do, especially when we're out on tour. The parties we have after our shows sometimes... well, you've read the reports."

"They are somewhat exaggerated by the press, I hope," Tom said.

"Somewhat," Jake said, although, in actuality, the press didn't know the half of it. "It's a recreational drug, just like the pot and the alcohol. A little more dangerous I will agree, and a lot more expensive, but that's all I use it for. When we're off tour, I pretty much leave it alone."

"That's the truth?"

It wasn't, not entirely. Jake still snorted up once or twice a week during the off periods—usually when he was going out—but his dad didn't need to know that. "It's the truth," he said. "At least for me and Bill. Matt uses it considerably more, even off-tour, but then Matt goes out a lot more than Bill and I."

"What about Darren and Coop?" Tom asked. "I understand Darren was quite intoxicated when he was injured in that explosion."

Jake nodded. "He was. That's one of the problems we're having in relation to our contract. He and Coop are into things a little worse than cocaine now."

Tom looked shocked. "Heroin?" he asked.

"We think so."

"Jake, you're not using *that* shit, are you?"

"No," Jake said. "Absolutely not. I may be a bit reckless but I'm not a complete moron."

"And Bill?"

"He's not doing it either. Neither is Matt for that matter. It's those two idiots. It started with the painkiller shots they gave Darren after he got burned. They ended up shooting him up before every concert after that. Sometime when the tour was over they started replacing the Demerol with heroin."

"The record company is actually supplying them with this drug?"

"They supply us with everything, Dad. From the food we eat to the houses we stay in to the booze we drink. We're owned by the company store right now."

"And you're going to try to change this?"

"We are *going* to change it," Jake said firmly. "Come hell or high water, I'm not going to keep living this way. That's a promise."

Tom smiled respectfully at his son. "Good," he said.

*****

Mary Kingsley hugged her only son for the better part of a minute as soon as he walked in the door. She cried on his shoulder she was so glad to see him safe and sound and in his family home without any news helicopters hovering overhead or reporters peeking in their window.

When she finally released him, Jake saw an exchange of glances between his two parents, a form of silent communication that only long-married couples could accomplish. Jake, having grown up observing such glances, was able to loosely interpret what they were not saying to each other.

Did you talk with him? his mother asked.

Yes, his father responded, *and it's not as bad as we thought.*

He carried his luggage upstairs, leaving them alone in the living room to confirm their silent communication with real communication. When he came back down, both of them seemed a little more at ease. His mother's tears had disappeared and his father handed him a cold bottle of beer. They sat down on the couch and talked, Tom and Jake smoking cigarettes, Mary giving her motherly disapproval at what she considered a nasty habit. Now that Tom had addressed the subject of drug abuse, Mary gradually brought the conversation around to another concern that had been lodged in their heads by the local media: the subject of girlfriend abuse.

"What exactly happened between you and Mindy Snow?" she asked him. "She seemed like such a nice girl when you brought her home to meet us."

"We broke up, Mom," Jake said with a shrug. "It was fun while it lasted but it just wasn't meant to be."

"The papers and the news," Mary said, "all reported that you were... you know... not very nice to her. And she told Frank Wilson that you were... uh... abusive. You weren't... you know... hitting her or anything, were you, Jake? Because we certainly didn't raise you to be like that."

Jake sighed. He had hoped his mother would let the subject drop but apparently, she wasn't going to. "No, Mom," he said. "I never hit her or any other woman. And I was never abusive to her either."

"Well why would she say such things?"

Jake explained it to her, telling her about the importance of image in Mindy's mind, about how she had started the relationship in the first place so she could shed her good girl image and get more adult roles, about the manipulation she had put him through, about how she had tipped off the photographer so he could take pictures of them in compromising positions.

"She told that photographer where you would be?" Mary asked, appalled. "And then she goaded you into being... you know... naked?"

"She did," Jake confirmed. "And then, when it was time for us to go back out on tour, she decided it was time to break up with me. I guess she figured it would help her get her role in *Handle With Caution* if she herself had been the victim of abuse, so she implied that I had been abusive to her."

"Why that manipulative little bitch!" Mary cried.

Jake nodded. "So that's the story of Mindy," he said. "She's in the middle of filming her movie and I haven't spoken a word with her since that last phone conversation while we were on tour. She's still dating John Carlisle and probably manipulating him just as badly."

"What a horrible person," Mary said.

"She's kind of typical for Hollywood," Jake said.

"I certainly hope you never get like that, Jake," she said.

"Me too, Mom," he said. "Me too."

*****

The Thanksgiving get-together filled Jake with a strong sense of pleasant nostalgia. It was the first time in four years he had been able to participate in the celebration with his family and it was just like it had always been while growing up. Stan and Lorraine Archer were there with Bill. Pauline was there. The men watched football and drank beer while the women gossiped and prepared food. At 2:00 PM the turkey was removed from the oven and Tom meticulously carved every last bit of meat from it, leaving a shredded carcass. They feasted on the meat, on Mary's homemade cornbread stuffing, on mashed potatoes and homemade gravy, on Lorraine's candied yams and fresh corn and green bean casserole, on Pauline's fruit salad. They drank several bottles of expensive Chardonnay that Jake had brought and put in the refrigerator to chill the night before. And they engaged in the pleasant exchange of family, talking of the upcoming Christmas season, the past year and all the good things that had come from it.

It was only as the get-together was winding down, after the dishes had been done and they were sitting in the living room eating homemade pumpkin and cherry cream cheese pie with strong coffee, that the subject of Jake and Bill's profession entered the conversational stream.

"Your success as rock musicians has done wonders for the Philharmonic," said Lorraine.

"Oh?" said Jake.

"Oh yes," Lorraine said. "Over the past two years attendance at our performances is up by more than a hundred and twelve percent. We've actually sold out the auditorium on more than a dozen occasions."

"That's stupendous," Bill said. And it was. For as long as their children could remember, both Mary and Lorraine had complained about the lack of interest the community held for the Philharmonic Orchestra and how the threat of bankruptcy and being disbanded was always hanging over their heads.

"What do *we* have to do with that?" Jake asked.

"Yes," said Bill, "I would think your recently realized attendance improvement would be a result of your own appeal to the musical tastes of the populace."

"No," said Mary, "it's mostly because I'm the mother of Jake Kingsley and Lorraine is the mother of 'Nerdly' Archer that's doing it."

"Oh, please don't call him that, Mary," Lorraine said with a wince. She detested Bill's nickname.

"Sorry," Mary said, "but you know what I mean."

"Yeah," she said with a hint of bitterness. "I guess I do."

Neither Jake nor Bill bothered asking how the populace knew that the lead violinist and the piano player for the Heritage Philharmonic Orchestra were the mothers of Jake Kingsley and Bill "Nerdly" Archer, respectively. It was common knowledge throughout the northern California region thanks to multiple *Heritage Register*, *Sacramento Bee*, and *San Francisco Chronicle* articles. Reporters for all of these publications, as well as all of the local television station news programs in all of these cities, knew the address of every *Intemperance* member's parents as well as their phone numbers, regardless of how many times said phone number was changed. Though Coop and Darren's parents had been pretty much spared, Bill's, Matt's, and Jake's parents were frequently contacted either by phone or in person by various reporters wishing to do sidelines on some issue of family life or to get reaction when the band or a band member did something outrageous. The subject of Bill and Jake's musical roots had been done to death back in the early days of the *Descent Into Nothing* success.

"What makes you think the increased attendance is because of us?" Jake asked.

"Oh, it's not too hard to figure out," Mary said. "Whenever we do a show these days, half the audience are young college kids and teenagers with long hair and wearing *Intemperance* T-shirts."

"Really?" Jake asked, surprised at the thought of their fans going to a classical music performance.

"Oh yes," agreed Lorraine. "And until you boys made a success of your band there was never a haze of marijuana smoke over the auditorium when we performed. Now it's so common that I don't even notice it anymore."

"They hold up their lighters for us too," said Mary.

Jake wasn't sure whether to apologize for this or not but both of the mothers assured him that they didn't mind, that they in fact appreciated the strange crossover of musical appreciation.

"As far as I'm concerned, you've done us a great service," Mary said. "Anything that helps introduce young people to classical music is a good thing."

"And we're operating in the black for the first time in ten years as well," said Lorraine.

Later, as the pie dishes were being washed and the leftovers distributed between the two families, Jake found occasion to pull Pauline to the side.

"Are you doing anything tomorrow?" he asked her.

"Well," she said, considering, "seeing as how my social calendar is about as full as it always is... no, I'm not doing a damn thing. Why?"

"Do you mind if Bill and I stop by for a little bit in the afternoon?"

"Sure," she said. "What's up?"

"We've got a little idea about how we can get our contract changed. We'd like to run it by you."

Her look became immediately cynical. "There's no way to change your contract, Jake. I've told you that before. You're locked into it until it expires."

"Unless National decides to re-negotiate with us," he said.

"Why would they do that?"

"That's what we want to talk to you about. We think we found a way."

The cynical look did not disappear. "This I've gotta hear," she said. "How about noon?"

*****

"No," Pauline said the next day at 12:10 PM. "It won't work."

They were sitting at her dining room table, turkey sandwiches and bottles of imported beer spread out before them. The well-worn copy of their contract sat in the center of the table, but Pauline had not even consulted it before making her assessment of their plan. Jake's face fell as he heard this. He had been confident that his plan not only had merit but was unimpeachable.

"Why not?" he asked. "If we refuse to compose or record for them, they'll be left with only two choices: either sue us for breach of contract or open renegotiation meetings. Their history proves they will go with the option that produces the most money for them."

Pauline was shaking her head through his entire statement. "Your plan would be a *blatant* breach of your contract," she said. "You can't just refuse to make music for them."

Now it was Jake that was shaking his head. "Maybe you didn't understand what I was saying," he told his sister. "I *know* we're violating the contract by doing this. That's the whole point. We're challenging them. We're defying them. We're going on strike. They can either sue us for breach of contract—which we understand they will win if they choose that option—or they can come to terms with us and continue to make money off of us."

"Just not as much as they're making now," Bill said.

"Right," said Jake. "But they'll still be pulling in millions of dollars per album. That's better than suing us and ruining us and getting nothing but what they manage to garnishee from us in the future."

"Jake, Bill," Pauline said, "I understand perfectly what you're saying. What you don't seem to understand is that it won't work. Your 'crossing the line' scenario is crossing much too far over the line. They'll have you by the balls if you pull a stunt like this."

"What do you mean?" Jake asked.

"Do you remember when you were having the dispute with them about choreographing your concerts?" she asked.

"Yes," Jake said. "That's part of what I'm basing this on."

"You were in the right there," Pauline said. "It doesn't say anywhere in your contract that they can dictate dance moves and choreography for your shows. They can make an argument, perhaps, that the order of musical performance clause allows such dictation but it's a precarious argument at best. In all likelihood, a judge would have ruled that they do not have that right based on the wording of your contract. In any case, the burden of proof would be resting on them. You told their lawyers that you would submit to the choreography if they got a judge to order you to, right?"

"Right," said Jake. "That was on your advice."

"And it was good advice," she said. "They caved in, didn't they?"

"Right," said Jake. "Wouldn't they cave on this issue as well?"

"No," she said. "You're not seeing the difference here. With the choreography issue, it wasn't specifically spelled out that they could force you to do that. The challenge to take it to a judge was a good one because they knew that if they did, he would more than likely tell them to take a flying fuck. But your contract *does* specifically state that you have to come up with new material for each contract period. If you refuse to do that, there is no argument or ambiguity about a breach of contract occurring. The terms are plainly spelled out."

"What difference does it make if there is no argument?" Jake asked. "I don't understand what that has to do with anything. We're not trying to hide the fact that we're in breach of contract. We want them to know it. We're gambling on their greed here. We refuse to make music and National is forced to choose between renegotiation and suing us for breach of contract."

"Uh huh," Pauline said. "And suppose they choose to go breach of contract? What then?"

"Then we lose," Jake said.

"And if you lose, you'll produce music for them like they want?"

"No!" Jake said. "We are absolutely firm on this point. None of us... that is, none of us in the core—me, Bill, and Matt—will produce so much as a note for them under this contract. We are prepared to go down with the ship if that's what is necessary."

"Exactly," said Bill. "The fundamental iniquitousness of this legal situation is both intolerable and unsustainable."

"Uh huh," Pauline said again. "I'm assuming you understand the ramifications of 'going down with the ship', as you put it?"

"Yes, of course," Jake said. "We're not allowed to make any more music for the duration of the contract. That's 1988. National will take us to court and sue us for what they could have expected to make from us during the terms of the contract. That will be a significant amount of money. Tens of millions, perhaps."

"Tens of millions that we do not have," Bill added. "They will be trying to get the proverbial blood out of the proverbial turnip."

"I really don't think they'll let it go to that," Jake told her. "They stand to make much more money by renegotiation than they do by breaching us."

Pauline frowned. "I'm not so convinced it's as simplistic as you're presenting it," she said. "And even if it is, there is no way they're going to cave into you immediately. And it's the immediate future that I'm talking about when I asked if you understood the ramifications. It seems clear to me that you do not."

"What do you mean?" Jake asked.

"If you refuse to make music for them you are in immediate and indisputable breach of your contract," she explained. "That means that National will no longer be under obligation to honor their end of the contract. That means your money flow will stop. That means your groceries will stop. That means they will evict you from your condos. Now with the housing, the law is a little sticky. If you absolutely refuse to leave they will be forced to go through a formal eviction process to remove you and that could take as much as six months before a judge orders some cops over there to boot you out."

"Six months is a long time," Jake said.

"It is," she agreed. "It's a long time to go without groceries, or transportation, or any of the basics of life. Without National providing those things, how are you going to eat?"

"Uh... well..." Jake stammered. Maybe he hadn't thought this all the way through.

"We could do gigs," Bill suggested. "If we're in breach of contract anyway, why not do some gigs around LA and pocket the money. Sure, National will add it to the lawsuit and we'd eventually have to give it to them, but..."

Pauline was shaking her head again. "That would never work," she said.

"Why not?" Jake asked.

"The moment you even announced you were planning a gig, National's lawyers would go before a judge and get him to issue a preliminary injunction. Your concert would be cancelled before you even set foot in the venue."

"Is there any way around that?" Jake asked.

"Around a judge issuing a preliminary judgement against you performing? No, not at all. If you defied such an order, two things would happen. One, National would get the judge to garnishee any income you gained from the performance, so you wouldn't get to keep it anyway."

"Well... that sucks," Jake said.

"And... two," Pauline continued, "you would be in contempt of court. There's a better than even chance the judge you defied would throw your asses into some LA county jail to rot for a few weeks."

"Jail?" Jake asked. "They would send us to jail for that?"

"You can't defy a judge, Jake," she said. "If he orders you not to perform and you do it anyway, that tends to piss a judge off. Judges are not the sort of people you want to piss off."

Nerdly did not like the direction this conversation was heading. He did not like it one bit. "I don't want to rot in some jail cell, Jake," he said. "You know what happens in those places. There are people in there who engage in anal intercourse by means of force and fear."

"Yeah," Jake said. "I've heard that."

"I don't *want* to engage in anal intercourse, with or without force or fear. So far I've kept that particular orifice as an outlet only."

"Well, except for that one groupie in Cincinnati," Jake reminded him. "Remember, she did that thing with that dildo she had?"

"Oh... yeah," Bill said, blushing.

"I don't really need to hear about this, do I?" Pauline said, rolling her eyes.

"No, probably not," Jake said.

"Definitely not," Bill agreed.

"So, you're saying," Jake summarized, "that because refusing to produce music for them is a flagrant violation of our contract, they can cut off our groceries, cut off our allowances, and evict us from our homes?"

"That's exactly what I'm saying," Pauline said. "I don't see any way around it."

"But what about when Matt refused to play that Brogan guitar onstage?" Jake asked. "And what about when we refused to do those hacker songs they wanted us to do?"

"Let's take those issues one by one," Pauline said. "With the guitar issue, Matt was clearly in the wrong. Your contract explicitly states that you will play the brand of instrument that they tell you to play. They could have gone to a judge and they could have gotten a court order for Matt to play the Brogan if they had chosen to do that. And if he defied them and played the Strat anyway, they could have breached you right there and kicked you out of your houses and cut everything off. They caved to him in that instance because of the money issue you're using to try to justify this plan. In that case, you were correct. In the great scheme of things, they decided it wasn't really that big of a deal, so they let it go in the name of not alienating you too much."

"Okay," Jake said. "I can buy that. But what about the hacker songs?"

"Things were not as clear on that issue," she said. "Your contract does not say they can force you to do a particular kind of song, it just says you have to have a certain amount of material available for recording by a certain date. In other words, you have to have a 'reasonable number of new recordings available for approval' by the deadline for each contract period. Now, since you had songs available for that—namely the tunes they rejected, which they have the right to do—their position was not as clear. They could have breached you for not having acceptable material, but *you* might have been able to get a preliminary injunction against *them* preventing them from enforcing the terms of the breach because you'd made a good faith effort to provide the material for them."

Jake looked sharply at her. "Say that again," he said.

"What do you mean?" she asked.

"I mean clarify a little," he said. "You're saying that if we made a good faith effort to provide a reasonable number of tunes for them, they can still reject them and breach us, but we can get a judge to order they don't evict us and don't cut off our allowances?"

"Well... in theory," she said. "You would need a good lawyer arguing for you, and a judge who interprets the contract loosely, but yes. If you make a good faith effort to fulfill your part of the bargain and they try to breach you anyway, and you convince a judge of that, he might be inclined to order National to hold up their end of the contract to provide money and housing to you until such time as the lawsuit for breach of contract is tried in front of a jury. Of course, you would lose at that point without question, but..."

"But that could take a year or more before a jury even heard it," Jake said.

"Probably even longer than that, as slow as our civil court system is," Pauline said. "Again, I don't know where you're going with this. You're not proposing to make a good faith effort. You're talking about a blatant breach that will allow them to immediately enforce the breach of contract provisions."

"Hmmm," Jake said slowly. "I think I'm starting to understand this."

"Then you're starting to see that you can't pull this off?"

"Maybe," he said, his mind spinning a mile a minute, a new idea forming. "At what point does a song become officially submitted to National? When does it become *their* property and therefore count as material offered for them?"

She looked at him strangely for a minute. "Why do you ask?"

"I'll tell you when you answer me," he said. "So, what's the answer?"

She picked up the contract for the first time and started flipping through it. Jake and Bill watched her in silence as she did so. Jake lit a cigarette and took a few drags. Bill sipped from his beer and chewed his fingernails. Finally, she found the section she was looking for.

"When you submit the official demo recording to National," she said, "the tune officially becomes their property and they can order you to record it or they can reject it."

"So, as soon as we do our half-assed recording of a song in the warehouse and give it to Crow," Jake said, "that qualifies as a submission for consideration?"

"That's right," she said.

"And when we were having the dispute with them over the hacker tunes," Jake said, "it was those recordings of our early stuff—the stuff they didn't like—that kept them from being able to argue that we were in immediate breach of contract and would have made it possible to get one of these preliminary judgements preventing National from enforcing an immediate breach of contract?"

"Right," she said. "You made a good faith effort to meet your deadline. As long as you do that, they can still reject the tunes and they can still breach you if you don't come up with tunes acceptable to them, but they would likely have to wait until a jury actually ruled in National's favor before they could kick you out of your homes and cut off your allowances."

Jake was smiling now. "One last question," he said. "What exactly constitutes a 'good faith' effort?"

She was starting to see where he was coming from. She smiled as well. "That's a term that is very much open to interpretation," she replied.

"That's what I thought," Jake said. "And how many of those superior court judges in the Los Angeles area do you suppose are fans of modern rock music?"

"I can get a list of names and ages," Pauline said, "but I wouldn't think that any of them are. If there's a single judge under the age of forty, I would be surprised."

"Are you thinking what I think you're thinking?" asked Bill, who had been watching the conversation go back and forth like he was watching a tennis match.

"I think I am," Jake said.

"Yes," agreed Pauline. "And I think you're on to something."

CHAPTER 15

CROSSING THE LINE

December 17, 1984
Los Angeles, California

It was Monday morning and Steve Crow was going over the music sales reports from the previous week. He was dismayed to see that *La Diferencia*'s debut album *The Difference* had moved into the number two spot on album sales, selling only six hundred fewer copies than *The Thrill Of Doing Business*, which was holding at number one for the eighteenth consecutive week. At this rate it was entirely possible that *The Difference* would take over the number one spot within a few weeks, dislodging *Intemperance*'s album as neatly as *I Love To Dance* had aced out *Crossing The Line* and *Young Love* had aced out *Rules Of The Road* in singles sales. *Young Love* was, in fact, still holding strong at number one on the singles chart and would probably continue to for another few weeks. And from what he had heard, *La Diferencia* was slated to release yet another single—*Serenade Of The Heart*—the moment *Young Love* started to fall.

"I wish we would've signed those fucking spics," Crow said enviously as he mentally calculated how much revenue that would have brought in and as he imagined how much less of a pain in the ass third world Venezuelan musicians would be compared to the lowlife antagonists *he* was being paid to manage.

And speaking of those pains in the asses, where the hell were they? It was ten minutes past nine. They had promised him they would be in his office, demo tape in hand, at nine o'clock sharp. It was just like them to show up late for a meeting. These days they seemed to do everything within their power to antagonize or generally annoy him. He wondered if they really had a demo tape for him or if they were just blowing smoke up his ass.

Crow had a respectable network of spies who kept an eye on the members of *Intemperance* for him. There were the manservants who lived with each band member and there were the limousine drivers who transported them from place to place (except for Jake, ever since that goody two-shoes bitch Mindy Snow bought him the Corvette, that particular avenue of information had been severely curtailed). There were the bouncers and the bartenders at the clubs they hung out in. And just lately there was Darren and Coop themselves. Both were so strung out on heroin these days they would tell him anything just to keep the supply coming. From this network came the information that, upon returning from their Thanksgiving vacation, Jake, Matt, and Bill suddenly decided to abandon the six songs they had been initially working on and start completely fresh. This had alarmed Crow greatly, enough that he had called Jake and demanded an explanation.

"They just weren't good enough," Jake told him, not even bothering to ask how Crow knew that they had abandoned the six songs, something that immediately triggered Crow's suspicions that a game was afoot.

"You said they were quality tunes," Crow said. "The best you've done so far. You said they were the tunes we would probably want to release as singles."

"We were overconfident in them," Jake said. "You know how it is. When we stepped away from them and gave them some honest analysis we found that they really kind of sucked."

"But Coop and Darren said they were bad-ass tunes," Crow protested, not even caring that he was naming one of his information sources. "They told me I would love them."

"Well... you know that Coop and Darren have been suffering from... oh... shall we say, impaired judgment, lately."

Crow had to admit that this was true. Since he had allowed Cedric to introduce Darren to the effects of China White heroin—that magic white powder that had kept many a rock musician under control—both he and Coop had taken to it with perhaps a little more enthusiasm than was desired. They were both mainlining the shit now and spending all day, every day, in a state of near catatonia, a state that was quickly becoming counter-productive to musical composition. And Jake and Matt, the two band members that he really needed to get under control, weren't using the shit at all, despite repeated attempts to introduce them to it.

"I understand," he told Jake, "but the deadline is coming up fast and we need at least three quality tunes out of you for single release and another seven for filler. Can't you at least use the six you started as the filler tunes?"

"They're not even good enough for that," Jake told him. "Trust me, they really suck."

"But..."

"Don't worry," Jake assured him. "We'll have twelve tunes for you on schedule. We know how to work under pressure."

And, if last Friday's phone call were to be believed, they had come through. According to Jake and Matt, they had thirteen original songs recorded and ready for submission. Conversations with Darren and Coop seemed to confirm this although both of them had been blasted to the gills when they'd talked.

"Yeah, man, it's like some good shit," Darren told him on the phone at one point. "I mean, I like wasn't so sure about it at first... it's a little different than our normal shit, you know, but the more we jammed, the more I liked it."

"It's different," Coop said later that same day. "But progressive, you know? It's the next level in *Intemperance* music."

Crow wasn't so sure he liked the terms "progressive" and "different" all that much. After all, formulation was the name of the game when you wanted to keep consecutive albums on the chart. Experimentation was strongly frowned upon since the general rule of thumb was that a band's core fans didn't like change in musical style (the ongoing success of *Van Halen*'s *1984* album was the exception to this rule). But at this point in the game he was approaching desperation anyway. The band needed to be in the studio in less than three weeks and because they refused to do covers or pre-written material (and because no one had thought to put a clause in their contract specifically demanding National's right of musical dictation) Crow was pretty much stuck with accepting whatever they came up with.

"How bad could it be, really?" he asked himself. After all, despite being big pains in his ass and despite their rebellious ways, they were talented musicians and composers. Even their worst efforts would still sound palatable, wouldn't they?

His intercom buzzed and his secretary let him know that Matt, Jake, and Bill had finally arrived. Crow did not have them come in right away. Instead, he said he was busy with something and made them wait for ten minutes just to show them his time was important as well. He spent the time flipping through the photographs of Jake and Mindy naked on the boat and in the water. He had used one of his connections to score a set of duplicate prints from Paul Peterson—prints that did not have the black line across the good parts. As a committed bisexual he became equally aroused by both Jake and Mindy. Finally, he put the photos back in their envelope and stowed them in his desk once again. When his hard-on deflated to normal he buzzed his secretary and had her send them in.

The three band members seemed in a jovial mood as they trooped into his office and took seats before his chair. He greeted them pleasantly, asked the normal questions about their health and welfare and they gave him the normal jerk-off answers. He offered them drinks and a few lines of cocaine like normal and this time they surprised him by taking him up on the offer.

"This ain't an official meeting," said Matt, "so why the fuck not? I'll have a Chivas and coke, heavy on the Chivas."

"You got any wine?" asked Jake. "I could go for a little French Chardonnay."

"How about Cognac?" asked Bill. "You have any of that?"

"Of course," said Crow.

"Copacetic," said Bill. "I'll have a double shot of Cognac on the rocks with seven-up and a cherry."

Crow actually winced at this last order, but he passed it, as well as the others, on to his secretary.

"How about those lines?" asked Matt once the drink orders were off. "Let's get blown, shall we?"

"Uh... sure," said Crow and proceeded to set them up with two lines of high-grade blow apiece. By the time they had all snorted up, their drinks had arrived and they all took a few sips.

"Here you go," said Jake, setting a large brown envelope on his desk. "The latest collection of masterpiece tunes from your favorite band."

Crow used a sterling silver envelope opener to cut open the top. He reached in and pulled out a cassette tape and a sheet of paper listing the titles of the tracks on the tape. He frowned a little and looked in the envelope again, seeing nothing but emptiness. "Where are the lyric sheets?" he asked.

"They're not in there?" Matt asked.

"No, there's just the track sheet."

"Well, fuck my mother with a two by four," Matt said. "I must've forgotten to put them in."

"You did make lyric sheets though, didn't you?" asked Crow. "We need those for copyright paperwork."

"Yeah, we made 'em," Matt said. "I bet I left them sitting on my desk at home. I'll send them over to you with the limo driver after he drops me off."

Crow shrugged and picked up the track sheet. He looked at the titles there. The very first one caught his eye: *Fuck the Establishment* by Jake Kingsley. "Fuck the establishment?" he asked.

"Hell yes," Jake said. "It rocks, man. It's one of our tightest tunes ever. And you gave me the idea for it. Remember when we were in here last month and you said you didn't care if we yelled 'fuck the establishment' over and over? That inspired me."

"We can't write 'Fuck the Establishment' on an album cover," Crow said. "And if you actually say that in the tune, they won't play it on the radio."

"We can write F, star, star, star, can't we?" Matt asked. "And if you do want to release it as a single, they can edit it so 'fuck' doesn't come through."

"Yeah," said Jake, "like that hacker band *WASP* did with that fuck like a beast tune."

"Well... we'll see," Crow said, already three quarters of the way to rejecting *Fuck the Establishment* without even hearing it. He looked at the next title. It was another one penned by Jake. "*So Many Choices*. Now that sounds better... in title anyway."

"It fuckin' rocks," Matt agreed.

"Oh yes," said Jake, "I think it's some of my best work actually. It's an examination of the dilemmas that we're all faced with on a daily basis, not just the complex ones, but the simple ones."

Crow nodded. He didn't give a rat's ass what the song was about, as long as people would like it. "Do you think it has potential for release as a single?"

"It's more than that," Matt said. "I think it might take a Grammy next year."

Crow liked the sound of that indeed. He looked at the rest of the titles, seeing nothing that reached out and touched him in any way. He wished they had remembered to bring the lyric sheets so he could get a better idea of what was waiting for him. Oh well. What could you do? At least they remembered the cassette and that was the important part.

The band finished their drinks and then said their goodbyes. Crow, feeling magnanimous now that he had the tape in his possession, told them to take the next two days off and relax.

"Thanks, Stevie," Matt said. "We'll do that. I think another fishing trip is in order."

"I think I'll just get drunk," said Jake.

"And I'm going to get back on CompuServe," said Bill. "You wouldn't believe what you can do on there."

"CompuServe?" asked Matt, shaking his head. "You still playing around with that nerdy shit?"

"I'm a nerd," said Bill. "What else should I do?"

"So, you like that service?" asked Crow, who had authorized the software purchase and the monthly charges when Bill had requested it two weeks ago.

"Oh yes," Bill replied. "It's the wave of the future."

"Wave of the fucking future," Matt scoffed. He looked at Crow. "Nerdly here thinks that in the next ten years every fucking computer in the world is going to be connected together and that we'll be able to send mail to each other that way, and pay our fucking bills, and get porn."

"Get porn?" asked Jake.

Bill nodded solemnly. "Historically the pornography industry had been quick to take advantage of fledgling technology and, in a few cases, has even contributed to the technology's success. Look at photography. No sooner had the camera been invented that the first nudie magazines and adult nickelodeons came into existence. Look at the movie camera. Before they even developed practical audio coordination for the technology, sex films were circulating via the black market. And with the computer, my guess is that pornography will be what drives the success and makes it a global phenomenon. Nobody will admit they signed up for CompuServe or this new service that's coming out, Prodigy, for the pictures of naked women, but that's why they'll be doing it."

"Now you're talking my language, Nerdly," Matt told him. "When it gets to the point that I can turn on my computer and pull up a beaver shot at will, you let me know. That's when I'll join the technological revolution."

"Agreed," said Bill.

They left Crow's office a minute later, still chatting about the pros and cons of computer porn and at what point they could expect to start encountering it. The second the door closed behind them Crow got on the phone to Doolittle. "I got the tape," he said. "They forgot to give me the lyric sheets, but I'll make copies of the title sheet."

"Good," his boss responded. "I'll get Bailey and we'll meet in my office in twenty minutes to give these tunes a listen."

*****

The second the elevator doors closed on them, Bill, Jake, and Matt started cracking up. It went on for the better part of thirty seconds, a much-needed release after twenty minutes of fighting to keep straight faces.

"Oh man," said Matt as the elevator reached the lobby level and they headed for the doors. "You were killin' me in there, Jake. A fucking 'examination of the dilemmas we're faced with on a daily basis'? Jesus Christ."

"Well, that *is* what the song is about," Jake said, causing another round of laughter to erupt.

"I'd love to be a fly on the wall of that office when he listens to that tape for the first time," Bill said.

"You ain't shittin'," Matt agreed. "The shock may just kill him."

"But remember," warned Jake, "this was a 'good faith' effort to produce music for the next album. They'll be calling us on this within the next two hours and they're really going to be throwing the accusations around. No matter what happens, no matter what they say, we *cannot* admit that this was anything less than our best efforts. If we do, the whole good faith concept comes crashing down and no judge is going to grant a preliminary injunction against them."

*****

"Fuck the establishment, huh?" said Doolittle as he perused his copy of the track sheet for the first time.

"Well... yeah," said Crow apologetically. He was plugging a boombox into the electrical outlet next to Doolittle's desk. "I'm a little leery of that one, song unheard. Unless it's absolutely ground-breaking in some way, I'm inclined to think that including it on the album—even as a filler tune not intended for airplay—would be more trouble than it's worth. Those censorship groups are already sniffing up *Intemperance*'s ass pretty hard. Putting a song with the word 'fuck' in the title might just give them the ammo they need to get some sort of a legal ruling in favor of their goals."

"I agree," Doolittle said. "But still, let's give it a listen. Maybe it is groundbreaking."

"And even if it's not," said Bailey, "maybe we can get them to change the lyrics to 'screw the establishment', or something like that."

"Good luck on that," Crow said sourly. He was a veteran of many battles with Jake and Matt over the subject of their songs and so far, they had given him nothing more than an ulcer.

Crow put the cassette into the boombox and closed the door. After a check to make sure it was properly rewound (it was) he pushed play. A slight hissing came out of the speakers and then the lead-in to the song began. It was a bass intro, starting slow and gradually picking up tempo. As with all of the recordings the band had given them in the past, the quality was quite impressive considering the primitive equipment that had been utilized to make it.

"So far, so good," Doolittle said as the bass reached top intensity and Matt's guitar sounded in. He ground out a furious, fast-paced opening riff and then settled in to what seemed the main riff, with Jake backing and Bill chiming in just between them. And then Jake's voice began to sing, the tone angry and hateful.

"There comes a time when you have to say,"
"Fuck this shit, I'm doin' it my way."
"There comes a time when you have to say,"
"Fuck this shit, I'm doin' it my way!"

"Wow," said Doolittle, as he listened to this opening verse sung over and over again. "That's pretty harsh, isn't it?"

"And what's with the repetitive lyrics?" asked Bailey. "I thought Jake and Matt both hated that formula?"

Jake sang the opening verse a total of twelve times while the guitars and the piano ground out an angry, spiteful, repetitive, but strangely appealing melody. At last, the tempo slowed down and the lyrics changed to a different style, though no less angry.

"You fucked with me, you fucked me hard."
"For my sense of worth, you've no regard."
"You cheat me blind, you exploit my name."
"My hopes and dreams, you set aflame!"

After this there was a pounding, heavy metal instrumental session followed by a transition back to the main riff and what was apparently the main verse—the line about there comes a time when you have to say, fuck this shit, I'm doin' it my way! This was repeated another twelve times and then there was a guitar solo lasting almost a minute. After this, another verse.

"So, fuck you all, time to do it my way."
"Get out of the palace, it's Bastille Day!"
"Fuck the establishment! Fuck you all!"
"I'll see your heads on spikes on the wall!"

From there, the tempo picked up again, the guitars grinding in a dual riff, the drums pounding, the piano keys being hammered. And Jake was now screaming the same lyrics over and over.

"Fuck the establishment! Fuck you all!"
"Fuck the establishment! Fuck you all!"
"Fuck the establishment! Fuck you all!"

He sang this out a grand total of twenty-eight times. On the final recital he stretched out "Fuck you all" for a good twenty seconds, strongly emphasizing each individual word as a crescendo of drums and cymbals and guitar solos ended the tune. As the last sound faded away, Crow reached over and pushed the stop button. He looked at his boss, who seemed a bit stunned by what he'd just heard.

"It's a very powerful song," Doolittle said.

"I agree," said Bailey."

"I mean, did you hear the anger and hatred that Jake managed to convey? Not just with the lyrics themselves, but with the way he sang it. He actually sounded like he was infuriated."

"Even the instrumental sections sounded angry," Crow said.

"Who do you suppose they're so pissed off at?" asked Bailey.

"I don't know," said Crow, "but I'd sure hate to be on the receiving end of that much hostility."

"No kidding," said Doolittle. "So anyway, what do we think about it?"

"It would sell like mad if we actually released it," said Crow, "but I'm inclined to go with my first impression and reject it."

"I reluctantly agree," said Doolittle. "I mean, he must've said the word 'fuck' a hundred times. That's way more than Blackie Lawless in *Fuck Like A Beast*. If we actually put that on an album the censorship freaks would murder us. They'd get a law passed that only eighteen and older could buy the album and that would kill sales to a good portion of *Intemperance*'s core audience."

"Not to mention opening the door to censorship of other albums," said Crow.

"I'm in agreement with you as well," said Bailey. "And even if we did get him to change the lyrics to 'screw the establishment' and 'screw you all', it would rob the tune of its raw power and make it sound phony."

"Well, that's too bad," said Doolittle. "Maybe in a more progressive age we can use it. Let's be sure to keep in on file."

"Right," said Crow. "Shall we listen to the next one?"

Doolittle picked up the title sheet and looked at it. "Hmm," he said. "Another one by Jake. '*So Many Choices*'." He nodded. "Sounds a little more reasonable."

"Jake said it's about the dilemmas we face in everyday life," Crow told him.

"Yeah," said Doolittle, "Jake is good at writing about that sort of thing. Let's hear it. If it's got the same power as that first tune, I'm sure we'll like it."

Crow pushed the play button. There was another hiss and then the song started with a standard three chord riff backed by acoustical sound from Jake and a solid piano melody.

"So far, so good," Doolittle said, liking the rhythm.

And then the singing began. Their mouths dropped as they heard it.

"I went down to the store today,"
"I needed some soup to eat."
"I like the kind in the red can."
"Easy to open, easy to heat."

"But there's a whole lot of red cans,"
"In your average grocery store aisle."
"From top to bottom, side to side."
"I knew I'd be here awhile."

"What the fuck?" said Doolittle.

Crow and Bailey both shook their heads, astounded.

There was a brief instrumental bit and then what was apparently the chorus of the tune kicked in.

"There's so many choices, too many to count."
"It's one of life's obstacles I must surmount."
"Should I go with chicken noodle, or perhaps bacon and bean?"
"Should I go with fulfillment, or the one that's healthy and lean?"

Doolittle reached over and hit the stop button. They all stared at each other for a moment.

"Am I insane," Doolittle asked, "or is he singing about picking out a can of soup in a grocery store?"

Crow licked his lips nervously. "That does sound like what he was talking about," he allowed.

"Maybe it's deep symbolism," Bailey suggested. "Jake writes like that sometimes. Maybe the soup is representing... oh... the decision of a country to go to war or not go to war."

"Symbolism in soup?" Doolittle asked. "Are you kidding?"

"That could be it," Bailey insisted. "Remember how Jake used to go on and on about all that shit happening in Beirut? Maybe the chicken noodle represents the decision to pull the marines out after the bombing. It's healthy and lean, right? But maybe the bean and bacon represents the idea of remaining committed to your ideals."

Doolittle stared at him. "I think you're a fucking idiot," he said. "The man is talking about buying soup in a grocery store. Soup!"

"Maybe we should listen to the rest of the song," Crow suggested.

Doolittle rolled his eyes and hit the play button. The song continued. The second verse was not about soup. It was about what kind of bread to buy—white or wheat, stone ground, or rye, you can't decide until you know which meat to apply.

"Fucking bread?" Doolittle growled. "What is the meaning of this, Crow? Is this a joke?"

"I don't know," Crow said. "This is the first I've heard of their submissions."

There was a bridge to the song dealing with cost versus nutrition, pleasing packaging versus quality, and the dilemma of picking out one's ingredients in order to assemble a complete meal. There was then a third verse. This one dealt with the issue of how to pick out the proper lunchmeat to go with the bread and the soup.

Doolittle hammered the stop button again. "This song is not about the fucking marines in Beirut! It's a song about going to the fucking grocery store! The grocery store! We can't put something like this on an album! It's not even good filler material!"

Crow was perplexed. "I'm not sure what the boys were thinking when they came up with that one," he admitted. "But I'll agree it's a definite reject."

"I still think it might be about Beirut," Bailey said.

They ignored him. "Let's see what the next one is about," said Doolittle, consulting the title sheet again. "Track three is called *The Switch*."

"That could be intriguing," Bailey said.

Crow hit the play button. The song started. They knew right away that something was terribly amiss with it. It opened with a piano solo, but it was quite far from Bill's normal style. It sounded almost like a beginner trying to follow along with a song sheet, and frequently failing to do so. Then the bass kicked in. It too sounded forced and out of practice, with frequent mistakes. The lead guitar started up and it sounded downright horrible even though it was only a two-chord riff. The backing guitar sounded even worse. The drumbeat was slow and uncoordinated with the bass beat and the overall rhythm.

"This is atrocious!" Doolittle cried. "What the hell are they doing?"

The vocals started. It wasn't Jake's voice that came out of the speaker however. It was a high-pitched, reedy voice, out of key and with a flat, monotone timbre.

"Is that Bill singing?" asked Crow.

"It sounds like him," Bailey agreed.

"He's horrible at it," Doolittle said. "Why in the hell is he singing lead?"

"I think I get it," said Crow, who was perusing the title sheet. "Look at this tiny notation they added at the bottom of the sheet."

Doolittle and Bailey both had to hold the sheet very close in order to read the miniscule printing in the bottom right corner. It was in Jake's neat handwriting and read: *In keeping with the spirit of the lyrics of* The Switch, *that song was performed with the band members swapping roles as follows. Jake Kingsley on bass guitar, Darren Appleman on lead guitar, Bill Archer on lead vocals and rhythm guitar, John Cooper on piano, and Matt Tisdale on drums.*

"They swapped instruments?" Doolittle yelled. "What the hell is that about?"

"Can they do that?" Bailey asked.

"Well... there's nothing in their contract that says they *can't*," Crow allowed.

"They can't play each other's instruments!" Doolittle said. "It sounds like shit. Bill can't sing, Coop doesn't know how to play the piano, Darren sure as shit can't play a lead guitar, and Matt has never held a set of drumsticks in his life! And while I'm sure that Jake could play the bass if he really wanted to, he doesn't seem to be making much of an effort here."

"No, he really doesn't," said Crow.

"Do you really think they thought this was a good idea?" asked Bailey. "Are they that taken with themselves?"

"No," said Doolittle. "They're not. They're fucking with us deliberately."

"What do you mean?" asked Bailey. "Why would they do that?"

"Their contract," said Crow.

"Right," said Doolittle. "They're firing a shot across our bow."

"Huh?" asked Bailey, not quite catching the analogy.

"They're giving us crappy tunes, knowing that we'll reject them," said Doolittle. "They're unhappy with their contract and they think that playing this little game with us is going to make us renegotiate with them."

"They can't do that!" Bailey exclaimed. "We've got them scheduled to go into the studio the first week in January."

"And they will go into the studio the first week in January," Doolittle said. "You can mark my fucking word on that."

"Let's listen to the rest of the tunes," Crow suggested. "Maybe we're jumping to conclusions here."

"I don't think so," Doolittle said, "but go ahead." He waved at the boombox.

Crow pushed the play button and then fast-forwarded to the next song. It was penned by Matt and called *The Discovery*. The instrumentation was half-assed and the lyrics seemed to be dealing with the subject of finding lint in one's belly button. The song after that was another piece by Matt called *Lighting Up*. It was lengthy dissertation with four verses and two bridges on the mechanics of lighting a cigarette. The next four songs were all in the same genre. There was one by Jake about fluffing his pillow before retiring for the night. There was one by Matt about moving his bowels the first thing in the morning. Another by Jake dealt with the age-old concept of picking one's nose and what to do with the booger once it was extracted. And then Matt touched upon the subject of proper condom disposal after a sexual encounter. For the last three songs, two of which were Matt's and one Jake's, they switched back to the genre of *Fuck The Establishment* by submitting angry, profanity-ridden tunes about getting fucked by corporations and contracts and rich white guys in suits. Though these tunes had decent instrumentation, the lyrics were quite outside the realm of what could reasonably be put on a mass-produced piece of vinyl that would be sold to teens.

"Yep," said Crow when the last of the songs—*White Suits*—was finally finished. "They're playing games with us all right."

"They're going to regret this," vowed Doolittle. He picked up his phone and got his secretary on the line.

"Yes, Mr. Doolittle?" she asked.

"I want to know where every member of *Intemperance* is right now," he told her.

"Yes, Mr. Doolittle," she replied.

It took her less than two minutes to check with the various resources they had to keep track of that information—namely the limo drivers and doormen of the buildings they lived in and, especially, the manservants. The phone buzzed and Doolittle picked it up.

"Where are they?" he asked.

"Darren and Coop are at Darren's house," she reported. "They've just shot up some heroin and are watching MTV."

"And the rest?"

"They're all at Jake's house, shooting pool," she said.

"Are they intoxicated?"

"According to Manny they've been doing nothing but drinking soda and smoking a lot of cigarettes. They're cold sober."

Doolittle nodded. "Yep," he said. "They know we're going to be calling them soon." He thanked his secretary and then hung up. He then consulted his Rolodex and looked up Jake's phone number. "Let's get this shit over with," he said. He picked up the phone and began to dial.

*****

"I swear to God, Nerdly," said Matt. "You are un-fucking-natural at this shit."

Bill smiled. He had just successfully sunk the eight ball into the corner pocket by making the cue ball bank three times off the rails, slide neatly between groups of Matt's solids still left on the table, passing by one with less than a quarter of an inch to spare, but never touching anything until contacting the eight with just enough force to push it into the pocket. "It's all a matter of simple geometry," Bill told him. "You see, the angles of a pool ball bouncing off the rail and imparting momentum to the other balls on the table are a perfect example of both geometric formula and Newtonian principles in action. When I make a shot, I simply check my angles, calculate the action and reaction of the spheres and adjust accordingly. It's a mathematic certainty that my shot will be true. The only real variable is my aim, which, as you've seen, is also quite true. You owe me five bucks. Pay up."

"I got your fuckin' Newtonian principles right here," Matt muttered. He pulled a five-dollar bill out of his wallet. He rubbed it across the back of his jeans as if wiping his ass with it and then handed it over.

"Thank you," Bill said, pocketing it. He turned to Jake. "Ready for another?"

"What the hell?" Jake asked, lighting another cigarette. "I still got twenty bucks on me. That's four more games I can lose."

While Matt, as loser, went about the process of gathering the balls and pushing them to the center of the table and Jake, the challenger, went about the process of racking them up so Bill could break for the new game, they talked of the tape they had just submitted, their voices low to avoid being overheard by the spy Manny.

"I think *The Switch* is going to be what clues them in," said Jake. "That was an absolutely horrible song."

"Except for the singing, right?" asked Bill. "I mean, my voice ain't that bad, is it?"

"You got a good back-up voice, Nerdly," said Matt, "but when you sing lead you sound like a fuckin' train full of cattle colliding with a chicken truck."

Bill looked hurt at this.

"Of course, you were *trying* to sound bad on the recording, weren't you?" asked Jake. "The way I was on the bass guitar?"

"Uh... yeah, of course," said Bill, who had thought he'd been singing his best.

"And you succeeded," said Matt. "But anyway, I think you're giving them more credit than they deserve, Jake. They'll probably get all the way to *Bedtime Ritual* before it starts to occur to them that something is wrong."

"You ever thought about what would happen if they actually like those songs?" asked Bill. "What if they really want us to record them?"

"Like them?" said Jake. "I seriously doubt that."

"Well, maybe not like them," said Bill. "But what if they think they're acceptable?"

"I wrote a song about taking a shit, Nerdly," Matt said. "And Jake wrote one about slinging a green booger against the wall. You don't really think they're gonna deem that recordable, do you?"

"I suppose you have a point there," Bill allowed.

All three of them were a bit giddy as they waited for the phone call from Crow or Doolittle that they knew had to be coming. The proverbial line had been crossed and their bosses were sure to be pissed off once they realized what was taking place. At the same time, they were absurdly proud of the considerable effort that had gone into composing and producing such horrible songs in the first place while keeping the master plan of what they were doing secret from Darren and Coop, who they knew were now nothing more than another set of spies for National Records.

The first part of the plan had been the easy part. It had been with considerable glee that Matt and Jake, the songwriters and melody composers of the group, had come up with the tunes in the first place. Once the plan had been agreed to after Jake and Bill's return from the visit with Pauline, they had each sat down and simply started strumming and playing, coming up with an average of two songs per night by simply picking a random subject out of the air and setting it to music. They rejected anything that could have remotely been classified as musical or deep or acceptable and had utilized rhythms and riffs that encompassed everything they hated about pop music.

The second part of the plan—keeping Darren and Coop from realizing what they were doing—had been a little more difficult but was aided by the fact that the two of them were so strung out on heroin that they paid little attention to things like musical quality and lyrical depth. It pained all three of them to see the drummer and the bassist in this state—after all, they were very close friends who had been through a lot with them—but they took advantage of this state to the full extent they were capable of.

"Is this a song about picking out soup, man?" Darren had asked when *So Many Choices* had first been introduced.

"Naw," Jake had told him. "It just *seems* like that. Actually, it's a deeply symbolic piece about the dilemmas of life as we know it, transcribed into a Zen-like representation of simplistic tasks."

"Ohhhh," Darren replied, nodding wisely. "That's fuckin' tight, Jake. Really tight. And not many tempo changes either."

"Yeah," said Coop. "You're really maturing musically, Jake. Seriously, man."

"Thanks," Jake had said. "Now let's go through it again."

It was through such discussions that they managed to convey to Crow and Doolittle that they were in fact working on new material at a furious pace and that they considered it to be "progressive" musically. As for the actual details of the songs or their composition—such as the fact that they were swapping roles for *The Switch*, or that *Fuck The Establishment* was full of angry profanity—they had simply asked Darren and Coop to keep that information to themselves for the time being.

"We want them to experience the full effect of our new style when they listen to the tape for the first time," Jake had explained. "If they hear about it in advance it'll spoil some of the surprise."

"I can dig that," Darren agreed.

"Yeah, me too," said Coop. "It's like a surprise party and shit."

Presumably, since none of the record company executives had called them during the rehearsal and recording process demanding to know what they thought they were doing, this plan had worked. They knew that Crow made a habit of calling both Coop and Darren at least once a day and that their respective manservants probably interrogated them every time they came home, but their answers about the musical quality and content must have been vague enough to keep from spilling the beans before the pot was boiling.

But the pot was surely boiling now and when Jake heard the phone ringing as Bill lined up to shoot his break shot, he knew it had finally boiled over.

The door opened and Manny stuck his head inside. He looked worried. "Jake," he said, "Mr. Doolittle is on the phone. He would like to speak with you."

"Mr. Doolittle?" Jake said, as if surprised. "Why whatever could he want?"

"Yeah," said Matt. "Crow told us we had the next two days off, didn't he?"

"He did," said Jake. He turned to Manny. "Take a message," he told him. "Tell him we're busy."

This served to fluster Manny. "Jake," he told him, "I think this might be important."

"You're not paid to think now, are you?" Jake responded. "Take a message."

His flustering grew worse, but he pulled his head back from the door and disappeared. He came back less than thirty seconds later. "Jake," he hissed, "Mr. Doolittle insists upon talking to you right now. He is not taking no for an answer."

"Oh, he's not, is he?" Jake said. "And what if I absolutely refused to come to that phone? Wouldn't he then be forced to take no for an answer?"

Manny actually started to tremble all over, his face turning a bright shade of red. "This is Mr. Doolittle we're talking about here," he said. "He is the second most powerful person at National Records. You can't say no to him, Jake. You can't!"

"I can't?"

"No," Manny said. "I must insist you come to the phone and speak to him immediately."

Jake looked up at the ceiling for a moment, as if lost in thought. Finally, he looked over at Manny again. "Well... if you insist," he said. He turned to Bill and Matt. "Shall we?"

"We shall," said Matt.

They followed Manny back into the living room, where the phone extension was sitting on one of the end tables. Jake sat on the couch. Matt and Bill sat next to him. Jake picked up the phone and put it to his ear.

"What's up, boss?" he said.

"Jake," Doolittle said, his voice low and controlled. "We just got done listening to that demo tape you submitted for us."

"Did you?" Jake asked. "We're rather proud of our efforts on that tape. What did you think?"

"I think you know what we think," he said. "It was horrible. Every one of those songs is non-recordable, but then that's just what you intended, isn't it?"

"Non-recordable?" Jake asked, making no effort to sound surprised. "Whatever do you mean?"

"Let's cut the shit, Jake. Your little plan is not going to work."

"Little plan? What plan might that be?"

"You submit horrible songs to us knowing that we'll reject them and try to pressure us into renegotiating your recording contract. It won't work. You're stuck with the contract you signed and you will be in that recording studio on schedule with songs that we can actually sell."

"We've given you all the songs we have, boss," Jake told him. "If you don't like the ones we submitted we can come up with some more, I suppose, but it'll take quite a while. Maybe three or four months."

"You will be in that recording studio on January 3," Doolittle said forcefully. "And you will have songs that are acceptable to us by that time. If you do not, you will be in breach of contract."

"I guess we'll have to be in breach of contract then, Mr. Doolittle," Jake told him, "because we've given you the songs we have, and we don't have anymore."

"Jake, this is not going to work," Doolittle told him. "I know what you're thinking. I've been dealing with punk musicians like you for twenty-five years and there is nothing that hasn't been tried. You're thinking that because we caved into you on some little things like what kind of guitar Matt plays or what songs you are going to do or what kind of moves you do on stage, that we'll cave on this too. But it won't work this time. This is too serious of an issue. You signed that contract and you are stuck with it. We will not renegotiate with you or change any of the terms of that contract and we will destroy your musical career if you're not in that studio on schedule."

"We never said we wouldn't be in the studio on schedule," Jake said. "We just submitted an entire tape of music that we are fully prepared to record."

"You submitted a tape full of crap," Doolittle told him.

"Crap is in the eye of the beholder," Jake said. "We have made a good faith effort to provide you with material for our next album. We have made this good faith effort by the deadline set in the contract. We are prepared to record these tunes we submitted and put our good name upon."

"Those tunes are not acceptable to us," Doolittle told him. "Your contract requires that we accept the tunes in order to avoid a breach of contract charge."

"Well I guess you'll just have to go ahead and charge us with that then," Jake told him. "We made our good faith effort and you rejected it. There is no way we could possibly come up with anything else before the deadline."

"Jake, this is not going to work!" Doolittle yelled, losing his cool for the first time. "We are not going to cave on this! If we renegotiated contracts every time some punk-ass band tried a stunt like this, we'd be bankrupt in no time. You may think we'll decide to settle with you just so we can keep making money off of you, but we won't. We'll lose millions by ruining your ass just to avoid setting a precedent that this sort of behavior is effective."

This speech actually got to Jake a little—he had not considered that they might go to the wall on this in order to avoid setting a precedent—but he didn't let Doolittle know that. He stood firm. "You do what you need to do, boss," he told him, "but we've made our good faith effort, we've submitted the tape to you, and there is no way we'll be coming up with anything else for at least three months. And even if we do come up with some new material, it will probably sound a lot like the material you already have. We kind of like this new style of ours, you know what I mean?"

"You're making a big mistake, Jake," Doolittle warned. "The biggest."

Jake said nothing in reply. He simply hung up the phone.

*****

Jake, Matt, and Bill all received multiple phone calls over the next two days. They received them from Doolittle, from Crow, from Shaver, even from William Casting, CEO of National Records—the big guy himself. These phone calls were all in the same vein, demands to submit recordable music by the deadline, threats of what would happen if they didn't, promises that National would not cave on this issue no matter what, that they would sacrifice the millions they stood to make even if they did renegotiate the *Intemperance* contract just to avoid setting a precedent other bands might try to take advantage of in the future. In addition to the phone calls, they began to get the same speeches from

Darren and Coop, both of whom had been told by Doolittle and Crow that they had been used to hatch an insidious plot against the record company that was providing them with food, shelter, and, most importantly, heroin.

"Dudes, that was like totally uncool of you to make us submit that crappy music," said Coop to Jake and Matt.

"Yeah, dudes," agreed Darren. "We're not like pawns on a chessboard and shit. I thought we were friends!"

Through all this Bill, Jake, and Matt stood firm in their convictions and refused to even acknowledge that there *was* a plot in progress. They made no demands of National Records and made no admissions of deliberately sabotaging their music to Darren or Coop. To do so would have destroyed the legal basis of their "good faith" argument. The demands, when they came, would have to come from a mouth other than theirs and even then, would have to be circumspect.

National, however, certainly had no problems making demands. On Thursday afternoon Manny once again handed the phone to Jake.

"Who is it this time?" Jake asked. "Doolittle, Crow, Shaver, or Casting?"

"It's Mr. Casting," Manny whispered, obviously in awe of having talked to the head of one of the largest record companies in the world.

Jake nodded and took the phone. He lit a cigarette and took a few puffs and then finally put it to his ear. "Wassup, Cassie?" Jake asked him.

"That's Mr. Casting to you, Kingsley," Casting said icily. "What are you doing at home?"

"Well," said Jake, "right now I'm enjoying a cigarette. After that I'm going to go into my bedroom and check out the new issue of *Hustler* and probably jack off. What are you doing?"

"Why aren't you in the warehouse producing new music for us?" Casting asked.

"Why would we do that?" Jake asked. "We submitted new material to you, you rejected it, and you don't want to wait three or four months for us to come up with something else. There's no reason for us to be in the warehouse."

"Oh, but there is," Casting said. "I'm told you had six songs in progress before you decided to pull this little stunt of yours."

"We're not pulling any stunts," Jake replied, "but your spies do have their facts correct about the six songs. We were working on them, but we decided they sucked ass and abandoned them."

"I'm told by two of your bandmates that they didn't 'suck ass', as you put it. In fact, I'm told they were quite good."

"As I said before, sucking ass is in the eye of the beholder. Darren and Coop are so strung out on that heroin you assholes are pushing off on them that they wouldn't know a good song if it reached out and took their syringes away from them."

"Nevertheless," Casting said, "I want you in that warehouse rehearsing those six tunes. We're going to record them."

"Oh, we are, are we?" Jake asked.

"Yes," Casting said. "Since you're refusing to submit acceptable material to us for your next album, we're going to have you record all of the rejects you previously submitted—with the exception of that anti-bible piece—and those six songs. That will give us ten for the album."

"Sorry," Jake said. "We rejected those six songs. We're not going to do them."

"I'm ordering you to do them," Casting said. "You have material available to you and we have the right to order you to record it."

"That would be true if we had ever recorded those six songs and submitted them to you and your boys on an audio cassette. We did not do that, however, so those songs do not yet belong to you."

"You rehearsed them in *our* warehouse," Casting said. "We know you composed them and that they're viable. That makes them our property."

"Really?" asked Jake. "Do you have a lyric sheet on them?"

"No," said Casting. "But that doesn't matter."

"Do you have a written composition of the basic melody?"

"No, but that doesn't matter either."

"Okay then," Jake said. "Here's the most important question. Have we ever recorded those tunes in any form?"

"You know you haven't."

"Then, according to my legal source—you might want to check with yours to confirm this—those tunes do not belong to you, they still belong to us, the songwriters. They only become your property when we actually record them and submit them to you or one of your representatives. We have not done that, so we still retain the rights to those songs. And as the songwriters of un-submitted pieces, we still retain the absolute right to do with our compositions as we please. And what we please is to not record them or to offer them to any entity. We've rejected them."

"Jake, I'm ordering you to record those songs!" Casting yelled.

"And I'm ordering you to rip your cock off and shove it up your ass," Jake replied. He then shook his head. "Jesus, I've been hanging out with Matt too much."

His conciliatory statement did not mollify Casting much. He was infuriated. "All right," he said, sounding like he was speaking through gritted teeth. "You want to play hardball? We'll play hardball. We're done screwing around with you. As of this moment, your weekly allowance is cut off, your limousine service is cut off, your nightclub privileges are cut off, everything is cut off! Do you hear me?"

"I hear you," Jake said mildly. He hung up the phone.

*****

When Casting said "everything", he literally meant everything. The phone rang again less than a minute after Jake hung up and Manny answered the kitchen extension, but he did not tell Jake to pick up. Instead, about ten minutes later, Jake heard him shuffling around, making lots of noise. He went into the kitchen and found him taking food out of the refrigerator and putting it in boxes.

"What you doing, Manny?" Jake asked him.

Manny was in quite the state. "I'm taking all of the food out of the house," he responded.

"Why would you do something like that?" Jake asked.

"Mr. Casting ordered me to," he said. "He apparently means to starve you into submission." He shook his head fretfully. "This is just such a mess. I'm sorry, Jake. Why don't you just do what they want?"

"For the same reason you don't go out and score yourself some pussy," Jake told him.

"Huh?" Manny asked.

"Because I'm just not into it," Jake clarified. "You know what I mean?"

Manny didn't know what he meant. He picked up a jar of mayonnaise and put it in the box.

"Oh, and Manny," Jake said.

"Yes?"

"Put all that shit back right now."

Manny shook his head. "Jake, I have to take everything out of here. Mr. Casting ordered me to. All the food, all the liquor, all the cigarettes, all the stuff in the safe—the drugs and that envelope full of money you have in there."

Jake didn't ask how Manny knew what was in the safe. He had the combination to it and it was undoubtedly part of his daily duties to snoop through it and report on its contents. Knowing that this was coming (although not suspecting that National would actually try to remove the food from the building) Jake had saved most of his allowance over the past few weeks. The envelope that Manny was referring to contained almost three thousand dollars in cash.

"You're taking none of that," Jake told him. "None, do you hear me? Especially not the contents of the safe."

"Jake, I've been ordered to," Manny insisted. "Everything in this condo came from National and now they want it back."

"Too bad," Jake said. "They can't have it."

"I'm taking it, Jake," Manny said nervously. "National is my boss, not you."

"But I'm the one who will throw your ass off the fucking balcony if you put so much as one more condiment container in that box."

"Jake," Manny said, his nervousness increasing but his determination steadfast, "I'll call the cops if I have to."

Jake smiled. He was not a legal expert by any means but, having grown up in a household headed by an ACLU lawyer, he did possess a bit more than the layman's knowledge of the laws regarding personal privacy, search and seizure, and landlord/tenant disputes. "Why don't you do that, Manny? Let's get them over here so we can hash this thing out in a proper manner."

Manny looked at him as if this were some kind of a trick. "I will, Jake," he said. "I'm not kidding. I have my orders and I intend to follow them."

"And I intend to solidly kick your ass and possibly throw you off the balcony if you try to remove one more thing from this condo. So, instead of resorting to physical violence, how about we get a legal opinion? Call them."

Manny sighed. "All right," he said. "I guess you're forcing me. But don't say I didn't warn you."

"I would never say that, Manny."

Manny walked across the kitchen and picked up the phone extension. While he was dialing, Jake went quickly into the office and opened the safe. He left the envelope full of money where it was but took out the bags of marijuana, the cocaine kit, and all of the pill bottles. He carried this into his bedroom and put it in a shoebox in his closet. When he returned to the kitchen Manny was still on the phone, his conversation indicating he had just made contact with the police dispatcher. Jake suspected he had not called the police outright but had called Casting first to clear it with him.

"They on their way?" Jake asked, lighting a cigarette.

"Yes," he replied. "I'm sorry it had to come to this, Jake. It would be so much easier if you would just do what they told you."

"Uh huh," Jake replied. He went back in the living room and sat down to wait.

It took less than fifteen minutes before there was a knock on the door. Manny answered it and two uniformed LAPD officers came in, their mannerisms and expressions telling Jake they were somewhat less than thrilled to be here.

"What seems to be the problem?" asked the lead cop, whose name was Officer Yamata.

Manny told his side of the story and then Jake told his. The cops listened carefully and then asked a few questions about who the condo was actually leased to. Jake produced the paperwork from his desk and showed it to them.

"So, it's leased by National Records and they pay the rent," Yamata said after skimming the documents, "but Mr. Kingsley here is listed as the tenant in occupancy of the residence."

"Yep," said Jake.

"And nowhere in here does it mention your name," Yamata said, looking over at Manny.

"That's true," Manny said, "but I'm an employee of National Records and I'm authorized by them to oversee everything that takes place in this condo. In effect, I'm Jake's immediate supervisor."

"It doesn't say anything about that in the lease," Yamata said. "You need to leave his stuff alone. You can't remove anything from this residence except for the contents of your own bedroom."

"But everything in here is National Records property!" Manny insisted.

"But it's in Mr. Kingsley's residence," Yamata returned. "If National Records wants anything in here back, they'll have to go to court and get a judge to say they can have it back."

"Hey," said Jake, as something occurred to him. "Since it's my residence and all, can I kick his ass out of here? He is here against my will after all."

Yamata shook his head. "In that case the landlord/tenant laws work in his favor. He has established residency here. If you want to kick him out, you'll have to go through the eviction process. That can take as much as six months."

"Oh well," Jake said. "It was a thought. On that same note, those same laws mean that National can't just kick *me* out of here either? If they want me out they'll have to go through the same eviction process?"

"That's correct," said Yamata's partner, a cute bleach blonde female cop named Rogan.

"Well, that gives me some leeway," Jake said thoughtfully.

"All right," said Manny, "I was really hoping it wouldn't come to this, but I'm left with no choice."

"What are you talking about?" Yamata asked.

Manny took a deep breath. "Mr. Kingsley has drugs in this condo," he said. "In the safe. He has cocaine, marijuana, illegally acquired prescription drugs, and a large amount of cash."

Neither Yamata nor Rogan reacted strongly to this information. Neither did Jake, for that matter.

"Is that true, Mr. Kingsley?" Yamata asked.

"There is a couple thousand in cash in there," Jake said, "but it's not drug money. I'm a rich rock star, remember?"

"I'm telling you, there are drugs in there," Manny said. "I'll open the safe for you." He started to walk in that direction.

"Mr. Kingsley," Rogan said. "Do you *want* him to open your safe? He really doesn't have the right to access it under this lease."

"Is that so?" Jake asked.

"That's so," she said.

"If I say no and he tries it anyway, will you shoot him?"

Rogan smiled. "If necessary," she said.

"Then no, I don't want him to open the safe."

The two cops went after Manny and caught him just as he was starting to spin the dial.

"What the hell are you doing?" Manny asked. "He has drugs in here! I'm trying to show them to you."

"That is Mr. Kingsley's safe," Yamata said. "He has told us he doesn't want you opening it."

"But there are drugs in there!" Manny yelled. "Don't you care about that?"

"Not really," Rogan said. "And even if we did, you are not authorized to open that safe. If you did, and there were drugs in there, we wouldn't be able to use that as evidence against Mr. Kingsley because he didn't authorize you to open the safe for us. It would be an illegal search and seizure."

"That's insane!" Manny said.

"That's the American justice system," Rogan said.

"Why does he have access to your safe?" Yamata asked Jake.

"National Records sticking their nose in where it doesn't belong," Jake said. "They provided the safe for me and he's here to spy on me. You know how it is."

"Why don't you just change the combination so he doesn't know it?" Yamata asked.

"Can I do that?"

"Well, I'm not sure if you're talking legally or physically," said Yamata, "but the answer to both questions is yes. It's your safe in your residence. You can do whatever you want with it."

"Do you guys know how to do it?" Jake asked.

They looked at each other and shrugged. "I'm sure we could figure it out," Rogan said. "You'd have to open it for us first though so we could see the mechanism."

"Right," said Yamata. "And if you did have anything illegal in there and we saw it after you voluntarily opened it for us... well... then we'd be forced to act on that."

"I see," Jake said as if contemplating. He looked over at Manny. "Manny, go ahead and open that thing up."

Manny had already figured out that Jake had moved anything incriminating. "Open it yourself," he said, stepping away.

Jake shrugged and opened the safe. As soon as it swung open and Manny saw that the drugs were indeed gone, he said, "The drugs are probably in his room somewhere now."

"Very nice," said Yamata as he stepped up to look at the mechanism of the safe.

"If you looked, I'm sure you'd find them," Manny hissed.

"We have no probable cause to search through Mr. Kingsley's bedroom," Rogan said. "The only way we could look in there is if Mr. Kingsley granted us voluntary consent for a search."

"Do you guys really want to search my room?" Jake asked.

"Not really," said Rogan.

"Okay then. I guess I won't give you consent then."

Manny stormed towards the door. Before he made it there, Rogan stopped him. "Oh, by the way," she said. "If you were to go into Mr. Kingsley's bedroom yourself and come out with drugs in your hand, not only would you be subject to a trespassing charge, but we would probably conclude that any drugs found were actually yours and that you were trying to frame him." She smiled. "Keep that in mind."

Manny's neck was now bright red. He walked out of the office and disappeared.

"This is what being a rock star is like, huh?" asked Rogan, her blue eyes shining at Jake.

"Not quite what you expected, huh?" he asked her.

"Not at all," she said. "And by the way..." She blushed a little. "I love your music."

"Thank you," he said.

It took them less than five minutes to figure out how to change the combination on the safe. Jake learned the procedure and then followed it, changing it to something Manny would never guess.

"Anything else we can help you with?" Rogan asked when they were done.

"Yeah," Jake said, looking at her. "You ever date a musician?"

She shook her head. "I never have."

"I never dated a cop either. Maybe we should do a couple of firsts?"

She was blushing quite strongly now, her confident demeanor driven underground. "I wouldn't be opposed to that," she said.

Before she left she handed him a business card with her name and current assignment printed on it. Below that, in a neat, feminine hand, she printed her home telephone number.

*****

Jake managed to call both Matt and Bill in time to prevent their respective manservants from removing all property from their condos. In the case of Bill, another call to the police was required to physically enforce the prevention. In the case of Matt, a threat to perform an emergency tracheotomy on the manservant with a butter knife and then fornicate with the resulting hole was enough. Jake also called Coop but Coop wasn't home, he was at Darren's. When Jake called Darren's, he got Cedric, who was undoubtedly already in the process of removing everything. Cedric informed him that both Darren and Coop were "indisposed" at the moment, which meant they were flying high on their latest shots of heroin. No matter how much Jake threatened and yelled, Cedric refused to put either of them on the phone.

"It is against the law for you to remove anything from their condo, Cedric," Jake warned. "You better leave their shit alone."

"I'll keep that in mind, Mr. Kingsley," Cedric replied in his cultured, pompous tone. He then hung up. And, of course, he removed everything he had been told to remove—all the groceries, all the booze, and all the drugs, up to and including their beloved China White.

It was only twelve hours later when Jake received the first phone call. It was from Darren and he was angry—murderously angry—that Jake's actions had resulted in the loss of "all my shit". He threatened to come over and kick Jake's ass if he didn't agree to settle this dispute with the record company immediately and convince Bill and Matt to do the same.

"We're not having a dispute with the record company, Darren," Jake told him, keeping with the plan of admitting nothing. "They didn't like our tunes and now they're playing games with us."

There were a few more threats and then Darren hung up. A few minutes later, Coop called threatening to kick Jake's ass as well.

Twelve hours after that, neither one of them were in any kind of shape to kick anyone's ass. For the next three days both of them went through the hell of heroin withdrawal. Their bodies ached and trembled and shook and sweated. They suffered explosive diarrhea. They vomited up everything they attempted to put in their stomachs, which wasn't much since they had no appetites whatsoever, nor did they have much food available in their condos. On the fourth day, these physical symptoms began to subside a bit but the mental symptoms—depression, suicidal thoughts, self-pity, anger, shame— were only just beginning. The phone calls began again, both of them calling Jake, Matt, and Bill in turn. They would beg pitifully for their fellow band members to end this thing and then angrily threaten when they were told there was nothing to end. The three core members did what they could. They used some of their squirreled away money to buy basic groceries for Darren and Coop so at least they wouldn't starve to death. They instructed them to call the cops if either of their manservants attempted to remove or sabotage these groceries. But as for getting their heroin and their pot and their booze and their limousines back, they simply told them to hang in there until National was done having their little fit. This did not make Darren or Coop feel better.

Christmas day came. The entire band spent it together at Jake's condo. They ate a roast turkey dinner that Jake had bought and prepared himself (Manny was forbidden by the record company to lift a finger to do any cleaning or cooking or other chores—he spent the majority of each day in his room). They sipped from glasses of white wine and drank liquor from the still reasonably stocked bar. Coop and Darren didn't eat much and both were more than a little whiny but they kept to their manners for the most part. It wasn't the greatest Christmas Jake had ever spent, but it wasn't the worst either.

The next day was a Wednesday and throughout the Los Angeles region, business as usual resumed. At 9:00 AM sharp, there was a knock on Jake's door. This was unusual in and of itself since the doormen downstairs were supposed to be controlling access to the residential floors and calling him when unexpected visitors showed up. Jake was unshaven, slightly hung over, and wearing a pair of tattered sweat pants and no shirt. His long hair was ragged and unkempt. He walked across the living room and opened the door, finding a neatly dressed man of about thirty standing outside.

"Can I help you?" Jake asked him.

"Are you Jake Kingsley?" the man asked.

"I am."

The man dropped an envelope at his feet. "You've been served, my friend. Have a nice day."

"But..." Jake started, but the man had already turned and walked away.

Jake reached down and picked up the envelope. He opened it and found an official paper notifying him that he had been subpoenaed to appear before the Honorable Joseph Cranford on January 3, 1985 in regards to a breach of contract charge filed by National Records Corporation.

He called each of the other band members, finding that they had all been served as well, pretty much at exactly the same instant he had. He then placed a phone call to an office building in Heritage and asked to speak to Pauline Kingsley. He was put on hold and forced to listen to the Muzak version of Elton John's *Daniel* for the next three minutes. Finally, his sister came on the line and he explained what had just happened. She had him read the entire subpoena to her.

"Just what I thought they would do," she said. "They're going to try to get this judge to declare you in breach of contract. If this effort is successful, the eviction proceedings will start immediately."

"This is where the good faith effort saves our asses, right?" Jake asked.

"Right," she said. "I'm going to file a motion for a preliminary injunction against enforcement of the contract. It will probably be granted if this judge deems the music you submitted as a good faith effort. If he feels that you were deliberately making sub-standard music, however, then good faith goes out the window."

"And how likely is that?"

She sighed into her phone. "Of all the potential judges to hear this case, Joseph Cranford is the worst."

"He is?"

"Yes," she said. "He's only forty-five. The youngest superior court judge in the Los Angeles area. If there's anyone who can even remotely appreciate rock music, he's the one. This is kind of worrisome."

"How worrisome?"

She didn't answer this question. "It's also kind of suspicious," she said instead.

"What do you mean?"

"Of all the superior court judges in the Los Angeles district, how did he, the only one I was truly worried about, just happen to get picked for this? This seems like more than a coincidence."

"You think National had some pull in what judge was picked?" Jake asked. "I thought that was impossible."

"Nothing's impossible when you have enough money," Pauline told him. "This is America after all. Look, let me dig into this thing a little. I'll get back to you as soon as I can."

"How worried should we be about this?" Jake wanted to know.

Silence, stretching out for almost ten seconds. Finally, "I'll get back to you, Jake."

*****

It was the following Monday before she got back to him, December 31, the last business day of 1984. She called at 10:30 in the morning and Jake knew from the tone of her voice in her initial greeting that she did not have good news to share.

"What's wrong?" he asked her.

"Judge Cranford is wrong," she told him. "It's even worse than I thought."

"What do you mean?"

"I've had our investigations department looking into Cranford for me over the last few days."

"You were investigating a superior court judge?" he asked. "Jesus, Pauline. Can't you get into trouble for that?"

"We do it all the time," she said. "That's what our investigations department is for. They research judges and jury members and opposing lawyers and opposing clients. There's nothing illegal about it. Well, not usually anyway. Most of what they gather is all public record stuff. All law firms do it."

"Okay," he said, feeling a little better—a little—now that he knew she hadn't been wiretapping or bugging a judge. "What did you find out?"

"Well, I think I solved the mystery of how he just happened to be picked for this particular case. He volunteered for it."

"Volunteered? Can he do that?"

"Not in general," she said. "But he offered to take it from Judge Stinson, who had been assigned to it originally. No explanation was given or asked for."

"Okay," said Jake. "What does that mean?"

"It didn't mean anything until our guys dug a little deeper. But when they did, they found out that Joseph Cranford went to law school with a man named Eric Frowley."

That name sounded familiar to Jake, though he couldn't quite place it at first. Pauline quickly gave him the clue that brought it home, however.

"Eric Frowley is lead counsel for National Records," she said.

"Holy shit," Jake said, suddenly remembering. He was one of the lawyers they'd met with during their last major dispute—the one over choreography of the concerts. It was upon his desk that Matt had rolled a joint and Jake had critiqued its engineering.

"They were fraternity brothers in Phi Delta Phi," Pauline told him. "They used to do circle jerks and date-rape freshmen girls together. And now he's the judge in charge of your case."

"Isn't that illegal?" Jake asked. "I mean, shouldn't he remove himself from the case because he knows this lawyer?"

"No," Pauline said. "A judge does not have to recuse himself merely because he's an acquaintance of one of the lawyers in the case. He only has to do that if he has some sort of business interest in the case or if there is some evidence of impartiality. And in this case, we don't even have any evidence that these two are still acquaintances. For all we know, they haven't talked to each other since law school."

"But doesn't the fact that he personally asked to take this case mean anything?" Jake asked.

"Well, it does to you and me," she said. "Common sense says that its quite obvious they know each other and that this is a set-up, but as far as legalities go, no, it doesn't mean anything."

"Then what do we do?"

A long pause. Finally, "I don't know."

This was perhaps the most distressing thing Jake had ever heard her say. "You don't know?"

"Look," she said, "I'll fly down and I'll be there with you when it's time to go to court. I'll do my best and my best is pretty damn good, but..."

"But?"

"But I think that maybe they outmaneuvered us," she said. "I'm sorry."

Jake sighed. "Yeah. Me too."

*****

Jake was not really in the mood for a New Year's Eve party that night but nevertheless he put on his partying clothes at 8:30 PM, put $400 of his rapidly dwindling supply of cash in his wallet, and went down to the parking garage to retrieve his Corvette. He had promised Kelly Rogan—the LAPD officer who had come to his house the night National had cut them off—that he would take her to the annual Flamingo Club New Year's Gala and he was a man who prided himself on keeping his promises.

He already knew that the relationship with Kelly wasn't working and wasn't working on many different levels—political, personal, and even sexual. She, like most cops, was a staunch, ultra-conservative right-winger and he was a screaming liberal left-wing musician. He did illegal drugs and she arrested people who did illegal drugs. He believed that all private citizens should be banned from owning firearms and she believed that every law-abiding citizen should be allowed to own their own assault weapon if they wished. He believed that religious teachings had no place in public schools and she believed that the worst mistake this country had ever made was removing prayer from public schools. He believed the government stuck their long nose far too far into the business of its citizens and she believed they didn't stick it in nearly far enough. Their conversations were usually nothing more than arguments over political issues politely disguised as friendly debates. Their second date, in fact, had consisted mostly of a lengthy discussion about his arrest in New York City on possession of cocaine charges.

"I'm glad you got off, you know, because I like you," she told him as they'd sipped drinks at a Flamingo Club table, "but that technicality you got off on is a perfect example of what's wrong with our system."

"Technicality?" Jake asked, raising his eyebrows. "They completely fabricated their probable cause writ. They had no legal reason to raid our hotel room so they made up a bunch of crap to get a judge to allow them to."

"Yes," she agreed. "They did step a bit over the line, but you did have eight grams of cocaine in your possession, didn't you?"

"That's not the point," he said. "They had no reason to enter our private area and look for it. They invaded our privacy."

"But you were doing something wrong and they caught you at it. Just because their reasons for gaining entry to your hotel room were a little questionable doesn't mean that the evidence of your wrongdoing should be thrown out."

"Actually, it *does* mean that," said Jake. "I have a reasonable expectation of privacy in my hotel room. How was what we were doing in there hurting anyone?"

"You were using drugs," she said. "That hurts everyone."

This was typical of their conversations. Jake never accused her of being wrong, and she never accused him of being wrong, but they were simply at different ends of the spectrum, unable to even hope to see eye to eye on most issues.

This concern in and of itself would not have been sufficient to make Jake begin to despise her as much as he was starting to despise her if that had been the only problem. He did, after all, enjoy a good debate of his political views with those who could debate intelligently and well, as Kelly sometimes could. The true reason he viewed his entire involvement with her as a big mistake was her attitude towards him. She was not dating him because he was Jake Kingsley, the man, someone she liked to intelligently debate with. She was dating him because he was Jake Kingsley, the famous musician, and she wanted to be with him on that basis alone, regardless of his differing opinions. She knew as well as he by their second date that they were incompatible as a couple but still she continued to pursue him because she wanted to be seen with him, to have the newspapers and the tabloids print stories about them, because she thought he was a rich and famous person and she wanted to be associated with him despite the perceived character flaws she felt he had. She was, in fact, exactly the sort of woman he had always tried to stay away from.

She made little effort to conceal what she was all about. She had no desire to spend time with him alone, on picnics, at the movies, or taking walks on the beach. Such things were not public enough for her. What she wanted was to be taken to the Flamingo Club or one of the other clubs frequented by the stars. She wanted exposure. She wanted to be seen in the company of Jake Kingsley and photographed in the company of Jake Kingsley and to be catered to by Jake Kingsley.

"How come nobody is taking pictures of us?" she'd asked less than thirty minutes into their first date, as they'd taken to the dance floor of The Flamingo for the first time.

"They're not all that interested in me anymore," Jake explained with a shrug. "Ever since Mindy Snow and I broke up, the photographers have hardly given me a second look."

"That's awful," she said, genuinely appalled.

"Not really," Jake answered honestly. "I kind of prefer the privacy."

This was a concept Kelly had been completely unable to grasp. Why wouldn't one want one's picture constantly appearing on nationally syndicated publications?

She fucked him after that first date, mostly because she seemed to think she was obligated to. And an obligation was exactly how she'd treated it. They went back to Jake's place after the Flamingo closed, she kissed him for a few minutes, and then mechanically removed her clothing and put herself upon his bed. Jake considered himself to be a much better than average lover. He had had lots of practice at the art during his lifetime and had always made the pleasure of his partner (or partners) his main consideration. But Kelly simply lay in place during the entire event, groaning mechanically when it seemed expected of her, and moving in a manner that seemed designed to get things over with as quickly as possible. He had licked and sucked at her vagina for the better part of twenty minutes but had been unable to draw anything other than a few obviously fake orgasms from her. He had pounded into her body using his best strokes, utilizing every bit of knowledge he'd gained and all this managed was a few more faked orgasms. Finally, when it seemed like she was actually going to go to sleep from boredom, he'd given up and let himself go. Very rare was the sexual episode where he felt he would have had a better time simply masturbating while looking at her body, but this was one of those times.

She fucked him after every other date they shared in pretty much the same manner, although it seemed her impatience with the act grew with each encounter. During their last encounter—after rutting against her for better than twenty minutes and enduring six fake orgasms—he'd simply given up. He stopped mid-thrust, pulled out of her, ripped off his condom and thrown it across the room, and started jacking off over her heaving breasts.

"What the fuck are you doing?" she yelled, disgusted.

He didn't answer, he simply sprayed his semen all over her, an act that infuriated her and made her rush to the shower to cleanse herself. She'd stormed out without saying a word and Jake had thought he'd seen the last of her but she'd called him later that evening, acting as if nothing had happened, and had asked if they were still going to the Flamingo for the New Year's Eve party. He said he would. After all, he'd promised.

He pulled his Corvette into a visitor spot in front of her West Hollywood complex now, carefully locking up and making his way to her upstairs apartment. She answered the door to his knock and greeted him politely, giving him a brief, emotionless kiss on the lips and inviting him inside.

"You look very nice tonight," he told her. And she did. She was wearing a strapless royal blue dress that clung to her curvy body in a most appetizing way and showed off a little more cleavage than was exactly fashionable.

"Thanks," she said, flashing a phony smile. "Do you think there will be photographers there tonight? I mean, with it being New Year's Eve and all?"

"Probably," he said, and there would. Of course, they probably wouldn't be all that interested in Jake Kingsley or the cute cop he was with. Jake was below the radar at the moment and would continue to be as such until something newsworthy happened with him.

"I certainly hope so," she huffed. "I've told all my friends I'm going to be there tonight with you so there'd better be some pictures of it in the entertainment magazines next week."

"Anything is possible," he said, suppressing a sigh, wishing that the evening was already over.

"Be sure to give me a big kiss at the stroke of midnight," she said. "Maybe they'll take a picture of that."

"Maybe they will."

She went to the television set and picked up her matching royal blue purse. As she hefted it onto her shoulder something seemed to occur to her. "Oh yeah," she said, opening it. "I got that information you asked me for. The stuff on that Hadley bitch."

Jake's interest perked up immediately. "You do?"

That "Hadley bitch" she was referring to was Angelina Hadley, or, Angie, as he had known her. Though he had not spoken to her or heard from her in any way since that day he'd climbed on the bus for the *Descent Into Nothing* tour, she had never quite left his mind. She had been someone he had loved, someone he had enjoyed being with, someone he had abandoned without explanation, and he had always felt guilty about that, had never been able to put her memory to rest. When he started dating Kelly it had occurred to him that she was a potentially valuable source of information about Angie's current whereabouts. Kelly was, after all, a Los Angeles police officer and had access to computerized information that mere citizens—even famous ones—could never hope to see. So, on their third date, during one of the more sedate portions of the evening (which had been right after they'd finished fucking) Jake had asked Kelly if she could look Angie up in that system and learn what there was to learn about her.

"Who is she?" Kelly asked, as she lay naked on his bed, smoking a cigarette and sipping from a bottle of beer.

"Just someone I used to hang out with," he replied. "I haven't seen her in a while and I'm just curious what's she's doing."

Kelly shrugged. "Sure. Why not? What's her name, date of birth, and last known address?"

He'd given it to her and had mostly forgotten the request until now, figuring that Kelly had just been jerking him off when she'd said she would do it. But apparently, she had not been.

"Yeah," Kelly said. "She's a real skank-o-rama, ain't she? You didn't used to fuck her or anything, did you?"

"Skank-o-rama?" Jake asked. "What does that mean?"

"It means she's a whore," Kelly said. "And a druggie too. She's been busted three times for prostitution and twice for possession of rock cocaine, all in the last six months."

Jake swallowed, feeling almost sick to his stomach. "Are you sure you have the right Angelina Hadley?" he asked slowly.

"It's her all right," she said. "Brown and brown, one-twenty, DOB of whatever it was you gave me, previous address that matches what you gave me. They had that restaurant you were telling me about listed in the system but she ain't working there anymore, hasn't in more than a year. She was living in some shithole motel up until about a month ago but now she's living in the county jail. Her last bust bought her a hundred and twenty days in the slam."

Jake felt like someone had punched him in the stomach. He was worried for a moment that he might actually vomit. "My god," he whispered.

"What's the big deal?" Kelly asked. "I mean, you knew she was a skank, right?"

Jake shook his head, numb, still trying to process this.

"So, are we going, or what?" Kelly said. "I want to get there early enough to watch everyone else come in."

"No," Jake said. "I need to go home."

Kelly looked at him like he was joking. "Are you serious?"

"I'm serious," he said. "Goodbye, Kelly."

He walked out the door and went back to his car, barely hearing her screams and curses from behind him.

CHAPTER 16

PAULINE

January 2, 1985
Heritage, California

It was well past 9:00 PM and Pauline was sitting behind her desk on the sixteenth floor of the Markley Building. The ultra-modern, thirty-two story building was the tallest, most exclusive high rise in Heritage. Situated directly adjacent to the Sacramento River, its westward facing offices featured spectacular views of the waterfront. Pauline didn't have one of these offices. In fact, she had no view at all. Her office featured no windows and was less than two hundred square feet, but at least she *had* an office now. Eight months ago, after four years of ninety-hour weeks, the firm had rewarded her dedication by replacing her cubicle with four stationary walls and a door. She had her own paralegal now too, and a secretary she only had to share with three other lawyers.

She was tired and out of sorts. She was also depressed because she knew there was at least two more hours of work to do on the contract draft she was assigned before her boss would be mollified enough to not hold it against her that she was taking tomorrow off. That meant she would be in bed by midnight at the earliest and would have to get up at 5:30 in order to make her 7:20 flight to Los Angeles where she would represent her brother and his band before Judge Cranford at one o'clock.

And more than likely lose, a part of her brain insisted upon reminding her. *You're busting your ass for nothing.*

She sighed, taking a sip out of her eleventh cup of coffee of the day. That was too depressing of a thought to contemplate very deeply but she could hardly help herself. She had no experience with music contracts and would be going up against seasoned music industry lawyers defending the very livelihood of their clients. And if that wasn't bad enough, the judge who would be ruling in the matter was at best a crony of the lead counsel for the other side, at worst, owned lock, stock, and barrel by the other side.

The more she allowed this to command her attention, the less of the work she was actually being paid for was getting done and the longer she would have until bedtime which translated into less sleep before she would be facing her foes. But she was nothing if not dedicated to her work, even if it was work she was doing for free, and her determination remained strong. She would go in there tomorrow and do her very best and who knew? Maybe it wasn't really as bad as she thought. Maybe Cranford wasn't corrupt and didn't know the difference between good music and crappy music. Anything was possible, wasn't it?

A knock on the side of her office door pulled her from these thoughts. The door, as usual, was open and standing there, his suit jacket missing, his tie loosened and hanging free, was Steve Marshall, head of Standforth and Breckman's investigations department. Steve was forty-five years old and had worked as a Heritage County sheriff's deputy and an investigator for the Heritage County District Attorney's office before being lured into private practice six years before. He was clean-cut, always well groomed, very good at what he did, and had the major hots for Pauline. He was also very married, with kids and all, a factor that did not preclude Pauline from shamelessly flirting with him, but did preclude the relationship from going any further. This was Pauline's decision, of course, not Steve's.

"Hey, beautiful," he haled. "Mind if I come in?"

"Sure," she said. "I'm not making much progress here anyway. What are you still doing here?" Unlike most of the junior lawyers, who could be found at their desks at any hour of any day or night, Steve was usually a strict nine to fiver.

"I was waiting for the office to empty enough so we could sneak up to Breckman's office and have a steamy sexual encounter on his desk."

She smiled. "I like the way you think. Why don't you run on up and get started without me? I'll be up in no time."

"Ahhh, the way you reject me," he said, taking a few steps into her office. "You'll be sorry someday."

"Will I?"

"You will. In fact, someday just might be today when I tell you why I really stayed late."

"Oh?"

"I've been doing some follow-up work on that little matter you had me check into for your brother. The Judge Cranford thing."

She was surprised. "You stayed four extra hours to follow up on something for me?" she asked.

He shrugged. "My actual workday today was taken up with actual firm business—strange but true—and I hate to leave loose strings dangling on anything, even if I was doing it under the table. That whole work ethic thing."

"*And* you want to get into my pants," she said, not unkindly.

"Well... yeah, there is that too." He grinned widely. "And what I discovered tonight in my sneaky, underhanded way just might get me there."

"What did you discover?" she asked, intrigued, catching a little of his enthusiasm.

He told her. She didn't let him into her pants—especially since she was wearing a dress—but she did give him a huge kiss right on his mouth.

*****

The hearing convened fifteen minutes late in a mostly empty courtroom. Judge Cranford, a handsome man with neatly styled salt and pepper hair, resplendent in his black robe, sat on his elevated podium and declared the proceedings in progress. A court reporter sat before her machine just in front of him. A Los Angeles sheriff's deputy, serving as bailiff, stood in the corner. At the defendant's table sat Jake, Matt, and Bill, all of whom were decked out in their best suits. Pauline sat between Jake and Bill, dressed in a conservative business dress, her dark hair tied tightly into a bun. At the plaintiff's table sat four power-suited lawyers, Eric Frowley chief among them. No one who actually worked for National Records was present.

"It is my understanding," said Judge Cranford, "that National Records has filed suit against the musical band *Intemperance* charging breach of contract. Is that correct, counsel?"

"Yes, Your Honor," Frowley replied.

"And furthermore," His Honor continued, "since this lawsuit will take some time to work its way through the system and since National Records believes that *Intemperance* is engaging in a blatant and deliberate work slowdown in violation of their contract, you have requested this hearing that I might issue a court order granting an immediate enforcement of the terms of the contract if the band refuses to make a good faith effort to abide by the contract."

"That is correct, Your Honor," Frowley agreed. "We will show that the band is currently and deliberately in flagrant violation of the contract and did not act in good faith, as required of them, when they produced and submitted a demo tape of music to National Records."

Cranford then looked over at Pauline. "It is also my understanding that council for the defense has filed a motion requesting a preliminary injunction on enforcement of the terms of the contract until such time as a jury trial can be conducted on the basis that the band did, in fact, act in good faith and submit a demo tape of music for acceptance by the plaintiff and the plaintiff is, in fact, being unreasonable in rejection of this effort."

"That is correct, Your Honor," Pauline said.

"Okay," Cranford said. "Good enough." He looked at the defendant's table. "Welcome to my courtroom, gentlemen. I trust you won't find it inappropriate if I tell you I have enjoyed the music you have recorded so far and I sincerely hope I can help alleviate this dispute so you can continue to produce such fine music in the future."

"Thank you, Your Honor," Jake said, "but there really is no dispute to mediate."

Cranford frowned a little but said nothing. He looked at Pauline. "Ms. Kingsley, let me take this opportunity to welcome you to Los Angeles. It's always nice to see fresh, young faces in my courtroom."

"Thank you, Your Honor," she replied.

"Any opening remarks before we get started?"

"Yes, Your Honor," Pauline said. "I'm afraid I must respectfully request that you recuse yourself from this case on grounds of conflict of interest."

There was some minor uproar from the plaintiff's table at her words but Cranford himself merely blinked. "Conflict of interest?" he asked. "That is a fairly serious accusation, Ms. Kingsley. Perhaps you would explain yourself?"

"Most certainly," she said. "I have information that you have financial interests in National Records Corporation, specifically that you own more than one thousand shares of National Records stock."

Again, Cranford did little more than blink. "And where," he enquired, "might you have acquired information such as that?"

"My source prefers to remain anonymous," Pauline told him. "In fact, he will refuse to testify to this knowledge."

"This is ridiculous," said Frowley. "She's an amateur trying to make demands based on unverifiable hearsay."

"That's correct," Pauline said. "I cannot produce a single document at this moment to verify my accusation. But we're not talking about the admissibility of evidence here, are we? I am simply stating a concern that has been brought to my attention. If this concern is groundless then I have no objection to Judge Cranford remaining in charge of this case. But if it is true, then I would ask, quite correctly, that His Honor recuse himself as required under the law."

Cranford smiled and, with a straight face, said, "As far as I know, I own no shares of National Records stock and have no financial interests in National Records."

Jake saw Matt tense up, knew he was about to scream out, "You fucking lying piece of shit!" or something equally contemptible. He put his hand on Matt's wrist, giving it a firm squeeze. Matt remained silent.

"Okay then," Pauline said politely. "I'll withdraw my request."

"I'll consider it withdrawn," Cranford said.

"However," she added, "considering the gravity of the decisions likely to result from this case, both in this hearing and in the long term, and, since I do have information, albeit unverified, that you might possibly own shares of National Records stock, I will find it necessary to request a formal investigation into this issue by the judicial review board."

"Oh, you will, will you?" he asked.

"Yes, Your Honor," she said. "I will. And I'm sure I don't have to explain to you that if you did, in fact, own shares of National Records stock and if you did not recuse yourself from this case based on that, you would be in blatant violation of section 170.3 of the California Code of Civil Procedure and subject to severe sanction by the board, up to and including removal from the bench."

Cranford actually paled as she made this statement. Frowley and his fellow mouthpieces did the same. Jake simply looked at his sister in awe, seeing her as he had never seen her before. Sure, he knew she was a lawyer, had suspected she was a good one, had taken more than his share of legal advice from her, but this was the first time he had ever seen her *act* like a lawyer. She had just crammed it home to a judge—a fucking superior court judge!—in his own courtroom and she had done it in a way that would not leave her open for charges of contempt or misconduct or unprofessionalism.

"Well now," Cranford said slowly, "I would certainly hate to have my name dropped on the judicial review board, and, since I have stockbrokers and accountants who handle most of my investment money for me, I suppose it is *theoretically* possible I might have unknowingly acquired a few shares of National Records stock at some point. In the interests of fair and impartial proceedings I will call a brief recess and make an inquiry with my accountant just to make sure."

He pounded his gavel and retreated to his chambers. Over at the plaintiff's table a furious whispered discussion was taking place. At the defendant's table Matt was grinning and being restrained from shouting insults at Frowley and his boys by Jake's hand on his arm. Pauline, who already knew she'd won this round, was keeping her game face firmly in place. Bill wrote something on one of her legal pads. He ripped it off and passed it to her. It read, *I've never been so aroused in my life. Will you mate with me?* She took the pen from his hand and scrolled back, *Ask me again when we're both rich.*

Five minutes went by and Judge Cranford reemerged from his chambers. He sat back at the bench and banged his gavel, officially ending the recess and prompting the court recorder to resume transcription.

"Well now," he said, "I would certainly like to thank Ms. Kingsley for bringing this matter to my attention. I spoke with my accountant and it turns out that I *do*, in fact, own a number of shares of National Records stock. I guess this will teach me to keep a little closer eye on my investments. In any case, since I do have a so-called 'business interest' with one of the principals in this case I must, under the law, recuse myself from it. The case will be reassigned and the attorneys of record will be notified of the new judge and the new time and place of the hearing." He pounded his gavel and left the courtroom.

Eric Frowley and his cohorts showed no expression as they gathered their papers and notebooks, placed them in their briefcases, and filed out of the courtroom.

Jake, Pauline, Bill, and Matt gathered their own materials and followed them out. Once in the hallway Matt yelled after the retreating group. "Hey, Frowley!"

Frowley turned and looked at them. His companions did the same.

"In your face, ass breath!" Matt yelled, triumphantly squeezing his crotch. "In your fuckin' face!"

Frowley's face darkened but he said nothing. He turned and walked out the door, disappearing.

*****

The Honorable Anthony Remington was chosen to take over the case of National Records vs. *Intemperance*. A new hearing was scheduled for January 11, the following Friday.

"Is he good or bad?" Jake asked Pauline when she called him the Monday following Cranford's recusal to tell him the news.

"He's better than Cranford, so there's a victory right there, but he's not as good as Allanstand would have been. Allanstand is seventy-eight years old and grew up in an era where Edison's original phonograph was still all the rage."

"How old is Remington?"

"Sixty-two," she said. "Born in 1923, grew up in Redding, California solidly upper middle class. Graduated high school with honors and went to UCLA until Pearl Harbor, at which point he enlisted in the marines. He fought with distinction at Iwo Jima and Okinawa. After the war, he returned to UCLA and finished his undergraduate degree and then went to Stanford School of Law. He served ten years with the LA County District Attorney's office and five in private practice before being appointed to the bench by Governor Ronald Reagan. He is very conservative and is considered a stickler for courtroom propriety and discipline. He has handed down more contempt of court rulings than any other judge in the region, including Allanstand, who has been on the bench for thirty plus years. That means we need to keep Matt's mouth stapled firmly shut."

"Stapled shut. Got it. What about propensities toward the record company?"

"He's never handled a music industry suit before," she replied. "At least not that we've been able to uncover. As far as his leanings go, however, his rulings tend to fall back on strict letter of the law. So, in short, if he feels that you genuinely made a good faith effort to produce acceptable music he'll grant our request for a preliminary injunction. If he feels you were deliberately not producing a good faith effort, he'll land on us like a ton of bricks and give National anything they ask for."

"So, that's kind of good, right?" Jake asked.

"I suppose," she said. "At least it's fair and that's about all we can ask at this point."

*****

The hearing convened exactly on time. Judge Remington was a tough looking man, the epitome of the fighting marine he had once been. His face was stern, his eyes unforgiving. As Jake rose in honor of His Honor, he thought he'd never seen a man who looked less thrilled to be facing a bunch of longhaired, ass-crack sniffing rock and roll musicians.

"You may be seated," Remington grunted once he was settled into his own chair.

They sat, their grouping the same as the previous hearing—Jake, Matt, Bill, and Pauline at one table, Frowley and his entourage at the other. Remington did not greet anyone or welcome anyone to his courtroom. He did not engage in any banter, friendly or unfriendly. He simply read his summary of the case and the purpose of this emergency hearing and asked Frowley if the information was correct.

"Yes, Your Honor," Frowley replied.

"So, you are alleging," Remington said, "that these... *musicians* here, who are under contract to provide you with new material for the next contractual period, have deliberately submitted sub-standard material with the intention it would be rejected, thus placing them in immediate breach of contract?"

"That is correct, Your Honor."

Remington nodded, made a brief note on a pad before him, and took a sip from his water glass. He looked at Pauline. "Ms..... Kingsley, is it?"

"Yes, Your Honor."

"Are you related to the Mr. Kingsley who is listed as one of the principals in the case?"

"Yes, Your Honor. He is my brother."

Remington frowned in disapproval at this. "I see you are at least a member of the Bar," he said. "Are you the least bit familiar with the subject of entertainment contract law?"

"Not entertainment contract law as such," she said, "but I do specialize in corporate contract law."

Remington yawned, seemingly tired of this subject. "All right then, I guess you'll have to do. Let's get to the meat of this little spat. Are your clients deliberately making sub-standard music?"

"My clients emphatically deny this, Your Honor. They worked long and hard and under constant pressure by National Records executives in order to compose this new material, record it in base form, and submit it to National Records by the deadline imposed upon them. The work on the tape they submitted represents their very best musical efforts. They are shocked and dismayed that National believes it is not a good faith effort."

"Uh huh," Remington grunted. "So, your clients are not deliberately making sub-standard music then?"

"No, Your Honor, they are not."

"That is all I asked. Next time I ask a yes or no question, spare me the long-winded explanation and just answer yes or no."

Pauline flushed a little. "Yes, Your Honor."

Remington looked back at the plaintiff's table. "Mr. Frowley, what is it that makes your clients believe the music the defendants submitted is not a good faith effort?"

"Your Honor, it is quite obvious if you listen to it. There are songs full of unacceptable profanity, songs about defecation and mucous removal from the nostrils. There is even a song about picking out a can of soup in a grocery store."

"What is wrong with a song about picking out a can of soup?" His Honor enquired.

"It is a marked deviation from the sort of material the fans of *Intemperance* have come to expect."

"Uh huh," Remington grunted again, making a few more notes. He sighed. "Well, as much as I was hoping to avoid this, I guess we'll have to take a listen. I trust you brought a copy with you?"

"Yes, Your Honor," Frowley said. "I have a copy of the demo tape the defendants submitted and copies of the lyric sheets. So that you may compare the recently submitted material with their previous material, I have also brought cassette tapes of the first two *Intemperance* albums."

"Your Honor, if I may?" said Pauline.

"Yes, Ms. Kingsley. What is it?"

"The cassette tapes that Mr. Frowley is offering for use as a comparison with the efforts my clients have recently submitted are commercial audio cassettes made from the master recordings produced in the National Records studio. In other words, they are the high-quality tapes the fans purchase."

"Yes, that is my understanding," Remington said. "What about them?"

"If it please the court, I have brought copies of the original demo tapes my clients submitted to National Records for those first two albums. It is my belief that these tapes would be a better comparison to the current tape since both were produced using the same primitive equipment."

"I fail to see why the recording method would make a difference, counselor."

"The difference, Your Honor, is that the commercial tapes were produced with all the resources of the National Records studio equipment and technicians over a period of months. They were subjected to mixing, redubbing, filtering, and remixing of each individual instrument and vocalization. It is only natural that this will sound much better than a demo tape created in a matter of days on a small mixing board."

Jake thought this was an ironclad argument. His Honor, however, did not seem impressed by it. In fact, he seemed insulted.

"Are you suggesting," he asked, "that I would allow myself to be swayed in judgment by a few fancy flourishes thrown in by studio technicians?"

"No, Your Honor," Pauline replied. "Not at all. I was merely suggesting that comparing a commercial quality album release and a crude demo tape is like comparing apples to oranges. To compare a demo tape with a demo tape is comparing apples to apples."

"And I disagree," Remington said. "I am a great lover of music, Ms. Kingsley, and I hardly think I would be swayed by the type of recording technique used to present that music to me. You can keep your demo tapes in your briefcase."

Jake saw Matt tense up, saw his mouth open to shout something out. He quickly and circumspectly elbowed him in the side, keeping his mouth stapled shut.

"Yes, Your Honor," Pauline said professionally.

"Okay," said Remington. "Let's get this over with." He turned toward the uniformed sheriff's deputy. "Tim, let's hear the new demo tape first."

Tim collected the tape from one of Frowley's associates and carried it over to a small stereo cassette player on the witness stand. He popped it in and turned it on. All that came out for a moment was hissing. Then came the intro to *Fuck The Establishment.*

Jesus, thought Jake as the instrumental intro kicked into high gear. *This isn't a copy of the demo, it's a copy of a copy of a copy of a copy—at least.* It sounded horrible indeed, much worse than they'd originally intended, the obvious victim of multi-generational recording. Remington listened to the first two minutes of the song, long enough to hear the word "fuck" twenty-four times. He then made a throat-cutting gesture at Tim. The stop button was pushed.

"Which one of you wrote that song?" Remington asked, his eyes glaring at the musicians.

"I did, Your Honor," Jake replied.

"And you are? Identify yourself for the record."

"Jake Kingsley, Your Honor. Lead singer for *Intemperance.*"

"You consider this to be an honest effort at producing music, Mr. Kingsley?" he asked. "And I might remind you that you have been sworn and are under oath."

"Yes, Your Honor," Jake said with a perfectly straight face. "I consider *Fuck The Establishment* to be one of my best efforts."

The glare continued. "You will refrain from using profanity of any kind in my courtroom, Mr. Kingsley," he said. "If you do it again, I will cite you for contempt of court and throw you in the county jail for thirty days where you can cuss all you want."

Jake blanched. This did not seem to be going well at all. "My apologies, Your Honor, but that *is* the title of the song."

"I hardly think that 'song' is the proper word for that ranting, obscenity-laced composition. That was quite possibly the most horrible effort at music I have ever heard."

Jake said nothing further. It seemed safer. Presently, Remington ordered the next song played. He listened to this one until the last verse before making the throat-cutting gesture again.

"At least it wasn't profane," he said. "Although calling it music is still quite a stretch. Next."

Tim played *The Switch*. Frowley took a moment to explain that the band had chosen to switch instruments for this particular piece.

"Really?" Remington asked, looking like he was going to vomit. "How could you tell?"

They went through the rest, one by one, with His Honor listening for an average of ninety seconds each time before making a sarcastic comment and ordering up the next. When the demo tape was finally over he looked at Jake, his eyes probing.

"That was grotesque," he said. "Absolutely and completely grotesque. You really consider this abortion of pseudo-musical composition, this symphony of all that is horrible and loathsome, to be your best musical effort?"

"Yes, Your Honor, we do," Jake replied.

Remington shook his head in disgust. "That noise is not fit to play to pigs during mating season."

Jake wasn't sure how to reply. Eventually he simply said, "I disagree, Your Honor."

"Uh huh," Remington said. "Let's hear your previous works now. Tim, get the cassettes please."

Tim got them. Jake saw, without surprise, that they were pristine copies of *Descent Into Nothing* and *The Thrill Of Doing Business*, both still in their factory wrappers.

"Does it matter which one goes first?" Remington asked.

"No, Your Honor," Frowley replied. "I think you'll find any song on either of these cassettes to be a stark contrast to the atrocities you just heard."

"Uh huh," Remington said. "Let's do the first album first. Tim, go ahead and play it."

Tim put *Descent Into Nothing* in and pushed play. The rich, melodic sound of *Intemperance*'s first hit poured out into the courtroom in all its glory. Remington listened to it all the way through and then listened to the next song. He cut that one off thirty seconds in and then listened to *Who Needs Love?* all the way through. He then motioned Tim to stop the tape.

"Put in the next album," Remington told him.

The Thrill Of Doing Business was soon blaring through the speakers. Remington listened to about three quarters of the title cut and then ordered a halt.

"Who wrote that one?" he demanded.

"I did, dude... uh... I mean, Your Honor," Matt said. "Something wrong with it?"

Remington's glare was almost murderous this time. "And you are?"

"Matthew Tisdale. Lead guitarist for *Intemperance*."

"I see," Remington said. "And was that song about buying illegal drugs and consorting with prostitutes?"

"Yes, Your Honor," Matt said proudly. "It was."

"And you consider that an acceptable topic in which to compose musical lyrics about and distribute in a mass media format?"

"Yes, Your Honor," Matt responded. He shrugged. "I mean, we *all* do those things, don't we? I mean, we might not talk about them, but, you know, it's a part of everyday life in America."

Remington actually turned red in the face this time. "I am a married man, Mr. Tisdale and a Christian man as well. If you make any more suggestions in this courtroom that I engage in a lack of fidelity or illicit drug use you'll find yourself rotting in a jail cell for the next two months. Is that clear?"

"Uh... sure," Matt said.

"Uh... sure what?" Remington spat.

"Uh... sure, Your Honor?" Matt squeaked.

Remington's eyes continued to drill into Matt's for a few more seconds. Finally, he turned back to the plaintiff's table. "Mr. Frowley," he said, "is it true that these two albums we have just listened to have sold over two million copies apiece?"

"Yes, Your Honor," Frowley said. "*Descent Into Nothing* is actually approaching three million now."

Remington shook his head. "That's the best argument for censorship I've ever heard in my life. I hear no appreciable difference between this demo tape the so-called band has submitted and the previously released selections. They are all appalling garbage and when this great country of ours finally collapses to rubble like the Roman Empire, every one of you standing before me today will be partially responsible. Music? This is garbage! All of it! I find no evidence the band *Intemperance* has failed to make a good faith effort to produce new material. Plaintiff's motion for a court order demanding immediate enforcement of breach of contract terms is denied. Defendant's petition for a preliminary injunction preventing enforcement of the breach of contract terms is granted."

Frawley let his game face slip a little. He frowned, his face turning red. "Your Honor, I must respectfully disagree."

Remington gave him a look that might've melted steel. "If you don't like what they're giving you, counselor, you'll just have to wait until trial to resolve it. You will continue to abide by the terms of the contract until such time as a jury decides whether or not a breach has occurred."

"But your honor," Frawley said, "it could take years before this comes to trial."

"Such is the American justice system," Frawley said with a shrug. "Is there anything else we need to discuss?"

"Yes, Your Honor," Pauline said. "There is one other thing."

Remington sighed. "Will I have to listen to any more of that noise?"

"No, Your Honor," she said. "I would just like to stipulate which provisions of the contract that National Records is not abiding by—you know, so we can avoid coming back in here and having to argue this point again."

"What provisions are those?" His Honor asked.

"You'll note in section six, subsection eight through twelve, that National is required to provide necessary food, clothing, housing, and transportation to each member of *Intemperance* if they are not receiving sufficient funding from royalty payments to make such acquisitions themselves."

Remington flipped to that section in his copy of the contract and read it over for a few moments. "Yes," he finally said. "It says National will provide housing analogous with public perception, all necessary food, all necessary clothing, and all necessary transportation costs in a manner befitting successful musicians. Are they not doing this?"

"They are not, Your Honor. National Records has cut off the band members from their groceries, clothing allowances, and limousine service since this dispute began. This is a blatant violation of the contract and I would ask at this time that you order National Records to immediately reinstate these allowances in the manner in which they were previously distributed."

"Objection, Your Honor," Frowley nearly shouted. "This was a hearing to determine good-faith effort and whether or not we could begin initiating the terms of contract breach, not which terms must be continued and enforced."

"Overruled," Remington said. "This is a hearing to determine whether or not there is sufficient evidence of a contract breach and whether or not a court order should be issued to help resolve such a breach. If I don't rule on this now, Ms. Kingsley will be right back in here tomorrow filing for another emergency hearing and I'll have to waste more valuable time of the court system and myself scheduling for it and listening to it. Let's just get it over with now."

"But, Your Honor..." Frowley started.

"There are no 'buts' in my courtroom, counselor. My word is final. It's one of the perks of this job, you see. Now tell me, did National Records cut off the food, clothing, and transportation allowances they are contractually required to provide to the members of *Intemperance*?"

"Your Honor," Frowley said, "the members of *Intemperance* are in breach of contract. Under the circumstances..."

"Whether the members of *Intemperance* are in breach or not is for a jury to decide," Remington cut in. "I believe I have already ruled on that. Now I will ask you one more time, counselor, and if you do not give me a simple yes or no answer, I will charge you with contempt of court. Did National Records cut off the contractually required food, clothing and transportation allowances for the members of *Intemperance*?"

Frowley sighed. "Yes, Your Honor. They did."

"That wasn't so hard now, was it?" Remington asked. "I'm ordering National Records to reinstate these allowances immediately, by the end of business hours today, at the levels they were previously set at." He glared at Frowley. "And don't try to play games with me on this. Games do not amuse me. Not in the least."

"It will be done, Your Honor," Frowley said through gritted teeth.

"I have utmost confidence in you," Remington said. "Now then, is there anything else?"

There was nothing else.

"Okay then," Remington said. "This hearing is adjourned. And I will ask both parties in this dispute to please come to a settlement before this comes to trial. It is my sincere wish to see none of you in my courtroom ever again." He banged his gavel and left the courtroom. Once in his chambers he put on a Gershwin album from his collection and spent the next twenty minutes cleansing his auditory canals of that rock and roll trash they had been contaminated with.

Meanwhile, out in the hallway, Matt made a point to call out to Frowley again.

"Round two to the band, bitch!" Matt yelled at him, showing both middle fingers. "To the fuckin' band!"

*****

Frowley was still infuriated when Pauline called him two hours later. She was forced to endure a five-minute lecture about lack of decorum and uncouth behavior and proper legal procedures and judges who didn't know their ass from a hole in the ground.

"That's all very interesting, Frowley," she said when he finally wound down. "Now, if we could get to the point of my phone call?"

"What do you want?"

"I would like to arrange a meeting between you, myself, and at least one member of National Records management with decision-making capabilities. I would like for this meeting to take place today, preferably before the close of business hours."

"You're out of your mind," he replied. "We'll meet you in court. Round two might have gone to you but the fight will go to us and you know it."

"This meeting," Pauline said, ignoring his speculation about what she did or did not know, "will be to discuss a possible settlement to this matter, something that will get the band back to work and the next *Intemperance* album back in production."

There was a long pause. Finally, "If your settlement involves changing the band's contract in any way, you can forget it."

"I will discuss the terms of the settlement during the meeting and only during the meeting, and only if National management is present."

On his end of the phone line, Frowley opened his mouth to tell Pauline to take a flying fuck. He closed it before anything could come out. Something occurred to him. If they did meet and this so-called lawyer from Bum-fuck Egypt actually admitted that the band was producing sub-standard material—something it seemed quite likely she would be dumb enough to do—they would be able to go back to Judge Remington and get the preliminary judgement lifted. He smiled. "Let me see what I can do," he told her. "Is there a number I can call you back at?"

*****

They met at the National Records Building at four o'clock. Hoping to impress and overwhelm Pauline—who they viewed as a small-town, small-time, hick lawyer similar to Gregory Peck's character in *To Kill A Mockingbird*—the meeting took place in the executive briefing room on the top floor. Both Casting and Doolittle were present, backed up by Frowley and his entire entourage. The lawyers and the executives were all decked out in their best power suits. They greeted Pauline warmly and sat her in a small chair that faced all of them in their raised chairs, forcing her to look upward just to talk to them.

"Is there anything we can get you before we begin?" asked Casting, ever the perfect host. "A drink perhaps?"

"No, thank you," Pauline replied.

"How about a line or two of our best cocaine? I've found that these things sometimes go smoother if everyone is a little relaxed."

"Again, no, thank you," Pauline said. "I have a nine o'clock flight back to Heritage so I'd just assume get this over with."

"As you wish," Casting said.

"Do you have any objection to the meeting being recorded?" asked Frowley.

"None at all," Pauline said. "In fact, I was going to ask you the same thing." With that, she opened her briefcase and removed a small micro-cassette recorder. She gave it a quick check, turned it on, and spoke softly into it, reciting the time, date, place, participants, and purpose of the meeting. She then sat it on the table before her, leaving it running.

Frowley gave her an isn't-that-cute look and then repeated the procedure with his own micro-cassette recorder.

"Now then," Frowley said. "It is my understanding that you have come here today with a settlement proposal. Is that correct?"

"Yes, it is," Pauline said.

"Well, let's hear what you have to say and we'll consider it."

"Very well." She took a deep breath. Her wording here would have to be very cautious and very precise. To make an admission of any kind that the band was doing any of this purposefully would be an automatic disqualification from the game now afoot. Yet she still had to convey her demands to them and offer them reassurance that if they played ball things would return to normal. As such, she had carefully composed and rehearsed the manner in which she was about to present her case to them. "My clients seem to be suffering from a very bad case of creativity block, wouldn't you say?"

Frowley fielded her serve and neatly volleyed it back to her. "That is one way of putting it," he said.

"I can't think of any other way," Pauline told him. "That tape they submitted to you was awful. It was the worst thing they've ever done."

Frowley raised his eyebrows a tad. Was it really going to be this easy? "Then you admit they are deliberately sabotaging their music?"

She smiled, letting him know that it wasn't really going to be that easy. "No, of course not," she said. "They are not deliberately sabotaging their music. Quite the contrary. They honestly tried their best to be creative in their latest endeavor. They are very upset that you do not consider it to be acceptable. I'm afraid they've lost confidence in their abilities to produce any more music."

"I see," Frowley said. "So, this is a crisis of confidence, is it?"

"Partly," she said. "Although I think this current crisis is simply a symptom of a much larger problem."

"And what might this much larger problem be?"

"Stress," said Pauline. "Stress caused by the way they have been treated by National Records under their current contract."

Frowley rolled his eyes. "Stress caused by the contract, huh? I knew it would come down to this. My clients will not renegotiate the *Intemperance* contract in any way, shape, or form. That is set in concrete, my dear. We will reject any settlement offer in which that is one of the terms."

Pauline simply shrugged. "Your contract is exploiting the band quite dreadfully. You are making millions of dollars in album sales, singles sales, concert revenue, and merchandising revenue while the band is going hundreds of thousands of dollars into debt to you. They are being treated in a manner that is frightfully unfair and they are resentful of this. I, for one, know that Jake, my brother, has a particular hatred of being treated unfairly."

"So, he decided to sabotage his music in response to this perceived unfairness?" Casting asked.

"No," Pauline said. "I don't believe that to be the case at all. I believe the stress and humiliation of being little better than indentured servants to a greedy corporation has caused the band to lose their creative edge."

Frowley gave her another eye roll, a bigger one this time. "And whatever might we do, Ms. Kingsley, to give these poor boys their creative edge back?"

"It's quite simple," she said. "You need to start treating them fairly."

"And how, may I ask, might we do that?"

Pauline smiled sweetly. "Well, I think renegotiating their contract might just do the trick."

Casting and Doolittle groaned. Frowley shook his head in disgust.

"This meeting is now over," Casting said. "I should have known better than to agree to it in the first place."

"I quite agree," said Doolittle.

"Your clients have two choices, Miss," Frowley said. "They can submit acceptable material in the next two weeks and record it at National's direction or they can be sued for breach of contract. I'm sure even a small-timer like yourself knows they don't have a chance in hell of winning a breach of contract suit at trial."

"Yes," Pauline said. "I am aware of that. But if that happens they won't be the only losers now, will they?"

"We're not renegotiating," Frowley said.

Pauline looked over at Casting. "Mr. Casting, if you sue *Intemperance* for breach of contract and win you will get next to nothing out of them. They are musicians and musicians only. They do not know how to do anything else. If they can't play their music, they are not going to become stockbrokers and make millions buying and selling. They are not going to go to medical school or law school or engineering school. They'll end up working at gas stations and convenience stores making minimum wage. You can garnish their wages for the rest of their lives and you won't get enough to pay for a month's retainer on Mr. Frowley's firm. You understand that, don't you?"

"We understand," Casting said. "And we don't care."

"Really?" she asked. "You don't care that you'll be losing somewhere in the vicinity of eighty million dollars in revenue?"

"That argument won't work," Casting said. "We've already told your little brother this but he didn't seem to get it. So now, we'll tell you. You seem to be the smart one in the family so maybe you'll be able to grasp this. If push comes to shove we will eat that eighty million dollars and destroy *Intemperance* forever. We will do this without hesitation in order to avoid setting a precedent. Do you know what a precedent is, hon? Did they go over that term in whatever rural law school you attended? If we renegotiated the *Intemperance* contract because of this asinine and illegal stunt your clients pulled, we'd have twenty other bands in here before the ink was even dry trying to pull the same thing. That would end up costing us a hell of a lot more than eighty million in the long run. The answer is no. No way, no how are we going to allow a band—no matter how successful or profitable they are—to blackmail us like this. It will not happen. Never!"

Pauline sat, expressionless, throughout this tirade. She had been hoping they would give in once they realized that Jake and Matt and Bill, the heart, soul, and creativity of the band, were truly prepared to go to the wall on this issue. After all, eighty million dollars was a lot of money for a corporation to throw away. But now it seemed that National was prepared to go to the wall as well. It was time to play her final card, a card that was, at least in part, bluff and bluster.

"You seem to be fond of the word 'precedent', Mr. Casting," she said. "Let's talk about that for a minute."

"I have nothing more to talk about," Casting said. "As I told you, this meeting is now over."

"Oh, I think you might want to listen to this last little bit I have to say. After that, I'll leave peacefully and quietly."

"Fine," Casting said. "But we're not changing our position."

"Understood," she said. "Now we were talking about precedent, weren't we? They did teach me about that word at that little old law school I attended and it's a very good word, a very good concept. In this particular matter it ties neatly into another little legal term I learned there, something called 'unenforceable provisions'. Have you ever heard of that one, Mr. Casting?"

Casting hadn't, but Frowley had. "Oh please," he said. "Your unsophistication at the study of law is really showing now. There is no way on God's green earth unenforceable provisions could possibly fly in this case. Not even with that drooling moron who sat in judgment this morning."

"Don't think so?" Pauline asked.

"I *know* so," Frowley said.

"What exactly is this 'unenforceable provisions' thing we're talking about here?" asked Casting.

"It's nothing, sir," Frowley said. "Absolutely nothing but this ambulance chaser grasping at straws. There is no way it could even remotely be applied here."

"Probably not on initial judgment," Pauline allowed. "But on appeal... well, that could get interesting now, couldn't it?"

"You would be laughed out of the courtroom," Frowley said.

"Excuse me," Casting said, "but what exactly are we talking about here?"

"It's a pipe dream," Frowley said. "An area of the law that has no relationship to a music contract."

"Since Mr. Frowley doesn't seem to want to explain 'unenforceable provisions' to you," Pauline said, "perhaps you would allow me?" She paused and when no one spoke up to tell her no, she explained it. "An unenforceable provision is a clause or clauses put into a written contract that is considered so contrary to acceptable behavior that even if the party to the contract voluntarily signed off on it and understood it, the law will not allow the enforcement of it. In effect, by its very nature, the provision is considered unenforceable. The most obvious application of this concept is when someone inserts an illegal act into a contract. For instance, if you had put in that if *Intemperance* does not sell enough albums to cover your initial outlay of funds, they would have to smuggle two hundred pounds of cocaine across the border for you."

"We have no such clause in our contract," Casting said.

"That was just a simplified example of illegal provisions," Pauline said. "I made it so you would understand the concept. Another example would be outrageous acts. The example they like to give in law school—at least at the hick law school I went to—is a company puts in a clause that says if a supplier does not deliver on schedule, he has to cut off his right arm. Just because the supplier signed and consented to such a clause does not make it enforceable."

"We have nothing like *that* in our contract either," Casting said.

"Of course you don't," said Frowley. "I told you she was grasping at straws."

"Again," said Pauline, "those were just simplified law school examples used to teach the basic concept of unenforceable provisions. Why don't we talk real world here for a minute? I personally have worked on three unenforceable provisions cases in my career and have taken two to litigation, one of which I won, the other I lost. In the first case, a fertilizer firm—I know, that hick thing again—put into its supply contract with one of our farming conglomerates that if they, the supplier, failed to deliver the promised amount of fertilizer on time and in the proper amount, they were still entitled to payment in full. The conglomerate signed this contract voluntarily—this was before my time or I would have advised against it—and then, one day, a train derailed and destroyed an entire shipment. The supplier demanded full payment under the contract. The conglomerate refused and I challenged the clause on the grounds it was an outrageous concept for a client to have to pay for a lack of delivery that was in no way their fault. The judge agreed and the clause was stricken from the contract."

Frowley clapped his hands contemptuously. "Bravo for you. You've wiped out injustice at the hands of those dreaded fertilizer cartels and made the state safe for good farming. But that has absolutely nothing to do with the *Intemperance* contract."

"It has more to do with it than you think, Mr. Frowley, but let me tell you about the other case I litigated... and lost. It will perhaps hit a little closer to home. You see, one of our clients is a large warehouse type of store. I'm sure you'd know the name if you heard it. Well, in northern California a few years ago there was this amateur inventor who designed and built these little brown gardening wagons."

"Gardening wagons?" Frowley cried. "How much more of this backwoods pseudo-law do we have to listen to?"

"Just this one more," Pauline said. "I promise."

"Sir," Frowley said to Casting, "she's trying to bluff you because that's all she has left."

"Maybe," Casting said thoughtfully. "But let's hear her out. Continue, Ms. Kingsley."

"Thank you. Anyway, this amateur inventor showed his little brown gardening wagon to some folks at the local warehouse store and they agreed to sell it for him. He delivered ten of them and apparently people really liked them. They snatched them up inside of a week. The store was intrigued and they asked him to make ten more. These too were snatched up. The store manager realized he was onto something here so he told his boss about the little brown gardening wagon. His boss told his boss and soon this warehouse store offered the inventor a contract to produce sixty of these wagons a week to be sold in eight stores throughout the region. The inventor's cost for materials for each wagon, at the time, was six dollars. The store promised to pay him twenty dollars for each wagon and they sold them for forty-five dollars.

"This went on for almost a year and then along came that whole spotted owl issue. I'm sure you've heard about that. The spotted owl is an endangered species and it just happens to live in some of the most productive timberland in the United States. Vast tracts of this timberland were placed off-limits to logging, thus ensuring that there was not as much timber available on the market. This, according to the law of supply and demand, drove up the price of timber, particularly the prime cuts our inventor needed, and it was now costing him almost twelve dollars to produce each wagon instead of six. This brought the inventor's profit margin down from \$840 per week to \$420. This was not enough for the inventor to live on. He asked the warehouse store to please increase his per-unit fee so he could offset the cost of timber, but they refused, stating it was not in his contract to do so.

"So, since he could not live on \$420 per week, he stopped making little brown gardening wagons for the warehouse store and went back to his old job. The warehouse store then claimed he was in breach of contract and activated another clause their shifty lawyers—of which I was one—had put into his contract. It was a clause that said if the inventor failed, for whatever reason, to live up to his end of the contract and give them sixty wagons per week, the warehouse store would then assume all patent and marketing rights to the little brown gardening wagon. With our blessing, the warehouse store shipped the design for this wagon to Taiwan, where they were able to make cheap copies of it for three dollars a unit, including overseas shipping, and sell them in every warehouse store in the nation at the same forty-five dollars, which amounted to forty-two dollars of profit per unit nationwide. A pretty good coup for the warehouse store, isn't it?"

Nobody said anything. They just continued to stare at her.

"Sometimes," she said, "I'm not real proud of what I do for a living. This was one of those times. There is a reason why we lawyers are vilified in our society. There is a reason why my own brother wrote a song called *Living By The Law*—a song you folks put on the first *Intemperance* album—bashing everything lawyers stand for. You see, when we wrote that contract with that small-time inventor— someone who just wanted to sell one of his inventions, to get something he'd produced with his own hands and brain on the market—we put those clauses in there with the express hope and intention that something like rising timber costs or sickness or getting tired of working for 'The Man' would make him breach. We *wanted* him to breach so we could obtain the rights to his invention and market it to Taiwan and make millions from it instead of hundreds. That was why we wouldn't let him raise the price. We deliberately skewed this contract so it was outrageously in our favor and so the small-time inventor, not knowing better and with no other choice anyway, would sign off on it no matter what we put in there. Is any of this starting to sound familiar, gentlemen?"

"No," Frowley said. "You screwed a backwoods small-timer. Bravo for you. You are indeed a credit to the profession. Your brother and his band, however, signed a standard industry recording contract no different than that signed by first time acts for more than thirty years."

"Exactly," Pauline said. "You're making my point for me."

"Excuse me?" Frowley said, not getting her.

"We'll come back to that," Pauline said. "Let me finish my little story first. You see, this small-time inventor soon found out that the warehouse store in question had marketed his invention and was selling it nationwide. He protested. We told him that he was shit out of luck and pointed to the contract he had signed. This inventor went and got himself one of those lawyers who advertise in the yellow pages of the Heritage phone book. Now you can joke all you want, Mr. Frowley, about my city, my firm, my education, but the fact is I went to a first-rate law school, graduated at the top of my class, and I work for the most prestigious law firm in the northern Central Valley of California. We accept only the best of the best from our little neck of the woods and we bill hundreds of millions each year from some of the biggest corporations on the planet. We are the epitome of the corporate law firm and we are damn good at what we do. And do you know what happened? This shyster lawyer who graduated one hundred and twelfth in his class, a true ambulance chaser who had collected less than ten thousand in sleazy settlements the year before this case, he took us to court on the basis of unenforceable provisions claiming that it was outrageous for the warehouse store to not allow the inventor to increase price in response to increased materials cost and that it was especially outrageous for us to demand he sign over the rights to his invention if he failed to deliver."

"And what happened?" Casting asked.

"He lost like a motherfucker when it went to trial," Pauline said.

"Jesus Christ," Frowley said. "She's rambling."

"No, I'm not," she said. "Because he then appealed the case and the appellate court ruled in his favor. That warehouse store was forced pay that inventor and his sleazy lawyer two million, nine hundred and twenty thousand dollars and to give him a rather large cut of any future sales."

"And you think that same thing will work here?" Frowley asked. "I think not. As I told you before, your brother and his band of degenerates signed a standard industry contract. We didn't just whip that thing out of thin air just for them."

"That is true," Pauline said. "But no one has ever challenged one of your standard industry contracts on grounds of unenforceable provisions before, have they?"

"No," Frowley said, "they haven't, and that's because the very idea is absurd."

"Is it?" she asked. "I would think that a contract which virtually guarantees that the band signing it goes into debt while the corporation sponsoring them makes outrageous profit, that a contract that makes the band pay for all of the costs of producing the album and marketing it, that a contract that allows the band's name to be exploited for merchandising purposes but shares none of the profit from such an endeavor, that such a contract would be prime fodder for an unenforceable provisions ruling if it were challenged."

"It would never fly," Frowley said. "Never. You would lose so badly you would never show your face in a courtroom again."

"I have no doubt that we would lose quite handily at the trial level," Pauline admitted. "I'm reasonably sure we would lose on first appeal as well. I've already researched the judges on the Court of Appeals for this district and they are a tight-assed, ultra-conservative bunch for sure. But what about the next appeal? That one goes straight to the California Supreme Court itself."

Frowley scoffed quite audibly at this suggestion. "They would never hear something like this."

"Are you sure about that?" Pauline asked him. "Remember who we're talking about here. The Supreme Court of this great state is headed by Rose Bird, perhaps the most liberal, anti-corporate judge to ever don a robe. Her cohorts are Cruz Reynoso and Joseph Grodin, both of whom have been accused of being so far to the left they may be members of the communist party. I think a broad-reaching case dealing with gross exploitation of popular entertainers might be just up their alley, especially since we will be doing everything within our power to draw attention to this issue while we're waiting for it to make its way through the system."

Casting looked alarmed for the first time. "Attention?" he asked. "What do you mean by that?"

"Media attention of course," Pauline said. "There doesn't seem to be any sort of non-disclosure clause in your standard industry contract, does there? We'll talk to every reporter we can find and tell them all about how much money you're making and how much the band is making. We'll give them copies of the band's quarterly reports. We'll tell them about the drug pushing and the whoremongering and the assigned housing and the spies. We'll tell them every dirty little secret the band has been witness to from the time they signed to the present."

"We'll get a gag order," Frowley said. "They won't be able to say anything."

"That might work," Pauline replied with a shrug. "I'd give you about a fifty-fifty chance of Remington granting such a request in order to avoid contaminating the jury pool. Remington is kind of a wild card in this whole thing, wouldn't you say? But even if he *did* grant a gag order, it will only be in effect until the jury returns a verdict in the initial trial. We're fully prepared to lose the initial trial anyway. Once the appeal process begins there is no more jury pool to worry about and the gag order would no longer be in effect. We'll be free to start spouting our mouths off to anyone about anything we want. The public will be outraged at the way you people operate. They'll demand reform. And by the time the case gets dropped on our good friend Rose Bird's desk, she'll probably be quite inclined to hear it."

Casting was now visibly worried by what he was hearing. "Frowley," he said. "What would happen if the Supreme Court ruled in favor of *Intemperance*? What exactly would that mean for us?"

"Nothing," Frowley said. "She's trying to blow smoke up our asses. There is no way any of that will happen."

"He may be right, Mr. Casting," Pauline said. "I'll be the first to admit that lots of things could go wrong with my little plan. The Supreme Court might refuse to hear it. Their composition might change to something a little more conservative before the case makes it to them. Rose Bird and her cohorts are all up for confirmation by the voters in 1986 and the people of California are a bit peeved with them regarding their death penalty rulings. In fact, my own law firm is contributing a fair amount of money to a campaign to remove those three from the bench. Their business related rulings are as infuriating to the state's large corporations as their death penalty rulings are to the average law and order type. So yes, there are many things that could derail us before the case reaches this level. But if the court *does* hear the case and it *does* rule in favor of *Intemperance...*" She smiled. "Well, what would happen then is that the entire *Intemperance* contract would be rendered null and void and you would quite possibly be subjected to a heavy monetary penalty. The band itself would then be free to renegotiate a new contract with whomever they wished. You would no longer own the rights to any *Intemperance* song."

"Is that true, Frowley?" Casting asked.

"Well... theoretically," he said. "But nothing like that is going to happen. She's just trying to scare you."

"Indeed, I am," Pauline said. "And I haven't even told you the really scary part yet. Do you want to hear the really scary part, Mr. Casting?"

"No, he doesn't," Frowley said. "This has gone on long enough."

"Shut up, Frowley," Casting said. He turned back to Pauline. "Go ahead."

"Thank you, I think I will," she said. "Do you remember a few minutes ago when we were talking about precedent? I seem to recall you asking me in a sarcastic tone if I knew what that meant and I explained to you that I did, in fact, know what it meant. The question is, do *you* really know what it means? You see, when the California Supreme Court rules in a case, a precedent is what is set by that ruling. That means if they do end up ruling that *Intemperance*'s contract is invalid under unenforceable provisions and should therefore be rendered null and void, every similar contract that was signed with every other band in the State of California will also be rendered null and void. How many of your contracts were signed in the State of California, Mr. Casting? Could it be that *all* of them were? How many of your money making bands are still operating under those contracts? Would forty percent be a realistic estimate?"

"That's none of your business," Frowley said.

Pauline shrugged. "I can think of ten or so just off the top of my head. *Intemperance*, *Earthstone*, *Birmingham*, Rob Stinson, *Puerto Vallarta*, Lucy Loving, *The Buttmen*, Rhiannon George, *Ground Zero*—need I go on? I'm sure there are dozens more, some of the most profitable rock, pop, and country acts in the world. If they signed a contract with you in the last five years, that contract will be in jeopardy, all the rights to all of those songs will be in jeopardy, the entire music industry of California will be in jeopardy. Now we're starting to talk about something a little more significant than a mere eighty million dollars, aren't we?"

"Yes," Casting said slowly, his face pale, his mind undoubtedly performing lightening bursts of arithmetic, all of it negative.

"In fact," Pauline said, giving the knife a little extra twist, "wouldn't the mere possibility of a good portion of your profits going into the proverbial shitter have an effect on the price of National Records stock? Wouldn't it really take a nosedive if the Supreme Court actually agreed to hear the case? Would it spin down and crash if they actually ruled in our favor?"

"Yes," Casting said. He was now looking physically ill, like someone had kicked him in the groin. "It would."

"None of that will happen, Mr. Casting," Frowley said, although even he didn't look all that confident any more.

"As I said," Pauline told them, "that is entirely possible, likely even. I'll be honest with you—a rarity for a lawyer, I know—and admit that we probably have no more than a thirty percent chance of success with all this. That gives you odds that are a little better than two out of three. For a gambling man, that's not too bad. In fact, it's damn good. You won't get odds like that at a casino. But we're not playing for mere casino chips here, are we? You have an awful lot to lose by playing those odds and not a whole hell of a lot to win. Are you sure you want to take the chance?"

"The odds are not that high," Frowley said. "She's trying to bluff you."

"What would you say the odds are?" Casting asked him.

"One in a hundred," he said. "Probably less."

"One in a hundred," Casting asked. "What happened to impossible?"

"You can't completely rule anything out," Frowley said. "It would be disingenuous of me to say that. But my advice as lead counsel for this corporation is to reject her offer and call her bluff. She knows the odds are stacked grossly in our favor and I believe the band will stop this ridiculous work action and go back to work once they realize we are not going to budge on this."

"The band is suffering from creativity block," Pauline reminded. "I'm quite certain that nothing will break this block until they're treated a little more fairly. Quite certain."

"And what exactly does 'a little more fairly' mean, Ms. Kingsley?" Casting asked.

"It means just that," she replied. "They're not asking for the world here, just the illusion of fairness, just to lose the overwhelming sensation that you people are fucking them raw with an unlubed sandpaper dildo—if I might quote Mr. Tisdale."

"The illusion of fairness, huh?" Casting said, pondering that.

"Such an illusion can foster great creativity, I'm told."

Casting grunted. "We need to discuss this in private," he said. "Where can we reach you?"

"I'll be at Jake's house until it's time for me to go to the airport. Will you need to discuss it longer than that?"

"Probably not," Casting told her. "Probably not."

*****

"Awesome," Jake declared. "Absolutely awesome, sis." He, Bill, and Matt had just listened to the tape recording of the meeting held on their behalf. He was once again respectfully awed by the notion that his sister really was a lawyer, and a damn good one.

"Fuck yeah," Matt agreed, holding up his beer in a toast to her. "You know, I always thought you were a tight-assed prude, Pauline."

"Oh yeah?" she asked.

"Yeah," he said. "And I still think that, but at least I now know you're *our* tight-assed prude. And you fuckin' rock."

"Uh... thanks, Matt," she said. "From you, I'm sure that is the deepest, most heartfelt compliment you are capable of."

"That's the way I mean it, hon," he assured her.

"I too must agree with my bandmates' assessment of your legal maneuvering," said Bill. "It was both effective and erotic."

"Erotic?" asked Pauline.

"Yes indeed," Bill said. "I, for one, fully intend to masturbate to your image at the first available opportunity."

"Uh... thank you too, Bill," she said. "Let me know how I do."

"I'll write out a summary of activities for you if you wish," he offered.

"Thanks, but that really won't be necessary."

"You sure?" Jake asked. "He's probably got a few pre-printed."

"Some other time perhaps," she said. "How about another drink though?"

"Fuckin' A," said Matt. "Mine's been empty almost two minutes now."

"I'm on it," said Jake. He turned toward the kitchen. "Yo, Manny! Get your ass out here! My guests are thirsty!"

Manny appeared a moment later, his face drawn and hiding considerable unhappiness. Living up to the court order issued by Remington, all services and supplies had been reinstated that afternoon, including the alcohol and drugs—which they easily could have gotten away with not reinstating—and the use of Manny as a servant. He had spent the day grocery shopping and cleaning, pausing only long enough to bring fresh drinks or work on the chicken cacciatore he had served for dinner. Jake had long since dropped any pretense of politeness toward him.

"Another round," Jake told him. "And be quick about it. Our buzzes are trying to fade on us as we speak."

"Yes, sir," Manny replied. "The same for everyone?"

"Naw, too easy," Matt said. "Fire me up a double martini this time. With two olives and an onion slice."

"I'll have some of Jake's chardonnay," Bill said. "Pour it on ice with 7-up and a cherry."

"Nerdly," said Matt, "that might be the faggiest thing I've heard you order yet."

Bill simply shrugged and picked up the marijuana pipe on the table. He took a large hit.

Jake and Pauline cut Manny a small break and simply requested more beer. Manny headed over to the bar and started mixing. About halfway through the process the phone rang. Manny looked at Jake.

"Don't just stand there," Jake told him. "Get the fuckin' phone!"

Manny stiffened but did what he was told. He trudged over and picked up the handset, which was located less than four feet from the couch where Jake was sitting. "Kingsley residence," he said. "May I help you?"

"It's so hard to get good help these days," Jake commented, taking the pipe from Bill and sparking up a hit of his own.

"Yes, Mr. Casting," Manny said into the phone. "She is here. Would you like to speak to her?" He paused, made a sour face, and then looked at Pauline. "It's Mr. Casting, Ms. Kingsley. He would like to speak with you."

Pauline smiled and took the phone from him. She was full of tension and trying not to show it. Would he agree to the terms? Would he tell her to fuck off? Had Frowley been able to convince him that the odds of her scheme succeeding were actually a lot longer than she was letting on? "Mr. Casting," she said, her voice calm and professional.

"Ms. Kingsley," he said, his voice the same. "I'm glad I was able to catch you before you left."

"So, what's the verdict?" she asked, cutting to the chase.

"The advice of my counsel is to reject your offer and fight this out with you," he said.

"That's what I gathered. Will you be following the advice of your counsel?"

"I'm a man in charge of a large, profitable corporation, Ms. Kingsley," he said. "My job is to make money for this corporation, not to lose it. As you so eloquently pointed out, it would behoove me not to put the assets of my corporation—namely the recording contracts that produce a good portion of our income—at undue risk. If there is even a miniscule chance of the scenario you outlined coming to pass, I must take the option that protects those contracts."

"Then you're agreeing to renegotiate the *Intemperance* contract?" she asked, daring to hope a little.

"If I did agree to such a thing," he said, "I could potentially be putting those very same recording contracts at even greater risk if word got out that we gave into you and allowed a first-time contract to terminate. I would be swamped by other bands attempting the same thing. I cannot allow that to happen either."

"What are you saying?" she asked.

"If we do this, it has to be completely secret. Completely. If a single word, a single rumor gets out, we will deny it emphatically, cease all negotiations immediately, and go forth with the breach of contract suit for better or for worse. Do you think you and your clients can keep this a secret?"

"I guarantee it," she said, giving a thumbs-up to Jake, Bill, and Matt, all of whom were listening intently.

"All right then," Casting told her. "The lawsuit remains active until we come to a mutual agreement, *if* such a thing is possible. I'm warning you, however, we're not going to give much ground."

"I understand," Pauline said. "When would you like to start negotiations?"

"As soon as possible," he told her. "We want to get this done and over with and get those boys back in the studio where they belong."

CHAPTER 17

BALANCE OF POWER

Los Angeles, California
February 19, 1985

The back of the stretch limousine was filled with a thick, pungent cloud of marijuana smoke, a cloud so dense the passengers could barely see from one end to the other. All five members of *Intemperance* were back there, as well as Janice Boxer, their publicity manager, and Steve Crow, the man identified as the producer of *The Thrill Of Doing Business* album and all the songs featured on it. There were two fat joints going around, the band members smoking them with enthusiasm, the two management types trying everything in their power to stop them.

"This really isn't proper," cried Janice, who had never smoked marijuana in her life (although she was suddenly starting to feel a little dizzy and thirsty). "We're on our way to the Grammy party! One of the most prestigious, exclusive black-tie events in Hollywood!"

"We're dressed in black ties, aren't we?" asked Jake, who took the remainder of the first joint from Coop and inserted it into a sterling silver roach clip. He put it to his lips, inhaled deeply, and then deliberately blew the majority of the smoke out into the confined space after holding it in less than five seconds.

"We're all going to be reeking of this stuff," said Crow. "They're going to think I was smoking it too."

"You say that like anyone gives a monkey's cock who you are," said Matt.

"I'm the producer of *Crossing The Line*," Crow said angrily. Obviously, this was a sore spot with him. "I'm just as much nominated for Record of the Year as you guys are."

"Yeah," said Matt. "You are. And that just goes to show how much of a fuckin' farce this whole Grammy Award concept is."

Janice and Crow both gasped as if his words constituted a blasphemy, which, to them, it did.

"A farce?" Janice said. "How can you say such a thing? The Grammy Award is the most coveted, most *sacred* of all musical honors!"

"It's nothing but a bunch of shit," Matt insisted. "It's a big promotional gambit put on, run, and voted on by you record industry assholes. The artists who make the songs have no input into it at all, nor do the fans who buy the music."

"Matt speaks truly," said Bill, who was sipping from his second cognac and 7-up (with two cherries and an olive). "If the award nomination and selection process was a true reflection of the popularity of an artist's music with the American public, *Thrill*, the album, would have been nominated for Album of the Year. After all, it was the third best selling LP of 1984, wasn't it?"

"You would think you would be grateful for being nominated for anything at all," Janice admonished. "*Crossing The Line* is up for Song of the Year and Record of the Year. Those are the top awards! The top!"

"And there's no way in hell we're going to win them," Jake said. "You do know that, don't you?"

"I'll admit that the ballots will probably favor either Tina Turner or *La Diferencia*," she said, "but Jake stands a good chance of taking the Best Rock Vocal Performance. A *very* good chance."

"Over Bruce Springsteen?" Jake asked. "Mr. Patriotism himself? I don't think so."

"All this shit has already been decided anyway," said Matt. "The fuckin' ceremony is still a week away and you people have already picked which ass-sucking bands you're going to promote the next cycle, haven't you?"

"You guys are so frustrating!" Crow suddenly yelled. "Why are you so negative about everything that has anything to do with our industry? Why do you think everything is a conspiracy?"

"The track record of your industry merits the suspicion that everything *is* a conspiracy," said Bill.

"Yeah," agreed Coop righteously. "It's the way the fuckin' world works, man!"

"Goddamn right," said Darren, who had just shot up with a healthy dose of heroin thirty minutes before and had no idea what anyone was even talking about.

"That is just ridiculous," said Crow. "We stand just as good a chance as Tina Turner or those improbably successful Mexicans of taking that award."

"They're Venezuelan," said Bill.

"A beaner is a beaner!" Crow yelled. "I don't even know why they were nominated! They're not an American band. Why are they in an American awards show?"

"Because an American record label recorded their album," said Jake. "Jesus, don't you even know how your own business works?"

"And what's up with this 'we' shit?" asked Matt. "Why the fuck are you included in the nomination for Record of the Year with us? What the hell did you do?"

"I produced the record!" Crow cried.

"You mean you threatened and tried to intimidate us throughout the entire process," said Jake. "Is that what producing is? And if you'll recall, you originally rejected that song in favor of some of that crap your ass-kissing songwriters came up with."

"Irregardless," said Crow. "I am producer of the record and just as entitled to the award as you are, maybe even more so."

"Regardless," Bill said.

"What?" asked Crow.

"Irregardless isn't a word. The way you use it means the same thing as 'regardless'. I hope you didn't insert that into your acceptance speech."

"Irregardless is too a word!" Crow said. "I hope you don't think you can..."

"There's the ballroom," Janice interrupted. "We're almost there."

"Shit," said Matt. "We'd better finish these roaches quick."

"Right," said Jake.

He and Matt each took a final hit and then blew out the smoke, adding a fresh layer of haze to the compartment. They then removed the smoldering remains of the roaches from the clips and popped them into their mouths, swallowing them.

"That's disgusting!" said Janice.

"Hey," said Matt, "there's no sense wasting even a fragment of good bud. Remember that and you'll go far in life."

The limo slid into the circular entryway to the Hollywood Grand Ballroom where the pre-Grammy party for 1985 was being held. This was an invitation-only event and, since the majority of the nominees were to be in attendance, a large contingent of the press corps was camped out in front to film the arriving stars. As the limo came to a stop more than a hundred video and still cameras were aimed at it. Camera lights blared brightly, lighting them up like they were on stage. Reporters doing live shots spoke into their microphones, speculating on who this latest arrival might be.

"Now remember," said Janice. "There will be reporters and camerapersons inside as well as out here. This is a very high profile event. No shenanigans like you pulled at the movie premier."

"Of course not," Jake promised.

"We've matured since then," said Matt.

The driver opened the back door of the limo and a large cloud of smoke, plainly visible in the light, went billowing out. Matt was the first person to exit the vehicle. He gave a nod to the gathered media and then turned to head up the red carpet towards the entrance. As he took his first step he belched and a large plume of marijuana smoke, formed in his stomach after he'd swallowed the still burning roach, ejected forcibly from his mouth.

"Oops," he said, grinning. "Excuse me."

Janice buried her head in her hands and wondered just how bad this one was going to be.

*****

Steve Billings, the legendary pop-country singer who would be the host of this year's Grammy Awards was also the host of the pre-Grammy party. He stood in the reception area of the main ballroom, dressed in a perfectly fitted tuxedo, his signature wire-rim glasses perched upon his face. A gaggle of reporters and cameramen flanked him. The band was led directly to him for the formal introduction and welcome. They all shook his hand as he greeted them by name. He wrinkled his nose a little as he caught a good whiff of the odor they were exuding.

"It smells like you boys have been engaging in a little High Mountain Thrill of your own this evening," he said lightly, referencing one of his most popular songs.

"Fuckin' A," said Matt. "Some good shit too. You wanna burn one with us?"

"Hell yeah!" said Coop. "That'd be a trip, wouldn't it? Gettin' stoned with Steve fuckin Billings?"

"Uh... some other time, perhaps," Billings said. "I've heard a few selections from your album. I'm not much of a fan of hard rock music but I must say, Jake, you play an impressive acoustic guitar."

"Thanks," Jake said. "You're not too bad at it yourself. My mom and dad listen to your music all the time."

"I see," he said slowly. "Well, welcome to..."

"Hey," said Coop, "tell us some stories from Vietnam, dude."

"Vietnam?" Billings said.

"Yeah, when you used to be a sniper. Who would've thought that someone as candy-ass as you used to pick off gooks back in the jungle."

"Well, actually..." started Billings.

"You and Mr. Rogers used to be in the same squad, didn't you?" asked Darren. "Which one of you had more kills?"

"You fuckin' idiots," said Matt. "He wasn't really a sniper in Vietnam. That's just one of those urban legend things." He looked at Billings. "Uh... isn't it?"

"I was never a sniper in Vietnam," Billings assured them.

"No shit?" asked Coop, disappointed.

"No shit," Billings said.

"What about Mr. Rogers though?" asked Darren. "*He* was a sniper, wasn't he?"

Billings thought this over for a second and then nodded. "Yes," he said. "Mr. Rogers was one of the best."

"Uh... why don't we mingle for a bit?" asked Janice, who was blushing bright red. "Thank you, Mr. Billings. It was lovely meeting you." With that, she whisked her musicians away and they quickly found the nearest bar.

For the next two hours, they mingled, sometimes together, sometimes separately. Janice tried to keep track of them—and thus keep them in line—but this task was made difficult by a sudden but insistent interest she developed in the appetizer table. She spent her first twenty minutes piling plateful after plateful of salami, cheese, crackers, and stuffed mushrooms onto the china and devouring them.

Jake talked to several musicians and other celebrities who had either been nominated for Grammy awards or were slated to be guests at the ceremony show. Weird Al Yankovich—who struck Jake as decidedly un-weird in person—discussed politics with him for almost twenty minutes. He held a five-minute conversation with Lionel Richie on the subject of the dress Sheila E. was wearing. He found himself next to B.B. King at one point and they talked for more than half an hour about the Les Paul guitar and the best means of reproducing sound through an amplifier with it.

After B.B excused himself and headed off towards the men's room, Jake lit a cigarette and headed for the bar to get another drink. Halfway across the room he was intercepted by a tall, heavily made-up brunette. He recognized her as Audrey Williams, a reporter for the *Hollywood Reporter* news show. Her cameraman and sound technician trailed behind her, shooting and recording.

"Jake? How are you doing?" she asked, stepping neatly in front of him and blocking his path.

"Just fine," he said, trying to step around her. She didn't allow it. She simply moved to keep her body in front of him.

"How about a brief word about the upcoming awards?" she asked.

He suppressed a sigh. He really hated dealing with reporters of any kind and the gossip show reporters were the worst. "Sure," he said. "What do you want to know?"

"There are many people who say that an act such as yours—you know, with the way you rampantly advocate immoral sexuality and drug use—should be banned from participation in the awards. What do you think about that?"

He shrugged. "I think some people worry too much about stuff like that. Obviously two million people liked our album enough to buy it."

"Then you think you're actually in the running to collect one of the coveted gramophones?" she asked.

"I don't know," he said. "You tell me. What do you think our chances are?"

This threw her off stride. She was not used to people asking her questions.

"Well, if there's nothing else," Jake said when she failed to answer him, "the call of the spirits is beckoning to me."

"The call of the spirits?" she said, her brow wrinkling in confusion.

"The bar," he clarified, holding up his empty glass to her.

"Oh... I get it," she said and then gave a dutiful giggle. "Actually, there is one more thing."

Of course there was, Jake thought. There's always one more thing with these people. "And what might that be?"

"It's about the lawsuit that National Records filed against you and your band," she said.

Jake sighed, completely unsurprised. The plan that the dispute between *Intemperance* and their record label would remain secret had turned out to be quite naïve. As soon as it was realized that the band had not entered the recording studio on the date that National publicists said they were going to, the reporters began flocking around, demanding to know why. The pat answer—that the band was unhappy with a few of their songs and we're taking the time to rework them—satisfied the enquirers for less than a week. At that point an investigative reporter for the *American Watcher* tabloid got wind of the lawsuit somehow (probably from a court clerk, Pauline speculated—they were notorious for blabbing information to reporters for money). Once alerted to the possibility that National was suing its most profitable band, it took the reporter less than a day to dig up the actual filing paperwork which was, of course, a matter of public record. They broke the story the first week of February with a copy of the lawsuit reproduced within their pages. Fortunately, they had been unable to get their hands on the actual transcript of the hearings that had taken place since both parties had agreed to keep them sealed.

As soon as it became public knowledge that a lawsuit had been filed, the reporters and paparazzi began hounding the band almost as badly as they'd done during the peak of the Jake and Mindy relationship. National cried foul before negotiations for the new contract could even get properly started. Now that the word was out about the dispute, they said, there was no point in negotiating anything since one of the key terms of the agreement had been violated. Frowley told Pauline they were back to square one. Either the band honor their existing contract immediately or they would go forth and sue the band for breach of contract.

Pauline got them back to the table by pointing out that the media discovering the lawsuit was not the fault of either her or the band, that just because they knew there was a lawsuit didn't mean they knew the band and the label were renegotiating, and, most important, that if they did go back to square one there was still the significant possibility of a future California Supreme Court ruling in the band's favor. This argument didn't sway Frowley, who had been against renegotiation from the start and still was, but it did sway Casting, the National Records CEO who feared such a precedent-setting Supreme Court ruling the same way medieval Europeans used to fear the black plague. A press conference, attended by Jake, Matt, and Pauline as well as himself, was held, and it was announced that, yes, there were some disagreements about new material that would be recorded for the next *Intemperance* album, and yes, these disagreements had led to the filing of a lawsuit when the band did not present enough acceptable material by their contractual deadline, but that both parties were working hard to settle these disagreements so the lawsuit could be dropped and the band could get back into the studio.

"That should hold them for a little while," Casting said after the press conference. "But there had better not be any leaks about the negotiations we're having. If they get confirmation we're doing that, the whole deal is off and we'll take our chances with Rosie and The Supremes."

And so far, no word had leaked. The gossip press enquired almost daily as to what exactly was going on between the warring factions but they were given nothing but vague answers and reassurances that reconciliation was "progressing". There were rumors of a contract renegotiation—that was pretty much inevitable under the circumstances—but both parties emphatically denied this when they were asked. Even Coop and Darren, both potential weak links in the secrecy agreement, managed to keep this to themselves, mostly because both were back on the heroin and spent most of their time shut up in one of their condos instead of going out to get drunk in the clubs where a wily reporter posing as a groupie might be able to loosen their lips.

Jake himself hardly thought of it as a lie when he denied that a contract renegotiation was in the works because to him it seemed the entire thing was a farce anyway, a huge exercise in frustration that would probably end up leading nowhere. Twice a week Pauline, himself, Matt, and Bill would meet with Casting, Doolittle, Crow, and Frowley for eight hours and toss terms of an agreement back and forth. This had been going on for almost a month now and so far, the two parties had not agreed to a single thing.

Neither side had even progressed to bargaining in good faith yet. Pauline would demand that the band's royalty rate be increased from ten percent to thirty percent. National would call this ridiculous and offer to increase the rate to eleven percent. Pauline would demand the band's royalties be based on full retail album price plus two dollars. National would say that since they were willing to increase the royalty rate to eleven percent the band should accept the wholesale album price as the base. National would demand that any new contract signed be extended to eight more contract periods and Pauline would say that they would only accept a single album and tour contract only. They would argue and bicker about these points all day long and get nowhere at all and at the next meeting they would do more of the same.

"Why?" Jake asked Pauline after the last session of negative progress only two days before. "Why are both of you making such ridiculous offers? You know they're not going to accept thirty percent royalties. They know we're not going to accept wholesale album rate. So why the hell are either one of you even making those offers? We've done nothing but waste everyone's time."

"It's the way the game is played, Jake," Pauline told him, her eyes with large bags beneath them, her skin color unnaturally pale from the constant fatigue she was forcing upon herself. "Have patience. Eventually we'll get around to tossing some real figures onto the table. That's when the fun really begins."

"How long?" Jake asked. "Jesus, look at what you're doing to yourself. You never get any sleep, you're flying back and forth twice a week to go to these worthless meetings, and you're probably pissing your bosses off something awful."

"That ain't no shit," she said. "They are definitely not happy with me lately."

"Pauline, you're going to get fired," he said. "I don't want that on my conscience. I appreciate everything you're doing for us, but you're destroying your career."

"I'm not doing it entirely out of the kindness of my heart, little brother," she said. "Did you forget that? If this thing works out the way I'm hoping, I won't need that career anymore anyway."

"But you're burning your bridge behind you," he told her.

"Sometimes that's the only thing you can do," she said. "Don't worry about me or my job. We started this thing and we'll see it through, one way or another."

And off she'd flown, to go put in another seventy hours in her corporate law office and do another twenty or so of research on her own on the subject of entertainment contract law.

"I have nothing new to add about the lawsuit filed against us," Jake told Audrey Williams now, his voice a little testier than it usually was when dealing with these types. "We're working to resolve the issue and making progress on it."

"Then there will be another *Intemperance* album this year?" she asked.

"Yes," he said. "There will."

"That's good to know," she said and then abruptly changed gears. "Have you seen *Handle With Caution* yet?"

She was the first reporter to ask him this question. *Handle With Caution* was the critically acclaimed film, just released the previous week, starring Mindy Snow as an abused wife trying to break free of the relationship. Jake had actually been hoping that the media, with its attention span similar to that of your average houseplant, might have actually forgotten that he used to date Mindy Snow. No such luck apparently.

"No," he said. "I've been rather busy lately and I haven't had a chance to take in any movies."

"Were you hurt that you weren't invited to the premier?" she asked. "After all, you and the star of the film used to be in an intimate relationship and Mindy herself has said that her experience with you helped her prepare for the role. Don't you think you were *owed* an invitation?"

"No, I wasn't hurt at all," Jake said. "Have you seen the movie?"

Again, asking her a question served to throw her off stride. "Uh... well... no, actually, I haven't." She recovered quicker this time. "What about the news that Mindy and John Carlisle are now engaged? Any comments on that?"

"None at all," he said. "I wish them nothing but the best. Now, if you'll excuse me, the bar is calling."

Before she could formulate another annoying, intrusive question, he quickly sidestepped around her and made his escape. He did not make it to the bar, however. Before he could get there, Darren waved him over to a corner of the room where he and Coop were talking to two other musicians. Jake went over to them.

"Dude," Darren said, "you remember Mike and Charlie, don't you?"

"Of course," Jake said, shaking their hands. Mike Landry and Charlie Meyer were the lead singer and bass player for *Birmingham*, the southern rock group who had opened for them on the *The Thrill Of Doing Business* tour. "How you guys doing?"

"Not bad," said Mike, who was sipping out of what appeared to be mineral water.

"Hangin' in here," said Charlie.

"Congratulations on your nomination," Jake said. *Birmingham* had been nominated for the Best New Artist award. The fact that their album had barely gone gold was, to Jake, further proof of the heavy-handed involvement of the record companies in the whole Grammy process. True, their single, *Texas Hold-em*, had done pretty well, parking itself at number one for a single week and selling well over a million copies, but it had done nowhere near as well as the other nominees in the bunch. National had simply pulled the strings they had to pull to get one of their acts into the show, the same thing they had done with *Intemperance.*

"Thanks," said Charlie, who was smoking a cigarette in an inexpert manner and sipping from a fruity looking drink. "I really hope we win it."

"Me too," said Mike. "You think we have a chance?"

Jake knew they didn't have a chance in hell of taking that Grammy. "Well," he said, "the competition is pretty stiff for that award. You got Cyndi Lauper, Sheila E., *The Judds*, even that MTV weirdo Corey Hart, all going up against you for it. They all sold quite a few albums." *A lot more than you did*, he did not add.

The dejection in their faces was a little more than he'd expected.

"What's the big deal?" he asked. "It's just a stupid award that doesn't really mean anything. At least that's my take on all of this."

"They have to win the award if they wanna do another album," Darren said.

"How's that?" asked Jake.

"National said we didn't sell enough of our first album," Charlie explained. "They said they made a small profit from us but they don't anticipate a second album doing the same unless we pull in one of the Grammy awards."

"They're not going to utilize the second contract period?" Jake asked. That was, actually, well within their rights, assuming *Birmingham* had signed the same contract *Intemperance* had.

"Not unless we take a Grammy," Mike said.

"And if we don't," said Charlie, "and they don't pick us up for another album, we won't be able to go sign with another record company. In fact, they told us we won't be able to work as musicians at all until the contract we have is expired."

"That's six years, man," Mike said. "Six fuckin' years. Is that shit legal?"

"Unfortunately, at this point in time, it is," said Jake. "These record contracts are like indentured servitude, aren't they?"

"Yeah," Charlie said, taking a sip. "That's what we're finding out."

"You oughtta do what we're doing," Darren suddenly blurted.

"What do you mean?" asked Charlie.

"We threatened those fuckers with..." He got no further because Jake's elbow drove into his side nearly hard enough to break a rib. "Damn, Jake!" he yelled. "What the fuck did you do that for?"

Jake pulled him to the side, out of earshot of the two *Birmingham* musicians. "You need to keep your mouth shut about what is going on between us and National," he whispered to him. "You can't tell anyone anything. I thought you understood that."

"Aww, man," Darren scoffed. "That just means reporters and shit, doesn't it? Mike and Charlie are cool. They're brother band members, man! They're getting fucked just like we are."

"It means *everyone*," Jake said. "It doesn't matter if they're cool or not. You can't even tell your mom about it."

"That's fucked up," Darren said, shaking his head at the injustice of it all.

"Besides," Jake said, "it wouldn't do them any good anyway. They barely made gold. We're double and triple platinum, you know what I mean? It's only because we're so fuckin' good that we're able to pull this off."

This argument seemed to carry more weight with Darren. "Ohhhh," he said. "I guess that makes sense. You gotta be important to The Man before The Man will start taking you seriously. That's what Coop always says."

"Coop is indeed a wise man," Jake said. "Now keep your mouth shut about it or you'll risk ruining everything. You dig?"

"I dig," Darren said. "But you didn't have to hit me so hard. That shit hurt, man."

"Sorry," Jake said, finishing the process of mollifying him.

They stepped back over to Charlie and Mike, both of whom were giving them strange looks.

"Excuse us," Jake said. "A little band talk, you know?"

"No problem," Mike said.

"What was that you were saying, Darren?" Charlie asked. "About what you threatened them with?"

"It's nothing," Darren said. "Forget I said anything."

"But..."

"It's nothing," Jake said. "Nothing at all."

"Yeah," Darren said. "And I gotta go to the bathroom again. You coming, Coop?"

"Oh... yeah," said Coop. "Good idea. I really gotta go."

They wandered off, undoubtedly to shoot another load of China White into their veins in one of the stalls.

"You guys *are* renegotiating your contract, aren't you?" asked Charlie.

"No," Jake said. "Not at all. You should know that National would never do that."

Charlie didn't look like he believed him, but he said nothing further. Jake wished them the best of luck and then excused himself. He headed for the bar again, this time arriving safely and unmolested.

"Another triple rum and coke?" the bartender asked, his voice more than a little condescending. He, like most of the serving staff, was a frustrated actor (although some were frustrated musicians). He also seemed to think he had been appointed etiquette guardian and his disapproval at the members of *Intemperance* reeking of marijuana and ordering jumbo-sized drinks in water glasses was quite plain with every word he spoke, every piece of body language he communicated.

Jake didn't really care whether the man approved of him or not. "You know it," he said. "It's a night for celebration, isn't it?"

"Fuckin' A it is," said a voice behind him. It was Matt, who had just appeared out of the crowd for a drink of his own. "Hey, loser-boy," he told the bartender. "Fire me up with another quadruple Chivas and coke, will ya? And not so much fuckin' ice this time."

"Do you have any idea," the bartender asked with a glare, "just how expensive this Chivas you're swilling down is?"

"Do *you* have any idea," Matt returned, "just how much I'm going to kick your snooty ass if that drink isn't sitting before me in the next forty-five seconds?"

"Are you threatening me?" the bartender demanded.

"Yes," Jake said mildly, "he is. And he will follow through with that threat too."

The bartender looked in Jake's eyes, spared a quick glance at Matt, and then apparently decided that the two of them were telling the truth. He mumbled something under his breath and took down two water glasses. He filled them with ice, poured four shots of Chivas into one, three shots of Jamaican rum into the other, and then topped both off with coke from his tap. He pushed the drinks at the two musicians and then headed off to the other end of the bar to serve one of the members of Bruce Springsteen's E Street Band.

"Prick," Matt said, sipping from his drink. "I oughtta kick his ass anyway just for the sheer enjoyment of it."

"He does seem to be a man who could use a good ass-kicking," Jake agreed.

"Imagine that shit, a fuckin' waiter looking down his snooty nose at *us*." He shook his head in disgust. "Oh well. Fuck it." He brightened. "Hey, you know who I was just talking to?"

"Who?" Jake asked.

"Sammy Hagar. Now there's a dude that knows how to party. We were talking for almost half an hour."

"Is he cool?" Jake asked. He had found, since becoming famous and meeting other famous people, that many celebrities were not cool, that they were, in fact, arrogant, stuck-up assholes.

"Way cool," Matt assured him. "He's into fishing, just like I am. He was telling me about this place he found down in Mexico on the Baja peninsula. It's called Cabo San Lucas."

"Cabo San Lucas? Never heard of it."

"Me either," Matt said. "He said it's a small little village right on the ocean where the Pacific and the Sea of Cortez come together. The weather is nice and warm in the winter and they have the best sport fishing he's ever found. Marlin the size of fuckin' Volkswagons. Once this contract shit is all settled and we start pulling in some legal tender I'm gonna fly down and check it out. Shit, if it's as good as he says maybe I'll buy myself a house down there."

"Sounds like your kind of place," Jake said.

A woman walked up and stood at the bar next to them. Jake first saw her with his peripheral vision and even with only that as input he could tell she was attractive. He turned to look more fully at her and recognized her as Celia Valdez, lead singer and acoustic guitarist for *La Diferencia*, the band whose singles had aced them out of two number one spots over the last year and whose album had bumped *The Thrill Of Doing Business* from the top of the album chart.

She was bigger than he expected, not fat or out of proportion in any way, but definitely not petite. She stood nearly six feet tall, only a few inches shorter than Jake himself, and, unlike many female celebrities, who tended to resemble anorexia victims in real life, she had an appetizing amount of meat on her bones. She was dressed in a conservative royal blue gown, her brunette hair cascading alluringly over her shoulders, only the very top portion of her ample cleavage revealed. Modest diamond earrings were in her lobes and an expensive looking diamond bracelet adorned her left wrist. Jake caught a scent of vanilla wafting off of her, noticeable mostly because it was not Chanel #5 or some other ritzy scent favored by the rich and famous.

The bartender saw her standing there and practically fell all over himself rushing to serve her. "Yes, Ms. Valdez?" he said graciously. "What can I get for you?"

"A glass of chardonnay," she said, her accent considerably thicker than it was on her album. "Do you have Snoqualmie Vineyards?"

"Of course," he said. "Let me go open a bottle for you."

"Thank you," she said. He disappeared, nearly running towards the back room. She turned and looked at Jake and Matt. A smile appeared on her face. "Hi," she said, speaking to both of them. "You're Jake Kingsley and Matt Tisdale, aren't you?"

"And you're the current, though undoubtedly short-lived queen of feel-good pop, aren't you?" asked Matt, his voice sounding very much like that of the bartender when he'd been talking to Jake.

The smile disappeared from her face, a slight frown replacing it. "I suppose you could call me that," she said. "Although it would be rather rude of you to do so, don't you think?"

Matt shrugged, his eyes fixed on her. "Shouldn't you be out dancing?" he asked. "Since you love it so much. Oh... that's right, you didn't write that song, did you? Some Aristocrat Records hacker pumped it out for you."

Her frown deepened, her eyes flashing anger, but just for a brief second. "You and your band compose your own music, don't you, Mr. Tisdale?" she asked.

"Damn right," he said. "We're *real* musicians."

"As I recall," she said, "*Crossing The Line* and *Rules Of The Road* were both outsold and out-charted by our songs *I Love To Dance* and *Young Love*. Our album also sold a quarter million more copies than yours. So, if our songs were composed by hackers, what does that make you and your band?"

Matt was actually rendered speechless. He stumbled and stammered and his face turned bright red but he was unable to formulate a single word. Finally, he took a deep breath and composed himself.

"I'll see you later, Jake," he said. "Something stinks around here." With that, he walked away, taking his drink with him and quickly becoming lost in the crowd.

"Wow," Jake said once he was gone. "I don't think I've ever seen anyone pull his chain like that before, not even when those cops in Texarkana gave him the phone book treatment."

"The phone book treatment?" Celia asked.

"Never mind," Jake said. He held out his hand to her. "I'm pleased to meet you, Celia, even if my bandmate isn't."

She shook with him. Her hand was larger than the average female's but no less soft, except for her fingertips, which were covered with the hard calluses indicative of a long time guitar player.

"Thank you," she said. "It would seem that your guitar player does not have much respect for a band that performs songs written by others?"

"Well, Matt's kind of a musical purist. He believes you're not truly a musician unless you're composing your own material."

"I see," she said, her eyes flitting downward and looking at the bar. "And do you feel the same?"

"Perhaps not as deeply as Matt feels," he replied. "But yes, I do tend to be prejudiced in favor of the classic singer/songwriter combination."

"Then you don't care for our music too much, I assume?"

"It's catchy," he said. "I actually found myself singing along with *I Love To Dance* a few times."

"Really?"

"Really," he confirmed. "There are some impressive elements to the composition."

"Such as?"

He looked at her. Her brown eyes were locked once again onto his face, inquisitive, intelligent. "Your voice is beautiful," he told her.

"Thank you," she said. "I think I have a fairly good command of it."

"That's an understatement," she said. "You're naturally talented with your singing and it's evident by listening to you on your songs that you've had considerable training as well."

She smiled again. "I'm flattered," she said. "And yes, I have had considerable training. I started out singing in the church choir in Barquisimeto when I was only eleven years old."

"Bar-what?" Jake asked.

"Barquisimeto," she said, pronouncing it slowly and phonetically as 'Bar-keys-a-meto'. "It's the city I grew up in. It's the capital of the Venezuelan state of Lara, a farming city mostly. My family is very active in the church and my mother put me in the choir at an early age. That was where I first learned to use my voice effectively. Since then I've had some professional lessons."

"They paid off," he told her. "Your singing voice is well-honed. It reminds me of Karen Carpenter with an accent."

"You like Karen Carpenter?" she asked, surprised.

"Well, *The Carpenters* music itself is kind of saccharin don't you think?"

"Perhaps," she agreed.

"But you don't have to like them to appreciate that Karen Carpenter's voice was exquisite, almost perfection in fact."

"And you're comparing me to her?" she asked. "That sounds like a pickup line."

He smiled. "I can't say that I'm not trying to pick up on you, because you yourself are every bit as beautiful as your voice, and I can't say that I haven't told the occasional fib before in the cause of picking someone up."

"No?"

"No," he said. "The most common one I hit them with is that I'm rich. It's an easy one to pull off when you're a famous musician, isn't it? However, since you are undoubtedly operating under a standard industry first-time contract like I am, I'm sure you already know I'm not really rich, don't you? In fact, I'm in considerable debt at the moment."

She smiled again. "Lord, don't I know it."

"But anyway, one thing I do not lie about, that I would *never* lie about, even to further my own sexual gratification, is someone's musical ability. I am sincere in my assessment of your voice. It is absolutely beautiful, a near-perfect contralto that Karen Carpenter herself would have been envious of."

This time she actually beamed at him. "You are a smooth talker indeed," she said.

"Thank you. Am I having an effect?"

"A minor one," she admitted. "If I didn't already have a boyfriend, and if you didn't work for a competing record company, and if I was the least bit inclined to date bad boys with a reputation for hosting orgies and drug parties, I might have agreed to go out with you."

"Did I mention your guitar playing is first rate too?"

She laughed. "No, but I'll forgo questioning your sincerity on that one and just thank you."

"You're welcome," he said, sipping from his drink. "And don't worry. I know when I've been shot down."

"Do you?" she asked. "That is certainly a rarity among men, especially men who happen to be famous musicians used to having women cater to their every whim."

"I must admit, I don't get shot down often so the experience is probably good for my humility factor. I do appreciate your use of force doctrine in performing the shoot down."

"My use of force doctrine?"

"You went with the guns instead of the nuclear-tipped missiles," he said. "My ego appreciates that."

"Your ego is welcome as well. And while we're talking about your ego, can I stroke it just a bit?"

"Stroke away," he said, grinning semi-lasciviously.

She shook her head in amusement. "I'm not much of a hard-rock fan," she said, "but I find your voice and your guitar playing to be quite impressive as well. You're also quite the lyricist. I've only listened to the songs that have been in competition with ours, but I do like them. You should do more ballads and less of the heavy stuff."

"Our fans like the heavy stuff," he said. "We like it too. Our inclusion in this little production of the Grammy Awards is almost accidental."

"It seems if you made it more purposeful you might stand a better chance of getting the nominations."

"That would be selling out," he said. "We try to make our music from the heart, not from the pocketbook."

She nodded respectfully at this. "Well then, I guess that puts me in my place, doesn't it?"

"Gently, I hope," he said. "We take our music very seriously and I think that's why we're so popular. It's an effort of love that pays off quite handsomely in the end."

"Well put," she said.

The bartender returned, making a big production out of setting Celia's glass of wine before her. "My apologies for taking so long, Ms. Valdez," he said. "I had to go to the lower store room to find one of the chilled bottles of Snoqualmie Vineyards. It's an eighty-four, unfortunately, not quite as good as the eighty-three. Is that all right?"

"I think I can choke it down," she said. "Thank you for getting it for me." She dropped a dollar bill into his tip jar.

"Thank you, Ms. Valdez," he said. He then shot a distasteful look in Jake's direction. "I do hope you didn't find the company you were forced to keep in my absence to be *too* unpleasant?"

Celia looked from Jake to the bartender for a moment and then smiled sweetly. She plucked her dollar bill back out of the jar. "I found it much more pleasant than when *you* were here," she said. "Mr. Kingsley was merely trying to pick me up. He's not a brown-nosing snob like you are."

The pretentious little smile on the bartender's face withered and died. "Well!" he said huffily. "I can see how grateful some people are when you go out of your way for them!" He stormed off, going as far to the other side of the bar as possible.

"Fuckin' prick," Celia said.

Jake laughed. "I can see your impressive command of English includes some of our more popular slang terms as well."

She blushed, embarrassed. "The English comes from the Venezuelan public school system," she said. "It's a requirement for the college prep classes. The profanity... well... that's from hanging out with the American roadies out on tour. That Latin American temper we're so famous for makes it slip out on occasion."

"I appreciate you letting it slip out on my behalf. I had a witty and equally profane retort of my own all ready to go, of course, but you beat me to the punch."

"Don't tell my mother I said that," she said. "She'd wash my mouth out with soap. So would Bobby for that matter."

"Your manager?" Jake asked.

She nodded. "And the boyfriend I mentioned earlier. He really hates it when I cuss in public. It spoils the wholesome *I Love To Dance* image."

"Yes," said Jake, "our manager is the same, except he hates it when we *don't* cuss in public."

"Then you're not really the sex-maniac, drug addicted bad boy you're supposed to be?"

"Not at all," he said. "I'm as pure as the driven snow. In my spare time I like to study the scriptures and write get well cards to crippled children."

"Of course," she said with a smile. "And that story about you and the cocaine-filled butt crack?"

"All to enhance the image," Jake said. "My pastor was quite shocked by it."

She laughed again, her brown eyes sparkling. "You're funny," she said.

"And cute?"

"Mildly," she said. "Kind of like an alpaca just after shearing."

This line impressed Jake. "Is that a Venezuelan insult?" he asked.

"Peruvian actually, but since it seemed to fit the situation, I borrowed it."

"You're funny too," he said.

"And cute?" she enquired, dimples forming on her face.

"Almost sickeningly cute," he allowed.

She smiled and took a sip of her wine. Jake took a sip of his rum and coke. Both realized that the other had demonstrated a little more character than had been expected, that the encounter between them was a little more pleasant than would have been thought. A silence, not quite uncomfortable but not quite comfortable either, developed.

"So seriously," she said, finally breaking it. "Did you really do it?"

"Did I really do what?"

"Snort coke out of a girl's butt crack?"

Jake had never answered this question truthfully to any other woman before except Pauline. Not even Mindy, who he had once thought he was in love with, not even his own mother, who he really was in love with, had ever gotten an admission from him on the butt-crack issue. But, for some reason, he found himself coming clean to Celia. "Yeah," he said. "I did it. Guilty as charged."

"I see," she said. "That's an interesting recreational pursuit. You managed to combine the deviant sexual aspect of your image with the rampant drug use aspect with one single act. You are to be congratulated I suppose."

Jake shrugged. "It seemed like a good idea at the time."

"I suppose I can see the appeal of something like that to the drunken male psyche. I assume you were drunk when you did it?"

"Plastered," he said. "It's kind of what we do after our shows."

"To enhance your image, right?"

"Of course," he said. "You don't think we actually *enjoy* doing all that, do you?"

"No," she said, laughing, "I would never think something like that."

"What do you do after your shows?" Jake asked her. "Enlighten me on the *La Diferencia* post-show party."

"We have a sensible dinner, share a bottle of chilled chardonnay, say our evening prayers to the Virgin Mary, and then go to bed by ten-thirty."

"Really?" he asked. She had said that with the air of utmost sincerity.

She held her serious expression for maybe six seconds before laughter came bursting out of her mouth. "No," she said. "Not really."

Jake laughed with her, finding himself enjoying it. "What do you do then?" he asked. "Don't tell me they have a collection of male groupies meet you in the shower?"

She didn't get a chance to answer. A tall, neatly groomed man suddenly appeared beside her. He was smiling—a phony, manager type of smile if Jake had ever seen one—but his eyes were looking at Jake with unmasked suspicion and distaste.

"Hey, Bobby," Celia said cordially. "Do you know Jake Kingsley from *Intemperance*?"

"I've never had the pleasure," he said. "How are you doing, Jake? I'm Bobby Macintyre."

"Nice to meet you, Bobby," Jake said, holding out his right hand for a shake.

They shook. Bobby seemed to feel that the harder he squeezed a person's hand, the more respect he would garner. He was going for broke in the respect department.

"Whoa there, Bobby," Jake said, twisting his hand and removing it from the grip. "I kind of need that hand to hold a guitar pick with on occasion."

"Sorry," Bobby said, sounding anything but. He turned to Celia. "Why don't we do some more mingling? The press is starting to notice your extended discussion with Jake here. It won't be long until they start speculating about it."

"Bobby!" Celia said, a bit of that anger flashing in her eyes.

"I'm sure Jake understands the need to protect one's image," Bobby said. "Don't you, Jake?"

"Oh, you bet," Jake said. "We can't have them thinking that the queen of pop and the king of raunch were having a discussion."

"You see?" Bobby asked her. "Even Jake agrees. I saw Tina Turner heading to the bathroom a minute ago. Let's get positioned so we can talk to her when she comes back out."

"We're going to stake out a bathroom?" she asked.

"I wouldn't exactly put it that way," he said.

"How would you put it?" she replied.

He shook his head, a little temper flaring in his own eyes now. "Just follow me," he told her. "And leave that wine there. How many times have I told you that you shouldn't be seen drinking alcohol in public?"

She went with him but didn't leave the wine. As they walked off she stopped and turned to Jake once more. "Nice talking to you, Jake," she said. "Good luck next week."

"The same to you," he said.

Bobby nearly jerked her away, leading her into the crowd. Jake watched her go until she was out of sight. The scent of her vanilla perfume seemed to remain behind.

*****

The twenty-seventh annual Grammy awards took place on February 26, 1985. *Intemperance* once again hot-boxed the limousine with marijuana smoke as they made the trip and were stoned out of their minds as they walked up the red carpet and entered the building.

In all, there were three nominations associated with *Intemperance*. The band itself and Crow, the producer, were both nominated for Record Of The Year for *Crossing The Line*. Jake was nominated for Song Of The Year for writing *Crossing The Line*. And the band alone was nominated for Best Rock Performance By A Duo Or Group With Vocal for *Crossing The Line*.

In general, Jake found the ceremony incredibly boring and endless. For hours they sat through such mundane awards as Best Spoken Word Recording, Best Reggae Recording, Best Production and Engineering. Only the frequent trips to the restroom to improve their marijuana high kept him sane. And in the end, *Intemperance* didn't win a single award. Though he'd known in his heart this was going to be the case, Jake was surprised to find himself on the edge of his seat when the envelope was opened during each of the awards they were nominated for. He was also surprised by the black disappointment he felt when *Prince and The Revolution* took the Best Rock Performance By A Duo Or Group, when Terry Britten and Graham Lyle took Song Of The Year, and when Tina Turner and Terry Britten took the top award of Record Of The Year for *What's Love Got To Do With It?*

"Fixed," said Matt, who was sitting next to him, each time they weren't announced as the winner. "This whole thing is nothing but a big fuckin' fix."

"Yep," agreed Jake.

Cyndi Lauper took the Best New Artist award, barely acing out *La Diferencia* and completely smashing the last hope of the members of *Birmingham*. *La Diferencia* had also been nominated for Record Of The Year and Album Of The Year. Celia Valdez had been nominated for Best Pop Vocal Performance – Female. Their songwriting team had been nominated for Song Of The Year for *I Love To Dance*. They walked away with nothing as well.

The two bands ran into each other after the ceremony while waiting in the queue to board their limousines. It started out civil enough when Celia and Jake greeted each other and commiserated on their mutual losses. She and Matt glared at each other but otherwise kept their comments to themselves, at least until she introduced the rest of the band.

"This is Eduardo, my brother," she said. "He's our lead guitarist."

Eduardo, like his sister, was quite tall, standing quite close to six and a half feet. "Nice to meet you," Jake said, shaking with him.

"Nice to meet you as well," he said and then turned to Matt. He held out his hand to him. "You need no introduction, Mr. Tisdale. I am a great admirer of your technique."

Matt didn't shake with him. "Then maybe you'd like to hear one of the secrets of the electric guitar," he said. "Check this out, this is way cool." He leaned closer, as if passing on confidential information. "There are more than two chords you can play on a guitar. I know it sounds crazy, but it's true. You should look into this and someday you might qualify as a full-blown hacker."

Eduardo's face darkened but he said nothing. He turned the other cheek and stepped back a bit.

Celia frowned and shot Matt another glare. She turned to a shorter man standing next to her. "This is Miguel," she said, speaking to Jake. "He's the bass player. We went to high school together and formed our first band."

"You're the bass player?" Matt spoke up, stepping over. "I'll shake with you, my friend. *You* are all right."

"Uh... thank you," Miguel said, surprised. They shook.

"You're welcome," said Matt. "Hey, the word on the street is you're sliding your chorizo into Miss Pop Queen here. That true?"

Miguel's face turned beet red. His eyes actually bulged out of their sockets for a moment. "You are a disgusting pile of shit," he told Matt, his words heavily accented.

"Yep," Matt agreed. "So anyway, how is she in the sack? Does she swallow like a good little senorita?"

This pushed Miguel over the edge. "*To voy a romper el orto!*" he yelled angrily. His fist came up, heading for Matt's head. Matt blocked the punch easily but before he could launch a counter-strike another fist, this one belonging to Eduardo, came flying in from his blind side. It struck Matt on his left temple, snapping his head to the side and sending him reeling into Diana Ross and her entourage, who were in the queue behind them.

"Motherfucker!" Matt yelled, shaking himself free from Diana. "You're dead!"

"Matt!" Jake, Crow, and Janice all yelled at the same time.

Matt didn't hear them. He waded in and threw a punch directly into Eduardo's stomach, doubling him over. Before he could land another, Jake grabbed him from behind, pulling him backwards. Celia and Bobby grabbed Eduardo, keeping him from attacking Matt again. But nobody grabbed Miguel. He stepped forward and threw another punch at Matt's face. Matt ducked down and it hit Jake instead, crashing in just above his right cheek with enough force to momentarily daze him. Stars erupted before his eyes and he fell backwards, his grip on Matt releasing. He hit the floor with a thud.

"All right, chili-picker!" Matt yelled. "That's your ass!" He went after Miguel and landed two punches on the side of his face before three security guards grabbed hold of him and pulled him off. Another two grabbed Miguel and dragged him in a separate direction.

"*Chinga tu madre, cabron!*" Miguel yelled at Matt. "*Chinga tu madre!*"

"What the fuck does that mean?" Matt yelled back. "You're in fucking America, asshole! Speak fucking English!"

"It means 'fuck your mother'," Celia shouted at him. "You don't want to know what 'cabron' means, *cabron!*"

"I'll fuckin' kill his ass!" Matt yelled. "Let me go, you fucks!"

They didn't let him go. He was dragged off in one direction and Miguel was dragged off in another. Soon they were out of sight. Several more security guards had arrived by this point and adroitly positioned themselves between Jake, who was just pulling himself to his feet, and Eduardo, who had been released by Celia and Bobby.

"It's cool," Jake said, holding up his hands appeasingly. "I ain't going after anyone."

Eduardo glared at him for a few moments and then finally nodded that he was cool as well. He turned and headed for the door, where a corridor had been cleared to allow them outside and out of sight. Bobby and the rest of the band and their entourage followed after him—all except Celia. She walked over to Jake.

"Are you okay?" she asked him.

"I think so," he said, rubbing his cheek and wincing a little. "It's not the first time Matt's mouth got me punched in the face and it probably won't be the last."

"He's an asshole," she said. "You know that, don't you?"

Jake shrugged. "He does have his moments. Your boyfriend there packs a pretty good punch. Not as good as the NYPD, but respectable."

"He's *not* my boyfriend," she said forcefully. "He's always had a crush on me but it never went anywhere. Bobby is my boyfriend."

"I see," Jake said. "Maybe you should reconsider your choice. I notice Bobby was the only one who didn't defend your honor."

"He's a lover, not a fighter," she said.

Jake chuckled. "Of course," he said. "Well, it's been nice seeing you again, Celia. Well... not really, but you know what I mean."

"Yeah," she said. "I know what you mean."

"Celia!" barked Bobby. "Get away from that... that *man*! Come on. They brought our limo out front so we can get out of this madhouse."

"I'm coming!" she yelled back at him. She turned back to Jake. "I'll see you here next year?"

"You bet," he told her. "We'll get rejected together again. It'll be fun."

She smiled and turned away.

"Hey," Jake called after her. She turned. "What does 'cabron' mean anyway?"

"It has many different meanings," she said, "none of them polite. I believe that Miguel was using the one that tells your friend he is an incestuous cuckold who cannot obtain an erection."

"Wow," Jake said. "All that in one word?"

"It's a very versatile insult," she said. "Goodbye, Jake."

"Goodbye, Celia," he said.

She gave him one last smile and then turned away. A moment later she was gone.

*****

Pauline's flight landed at LAX at 7:05 the next morning. Jake, dressed in his dark shades, his hair tucked under a baseball cap, was there to pick her up. He noticed right away that she was toting two large suitcases instead of the normal carry-on.

"What's with the baggage?" he asked her.

"I'll tell you in the car," she said. "Here come some of your fans."

Like usual, the hat and sunglasses routine only kept him from being recognized for a short period of time. Within minutes, adoring fans and hostile religious types swarmed him. He signed a few autographs, deflected a few insults, and finally extricated them and led them out to the parking area. Pauline's luggage barely fit into Corvette but somehow, they managed it.

"Sorry you didn't win a Grammy," Pauline told him as they pulled out onto the access road. "What happened to your eye?"

He removed his sunglasses and showed her the black and blue shiner Miguel's punch had produced. "It's a good one, isn't it? Not as impressive as the one in Texarkana, but up there."

"What happened?" she asked.

"Oh... you know, the usual," he said. "We got in a fight with *La Diferencia* after the Grammy Awards."

"You got in a fight with a pop band?" she asked, shaking her head in disbelief.

"Matt did actually. I just got caught in the crossfire. But it's cool now."

"It's cool?" she asked incredulously. "Jake, what the hell happened?"

"It'll be in all the gossip columns this morning if you want to read about it. Let's talk about you for a minute. What's with the luggage? Are you staying awhile?"

"Looks like it," she said. "I was called to a meeting with three of the partners yesterday. They gave me an ultimatum. Either I stop my outside work and go back to devoting all my energy to the firm or I'm fired."

Jake sighed. "And you chose the second option?"

She nodded. "The time came to burn that bridge behind me. Do you think I can stay with you until we work this thing out?"

"Pauline, why don't we stop this?" he said. "You go back to your job, right now, today, and we'll find an entertainment lawyer to represent us in the negotiations."

She shook her head. "You would be violating the agreement we have just by consulting another lawyer. I'm in for the long haul, Jake. Nothing has changed except the time I'll have to devote to you guys."

"But..."

"No buts," she said. "I made my decision and I don't regret it a bit. This will work out and I'll get my reward when it does. Besides, they didn't just kick me out on the street. I got a severance package. Six thousand dollars and benefits paid until June 1. You can't beat that, can you?"

"Employment beats that," he said.

"Not in my eyes, little brother. Now can I stay with you, or what?"

"Yeah," he said. "You can sleep in the office. The couch folds out into a bed."

*****

It was not surprising to find out that National already knew Pauline had moved in with Jake by the time they made it to the negotiation session that morning at nine o'clock. After all, Manny had seen her carry two suitcases into the condo and set them up in the office and Manny was still a pipeline of information. What was surprising, and a little disconcerting as well, was the fact that they also knew *why* Pauline had moved her stuff in. They scoffed at the explanation that she had taken a leave of absence until the negotiations were complete and told her point-blank that they knew she'd been fired.

"You have very good sources," Pauline replied, keeping her poker face firmly affixed. "But none of that has any bearing on our negotiations. So how about we get down to it?"

They didn't get down to it. Instead, they spent the first four hours arguing back and forth about whether the current contract allowed Pauline to stay in Jake's condo. National claimed that she couldn't, that Jake allowing her to stay overnight in the past had been a technical violation of the rules they'd been graciously willing to overlook but that moving in was absolutely out of the question. Pauline countered by telling them there was nothing in the contract about guests in Jake's condo and therefore, under the law, what was not forbidden was implicitly allowed.

Back and forth they went, sometimes politely, sometimes rudely, never coming close to anything like an agreement on the issue. It was obvious that Frowley and his sharks smelled blood in the water and were hoping to bankrupt the band's lawyer by forcing her to stay in a hotel and burn up her savings. It was Jake who finally managed to break this particular impasse.

"Look," he told Frowley and Casting, "we have already established that my condo is my home. We established that back when your spy tried to take all the shit out, remember? Now, since that condo is my home I have the right to invite anyone I want into my home. I have invited my sister there and she will be staying there whether you like it or not."

"She will *not!*" Frowley said. "If she establishes residence there you'll be in violation of..."

"If you don't like her staying there," Jake interrupted, "then call the cops and try to have her thrown out. When that fails, you can try to evict her through the normal legal process. That'll take what? About six months? Assuming that you're even successful? So why don't we take it as a given that she'll be staying there for the next six months and get on with the negotiations in the meantime?"

After only twenty more minutes of discussion they finally decided that what Jake said made sense. They took a short break and then resumed negotiations. As had been the case at every meeting before, they went nowhere.

For the next two weeks they continued to go nowhere even though they increased the meeting days to three times a week instead of two. Ridiculous demands were thrown down on the table by both sides, rejected, and then countered with equally ridiculous demands.

"Jesus fucking Christ!" Jake yelled as they entered the National Records building on the last Monday in March. "We are getting nowhere! Eight fucking weeks of this shit and we're still at square one!"

"It takes time," Pauline said for perhaps the thousandth time. "Trust me. We'll get there."

"When?" Jake asked. "Not a goddamn thing has been done yet. You keep putting the same figures on the table and they keep putting the same figures on the table. Why don't you just cut the bullshit and give them a legitimate offer on something? On anything?"

"We can't," she said. "Not until they do it first. That's what all of this is about."

"What?" Jake asked.

"Whoever throws down the first legitimate compromise in the negotiations will be surrendering the initiative."

"What the fuck does that mean?" Matt asked. If Jake's patience was being tried, Matt's was being burned and skinned alive.

"Yes," said Bill. Even he was starting to get a bid edgy about the lack of progress despite the fact that each session kept him in close contact with the woman whose image he most frequently masturbated to. "I fail to see the benefit of sitting in here day after day without advancing our agenda in any way."

"Look, guys," Pauline said. "It's like a staring contest here, okay? National and us are both looking at each other, eyes open, trying to stare each other down. Whoever blinks first is ceding the advantage in the rest of the negotiations. We cannot be the ones to blink first or they'll know we're more desperate than they are."

"And aren't they in there saying the same goddamn thing?" Jake asked.

"Yes, they are," she said. "That's what makes the game so interesting. It's corporate law at its finest."

"Blink?" Matt said. "Is that what you want them to do? I'll make 'em fucking blink! I'll throw a goddamn fist in their faces! That oughtta do it!"

"Patience," Pauline said. "Keep playing the game with me and we'll get through this in no time."

"Fucking lawyers," Matt muttered. "All of you should've been outlawed by the constitution back in the beginning."

They went upstairs and spend another day accomplishing nothing. The next session was pretty much the same. But finally, on Friday, April 1, 1985—April Fools Day—National blinked.

*****

It wasn't much of a blink. Jake, Bill, and Matt didn't even notice it when it happened. It was late in the session, just before they called an end to the day. They returned from a break and Frowley asked for and received the floor.

"On the subject of royalty rate," he said, "National Records is prepared to offer *Intemperance* the rate of twelve percent."

"Twelve percent?" Pauline said, rolling her eyes upward. "You've offered this before, Frowley, but always in conjunction with wholesale album rate for calculation. As I've told you, this is unacceptable. It's less than they're making now."

"We'll give them twelve percent royalties and keep the calculation rate where it's at, at an assumed retail rate of five dollars per album."

Pauline gave no facial expression. "We'll take that under consideration," she said. "Now about the tour costs. Let's go over that again. We want National to pay one hundred percent of the costs, including band and crew entertainment expenses, and give eighty percent of tour profits to the band."

"That is *not* a good faith offer," Frowley said. "How many times do we have to go over this?"

They spent the remainder of the day arguing about tour expenses and achieving nothing. When they called an end to the session Pauline kept her game face on until they were in the elevator. At that point she cheered in triumph.

"Yes!" she said. "We did it. We fucking did it!"

"We did what?" Jake asked. "What the hell are you talking about?"

"They ceded the advantage to us," she said.

"They did?" asked Matt. "When did that happen?"

"When they offered us twelve percent royalties at five dollars an album," she said. "They changed their offer! They blinked!"

"Twelve percent royalties ain't shit," Matt said. "Not on a five dollar an album wholesale rate."

"That's not nearly enough to reverse the debt cycle we're in," said Bill.

"Of course it's not," Pauline said, "but that's not the point. They changed the offer! It's still not a good faith offer, of course, but it's more than they were offering before. It's the first chink in their armor. Now we can start prying at it."

"So... things will start to move now?" Jake asked.

"That was the hard part," Pauline said. "The rest of the negotiations will practically fly by."

*****

Jake should have known that practically flying by was a relative term that meant something very different to the lawyer mind than it did to the professional musician mind. At the next session Pauline, acting in accordance with an unwritten set of rules that governed such negotiations, countered National's blink with a blink of her own. She allowed that the band would be willing to accept twenty-five percent royalties on going retail album rate plus one dollar. This led to another two sessions of back and forth arguing before National upped their offer to thirteen percent on a four dollar and fifty cent retail rate.

"Jesus fucking Christ," Jake said. "We're back where we started!"

"This does seem entirely counterproductive," Bill agreed.

"Patience," Pauline said. "We're moving forward. Trust me on this."

As it turned out, she was right. The two sides concentrated fully on the royalty rate and the album rate it would be based upon and stopped talking about anything else. The offers went back and forth, slowly but surely closing in towards the middle. Finally, on April 17, 1985, they declared agreement on eighteen percent royalties at going retail rate—which currently stood at eight dollars per album and one dollar per single. After thirty-seven sessions, after 260 hours of negotiation, they had reached their first agreement. Now there were only sixty or seventy other points that needed to be hashed out.

The tedium dragged on, with each new issue starting the whole process anew. Ridiculous offers would be placed on the table by both sides and hours beyond counting would be spent waiting for someone to blink first. As Pauline had told them though, once the precedent was set, most of the time it was National that blinked first. Album production costs and promotion costs, which had been one hundred percent recoupable under the old contract, were slowly whittled down to only fifty percent recoupable. The ten percent breakage fee and the twenty-five percent packaging fee were completely eliminated, though not without a vicious fight.

National absolutely refused to budge, however, on the issues of fifty percent for tour costs and fifty percent for video costs. The band would have to continue paying for half of everything. The band did win some non-monetary concessions on these issues, however. After much bickering and many wasted sessions, they got National to agree to allow them much greater input in both the tour production and the video production. The way the wording turned out in the end, *Intemperance* would have creative control over both with veto power being reserved by National and by the band itself. So, in other words, if both parties did not agree on the content of a video or how the tours would be presented, either could kill it.

On the issue of "entertainment costs" for the band on tour, National would not budge on the one hundred percent recoupable rate. The band finally agreed to this with the stipulation that "entertainment costs" for the crew would be only fifty percent recoupable and "entertainment costs" for National management—namely Greg and his three hundred dollar a day cocaine habit—would be fully paid for by National itself. They reluctantly agreed to this and then moved on to the subject of tour revenue and merchandising revenue, eventually agreeing to share fifty percent of this income with the band.

These were all issues that were agreed to in a relatively timely and civilized manner, which meant that all of this was hammered out by mid-May. From there, they started working on the points that were *really* sticklers.

The first of these points had to do with endorsements. Throughout the first two albums National had been raking in a considerable amount of endorsement fees by forcing the band to play instruments onstage and in the studio that had been supplied by companies they had contracts with. The band had been given no choice in any of this (with the exception of Matt's stubborn insistence on playing his Strat onstage) and had been given none of the revenue. The band wanted to change that. National didn't want this to change. For more than five sessions they went over this particular subject before finally coming to an agreement that the band would play whatever instruments they wished onstage as long as they provided them on their own. They would be free to collect whatever endorsement fees they could garner from whatever company they could garner them from. In the studio, however, National insisted upon retaining their rights to the endorsement fees and choice of instruments. They absolutely refused to give up any of these rights or any of the money. Reluctantly, and after much infighting among themselves, the band agreed to this and it went into the contract.

That was only the warm-up for the contention points. The next had to do with creative license and how it would be decided which songs would appear on *Intemperance* albums. It was here that Frowley and his crew truly tried to screw *Intemperance* to the best of their abilities. They tried inserting language that would allow National to choose what songs would be on the albums, to reject any song they didn't like, to demand new songs if the submissions weren't deemed acceptable, to force the band to accept songs from other songwriters or to do covers of existing songs. They thought that since Pauline was new to this entertainment contract thing and was a bumpkin to boot, that she wouldn't notice the language. She did.

Pauline caught and rejected each effort to slip something in and eventually, after more than eight sessions of negotiation, managed to convince them that the entire process would be for nothing if the band weren't given the majority of the control over what would be put on their albums. They ended up with language very similar to that of the video and tour clauses. The band would be given creative control over the content of their albums, deciding which songs would be eventually appear there, in what order, what the name of the album would be, and what the artwork of the album cover would consist of. National would retain veto power over any song the band proposed to put on the album but they would give up the right to sue for breach of contract if they rejected too many songs. It was early July by the time this issue was worked out.

That brought them to the final major issue, that of band discipline. This was something that Pauline and Jake thought could be worked out in half a session or so. As it turned out, National did not want to give up the chokehold they had by effectively making each band member an equal and retaining employer powers over the entire group. For the longest time they refused to budge on this issue.

"*Intemperance* will remain our employees and discipline will be our responsibility," Casting insisted. "We can't have the band itself deciding who goes and who stays. If someone needs to be talked to or even removed, we will be the one who make that decision."

"The band works best the way they were before signing with you," Pauline countered. "I cannot even begin to tell you how much you've hurt their productivity by removing the ability of Matt to keep control over the other members."

"Matt is a sadistic, drug-addicted tyrant," Casting shot back. "He's prone to irrational fits of rage and even violence. You saw what happened at the Grammy Awards, didn't you? We are the ones who need to keep this band under control, not him."

"And you are the ones who turned Darren and Coop into fucking heroin addicts!" Matt yelled back, barely restraining those violent tendencies of which they spoke. "Right now, they're in their condo, oblivious to everything that's going on in this room because of that white powder you pushed on them. It's doubtful that they will ever be productive again under your rules."

"We will not give up control of the band," Casting said. "It won't happen. We'll throw out this entire contract before we do that!"

"You can throw out the entire fucking contract," Matt said, "because we won't be able to make any new music anyway if we can't get those addicts back under control."

July stretched towards August. National offered to put rules in place similar to what had existed before, but the band rejected this on grounds that they didn't trust National to enforce them.

"Your track record on this isn't that great," Jake said. "You were the ones who encouraged Darren and Coop to start using drugs before performances in the first place. You're the ones who send that coke-sniffing hypocrite out on tour with us to arrange for all these drugs. You made a mockery of our rules for whatever twisted reason and now you expect us to believe you'll enforce them? No, afraid not. We need real authority over our members, authority that is completely separate and independent from any interference by you or yours."

"We're not going to give Matt the authority to fire someone just because he got in a pissing match with him," Casting said. "That puts too much instability in the group. What if he fires you, Jake? Or you, Bill? This contract wouldn't be worth a shit to us if any one of you three goes."

Gradually, like a stream eroding a rock, they came to an agreement on the issue. It was decided that band discipline would be the responsibility of the entire band. No one person could fire a band member, but a majority vote of all five members could. National tried to get a veto clause thrown in but it was soundly rejected. National itself could fire the entire band if it wanted, but could not fire an individual member without consent of a majority of the band. And then there was the matter of replacing a member if he were fired or quit or died. National wanted the right to find the new member themselves. *Intemperance* wanted the same. Eventually they agreed that the band would recruit any new member but National would have to agree to the choice in advance.

That was the final major issue to be fought over. Though they weren't done yet, they all began to see the light at the end of the tunnel. Over the next few sessions they hammered out the rest of the details. The band would receive an advance of half a million dollars payable as soon as the contract was signed. Fifty percent of the debt from the previous contract would be forgiven, the other fifty percent would be paid off in quarterly installments by taking twenty percent out of their royalty checks. There was no need for housing clauses or transportation clauses or grocery clauses or manservant clauses since the band would be able to provide all of those things for themselves once the money started coming in. The band would retain the right to audit National Records at any time for any or no reason in regard to their album sales and expenses. National fought and kicked a bit on this issue but finally gave in. And then there was the issue of how many contract periods the contract would encompass. Pauline fought hard to hold it to only two but eventually agreed to four, which would make it go one album further than *Intemperance*'s original contract had.

"Well then," asked Pauline. "Do we have a contract?"

"It would seem we do," Frowley said.

"Let's get it printed up and signed," Pauline said.

This took another two days to accomplish but on August 28, 1985, they dragged Darren and Coop out of their drug-haze and took them down to the National Records Building. All five of them put their signatures on the paper and it became official.

*****

They went to Jake's condo after the signing ceremony and opened several bottles of champagne to celebrate. The festive mood didn't last very long, however. There was still serious business to attend to. Jake and Matt called Darren and Coop into Jake's office and sat them down.

"We need to talk, guys," Jake told them.

"No problemo, Jake," Darren said. "You gonna tell us when our money is coming in?"

"Fuck yeah," agreed Coop. "They're actually going to cut us a fuckin' check for eighty grand? I mean, like really?"

"It's not a check," Matt said. "They're going to wire the money into your account. Should be done by tomorrow morning."

"That's fuckin' bitchin," Darren said. "I'm gonna go buy me a new car, first fuckin' thing!"

"Me too," said Coop. "I want a Porsche nine-two-fucking-four."

"Fuck yeah!" said Darren. "With one of them new CD players in it!"

"Yeah!"

"Uh... guys," Jake interrupted.

They looked up at him.

"You understand that you need to start finding your own housing tomorrow, don't you? Now that we're under the new contract, National isn't paying for your pad anymore."

Their faces fell. "No shit? You mean we gotta pay rent and shit?"

"That's why you have your own money now," Matt told them. "The advance is to cover your expenses until the royalty checks start rolling in."

"That's fucked up!" Darren said.

"And they're not going to be paying for your food or your drinks anymore either," Jake said.

"They're not?" Coop asked.

A horrible thought occurred to Darren. "What about our... I mean... the pain medicine we take? Are they gonna keep paying for that?"

"You mean your fucking heroin," Matt said. "That shit you put in your arm three or four times a day? And the answer to that is no, they aren't going to paying for it anymore."

Darren and Coop looked at each other in a panic.

"Dude," Darren said, "what the fuck kind of contract did we sign? What is this shit?"

"I thought you said this was a better contract!" said Coop.

"We've kept you informed the whole time we were negotiating it," Jake said. "And we also gave you copies of it to look over two days ago. Did you read them?"

"No," said Darren. "Why the fuck would we read them? You told us it was a good contract!"

"It is a good contract," Matt said. "It's going to let us take control of our own lives and get rich in the process... as long as we make good music."

"And that's what we need to talk to you about now," said Jake.

"What do you mean?" asked Coop.

Matt and Jake looked at each other, drawing strength for this from each other. Both had vowed to stick to their guns on this issue but it was hard. Despite all the chaos these two had caused over the past year they were still close friends and band mates. There was a deep bond between all of them and it was hard to pull on that bond and risk breaking it.

"It's like this, guys," Jake said. "The new contract has put band discipline back into the hands of the band. National no longer has the right to override decisions made by the band or to change the rules of the band. As of the moment you put your signatures on that piece of paper, you can now be removed from the band by a majority vote of the five of us."

"What the fuck you talking about?" Coop demanded.

"It means if Nerdly, Jake, and I all say you should be fired, you're fired and we'll replace you with someone else."

They looked shocked at this statement.

"Fired?" Darren said. "What the fuck do you mean?"

"Why would you fire us?" asked Coop.

"Because you're a couple of heroin addicts," Matt said. "Why the hell do you think?"

"We're not heroin addicts!" they both cried in unison.

"Let's not mince words here," said Jake. "You both shoot heroin into your veins at least three times every day. If you fail to do this, you start puking and shaking. In my book, that's the definition of a heroin addict."

"It's for *pain*, man!" Darren cried. "Ever since that explosion onstage, my fuckin' ear hurts all the time."

"Uh huh," said Matt. "And what's your excuse, Coop? You got a bad ear too?"

"No," he said. "I just use it to get high, but it ain't that bad. I got it under control."

"You ain't got shit under control," Matt said. "Either one of you. When we were rehearsing, you guys were showing up loaded on that shit and falling asleep at your instruments. You stopped contributing to the production. You were useless."

"We can't produce music that way," Jake said, "and we can't perform music that way. It has to stop. Both of you need to make a choice."

"What choice?" Darren asked.

"As of this moment," Matt said, "we are reinstating the rules of the band as they existed back in the D Street West days. There will be no more drug use or alcohol use for four hours prior to any rehearsal or performance."

Darren and Coop looked at each other, both licking their lips nervously.

"I guess we can live with that," Coop said.

"Yeah," Darren muttered. "I guess."

"That's not all though," Matt said.

"It's not?" asked Darren.

"No," Matt said. "That only applies to the normal drugs like coke and pot, and to the booze and beer. You can keep doing those things as much as you want on your own time. If it becomes a problem, we'll discuss it then. But the heroin, you need to give that up completely."

"Completely?" Darren said.

"You mean, like, for good?" Coop asked.

"For good," Jake said. "It's a little too heavy-duty of a drug. You guys can't control yourselves when you're on it. It has to go."

"But the pain in my ear..." Darren started.

"Take some fuckin' aspirin like everyone else," Matt said.

"Aspirin doesn't help!"

"Look," said Jake. "It's very simple. You can keep doing heroin if you want, but you're not going to be a member of this band if you do. We had a little something thrown into the new contract with you two in mind. National will pay for rehab services for any band member who needs it. You two definitely need it. We've made arrangements for both of you to check into the Betty Ford Center day after tomorrow and go through their heroin program. They'll give you methadone and wean you through the worst of the withdrawals. When you get out you can go back to smoking weed and snorting coke and drinking booze, you can even drop acid if you want, as long as you don't do it in the four hour window before a rehearsal or a show. But you need to stay away from the heroin. Forever. If you go back to it we'll find out and we'll kick you out. That's the deal."

"That's totally fucked up!" Darren yelled, enraged.

"Yep," said Matt, "but then life is pretty fucked up, isn't it?"

*****

The next morning Jake drove over to Matt's condo and picked him up for their next post-contract mission, one that both of them were looking forward to. Jake found Matt drinking a bottle of beer and using the liquid to wash down half a dozen small orange pills.

"What are you taking?" he asked, slightly alarmed by the sheer number of the pills Matt had ingested.

"I ain't offing myself," Matt said. "It's a urinary tract analgesic."

"A urinary tract analgesic? What are you taking that for? You got the clap again?"

"No, I ain't got the fuckin' clap. I learned from the first time. This shit is a real interesting drug though. It's called Pyridium."

"Pyridium?" Jake asked. "What does it do?"

"I got it from this bitch I was fucking last month," he said. "She had a bladder infection."

"You were fucking a girl with a bladder infection?" Jake asked, appalled.

Matt shrugged. "What's the difference? A pussy is a pussy. You just don't eat her out."

"I suppose," Jake said. "So, did she give you her bladder infection?"

"No, I used a rubber, like always. It's the side-effect of the pill that I'm after."

"What side effect? Does it get you high?"

"Naw," he said. "It turns your piss bright orange."

Jake nodded slowly. "And you want your piss to be bright orange for what reason?"

"You'll see," he said. "I've been taking six of them every four hours since yesterday. It's working real well."

"Uh huh," Jake said, shaking his head. Sometimes Matt's train of thought was just a little too winding for him to follow. "Well, should we go then?"

"Yep," Matt agreed. "Let's fuckin' do it."

They drove to Hollywood, parking in front of the Hedgerow Building where Ronald Shaver, their so-called manager, kept his office. They rode up to the twenty-second floor and checked in with Trina, his beautiful secretary. She told them to go right in. Mr. Shaver was expecting them.

"Boys," he greeted as they closed the office door behind them. "Good to see you. I was kind of surprised when Trina told me you'd asked for an appointment. What brings you out here today?"

They hadn't talked to Shaver in months, not since he'd called them several times, at National's request, to try to convince them to drop their little plan of blackmailing the record company into renegotiating. Once the actual renegotiation began, they hadn't heard word one from him.

"We have good news, Shaver," Jake said. "We just signed a new contract with National Records yesterday."

"A new contract?" he asked, surprised. He then smiled. "I heard rumors about that but every time I called my contacts at National they denied them. It was true? You really did get them to renegotiate?"

"We really did," Matt said. "They caved into us and revamped the whole fuckin' deal."

"Yep," said Jake. "We're gonna be pulling in eighteen percent royalties now based on full retail rate. What do you think about that?"

"Outstanding!" Shaver said, delighted, his mind undoubtedly already going over his cut of that. "When does it take effect?"

"It took effect yesterday afternoon," Jake said. "Our advances should be wired to our accounts by noon."

"What kind of advance did you secure?" Shaver asked them.

"Half a million," Matt said. "Not bad for a bunch of amateurs, huh?"

Shaver nodded appreciatively. "Not bad at all," he said. "Although I really wish you would have had me sit in on your negotiations. I know we've had our differences, but if they were willing to give you half a million in advance money without my presence, they might've gone a million *with* my presence."

"Well," said Matt, "we *would've* invited you to participate, but there was this whole thing about how you fucked us over the first time. Do you remember that?"

"Yes," said Jake. "It seems you were looking more out for your interests than ours."

"Now, guys," Shaver said. "I've told you this in the past; the contract you signed with me was a standard industry representation contract. I know you didn't like it, but it was no different than the one I signed with *Earthstone* or *The Two Lips*."

"Yes, we're now well versed on that whole standard industry concept," Jake said. "But you know what? All is forgiven."

"It is?" Shaver asked.

"Yep," said Matt. "Because it doesn't fucking matter anymore."

"What do you mean?"

"I'll tell you in a minute," Matt said. "But first, do you have any of that premo blow on you? I could use a couple lines about now. How about you, Jake?"

"Definitely," Jake said. "I haven't done any coke in a week."

"Uh... sure," Shaver said. He quickly produced his kit and started crunching up lines. "Would you like a drink?"

"Fuckin' A," said Matt. "We'll have the usual."

Shaver nodded and hit the intercom button. "Trina," he said, "two Chivas and cokes for my guests, please?"

"Make them doubles," Jake said.

"Doubles," Shaver dutifully repeated.

While they were waiting, Jake and Matt took turns expounding upon the contract they'd just signed. Shaver listened respectfully as he heard some of the more lucrative terms. Trina came in and gave them their drinks. She then retreated. Shaver put the mirror before them and they each snorted up their two lines plus one of Shaver's, leaving him with nothing. He frowned but didn't comment.

"Goddamn," Jake said, sniffing, feeling the drug go to his head. "You always did have the best blow, Shaver."

"Yep," said Matt, downing three-quarters of his drink in one gulp. "I'll always remember that about you."

"Remember?" asked Shaver, who had dumped out some more coke and was making a few fresh lines for himself. "What do you mean?"

"Ahh," said Jake, "that's what we actually came here for. You see, your contract with us was for the duration of the contract we signed with National, remember?"

"Uh... yes," said Shaver, his eyes clouding a bit.

"Our contract with National," said Jake, "the one we signed with your assistance, the one that bound us to you, well... it's no longer in effect. It has been superseded by the new contract. So that means we are free to sign a contract with another manager now."

Shaver stopped in mid-chop. "Oh, I see," he said. "You're here to renegotiate your terms with me."

"No, not really," Jake said. "We've already got ourselves another manager."

Shaver shook his head. "What's he charging you? Let's talk about this, guys. I'm open to negotiation. I would be willing to go down as low as fifteen percent for you."

"She is charging us twenty percent and we're glad to pay it," Jake said. "You see, we know she's not going to screw us like you did."

"She?" he asked. "A woman? A woman wants to be your manager?"

"*Is* our manager," Matt said. "It's Jake's sister, Pauline. The bad-ass bitch who helped us score this new contract, who fuckin' fought for us and lost her job for us and stood by us."

"But she doesn't know anything about managing a band!" Shaver said. "You'll sink if you don't have me!"

"You never did shit for us, Shaver," Matt said.

"I got you that first contract!" Shaver yelled. "If it wasn't for me you'd still be playing at those shitty clubs in Heritage!"

"That is true," Jake allowed, "and we are grateful to you for giving us that first break, but you also screwed us. We don't take kindly to being screwed. I think the several million dollars you've collected on our behalf is more than compensation for you getting us into the business."

"Besides, you'll still be making money off us," Matt said bitterly. "You'll still be collecting twenty percent of our royalties for the first two albums."

"Jake, Matt," Shaver said, "we can work this out, can't we? You don't want an inexperienced manager. You *need* me."

"We don't need shit," said Matt. "Now, if you don't mind, I will now put in writing the official severance of our relationship with each other."

"What?" asked Shaver. "Writing? What are you talking about?"

Matt didn't answer. Instead, he stood up and took two steps towards the wall. He unbuttoned his jeans and took out his penis. He began to piss, the urine coming out an unnaturally bright, almost fluorescent orange color. It sprayed over Shaver's white wall, staining everything it touched. Matt began to move up and down, back and forth, forming words with the stream of orange urine. When he was done, the message showed up clearly: UR FIRED.

*****

Two days later, Jake was sitting in his living room, sipping a rum and coke and flipping through a collection of apartment brochures that had been sent to him. Manny was already gone, his fate unknown to Jake and uncared about. Jake himself had thirty days to find new lodging.

He now had $79,780 in his bank account, his share of the $500,000 advance minus Pauline's twenty percent and the amount he'd spent on groceries for himself and the monthly insurance payment for his Corvette. On Pauline's advice he was already considering another thirty thousand of it to be gone as well, earmarked for federal and state income taxes, which he alone would be responsible for calculating and paying. That left him with about fifty grand to pay for housing, gas, insurance, groceries, clothing, and everything else he would need to buy until their first royalty payments started to come in. The best they could hope for there was next July, assuming they got an album out by December and assuming that album went platinum very quickly. If not, it would be after the third quarter of next year, October, before they saw more revenue since their advance money and all the other expenses would be recouped first. That fifty grand was going to have to stretch thirteen months.

Granted, this left him with about $3800 a month to spend free and clear. That was considerably more than the average middle-class citizen of the United States enjoyed at this particular point in history, but the average middle-class citizen did not live in Los Angeles and was not used to living in a luxury condo. Jake simply did not have enough money to continue living in the lifestyle to which he'd become accustomed. Comparable apartments went for around $2500 a month. He figured his budget would allow only about $1500, $1700 at the most, for housing. In that price range he could find nothing in the downtown area that was livable to his standards. If he wanted to keep up something of an air of luxury, he would have to travel outward, to the suburbs.

"Oh well," he said to himself as he lit a cigarette and took a sip from his drink. "I suppose there are people who would kill to have my problems."

He took a moment to worry about Darren and Coop. Both had checked into the Betty Ford Center, as scheduled, and were currently enjoying their first twenty-four hours without heroin. He hoped they would come out clean and stay clean but even if they did, they were already setting themselves up for big problems down the line. Jake and Bill had both offered to find new housing for them while they were in rehab but both had refused. National had stuck their noses in and offered to continue leasing their current condos to them, something that would eat up their advance money long before the first royalty check, even if it did come in July. Those condos went for three grand a month, plus dues.

The phone rang, interrupting his thoughts. He actually sat for three rings before remembering that Manny was no longer there to act as phone secretary. He got up and answered it.

"Mr. Kingsley?" a vaguely familiar voice said.

"Who is enquiring?" Jake asked.

"Ted Perkins," the voice said. "I'm in charge of the endorsements department at Brogan Guitars. We met a few years ago while you were recording your first album, remember?"

"Yes, I do," Jake said, and he did. Perkins was the rep who had pushed the Brogan guitars on them during the recording and touring stages of *Descent Into Nothing*. He was also one of the people who had called and threatened Matt with contract violation when he refused to play one on stage. "How did you get my number?"

"Mr. Crow over at National gave it to me," he said. "It is my understanding that the endorsement contract we held with National regarding the guitar you play onstage during your tour is no longer valid."

"That's your understanding, huh?" Jake said suspiciously, not volunteering anything further. The contract they had just signed contained a strict non-disclosure clause about its very existence.

"This is information Mr. Crow gave to me," Perkins said. "I am told that you and all of the other guitar players of the group are now independent agents for touring contract endorsements."

"Yes," he said carefully. "I suppose we are. What exactly is it that you want, Mr. Perkins?"

"Please," he said, "call me Ted."

"Ted," Jake said. "What is it that you want?"

"Well, I want to offer you an endorsement contract," he said. "I know you like our guitars, Mr. Kingsley, and it is our hope that you will continue to play them onstage."

"What kind of endorsement contract?" Jake asked.

"We should probably discuss this in person. Would nine o'clock tomorrow morning be convenient?"

"Tomorrow?"

"I could send a limousine to your residence to pick you up if you wish."

"Uh... why don't you just give the basics of what you're offering right now?" Jake asked. "And then we'll go from there."

Perkins didn't seem to like this but he went forth anyway. "We are prepared to offer you a five hundred thousand dollar endorsement fee if you would agree to exclusively play Brogan guitars on your upcoming tour and another five hundred thousand on any subsequent tours. In addition, we will provide you with free instruments for the duration of this contract."

"Half a million bucks a tour?" Jake asked. "Is that what you were paying National before?"

"I'm afraid I am not allowed to discuss the details of contracts with other clients," Perkins said.

"When would I get that money?" Jake asked.

"It would payable upon the signing of the contract," Perkins said. "Of course, if you were to not go out on tour for whatever reason, or if you were to play different guitars on stage, you would be obligated to return that money to us along with a moderate breach of contract fee."

"Of course," Jake said. "Look, Perkins, let me think this thing over for a bit. I'll get back to you."

"Uh... well... sure," he said. "But how about that meeting tomorrow? Are we still on for that?"

"I'll let you know," Jake said. "What's your number?"

He recited his telephone number and Jake wrote it down. Before he could say anything further, Jake hung up on him. He consulted a sheet of paper and dialed the number for the Hyatt Hotel. Pauline had moved in there the moment her hundred grand had been deposited in her account. She too was now looking for luxury apartments in the LA area.

"What's up?" she asked when she came on the line.

"I just got this phone call," Jake said. He then told her about his conversation with Perkins.

"Half a million bucks, huh?" she said, whistling appreciatively. "Not bad for just playing a certain guitar. I bet you can do better though."

"You think so?"

"It's worth a shot anyway. Didn't you always say you loved your Les Paul but you only liked the Brogan?"

"Yeah," he said. "I did say that." This too was true. Though the Brogan was actually a little bit sturdier of an instrument with more modern components, a Les Paul was a classic, the kind of guitar a musician could bond with.

"Why don't we call up Gibson and see if maybe they are interested in an endorsement contract? It can't hurt, can it?"

"No," Jake agreed. "I guess it can't. Will you talk to them for me?"

"What are big sisters for?"

As it turned out, Gibson was very interested in an endorsement contract with Jake Kingsley. They offered him a million dollars per tour and free instruments for life if he would exclusively play the Les Paul onstage. Pauline told them they would check with Brogan to see if they were willing to make a counter offer. Gibson then upped the offer to $1.5 million per tour and, in addition, they promised to release a Jake Kingsley signature model Les Paul for sale to the general public and they would give Jake a commission of twenty dollars for each one that was sold.

"Where do I sign?" Jake asked.

"But, Jake," Pauline said, "shouldn't we run this offer through a few more guitar makers first? There's a good chance that Brogan or Fender might up it."

"Nope," Jake said. "The deal couldn't get any better for me. I was planning on playing my Les Paul onstage for free anyway. Let's wrap it up and get it signed."

They wrapped it up and got it signed. Since Pauline had brokered the deal, she received $300,000 of the $1.5 million and would get four dollars for each guitar sold. Jake looked at his bank balance the day the money was wired and stared at the amount for almost fifteen minutes. There was now $1,279,203 in there. It was now official. He was a millionaire.

Matt was the next to become a millionaire. Learning from Jake's experience and utilizing the negotiation skills of Pauline, he signed an endorsement contract with Fender to do exactly what he had already been doing: play his Stratocaster onstage. They gave him two million dollars per tour and promised him thirty dollars for each Matt Tisdale signature model that was sold to the public.

This led to the rest of the band signing endorsement deals of their own. Bill accepted $750,000 to play a Steinway Concert grand piano while on tour. The Steinway people even promised to install high-fidelity pick-up microphones for optimum sound reproduction. Coop, from within the walls of the Betty Ford Center, actually got a bidding war going between Ludwig, Pearl, Lexington, and Yamaha, with Yamaha finally offering him half a million per tour and giving him a commission of twelve dollars per John "Coop" Cooper signature starter set that was sold. Darren was the only one who didn't get a six-figure deal. Brogan ended up offering him a relatively paltry $75,000 to continue playing their bass guitar during tours and to appear in advertisements in various rock music magazines. There was no Darren Appleman signature bass proposed and, thus, no commission. Part of the reason Darren didn't fare as well as the others in the endorsement game was because he was a bass player and that was simply not perceived to be as glamorous as the other positions in the band. A bigger part of the reason, however, was that he chose not to use Pauline as a negotiator and mouthpiece for brokering the deal.

"I ain't paying her twenty percent to get me a fuckin' deal with a guitar company," he said stubbornly when Jake—during one of his visits to the Betty Ford Center—suggested that it might be a good idea. "It's bad enough I had to give her twenty percent of the hundred grand we got for signing the contract."

This was typical of Darren's attitude toward the rest of the band during this period. While Coop seemed to be responding well to the treatment and seemed genuinely happy to be shaking off his heroin addiction, Darren was full of excuses and resentment. Counselors told Jake on several occasions that he hadn't even acknowledged the first and most important step of the therapy, which was to admit that he was addicted and had a problem. As a result of this stubbornness, Ted Perkins met with Darren on day 24 of his stay at the Betty Ford Center and put an endorsement contract before him that offered perhaps half of what he would've got with Pauline's help and was chock full of loopholes such as the magazine advertisement requirement, a rider that dictated he would not get paid until the tour actually started, and that he would have to reimburse Brogan a proportionate amount for any tour dates that were missed.

"We're gonna keep having problems with him," Jake opined on day thirty of the rehab, the final day.

"Yep," Matt agreed. "The best we can hope for is to keep him in line through the recording process and the tour."

*****

On October 3, 1985, *Intemperance* entered their rehearsal warehouse (the rent on which was now entirely paid by National Records instead of being recouped from band profits) for the first time since recording the atrocious demo tape that had kicked off the dispute and eventual renegotiation. Their instruments were dusty and out of tune, requiring two hours of cleaning and maintenance before they could even begin playing.

"Jake and I have both been working on new tunes during this whole thing we've been going through," Matt said. "I have about six and Jake has seven or eight, right, Jake?"

"Probably seven," Jake said. "I'm not really sure about that last one I was working on."

"Fair enough," Matt said. "But for now, how about we start by refreshing ourselves on the three main tunes we did before this whole thing started? Does everyone remember them?"

"You mean the ones you said sucked ass?" asked Darren. "The ones you replaced with that crappy shit we put on the tape?"

"You know why we did that," said Jake. "That got us the new contract we're under, remember?"

"I kind of liked the old contract," Darren said. "Nobody asked me or Coop if we wanted to change it."

"You liked it because it let you shoot heroin to your heart's content," Jake told him. "You didn't even care that it was bankrupting you."

"Hey, fuck off, Jake!" Darren shouted. "Just because you scored a fucking million and a half endorsement contract off this new deal doesn't mean the rest of us have to like it!"

"Hey!" Matt yelled. "Knock it off, both of you. We ain't going there. We're here to play some music and get an album together, so let's fuckin' do it."

Jake and Darren both glared at each other for a moment and then nodded.

"Let's do it," Darren said.

"Yeah," Jake agreed. "Let's see if we still got it."

"That's the fuckin' spirit," Matt said. "Let's do *Service Me* first.

They didn't still have it, not at first anyway. One or the other of them would constantly miss a cue or play the wrong piece or flat out forget what they were supposed to be doing. Jake screwed up the lyrics, letting entire sections go unsung. The harmony of the rest of the members during the chorus was unharmonious at best. But they kept at it, referring to music sheets and lyric sheets and starting over again and again. Finally, after almost two hours, they managed to play the entire song all the way through without having anyone screw up.

"All right," said Matt, nodding in satisfaction. "That was almost un-shitty. Now let's do it again. From the beginning."

They did it again, almost flawlessly. And then they did it again. And as they played and sang, gripping their instruments, pounding their drums and piano keys, letting their voices be heard, the magic of making music slowly overtook them. They let their fears and resentments, their worries and anxieties, slip away from them, floating out on a stream of electrons through wires, pounding out as vibrations through the air emitted by amplifiers. They became a band again, doing what they did best: playing their music. By the time they called it a day at six o'clock that evening, they'd dialed in two of their previous tunes and were well on their way to dialing in the third. They left the warehouse in much better moods than they'd entered it with, even Darren, who was still pondering how good it would feel to drive a needle full of heroin into his vein and wondering when the scrutiny would be off of him enough that he could start doing it again.

*****

There wasn't a day that went by that Steve Crow didn't call either Jake or Matt to hound them about when he could expect a demo tape on his desk.

"We're already out of the Grammy Awards for next year since there's no way in hell we're going to get an album out by January 1," he complained to Jake one day. "And that fucking band of spics you got in a fight with released their new album three weeks ago. Have you heard that shit? They're already tearing up the charts! They're going to go gold in less than a month!"

"What does that have to do with us?" Jake asked.

"It means they're going to be in the awards and you are not," Crow said. "Do you have any idea how much free publicity we're missing out on by not being in the awards?"

"We're going as fast as we can, Steve," Jake said. "Have patience."

"If you would've been working on this new material during the contract negotiations you could've gone right into the studio once it was signed."

"Steve, think about that for a minute," Jake told him. "If we would've done that, our entire negotiating position would have been compromised. You're lucky that Matt and I were even composing new tunes during all that. We could've just been sitting on our asses."

"I suppose," he said. "I'm just letting you know that you're in danger of obscurity. It's been almost two years since *Thrill* was released. A lot of your fans might have forgotten about you."

"Is that why *Thrill* is still in the top ten album chart?" Jake asked. "Is that why three of the songs on *Thrill* are still the most requested on rock radio stations nationwide?"

"That's now," Crow said. "It'll still take at least three months to record your tunes once they're submitted. A lot can change in three months."

"We will record no tune before its time, Steve," Jake told him. "We're getting there, okay? When we have the demo tape ready for you, we'll submit it."

"Three good songs and seven filler tunes," Crow pleaded. "That's all we ask, Jake."

"We don't do filler tunes," Jake replied. "You'll get ten good tunes and the album will sell like mad. Don't worry."

But, of course, he continued to worry and continued to hound. The band did their best to ignore him and continued with their composition, working at least six hours, five days a week, composing and perfecting, honing and rejecting. By mid-October they were well into the rhythm during their sessions, even Darren and Coop, and it was almost like old times. The suggestions flew and the changes were tried and incorporated. New songs were introduced one by one and then perfected. Finally, on November 7, they had twelve songs ready for submission—five by Matt and seven by Jake. Putting themselves under Bill's direction, they recorded a demo tape over a period of three days, working through the weekend. On November 11, the following Monday, they put the demo tape, the lyric sheets, and the music sheets on Steve Crow's desk.

"This is the real thing this time?" he asked as he opened the envelope and removed the contents.

"The real fuckin' thing," Matt said. "Some of the best tunes we've ever done are on that tape."

"Okay then," he said. "Let's give it a listen."

They gave it a listen. For the first time since being assigned to *Intemperance*, Steve Crow found himself in awe of them. Rich, melodic, and most of all, complex rock and roll music poured out of his speakers for more than fifty minutes and he drank it in. When the tape finally ended he looked up at them, respect showing in his eyes.

"This album is going to sell a lot of copies," he said.

"That's the idea," Jake said. "When do we go into the studio?"

"Soon," he said. "As soon as I can book the time. Meanwhile, let's get Doolittle in here and we'll start working on the production list."

*****

National was so desperate to get the album into production they fought very little with the band on which songs would be included and in what order they would be played. The only time they used their veto power was when Jake suggested they record *It's In The Book* and name the album that. The band didn't fight the issue. Eventually they settled on ten of the new songs, six of Jake's and four of Matt's. Two of the songs were ballads, which National was particularly fond of since those tended to translate into best-selling singles. The title cut of the new album was to be *Balance Of Power*, one of Jake's songs that dealt with the subject of asserting yourself and taking control of your own destiny—a subject that no one at National seemed to realize was about the whole dispute they'd just had with their best-selling band.

They entered the recording studio on December 6 amid much gossip media coverage. Throughout the entire negotiation process the reporters had continued to hound both the band and the National executives about rumors of a new contract and the fact that a lawsuit was still on record. This attention increased to a frenzy once it was reported that National had dropped the lawsuit. Now, on the day the band actually started recording, National triumphantly announced that fact to the world, stating that since two of the members had successfully completed rehab at the Betty Ford Center for drug addiction, the band was now on track and anticipated finishing their new album by spring.

"What about the rumors of a new contract?" asked several reporters.

"There is no new contract," Crow replied. "The band is operating under their current contract and will remain so until it expires."

*****

Recording, including remixes, dubs, and overdubs, for *Balance Of Power* was finished on March 3, 1986. National rushed the album into production as quickly as possible, with plans to get the first single—*I've Found Myself Again*—on the radio by the first day of spring and to put the album itself into record stores by April 1.

"Now it's time to get the video for *Found* into production," Crow told them on March 4. "It needs to be on MTV simultaneous with the release of the single. That doesn't give us much time."

The filming of the video turned out to be the first major test of the new contract and the powers that had been granted to *Intemperance* under it. The band met with Norman Rutger, the man who had produced and written all of their previous videos. His idea was to continue the Satanist theme started in the other videos. He envisioned the band dressed in black leather and roaming through dank underground catacombs, searching through rooms full of torture equipment and splattered with blood. During the chorus of the song Jake would find a smiling duplicate of himself in an embrace with a winged demon in one of the more hideous rooms.

"No fucking way," Jake said when he first heard this. "That is not what the song is about and I will not sign off on any video that represents one of my songs incorrectly."

Rutger, of course, started his whole spiel about how he couldn't work under such conditions and how the "visionless buffoons" had a lot of nerve questioning his inspired imaginings.

"We'll do it my way or we'll use our veto power," Jake told Crow and Doolittle when he was called into their office.

"But Rutger is the premier video producer," Doolittle said. "He refuses to take direction from a musician."

"He does have a good sense of what the audience is looking for in a video," Crow said. "Two of your other videos were almost nominated for awards."

"I don't give a shit about videos or video awards," Jake told them. "I think videos are destroying music and perverting this entire industry. The music world would be much better off without them. But if you insist upon us making one, it is going to be a video that is true to the meaning of the song. I will not compromise on this. *I've Found Myself Again* is a song about being on the road, about the frustrations and the boredom and the burnout and about how all that disappears when we hit the stage each night. We make a video about that or we don't make a video at all. It's your choice."

"But Rutger refuses to take input on the content of his videos," Crow said.

"Then find someone else to produce it," Jake said. "Someone who *does* take input."

Left with no other choice, they did as Jake asked (cursing the new *Intemperance* contract all the while). They found an unknown producer named Erica Wilde, a woman in her mid-thirties who held a degree from a prestigious filmmaking school but who had spent her entire career making commercials for auto makers and soap manufacturers. She had never done a video before but she was eager to give it a shot.

Erica was an overweight, bespectacled librarian-looking woman who had very little fashion sense. But she proved to be an intelligent and open-minded filmmaker. "What are we going for, here?" she asked Jake at their first meeting. "My understanding is that you have specific imagery you wish to convey with this video and that I am to follow your suggestions to the best of my ability. So, what are we talking?"

"Look," Jake said, "I'm not trying to control your production of the video. I am a musician and I know next to nothing about filmmaking. All I want is a video that is true to the theme of the song. Do you think you can do that?"

"What's the song about?" she asked.

Jake popped an advanced copy of the master recording into a cassette player. "I just happen to have the song with me," he said. He pushed play. "You tell me what it's about."

She listened to it and then had him rewind it and listened to it again. "Not bad," she said. "I'm more of a soft rock fan but that is good music."

"Thank you," he said. "So, what is it about?"

"Well, it's a road song, obviously. That's a fairly common staple of musical recordings, isn't it? *Wheel In The Sky* by *Journey*, *Homeward Bound* by Simon and Garfunkle, *Turn The Page* by Bob Seger. It's in the same genre as those tunes. Yours is a little different though. It describes the boredom and the long hours and the fatigue and the nameless groupies but it also expounds upon the reason you're out there in the first place, the thrill you get when you step out onto the stage and hear the crowd screaming for you."

Jake was grinning as he listened to her words. "I think you know a little bit more about music than you're letting on," he told her.

"Maybe," she said. "Do I pass your little test?"

"You do," he said. "Now let's talk about what we're gonna do with this song, shall we?"

They talked, and as they did, Jake started to like this mousy, unassuming woman more and more. When Jake told her that National had some fifty hours of video that had been taken during the *Thrill* tour, footage that included activities during the bus trips, activities back stage, and activities onstage, her interest perked up considerably.

"I'd like to see all of that footage," she said. "Do you think they'll let me?"

"If it will get their video shot by March 20, they'll let you," Jake told her.

They let her. And from those randomly shot tapes she formed the basis of the video, taking cut scenes of actual tour life and mixing them with other scenes that she carefully directed in the video studio rented for her use. The final result was a moving and very deep representation of the rigors of life on the road and the animation that filled the band when they actually stepped out onto the stage each night.

"It's a fucking work of art," Matt proclaimed when a copy was screened for them on March 16.

"You are a true talent, Erica," Jake said. "You captured the essence of my song perfectly."

Even Darren agreed that it rocked, although he complained that there wasn't enough footage of him and his bass.

When they screened it for Crow and Doolittle, however, they only grunted.

"I guess it'll do," Crow said.

"Yes," agreed Doolittle. "It's better than nothing, but will you let Mr. Rutger produce the video for *Service Me* when the time comes?"

"No," said Matt. "I want this fine-ass filming bitch here to do all the videos for my songs as well. She fuckin' rocks."

Erica beamed at his praise. The two executives rolled their eyes upward but didn't disagree. After all, the alternative was no video at all.

*****

Tour planning began two days before the first single from *Balance Of Power* was released. The band and National butted heads in the first ten minutes.

"What the fuck is this shit?" asked Matt as he looked at the first piece of paperwork that had been handed to him.

"It's the tour schedule," Crow said. "Is there something wrong with it?"

"We're starting on the west coast," Matt said. "That's all cool. It means we won't have to drive all the way across the fuckin' country just to hit the first date, but Heritage isn't on this list."

"We're anticipating much greater response to this album than the last," Crow said. "That means you'll be playing top venues on the tour. Heritage doesn't have a large enough arena to justify stopping there."

"Heritage is our home town," Jake said. "We *have* to play there."

"The Heritage fans can come to one of the shows in Sacramento," Crow said. "We're doing two of them there and its only sixty miles away."

"We will do a show in Heritage or we won't do any shows anywhere," Jake said. He pushed the piece of paper back across the table. "It's our home town and the people who live there are the ones who made us what we were when we first signed. We will not skip them on any tour, ever. Add Heritage in."

"Preferably first," Matt added. "I think they should get that benefit."

Crow fumed and blanched and gritted his teeth for a few moments but he finally took the paper. "I'll see what I can do," he finally said. "Now let's go over the rest of the production."

They did, and the band didn't like what they heard. National was proposing an extravagant production that involved multiple pyrotechnics, six separate laser shows, and a harness and pulley arrangement that would make Jake fly across the audience for the closing number. In addition, the wardrobe department had them dressed in the same leather clothing they'd hated so much on the first two tours.

"No, no, no!" Matt said. "We ain't doing none of this shit!"

"None of what shit?" Crow cried.

"None of the lasers, none of the pulleys, none of the fuckin' leather, none of the pyrotechnics," he said.

"Especially none of the pyrotechnics," Darren added with a shudder.

"This is standard industry production!" Crow cried. "Your fans expect to see you in leather! They expect to see lasers and explosions! You can't pull that off on the last tour and then not do it one better on the next!"

"Why not?" Jake asked.

"Because you can't!" Crow said. "Each tour has to be better than the one before it."

"And it will be," Jake said. "It will be a concert, just like we used to do back in the day."

"You got that shit right," Matt said. "No leather, no lasers, no fucking bombs blowing people through the air, just music. That's what we're about."

"We'll do a ninety minute set," Jake said. "We'll open with *Found* and close with *CTL*. There will be two encore tunes after that. The lighting will be standard and there will be no lasers, pyrotechnics, or any other freaky-ass, high-tech shit. That is not what the fans come to see."

"And no fucking leather," Matt added. "I will never don another pair of leather pants as long as I live. I started out in this business wearing simple blue jeans onstage and that is how I will finish out my career."

"Guys," Crow said, "I think you're letting the tour profits go to your head. Sure, it's nice if you make money off a tour, but the purpose of touring is to get people to buy your albums. Don't start trying to eliminate the expensive items like lasers and pyrotechnicians in the name of profit. That's a big mistake."

"That's not why we're doing it," Jake said. "A concert is about the music and the band that plays it. We put on a good show. We always have. People won't be coming to see us because of the lasers or the lights, they'll be coming to see us because we're *Intemperance*."

"And they know that *Intemperance* knows how to fucking rock," Matt added.

They fought and bickered about this for nearly two days but eventually National had little choice but to give in. After all, with the new contract, the band had the right to veto any tour schedule or production detail they didn't like. The alternative was no tour at all.

"You're destroying your career," Crow warned them. "I just want you to know that."

"We still have the option of not picking you up for the next contract period," Doolittle warned, upping the ante a little.

"You'll be eating your fucking words when this is over," Matt replied. "So, should we start putting this thing together, or what?"

Crow sighed. "Yeah," he said. "I guess we should."

*****

The rehearsals started. The show the band planned to do in cities across America and Canada from May 1 through November 11 was a simple show, consisting of little more than the band taking the stage and playing their asses off. They had a song list and an encore list that they would religiously follow but other than that, there was nothing in the way of lighting effects or acrobatics or choreography rehearsed. They would simply keep the lights shining brightly on them and use their own instincts when they hit the stage.

On March 21, 1986, the single of *I've Found Myself Again* was released to radio stations across the country. Within two days it was the most-requested song nationwide. On April 1, 1986, *Balance Of Power*, the album, was released for sale in record stores. It set an all-time record for most sales in twenty-four hours, with a staggering 83,429 copies purchased.

"It seems that people don't think it's *too* shitty," Matt told Crow after a rehearsal on April 2.

"Let's hope you're right," Crow returned.

He was. In the thirty days between the release of the album and the start of the tour, *I've Found Myself Again* shot up the singles chart to number six and showed every sign of continuing its climb, and *Balance Of Power*, the album, actually debuted at number one. Reviews came out and the album was declared "the best effort by *Intemperance* yet". Tickets for upcoming shows went on sale all along the west coast and sold out within minutes. Scalpers were reportedly asking more than ninety dollars a ticket for the shittiest seats. Even Matt, Jake, and Bill were surprised.

April 30 came and the band climbed on the same old tour bus. They drove upstate to Heritage and on the evening of May 1 they stepped out on the stage, knowing that Jake's parents and sister, Bill's parents, and many thousands of people who used to pay the cover charge and come to their shows at D Street West were out there watching them.

The lights came up and the music began to play. Jake knew, when he heard the cheers, that he'd found himself again.

They began to play.

THE END (of volume one)

Printed in Great Britain
by Amazon